THE HAMMER OF EDEN
and
TRIPLE

Ken Follett was only twenty-seven when he wrote the award-winning *Eye of the Needle*, which became an international bestseller. He has since written several equally successful novels, including *World Without End*, the long-awaited sequel to the worldwide bestselling *The Pillars of the Earth*, an epic of family drama, violent conflict and vaulting ambition set around the building of a great cathedral. Ken Follett is also the author of the non-fiction bestseller *On Wings of Eagles*. He lives with his family in London and Hertfordshire.

www.ken-follett.com

Also by Ken Follett

KEN FOLLETT

THE HAMMER OF EDEN

and

TRIPLE

PAN BOOKS

The Hammer of Eden first published 1998 by Macmillan
First published by Pan Books 1999
Triple first published 1979 by Macdonald and Jane's
First published in paperback 1979 by Raven Books
First published by Pan Books 1998

This edition published 2010 by Pan Books
an imprint of Pan Macmillan, a division of Macmillan Publishers Limited
Pan Macmillan, 20 New Wharf Road, London N1 9RR
Basingstoke and Oxford
Associated companies throughout the world
www.panmacmillan.com

ISBN 978-0-330-51757-7

1 3 5 7 9 8 6 4 2

A CIP catalogue record for this book is available from
the British Library.

Printed in the UK by CPI Mackays, Chatham ME5 8TD

THE HAMMER OF EDEN

PART ONE

FOUR WEEKS

When he lies down to sleep, this landscape is always on his mind:

A pine forest covers the hills, as thick as the fur on a bear's back. The sky is so blue, in the clear mountain air, that it hurts his eyes to look up. Miles from the road there is a secret valley with steep sides and a cold river in its cleft. Here, hidden from strangers' eyes, a sunny south-facing slope has been cleared, and grapevines grow in neat rows.

When he remembers how beautiful it is, he feels his heart will break.

Men, women and children move slowly through the vineyard, tending the plants. These are his friends, his lovers, his family. One of the women laughs. She is a big woman with long, dark hair, and he feels a special warmth for her. She throws back her head and opens her mouth wide, and her clear high voice floats across the valley like birdsong. Some of the men quietly speak a mantra as they work, praying to the gods of the valley and of the grapevines for a good crop. At their feet, a few massive tree stumps remain, to remind them of the back-breaking work that created this place twenty-five years ago. The soil is stony, but this is good, because the stones retain the heat of the sun and warm the roots of the vines, protecting them from the deadly frost.

Beyond the vineyard is a cluster of wooden buildings, plain but well built and weatherproof. Smoke rises from a cookhouse. In a clearing, a woman is teaching a boy how to make barrels.

This is a holy place.

Protected by secrecy and by prayers, it has remained pure, its people free, while the world beyond the valley has degenerated into corruption and hypocrisy, greed and filth.

But now the vision changes.

Something has happened to the quick cold stream that used to zigzag through the valley. Its chatter has been silenced, its hurry abruptly halted. Instead of a rush of white water there is a dark pool, silent and still. The edges of the pool seem static, but if he looks away for a few moments the pool widens. Soon he is forced to retreat up the slope.

He cannot understand why the others do not notice the rising tide. As the black pool laps at the first row of vines, they carry on working with their feet in the water. The buildings are surrounded, then flooded. The cookhouse fire goes out, and empty barrels float away across the growing lake. Why don't they run? he asks himself; and a choking panic rises in his throat.

Now the sky is dark with iron-coloured clouds, and a cold wind whips at the clothing of the people, but still they move along the vines, stooping and rising, smiling at one another and talking in quiet, normal voices. He is the only one who can see the danger, and he realizes he must pick up one or two or even three of the children, and save them from drowning. He tries to run toward his daughter, but he discovers that his feet are stuck in the mud and he cannot move; and he is filled with dread.

In the vineyard the water rises to the workers' knees, then their waists, then their necks. He tries to yell at the people he loves, telling them they must do something now, quickly, in the next few seconds, or they will die, but though he opens his mouth and strains his throat, no sounds will come out. Sheer terror possesses him.

The water laps into his open mouth and begins to choke him.

This is when he wakes up.

CHAPTER ONE

A MAN called Priest pulled his cowboy hat down at the front and peered across the flat, dusty desert of south Texas.

The low dull-green bushes of thorny mesquite and sagebrush stretched in every direction as far as he could see. In front of him, a ridged and rutted track ten feet wide had been driven through the vegetation. These tracks were called *senderos* by the Hispanic bulldozer drivers who cut them in brutally straight lines. On one side, at precise fifty-yard intervals, bright-pink plastic marker flags fluttered on short wire poles. Moving slowly along the sendero was a truck.

Priest had to steal the truck.

He had stolen his first vehicle at the age of eleven. It was a brand-new snow-white 1961 Lincoln Continental parked, with the keys in the dash, outside the Roxy Theater on South Broadway in Los Angeles. Priest, who was called Ricky in those days, could hardly see over the steering wheel. He had been so scared he almost wet himself, but he drove it ten blocks and handed the keys proudly to Jimmy 'Pigface' Riley, who gave him five bucks then took his girl for a drive and crashed the car on the Pacific Coast Highway. That was how Ricky became a member of the Pigface Gang.

But this truck was not just a vehicle.

As he watched, the powerful machinery behind the driver's cabin slowly lowered a massive steel plate, six feet square, to the ground. There was a pause, then he heard a low-pitched rumble. A cloud of dust rose around the truck as the plate began to pound the earth rhythmically. He felt the ground shake beneath his feet.

This was a seismic vibrator, a machine for sending shock waves through the earth's crust. Priest had never had much education, except in stealing cars, but he was the smartest person he had ever met, and he understood how the vibrator worked. It was similar to radar and sonar. The shock waves were reflected off features in the earth—such as rock or liquid—and they bounced back to the surface, where they were picked up by listening devices called geophones, or jugs.

Priest worked on the jug team. They had planted more than a thousand geophones at precisely measured intervals in a grid a mile square. Every time the vibrator shook, the reflections were picked up by the jugs and recorded by a supervisor working in a trailer known as the doghouse. All this data would later be fed into a supercomputer in Houston to produce a three-dimensional map of what was under the earth's surface. And the map would be sold to an oil company.

The vibrations rose in pitch, making a noise like the mighty engines of an ocean liner gathering speed;

then the sound stopped abruptly. Priest ran along the sendero to the truck, screwing up his eyes against the billowing dust. He opened the door and clambered up into the cabin. A stocky black-haired man of about thirty was at the wheel. 'Hey, Mario,' Priest said as he slid into the seat alongside the driver.

'Hey, Ricky.'

Richard Granger was the name on Priest's Commercial Driving License (Class B). The licence was forged but the name was real.

He was carrying a carton of Marlboro cigarettes, the brand Mario smoked. He tossed the carton onto the dash. 'Here, I brought you something.'

'Hey, man, you don't need to buy me no cigarettes.'

'I'm always bummin' your smokes.' He picked up the open pack on the dash, shook one out, and put it in his mouth.

Mario smiled. 'Why don't you just buy your own cigarettes?'

'Hell, no, I can't afford to smoke.'

'You're crazy, man,' Mario laughed.

Priest lit his cigarette. He had always had an easy ability to get on with people, make them like him. On the streets where he grew up, people beat you up if they didn't like you, and he had been a runty kid. So he had developed an intuitive feel for what people wanted from him—deference, affection, humour, whatever—and the habit of giving it to them quickly. In the oilfield, what held the men together was humour: usually mocking, sometimes clever, often obscene.

Although he had been here only two weeks, Priest had won the trust of his co-workers. But he had not figured out how to steal the seismic vibrator. And he had to do it in the next few hours, for tomorrow the truck was scheduled to be driven to a new site, seven hundred miles away, near Clovis, New Mexico.

His vague plan was to hitch a ride with Mario. The trip would take two or three days—the truck, which weighed forty thousand pounds, had a highway speed of around forty miles per hour. At some point he would get Mario drunk, or something, then make off with the truck. He had been hoping a better plan would come to him, but inspiration had failed so far.

'My car's dying,' he said. 'You want to give me a ride as far as San Antonio tomorrow?'

Mario was surprised. 'You ain't coming all the way to Clovis?'

'Nope.' He waved a hand at the bleak desert landscape. 'Just look around,' he said. 'Texas is so beautiful, man, I never want to leave.'

Mario shrugged. There was nothing unusual about a restless transient in this line of work. 'Sure, I'll give you a ride.' It was against company rules to take passengers, but the drivers did it all the time. 'Meet me at the dump.'

Priest nodded. The garbage dump was a desolate hollow, full of rusting pickups and smashed TV sets and verminous mattresses, on the outskirts of Shiloh, the nearest town. No one would be there to see Mario pick him up, unless it was a couple of kids shooting snakes with a .22 rifle. 'What time?'

'Let's say six.'

'I'll bring coffee.'

Priest needed this truck. He felt his life depended on it. His palms itched to grab Mario right now and throw him out and just drive away. But that was no good. For one thing, Mario was almost twenty years younger than Priest, and might not let himself be thrown out so easily. For another, the theft had to go undiscovered for a few days. Priest needed to drive the truck to California and hide it before the nation's cops were alerted to watch out for a stolen seismic vibrator.

There was a beep from the radio, indicating that the supervisor in the doghouse had checked the data from the last vibration and found no problems. Mario raised the plate, put the truck in gear, and moved forward fifty yards, pulling up exactly alongside the next pink marker flag. Then he lowered the plate again and sent a ready signal. Priest watched closely, as he had done several times before, making sure he remembered the order in which Mario moved the levers and threw the switches. If he forgot something later, there would be no one he could ask.

They waited for the radio signal from the doghouse that would start the next vibration. This could be done by the driver in the truck, but generally supervisors preferred to retain command themselves and start the process by remote control. Priest finished his cigarette and threw the butt out of the window. Mario nodded toward Priest's car, parked a quarter of a mile away on the two-lane blacktop. 'That your woman?'

Priest looked. Star had got out of the dirty light-blue Honda Civic and was leaning on the hood, fanning her face with her straw hat. 'Yeah,' Priest said.

'Lemme show you a picture.' Mario pulled an old leather billfold out of the pocket of his jeans. He extracted a photograph and handed it to Priest. 'This is Isabella,' he said proudly.

Priest saw a pretty Mexican girl in her twenties wearing a yellow dress and a yellow Alice band in her hair. She held a baby on her hip, and there was a dark-haired boy standing shyly by her side. 'Your children?'

He nodded. 'Ross and Betty.'

Priest resisted the impulse to smile at the Anglo names. 'Good-looking kids.' He thought of his own children, and almost told Mario about them; but he stopped himself just in time. 'Where do they live?'

'El Paso.'

The germ of an idea sprouted in Priest's mind. 'You get to see them much?'

Mario shook his head. 'I'm workin' and workin', man. Savin' my money to buy them a place. A nice house, with a big kitchen and a pool in the yard. They deserve that.'

The idea blossomed. Priest suppressed his excitement and kept his voice casual, making idle conversation. 'Yeah, a beautiful house for a beautiful family, right?'

'That's what I'm thinking.'

The radio beeped again, and the truck began to shake. The noise was like rolling thunder, but more regular. It began on a profound bass note and slowly rose in pitch. After exactly fourteen seconds it stopped.

In the quiet that followed, Priest snapped his fingers. 'Say, I got an idea . . . No, maybe not.'

'What?'

'I don't know if it would work.'

'What, man, what?'

'I just thought, you know, your wife is so pretty and your kids are so cute, it's wrong that you don't see them more often.'

'*That's* your idea?'

'No. My idea is, I could drive the truck to New Mexico while you go visit them, that's all.' It was important not to seem too keen, Priest told himself. 'But I guess it wouldn't work out,' he added in a who-gives-a-damn voice.

'No, man, it ain't possible.'

'Probably not. Let's see, if we set out early tomorrow and drove to San Antonio together, I could drop you off at the airport there, you could be in El Paso by noon, probably. You'd play with the kids, have dinner with your wife, spend the night, get a plane the next day, I could pick you up at Lubbock airport . . . How far is Lubbock from Clovis?'

'Ninety, maybe a hundred miles.'

'We could be in Clovis that night, or next morning at the latest, and no way for anyone to know you didn't drive the whole way.'

'But you want to go to San Antonio.'

Shit. Priest had not thought this through, he was making it up as he went along. 'Hey, I've never been to Lubbock,' he said airily. 'That's where Buddy Holly was born.'

'Who the hell is Buddy Holly?'

Priest sang: '*I love you, Peggy Sue . . .* Buddy Holly died before you were born, Mario. I liked him better than Elvis. And don't ask me who Elvis was.'

'You'd drive all that way just for me?'

Priest wondered anxiously whether Mario was suspicious, or just grateful. 'Sure I would,' Priest told him. 'As long as you let me smoke your Marlboros.'

Mario shook his head, miming amazement. 'You're a hell of a guy, Ricky. But I don't know.'

He was not suspicious, then. But he was apprehensive, and he probably could not be pushed into a decision. Priest masked his frustration with a show of nonchalance. 'Well, think about it,' he said.

'If something goes wrong, I don't want to lose my job.'

'You're right.' Priest fought down his impatience. 'I tell you what, let's talk later. You going to the bar tonight?'

'Sure.'

'Why don't you let me know then?'

'Okay, that's a deal.'

The radio beeped the all-clear signal, and Mario threw the lever that raised the plate off the ground.

'I got to get back to the jug team,' Priest said. 'We've got a few miles of cable to roll up before nightfall.' He handed back the family photo and opened the door. 'I'm telling you, man, if I had a girl that pretty I wouldn't leave the goddam *house*.' He grinned, then jumped to the ground and slammed the door.

The truck moved off toward the next marker flag as Priest walked away, his cowboy boots kicking up dust.

As he followed the sendero to where his car was parked, he saw Star begin to pace up and down, impatient and anxious.

She had been famous, once, briefly. At the peak of the hippie era she lived in the Haight-Ashbury neighbourhood of San Francisco. Priest had not known her then—he had spent the late sixties making his first million dollars—but he had heard the stories. She had been a striking beauty, tall and black-haired with a generous hourglass figure. She had made a record, reciting poetry against a background of psychedelic music with a band called Raining Fresh Daisies. The album had been a minor hit and Star was a celebrity for a few days.

But what turned her into a legend was her insatiable sexual promiscuity. She had had sex with anyone who briefly took her fancy: eager twelve-year-olds and surprised men in their sixties, boys who thought they were gay and girls who did not know they were lesbians, friends she had known for years and strangers off the street.

That was a long time ago. Now she was a few weeks from her fiftieth birthday, and there were streaks of grey in her hair. Her figure was still generous, though no longer like an hourglass: she weighed a hundred and eighty pounds. But she still exercised an extra-ordinary sexual magnetism. When she walked into a bar, all the men stared.

Even now, when she was worried and hot, there was a sexy flounce to the way she paced and turned beside the cheap old car, an invitation in the movement of her flesh beneath the thin cotton dress, and Priest felt the urge to grab her right there.

'What happened?' she said as soon as he was within earshot.

Priest was always upbeat. 'Looking good,' he said.

'That sounds bad,' she said sceptically. She knew better than to take what he said at face value.

He told her the offer he had made to Mario. 'The beauty of it is, Mario will be blamed,' he added.

'How so?'

'Think about it. He gets to Lubbock, he looks for me, I ain't there, nor his truck either. He figures he's been suckered. What does he do? Is he going to make his way to Clovis and tell the company he lost their truck? I don't think so. At best, he'd be fired. At worst, he could be accused of stealing the truck, and thrown in jail. I'm betting he won't even go to Clovis. He'll get right back on the plane, fly to El Paso, put his wife and kids in the car and disappear. Then the police will be *sure* he stole the truck. And Ricky Granger won't even be a suspect.'

She frowned. 'It's a great plan, but will he take the bait?'

'I think he will.'

Her anxiety deepened. She slapped the dirty roof of the car with the flat of her hand. 'Shit, we have to have that goddam truck!'

He was as worried as she, but he covered it with a cocksure air. 'We will,' he said. 'If not this way, another way.'

She put the straw hat on her head and leaned back against the car, closing her eyes. 'I wish I felt sure.'

He stroked her cheek. 'You need a ride, lady?'

'Yes, please. Take me to my air-conditioned hotel room.'

'There'll be a price to pay.'

She opened her eyes wide in pretended innocence. 'Will I have to do something nasty, mister?'

He slid his hand into her cleavage. 'Yeah.'

'Oh, darn,' she said, and she lifted the skirt of her dress up around her waist.

She had no underwear on.

Priest grinned and unbuttoned his Levi's.

She said: 'What will Mario think if he sees us?'

'He'll be jealous,' Priest said as he entered her. They were almost the same height, and they fitted together with the ease of long practice.

She kissed his mouth.

A few moments later he heard a vehicle approaching on the road. They both looked up without stopping what they were doing. It was a pickup truck with three roustabouts in the front seat. The men could see what was going on, and they whooped and hollered through the open window as they went by.

Star waved at them, calling: 'Hi, guys!'

Priest laughed so hard he came.

*

The crisis had entered its final, decisive phase exactly three weeks earlier.

They were sitting at the long table in the cook-house, eating their midday meal, a spicy stew of lentils and vegetables with new bread warm from the oven, when Paul Beale walked in with an envelope in his hand.

Paul bottled the wine that Priest's commune made —but he did more than that. He was their link with the outside, enabling them to deal with the world yet keep it at a distance. A bald, bearded man in a leather jacket, he had been Priest's friend since the two of them were fourteen-year-old hoodlums, rolling drunks in LA's Skid Row in the early sixties.

Priest guessed that Paul had received the letter this morning and had immediately got in his car and driven here from Napa. He also guessed what was in the letter, but he waited for Paul to explain.

'It's from the Bureau of Land Management,' Paul said. 'Addressed to Stella Higgins.' He handed it to Star, sitting at the foot of the table opposite Priest. Stella Higgins was her real name, the name under which she had first rented this piece of land from the Department of the Interior in the autumn of 1969.

Around the table, everyone went quiet. Even the kids shut up, sensing the atmosphere of fear and dismay.

18

Star ripped open the envelope and took out a single sheet. She read it with one glance. 'June the seventh,' she said.

Priest said: 'Five weeks and two days from now.' That kind of calculation came automatically to him.

Several people groaned in despair. A woman called Song began to cry quietly. One of Priest's children, ten-year-old Ringo, said: 'Why, Star, why?'

Priest caught the eye of Melanie, the newest arrival. She was a tall, thin woman, twenty-eight years old, with striking good looks: pale skin, long hair the colour of paprika, and the body of a model. Her five-year-old son, Dusty, sat beside her. 'What?' Melanie said in a shocked voice. 'What is this?'

Everyone else had known this was coming, but it was too depressing to talk about, and they had not told Melanie.

Priest said: 'We have to leave the valley. I'm sorry, Melanie.'

Star read from the letter. ' "The above-named parcel of land will become dangerous for human habitation after June 7th, therefore your tenancy is hereby terminated on that date in accordance with clause nine, part B, paragraph two of your lease." '

Melanie stood up. Her white skin flushed red, and her pretty face twisted in sudden rage. 'No!' she yelled. 'No! They can't do this to me—I've only just found you! I don't believe it, it's a lie.' She turned her fury on Paul. 'Liar!' she screamed. 'Motherfucking liar!'

Her child began to cry.

'Hey, knock it off!' Paul said indignantly. 'I'm just the goddam mailman here!'

Everyone started shouting at the same time.

Priest was beside Melanie in a couple of strides. He put his arm around her and spoke quietly into her ear. 'You're frightening Dusty,' he said. 'Sit down, now. You're right to be mad, we're all mad as hell.'

'Tell me it isn't true,' she said.

Priest gently pushed her into her chair. 'It's true, Melanie,' he said. 'It's true.'

When they had quietened down, Priest said: 'Come on, everyone, let's wash the dishes and get back to work.'

'Why?' said Dale. He was the winemaker. Not one of the founders, he had come here in the eighties, disillusioned with the commercial world. After Priest and Star, he was the most important person in the group. 'We won't be here for the harvest,' he went on. 'We have to leave in five weeks. Why work?'

Priest fixed him with the Look, the hypnotic stare that intimidated all but the most strong-willed people. He let the room fall silent, so that they would all hear. At last he said: 'Because miracles happen.'

*

A local ordinance prohibited the sale of alcoholic beverages in the town of Shiloh, Texas, but just the other side of the town line there was a bar called the Doodlebug, with cheap draught beer and a country-western band and waitresses in tight blue jeans and cowboy boots.

Priest went on his own. He did not want Star to show her face and risk being remembered later. He wished she had not had to come to Texas. But he needed someone to help him take the seismic vibrator home. They would drive day and night, taking turns at the wheel, using drugs to stay awake. They wanted to be home before the machine was missed.

He was regretting that afternoon's indiscretion. Mario had seen Star from a full quarter of a mile away, and the three roustabouts in the pickup had glimpsed her only in passing, but she was distinctive-looking, and they could probably give a rough description of her: a tall white woman, heavy set, with long dark hair . . .

Priest had changed his appearance before arriving in Shiloh. He had grown a bushy beard and moustache, and tied his long hair in a tight plait which he kept tucked up inside his hat.

However, if everything went according to his plan, no one would be asking for descriptions of him or Star.

When he arrived at the Doodlebug, Mario was already there, sitting at a table with five or six of the jug team and the party boss, Lenny Petersen, who controlled the entire seismic exploration crew.

Not to seem too eager, Priest got a Lone Star longneck and stood at the bar for a while, sipping his beer from the bottle and talking to the barmaid, before joining Mario's table.

Lenny was a balding man with a red nose. He had given Priest the job, two weekends ago. Priest had spent an evening at the bar, drinking moderately, being friendly to the crew, picking up a smattering of seismic exploration slang, and laughing loudly at Lenny's jokes. Next morning he had found Lenny at the field office and asked him for a job. 'I'll take you on trial,' Lenny had said.

That was all Priest needed.

He was hardworking, quick to catch on, and easy to get along with, and in a few days he was accepted as a regular member of the crew.

Now, as he sat down, Lenny said in his slow Texas accent: 'So, Ricky, you're not coming with us to Clovis.'

'That's right,' Priest said. 'I like the weather here too much to leave.'

'Well, I'd just like to say, very sincerely, that it's been a real privilege and pleasure knowing you, even for such a short time.'

The others grinned. This kind of joshing was commonplace. They looked to Priest for a riposte.

He put on a solemn face and said: 'Lenny, you're so sweet and kind to me that I'm going to ask you one more time. Will you marry me?'

They all laughed. Mario clapped Priest on the back.

Lenny looked troubled and said: 'You know I can't marry you, Ricky. I already told you the reason why.' He paused for dramatic effect, and they all leaned forward to catch the punchline. 'I'm a lesbian.'

They roared with laughter. Priest gave a rueful smile, acknowledging defeat, and ordered a pitcher of beer for the table.

The conversation turned to baseball. Most of them liked the Houston Astros, but Lenny was from Arlington and he followed the Texas Rangers. Priest had no interest in sports, so he waited impatiently, joining in now and again with a neutral comment. They were in expansive mood. The job had been finished on time, they had all been well paid and it was Friday night. Priest sipped his beer slowly. He never drank much: he hated to lose control. He watched Mario sinking the suds. When Tammy, their waitress, brought another pitcher, Mario stared longingly at her breasts beneath the chequered shirt. *Keep wishing, Mario—you could be in bed with your wife tomorrow night.*

After an hour, Mario went to the men's room.

Priest followed. *The hell with this waiting, it's decision time.*

He stood beside Mario and said: 'I believe Tammy's wearing black underwear tonight.'

'How do you know?'

'I got a little peek when she leaned over the table. I love to see a lacy brassiere.'

Mario sighed.

Priest went on: 'You like a woman in black underwear?'

'Red,' said Mario decisively.

'Yeah, red's beautiful, too. They say that's a sign a woman really wants you, when she puts on red underwear.'

'Is that a fact?' Mario's beery breath came a little faster.

'Yeah, I heard it somewhere.' Priest buttoned up. 'Listen, I got to go. My woman's waiting back at the motel.'

Mario grinned and wiped sweat from his brow. 'I saw you and her this afternoon, man.'

Priest shook his head in mock regret. 'It's my weakness. I just can't say no to a pretty face.'

'You were *doing* it, right there in the goddam road!'

'Yeah. Well, when you haven't seen your woman for a while, she gets kind of frantic for it, know what I mean?' *Come on, Mario, take the friggin' hint!*

'Yeah, I know. Listen, about tomorrow.'

Priest held his breath.

'Uh, if you're still willing to do like you said . . .'

Yes! Yes!

'Let's go for it.'

Priest resisted the temptation to hug him.

Mario said anxiously: 'You still want to, right?'

'Sure I do.' Priest put an arm around Mario's shoulders as they left the men's room. 'Hey, what are buddies for, know what I mean?'

'Thanks, man.' There were tears in Mario's eyes. 'You're some guy, Ricky.'

*

They washed their pottery bowls and wooden spoons in a big tub of warm water and dried them on a towel made from an old work shirt. Melanie said to Priest: 'Well, we'll just start again somewhere else! Get a piece of land, build wood cabins, plant vines, make wine. Why not? That's what you did all those years ago.'

'It is,' Priest said. He put his bowl on a shelf and tossed his spoon into the box. For a moment he was young again, strong as a pony and boundlessly energetic, certain that he could solve whatever problem life threw up next. He remembered the unique smells of those days: newly sawn timber; Star's young body, perspiring as she dug the soil; the distinctive smoke of their own marijuana, grown in a clearing in the woods; the dizzy sweetness of grapes as they were crushed. Then he returned to the present, and he sat down at the table.

'All those years ago,' he repeated. 'We rented this land from the government for next to nothing, then they forgot about us.'

Star put in: 'Never a rent increase, in twenty-nine years.'

Priest went on: 'We cleared the forest with the labour of thirty or forty young people who were willing to work free, twelve and fourteen hours a day, for the sake of an ideal.'

Paul Beale grinned. 'My back still hurts when I think of it.'

'We got our vines for nothing from a kindly Napa Valley grower who wanted to encourage young people to do something constructive instead of just sitting around taking drugs all day.'

'Old Raymond Dellavalle,' Paul said. 'He's dead now, God bless him.'

'And, most important, we were willing and able to live on the poverty line, half-starved, sleeping on the floor, holes in our shoes, for five long years until we got our first saleable vintage.'

Star picked up a crawling baby from the floor, wiped its nose, and said: 'And we didn't have any kids to worry about.'

'Right,' Priest said. 'If we could reproduce all those conditions, we could start again.'

Melanie was not satisfied. 'There has to be a way!'

'Well, there is,' Priest said. 'Paul figured it out.'

Paul nodded. 'You could set up a corporation, borrow a quarter of a million dollars from a bank, hire a workforce, and become like any other bunch of greedy capitalists watching the profit margins.'

'And that,' Priest said, 'would be the same as giving in.'

*

It was still dark when Priest and Star got up on Saturday morning in Shiloh. Priest got coffee from the diner next door to their motel. When he came back, Star was poring over a road atlas by the light of the reading lamp. 'You should be dropping Mario off at San Antonio international airport around nine thirty, ten o'clock this morning,' she said. 'Then you'll want to leave town on Interstate 10.'

Priest did not look at the atlas. Maps baffled him. He could follow signs for I-10. 'Where shall we meet?'

Star calculated. 'I should be about an hour ahead of you.' She put her finger on a point on the page. 'There's a place called Leon Springs on I-10 about fifteen miles from the airport. I'll park where you're sure to see the car.'

'Sounds good.'

They were tense and excited. Stealing Mario's truck was only the first step in the plan but it was crucial: everything else depended on it.

Star was worrying about practicalities. 'What will we do with the Honda?'

Priest had bought the car three weeks ago for a thousand dollars cash. 'It's going to be hard to sell. If we see a used car lot, we may get five hundred for it. Otherwise we'll find a wooded spot off the interstate and dump it.'

'Can we afford to?'

'Money makes you poor.' Priest was quoting one of the Five Paradoxes of Baghram, the guru they lived by.

Priest knew how much money they had to the last cent, but he kept everyone else in ignorance. Most of the communards did not even know there was a bank account. And no one in the world knew about Priest's emergency cash, ten thousand dollars in twenties, taped to the inside of a battered old acoustic guitar that hung from a nail on the wall of his cabin.

Star shrugged. 'I haven't worried about it for twenty-five years, so I guess I won't start now.' She took off her reading glasses.

Priest smiled at her. 'You're cute in your glasses.'

She gave him a sideways glance and asked a surprise question. 'Are you looking forward to seeing Melanie?'

Priest and Melanie were lovers.

He took Star's hand. 'Sure,' he said.

'I like to see you with her. She makes you happy.'

A sudden memory of Melanie flashed into Priest's mind. She was lying face down across his bed, asleep, with the morning sun slanting into the cabin. He sat sipping coffee, watching her, enjoying the texture of her white skin, the curve of her perfect rear end, the way her long red hair spread out in a tangled skein. In a moment she would smell the coffee, and roll over, and open her eyes, and then he would get back into bed and make love to her. But for now he was luxuriating in anticipation, planning how he would touch her and turn her on, savouring this delicious moment like a glass of fine wine.

The vision faded and he saw Star's forty-nine-year-old face in a cheap Texas motel. 'You're not unhappy about Melanie, are you?' he asked.

'Marriage is the greatest infidelity,' she said, quoting another of the Paradoxes.

He nodded. They had never asked one another to be faithful. In the early days it had been Star who scorned the idea of committing herself to one lover. Then, after she hit thirty and started to calm down, Priest had tested her permissiveness by flaunting a string of girls in front of her. But for the last few years, though they still believed in the principle of free love, neither of them had actually taken advantage of it.

So Melanie had come as kind of a shock to Star. But that was okay. Their relationship was too settled anyway. Priest did not like anyone to feel they could predict what he was going to do. He loved Star, but the ill-concealed anxiety in her eyes gave him a pleasant feeling of control.

She toyed with her styrofoam coffee container. 'I

just wonder how Flower feels about it all.' Flower was their thirteen-year-old daughter, the oldest child in the commune.

'She hasn't grown up in a nuclear family,' he said. 'We haven't made her a slave to bourgeois convention. That's the point of a commune.'

'Yeah,' Star agreed, but it was not enough. 'I just don't want her to lose you, that's all.'

He stroked her hand. 'It won't happen.'

She squeezed his fingers. 'Thanks.'

'We got to go,' he said, standing up.

Their few possessions were packed into three plastic grocery bags. Priest picked up the bags and took them outside to the Honda. Star followed.

They had paid their bill the previous night. The office was closed, and no one watched as Star took the wheel and they drove away in the grey early light.

Shiloh was a two-street town with one stop light where the streets crossed. There were not many vehicles around at this hour on a Saturday morning. Star ran the stop light and headed out of town. They reached the dump a few minutes before six o'clock.

There was no sign beside the road, no fence or gate, just a track where the sagebrush had been beaten down by the tyres of pickup trucks. Star followed the track over a slight rise. The dump was in a dip, hidden from the road. She pulled up beside a pile of smouldering garbage. There was no sign of Mario or the seismic vibrator.

Priest could tell that Star was still troubled. He had

to reassure her, he thought worriedly. She could not afford to be distracted today of all days. If something should go wrong, she would need to be alert, focused.

'Flower isn't going to lose me,' he said.

'That's good,' she replied cautiously.

'We're going to stay together, the three of us. You know why?'

'Tell me.'

'Because we love each other.'

He saw relief drain the tension out of her face. She fought back tears. 'Thank you,' she said.

He felt reassured. He had given her what she needed. She would be okay now.

He kissed her. 'Mario will be here any second. You get movin', now. Put some miles behind you.'

'You don't want me to wait until he gets here?'

'He mustn't get a close look at you. We can't tell what the future holds, and I don't want him to be able to identify you.'

'Okay.'

Priest got out of the car.

'Hey,' she said, 'don't forget Mario's coffee.' She handed him the paper sack.

'Thanks.' He took the bag and slammed the car door.

She turned around in a wide circle and drove away fast, her tyres throwing up a cloud of Texas desert dust.

Priest looked around. He found it amazing that such a small town could generate so much trash. He saw twisted bicycles and new-looking baby carriages, stained couches and old-fashioned refrigerators, and at least ten supermarket carts. The place was a wasteland of packaging: cardboard boxes for stereo systems, pieces of lightweight polystyrene packing like abstract sculptures, paper sacks and polythene bags and tinfoil wrappers, and a host of plastic containers that had contained substances Priest had never used: rinse aid, moisturizer, conditioner, fabric softener, fax toner. He saw a fairy-tale castle made of pink plastic, presumably a child's toy, and he marvelled at the wasteful extravagance of such an elaborate construction.

In Silver River Valley there was never much garbage. They did not use baby carriages or refrigerators, and they rarely bought anything that came in a package. The children would use imagination to make a fairy-tale castle from a tree or a barrel or a stack of timber.

A hazy red sun edged up over the ridge, casting a long shadow of Priest across a rusting bedstead. It made him think of sunrise over the snow peaks of the Sierra Nevada, and he suffered a sharp pang of longing for the cool, pure air of the mountains.

Soon, soon.

Something glinted at his feet. A shiny metal object was half-buried in the earth. Idly, he scraped away the dry earth with the toe of his boot, then bent down and picked up the object. It was a heavy Stillson wrench. It seemed new. Mario might find it useful, Priest thought: it was about the right size for the large-scale machinery of the seismic vibrator. But, of course, the truck would contain a full tool kit with wrenches to fit every nut used in its construction. Mario had no need of a discarded wrench. This was the throwaway society.

Priest dropped the wrench.

He heard a vehicle, but it did not sound like a big truck. He glanced up. A moment later, a tan pickup came over the ridge, bouncing along the rough track. It was a Dodge Ram with a cracked windshield: Mario's car. Priest suffered a pang of unease. What did this mean? Mario was supposed to show up in the seismic vibrator. His own car would be driven north by one of his buddies, unless he had decided to sell it here and buy another in Clovis. Something had gone wrong. 'Shit,' he said. 'Shit.'

He suppressed his feelings of anger and frustration as Mario pulled up and got out of the pickup. 'I brought you coffee,' he said, handing Mario the paper sack. 'What's up?'

Mario did not open the bag. He shook his head sadly. 'I can't do it, man.'

Shit.

Mario went on: 'I really appreciate what you offered to do for me, but I gotta say no.'

What the hell is going on?

Priest gritted his teeth and made his voice sound casual. 'What happened to change your mind, buddy?'

'After you left the bar last night, Lenny gave me this long speech, man, about how much the truck cost, and how I don't gotta give no rides, nor pick up no hitchhikers, and how he's trustin' me, and stuff.'

I can just imagine Lenny, shitfaced drunk and maudlin

—he probably had you nearly in tears, Mario, you dumb son of a bitch.

'You know how it is, Ricky, this is an okay job— hard work and long hours, but the pay is pretty good. I don't want to lose this job.'

'Hey, no problem,' Priest said with forced lightness. 'So long as you can still take me to San Antonio.' *I'll think of something between here and there.*

Mario shook his head. 'I better don't, not after what Lenny said. I ain't taking nobody nowhere in that truck. That's why I brought my own car here, so I can give you a ride back into town.'

And what am I supposed to do now, for Chrissakes?

'So, uh, what do you say, you wanna get going?'

And then what?

Priest had built a castle of smoke, and now he saw it shimmer and dissipate in the light breeze of Mario's guilty conscience. He had spent two weeks in this hot, dusty desert, working at a stupid worthless job, and had wasted hundreds of dollars on air fares and motel bills and disgusting fast food.

He did not have time to do it again.

The deadline was now only two weeks and one day away.

Mario frowned. 'Come on, man, let's go.'

*

'I'm not going to give this place up,' Star had said to Priest, on the day the letter arrived. She sat next to him on a carpet of pine needles at the edge of the vineyard, during the mid-afternoon rest period, drinking cold water and eating raisins made from last year's grapes. 'This is not just a wine farm, not just a valley, not just a commune—this is my whole life. We came here, all those years ago, because we believed that our parents had made a society that was twisted and corrupt and poisoned. And we were right, for Christ's sake!' Her face flushed as she let her passion show, and Priest thought how beautiful she was, still. 'Just *look* at what's happened to the world outside,' she said, raising her voice. 'Violence and ugliness and pollution, presidents who tell lies and break the law, riots and crime and poverty. Meanwhile, we've lived here in peace and harmony, year after year, with no money, no sexual jealousy, no conformist rules. We said that all you need is love, and they called us naive, but we were *right* and they were *wrong*. We *know* we've found the way to live—we've *proved* it.' Her voice had become very precise, betraying her old-money origins. Her father had come from a wealthy family, but had spent his life as a doctor in a slum neighbourhood. Star had inherited his idealism. 'I'll do anything to save our home and our way of life,' she went on. 'I'll die for it, if our children can continue to live here.' Her voice went quiet, but her words were clear, and she spoke with remorseless determination. 'I'll kill for it, too,' she said. 'Do you understand me, Priest? *I will do anything.*'

*

'Are you listening to me?' Mario said. 'You want a ride into town, or not?'

'Sure,' Priest said. *Sure, you lily-livered bastard, you yellow dog coward, you goddam scum of the earth, I want a ride.*

Mario turned around.

Priest's eye fell on the Stillson wrench he had dropped a few minutes earlier.

A new plan unfolded, fully formed, in his mind.

As Mario walked the three paces to his car, Priest stooped and picked up the wrench.

It was about eighteen inches long and weighed four or five pounds. Most of the weight was at the business end, with its adjustable jaws for gripping massive hexagonal nuts. It was made of steel.

He glanced past Mario, along the track that led to the road. There was no one in sight.

No witnesses.

Priest took a step forward just as Mario reached to open the door of his pickup.

He had a sudden disconcerting flash: a photograph of a pretty young Mexican woman in a yellow dress, with a child in her arms and another by her side, and for a split second his resolve wavered as he felt the crushing weight of the grief he would bring into their lives.

Then he saw a worse vision: a pool of black water slowly rising to engulf a vineyard and drown the men, women and children who were tending the vines.

He ran at Mario, raising the wrench high over his head.

Mario was opening the car door. He must have seen something out of the corner of his eye, for when Priest was almost on him he suddenly let out a roar of fear and flung the door wide, partly shielding himself.

Priest crashed into the door, which flew back at Mario. It was a wide, heavy door and it knocked Mario sideways. Both men stumbled. Mario lost his footing and went down on his knees, facing the side of the pickup. His Houston Astros baseball cap landed on the ground. Priest fell backward and sat heavily on the stony earth, dropping the wrench. It landed on a plastic half-gallon Coke bottle and bounced a yard away.

Mario gasped: 'You crazy—' He got to one knee and reached for a handhold to pull his heavy body upright. His left hand closed around the door frame. As he heaved, Priest—still on his butt—drew back his leg and kicked the door as hard as he could with his heel. It slammed on Mario's fingers and bounced open. Mario cried out with pain and fell to one knee, slumping against the side of the pickup.

Priest leaped to his feet.

The wrench gleamed silvery in the morning sun. He snatched it up. He looked at Mario, and his heart filled with rage and hate toward the man who had wrecked his careful plan and put his way of life in jeopardy. He stepped close to Mario and raised the tool.

Mario half-turned toward him. The expression on his young face showed infinite puzzlement, as if he had no understanding of what was happening. He opened his mouth and, as Priest brought the wrench down, he said in a questioning voice: 'Ricky . . .?'

The heavy end of the wrench made a sickening thud as it smashed into Mario's head. His dark hair was thick and glossy, but it made no perceptible difference. His scalp tore, his skull cracked, and the wrench sunk into the soft brain underneath.

But he did not die.

Priest began to be afraid.

Mario's eyes stayed open and focused on Priest. The mystified, betrayed expression barely altered. He seemed to be trying to finish what he had started to say. He lifted one hand, as if to catch someone's attention.

Priest took a frightened step back. 'No!' he said.

Mario said: 'Man . . .'

Priest felt possessed by panic. He lifted the wrench again. 'Die, you motherfucker!' he screamed, and he hit Mario again.

This time the wrench sank in farther. Withdrawing it was like pulling something out of soft mud. Priest felt a surge of nausea when he saw the living grey matter smeared on the adjustable jaws of the tool. His stomach churned and he swallowed hard, feeling dizzy.

Mario fell slowly backward and lay slumped against the rear tyre, motionless. His arms became limp and his jaw slack, but he stayed alive. His eyes locked with Priest's. Blood gushed from his head and ran down his face and into the open neck of his checked shirt. His stare terrified Priest. 'Die,' Priest pleaded. 'For the love of God, Mario, please die.'

Nothing happened.

Priest backed off. Mario's eyes seemed to be begging him to finish the job, but he could not hit him again. There was no logic to it, he just could not lift the wrench.

Then Mario moved. His mouth opened, his body became rigid, and a strangled scream of agony burst from his throat.

It pushed Priest over the edge. He, too, screamed; then he ran at Mario and hit him again and again, in the same place, hardly seeing his victim through the haze of terror that blurred his eyesight.

The screaming stopped and the fit passed.

Priest stepped back, dropping the wrench on the ground.

The corpse of Mario fell slowly sideways until the mess that had been his head hit the ground. His grey brains seeped into the dry soil.

Priest fell to his knees and closed his eyes. 'Dear God Almighty, forgive me,' he said.

He knelt there, shaking. He was afraid that if he opened his eyes he might see Mario's soul going up.

To quiet his brain he recited his mantra: *Ley, tor, pur-doy-kor.* It had no meaning: that was why concentrating hard on it produced a soothing effect. It had the rhythm of a nursery rhyme he recalled from childhood:

> *One, two, three-four-five*
> *Once I caught a fish alive*
> *Six, seven, eight-nine-ten*
> *Then I let him go again.*

When he was chanting to himself, he often slipped from the mantra into the rhyme. It worked just as well.

As the familiar syllables soothed him, he thought about the way his breath entered his nostrils, went through his nasal passages into the back of his mouth, passed along his throat, and descended into his chest, finally penetrating the farthest branches of his lungs, before retracing the entire journey in reverse: lungs, throat, mouth, nose, nostrils, and back out into the open air. When he concentrated fully on the journey of the breath, nothing else came into his head—no visions, no nightmares, no memories.

A few minutes later he stood up, his heart cold, his face set in a determined expression. He had purged himself of emotion: he felt no regret or pity. The murder was in the past, and Mario was just a piece of garbage that he had to dispose of.

He picked up his cowboy hat, brushed off the dirt, and put it on his head.

He found the pickup's tool kit behind the driving seat. He took a screwdriver and used it to detach the licence plates, front and rear. He walked across the dump and buried them in a smouldering mass of garbage. Then he put the screwdriver back in the tool kit.

He bent over the body. With his right hand he grasped the belt of Mario's jeans. With his left he took a fistful of the check shirt. He lifted the body off the ground. He grunted as his back took the strain: Mario was heavy.

The door of the pickup stood open. Priest swung Mario back and forth a couple of times, building up a rhythm, then with one big heave he threw the body into the cabin. It lay over the bench seat, with the heels of the boots sticking out of the open door and the head hanging into the footwell on the passenger side. Blood dripped from the head.

He threw the wrench in after the body.

He wanted to siphon gas out of the pickup's tank. For that he needed a long piece of narrow tubing.

He opened the hood, located the windshield washer fluid, and ripped out the flexible plastic pipe that led from the reservoir to the windshield nozzle. He picked up the half-gallon Coke bottle he had noticed earlier, then walked around to the side of the pickup and unscrewed the gas cap. He fed the tube into the fuel tank, sucked on it until he tasted gasoline, then inserted the end into the Coke bottle. Slowly, it filled with gas.

Gas continued to spill on the ground while he walked to the door of the pickup and emptied the Coke bottle over the corpse of Mario.

He heard the sound of a car.

Priest looked at the dead body soaked in gasoline in the cab of the pickup. If someone came along right now, there was nothing he could say or do to conceal his guilt.

His rigid calm left him. He started to shake, the plastic bottle slipped from his fingers, and he crouched on the ground like a scared child. Trembling, he stared at the track that led to the road. Had

an early riser come to get rid of an obsolete dishwasher, or the plastic playhouse the kids had grown
out of, or the old-fashioned suits of a dead grandfather? The noise of the engine swelled as it came
nearer, and Priest closed his eyes.

Ley, tor, pur-doy-kor.

The noise began to fade. The vehicle had passed
the entrance and gone on down the road. It was just
traffic.

He felt stupid. He stood up, regaining control. *Ley,
tor, pur-doy-kor.*

But the scare made him hurry.

He filled the Coke bottle again and quickly doused
the plastic bench seat and the entire interior of the
cabin with gasoline. He used the remainder of the gas
to lay a trail across the ground to the rear of the truck,
then splashed the last of it on to the side near the fuel
cap. He threw the bottle into the cabin and stepped
back.

He noticed Mario's Houston Astros cap on the
ground. He picked it up and threw it into the cab with
the body.

He took a book of matches from his jeans, struck
one, and used it to light all the others; then he threw
the blazing matchbook into the cab of the pickup and
swiftly backed away.

There was a whoosh of flame and a cloud of black
smoke, and in a second the inside of the cabin was a
furnace. A moment later the flames snaked across the
ground to where the tube was still spilling gas from
the tank. There was another explosion as the gas tank

blew up, rocking the pickup on its wheels. The rear tyres caught light and flames flickered around the oily chassis.

A disgusting smell filled the air, almost like roasting meat. Priest swallowed hard and stood farther back.

After a few seconds the blaze became less intense. The tyres, the seats, and the body of Mario continued to burn slowly.

Priest waited a couple of minutes, watching the flames; then he ventured closer, trying to breathe shallowly to keep the stench out of his nose. He looked inside the cabin of the pickup. The corpse and the seating had congealed together into one vile black mass of ash and melted plastic. When it cooled down, the vehicle would be just another piece of junk that some kids had set fire to.

He knew he had not got rid of all traces of Mario. A casual glance would reveal nothing, but if the cops ever examined the pick-up, they would probably find Mario's belt buckle, the fillings from his teeth, and maybe his charred bones. Some day, Priest realized, Mario might come back to haunt him. But he had done all he could to conceal the evidence of his crime.

Now he had to steal the seismic vibrator.

He turned away from the burning body and started walking.

*

At the commune in Silver River Valley, there was an inner group called the Rice Eaters. There were seven of them, the remnants of those who had survived the desperate winter of 1972–73, when they had been isolated by a blizzard and had eaten nothing but brown rice boiled in melted snow for three straight weeks. On the day the letter came, the Rice Eaters stayed up late in the evening, sitting in the cookhouse, drinking wine and smoking marijuana.

Song, who had been a fifteen-year-old runaway in 1972, was playing an acoustic guitar, picking out a blues riff. Some of the group made guitars in the winter. They kept the ones they liked best, and Paul Beale took the rest to a shop in San Francisco where they were sold for high prices. Star was singing along in a smoky, intimate contralto, making up words, *Ain't gonna ride that no-good train.* She had the sexiest voice in the world, always did.

Melanie sat with them, although she was not a Rice Eater, because Priest did not care to throw her out, and the others did not challenge Priest's decisions. She was crying silently, big tears streaming down her face. She kept saying: 'I only just found you.'

'We haven't given up,' Priest told her. 'There has to be a way to make the Governor of California change his damn mind.'

Oaktree, the carpenter, a muscular black man the same age as Priest, said in a musing tone: 'You know, it ain't that hard to make a nuclear bomb.' He had been in the Marines but he deserted after killing an officer during a training exercise, and he had been here ever since. 'I could do it in a day, if I had some plutonium. We could blackmail the governor—if they don't do what we want, we threaten to blow Sacramento all to hell.'

'No!' said Aneth. She was nursing a child. The boy was three years old: Priest thought it was time he was weaned, but Aneth felt he should be allowed to suckle as long as he wanted to. 'You can't save the world with bombs.'

Star stopped singing. 'We're not trying to save the world. I gave that up in 1969, after the world's press turned the hippie movement into a joke. All I want now is to save *this*, what we have here, our life, so our children can grow up in peace and love.'

Priest, who had already considered and rejected the idea of making a nuclear bomb, said: 'It's getting the plutonium that's the hard part.'

Aneth detached the child from her breast and patted his back. 'Forget it,' she said. 'I won't have anything to do with that stuff. It's deadly!'

Star began to sing again. *Train, train, no-good train.*

Oaktree persisted. 'I could get a job in a nuclear power plant, figure out a way to beat their security system.'

Priest said: 'They would ask you for your résumé. And what would you say you had been doing for the last twenty-five years? Nuclear research at Berkeley?'

'I'd say, I been living with a bunch of freaks and now they need to blow up Sacramento, so I came here to get me some radio friggin' *activity*, man.'

The others laughed. Oaktree sat back in his chair

and began to harmonize with Star: *No, no, ain't gonna ride that no-good train.*

Priest frowned at the flippant air. He could not smile. His heart was full of rage. But he knew that inspired ideas sometimes came out of light-hearted discussions, so he let it run.

Aneth kissed the top of her child's head and said: 'We could kidnap someone.'

Priest said: 'Who? The governor probably has six bodyguards.'

'What about his right-hand man, that guy Albert Honeymoon?' There was a murmur of support: they all hated Honeymoon. 'Or the President of Coastal Electric?'

Priest nodded. This could work.

He knew about stuff like that. It was a long time since he had been on the streets, but he remembered the rules of a rumble: plan carefully, look cool, shock the mark so badly he can hardly think, act fast, and get the hell out. But something bothered him. 'It's too . . . like, low-profile,' he said. 'Say some big-shot gets kidnapped. So what? If you're going to scare people, you can't pussyfoot around, you have to scare them *shitless.*'

He restrained himself from saying more. *When you've got a guy on his knees, crying and pissing his pants and pleading with you, begging you not to hurt him any more, that's when you say what you want; and he's so grateful, he loves you for telling him what he has to do to make the pain stop.* But that was the wrong kind of talk for someone like Aneth.

At this point, Melanie spoke again.

She was sitting on the floor with her back against Priest's chair. Aneth offered her the big spliff that was going around. Melanie wiped her tears, took a long pull on the joint, and passed it up to Priest, then blew out a cloud of smoke and said: 'You know, there are ten or fifteen places in California where the faults in the earth's crust are under such tremendous, like, *pressure* that it would only take a teeny little nudge, or something, to make the tectonic plates slip, and then, BOOM. It's like a giant slipping on a pebble. It's only a little pebble, but the giant is so big that his fall shakes the earth.'

Oaktree stopped singing long enough to say: 'Melanie, baby, what the fuck you talking about?'

'I'm talking about an earthquake,' she said.

Oaktree laughed. *Ride, ride that no-good train.*

Priest did not laugh. Something told him this was important. He spoke with quiet intensity. 'What are you saying, Melanie?'

'Forget kidnapping, forget nuclear bombs,' she said. 'Why don't we threaten the governor with an earthquake?'

'No one can cause an earthquake,' Priest said. 'It would take such an enormous amount of energy to make the earth move.'

'That's where you're wrong. It might take only a small amount of energy, if the force was applied in just the right place.'

Oaktree said: 'How do you know all this stuff?'

'I studied it. I have a master's in seismology. I

should be teaching in a university now. But I married my professor, and that was the end of my career. I was turned down for a doctorate.'

Her tone was bitter. Priest had talked to her about this, and he knew she bore a deep grudge. Her husband had been on the university committee that turned her down. He had been obliged to withdraw from the meeting while her case was discussed, which seemed natural to Priest, but Melanie felt her husband should somehow have made sure of her success. Priest guessed that she had not been good enough to study at doctoral level—but she would believe anything rather than that. So he told her that the men on the committee were so terrified of her combination of beauty and brains that they conspired to do her down. She loved him for letting her believe that.

Melanie went on: 'My husband—soon to be my ex-husband, I hope—developed the stress-trigger theory of earthquakes. At certain points along the fault line, sheer pressure builds up, over the decades, to a very high level. Then it takes only a relatively weak vibration in the earth's crust to dislodge the plates, release all that accumulated energy, and cause an earthquake.'

Priest was captivated. He caught Star's eye. She nodded sombrely. She believed in the unorthodox. It was an article of faith with her that the bizarre theory would turn out to be the truth, the unconventional way of life would be the happiest, and the madcap plan would succeed where sensible proposals foundered.

Priest studied Melanie's face. She had an other-worldly air. Her pale skin, startling green eyes and red hair made her look like a beautiful alien. The first words he had spoken to her had been: 'Are you from Mars?'

Did she know what she was talking about? She was stoned, but sometimes people had their most creative ideas while doping. He said: 'If it's so easy, how come it hasn't already been done?'

'Oh, I didn't say it would be easy. You'd have to be a seismologist to know exactly where the fault was under critical pressure.'

Priest's mind was racing now. When you were in real trouble, sometimes the way out was to do some-thing so weird, so totally unexpected that your enemy was paralysed by surprise. He said to Melanie: 'How would you cause a vibration in the earth's crust?'

'That would be the hard part,' she said.

Ride, ride, ride
I'm gonna ride that no-good train.

*

Walking back to the town of Shiloh, Priest found himself thinking obsessively about the killing: the way the wrench had sunk into Mario's soft brains, the look on the man's face, the blood dripping into the footwell.

This was no good. He had to stay calm and alert. He still did not have the seismic vibrator that was going to save the commune. Killing Mario had been the easy part, he told himself. Next he had to pull the wool over Lenny's eyes. But how?

He was jerked back to the immediate present by the sound of a car.

It was coming from behind him, heading into town.

In these parts, no one walked. Most people would assume his car had broken down. Some would stop and offer him a ride.

Priest tried to think of a reason why he would be walking into town at six thirty on Saturday morning.

Nothing came.

He tried to call on whatever god had inspired him with the idea of murdering Mario, but the gods were silent.

There was nowhere he could be coming *from* within fifty miles—except for the one place he could not speak of, the dump where Mario's ashes lay on the seat of his burned-out pickup.

The car slowed as it came nearer.

Priest resisted the temptation to pull his hat down over his eyes.

What have I been doing?

—I went out into the desert to observe nature.

Yeah, sagebrush and rattlesnakes.

—My car broke down.

Where? I didn't see it.

—I went to take a leak.

This far?

Although the morning air was cool, he began to perspire.

The car passed him slowly. It was a late-model Dodge Neon with a metallic-green paint job and Texas plates. There was one person inside, a man. He could see the driver examining him in the mirror, checking him out. Could be an off-duty cop—

Panic filled him, and he had to fight the impulse to turn and run.

The car stopped and reversed. The driver lowered the nearside window. He was a young Asian man in a business suit. He said: 'Hey, buddy, want a ride?'

What am I going to say? 'No, thanks, I just love to walk.'

'I'm a little dusty,' Priest said, looking down at his jeans. *I fell on my ass trying to kill a man.*

'Who isn't, in these parts?'

Priest got in the car. His hands were shaking. He fastened his seat belt, just to have something to do to disguise his anxiety.

As the car pulled away, the driver said: 'What the heck you doing walking out here?'

I just murdered my friend Mario with a Stillson wrench.

At the last second, Priest thought of a story. 'I had a fight with my wife,' he said. 'I stopped the car and got out and walked away. I didn't expect her to just drive on.' He thanked whatever gods had given him inspiration again. His hands stopped shaking.

'Would that be a good-looking dark-haired woman in a blue Honda that I passed fifteen or twenty miles back?'

Jesus Christ, who are you, the Memory Man?

The guy smiled and said: 'When you're crossing this desert, every car is interesting.'

'No, that ain't her,' Priest said. 'My wife's driving my goddam pickup truck.'

'I didn't see a pickup.'

'Good. Maybe she didn't go too far.'

'She's probably parked down a farm track crying her eyes out, wishing she had you back.'

Priest grinned with relief. The guy had bought his story.

The car reached the edge of town. 'What about you?' Priest said. 'How come you're up early on Saturday morning?'

'I didn't fight with my wife, I'm going home to her. I live in Laredo. I travel in novelty ceramics—decorative plates, figurines, signs saying "Baby's Room", very attractive stuff.'

'Is that a fact?' *What a way to waste your life.*

'We sell them in drugstores mostly.'

'The drugstore in Shiloh won't be open yet.'

'I'm not working today, anyway. But I might stop for breakfast. Got a recommendation?'

Priest would have preferred the salesman to drive through town without stopping, so that he would have no chance to mention the bearded guy he had picked up near the dump. But he was sure to see Lazy Susan's as he drove along Main Street, so there was no point in lying. 'There's a diner.'

'How's the food?'

'Grits are good. It's right after the stop light. You can let me out there.'

A minute later the car pulled into a slantwise slot outside Susan's. Priest thanked the novelty salesman and got out. 'Enjoy your breakfast,' he called as he walked away. *And don't get into conversation with anyone local, for Chrissake.*

A block from the diner was the local office of Ritkin Seismex, the small seismic exploration firm he had been working for. The office was a large trailer in a vacant lot. Mario's seismic vibrator was parked in the lot alongside Lenny's cranberry-red Pontiac Grand Am.

Priest stopped and stared at the truck for a moment. It was a ten-wheeler, with big off-road tyres like dinosaur armour. Underneath a layer of Texas dirt it was bright blue. He itched to jump in and drive it away. He looked at the mighty machinery on the back, the powerful engine and the massive steel plate, the tanks and hoses and valves and gauges. *I could have the thing started in a minute, no keys necessary.* But if he stole it now, every highway patrolman in Texas would be looking for him within a few minutes. He had to be patient. *I'm going to make the earth shake, and no one is going to stop me.*

He went into the trailer.

The office was busy. Two jug team supervisors stood over a computer as a colour map of the area slowly emerged from the printer. Today they would collect their equipment from the field and begin to move it to Clovis. A surveyor was arguing on the phone in Spanish, and Lenny's secretary, Diana, was checking a list.

Priest stepped through an open door into the inner office. Lenny was drinking coffee with a phone to his ear. His eyes were bloodshot and his face blotchy after last night's drinking. He acknowledged Priest with a barely perceptible nod.

Priest stood by the door, waiting for Lenny to finish. His heart was in his mouth. He knew roughly what he was going to say. But would Lenny take the bait? Everything depended on it.

After a minute, Lenny hung up the phone and said: 'Hey, Ricky—you seen Mario this mornin'?' His tone was annoyed. 'He should of left here a half-hour past.'

'Yeah, I seen him,' Priest said. 'I hate to bring you bad news this friggin' early, but he's let you down.'

'What are you talking about?'

Priest told the story that had come into his mind, in a flash of inspiration, just before he picked up the wrench and went after Mario. 'He was missing his wife and kids so bad, he got into his old pickup and left town.'

'Aw, shit, that's great. How did you find out?'

'He passed me on the street, early this morning, headed for El Paso.'

'Why the hell didn't he call me?'

'Too embarrassed about letting you down.'

'Well, I just hope he keeps going across the border and doesn't stop until he drives into the goddam ocean.' Lenny rubbed his eyes with his knuckles.

Priest began to improvise. 'Listen, Lenny, he's got a young family, don't be too hard on him.'

'Hard? Are you serious? He's history.'

'He really needs this job.'

'And I need someone to drive his rig all the damn way to New Mexico.'

'He's saving up to buy a house with a pool.'

Lenny became sarcastic. 'Knock it off, Ricky, you're making me cry.'

'Try this.' Priest swallowed and tried to sound casual. 'I'll drive the damn truck to Clovis if you promise to give Mario his job back.' He held his breath.

Lenny stared at Priest without saying anything.

'Mario ain't a bad guy, you know that,' Priest went on. *Don't gabble, you sound nervous, try to seem relaxed!*

Lenny said: 'You have a Commercial Driver's License, Class B?'

'Since I was twenty-one years old.' Priest took out his billfold, extracted the licence, and tossed it on the desk. It was a forgery. Star had one just like it. Hers was a forgery, too. Paul Beale knew where to get such things.

Lenny checked it, then looked up and said suspiciously: 'So, what are you after? I thought you didn't want to go to New Mexico.'

Don't screw around, Lenny, tell me yes or no! 'Suddenly I could use another five hundred bucks.'

'I don't know . . .'

You son of a bitch, I killed a man for this, come on!

'Would you do it for two hundred?'

Yes! Thank you! Thank you! He pretended to hesitate. 'Two hundred is low for three days' work.'

'It's two days', maybe two and a half. I'll give you two-fifty.'

Anything! Just give me the keys! 'Listen, I'm going to do it anyway, whatever you pay me, because Mario's a nice kid and I want to help him. So, just pay me whatever you genuinely think the job's worth.'

'All right, you sly mother, three hundred.'

'You got a deal.' *And I've got a seismic vibrator.*

Lenny said: 'Hey, thanks for helping me out. I sure appreciate it.'

Priest tried not to beam triumphantly. 'You bet.'

Lenny opened a drawer, took out a sheet of paper, and tossed it over the desk. 'Just fill out this form for insurance.'

Priest froze.

He could not read or write.

He stared at the form in fear.

Lenny said impatiently: 'Come on, take it, for Chrissake, it ain't a rattlesnake.'

I can't understand it, I'm sorry, those squiggles and lines on the paper just jump and dance and I can't make them keep still!

Lenny looked at the wall and spoke to an invisible audience. 'A minute ago I would of swore the man was wide awake.'

Ley, tor, pur-doy-kor.

Priest reached out slowly and took the form.

Lenny said: 'Now what was so hard about that?'

Priest said: 'Uh, I was just thinking about Mario, do you suppose he's okay?'

'Forget him. Fill out the form and get going. I want to see that truck in Clovis.'

'Yeah.' Priest stood up. 'I'll do it outside.'

'Right, let me get to my other fifty-seven friggin' problems.'

Priest walked out of Lenny's room into the main office.

You've had this scene a hundred times before, just calm down, you know how to deal with it.

He stopped outside Lenny's door. Nobody noticed him; they were all busy.

He looked at the form. *The big letters stick up, like trees among the bushes. If they're sticking down, you got the form upside down.*

He had the form upside down. He turned it around.

Sometimes there was a big X, printed very heavy, or written in pencil or red ink, to show you where to put your name; but this form did not have that easy-to-spot mark. Priest could write his name, sort of. It took him a while, and he knew it was kind of a scrawl, but he could do it.

However, he could not write anything else.

As a kid he was so smart he did not need to read and write. He could add up in his head faster than anyone, even though he could not read figures on paper. His memory was infallible. He could always get people to do what he wanted without writing anything down. In school he managed to find ways to avoid reading aloud. When there was a writing assignment he might get another kid to do it for him, but if that failed he had a thousand excuses, and the teachers eventually shrugged and said that if a child really did not want to work they could not force him. He got a reputation for laziness, and when he saw a crisis approaching he would play hooky.

Later on, he had managed to run a thriving liquor

wholesaling business. He never wrote a letter, but did everything on the phone and in person. He kept dozens of phone numbers in his head until he could afford a secretary to place calls for him. He knew exactly how much money was in the till, and how much in the bank. If a salesman presented him with an order form, he would say: 'I'll tell you what I need and you fill out the form.' He had an accountant and a lawyer to deal with the government. He had made a million dollars at the age of twenty-one. He had lost it all by the time he met Star and joined the commune —not because he was illiterate, but because he defrauded his customers and failed to pay his taxes and borrowed money from the Mob.

Getting an insurance form filled out had to be easy.

He sat down in front of Lenny's secretary's desk and smiled at Diana. 'You look tired this morning, honey,' he said.

She sighed. She was a plump blonde in her thirties, married to a roustabout, with three teenage kids. She was quick to rebuff crude advances from the men who came into the trailer, but Priest knew she was susceptible to polite charm. 'Ricky, I got so much to do this morning, I wish I had two brains.'

He put on a crestfallen look. 'That's bad news—I was going to ask you to help me with something.'

She hesitated, then smiled ruefully. 'What is it?'

'My handwriting's so poor, I wanted you to fill out this form for me. I sure hate to trouble you when you're so busy.'

'Well, I'll make a deal with you.' She pointed to a

neat stack of carefully labelled cardboard boxes up against the wall. 'I'll help you with the form, if you'll put all those files in the green Chevy Astrovan outside.'

'You got it,' Priest said gratefully. He gave her the form.

She looked at it. 'You going to drive the seismic vibrator?'

'Yeah, Mario got homesick and went to El Paso.'

She frowned. 'That's not like him.'

'It sure ain't. I hope he's okay.'

She shrugged and picked up her pen. 'Now, first we need your full name, and date and place of birth.'

Priest gave her the information and she filled out the blanks on the form. It was easy. Why had he panicked? It was just that he had not expected the form. Lenny had surprised him, and for a moment he had given way to fear.

He was experienced at concealing his disability. He even used libraries. That was how he had found out about seismic vibrators. He had gone to the Central Library on I Street in downtown Sacramento—a big, busy place where his face probably would not be remembered. At the reception desk he had learned that science was up on the second floor. There, he had suffered a stab of anxiety when he looked at the long aisles of bookshelves and the rows of people sitting at computer screens. Then he caught the eye of a friendly looking woman librarian of about his own age. 'I'm looking for information on seismic exploration,' he had said with a warm smile. 'Could you help me?'

She had taken him to the right shelf, picked out a

book, and with a little encouragement found the relevant chapter. 'I'm interested in how they generate the shock waves,' he had explained. 'I wonder if this book has that information.'

She had leafed through the pages with him. 'There seem to be three ways,' she had said. 'An underground explosion, a weight drop, or a seismic vibrator.'

'Seismic vibrator?' he had said, with just the hint of a twinkle in his eye. 'What's that?'

She had pointed to a photograph. Priest stared, fascinated. The librarian said: 'It looks pretty much like a truck.'

To Priest it had looked like a miracle.

'Can I photocopy some of these pages?' he had asked.

'Sure.'

If you were smart enough, there was always a way to get someone else to do the reading and writing.

Diana finished the form, drew a big X next to a dotted line, handed the paper to him and said: 'You sign here.'

He took her pen and wrote laboriously. The 'R' for Richard was like a showgirl with a big bust kicking out one leg. Then the 'G' for Granger was like a billhook with a big round blade and a short handle. After 'RG' he just did a wavy line like a snake. It was not pretty, but people accepted it. A lot of folk signed their names with a scrawl, he had learned: signatures did not have to be written clearly, thank God.

This was why his forged licence had to be in his own name: it was the only one he could write.

He looked up. Diana was watching him curiously, surprised at how slowly he wrote. When she caught his eye, she reddened and looked away.

He gave her back the form. 'Thanks for your help, Diana, I sure appreciate it.'

'You're welcome. I'll get you the keys to the truck as soon as Lenny gets off the phone.' The keys were kept in the boss's office.

Priest remembered that he had promised to move the boxes for her. He picked one up and took it outside. The green van stood in the yard with its rear door open. He loaded the box and went back for another.

Each time he came back in, he checked her desk. The form was still there, and no keys were visible.

After he had loaded all the boxes, he sat in front of her again. She was on the phone, talking to someone about motel reservations in Clovis.

Priest ground his teeth. He was almost there, he nearly had the keys in his hand, and he was listening to crap about motel rooms! He forced himself to sit still.

At last she hung up. 'I'll ask Lenny for those keys,' she said. She took the form into the inner office.

A fat bulldozer driver called Chew came in. The trailer shook with the impact of his work boots on the floor. 'Hey, Ricky,' he said. 'I didn't know you were married.' He laughed. The other men in the office looked up, interested.

Shit, what's this? Priest said: 'Now where did you hear a thing like that?'

'Saw you get out of a car outside Susan's a while back. Then I had breakfast with the salesman that gave you a ride.'

Damn, what did he tell you?

Diana emerged from Lenny's office with a key ring in her hand. Priest wanted to snatch it from her, but he pretended to be more interested in talking to Chew.

Chew went on: 'You know, Susan's western omelette is really something.' He lifted his leg and farted, then looked up and saw the secretary standing in the doorway, listening. 'Scuse me, Diana. Anyhow, this youngster was saying how he picked you up out near the dump.'

Hell!

'You were walking in the desert alone at six thirty, on account of how you quarrelled with your wife and stopped the car and got out.' Chew looked around the other men, making sure he had their attention. 'Then she up and drove off and left you there!' He grinned broadly and the others laughed.

Priest stood up. He did not want people remembering that he was out near the dump on the day Mario disappeared. He needed to kill this talk dead. He put on a hurt look. 'Well, Chew, I'm going to tell you something. If I ever happen to learn anything about your private affairs, specially something a little embarrassing, I promise I won't shout about it all over the office. Now what do you think of that?'

Chew said: 'Ain't no call to get sensitive.'

The other men looked shamefaced. No one wanted to talk about this any more.

There was an awkward silence. Priest did not want to exit in a bad atmosphere, so he said: 'Hell, Chew, no hard feelings.'

Chew shrugged. 'No offence intended, Ricky.'

The tension eased.

Diana handed Priest the keys to the seismic vibrator.

He closed his fist over the bunch. 'Thank you,' he said, trying to keep the elation out of his voice. He could hardly wait to get out of there and sit behind the wheel. 'Bye, everyone. See you in New Mexico.'

'You drive safely, now, you hear?' Diana said as he reached the door.

'Oh, I'll do that,' Priest replied. 'You can count on it.'

He stepped outside. The sun was up and the day was getting warmer. He resisted the temptation to do a victory dance around the truck. He climbed in and turned over the engine. He checked the gauges. Mario must have filled the tank last night. The truck was ready for the road.

He could not keep the grin off his face as he pulled out of the yard.

He drove out of town, moving up through the gears, and headed north, following the route Star had taken in the Honda.

As he approached the turn-off for the dump he began to feel strange. He imagined Mario at the side of the road, with grey brains seeping out of the hole in his head. It was a stupid, superstitious thought, but he could not shake it. His stomach churned. For a moment he felt weak, too weak to drive. Then he pulled himself together.

Mario was not the first man he had killed.

Jack Kassner had been a cop, and he had robbed Priest's mother.

Priest's mother had been a whore. She had been only thirteen years old when she gave birth to him. By the time Ricky was fifteen, she was working with three other women out of an apartment over a dirty book-store on Seventh Street in the Skid Row neighbourhood of downtown Los Angeles. Jack Kassner was a vice squad detective who came once a month for his shake-down money. He usually took a free blow job at the same time. One day he saw Priest's mother getting the bribe money out of the box in the back room. That night the vice squad raided the apartment, and Kas-sner stole fifteen hundred dollars, which was a lot of money in the sixties. Priest's mother did not mind doing a few days in the slammer but she was heart-broken to lose all the money she had saved. Kassner told the women that if they complained he would slap them with drug-trafficking charges and they would all go down for a couple of years.

Kassner thought he was in no danger from three B-girls and a kid. But the next evening, as he stood in the men's room of the Blue Light bar on Broadway, pissing away a few beers, little Ricky Granger stuck a razor-sharp six-inch knife in his back, easily slicing through the black mohair suit jacket and the white nylon shirt and penetrating the kidney. Kassner was in so much pain he never got his hand on his gun. Ricky stabbed him several more times, quickly, as the cop lay on the wet concrete floor of the men's room vomiting blood; then he rinsed his blade under the tap and walked out.

Looking back, Priest marvelled at the cool assurance of his fifteen-year-old self. It had taken only fifteen or twenty seconds, but during that time anyone might have stepped into the room. However, he had felt no fear, no shame, no guilt.

But after that he had been afraid of the dark.

He was not in the dark very much, in those days. The lights usually stayed on all night in his mother's apartment. But sometimes he would wake up a little before dawn on a slow night, like a Monday, and find that everyone was asleep and the lights were out; and then he would be possessed by blind irrational terror, and would blunder around the room, bumping into furry creatures and touching strange clammy surfaces, until he found the light switch, and sat down on the edge of the bed, panting and perspiring, slowly recovering as he realized that the clammy surface was the mirror and the furry creature his fleece-lined jacket.

He had been afraid of the dark until he found Star.

He recalled a song that had been a hit the year he met her, and he began to sing:

Smoke on the water . . .

The band was Deep Purple, he recalled. Everyone was playing their album that summer.

It was a good apocalyptic song to sing at the wheel of a seismic vibrator.

Smoke on the water
A fire in the sky . . .

He passed the entrance to the dump and drove on, heading north.

*

'We'll do it tonight,' Priest had said. 'We'll tell the governor there'll be an earthquake four weeks from today.'

Star was dubious. 'We're not even sure this is possible. Maybe we should do everything else first, get all our ducks lined up in a row, *then* issue the ultimatum.'

'Hell, no!' Priest said. The suggestion angered him. He knew that the group had to be led. He needed to get them committed. They had to go out on a limb, take a risk, and feel there was no turning back. Otherwise, tomorrow they would think of reasons to get scared and back out.

They were fired up now. The letter had arrived today and they were all angry and desperate. Star was grimly determined; Melanie was in a fury; Oaktree was ready to declare war; Paul Beale was reverting to his street hoodlum type. Song had hardly spoken, but she was the helpless child of the group, and would go along with the others. Only Aneth was opposed, and her opposition would be feeble because she was a weak person. She would be quick to raise objections, but she would back down even faster.

Priest himself knew with cold certainty that if this place ceased to exist his life would be over.

Now Aneth said: 'But an earthquake might kill people.'

Priest said: 'I'll tell you how I figure this will pan out. I guess we'll have to cause a small, harmless tremor, out in the desert somewhere, just to prove we can do what we say. Then, when we threaten a second earthquake, the governor will negotiate.'

Aneth turned her attention back to her child.

Oaktree said: 'I'm with Priest. Do it tonight.'

Star gave in. 'How should we make the threat?'

'An anonymous phone call or letter, I guess,' Priest said. 'But it has to be impossible to trace.'

Melanie said: 'We could post it on an Internet bulletin board. If we used my laptop and mobile phone, no one could possibly trace it.'

Priest had never seen a computer until Melanie arrived. He threw a questioning glance at Paul Beale, who knew all about such things. Paul nodded and said: 'Good idea.'

'All right,' Priest said. 'Get your stuff.'

Melanie went off.

'How will we sign the message?' Star said. 'We need a name.'

Song said: 'Something that symbolizes a peace-loving group who have been driven to take extreme measures.'

'I know,' Priest said. 'We'll call ourselves the Hammer of Eden.'

It was just before midnight on the 1st of May.

*

Priest became tense as he reached the outskirts of San Antonio. In the original plan, Mario would have driven the truck as far as the airport. But now Priest was alone as he entered the maze of freeways that encircled the city, and he began to sweat.

There was no way he could read a map.

When he had to drive an unfamiliar road, he always took Star with him to navigate. She and the other Rice Eaters knew he could not read. The last time he drove alone on strange roads had been in the late autumn of 1972 when he fled from Los Angeles and finished up, by accident, at the commune in Silver River Valley. He had not cared where he went, then. In fact he would have been happy to die. But now he wanted to live.

Even road signs were difficult for him. If he stopped and concentrated for a while, he could tell the difference between 'East' and 'West' or 'North' and 'South'. Despite his remarkable ability to calculate in his head, he could not read numbers without staring hard and thinking long. With an effort, he could recognize signs for Route 10: a stick with a circle. But there was a lot of other stuff on road signs that meant nothing to him and confused the picture.

He tried to stay calm, but it was difficult. He liked to be in control. He was maddened by the sense of helplessness and bewilderment that came over him when he lost his way. He knew by the sun which way was north. When he felt he might be going wrong, he pulled into the next gas station or shopping mall and asked for directions. He hated doing it, for people noticed the seismic vibrator—it was a big rig, and the machinery on the back looked kind of intriguing— and there was a danger he would be remembered. But he had to take the risk.

And the directions were not always helpful. Gas station attendants would say things like: 'Yeah, easy, just follow Corpus Christi highway until you see a sign for Brooks Air Force base.'

Priest just forced himself to remain calm, keep asking questions, and hide his frustration and anxiety. He played the part of a friendly but stupid truck driver, the kind of person who would be forgotten by the next day. And eventually he got out of San Antonio on the right road, sending up prayers of thanks to whatever gods might be listening.

A few minutes later, passing through a small town, he was relieved to see the blue Honda parked at a McDonald's restaurant.

He hugged Star gratefully. 'What the hell happened?' she said worriedly. 'I expected you a couple of hours ago!'

He decided not to tell her he had killed Mario. 'I got lost in San Antonio,' he said.

'I was afraid of that. When I came through I was surprised how complicated the freeway system was.'

'I guess it's not half as bad as San Francisco, but I know San Francisco.'

'Well, you're here now. Let's order coffee and get you calmed down.'

Priest bought a beanburger and got a free plastic

clown which he put carefully in his pocket for his six-year-old son, Smiler.

When they drove on, Star took the wheel of the truck. They planned to drive nonstop, all the way to California. It would take at least two days and nights, maybe more. One would sleep while the other drove. They had some amphetamines to combat drowsiness.

They left the Honda in the McDonald's lot. As they pulled away, Star handed Priest a paper bag, saying: 'I got you a present.'

Inside was a pair of scissors and a battery-powered electric shaver.

'Now you can get rid of that damn beard,' she said.

He grinned. He turned the rear-view mirror toward himself and started to cut. His hair grew fast and thick, and the bushy beard and moustache had made him round-faced. Now his own face gradually re-emerged. With the scissors he trimmed the hair down to a stubble, then he used the shaver to finish the job. Finally he took off his cowboy hat and undid his plait.

He threw the hat out the window and looked at his reflection. His hair was pushed back from a high forehead, and fell in waves around a gaunt face. He had a nose like a blade, and hollow cheeks, but he had a sensual mouth—many women had told him that. However, it was his eyes they usually talked about. They were dark brown, almost black, and people said they had a forceful, staring quality that could be mesmerizing. Priest knew it was not the eyes themselves, but the intensity of the look that could captivate

a woman: he gave her the feeling that he was concentrating powerfully on her and nothing else. He could
do it to men, too. He practised the Look now, in the
mirror.

'Handsome devil,' Star said—laughing at him, but
in a nice way, affectionate.

'Smart, too,' Priest said.

'I guess you are. You got us this machine, anyway.'

Priest nodded. 'And you ain't seen nothing yet.'

CHAPTER TWO

I N THE Federal Building at 450 Golden Gate
Avenue in San Francisco, early on Monday morning, FBI agent Judy Maddox sat in a courtroom on the
fifteenth floor, waiting.

The court was furnished in blond wood. New courtrooms always were. They generally had no windows, so
the architects tried to make them brighter by using
light colours. That was her theory. She spent a lot of
time waiting in courtrooms. Most law enforcement
personnel did.

She was worried. In court she was often worried.
Months of work, sometimes years, went into preparing
a case, but there was no telling how it would go once
it got to court. The defence might be inspired or
incompetent, the judge a sharp-eyed sage or a senile
old fool, the jury a group of intelligent, responsible
citizens or a bunch of lowlife jerks who ought to be
behind bars themselves.

Four men were on trial today: John Parton, Ernest
'Taxman' Dias, Foong Lee, and Foong Ho. The Foong
brothers were the big-time crooks, the other two their
executives. In cooperation with a Hong Kong triad,
they had set up a network for laundering money from

the northern California dope industry. It had taken Judy a year to figure out how they were doing it and another year to prove it.

She had one big advantage when going after Asian crooks: she looked Oriental. Her father was a green-eyed Irishman, but she took more after her late mother, who had been Vietnamese. Judy was slender and dark-haired, with an upward slant to her eyes. The middle-aged Chinese gangsters she had been investigating had never suspected that this pretty little half-Asian girl was a hotshot FBI agent.

She was working with an assistant US attorney whom she knew unusually well. His name was Don Riley, and until a year ago they had been living together. He was her age, thirty-six, and he was experienced, energetic, and as smart as a whip.

She had thought they had a watertight case. But the accused men had hired the top criminal law firm in the city and put together a clever, vigorous defence. Their lawyers had undermined the credibility of witnesses who were, inevitably, from the criminal milieu themselves; and they had exploited the documentary evidence amassed by Judy to confuse and bewilder the jury.

Now neither Judy nor Don could guess which way it would go.

Judy had a special reason to be worried about this case. Her immediate boss, the supervisor of the Asian Organized Crime squad, was about to retire, and she had applied for the job. The overall head of the San Francisco office, the Special Agent in Charge, or SAC, would support her application, she knew. But she had a rival: Marvin Hayes, another high-flying agent in her age group. And Marvin also had powerful support: his best friend was the Assistant Special Agent in Charge responsible for all the organized crime and white-collar crime squads.

Promotions were granted by a career board, but the opinions of the SAC and ASACs carried a lot of weight. Right now the contest between Judy and Marvin Hayes was close.

She wanted that job. She wanted to rise far and fast in the FBI. She was a good agent, she would be an outstanding supervisor, and one of these days she would be the best SAC the Bureau had ever had. She was proud of the FBI but she knew she could make it better: with faster introduction of new techniques like profiling, streamlined management systems, and—most of all—by getting rid of agents like Marvin Hayes.

Hayes was the old-fashioned type of law enforcement officer: lazy, brutal, and unscrupulous. He had not put as many bad guys in jail as Judy, but he had made more high-profile arrests. He was good at insinuating himself into a glamorous investigation and quick to distance himself from a case that was going south.

The SAC had hinted to Judy that she would get the job, rather than Marvin, if she won her case today.

In court with Judy were most of the team on the Foong case: her supervisor, the other agents who had worked with her, a linguist, the squad secretary, and two San Francisco Police Department detectives. To her suprise, neither the ASAC nor the SAC was there. This was a big case, and the result was important to both of them. She felt a twinge of unease. She wondered if something was going on at the office that she did not know about. She decided to step outside and call. But before she got to the door, the clerk of the court entered and announced that the jury was about to return. She sat down again.

A moment later Don came back in, smelling of cigarettes: he had started smoking again since they split. He gave her shoulder an encouraging squeeze. She smiled at him. He looked nice, with his neat short haircut, dark blue suit, white button-down shirt, and dark red Armani tie. But there was no chemistry, no zing: she no longer wanted to muss his hair and undo his tie and slide her hand inside the white shirt.

The defence lawyers returned, the accused men were walked into the dock, the jury entered, and at last the judge emerged from his chambers and took his seat.

Judy crossed her fingers under the table.

The clerk stood up. 'Members of the jury, have you reached a verdict?'

Absolute silence descended. Judy realized she was tapping her foot. She stopped.

The foreman, a Chinese shopkeeper, stood up. Judy had spent many hours wondering whether he would sympathize with the accused because two of them were Chinese, or hate them for dishonouring the race. In a quiet voice he said: 'We have.'

'And how do you find the accused—guilty or not guilty?'

'Guilty as charged.'

There was a second of silence as the news sank in. Behind her, Judy heard a groan from the dock. She resisted the impulse to whoop with joy. She looked at Don, who was smiling broadly at her. The expensive defence lawyers shuffled papers and avoided each other's eyes. Two reporters got up and left hastily, heading for the phones.

The judge, a thin, sour-faced man of around fifty, thanked the jury and adjourned the case for sentencing in a week's time.

I did it, Judy thought. I won the case, I put the bad guys in jail, and my promotion is in the bag. Supervising Special Agent Judy Maddox, only thirty-six, a rising star.

'All stand,' the clerk said.

The judge went out.

Don hugged Judy.

'You did a great job,' she told him. 'Thanks.'

'You gave me a great case,' he said.

She could tell he wanted to kiss her, so she stepped back a pace. 'Well, we both did good,' she said.

She turned to her colleagues and went around them all, shaking hands and hugging and thanking them for their work. Then the defence lawyers came over. The senior of the two was David Fielding, a partner in the firm of Brooks Fielding. He was a distinguished-looking man of about sixty. 'Congratulations, Ms Maddox, on a well-deserved win,' he said.

'Thank you,' she said. 'It was closer than I expected. I thought I had it buttoned up until you got started.'

He acknowledged the compliment with a tilt of his well-groomed head. 'Your preparation was immaculate. Were you trained as a lawyer?'

'I went to Stanford Law School.'

'I thought you must have a law degree. Well, if you ever get tired of the FBI, please come and see me. With my firm you could be earning three times your present salary in less than a year.'

She was flattered, but she also felt condescended to, so her reply was sharp. 'That's a nice offer, but I want to put bad guys in jail, not keep them out.'

'I admire your idealism,' he said smoothly, and turned to speak to Don.

Judy realized she had been waspish. It was a fault of hers, she knew. But what the hell, she did not want a job with Brooks Fielding.

She picked up her briefcase. She was eager to share her victory with the SAC. The San Francisco field office of the FBI was in the same building as the court, on two lower floors. As she turned to leave, Don grabbed her arm. 'Have dinner with me?' he said. 'We ought to celebrate.'

She did not have a date. 'Sure.'

'I'll make a reservation and call you.'

As she left the room, she remembered the feeling she had had earlier, that he wanted to kiss her; and she wished she had invented an excuse.

As she entered the lobby of the FBI office she wondered again why the SAC and the ASAC had not come to court for the verdict. There was no sign of unusual activity here. The carpeted corridors were quiet. The robot mailman, a motorized cart, hummed from door to door on its predetermined route. For a law enforcement agency, they had fancy premises. The difference between the FBI and a police precinct house was like the difference between corporate head-quarters and the factory floor.

She headed for the SAC's office. Milton Lestrange had always had a soft spot for her. He had been an early supporter of women agents, who now numbered ten per cent of agents. Some SACs barked orders like army generals, but Milt was always calm and courteous.

As soon as she entered his outer office she knew something was wrong. His secretary had obviously been crying. Judy said: 'Linda, are you okay?' The secretary, a middle-aged woman who was normally coldly efficient, burst into tears again. Judy went to comfort her, but Linda waved her away and pointed to the door of the inner office.

Judy went in.

It was a large room, expensively furnished, with a big desk and a polished conference table. Sitting behind Lestrange's desk, with his jacket off and his tie loosened, was ASAC Brian Kincaid, a big, barrel-chested man with thick white hair. He looked up and said: 'Come in, Judy.'

'What the hell is going on?' she said. 'Where's Milt?'

'I have bad news,' he said, though he did not look too sad. 'Milt is in the hospital. He's been diagnosed with pancreatic cancer.'

'Oh, my God.' Judy sat down.

Lestrange had gone to the hospital yesterday—for a routine check-up, he had said, but he must have known there was something wrong.

Kincaid went on: 'He'll be having an operation, some kind of intestinal bypass, and he won't be back here for a while, at best.'

'Poor Milt!' Judy was shocked. He had seemed like a man at his peak: fit, vigorous, a good boss. Now he had been diagnosed with a deadly illness. She wanted to do something to comfort him, but she felt helpless. 'I guess Jessica's with him,' she said. Jessica was Milt's second wife.

'Yes, and his brother's flying up from Los Angeles today. Here in the office—'

'What about his first wife?'

Kincaid looked irritated. 'I don't know about her. I talked to Jessica.'

'Someone should tell her. I'll see if I can get a number for her.'

'Whatever.' Kincaid was impatient to get off the personal stuff and talk about work. 'Here in the office, there are some changes, inevitably. I've been made Acting SAC in Milt's absence.'

Judy's heart sank. 'Congratulations,' she said, trying for a neutral tone.

'I'm moving you to the Domestic Terrorism desk.'

At first Judy was just puzzled. 'What for?'

'I think you'll do well there.' He picked up the phone and spoke to Linda. 'Ask Matt Peters to come in and see me right away.' Peters was supervisor of the DT squad.

'But I just won my case,' Judy said indignantly. 'I put the Foong brothers in jail today!'

'Well done. That doesn't change my decision.'

'Wait a minute. You know I've applied for the job of supervisor in the Asian Organized Crime squad. If I get moved off the squad now, it's going to look like I had some kind of problem.'

'I think you need to broaden your experience.'

'And *I* think *you* want Marvin to get the Asian desk.'

'You're right. I believe Marvin is the best person for that job.'

What a jerk, Judy thought furiously. He gets made boss and the first thing he does is use his new power to promote a buddy. 'You can't do this,' she said. 'We have Equal Employment Opportunity rules.'

'Go ahead, make a complaint,' Kincaid said. 'Marvin is better qualified than you.'

'I've put a hell of a lot more bad guys in jail.'

Kincaid gave a complacent smile and played his trump card. 'But he's spent two years at headquarters in Washington.'

He was right, Judy thought despairingly. She had never worked at FBI headquarters. And although it was not an absolute requirement, headquarters experience was thought desirable in a supervisor. So there was no point in her making an Equal Opportunity complaint. Everyone knew she was the better agent, but Marvin looked better on paper.

Judy fought back tears. She had worked her socks off for two years and scored a major victory against organized crime, and now she was being cheated of her reward by this creep.

Matt Peters came in. He was a stocky guy of about forty-five, bald, wearing a short-sleeved shirt and a tie. Like Marvin Hayes, he was close to Kincaid. Judy began to feel surrounded.

'Congratulations on winning your case,' Peters said to Judy. 'I'll be glad to have you on my squad.'

'Thank you.' Judy could not think what else to say.

Kincaid said: 'Matt has a new assignment for you.'

Peters had a file under his arm, and now he handed it to Judy. 'The governor has received a terrorist threat from a group calling itself the Hammer of Eden.'

Judy opened the file but she could hardly make out the words. She was shaking with anger and an overwhelming sense of futility. To cover her emotions she tried to talk about the case. 'What are they demanding?'

'A freeze on the building of new power plants in California.'

'Nuclear plants?'

'Any kind. They gave us four weeks to reply. They say they're the radical offshoot of the Green California Campaign.'

Judy tried to concentrate. Green California was a legitimate environmental pressure group based in San Francisco. It was hard to believe they would do something like this. But all such organizations were capable of attracting nutcases. 'And what's the threat?'

'An earthquake.'

She looked up from the file. 'You're putting me on.'

Matt shook his bald head.

Because she was angry and upset, she did not bother to sweeten her words. 'This is stupid,' she said bluntly. 'No one can *cause* an earthquake. They might as well threaten us with three feet of snow.'

He shrugged. 'Check it out.'

Judy knew that high-profile politicians received threats every day. Messages from crazies were not investigated by the FBI unless there was something special about them. 'How was this threat communicated?'

'It appeared on an Internet bulletin board on the first of May. It's all in the file.'

She looked him in the eye. She was in no mood to take any crap. 'There's something you're not telling me. This threat has no credibility whatsoever.' She looked at her watch. 'Today is the twenty-fifth. We've ignored the message for three-and-a-half weeks. Now, suddenly, with four days left to the deadline, we're worried?'

'John Truth saw the bulletin board—surfing the Net, I guess. Maybe he was desperate for a hot new topic. Anyway, he talked about the threat on his show Friday night, and he got a lot of calls.'

'I get it.' John Truth was a controversial talk radio host. The show came out of San Francisco, but it was syndicated live on stations all over California. Judy became even angrier. 'John Truth pressured the governor to do something about the terrorist message. The governor responded by calling in the FBI to investigate. So we have to go through the motions of an investigation that no one really believes in.'

'That's about it.'

Judy took a deep breath. She addressed Kincaid, not Peters, because she knew this was his doing. 'This office has been trying to nail the Foong brothers for twenty years. Today I put them in jail.' She raised her voice. 'And now you give me a bullshit case like this?'

Kincaid looked pleased with himself. 'If you want to be in the Bureau, you'll have to learn to take the rough with the smooth.'

'I learned, Brian!'

'Don't yell.'

'I learned,' she repeated in a lower voice. 'Ten years ago, when I was new and inexperienced and my supervisor didn't know how far he could rely on me, I was given assignments like this—and I took them cheerfully, and did them conscientiously, and proved that I goddam well deserve to be trusted with real work!'

'Ten years is nothing,' Kincaid said. 'I've been here twenty-five.'

She tried reasoning with him. 'Look, you've just been put in charge of this office. Your first act is to give one of your best agents a job that should have gone to a rookie. Everyone will know what you've done. People will think you've got some kind of grudge.'

'You're right, I just got this job. And you're already telling me how to do it. Get back to work, Maddox.'

She stared at him. Surely he would not just dismiss her.

He said: 'This meeting is over.'

Judy could not take it. Her rage boiled over.

'It's not just this meeting that's over,' she said. She stood up. 'Fuck you, Kincaid.'

A look of astonishment came over his face.

Judy said: 'I quit.'

And then she walked out.

*

'You said that?' Judy's father said.

'Yeah. I knew you'd disapprove.'

'You were right about that, anyway.'

They were sitting in the kitchen, drinking green tea. Judy's father was a detective with the San Francisco police. He did a lot of undercover work. He was a powerfully built man, very fit for his age, with bright green eyes and grey hair in a ponytail.

He was close to retirement, and dreading it. Law enforcement was his life. He wished he could remain a cop until he was seventy. He was horrified by the idea of his daughter quitting when she did not have to.

Judy's parents had met in Saigon. Her father was with the army in the days when American troops there were still called 'advisers'. Her mother came from a middle-class Vietnamese family: Judy's grandfather had been an accountant with the Finance Ministry there. Judy's father brought his bride home and Judy was born in San Francisco. As a baby she called her parents

Bo and Me, the Vietnamese equivalent of Daddy and Mommy. The cops caught on to this and her father became known as Bo Maddox.

Judy adored him. When she was thirteen, her mother had died in a car wreck. Since then, Judy had been close to Bo. After she broke up with Don Riley, a year ago, she had moved into her father's house.

She sighed. 'I don't often lose it, you have to admit.'

'Only when it's really important.'

'But now that I've told Kincaid I'm quitting, I guess I will.'

'Now that you've cursed him like that, I guess you'll have to.'

Judy got up and poured more tea for both of them. She was still boiling with fury inside. 'He's such a damn fool.'

'He must be, because he just lost a good agent.' Bo sipped his tea. 'But you're dumber—you lost a great job.'

'I was offered a better one today.'

'Where?'

'Brooks Fielding, the law firm. I could earn three times my FBI salary.'

'Keeping mobsters out of jail!' Bo said indignantly.

'Everyone's entitled to a vigorous defence.'

'Why don't you marry Don Riley and have babies? Grandchildren would give me something to do in retirement.'

Judy winced. She had never told Bo the real story of her breakup with Don. The simple truth was that he had had an affair. Feeling guilty, he had confessed to Judy. It was only a brief fling with a colleague, and Judy had tried to forgive him, but her feelings for Don were not the same afterwards. Never again did she feel the urge to make love to him. She had not felt drawn to anyone else, either. A switch had been thrown somewhere inside her, and her sex drive had closed down.

Bo did not know any of this. He saw Don Riley as the perfect husband: handsome, intelligent, successful, and working in law enforcement.

Judy said: 'Don asked me to have a celebration dinner, but I think I'll cancel.'

'I guess I ought to know better than to tell you who to marry,' Bo said with a rueful grin. He stood up. 'I've got to go. We have a raid going down tonight.'

She did not like it when he worked at night. 'Have you eaten?' she asked anxiously. 'Shall I make you some eggs before you go?'

'No, thanks, honey. I'll get a sandwich later.' He pulled on a leather jacket and kissed her cheek. 'I love you.'

'Bye.'

As the door slammed, the phone rang. It was Don. 'I got us a table at Masa's,' he said.

Judy sighed. Masa's was very swanky. 'Don, I hate to let you down, but I'd rather not.'

'Are you serious? I practically had to offer my sister's body to the maître d' to get a table at this short notice.'

'I don't feel like celebrating. Bad stuff happened at the office today.' She told him about Lestrange getting cancer and Kincaid giving her a dumbass assignment. 'So I'm quitting the Bureau.'

Don was shocked. 'I don't believe it! You *love* the FBI.'

'I used to.'

'This is terrible!'

'Not so terrible. It's time for me to make some money, anyway. I was a hotshot at law school, you know. I got better grades than a couple of people who are earning fortunes now.'

'Sure, help a murderer beat the rap, write a book about it, make a million dollars . . . Is this *you*? Am I speaking to Judy Maddox? Hello?'

'I don't know, Don, but with all this on my mind, I'm not in the mood to go out on the town.'

There was a pause. Judy knew that Don was resigning himself to the inevitable. After a moment he said: 'Okay, but you have to make it up to me. Tomorrow?'

Judy did not have the energy to fence with him any more. 'Sure,' she said.

'Thanks.'

She hung up.

She turned on the TV and looked in the fridge, thinking about dinner. But she did not feel hungry. She took out a can of beer and opened it. She watched TV for three or four minutes before realizing the show was in Spanish. She decided she did not want the beer. She turned off the TV and poured the beer down the sink.

She thought about going to Everton's, the FBI agents' favourite bar. She liked to hang out there, drinking beer and eating hamburgers and swapping war stories. But she was not sure she would be welcome now, especially if Kincaid was there. She was already beginning to feel like an outsider.

She decided to write her résumé. She would go into the office and do it on her computer. Better to be out doing something than sitting at home getting cabin fever.

She picked up her gun, then hesitated. Agents were on duty twenty-four hours a day, and were obliged to be armed except in court, inside a jail, or at the office. *But if I'm no longer an agent, I don't have to go armed.* Then she changed her mind. *Hell, if I see a robbery in progress and I have to drive on by because I left my weapon at home, I'm going to feel pretty stupid.*

It was a standard-issue FBI weapon, a SIG-Sauer P228 pistol. It normally held thirteen rounds of 9mm ammunition, but Judy always racked back the slide and chambered the first bullet, then removed the clip and added an extra round, making fourteen. She also had a Remington model 870 five-chamber shotgun. Like all agents, she did firearms training once a month, usually at the sheriff's range in Santa Rita. Her marksmanship was tested four times a year. The qualification course never gave her any trouble: she had a good eye and a steady hand, and her reflexes were quick.

Like most agents, she had never fired her gun except in training.

FBI agents were investigators. They were highly educated and well paid. They did not dress for combat.

It was perfectly normal to go through an entire twenty-five-year career with the Bureau and never get involved in a shootout or even a fistfight. But they had to be ready for it.

Judy put her weapon into a shoulder bag. She was wearing the *ao dai*, a traditional Vietnamese garment like a long blouse, with a little upright collar and side-slits, always worn over baggy pants. It was her favourite casual wear because it was so comfortable, but she knew it also looked good on her: the white material showed off her shoulder-length black hair and honey-coloured skin, and the close-fitting blouse flattered her petite figure. She would not normally wear it to the office, but it was late in the evening, and anyway she had resigned.

She went outside. Her Chevrolet Monte Carlo was parked at the kerb. It was an FBI car, and she would not be sorry to lose it. When she was a defence lawyer she could get something more exciting—a little European sports car, maybe, a Porsche or an MG.

Her father's house was in the Richmond neighbourhood. It was not very swanky, but an honest cop never got rich. Judy took the Geary Expressway downtown. Rush hour was over and the traffic was light, so she was at the Federal Building in a few minutes. She parked in the underground garage and took the elevator to the twelfth floor.

Now that she was leaving the Bureau, the office took on a cosy familiarity that made her feel nostalgic. The grey carpet, the neatly numbered rooms, the desks and files and computers all spoke of a powerful, well-resourced organization, confident and dedicated. There were a few people working late. She entered the office of the Asian Organized Crime squad. The room was empty. She turned on the lights, sat at her desk, and booted up her computer.

When she thought about writing her résumé, her mind went blank.

There was not much to say about her life before the FBI: just school and two dull years in the legal department of Mutual American Insurance. She needed to give a clear account of her ten years in the Bureau, showing how she had succeeded and progressed. But, instead of an ordered narrative, her memory produced a disjointed series of flashbacks: the serial rapist who had thanked her, from the dock, for putting him in jail where he could do no more harm; a company called Holy Bible Investments that had robbed dozens of elderly widows of their savings; the time she had found herself alone in a room with an armed man who had kidnapped two small children, and she had persuaded him to give her his gun . . .

She could hardly tell Brooks Fielding about those moments. They wanted Perry Mason, not Wyatt Earp.

She decided to write her formal letter of resignation first.

She put the date, then typed: 'To the Acting Special Agent in Charge.'

She wrote: 'Dear Brian: This is to confirm my resignation.'

It hurt.

She had given ten years of her life to the FBI. Other

women had got married and had children, or started their own business, or written a novel, or sailed around the world. She had dedicated herself to being a terrific agent. Now she was throwing it all away. The thought brought tears to her eyes. *What kind of an idiot am I, sitting alone in my office crying to my damn computer?*

Then Simon Sparrow came in.

He was a heavily muscled man with neat short hair and a moustache. He was a year or two older than Judy. Like her, he was casually dressed, in tan chinos and a short-sleeved sports shirt. He had a doctorate in linguistics and had spent five years with the Behavioral Science Unit at the FBI Academy at Quantico, Virginia. His specialty was threat analysis.

He liked Judy and she liked him. With the men in the office he talked men's talk, football and guns and cars, but when he was alone with Judy he noticed and commented on her outfits and her jewellery the way a girlfriend would.

He had a file in his hand. 'Your earthquake threat is *fascinating*,' he said, his eyes glowing with enthusiasm.

She blew her nose. He had surely seen that she was upset, but he was tactfully pretending not to notice.

He went on: 'I was going to leave this on your desk, but I'm glad I've caught you.'

He had obviously been working late to finish his report, and Judy did not want to deflate his keenness by telling him she was quitting. 'Take a seat,' she said, composing herself.

'Congratulations on winning your case today!'

'Thanks.'

'You must be so pleased.'

'I should be. But I had a fight with Brian Kincaid right afterwards.'

'Oh, him.' Simon dismissed their boss with a flap of his hand. 'If you apologize nicely, he'll have to forgive you. He can't afford to lose you, you're too good.'

That was unexpected. Simon was normally more sympathetic. It was almost as if he had known beforehand. But if he knew about the fight, he knew she had resigned. So why had he brought her the report?

Intrigued, she said: 'Tell me about your analysis of the threat.'

'It had me mystified for a while.' He handed her a printout of the message as it had originally appeared on the Internet bulletin board. 'Quantico were puzzled, too,' he added. He would have automatically consulted the Behavioral Science Unit on this, Judy knew.

She had seen the message before: it was in the file Matt Peters had handed her earlier today. She studied it again.

May 1st
To the state governor
  Hi!
  You say you care about pollution and the environment, but you never do nothing about it; so we're going to make you.
  The consumer society is poisoning the planet because you are too greedy, and you got to stop now!

We are the Hammer of Eden, the radical offshoot of the Green California campaign.

We are telling you to announce an immediate freeze on building power plants. No new plants. Period. Or else!

Or else what, you say?

Or else we will cause an earthquake exactly four weeks from today.

Be warned! We really mean it!

—The Hammer of Eden.

It did not tell her much, but she knew that Simon would mine every word and comma for meaning.

'What do you make of it?' he asked.

She thought for a minute. 'I see a nerdy young student with greasy hair, wearing a washed-out Guns n' Roses T-shirt, sitting at his computer fantasizing about making the world obey him, instead of ignoring him the way it always has.'

'Well, that's about as wrong as could be,' Simon said with a smile. 'He's an uneducated low-income man in his forties.'

Judy shook her head in amazement. She was always astonished by the way Simon drew conclusions from evidence she could not even see. 'How do you know?'

'The vocabulary and sentence structure. Look at the salutation. Affluent people don't start a letter with "Hi", they put "Dear Sir". And college graduates generally avoid double negatives such as "you never do nothing".'

Judy nodded. 'So you're looking for Joe Bluecollar,

aged forty-five. That sounds pretty straightforward. What puzzled you?'

'Contradictory indications. Other elements in the message suggest a young middle-class woman. The spelling is perfect. There's a semicolon in the first sentence, which indicates some education. And the number of exclamation points suggests a female— sorry, Judy, but it's the truth.'

'How do you know she's young?'

'Older writers are more likely to use initial capital letters for a phrase such as "State Governor" and hyphenate words such as "offshoot" that young writers run together to make one word. Also, the use of a computer and the Internet suggest someone both young and educated.'

She studied Simon. Was he deliberately getting her interested to stop her resigning? If he was, it wouldn't work. Once she had made a decision, she hated to change her mind. But she was fascinated by the mystery Simon had posed. 'Are you about to tell me this message was written by someone with a split personality?'

'Nope. Simpler than that. It was written by two people: the man dictating, the woman typing.'

'Clever!' Judy was beginning to see a picture of the two individuals behind this threat. Like a hunting dog that scents game, she was tense, alert, the anticipation of the chase already thrilling in her veins. *I can smell these people, I want to know where they are, I'm sure I can catch them.*

But I've resigned.

'I ask myself why he dictates,' Simon said. 'It might come naturally to a corporate executive who was used to having a secretary, but this is just a regular guy.'

Simon spoke casually, as if this was just idle speculation, but Judy knew that his intuitions were often inspired. 'Any theories?'

'I wonder if he's illiterate?'

'He could simply be lazy.'

'True.' Simon shrugged. 'I just have a hunch.'

'All right,' Judy said. 'You've got a nice college girl who is somehow in the thrall of a street guy. Little Red Riding Hood and the big bad wolf. She's probably in danger, but is anyone else? The threat of an earthquake just doesn't seem real.'

Simon shook his head. 'I think we have to take it seriously.'

Judy could not contain her curiosity. 'Why?'

'As you know, we analyse threats according to *motivation*, *intent*, and *target selection*.'

Judy nodded. This was basic stuff.

'*Motivation* is either emotional, or practical. In other words, is the perpetrator doing this just to make himself feel good, or because he wants something?'

Judy thought the answer was pretty obvious. 'On the face of it, these people have a specific goal. They want the state to stop building power plants.'

'Right. And that means they don't really want to hurt anyone. They hope to achieve their aims just by making a threat.'

'Whereas the emotional types would rather kill people.'

'Exactly. Next, *intent* is either political, criminal, or mentally disturbed.'

'Political, in this case, at least on the surface.'

'Right. Political ideas can be a pretext for an act that is basically insane, but I don't get that feeling here, do you?'

Judy saw where he was heading. 'You're trying to tell me these people are rational. But it's insane to threaten an earthquake!'

'I'll come back to that, okay? Finally, *target selection* is either specific or random. Trying to kill the president is specific; going berserk with a machine-gun in Disneyland is random. Taking the earthquake threat seriously, just for the sake of argument, it would obviously kill a lot of people indiscriminately, so it's random.'

Judy leaned forward. 'All right, you've got practical intent, political motivation, and random targeting. What does that tell you?'

'The textbook says these people are either bargaining, or seeking publicity. I say they're bargaining. If they wanted publicity, they wouldn't have chosen to put their message on an obscure bulletin board on the Internet—they would have gone for TV or the newspapers. But they didn't. So I think they simply wanted to communicate with the governor.'

'They're naive if they think the governor reads his messages.'

'I agree. These people display an odd combination of sophistication and ignorance.'

'But they're serious.'

'Yeah, and I've got another reason for believing that. Their demand—for a freeze on new power plants—isn't the kind of thing you would choose for a pretext. It's too down-to-earth. If you were making it up, you'd go for something splashy, like a ban on air-conditioning in Beverly Hills.'

'So who the hell are these people?'

'We don't know. The typical terrorist shows an escalating pattern. He begins with threatening phone calls and anonymous letters; then he writes to the newspapers and TV stations; then he starts hanging around government buildings, fantasizing. By the time he shows up for the White House tour with a Saturday Night Special in a plastic shopping bag, we've got quite a lot of his work on the FBI computer. But not this one. I've had the linguistic fingerprint checked against all past terrorist threats on record at Quantico, but there's no match. These people are new.'

'So we know nothing about them?'

'We know plenty. They live in California, obviously.'

'How do you know that?'

'The message is addressed: "To the state governor". If they were in another state, they would send it to the Governor of California.'

'What else?'

'They're Americans, and there's no indication of any particular ethnic group: their language shows no characteristically black, Asian, or Hispanic features.'

'You left out one thing,' Judy told him.

'What?'

'They're crazy.'

He shook his head.

Judy said: 'Simon, come on! They think they can cause an earthquake. They have to be crazy!'

He said stubbornly: 'I don't know anything about seismology, but I know psychology, and I'm not comfortable with the theory that these people are out of their minds. They're sane, serious, and focused. And that means they're dangerous.'

'I don't buy it.'

He stood up. 'I'm beat. Want to go for a beer?'

'Not tonight, Simon—but thanks. And thanks for the report. You're the best.'

'You bet. So long.'

Judy put her feet up on her desk and studied her shoes. She was sure now that Simon had been trying to persuade her not to resign. Kincaid might think this was a bullshit case, but Simon's message was that the Hammer of Eden might be a genuine threat, a group that really needed to be tracked down and put out of action.

In which case, her career at the FBI was not necessarily over. She could make a triumph of a case that had been given to her as a deliberate insult. That would make her seem brilliant at the same time as it made Kincaid appear dumb. The prospect was enticing.

She put her feet down and looked at her screen. Because she had not touched the keys for a while, her screen saver had come on. It was a photograph of her at the age of seven, with gaps in her teeth and a plastic clip holding her hair back off her forehead. She was sitting on her father's knee. He was still a patrolman then, wearing the uniform of a San Francisco cop. She had taken his cap and was trying to put it on her own head. The picture had been taken by her mother.

She imagined herself working for Brooks Fielding, driving a Porsche, and going to court to defend people like the Foong brothers.

She touched the space bar and the screen saver disappeared. In its place she saw the words she had written: 'Dear Brian: This is to confirm my resignation.' Her hands hovered over the keyboard. After a long pause, she spoke aloud. 'Aw, hell,' she said. Then she erased the sentence and wrote: 'I would like to apologize for my rudeness . . .'

CHAPTER THREE

THE TUESDAY morning sun was coming up over I-80. Priest's 1971 Plymouth 'Cuda headed for San Francisco, its built-in roar making fifty-five miles per hour sound like ninety.

He had bought the car new, at the height of his business career. Then, when his wholesale drinks business collapsed and the IRS was about to arrest him, he had fled with nothing but the clothes he stood up in —a navy business suit, as it happened, with broad lapels and flared pants—and his car. He still had both.

During the hippie era, the only cool car to own was a Volkswagen Beetle. Driving the bright yellow 'Cuda, Priest looked like a pimp, Star used to tell him. So they gave it a trippy paint job: planets on the roof, flowers on the trunk lid, and an Indian goddess on the hood with eight arms trailing over the fenders, all in purple and pink and turquoise. In twenty-five years the colours had faded to a mottled brown, but you could still make out the design, if you looked closely. And now the car was a collectable.

He had set out at 3 a.m. Melanie had slept all the way. She lay with her head in his lap, her fabulously long legs folded on the worn black upholstery. As he drove, he toyed with her hair. She had sixties hair, long and straight with a part in the middle, although she had been born around the time the Beatles split up.

The kid was asleep, too, lying full-length on the back seat, mouth open. Priest's German shepherd dog, Spirit, lay beside him. The dog was quiet, but every time Priest looked back at him he had one eye open.

Priest felt anxious.

He told himself he should feel good. This was like the old days. In his youth he always had something going, some scam, a project, a plan to make money or steal money or have a party or start a riot. Then he discovered peace. But sometimes he felt that life had become too peaceful. Stealing the seismic vibrator had revived his old self. He felt more alive now, with a pretty girl beside him and a battle of wits ahead, than he had for years.

All the same, he was worried.

He had stuck his neck all the way out. He had boasted that he could bend the Governor of California to his will, and he had promised an earthquake. If he failed, he would be finished. He would lose everything that was dear to him, and if he was caught he would be in jail until he was an old man.

But he was extraordinary. He had always known he was not like other people. The rules did not apply to him. He did things no one else thought of.

And he was already halfway to his goal. He had stolen a seismic vibrator. He had killed a man for it, but he had got away with the murder: there had been no repercussions except for occasional nightmares in which Mario got out of his burning pickup, with his clothes alight and fresh blood pouring from his smashed head, and came staggering after Priest.

The truck was now hidden in a lonely valley in the foothills of the Sierra Nevada. Today Priest was going to find out exactly where to place it so as to cause an earthquake.

And Melanie's husband was going to give him that information.

Michael Quercus knew more than anyone else in the world about the San Andreas fault, according to Melanie. His accumulated data was stored on his computer. Priest wanted to steal his back-up disc.

And he had to make sure that Michael would never know what had happened.

For that, he needed Melanie. Which was why he was worried. He had known her only a few weeks. In that short time, he had become the dominant person in her life, he knew; but he had never put her through a test like this. And she had been married to Michael for six years. She might suddenly regret leaving her husband; she might realize how much she missed the dishwasher and the TV; she might be struck by the danger and the illegality of what she and Priest were doing; there was no telling what might happen to someone as bitter and confused and troubled as Melanie.

In the rear seat, her five-year-old son woke up.

Spirit, the dog, moved first, and Priest heard the click of his claws on the plastic of the seat. Then there was a childish yawn.

Dustin, known as Dusty, was an unlucky boy. He suffered from multiple allergies. Priest had not yet seen one of his attacks, but Melanie had described them: Dusty sneezed uncontrollably, his eyes bulged, and he broke out in itchy skin rashes. She carried powerful suppressing drugs, but she said they mitigated the symptoms only partially.

Now Dusty started to fret.

'Mommy, I'm thirsty,' he said.

Melanie came awake. She sat upright, stretching, and Priest glanced at the outline of her breasts in the skimpy T-shirt she wore. She turned around and said: 'Drink some water, Dusty, you have a bottle right there.'

'I don't want water,' he whined. 'I want orange juice.'

'We don't have any goddam juice,' she snapped.

Dusty started to cry.

Melanie was a nervous mother, frightened of doing the wrong thing. She was obsessive about her son's health, so she was overprotective, but at the same time her tension made her cranky with him. She felt sure her husband would one day try to take the boy away from her, so she was terrified of doing anything that would enable him to call her a bad mother.

Priest took charge. He said: 'Hey, whoa, what the heck is that coming up behind us?' He made himself sound really scared.

Melanie looked around. 'It's just a truck.'

'That's what you think. It's *disguised* as a truck, but really it's a Centaurian fighter spacecraft with photon torpedoes. Dusty, I need you to tap three times on the rear window to raise our invisible magnetic armour. Quick!'

Dusty tapped on the window.

'Now, we'll know he's firing his torpedoes if we see an orange light flashing on his port fender. You better watch for that, Dusty.'

The truck was closing on them fast, and a minute later its left side indicator flashed and it pulled out to pass them.

Dusty said: 'It's firing, it's firing!'

'Okay, I'll try to hold the magnetic armour while you fire back! That water bottle is actually a laser gun!'

Dusty pointed the bottle at the truck and made zapping noises. Spirit joined in, barking furiously at the truck as it passed. Melanie started to laugh.

When the truck pulled back into the slow lane ahead of them, Priest said: 'Whew. We were lucky to come out of that in one piece. I think they've given up for now.'

'Will there be any more Centaurians?' Dusty asked eagerly.

'You and Spirit keep watch out the back and let me know what you see, okay?'

'Okay.'

Melanie smiled and said quietly: 'Thanks. You're so good with him.'

I'm good with everyone: men, women, children, and pets.

I got charisma. I wasn't born with it—I learned. It's just a way of making people do what you want. Anything from persuading a faithful wife to commit adultery, all the way down to getting a scratchy kid to stop whining. All you need is charm.

'Let me know what exit to take,' Priest said.

'Just watch for signs to Berkeley.'

She did not know he could not read. 'There's probably more than one. Just tell me where to turn.'

A few minutes later they left the freeway and entered the leafy university town. Priest could feel Melanie's tension rise. He knew that all her rage against society and her disappointment with life some-how centred on this man she had left six months ago. She directed Priest through the intersections to Euclid Avenue, a street of modest houses and apartment buildings probably rented by graduate students and younger faculty.

'I still think I should go in alone,' she said.

It was out of the question. Melanie was not steady enough. Priest could not rely on her when he was beside her, so there was no way he would trust her alone. 'No,' he said.

'Maybe I—'

He allowed a flash of anger to show. 'No!'

'Okay, okay,' she said hastily. She bit her lip.

Dusty said excitedly: 'Hey, this is where Daddy lives!'

'That's right, honey,' Melanie said. She pointed to a low-rise stucco apartment building, and Priest parked outside it.

Melanie turned to Dusty, but Priest forestalled her. 'He stays in the car.'

'I'm not sure how safe—'

'He's got the dog.'

'He might get scared.'

Priest twisted around to speak to Dusty. 'Hey, Lieutenant, I need you and Ensign Spirit to stand guard over our spacecraft while First Officer Mom and I go inside the spaceport.'

'Am I going to see Daddy?'

'Of course. But I'd like a few minutes with him first. Think you can handle the guard duty assignment?'

'You bet!'

'In the space navy, you have to say "Aye, sir!", not "You bet".'

'Aye, sir!'

'Very good. Carry on.' Priest got out of the car.

Melanie got out, but she still looked troubled. 'For Christ's sake don't let Michael know we left his kid in the car,' she said.

Priest did not reply. *You might be afraid of offending Michael, baby, but I don't give a flying fuck.*

Melanie took her purse off the seat and slung it over her shoulder. They walked up the path to the building door. Melanie pressed the entryphone buzzer and held it down.

Her husband was a night owl, she had told Priest. He liked to work in the evening and sleep late. That was why they had chosen to get here before seven o'clock in the morning. Priest hoped Michael would be too bleary-eyed to wonder whether their visit had a hidden purpose. If he got suspicious, stealing his disc might be impossible.

Melanie said he was a workaholic, Priest recalled as they waited for Michael to answer. He spent his days driving all over California checking the instruments that measured small geological movements in the San Andreas and other faults, and the nights inputting the data into his computer.

But what had finally driven her to leave him was an incident with Dusty. She and the child had been vegetarian for two years, and they would eat only organic food and health-store products. Melanie believed the strict diet reduced Dusty's allergy attacks, although Michael was sceptical. Then one day she had discovered that Michael had bought Dusty a hamburger. To her, that was like poisoning the child. She still shook with fury when she told the story. She had left that night, taking Dusty with her.

Priest thought she might be right about the allergy attacks. The commune had been vegetarian ever since the early seventies, when vegetarianism was eccentric. At the time Priest had doubted the value of the diet, but had been in favour of a discipline that set them apart from the world outside. Their grapes were grown without chemicals simply because they had been unable to afford sprays, so they had made a virtue of necessity and called their wine organic, which turned out to be a strong selling point. But he could not help noticing that after a quarter-century of this life the communards were a remarkably healthy bunch. It was rare for them to have a medical emergency they could not cope with themselves. So he was now convinced. But, unlike Melanie, he was not obsessive about diet. He still liked fish, and now and again he would unintentionally eat meat in a soup or a sandwich, and would shrug it off. But if Melanie discovered that her mushroom omelette had been cooked in bacon fat she would throw up.

A grouchy voice came through the intercom. 'Who is it?'

'Melanie.'

There was a buzz, and the building door opened. Priest followed Melanie inside and up the stairs. An apartment was open on the second floor. Michael Quercus stood in the doorway.

Priest was surprised by his appearance. He had been expecting a weedy professorial type, probably bald, wearing brown clothes. Quercus was tall and athletic, around thirty-five, with a head of short black curls and the shadow of a heavy beard on his cheeks. He wore only a towel around his waist, so Priest could see that he had broad, well-muscled shoulders and a flat belly. *They must have made a handsome couple.*

As Melanie reached the top of the stairs, Michael said: 'I've been very worried—where the hell have you been?'

Melanie said: 'Can't you put some clothes on?'

'You didn't say you had company,' he replied coolly. He stayed in the doorway. 'Are you going to answer my question?'

Priest could see he was barely controlling his stored-up rage.

'I'm here to explain,' Melanie said. She was enjoying Michael's fury. *What a screwed-up marriage.* 'This is my friend Priest. May we come in?'

Michael stared at her angrily. 'This had better be pretty fucking good, Melanie.' He turned his back and walked inside.

Melanie and Priest followed him into a small hallway. He opened the bathroom door, took a dark blue cotton robe off a hook, and slipped into it, taking his time. He discarded his towel and tied the belt. Then he led them into the living room.

This was clearly his office. As well as a couch and a TV set, there was a computer screen and keyboard on the table, and a row of electronic machines with blinking lights on a deep shelf. Somewhere in those bland pale-grey boxes was stored the information Priest needed. He felt tantalized. There was no way he could get at it unaided. He had to depend on Melanie.

One wall was entirely taken up with a huge map. 'What the hell is that?' Priest said.

Michael just gave him a who-the-fuck-are-you look and said nothing, but Melanie answered the question. 'It's the San Andreas fault.' She pointed. 'Beginning at Point Arena lighthouse a hundred miles north of here in Mendocino county, all the way south and east, past Los Angeles and inland to San Bernardino. A crack in the earth's crust, seven hundred miles long.'

Melanie had explained Michael's work to Priest. His

speciality was the calculation of pressure at different places along seismic faults. It was partly a matter of precise measurement of small movements in the earth's crust, partly a question of estimating the accumulated energy based on the lapse of time since the last earthquake. His work had won him academic prizes. But a year ago he had quit the university to start his own business, a consultancy offering advice on earthquake hazards to construction firms and insurance companies.

Melanie was a computer wizard and had helped Michael devise his set-up. She had programmed his machine to back up every day between 4 a.m. and 6 a.m., when he was asleep. Everything on his computer, she had explained to Priest, was copied onto an optical disc. When he switched on his screen in the morning, he would take the disc out of the disc drive and put it in a fireproof box. That way, if his computer crashed or the house burned down, his precious data would not be lost.

It was a wonder to Priest that information about the San Andreas fault could be kept on a little disc, but then books were just as much of a mystery. He simply had to accept what he was told. The important thing was that with Michael's disc Melanie would be able to tell Priest where to place the seismic vibrator.

Now they just had to get Michael out of the room long enough for Melanie to snatch the disc from the optical drive.

'Tell me, Michael,' Priest said. 'All this stuff.' He

indicated the map and the computers with a wave of his hand, then fixed Michael with the Look. 'How does it make you *feel*?'

Most people got flustered when Priest gave them the Look and asked them a personal question. Sometimes they gave a revealing answer because they were so disconcerted. But Michael seemed immune. He just looked blankly at Priest and said: 'It doesn't make me *feel* anything, I use it.' Then he turned to Melanie and said: 'Now, are you going to tell me why you disappeared?'

Arrogant prick.

'It's very simple,' she said. 'A friend offered me and Dusty the use of her cabin in the mountains.' Priest had told her not to say which mountains. 'It was a late cancellation of a rental.' Her tone of voice indicated that she did not see why she had to explain something so simple. 'We can't afford vacations, so I grabbed at the chance.'

That was when Priest had met her. She and Dusty had been wandering in the forest and got completely lost. Melanie was a city girl and could not even find her way by the sun. Priest was out on his own that day, fishing for sockeye salmon. It was a perfect spring afternoon, sunny and mild. He had been sitting on the bank of a stream, smoking a joint, when he heard a child crying.

He knew it was not one of the commune children, whose voices he would have recognized. Following the sound, he found Dusty and Melanie. She was close to tears. When she saw Priest she said: 'Thank God, I thought we were going to die out here!'

He had stared at her for a long moment. She was a little weird, with her long red hair and green eyes, but in the cutoff jeans and a halter top she looked good enough to eat. It was magical, coming across a damsel in distress like that when he was alone in the wilderness. If it had not been for the kid, Priest would have tried to lay her right then and there, on the springy mattress of fallen pine needles beside the splashing stream.

That was when he had asked her if she was from Mars. 'No,' she said, 'Oakland.'

Priest knew where the vacation cabins were. He picked up his fishing rod and led her through the forest, following the trails and ridges that were so familiar to him. It was a long walk, and on the way he talked to her, asking sympathetic questions, giving his engaging grin now and again, and found out all about her.

She was a woman in deep trouble.

She had left her husband and moved in with the bass guitarist in a hot rock band; but the bassist had thrown her out after a few weeks. She had no one to turn to: her father was dead and her mother lived in New York with a guy who had tried to get into bed with Melanie the one night she had slept at their apartment. She had exhausted the hospitality of her friends and borrowed all the money they could afford to lend. Her career was a washout and she was working in a supermarket, stacking shelves, leaving Dusty with a neighbour all day. She lived in a slum that was so dirty it gave the kid constant allergy attacks. She needed to move to a place with clean air but she could not find a job outside the city. She was up a blind alley and desperate. She had been trying to calculate the exact overdose of sleeping pills that would kill her and the child when a girlfriend had offered her this vacation.

Priest liked people in trouble. He knew how to relate to them. All you had to do was offer them what they needed, and they became your slaves. He was uncomfortable with confident, self-sufficient types: they were too hard to control.

By the time they reached the cabin it was suppertime. Melanie made pasta and salad, then put Dusty to bed. When the child was asleep, Priest seduced her on the rug. She was frantic with desire. All her pent-up emotional charge was released by sex, and she made love as if it was her last chance ever, scratching his back and biting his shoulders and pulling him deep inside her as if she wanted to swallow him up. It was the most exciting encounter Priest could remember.

Now her supercilious handsome-professor husband was complaining. 'That was *five weeks* ago. You can't just take my son and disappear without even a phone call!'

'You could have called me.'

'I didn't know where you were!'

'I have a mobile.'

'I tried. I couldn't get an answer.'

'The service was cut off because you didn't pay the bill. You're supposed to pay it, we agreed.'

'I was a couple of days late, that's all! They must have turned it back on.'

'Well, you called when it was cut off, I guess.'

This family row was not bringing Priest closer to that disc, he fretted. *Got to get Michael out of the room, some way, any way.* He interrupted to say: 'Why don't we all have some coffee?' He wanted Michael to go into the kitchen to make it.

Michael jerked a thumb over his shoulder. 'Help yourself,' he said brusquely.

Shit.

Michael turned back to Melanie. 'It doesn't matter *why* I couldn't reach you. I couldn't. That's why you have to call me before taking Dusty away on vacation.'

Melanie said: 'Listen, Michael, there's something I haven't told you yet.'

Michael looked exasperated, then sighed and said: 'Sit down, why don't you.' He sat behind his desk.

Melanie sank into a corner of the couch, folding her legs beneath her in a familiar way that made Priest think this had been her regular seat. Priest perched on the arm of the couch, not wanting to sit lower than Michael. *I can't even figure out which of those machines is the disc drive. Come on, Melanie, lose the damn husband!*

Michael's tone of voice suggested he had been through scenes like this with Melanie before. 'All right, make your pitch,' he said wearily. 'What is it this time?'

'I'm going to move to the mountains, permanently. I'm living with Priest and a bunch of people.'

'Where?'

Priest answered that question. He did not want Michael to know where they lived. 'It's in Del Norte county.' That was in the redwood country at the northern end of California. In fact the commune was in Sierra county, in the foothills of the Sierra Nevada, near the eastern border of the state. Both were far from Berkeley.

Michael was outraged. 'You can't take Dusty to live hundreds of miles away from his father!'

'There's a reason,' Melanie persisted. 'In the last four weeks, Dusty hasn't had a single allergy attack. He's healthy in the mountains, Michael.'

Priest added: 'It's probably the pure air and water. No pollution.'

Michael was sceptical. 'It's the desert, not the mountains, that normally suits people with allergies.'

'Don't talk to me about *normally*!' Melanie flared. 'I can't go to the desert—I don't have any money. This is the only place I can afford where Dusty can be healthy!'

'Is Priest paying your rent?'

Go ahead, asshole, insult me, talk about me like I'm not here; and I'll just carry on fucking your sexy wife.

Melanie said: 'It's a commune.'

'Jesus, Melanie, what kind of people have you fallen in with now? First a junkie guitar player—'

'Wait a minute, Blade was not a junkie—'

'Now a godforsaken hippie commune!'

Melanie was so involved in this quarrel that she had forgotten why they were here. *The disc, Melanie, the damn disc!* Priest interrupted again. 'Why don't you ask Dusty how he feels about this, Michael?'

'I will.'

Melanie shot Priest a despairing look.

He ignored her. 'Dusty's right outside, in my car.'

Michael flushed with anger. 'You left my son outside in the car?'

'He's okay, my dog's with him.'

Michael glared furiously at Melanie. 'What the hell is wrong with you?' he shouted.

Priest said: 'Why don't you just go and get him?'

'I don't need your fucking permission to get my own son. Give me the car keys.'

'It's not locked,' Priest said mildly.

Michael stormed out.

'I told you not to tell him Dusty was outside!' Melanie wailed. 'Why did you do it?'

'To get him out of the goddam room,' Priest said. 'Now grab that disc.'

'But you've made him so mad!'

'He was angry already!' This was no good, Priest realized. She might be too frightened to do what was needed. He stood up. He took her hands, pulled her upright, and gave her the Look. 'You don't have to be afraid of him. You're with me now. I take care of you. Be cool. Say your mantra.'

'But—'

'Say it.'

'*Lat hoo, dat soo.*'

'Keep saying it.'

'*Lat hoo, dat soo, lat hoo, dat soo.*' She became calmer.

'Now get the disc.'

She nodded. Still saying her mantra under her breath, she bent over the row of machines on the shelf. She pressed a button and a flat plastic square popped out of a slot.

Priest had noticed before that 'discs' were always square in the world of computers.

She opened her purse and took out another disc that looked similar. 'Shit!' she said.

'What?' Priest said worriedly. 'What's wrong?'

'He's changed his brand!'

Priest looked at the two discs. They seemed the same to him. 'What's the difference?'

'Look, mine is a Sony but Michael's is a Philips.'

'Will he notice?'

'He might.'

'Damn.' It was vital that Michael did not know his data had been stolen.

'He'll probably start work as soon as we've gone. He'll eject the disc and swap it with the one in the fireproof box, and if he looks at them he'll see they're different.'

'And he's sure to connect that with us.' Priest felt a surge of panic. It was all turning to shit.

Melanie said: 'I could buy a Philips disc and come back another day.'

Priest shook his head. 'I don't want to do this again. We might fail again. And we're running out of time. The deadline is three days away. Does he keep spare discs?'

'He should. Sometimes a disc gets corrupted.' She

looked around. 'I wonder where they are.' She stood in the middle of the floor, helpless.

Priest could have screamed with frustration. He had dreaded something like this. Melanie had completely gone to pieces, and they had only a minute or two. He had to get her calmed down fast. 'Melanie,' he said, struggling to make his voice low and reassuring. 'You have two discs in your hand. Put them both in your purse.'

She obeyed him automatically.

'Now close your purse.'

She did that.

Priest heard the building door slam. Michael was on his way back. Priest felt perspiration break out in the small of his back. 'Think: when you were living here, did Michael have a stationery cupboard?'

'Yes. Well, a drawer.'

'Well?' *Wake up, girl!* 'Where is it?'

She pointed to a cheap white chest against the wall.

Priest yanked open the top drawer. He saw a package of yellow pads, a box of cheap ballpoints, a couple of reams of white paper, some envelopes—and an open box of discs.

He heard Dusty's voice. It seemed to come from the vestibule at the entrance to the apartment.

With shaking fingers, he fumbled a disc out of the packet and handed it to Melanie. 'Will this do?'

'Yes, it's a Philips.'

Priest closed the drawer.

Michael walked in with Dusty in his arms.

Melanie stood frozen with the disc in her hand.

117

For God's sake, Melanie, do something!

Dusty was saying: 'And you know what, Daddy? I didn't sneeze in the mountains.'

Michael's attention was fixed on Dusty. 'How about that?' he said.

Melanie regained her composure. As Michael bent to put Dusty down on the couch, she stooped over the disc drive and slid the disc into the slot. The machine whirred softly and drew it in, like a snake eating a rat.

'You didn't sneeze?' Michael said to Dusty. 'Not once?'

'Uh-uh.'

Melanie straightened up. Michael had not seen what she did.

Priest closed his eyes. The relief was overwhelming. They had got away with it. They had Michael's data— and he would never know.

Michael said: 'That dog doesn't make you sneeze?'

'No, Spirit is a clean dog. Priest makes him wash in the stream, and then he comes out and shakes himself and it's like a rainstorm!' Dusty laughed with pleasure as he remembered.

'Is that right?' his father said.

Melanie said: 'I told you, Michael.'

Her voice sounded shaky, but Michael did not seem to notice. 'All right, all right,' he said in a conciliatory tone. 'If it makes such a difference to Dusty's health, we'll just have to work something out.'

She looked relieved. 'Thanks.'

Priest allowed himself the ghost of a smile. It was

all over. His plan had moved another crucial step forward.

Now they just had to hope that Michael's computer did not crash. If that happened, and he tried to retrieve his data from the optical disc, he would discover that it was blank. But Melanie said that crashes were rare. In all probability, there would be no crash today. And tonight the computer would back up again, overwriting the blank disc with Michael's data. By this time tomorrow it would be impossible to tell that a switch had been made.

Michael said: 'Well, at least you came here to talk about it. I appreciate that.'

Melanie would much rather have dealt with her husband on the phone, Priest knew. But her move to the commune was a perfect pretext for visiting Michael. He and Melanie could never have paid a casual social call on her husband without making him suspicious. But this way it would not occur to Michael to wonder why they had come.

In fact, Michael was not the suspicious type, Priest felt sure. He was brainy but guileless. He had no ability to look beneath the surface and see what was really going on in the heart of another human being.

Priest himself had that ability in spades.

Melanie was saying: 'I'll bring Dusty to see you as often as you like, I'll drive down.'

Priest could see into her heart. She was being nice to Michael, now that he had given her what she wanted—she had her head on one side and she was smiling prettily at him—but she did not love him, not any more.

Michael was different. He was angry with her for leaving him, that was clear. But he still cared for her. He was not over her yet, not quite. A part of him still wanted her back. He would have asked her, but he was too proud.

Priest felt jealous.

I hate you, Michael.

CHAPTER FOUR

J UDY WOKE up early on Tuesday wondering if she had a job.

Yesterday she had said: 'I quit.' But she had been angry and frustrated. Today she was sure she did not want to leave the FBI. The prospect of spending her life defending criminals, instead of catching them, depressed her. Had she changed her mind too late? Last night she had left a note on Brian Kincaid's desk. Would he accept her apology? Or would he insist on her resignation?

Bo came in at 6 a.m. and she warmed up some *pho*, the noodle soup that the Vietnamese eat for breakfast. Then she dressed in her smartest outfit, a dark blue Armani suit with a short skirt. On a good day it made her sophisticated, authoritative, and sexy all at the same time. *If I'm going to be fired, I might as well look like someone they'll miss.*

She was stiff with tension as she drove to work. She parked in the garage beneath the Federal Building and took the elevator to the FBI floor. She went straight to the SAC's office.

Brian Kincaid was behind the big desk, wearing a

white shirt with red suspenders. He looked up at her. 'Good morning,' he said coldly.

'Morn—' Her mouth was dry. She swallowed and started again. 'Good morning, Brian. Did you get my note?'

'Yes, I did.'

Obviously he wasn't going to make this any easier for her.

She could not think what else to say, so she simply looked at him and waited.

Eventually he said: 'Your apology is accepted.'

She felt weak with relief. 'Thank you.'

'You can move your personal stuff into the Domestic Terrorism squad room.'

'Okay.' There were worse fates, she reflected. There were several people she liked in the DT squad. She began to relax.

Kincaid said: 'Get to work on the Hammer of Eden case right away. We need something to tell the governor.'

Judy was surprised. 'You're seeing the governor?'

'His cabinet secretary.' He checked a note on his desk. 'A Mr Albert Honeymoon.'

'I've heard of him.' Honeymoon was the governor's right-hand man. The case had taken a higher profile, Judy realized.

'Let me have a report by tomorrow night.'

That hardly gave her time to make progress, given how little she had to begin with. Tomorrow was Wednesday. 'But the deadline is Friday.'

'The meeting with Honeymoon is on Thursday.'

'I'll get you something concrete to give him.'

'You can give it to him yourself. Mr Honeymoon insists on seeing what he calls the person at the sharp end. We need to be at the governor's office in Sacramento at twelve noon.'

'Wow. Okay.'

'Any questions?'

She shook her head. 'I'll get right on it.'

As she left, she felt elated that she had her job back, but dismayed by the news that she had to report to the governor's aide. It was not likely she would catch the people behind the threat in only two days, so she was almost doomed to report failure.

She emptied her desk in the Asian Organized Crime squad and carried her stuff down the corridor to Domestic Terrorism. Her new supervisor, Matt Peters, allocated her a desk. She knew all the agents, and they congratulated her on the Foong brothers case, though in subdued tones—everyone knew she had rowed with Kincaid yesterday.

Peters assigned a young agent to work with her on the Hammer of Eden case. He was Raja Khan, a fast-talking Hindu with an MBA. He was twenty-six. Judy was pleased. Although inexperienced, he was intelligent and keen.

She briefed him on the case and sent him to check out the Green California Campaign. 'Be nice,' she told him. 'Tell them we don't believe they're involved but we have to eliminate them.'

'What am I looking for?'

'A couple: a blue-collar man of about forty-five who

123

may be illiterate, and an educated woman of about thirty who is probably dominated by the man. But I don't think you'll find them there. That would be too easy.'

'Alternatively . . .?'

'The most useful thing you can do is get the names of all the officers of the organization, paid or volunteer, and run them through the computer to see if any of them have any record of criminal or subversive activity.'

'You got it,' Raja said. 'What will you do?'

'I'm going to learn about earthquakes.'

*

Judy had been in one major earthquake.

The Santa Rosa earthquake had caused damage worth six million dollars—not much, as these things go—and had been felt over the relatively small area of twelve thousand square miles. The Maddox family was then living in Marin county, north of San Francisco, and Judy was in first grade. It was a minor tremor, she knew now. But at the time she had been six years old, and it had seemed like the end of the world.

First there was a noise like a train, but real close, and she came awake fast and looked around her bedroom in the clear light of dawn, searching for the source of the sound, scared to death.

Then the house began to shake. Her ceiling light with its pink fringed shade whipped back and forth. On her bedside table, *Best Fairy Tales* leaped up in the air like a magic book and came down open at *Tom Thumb*, the story Bo had read her last night. Her hair brush and her toy make-up set danced on the Formica top of the dresser. Her wooden horse rocked furiously with no one on it. A row of dolls fell off their shelf, as if diving into the rug, and Judy thought they had come alive, like toys in a fable. She found her voice at last and screamed once: 'DADDY!'

From the next room she heard her father curse, then there was a thud as his feet hit the floor. The noise and the shaking grew worse, and she heard her mother cry out. Bo came to Judy's door and turned the handle, but it would not open. She heard another thud as he shouldered it, but it was stuck.

Her window smashed, and shards of glass fell inwards, landing on the chair where her school clothes were neatly folded ready for the morning: grey skirt, white blouse, green V-neck sweater, navy blue underwear, and white socks. The wooden horse rocked so hard it fell over on top of the dolls' house, smashing the miniature roof; and Judy knew the roof of her real house might be smashed as easily. A framed picture of a rosy-cheeked Mexican boy came off its hook on the wall, flew through the air, and hit her head. She cried out in pain.

Then her chest of drawers began to walk.

It was an old bow-fronted pine chest her mother had bought in a junk shop and painted white. It had three drawers, and it stood on short legs that ended in feet like lions' paws. At first it seemed to dance in place, restlessly, on its four feet. Then it shuffled from side to side, like someone hesitating nervously in a doorway. Finally it started to move toward her.

She screamed again.

Her bedroom door shook as Bo tried to break it down.

The chest inched across the floor toward her. She hoped maybe the rug would halt its advance, but the chest just pushed the rug with its lions' paws.

Her bed shook so violently that she fell out.

The chest came within a few inches of her and stopped. The middle drawer came open like a wide mouth ready to swallow her. She screamed at the top of her voice.

The door shattered and Bo burst in.

Then the shaking stopped.

*

Thirty years later she could still feel the terror that had possessed her like a fit as the world fell apart around her. She had been frightened of closing the bedroom door for years afterwards; and she was still scared of earthquakes. In California, feeling the ground move in a minor tremor was commonplace, but she had never really gotten used to it. And when she felt the earth shake, or saw television pictures of collapsed buildings, the dread that crept through her veins like a drug was not the fear of being crushed or burned, but the blind panic of a little girl whose world suddenly started to fall apart.

She was still on edge that evening as she walked

into the sophisticated ambience of Masa's, wearing a black silk sheath and the row of pearls Don Riley had given her the Christmas they were living together.

Don ordered a white burgundy called Corton Charlemagne. He drank most of it: Judy loved the nutty taste, but she was not comfortable drinking alcohol when she had a semi-automatic pistol loaded with 9mm ammunition tucked into her black patent evening purse.

She told Don that Brian Kincaid had accepted her apology and allowed her to withdraw her resignation.

'He had to,' Don said. 'Refusing would be tantamount to firing you. And it would look real bad for him if he lost one of his best people on his first day as Acting SAC.'

'Maybe you're right,' Judy said, but she was thinking that it was easy for Don to be wise after the event.

'Sure I'm right.'

'Remember, Brian is KMA.' It stood for Kiss My Ass, and it meant the person had built up such a generous pension entitlement that he could retire comfortably at any time that suited him.

'Yeah, but he has his pride. Imagine where he explains to headquarters how come he had to let you go. "She said *fuck* to me," he says. Washington goes: "So what are you, a priest? You never heard an agent say *fuck* before?" Uh-uh.' Don shook his head. 'Kincaid would seem like a wimp to refuse your apology.'

'I guess so.'

'Anyway, I'm real glad we may be working together again soon.' He raised his glass. 'Here's to many more brilliant prosecutions by the great team of Riley and Maddox.'

She clinked glasses and took a sip of wine.

They talked over the case as they ate, recalling the mistakes they had made, the surprises they had sprung on the defence, the moments of tension and triumph.

When they were drinking coffee, Don said: 'Do you miss me?'

Judy frowned. It would be cruel to say no, and anyway it was not true. But she did not want to give him false encouragement. 'I miss some things,' she said. 'I like you when you're funny and smart.' She also missed having a warm body beside her at night, but she was not going to tell him that.

He said: 'I miss talking about my work, and hearing about yours.'

'I guess I talk to Bo now.'

'I miss him, too.'

'He likes you. He thinks you're the ideal husband—'

'I am, I am!'

'—for someone in law enforcement.'

Don shrugged. 'I'll settle for that.'

Judy grinned. 'Maybe you and Bo should get married.'

'Ho, ho.' He paid the check. 'Judy, there's something I want to say.'

'I'm listening.'

'I think I'm ready to be a father.'

For some reason that angered her. 'So what am I

supposed to do about it—shout hooray and open my legs?'

He was taken aback. 'I mean . . . well, I thought you wanted commitment.'

'Commitment? Don, all I asked was that you refrain from shtupping your secretary, but you couldn't manage that!'

He looked mortified. 'Okay, don't get mad. I'm just trying to tell you that I've changed.'

'And now I'm supposed to come running back to you as if nothing had happened?'

'I guess I still don't understand you.'

'You probably never will.' His evident distress softened her. 'Come on, I'll drive you home.' When they were living together she had always been the after-dinner driver.

They left the restaurant in an awkward silence. In the car, he said: 'I thought we might at least talk about it.' Don the lawyer, negotiating.

'We can talk.' *But how can I tell you that my heart is cold?*

'What happened with Paula . . . it was the worst mistake of my whole life.'

She believed him. He was not drunk, just mellow enough to say what he felt. She sighed. She wanted him to be happy. She was fond of him, and she hated to see him in pain. It hurt her too. Part of her wished she could give him what he wanted.

He said: 'We had some good times together.' He stroked her thigh through the silk dress.

She said: 'If you feel me up while I'm driving, I'll throw you out of the car.'

He knew she could do it. 'Whatever you say.' He took his hand away.

A moment later she wished she had not been so harsh. It was not such a bad thing, to have a man's hand on your thigh. Don was not the world's greatest lover—he was enthusiastic, but unimaginative. However, he was better than nothing, and nothing was what she had had since she left him.

Why don't I have a man? I don't want to grow old alone. Is there something wrong with me?

Hell, no.

A minute later she pulled up outside his building. 'Thanks, Don,' she said. 'For a great prosecution and a great dinner.'

He leaned over to kiss her. She offered her cheek, but he kissed her lips, and she did not want to make a big thing of it, so she let him. His kiss lingered until she broke away. Then he said: 'Come in for a while. I'll make you a cappuccino.'

The longing look in his eyes almost broke her will. How hard could it be, she asked herself? She could put her gun in his safe, drink a large heart-warming brandy, and spend the night in the arms of a decent man who adored her. 'No,' she said firmly. 'Good night.'

He stared at her for a long moment, misery in his eyes. She looked back, embarrassed and sorry, but resolute.

'Good night,' he said at last. He got out and closed the car door.

Judy pulled away. When she glanced in the rear-view mirror she saw him standing on the sidewalk, his hand half-raised in a kind of wave. She ran a red light and turned a corner, then at last she felt alone again.

*

When she got home, Bo was watching Conan O'Brien and chuckling. 'This guy breaks me up,' he said. They watched his monologue until the commercial break, then Bo turned the TV off. 'I solved a murder today,' he said. 'How about that?'

Judy knew he had several unsolved cases on his desk. 'Which one?'

'The Telegraph Hill rape-murder.'

'Who did it?'

'A guy who's already in jail. He was arrested a while back for harassing young girls in the park. I had a hunch about him and searched his apartment. He had a pair of police handcuffs like the ones found on the body, but he denied the murder, and I couldn't break him. Today I got his DNA test back from the lab. It matches the semen from the victim's body. I told him that and he confessed. Jackpot.'

'Well done!' She kissed the top of his head.

'How about you?'

'Well, I still have a job, but it remains to be seen whether I have a career.'

'You have a career, come on.'

'I don't know. If I get demoted for putting the Foong brothers in jail, what will they do to me when I have a failure?'

'You've suffered a setback. It's just temporary. You'll get over it, I promise.'

She smiled, remembering the time when she had thought there was nothing her father could not do. 'Well, I didn't make much progress with my case.'

'Last night you thought it was a bullshit assignment anyway.'

'Today I'm not so sure. The linguistic analysis showed that these people are dangerous, whoever they are.'

'But they can't trigger an earthquake.'

'I don't know.'

Bo raised his eyebrows. 'You think it's possible?'

'I've spent most of today trying to find out. I spoke to three seismologists and got three different answers.'

'Scientists are like that.'

'What I really wanted was for them to tell me firmly it couldn't happen. But one said it was "unlikely", one said the possibility was "vanishingly small", and the third said it could be done with a nuclear bomb.'

'Could these people—what are they called?'

'The Hammer of Eden.'

'Could they have a nuclear device?'

'It's possible. They're smart, focused, serious. But then why would they talk about earthquakes? Why not just threaten us with their bomb?'

'Yeah,' Bo said thoughtfully. 'That would be just as terrifying and a lot more credible.'

'But who can tell how these people's minds work?'

'What's your next step?'

'I have one more seismologist to see, a Michael Quercus. The others all say he's kind of a maverick but he's the leading authority on what causes earthquakes.'

She had already tried to interview Quercus. Late that afternoon she had rung his doorbell. He had told her, through the entryphone, to call for an appointment.

'Maybe you didn't hear me,' she had said. 'This is the FBI.'

'Does that mean you don't have to make appointments?'

She had cursed under her breath. She was a law enforcement officer, not a damn replacement window salesperson. 'It does, generally,' she said into the intercom. 'Most people feel our work is too important to wait.'

'No, they don't,' he replied. 'Most people are scared of you, that's why they let you in without an appointment. Call me. I'm in the phone book.'

'I'm here about a matter of public safety, Professor. I've been told you're an expert who can give me crucial information that will help in our work of protecting people. I'm sorry I didn't have the opportunity of calling for an appointment, but now that I'm here, I would really appreciate it if you would see me for a few minutes.'

There was no reply, and she realized he had hung up at his end.

She had driven back to the office, fuming. She did not make appointments: agents rarely did. She preferred to catch people off guard. Almost everyone she interviewed had something to hide. The less time they had to prepare, the more likely they were to make a revealing mistake. But Quercus was infuriatingly correct: she had no right to barge in on him.

Swallowing her pride, she had called him and made an appointment for tomorrow.

She decided not to tell Bo any of this. 'What I really need,' she said, 'is someone to explain the science to me in such a way that I can make my own judgement about whether a terrorist could cause an earthquake.'

'And you need to find these Hammer of Eden people and bust them for making threats. Any progress there?'

She shook her head. 'I had Raja interview everyone at the Green California Campaign. No one there matches the profile, none have any kind of criminal or subversive record, in fact there's nothing suspicious about them at all.'

Bo nodded. 'It always was unlikely the perpetrators would have told the truth about who they were. Don't be discouraged. You've only been on the case a day and a half.'

'True—but that leaves only two clear days to their deadline. And I have to go to Sacramento on Thursday to report to the governor's office.'

'You'd better start early tomorrow.' He got up off the couch.

They both went upstairs. Judy paused at her bedroom door. 'Remember that earthquake, when I was
six?'

He nodded. 'It wasn't much, by California standards, but it scared you half to death.'

Judy smiled. 'I thought it was the end of the world.'

'The shaking must have shifted the house a little,
because your bedroom door jammed shut, and I
nearly bust my shoulder breaking it down.'

'I thought it was you that made the shaking stop. I
believed that for years.'

'Afterwards you were scared of that damn chest of
drawers that your mother liked so much. You wouldn't
have it in the house.'

'I thought it wanted to eat me.'

'In the end I chopped it up for firewood.' Suddenly
Bo looked sad. 'I wish I could have those years back,
to live all over again.'

She knew he was thinking of her mother. 'Yeah,'
she said.

'Good night, kid.'

'Night, Bo.'

*

As she drove across the Bay Bridge on Wednesday
morning, heading for Berkeley, Judy wondered what
Michael Quercus looked like. His irritable manner
suggested a peevish professor, stooped and shabby,
peering irritably at the world through glasses that kept
falling down his nose. Or he could be an academic fat

cat in a pinstripe suit, charming to people who might donate money to the university, contemptuously indifferent to anyone not of use to him.

She parked in the shade of a magnolia tree on Euclid Avenue. As she rang his bell she had a horrible feeling he might find another excuse to send her away; but when she gave her name there was a buzz and the door opened. She climbed two flights to his apartment. It was open. She walked in. The place was small and cheap: his business could not be making much money. She passed through a vestibule and found herself in his office-cum-living-room.

He was sitting at his desk in khakis, tan walking boots and a navy blue polo shirt. Michael Quercus was neither a peevish professor nor an academic fat cat, she saw immediately. He was a hunk: tall, fit, good-looking, with sexy hair, dark and curly. She quickly summed him up as one of those guys who were so big and handsome and confident they thought they could do anything they liked.

He, too, was surprised. His eyes widened and he said: 'Are you the FBI agent?'

She gave him a firm handshake. 'Were you expecting someone else?'

He shrugged. 'You don't look like Efrem Zimbalist Junior.'

Zimbalist was the actor who played Inspector Lewis Erskine in the long-running television show *The FBI*. Judy said mildly: 'I've been an agent for ten years. Can you imagine how many people have already made that joke?'

To her surprise he grinned broadly. 'Okay,' he said. 'You got me.'

That's better.

She noticed a framed photo on his desk. It showed a pretty redhead with a child in her arms. People always liked to talk about their children. 'Who's this?' she said.

'Nobody important. You want to get to the point?'

Forget friendly.

She took him at his word and asked her question right out. 'I need to know if a terrorist group could trigger an earthquake.'

'Have you had a threat?'

I'm supposed to be asking the questions. 'You haven't heard? It's been talked about on the radio. Don't you listen to John Truth?'

He shook his head. 'Is it serious?'

'That's what I need to establish.'

'Okay. Well, the short answer is yes.'

Judy felt a frisson of fear. Quercus seemed so sure. She had been hoping for the opposite answer. She said: 'How could they do it?'

'Take a nuclear bomb, put it at the bottom of a deep mineshaft, and detonate it. That'll do the trick. But you probably want a more realistic scenario.'

'Yeah. Imagine *you* wanted to trigger an earthquake.'

'Oh, I could do it.'

Judy wondered if he was just bragging. 'Explain how.'

'Okay.' He reached down behind his desk and

picked up a short plank of wood and a regular house brick. He obviously kept them there for this purpose. He put the plank on his desk and the brick on the plank. Then he lifted one end of the plank slowly until the brick slid down the slope on to the desk. 'The brick slips when the gravity pulling it overcomes the friction holding it still,' he said. 'Okay so far?'

'Sure.'

'A fault such as the San Andreas is a place where two adjacent slabs of the earth's crust are moving in different directions. Imagine a pair of icebergs scraping past one another. They don't move smoothly: they get jammed. Then, when they're stuck, pressure builds up, slowly but surely, over the decades.'

'So how does that lead to earthquakes?'

'Something happens to release all that stored-up energy.' He lifted one end of the plank again. This time, he stopped just before the brick began to slide. 'Several sections of the San Andreas fault are like this —just about ready to slip, any decade now. Take this.'

He handed Judy a clear plastic twelve-inch ruler.

'Now tap the plank sharply just in front of the brick.'

She did so, and the brick began to slide.

Quercus grabbed it and stopped it. 'When the plank is tilted, it takes only a little tap to make the brick move. And where the San Andreas is under tremendous pressure, a little nudge may be enough to unjam the slabs. Then they slip—and all that pent-up energy shakes the earth.'

Quercus might be abrasive, but once he got on to

his subject he was a pleasure to listen to. He was a clear thinker and he explained himself easily, without condescending. Despite the ominous picture he was painting, Judy realized she was enjoying talking to him, and not just because he was so good-looking. 'Is that what happens in most earthquakes?'

'I believe so, though some other seismologists might disagree. There are natural vibrations that resound through the earth's crust from time to time. Most earthquakes are probably triggered by the right vibration in the right place at the right time.'

How am I going to explain all this to Mr Honeymoon? He's going to want simple yes–no answers. 'So how does that help our terrorists?'

'They need a ruler, and they need to know where to tap.'

'What's the real-life equivalent of the ruler? A nuclear bomb?'

'They don't need anything so powerful. They have to send a shock wave through the earth's crust, that's all. If they know exactly where the fault is vulnerable, they might do it with a charge of dynamite, precisely placed.'

'Anyone can get hold of dynamite if they really want to.'

'The explosion would have to be underground. I guess drilling a shaft would be the challenge for a terrorist group.'

Judy wondered if the blue-collar man imagined by Simon Sparrow was a drilling rig operator. Such men would surely need a special licence. A quick check with the Department of Motor Vehicles might yield a list of all of them in California. There could not be many.

Quercus went on: 'They would obviously need drilling equipment, expertise, and some kind of pretext to get permission.'

Those problems were not insurmountable. 'Is it really so simple?' Judy said.

'Listen, I'm not telling you this would work. I'm saying it might. No one will know for sure until they try it. I can try to give you some insight into how these things happen, but you'll have to make your own assessment of the risk.'

Judy nodded. She had used almost the same words last night in telling Bo what she needed. Quercus might act like an asshole sometimes but, as Bo would say, everyone needs an asshole now and again. 'So knowing where to place the charge is everything?'

'Yes.'

'Who has that information?'

'Universities, the state geologist . . . me. We all share information.'

'Anyone can get hold of it?'

'It's not secret, though you would need to have some scientific knowledge to interpret the data.'

'So someone in the terrorist group would have to be a seismologist.'

'Yes. Could be a student.'

Judy thought of the educated thirty-year-old woman who was doing the typing, according to Simon's theory. She could be a graduate student. How many geology students were there in California? How long would it take to find and interview them all?

Quercus went on: 'And there's one other factor: earth tides. The oceans move this way and that under the gravitational influence of the moon, and the solid earth is subject to the same forces. Twice a day, there's a seismic window, when the fault line is under extra stress because of the tides; and that's when an earthquake is most likely—or most easy to trigger. Which is my specialty. I'm the only person who has done extensive calculations of seismic windows for California faults.'

'Could someone have gotten this data from you?'

'Well, I'm in the business of selling it.' He gave a rueful smile. 'But, as you can see, my business isn't making me rich. I have one contract, with a big insurance company, and that pays the rent, but unfortunately that's all. My theories about seismic windows make me kind of a maverick, and corporate America hates mavericks.'

The note of wry self-deprecation was surprising, and Judy started to like him better. 'Someone might have taken the information without your knowledge. Have you been burgled lately?'

'Never.'

'Could your data have been copied by a friend, or relative?'

'I don't think so. No one spends time in this room without my being here.'

She picked up the photo from his desk. 'Your wife, or girlfriend?'

He looked annoyed, and took the picture out of her hand. 'I'm separated from my wife, and I don't have a girlfriend.'

'Is that so?' said Judy. She had got everything she needed from him. She stood up. 'I appreciate your time, Professor.'

'Please call me Michael. I've enjoyed talking to you.'

She was surprised.

He added: 'You pick up fast. That makes it more fun.'

'Well . . . good.'

He walked her to the door of the apartment and shook her hand. He had big hands, but his grip was surprisingly gentle. 'Anything else you want to know, I'll be glad to help.'

She risked a gibe. 'So long as I call ahead for an appointment, right?'

He did not smile. 'Right.'

Driving back across the bay, she reflected that the danger was now clear. A terrorist group might, conceivably, be able to cause an earthquake. They would need accurate data on critically stressed points on the fault line, and perhaps on seismic windows, but that was obtainable. They had to have someone to interpret the data. And they needed some way to send shock waves through the earth. That would be the most difficult task, but it was not out of the question.

She had the unwelcome task of telling the governor's aide that the whole thing was horrifyingly possible.

CHAPTER FIVE

PRIEST WOKE at first light on Thursday.

He generally woke early, all the year round. He never needed much sleep, unless he had been partying too hard, and that was rare now.

One more day.

From the governor's office there had been nothing but a maddening silence. They acted as if no threat had been made. So did the rest of the world, by and large. The Hammer of Eden was rarely mentioned in the news broadcasts Priest listened to on his car radio.

Only John Truth took them seriously. He kept taunting Governor Mike Robson in his daily radio show. Until yesterday, all the governor would say was that the FBI was investigating. But last night Truth had reported that the governor had promised a statement today.

That statement would decide everything. If it was conciliatory, and gave at least a hint that the governor would consider the demand, Priest would rejoice. But if the statement was unyielding, Priest would have to cause an earthquake.

He wondered if he really could.

Melanie sounded convincing when she talked about

the fault line and what it would take to make it slip. But no one had ever tried this. Even she admitted she could not be one hundred per cent sure it would work. What if it failed? What if it worked and they were caught? What if it worked and they were killed in the earthquake—who would take care of the communards and the children?

He rolled over. Melanie's head lay on the pillow beside him. He studied her face in repose. Her skin was very white, and her eyelashes were almost transparent. A strand of long ginger-coloured hair fell across her cheek. He pulled the sheet back a little and looked at her breasts, heavy and soft. He contemplated waking her. Under the covers, he reached out and stroked her, running his hand across her belly and into the triangle of reddish hair below. She stirred, swallowed, then turned over and moved away.

He sat up. He was in the one-room house that had been his home for the last twenty-five years. As well as the bed, it had an old couch in front of the fireplace and a table in the corner with a fat yellow candle in a holder. There was no electric light.

In the early days of the commune, most people lived in cabins like this, and the kids all slept in a bunkhouse. But over the years some permanent couples had formed, and they had built bigger places with separate bedrooms for their children. Priest and Star had kept their own individual houses, but the trend was against them. It was best not to fight the inevitable: Priest had learned that from Star. Now there were six family homes as well as the original fifteen cabins.

Right now the commune consisted of twenty-five adults and ten children, plus Melanie and Dusty. One cabin was empty.

This room was as familiar as his hand, but lately the well-known objects had taken on a new aura. For years his eye had passed over without registering them: the picture of Priest that Star had painted for his thirtieth birthday; the elaborately decorated hookah left behind by a French girl called Marie-Louise; the rickety shelf Flower had made in woodwork class; the fruit crate in which he kept his clothes. Now that he knew he might have to leave, each homely item looked special and wonderful, and it brought a lump to his throat to look at them. His room was like a photograph album in which every picture unchained a string of memories: the birth of Ringo; the day Smiler nearly drowned in the river; making love to twin sisters called Jane and Eliza; the warm, dry autumn of their first grape harvest; the taste of the '89 vintage. When he looked around, and thought of the people who wanted to take it all away from him, he was filled with a rage that burned inside him like vitriol in his belly.

He picked up a towel, stepped into his sandals, and went outside naked. His dog, Spirit, greeted him with a quiet snuffle. It was a clear, crisp morning, with patches of high cloud in the blue sky. The sun had not yet appeared over the mountains, and the valley was in shadow. No one else was about.

He walked downhill through the little village, and Spirit followed. Although the communal spirit was still strong, people had customized their homes with individual touches. One woman had planted the ground around her house with flowers and small shrubs: Priest had named her Garden in consequence. Dale and Poem, who were a couple, had let their children paint the outside walls, and the result was a colourful mess. A man called Slow, who was retarded, had built a crooked porch on which stood a wobbly home-made rocking chair.

Priest knew the place might not be beautiful to other eyes. The paths were muddy, the buildings were rickety, and the layout was haphazard. There was no zoning: the kids' bunkhouse was right next to the wine barn, and the carpentry yard was in the midst of the cabins. The privies were moved every year, to no avail: no matter where they were sited, you could always smell them on a hot day. Yet everything about the place warmed his heart. And when he looked farther away, and saw the forested hillsides soaring steeply from the gleaming river all the way to the blue peaks of the Sierra Nevada, he had a view that was so beautiful it hurt.

But now, every time he looked at it, the thought that he might lose it stabbed him like a knife.

Beside the river, a wooden box on a boulder held soap, cheap razors, and a hand mirror. He lathered his face and shaved, then stepped into the cold stream and washed all over. He dried himself briskly on the coarse towel.

There was no piped water here. In winter, when it was too cold to bathe in the river, they had a commu-nal bath night twice a week, and heated great barrels of water in the cookhouse to wash one another: it was quite sexy. But in summer only babies had warm water.

He went back up the hill and dressed quickly in the blue jeans and work shirt he always wore. He walked over to the cookhouse and stepped inside. The door was not locked: no doors had locks here. He built up the fire with logs and lit it, put a pan of water on for coffee, and went out.

He liked to walk around when the others were all abed. He whispered their names as he passed their homes: 'Moon. Chocolate. Giggle.' He imagined each one lying there, sleeping: Apple, a fat girl, lying on her back with her mouth open, snoring; Juice and Alaska, two middle-aged women, entwined together; the kids in the bunkhouse—his own Flower, Ringo, and Smiler; Melanie's Dusty; the twins Bubble and Chip, all pink cheeks and tousled hair . . .

My people.

May they live here for ever.

He passed the workshop, where they kept spades and hoes and pruning shears; the concrete circle where they trod the grapes in October; and the barn where the wine from last year's harvest stood in huge wooden casks, slowly settling and clarifying, now almost ready to be blended and bottled.

He paused outside the temple.

He felt very proud. From the very beginning they had talked of building a temple. For many years it had seemed an impossible dream. There was always too much else to do—land to clear and vines to plant, barns to build, the vegetable garden and the free shop and the kids' lessons. But five years ago the commune had seemed to reach a plateau. For the first time, Priest was not worried about whether they would have enough to eat through the coming winter. He no longer felt that one bad harvest could wipe them out. There was nothing undone on the list of urgent tasks he carried in his head. So he had announced that it was time to build the temple.

And here it was.

It meant a lot to Priest. It showed that his community was mature. They were not living hand to mouth any more. They could feed themselves and have time and resources to spare for building a place of worship. They were no longer a bunch of hippies trying out an idealistic dream. The dream worked; they had proved it. The temple was the emblem of their triumph.

He stepped inside. It was a simple wooden structure with a single skylight and no furniture. Everyone sat cross-legged in a circle on the plank floor to worship. It was also schoolhouse and meeting room. The only decoration was a banner Star had made. Priest could not read it, but he knew what it said:

> *Meditation is life: all else is distraction*
> *Money makes you poor*
> *Marriage is the greatest infidelity*
> *When no one owns anything, we all own everything*
> *Do what you like is the only law*

These were the Five Paradoxes of Baghram. Priest said he had learned them from an Indian guru he studied under in Los Angeles, but in fact he had made them up. *Pretty good for a guy who can't read.*

He stood in the centre of the room for several minutes, eyes closed, arms hanging loosely at his sides, focusing his energy. There was nothing phoney about *this*. He had learned meditation techniques from Star, and they really worked. He felt his mind clarify like the wine in the casks. He prayed that Governor Mike Robson's heart would be softened and he would announce a freeze on the building of new power plants in California. He imagined the handsome governor in his dark suit and white shirt, sitting in a leather chair behind a polished desk; and in his vision the governor said: 'I have decided to give these people what they want—not just to avoid an earthquake, but because it makes sense anyway.'

After a few minutes, Priest's spiritual strength was renewed. He felt alert, confident, centred.

When he went outside again, he decided to check on the vines.

There had been no grapes originally. When Star arrived there was nothing in the valley but a ruined hunting lodge. For three years the commune had lurched from crisis to crisis, riven by quarrels, washed out in storms, sustained only by begging trips to towns. Then Priest came.

It took him less than a year to become Star's acknowledged equal as joint leader. First he had organized the begging trips for maximum efficiency. They would hit a town like Sacramento or Stockton on a Saturday morning, when the streets were crowded with shoppers. Each individual would be assigned a different corner. Everyone had to have a pitch: Aneth would say she was trying to get the bus fare home to her folks in New York, Song would strum her guitar and sing 'There but for Fortune', Slow would say he had not eaten for three days, Bones would make people smile with a sign saying: 'Why lie? It's for beer.'

But begging was only a stopgap. Under Priest's direction, the hippies had terraced the hillside, diverted a brook for irrigation, and planted a vineyard. The tremendous team effort made them into a strongly knit group, and the wine enabled them to live without begging. Now their Chardonnay was sought after by connoisseurs.

Priest walked along the neat rows. Herbs and flowers were planted between the vines, partly because they were useful and pretty, but mainly to attract ladybirds and wasps that would destroy greenfly and other pests. No chemicals were used here: they relied on natural methods. They grew clover, too, because it fixed nitrogen from the air, and when they ploughed it into the soil it acted as a natural fertilizer.

The vines were sprouting. It was late May, so the annual peril of frost killing the new shoots was past. At this point in the cycle, most of the work consisted of tying the shoots to trellises to train their growth and prevent wind damage.

Priest had learned about wine during his years as a liquor wholesaler, and Star had studied the subject in books, but they could not have succeeded without old Raymond Dellavalle, a good-natured wine grower who had helped them because, Priest guessed, he wished his own youth had been more daring.

Priest's vineyard had saved the commune, but the commune had saved Priest's life. He had arrived here a fugitive—on the run from the Mob, the Los Angeles police and the Inland Revenue Service all at once. He was a drunk and a cocaine abuser, lonely, broke and suicidal. He had driven down the dirt road to the commune, following vague directions from a hitch-hiker, and wandered through the trees until he came upon a bunch of naked hippies sitting on the ground chanting. He stared at them for a long while, spell-bound by the mantra and the sense of profound calm that rose up like smoke from a fire. One or two smiled at him but they continued their ritual. Eventually he had stripped off, slowly, like a man in a trance, discarding his business suit, pink shirt, platform shoes and red-and-white jockey shorts. Then, naked, he had sat down with them.

Here he had found peace, a new religion, work, friends, and lovers. At a time when he was ready to drive his yellow Plymouth 'Cuda 440–6 right over the edge of a cliff, the commune had given meaning to his life.

Now there would never be any other existence for him. This place was all he had, and he would die to defend it.

I may have to.

He would listen to John Truth's radio show tonight. If the governor was going to open the door to negotiation, or make any other concession, it would surely be announced before the end of the broadcast.

When he came to the far side of the vineyard, he decided to check on the seismic vibrator.

He walked up the hill. There was no road, just a well-trodden path through the forest. Vehicles could not get through to the village. A quarter of a mile from the houses, he arrived at a muddy clearing. Parked under the trees were his old 'Cuda, a rusty Volkswagen minibus that was even older, Melanie's orange Subaru, and the communal pickup, a dark-green Ford Ranger. From here a dirt track wound two miles through the forest, uphill and down, disappearing into a mudslide here and passing through a stream there, until at last it reached the county road, a two-lane blacktop. It was ten miles to the nearest town, Silver City.

Once a year the entire commune would spend a day rolling barrels of wine up the hill and through the trees to this clearing, there to be loaded on to Paul Beale's truck for transport to his bottling plant in Napa. It was the big day in their calendar, and they always held a feast that night, then took a holiday on the following day, to celebrate a successful year. The ceremony took place eight months after the harvest, so it was due in a few days' time. This year, Priest resolved, they would hold the party the day after the governor reprieved the valley.

In return for the wine, Paul Beale brought food for the communal kitchen and kept the free shop stocked with supplies: clothing, candy, cigarettes, stationery, books, tampons, toothpaste, everything anyone needed. The system operated without money. However, Paul kept accounts and, at the end of each year, he deposited surplus cash in a bank account that only Priest and Star knew about.

From the clearing, Priest headed along the track for a mile, skirting rainwater pools and clambering over deadfalls, then turned off and followed an invisible way through the trees. There were no tyre tracks because he had carefully brushed the carpet of pine needles that formed the forest floor. He came to a hollow and stopped. All he could see was a pile of vegetation: broken branches and uprooted saplings heaped twelve feet high like a bonfire. He had to go right up to the pile and push some of the brush aside to confirm that the truck was still there under its camouflage.

Not that he thought anyone would come here looking for the truck. The Ricky Granger who had been hired as a juggie by Ritkin Seismex in the south Texas oilfield had no traceable connection with this remote vineyard in Sierra county, California. However, it did occasionally happen that a couple of backpackers would lose their way radically and wander on to the commune's land—as Melanie had—and they would sure as hell wonder why this large piece of expensive machinery was parked out here in the woods. So Priest and the Rice Eaters had slaved for two hours concealing the truck. Priest was pretty sure it could not be seen even from the air.

He exposed a wheel and kicked the tyre, just like the sceptical purchaser of a used car. He had killed a man for this vehicle. He thought briefly about Mario's pretty wife and kids, and wondered whether they had realized yet that Mario was never coming home. Then he put the thought out of his mind.

He wanted to reassure himself that the truck would be ready to go tomorrow morning. Just looking at it made him edgy. He felt a powerful urge to get going right away, today, now, just to ease the tension. But he had announced a deadline, and timing would be important.

This waiting was unbearable. He thought of getting in and starting the truck, just to make sure everything was okay; but that would be foolish. He was suffering from dumb nerves. The truck would be fine. He would do better to stay away and leave it alone until tomorrow.

He parted another section of the covering and looked at the steel plate that hammered the earth. If Melanie's scheme worked, the vibration would unleash an earthquake. There was a pure kind of justice about the plan. They would be using the earth's stored-up energy as a threat to force the governor to take care of the environment. The earth was saving the earth. It felt right to Priest in a way that was almost holy.

Spirit gave a low bark, as if he had heard something. It was probably a rabbit, but Priest nervously replaced the branches he had moved, then headed back.

He made his way through the trees to the track and turned toward the village.

He stopped in the middle of the track and frowned, mystified. On the way here he had stepped over a fallen bough. Now it had been moved to the side. Spirit had not been barking at rabbits. Someone else was about. He had not heard anyone, but sounds were quickly muffled in the dense vegetation. Who was it? Had someone followed him? Had they seen him looking at the seismic vibrator?

As he headed home, Spirit became agitated. When they came within sight of the parking circle, Priest saw why.

There in the muddy clearing, parked beside his 'Cuda, was a police car.

Priest's heart stopped.

So soon! How could they have tracked him down so soon?

He stared at the cruiser.

It was a white Ford Crown Victoria with a green stripe along the side, a silver six-pointed sheriff's star on the door, four aerials, and a rack of blue, red, and orange lights on the roof.

Be calm. All things must pass.

The police might not be here for the vibrator. Idle curiosity might have brought a cop wandering down the track: it had never happened before, but it was possible. There were lots of other possible reasons. They could be searching for a tourist who had gone missing. A sheriff's deputy could be looking for a secret place to meet his neighbour's wife.

They might not even realize there was a commune here. Perhaps they need never find out. If Priest slipped back into the woods—

Too late. Just as the thought entered his head, a cop stepped around the trunk of a tree.

Spirit barked fiercely.

'Quiet,' Priest said, and the dog fell silent.

The cop was wearing the grey-green uniform of a sheriff's deputy, with a star over the left breast of the short jacket, a cowboy hat, and a gun on his pants belt.

He saw Priest and waved.

Priest hesitated, then slowly raised his hand and waved back.

Then, reluctantly, he walked up to the car.

He hated cops. Most of them were thieves and bullies and psychopaths. They used their uniform and their position to conceal the fact that they were worse criminals than the people they arrested. But he would force himself to be polite, just as if he were some dumb suburban citizen who imagined the police were there to protect him.

He breathed evenly, relaxed the muscles of his face, smiled, and said: 'Howdy.'

The cop was alone. He was young, maybe twenty-five or thirty, with short light-brown hair. His body in the uniform was already beefy: in ten years' time he would have a beer gut.

'Are there any residences near here?' the cop asked.

Priest was tempted to lie, but a moment's reflection told him it was too risky. The cop only had to walk a quarter of a mile in the right direction to stumble upon the houses, and his suspicions would be aroused if he found he had been lied to. So Priest told the truth. 'You're not far from the Silver River Winery.'

'I never heard of it before.'

That was no accident. In the phone book, its address and number were Paul Beale's in Napa. None of the communards registered to vote. None of them paid taxes because none had any income. They had always been secretive. Star had a horror of publicity that dated from the time the hippie movement had been destroyed by overexposure in the media. But many of the communards had a reason to hide away. Some had debts, others were wanted by the police. Oaktree was a deserter, Song had escaped from an uncle who sexually abused her, and Aneth's husband had beaten her up and swore that if she left him he would seek her out wherever she might be.

The commune continued to act as a sanctuary, and some of the more recent arrivals were also on the run. The only way anyone could find out about the place was from people such as Paul Beale who had lived here for a while then returned to the world outside, and they were very cautious about sharing the secret.

There had never been a cop here.

'How come I never heard of the place?' the cop said. 'I been a deputy here ten years.'

'It's pretty small,' Priest said.

'You the owner?'

'No, just a worker.'

'So what do you do here, make wine?'

Oh, boy, an intellectual giant. 'Yeah, that about sums

it up.' The cop did not pick up the irony. Priest went on: 'What brings you to these parts so early in the morning? We haven't had a crime here since Charlie got drunk and voted for Jimmy Carter.' He grinned. There was no Charlie: he was trying to make the kind of joke a cop might like.

But this one remained straight-faced. 'I'm looking for the parents of a young girl who gives her name as Flower.'

A terrible fear possessed Priest, and he suddenly felt as cold as the grave. 'Oh, my God, what's happened?'

'She's under arrest.'

'Is she okay?'

'She's not injured in any way, if that's what you mean.'

'Thank God. I thought you were going to say she'd been in an accident.' Priest's brain began to recover from the shock. 'How can she be in jail? I thought she was here, asleep in her bed!'

'Obviously not. How are you connected with her?'

'I'm her father.'

'Then you'll need to come to Silver City.'

'Silver City? How long has she been there?'

'Just overnight. We didn't want to keep her that long, but for a while she refused to tell us her address. She broke down an hour or so ago.'

Priest's heart lurched to think of his little girl in custody, trying to keep the secret of the commune until she broke down. Tears came to his eyes.

The cop went on: 'Even so, you were godawful hard to find. In the end I got directions from a bunch of damn gun-toting freaks about five miles down the valley from here.'

Priest nodded. 'Los Alamos.'

'Yeah. Had a damn big sign up saying: "We do not recognize the jurisdiction of the United States government." Assholes.'

'I know them,' Priest said. They were right-wing vigilantes who had taken over a big old farmhouse in a lonely spot and now guarded it with high-powered firearms and dreamed of fighting off a Chinese invasion. Unfortunately they were the commune's nearest neighbours. 'Why is Flower in custody? Did she do something wrong?'

'That is the usual reason,' the cop said sarcastically.

'What did she do?'

'She was caught stealing from a store.'

'From a *store*?' Why would a kid who had access to a free shop want to do that? 'What did she steal?'

'A large-size colour photograph of Leonardo DiCaprio.'

*

Priest wanted to punch the cop in the face, but that would not have helped Flower, so instead he thanked the man for coming here and promised that he and Flower's mother would appear at the sheriff's office in Silver City within an hour to pick up their daughter. Satisfied, the cop drove away.

Priest went to Star's cabin. It doubled as the commune's clinic. Star had no medical training, but she had picked up a great deal of medical knowledge from her physician father and nurse mother. As a girl she had got used to medical emergencies and had even assisted at births. Her room was full of boxes of bandages, jars of ointment, aspirins, cough medicines and contraceptives.

When Priest woke her and told her the bad news, she became hysterical. She hated the police almost as much as he did. In the sixties she had been beaten by cops with nightsticks on demonstrations, sold bad dope by undercover narcs, and, on one occasion, raped by detectives in a precinct house. She jumped out of bed, screaming, and started hitting him. He held her wrists and tried to calm her down.

'We have to go there now and get her out!' Star yelled.

'Right,' he said. 'Just get dressed first, okay?'

She stopped struggling. 'Okay.'

While she was pulling on her jeans he said: 'You were busted at thirteen, you told me.'

'Yeah, and a dirty old sergeant with a cigarette hanging from the corner of his mouth put his hands on my tits and said I was going to grow up into a beautiful lady.'

'It won't help Flower if you go in there mad and get yourself arrested too,' he pointed out.

She got control of herself. 'You're right, Priest. For her sake, we have to ingratiate ourselves with those motherfuckers.' She combed her hair and glanced in a small mirror. 'All right. I'm ready to eat shit.'

Priest had always believed it was best to be conventionally dressed when dealing with the police. He woke

Dale and got from him the old dark blue suit. It was communal property now, and Dale had worn it most recently, to go to court when the wife he had left twenty years ago finally decided to divorce him. Priest put the suit on over his work shirt and tied the twenty-five-year-old pink-and-green 'kipper' tie. The shoes had long worn out so he put his sandals back on. Then he and Star got in the 'Cuda.

When they reached the county road, Priest said: 'How come neither of us noticed she wasn't at home last night?'

'I went to say goodnight to her, but Pearl told me she had gone to the privy.'

'I got that story too! Pearl must have known what happened and covered up for her!' Pearl, the daughter of Dale and Poem, was twelve years old and Flower's best friend.

'I went back later but all the candles were out and the bunkhouse was in darkness so I didn't want to wake them up. I never imagined . . .'

'Why would you? The darn kid has spent every night of her life in the same place—no reason to think she was anywhere else.'

They drove into Silver City. The sheriff's office was next door to the courthouse. They entered a gloomy lobby decorated with yellowing news clippings of ancient murders. There was a reception desk behind a window with an intercom and a buzzer. A deputy in a khaki shirt and green tie said: 'Help you?'

Star said: 'My name is Stella Higgins and you have my daughter here.'

The deputy gave them a hard look. Priest figured he was appraising them, wondering what kind of parents they were. He said: 'Just one moment, please,' and disappeared.

Priest spoke to Star in a low voice. 'I think we should be respectable law-abiding citizens who are appalled that a child of theirs is in trouble with the police. We have nothing but profound respect for law enforcement personnel. We are sorry to have caused trouble to such hard-working folk.'

'Gotcha,' Star said tightly.

A door opened and the deputy let them in. 'Mr and Mrs Higgins,' he said. Priest did not correct him. 'Follow me, please.' He led them to a conference room with a grey carpet and bland modern furniture.

Flower was waiting.

She was going to be formidable and voluptuous like her mother, one day, but at thirteen she was still a lanky, awkward girl. Now she was sullen and tearful at the same time. But she seemed unharmed. Star hugged her silently, then Priest did the same.

Star said: 'Honey, have you spent the night in jail?'

Flower shook her head. 'At some house,' she said.

The deputy explained. 'California law is very strict. Juveniles can't be jailed under the same roof as adult criminals. So we have a couple of people in town who are willing to take charge of young offenders overnight. Flower stayed at the home of Miss Waterlow, a local schoolteacher who also happens to be the sheriff's sister.'

Priest asked Flower: 'Was it okay?'

The child nodded dumbly.

He began to feel better. *Hell, worse things can happen to kids.*

The deputy said: 'Sit down, please, Mr and Mrs Higgins. I'm the probation officer, and it's part of my job to deal with juvenile offenders.'

They sat down.

'Flower is charged with stealing a poster worth $9.99 from the Silver Disc Music Store.'

Star turned to her daughter. 'I can't understand this,' she said. 'Why would you steal a *poster* of a damn *movie star*?'

Flower was suddenly vocal. She yelled: 'I just wanted it, okay? I just wanted it!' Then she burst into tears.

Priest addressed the deputy. 'We'd like to take our daughter home as soon as possible. What do we need to do?'

'Mr Higgins, I should point out to you that the maximum penalty for what Flower has done would be imprisonment until the age of twenty-one.'

'Jesus Christ!' Priest exclaimed.

'However, I wouldn't expect such a harsh punishment for a first offence. Tell me, has Flower been in trouble before?'

'Never.'

'Are you surprised by what she has done?'

'Yes.'

'We're flabbergasted,' said Star.

The deputy probed their home life, trying to establish whether Flower was well cared for. Priest answered most of the questions, giving the impression that they were simple agricultural workers. He said nothing of their communal life or their beliefs. The deputy asked where Flower attended school, and Priest explained that there was a school at the winery for the children of workers.

The deputy seemed satisfied with the answers. Flower had to sign a promise to appear in court in four weeks' time at 10 a.m. The deputy asked for one of the parents to countersign, and Star obliged. They did not have to post bail. They were out of there in less than an hour.

Outside the sheriff's office, Priest said: 'This doesn't make you a bad person, Flower. You did a dumb thing, but we love you as much as we always did. Just remember that. And we'll all talk about it when we get home.'

They drove back to the winery. For a while Priest had been unable to think about anything except how his daughter was but, now that he had her back safe and well, he began to reflect on the wider implications of her arrest. The commune had never previously attracted the attention of the police. There was no theft, because they did not acknowledge private property. Sometimes there were fistfights, but the communards dealt with such situations themselves. No one had ever died there. They had no phone to call the police. They never broke any laws except the drug laws, and they were discreet about that.

But now the place was on the map.

It was the worst possible moment for this to happen.

There was nothing he could do about it other than

to be extra-cautious. He resolved not to blame Flower. At her age he had been a full-time professional thief, with an arrest record that stretched back three years. If any parent could understand, he should.

He switched on the car radio. At the top of the hour there was a news bulletin. The last item referred to the earthquake threat. 'Governor Mike Robson meets with FBI agents this morning to discuss the terrorist group the Hammer of Eden, who have threatened to cause an earthquake,' said the newsreader. 'A spokesman for the Bureau said that all threats are taken seriously but would not comment further ahead of the meeting.'

The governor would make his announcement after he met with the FBI, Priest guessed. He wished the radio station had given the time of the meeting.

It was mid-morning when they got home. Melanie's car had gone from the parking circle: she had taken Dusty to San Francisco to leave him with his father for the weekend.

There was a subdued air at the winery. Most of the group were weeding in the vineyard, working without the usual songs and laughter. Outside the cookhouse Holly, the mother of his sons Ringo and Smiler, grimly fried onions while Slow, who was always sensitive to atmosphere, looked frightened as he scrubbed early potatoes from the vegetable garden. Even Oaktree, the carpenter, seemed quiet as he bent over his workbench, sawing a plank.

When they saw Priest and Star returning with Flower, they all began to finish up the tasks they were doing and head for the temple. When there was a crisis they always met to discuss it. If it was a minor matter it could wait until the end of the day, but this was too important to be postponed.

On their way to the temple, Priest and his family were intercepted by Dale and Poem with their daughter, Pearl.

Dale, a small man with neat, short hair, was the most conventional one in the group. He was a key person because he was an expert winemaker and he controlled the blend of each year's vintage. But Priest sometimes felt he treated the commune as if it was any other village. Dale and Poem had been the first couple to build a family cabin. Poem was a dark-skinned woman with a French accent. She had a wild streak—Priest knew, he had slept with her many times—but with Dale she had become kind of domesticated. Dale was one of the few who might conceivably make the readjustment to normal life if he had to leave. Most of them would not, Priest felt: they would end up in jail or institutionalized or dead.

'There's something you should see,' Dale said.

Priest noticed a quick interchange between the girls. Flower shot an accusing glare at Pearl, who looked frightened and guilty.

'What now?' said Star.

Dale led them all to the one empty cabin. At present it was used as a study room by the older children. There was a rough table, some chairs, and a cupboard containing books and pencils. The ceiling had a trapdoor leading to a crawl space under the sloping roof. Now the trapdoor was open and a step-ladder stood beneath it.

Priest had a horrible feeling he knew what was coming.

Dale lit a candle and went up the ladder. Priest and Star followed. In the roof space, illuminated by the flickering candle, they saw the girls' secret cache: a box full of cheap jewellery, make-up, fashionable clothes, and teen magazines.

Priest said quietly: 'All the things we brought them up to consider worthless.'

Dale said: 'They've been hitch-hiking to Silver City. They've done it three times in the past four weeks. They take these clothes and change out of their jeans and work shirts when they get there.'

Star said: 'What do they do there?'

'Hang out on the street, talk to boys, and steal from stores.'

Priest put his hand into the box and pulled out a narrow-bodied T-shirt, blue with a single orange stripe. It was made of nylon, and felt thin and trashy. It was the kind of clothing he despised: it gave no warmth or protection and it did nothing but cover the beauty of the human body with a layer of ugliness.

With the shirt in his hand, he retreated down the stepladder. Star and Dale followed.

The two girls looked mortified.

Priest said: 'Let's go to the temple and discuss this with the group.'

By the time they got there, everyone else had assembled, children included. They were sitting cross-legged on the floor, waiting.

Priest sat in the middle, as always. The discussions were democratic, in theory, and the commune had no leaders, but in practice he and Star dominated all meetings. Priest would steer the dialogue towards the outcome he wanted, usually by asking questions rather than stating a point of view. If he liked an idea he would encourage a discussion of its benefits; if he wanted to squash a proposal he would ask how they could be sure it would work. And if the mood of the meeting was against him, he would pretend to be persuaded, then subvert the decision later.

'Who wants to begin?' he said.

Aneth spoke up. She was a motherly type in her forties, and she believed in understanding rather than condemning. She said: 'Maybe Flower and Pearl should begin, by telling us why they wanted to go to Silver City.'

'To meet people,' Flower said defiantly.

Aneth smiled. 'Boys, you mean?'

Flower shrugged.

Aneth said: 'Well, I guess that's understandable . . . but why did you have to steal?'

'To look nice!'

Star gave an exasperated sigh. 'What's wrong with your regular clothes?'

'Mom, be serious,' Flower said scornfully.

Star leaned forward and slapped her face.

Flower gasped. A red mark appeared on her cheek.

'Don't you dare speak to me that way,' Star said. 'You've just been caught stealing and I've had to get you out of jail, so don't talk as if I'm the stupid one.'

Pearl started to cry.

Priest sighed. He should have seen this coming. There was nothing wrong with the clothes in the free shop. They had jeans in blue, black, or tan; denim work shirts; T-shirts in white, grey, red, and yellow; sandals and boots; heavy wool sweaters for the winter; waterproof coats for working in the rain. But the same clothes were worn by everyone, and had been for years. Of course the children wanted something different. Thirty-five years ago, Priest had stolen a Beatle jacket from a boutique called Rave on San Pedro Street.

Poem said to her daughter: 'Pearl, *chérie*, you don't like your clothes?'

Between sobs she said: 'We wanted to look like Melanie.'

'Ah,' Priest said, and he saw it all.

Melanie was still wearing the clothes she had brought here: skimpy tops that showed her midriff, mini-skirts and short shorts, funky shoes and cute caps. She looked chic and sexy. It was not surprising the girls had adopted her as a role model.

Dale said: 'We need to talk about Melanie.' He sounded apprehensive. Most of them were nervous about saying anything that might be seen as a criticism of Priest.

Priest felt defensive. He had brought Melanie here and he was her lover. And she was crucial to the plan.

She was the only one who could interpret the data from Michael's disc, which had now been copied on to her laptop. Priest could not let them turn on her. 'We never make people change their clothes when they join us,' he said. 'They wear out their old stuff first, it's always been the rule.'

Alaska spoke up. A former schoolteacher, she had come here with her lover, Juice, ten years ago, after they had been ostracized in the small town where they lived for coming out as lesbians. 'It's not just her clothes,' Alaska said. 'She doesn't do much work.' Juice nodded agreement.

Priest argued: 'I've seen her in the kitchen, washing dishes and baking cookies.'

Alaska looked scared, but she persisted. 'Some light domestic chores. She doesn't work in the vineyard. She's a passenger, Priest.'

Star saw Priest coming under attack and weighed in on his side. 'We've had a lot of people like that. Remember what Holly was like when she first came?'

Holly had been a bit like Melanie, a pretty girl who was attracted first to Priest and then to the commune.

Holly grinned ruefully. 'I admit it. I was lazy. But eventually I started to feel bad about not pulling my weight. Nobody said anything to me. I just realized I'd be happier doing my fair share.'

Now Garden spoke. A former junkie, she was twenty-five but looked forty. 'Melanie's a bad influence. She talks to the kids about pop records and TV shows and trash like that.'

Priest said: 'Obviously we need to have a discussion

with Melanie about this when she gets back from San Francisco. I know she's going to be very upset when she hears what Flower and Pearl have done.'

Dale was not satisfied. 'What bugs a lot of us . . .'

Priest frowned. This sounded as if a group of them had been talking behind his back. *Jesus, have I got a full-scale rebellion on my hands?* He let his displeasure show in his voice. 'Well? What *bugs* a lot of you?'

Dale swallowed. 'Her mobile phone and computer.'

There was no power line into the valley, so they had few electrical appliances; and there had grown up a kind of puritanism about things like TV and video-tapes. Priest had to listen to his car radio to hear the news. They had come to look down on anything electrical. Melanie's equipment, which she recharged at the public library in Silver City by plugging into an outlet normally used for the vacuum cleaner, had drawn some disapproving stares. Now several people nodded agreement with Dale's complaint.

There was a special reason why Melanie had to keep her mobile and her computer. But Priest could not explain it to Dale. He was not a Rice Eater. Although he was a full member of the group and had been here for years, Priest could not be sure he would go along with the earthquake plan. He might freak.

Priest realized he had to end this. It was getting out of control. Discontented people had to be dealt with one by one, not in a collective discussion where they reinforced one another.

But before he could say anything, Poem weighed in. 'Priest, is there something going on? Something you're not telling us about? I never really understood why you and Star had to go away for two-and-a-half weeks.'

Song, supporting Priest, said: 'Wow, that's such a mistrustful question!'

The group was falling apart, Priest could see. It was the imminent prospect of having to leave the valley. There was no sign of the miracle he had hinted at. They saw their world coming to an end.

Star said: 'I thought I told everyone. I had an uncle who died and left his affairs in a tangle, and I was his only relative, so I had to help the lawyers straighten everything out.'

Enough.

Priest knew how to choke off a protest. He spoke decisively. 'I feel we're discussing these things in a bad atmosphere,' he said. 'Does anyone agree with me?'

They all did, of course. Most of them nodded.

'What do we do about it?' Priest looked at his ten-year-old son, a dark-eyed, serious child. 'What do you say, Ringo?'

'We meditate together,' the boy said. It was the answer any of them would give.

Priest looked around. 'Does everyone approve of Ringo's idea?'

They did.

'Then let's make ourselves ready.'

Each of them assumed the position they liked. Some lay flat on their backs, others bent into a foetal curl, one or two lay as if sleeping. Priest and several others sat cross-legged, hands loose on their knees, eyes closed, faces raised to heaven.

'Relax the small toe of your left foot,' Priest said in a quiet, penetrating voice. 'Then the fourth toe, then the third, then the second, then the big toe. Relax your whole foot . . . and your ankle . . . and then your calf.' As he went slowly around the body, a contemplative peace descended on the room. People's breathing slowed and became even, their bodies grew more and more still, and their faces gradually took on the tranquillity of meditation.

Finally Priest said a slow, deep syllable: 'Om.'

With one voice, the congregation replied: 'Omm . . .'

My people.
May they live here for ever.

CHAPTER SIX

THE MEETING at the governor's office was scheduled for twelve noon. Sacramento, the state capital, was a couple of hours' drive from San Francisco. Judy left home at nine forty-five to allow for heavy traffic getting out of the city.

The aide she was to meet, Al Honeymoon, was a well-known figure in California politics. Officially cabinet secretary, he was in fact hatchet man. Any time Governor Robson needed to run a new highway through a beauty spot, build a nuclear power station, fire a thousand government employees, or betray a faithful friend, he got Honeymoon to do the dirty work.

The two men had been colleagues for twenty years. When they met, Mike Robson was still only a state congressman and Honeymoon was fresh out of law school. Honeymoon had been selected for his bad-guy role because he was black, and the governor had shrewdly calculated that the press would hesitate to vilify a black man. Those liberal days were long gone, but Honeymoon had matured into a political operator of great skill and utter ruthlessness. No one liked him, but plenty of people were scared of him.

For the sake of the Bureau, Judy wanted to make a good impression on him. It was not often that political types had a direct personal interest in an FBI case. Judy knew that her handling of this assignment would for ever colour Honeymoon's attitude to the Bureau and to law enforcement agencies in general. Personal experience always had more impact than reports and statistics.

The FBI liked to appear all-powerful and infallible. But she had made so little progress with the case that it would be kind of difficult to play that part, especially to a hardass like Honeymoon. Anyway, it was not her style. Her plan was simply to appear efficient and inspire confidence.

And she had another reason for giving a good account of herself. She wanted Governor Robson's statement to open the door to a dialogue with the Hammer of Eden. A hint that the governor might negotiate could just persuade them to hold off. And if they responded by trying to communicate, that might give Judy new clues to who they were. Right now, it was the only way she could think of to catch them. All other lines of inquiry had led to dead ends.

She thought it might be difficult to persuade the governor to give this hint. He would not want to give the impression he would listen to terrorist demands, for fear of encouraging others. But there should be a way to word the statement so that the message was clear only to the Hammer of Eden people.

She was not wearing her Armani power suit. Instinct told her that Honeymoon was more likely to warm to someone who came on as a working Joe, so she had put on a steel-grey pantsuit, tied her hair back in a neat knot, and carried her gun in a holster on her hip. In case that was too severe, she wore small pearl earrings that called attention to her long neck. It never did any harm to look attractive.

She wondered idly whether Michael Quercus found her attractive. He was a dish: shame he was so irritating. Her mother would have approved of him. Judy could remember her saying: 'I like a man who takes charge.' Quercus dressed nicely, in an understated kind of way. She wondered what his body was like under his clothes. Maybe he was covered with dark hair, like a monkey: she did not like hairy men. Maybe he was pale and soft, but she thought not: he seemed fit. She realized she was fantasizing about Quercus in the nude, and she felt annoyed with herself. *The last thing I need is a bad-tempered matinée idol.*

She decided to call ahead and check the parking. She dialled the governor's office on her cellphone and got Honeymoon's secretary. 'I have a twelve noon meeting with Mr Honeymoon and I'm wondering if I can park at the Capitol building. I've never been to Sacramento before.'

The secretary was a young man. 'We have no visitor parking at the building, but there's a parking garage on the next block.'

'Where exactly is that?'

'The entrance is on Tenth Street between K Street and L. The Capitol building is on Tenth between L and M. It's literally a minute away. But your meeting isn't at noon, it's at eleven-thirty.'

'What?'

'Your meeting is scheduled for eleven thirty.'

'Has it been changed?'

'No, ma'am, it always was eleven thirty.'

Judy was furious. To arrive late would create a bad impression even before she opened her mouth. This was already going wrong.

She controlled her anger. 'I guess someone made a mistake.' She checked her watch. If she drove like hell she could be there in ninety minutes. 'It's no problem, I'm running ahead of schedule,' she lied. 'I'll be there.'

'Very good.'

She put her foot down and watched the Monte Carlo's speedometer climb to a hundred. Fortunately the road was not busy. Most of the morning traffic was headed the other way, into San Francisco.

Brian Kincaid had told her the time of the meeting, so he would be late too. They were travelling separately because he had a second appointment in Sacramento, at the FBI field office there. Judy dialled the San Francisco office and spoke to the SAC's secretary. 'Linda, this is Judy. Would you call Brian and tell him the governor's aide is expecting us at eleven thirty, not twelve noon, please?'

'I think he knows that,' Linda said.

'No, he doesn't. He told me twelve. See if you can reach him and warn him.'

'Sure will.'

'Thanks.' Judy hung up and concentrated on her driving.

A few minutes later she heard a police siren.

She looked in her mirror and saw the familiar tan paint job of a California Highway Patrol car.

'I do not fucking believe this,' she said.

She pulled over and braked hard. The patrol car pulled in behind her. She opened her door.

An amplified voice said: 'STAY IN THE CAR.'

She took out her FBI shield, held it at arm's length so the cop could see it, then got out.

'STAY IN THE CAR!'

She heard a note of fear in the voice and saw that the patrolman was alone. She sighed. She could just imagine some rookie cop pulling a gun and shooting her out of nervousness.

She held out her shield so he could see it. 'FBI!' she shouted. 'Look, for Christ's sake!'

'GET BACK IN THE CAR!'

She looked at her watch. It was ten thirty. Shaking with frustration, she sat in her car. She left the door open.

There was a maddeningly long wait.

At last the patrolman approached her. 'The reason I stopped you is that you were doing ninety-nine miles per hour—'

'Just look at this,' she said, holding out her shield.

'What's that?'

'For Christ's sake, it's an FBI shield! I'm an agent on urgent business and you've just delayed me!'

'Well, you sure don't look like—'

She jumped out of the car, startling him, and waved a finger under his chin. 'Don't you tell me I don't look like a fucking agent. You don't recognize an FBI shield, so how would you know what an agent looks like?' She put her hands on her hips, pushing her jacket back so that he could see her holster.

'Can I see your licence, please?'

'Hell, no. I'm leaving now, and I'm going to drive to Sacramento at ninety-nine miles per hour, do you understand?' She got back into the car.

'You can't do that,' he said.

'Write your congressman,' she said, and she slammed the door and drove off.

She moved into the fast lane, accelerated to a hundred then checked her watch. She had wasted about five minutes. She could still make it.

She had lost her temper with the patrolman. He would tell his superior, who would complain to the FBI. Judy would get a reprimand. But if she had been polite to the guy she would still be there. 'Shit,' she said feelingly.

She reached the turn-off for downtown Sacramento at eleven twenty. By eleven twenty-five she was entering the parking garage on 10th Street. It took her a couple of minutes to find a slot. She ran down the staircase and across the street.

The Capitol building was a white stone palace like a wedding cake, set in immaculate gardens bordered by giant palm trees. She hurried along a marble hall to a large doorway with 'GOVERNOR' carved over it. She stopped, took a couple of calming breaths, and checked her watch.

It was exactly eleven thirty. She had got there on time. The Bureau would not look incompetent.

She opened the double doors and stepped inside.

She found herself in a large lobby presided over by a secretary behind an enormous desk. On one side was a row of chairs where, to her surprise, she saw Brian Kincaid waiting, looking cool and relaxed in a crisp dark grey suit, his white hair neatly combed, not at all like someone who had rushed to get here. She was suddenly conscious that she was perspiring.

When Kincaid caught her eye, she saw a flash of surprise in his expression, swiftly suppressed.

She said: 'Uh . . . hi, Brian.'

'Morning.' He looked away.

He did not thank her for sending a message to warn him that the meeting was earlier.

She asked: 'What time did you get here?'

'A few minutes ago.'

That meant he had known the correct time for the meeting. But he had told her it was half an hour later. Surely he had not deliberately misled her? It seemed almost childish.

Before she had time to reach a conclusion, a young black man emerged from a side door. He spoke to Brian. 'Agent Kincaid?'

He stood up. 'That's me.'

'And you must be Agent Maddox. Mr Honeymoon will see you both now.'

They followed him along the corridor and around

a corner. As they walked, he said: 'We call this the Horseshoe, because the governor's offices are grouped around three sides of a rectangle.'

Halfway along the second side they passed another lobby, this one occupied by two secretaries. A young man holding a file waited on a leather couch. Judy guessed that was the way to the governor's personal office. A few steps on, they were shown into Honeymoon's room.

He was a big man with close-cropped hair turning grey. He had taken off the jacket of his grey pinstripe suit to reveal black suspenders. The sleeves of his white shirt were rolled, but his silk tie was fastened tight in a high pin-through collar. He removed a pair of gold-rimmed half-glasses and stood up. He had a dark, sculptured face that wore a don't-fuck-with-me expression. He could have been a police lieutenant, except he was too well dressed.

Despite his intimidating appearance, his manner was courteous. He shook their hands and said: 'I appreciate your coming here all the way from San Francisco.'

'No problem,' said Kincaid.

They sat down.

Without preamble, Honeymoon said: 'What's your assessment of the situation?'

Kincaid said: 'Well, sir, you particularly asked to meet with the agent at the sharp end, so I'll let Judy here fill you in.'

Judy said: 'We haven't caught these people yet, I'm afraid.' Then she cursed herself for beginning with an apology. *Be positive!* 'We're fairly sure they're *not* connected with the Green California Campaign—that was a weak attempt to lay a false trail. We don't know who they are, but I can tell you some important things we have found out about them.'

Honeymoon said: 'Go ahead, please.'

'First of all, linguistic analysis of the threat message tells us we're dealing not with a lone individual but with a group.'

Kincaid said: 'Well, two people at least.'

Judy glared at Kincaid, but he did not meet her eye.

Honeymoon said irritably: 'Which is it, two or a group?'

Judy felt herself blush. 'The message was composed by a man and typed by a woman, so there are at least two. We don't yet know if there are more.'

'Okay. But please be exact.'

This was not going well.

Judy pressed on. 'Point two: these people are not insane.'

Kincaid said: 'Well, not clinically. But they sure as hell aren't normal.' He laughed, as if he had said something witty.

Judy silently cursed him for undermining her. 'People who commit crimes of violence can be divided into two kinds, organized and disorganized. The disorganized kind act on the spur of the moment, use whatever weapons come to hand, and choose their victims at random. They're the real crazies.'

Honeymoon was interested. 'And the other kind?'

'The organized ones plan their crimes, carry their

weapons with them, and attack victims who have been selected beforehand using some logical criteria.'

Kincaid said: 'They're just crazy in a different way.'

Judy tried to ignore him. 'Such people may be sick, but they are not looney tunes. We can think of them as rational, and try to anticipate what they might do.'

'All right. And the Hammer of Eden people are organized.'

'Judging by their threat message, yes.'

'You rely a great deal on this linguistic analysis,' Honeymoon said sceptically.

'It's a powerful tool.'

Kincaid put in: 'It's no substitute for careful investigative work. But in this case, it's all we've got.'

The implication seemed to be that they had to fall back on linguistic analysis because Judy had failed to do the legwork. Feeling desperate, she struggled on. 'We're dealing with serious people—which means that if they can't cause an earthquake, they may attempt something else.'

'Such as?'

'One of the more usual terrorist acts. Explode a bomb, take a hostage, murder a prominent figure.'

Kincaid said: 'Assuming they have the capability, of course. So far we've nothing to indicate that.'

Judy took a deep breath. There was something she had to say, and she could not avoid it. 'However, I'm not prepared to rule out the possibility that they really could cause an earthquake.'

Honeymoon said: '*What?*'

Kincaid laughed scornfully.

Judy said stubbornly: 'It's not likely, but it's conceivable. That's what I was told by California's leading expert, Professor Quercus. I'd be failing in my duty if I didn't tell you.'

Kincaid leaned back in his chair and crossed his legs. 'Judy has told you the textbook answers, Al,' he said in a we're-all-boys-together tone of voice. 'Now maybe I should tell you how it looks from the perspective of a certain amount of age and experience.'

Judy stared at him. *I'll get you for this if it's the last thing I do, Kincaid. You've spent this entire meeting putting me down. But what if there really is an earthquake, you asshole? What will you say to the relatives of the dead?*

'Please go on,' Honeymoon said to Kincaid.

'These people can't cause an earthquake and they don't give a flying fuck about power plants. My instinct tells me this is a guy trying to impress his girlfriend. He's got the governor freaked out, he's got the FBI running around like blue-assed flies, and the whole thing is on the John Truth radio show every night. Suddenly he's a big shot and she's, like, wow!'

Judy felt totally humiliated. Kincaid had let her lay out her findings and then poured scorn on everything she had said. He had obviously planned this, and she was now sure that he had deliberately misled her about the time of the meeting in the hope that she would show up late. The whole thing was a strategy for discrediting her and at the same time making Kincaid look better. She felt sick.

Honeymoon stood up suddenly. 'I'm going to

advise the governor to take no action on this threat.'
He added dismissively: 'Thank you both.'

Judy realized it was too late to ask him to open the
door to dialogue with the terrorists. The moment had
passed. And any suggestion of hers would be nixed by
Kincaid anyway. She felt despairing. *What if it's real?*
What if they actually can do it?

Kincaid said: 'Any time we can be of assistance, you
just let us know.'

Honeymoon looked faintly scornful. He hardly
needed an invitation to use the services of the FBI.
But he politely held out his hand to shake.

A moment later, Judy and Kincaid were outside.

Judy remained silent as they walked around the
Horseshoe and through the lobby into the marble
hallway. There Kincaid stopped and said: 'You did just
fine in there, Judy. Don't you worry about a thing.'
He could not conceal his smirk.

She was determined not to let him see how rattled
she was. She wanted to scream at him, but she forced
herself to say calmly: 'I think we did our job.'

'Sure we did. Where are you parked?'

'In the garage across the street.' She jerked a thumb.

'I'm the opposite side. See you later.'

'You bet.'

Judy watched him walk away, then she turned and
went in the other direction.

Crossing the street, she saw a See's Candy store. She
went in and bought some chocolates.

Driving back to San Francisco, she ate the whole
box.

CHAPTER SEVEN

P RIEST NEEDED physical activity to keep him from going crazy with tension. After the meeting in the temple he went to the vineyard and started weeding. It was a hot day, and he soon worked up a sweat and took off his shirt.

Star worked beside him. After an hour or so she looked at her watch. 'Time for a break,' she said. 'Let's go listen to the news.'

They sat in Priest's car and turned on the radio. The bulletin was identical to the one they had heard earlier. Priest ground his teeth in frustration. 'Damn, the governor has to say something soon!'

Star said: 'We don't expect him to give in right away, do we?'

'No, but I thought there would be some message, maybe just a hint of a concession. Hell, the idea of a freeze on new power plants ain't exactly wacko. Millions of people in California probably agree with it.'

Star nodded. 'Shit, in Los Angeles it's already dangerous to breathe because of the pollution, for Christ's sake! I can't believe people really want to live that way.'

'But nothing happens.'

'Well, we figured all along we'd need to give a demonstration before they'd listen.'

'Yeah.' Priest hesitated, then blurted: 'I guess I'm just scared it won't work.'

'The seismic vibrator?'

He hesitated again. He would not have been this frank with anyone but Star, and he was already half-regretting his confession of doubt. But he had begun, so he might as well finish. 'The whole thing,' he said. 'I'm scared there'll be no earthquake, and then we'll be lost.'

She was a little shocked, he could see. She was used to him being supremely confident about everything he did. But he had never done anything like this.

Walking back to the vineyard, she said: 'Do something with Flower tonight.'

'What do you mean?'

'Spend time with her. Do something with her. You're always playing with Dusty.'

Dusty was five. It was easy to have fun with him. He was fascinated by everything. Flower was thirteen, the age when everything grown-ups do seems stupid. Priest was about to say this when he realized there was another reason for what Star was saying.

She thinks I may die tomorrow.

The thought hit him like a punch. He knew that this earthquake plan was dangerous, of course, but he had mainly considered the peril to himself and the risk of leaving the commune leaderless. He had not imagined Flower alone in the world at the age of thirteen.

'What'll I do with her?' he said.

'She wants to learn the guitar.'

That was news to Priest. He was not much of a guitarist himself, but he could play folk songs and simple blues, enough to get her started anyway. He shrugged. 'Okay, we'll start tonight.'

They went back to work, but a few minutes later they were interrupted when Slow, grinning from ear to ear, shouted: 'Hey, lookit who's here!'

Priest looked across the vineyard. The person he was waiting for was Melanie. She had gone to San Francisco to take Dusty to his father. She was the only one who could tell Priest exactly where to use the seismic vibrator, and he would not feel comfortable until she was back. But it was too early to expect her, and anyway Slow would not have got so excited about Melanie.

He saw a man coming down the hill, followed by a woman carrying a child. Priest frowned. Often a year went by without a single visitor coming to the valley. This morning they had had the cop; now these people. But were they strangers? He narrowed his eyes. The man's rolling walk was terribly familiar. As the figures got closer, Priest said: 'My God, is that Bones?'

'Yes, it is!' Star said delightedly. 'Holy Moley!' And she hurried toward the newcomers. Spirit joined in the excitement and ran with her, barking.

Priest followed more slowly. Bones, whose real name was Billy Owens, was a Rice Eater. But he had liked the way things were before Priest arrived. He enjoyed the hand-to-mouth existence of the early commune. He revelled in the constant crises, and liked to be drunk or stoned, or both, within a couple of hours of waking up. He played the blues harmonica with manic brilliance and was the most successful street beggar they had. He had not joined a commune to find work, self-discipline, and a daily act of worship. So after a couple of years, when it became clear that the Priest–Star regime was permanent, Bones took off. He had not been seen since. Now, after more than twenty years, he was back.

Star threw her arms around him, hugged him hard, and kissed his lips. Those two had been a serious item for a while. All the men in the commune had slept with Star, in those days, but she had had a special soft spot for Bones. Priest felt a twinge of jealousy as he watched Bones press Star's body to his own.

When they let each other go, Priest could see that Bones did not look well. He had always been a thin man, but now he looked as if he was dying of starvation. He had wild hair and a straggly beard, but the beard was matted and the hair seemed to be falling out in clumps. His jeans and T-shirt were dirty, and the heel had come off one of his cowboy boots.

He's here because he's in trouble.

Bones introduced the woman as Debbie. She was younger than he, no more than twenty-five, and pretty in a pinched-looking way. Her child was a boy about eighteen months old. She and the kid were almost as thin and dirty as Bones.

It was time for their midday meal. They took Bones to the cookhouse. Lunch was a casserole made with pearl barley and flavoured with herbs grown by Garden. Debbie ate ravenously and fed the child too, but Bones just took a couple of spoonfuls then lit a cigarette.

There was a lot of talk about the old times. Bones said: 'I'll tell you my favourite memory. One afternoon right on that hillside over there, Star explained to me about cunnilingus.' There was a ripple of laughter around the table. It was faintly embarrassed laughter, but Bones failed to pick up on that, and he went on: 'I was twenty years old and I never knew people did that. I was shocked! But she made me try it. And the taste! Yech!'

'There was a lot you didn't know,' Star said. 'I remember you telling me that you couldn't understand why you sometimes got headaches in the morning, and I had to explain to you that it happened whenever you got falling-down drunk the night before. You didn't know the meaning of the word "hangover".'

She had deftly changed the subject. In the old days it had been perfectly normal to talk about cunnilingus around the table, but things had changed since Bones left. No one had ever made an issue of cleaning up their conversation, but it had happened naturally as the children started to understand more.

Bones was nervy, laughing a lot, trying too hard to be friendly, fidgeting, chain-smoking. *He wants something. But he'll tell me what it is soon enough.*

As they cleared the table and washed the bowls, Bones took Priest aside and said: 'Got something I want to show you. Come on.'

Priest shrugged and went with him.

As they walked, Priest took out a little bag of marijuana and a pack of cigarette papers. The communards did not usually smoke dope during the day, because it slowed down the work in the vineyard, but today was a special day, and Priest felt the need to soothe his nerves. As they walked up the hill and through the trees, he rolled a joint with the ease of long practice.

Bones licked his lips. 'You don't have anything with, like, more of a kick, do you?'

'What are you using these days, Bones?'

'A little brown sugar now and again, you know, keep my head straight.'

Heroin.

So that was it. Bones had become a junkie.

'We don't have any smack here,' Priest told him. 'No one uses it.' *And I'd get rid of anyone who did, faster than you can say spike.*

Priest lit the joint.

When they reached the clearing where the cars were parked, Bones said: 'This is it.'

At first Priest could not work out what he was looking at. It was a truck, but what kind? It was painted with a gay design in bright red and yellow, and along the side was a picture of a monster breathing fire, and some lettering in the same gaudy colours.

Bones, who knew that Priest could not read, said: 'The Dragon's Mouth. It's a carnival ride.'

Priest saw it then. A lot of small carnival rides were mounted on trucks. The truck engine powered the ride in use. Then the parts of the ride could be folded down and the truck driven to the next site.

Priest passed him the joint and said: 'Is it yours?'

Bones took a long toke, held the smoke down, then blew out before answering. 'I been making my living from this for ten years. But it needs work, and I can't afford to get it fixed. So I have to sell it.'

Now Priest could see what was coming.

Bones took another draw on the joint but did not hand it back. 'It's probably worth fifty thousand dollars, but I'm asking ten.'

Priest nodded. 'Sounds like a bargain . . . for someone.'

'Maybe you guys should buy it,' Bones said.

'What the fuck would I do with a carnival ride, Bones?'

'It's a good investment. If you have a bad year with the wine, you could go out with the ride and make some money.'

They had bad years, sometimes. There was nothing they could do about the weather. But Paul Beale was always willing to give them credit. He believed in the ideals of the commune, even though he had been unable to live up to them himself. And he knew there would always be another vintage next year.

Priest shook his head. 'No way. But I wish you luck, old buddy. Keep trying, you'll find a buyer.'

Bones must have known it had been a long shot, but all the same he looked panicky. 'Hey, Priest, you want to know the truth of it . . . I'm in bad shape.

Could you loan me a thousand bucks? That'd get me straight.'

It would get you stoned out of your head, you mean. Then, after a few days, you'd be right back where you were.

'We don't have any money,' Priest told him. 'We don't use it here, don't you remember that?'

Bones looked crafty. 'You gotta have a stash somewhere, come on!'

And you think I'm going to tell you about it?

'Sorry, pal, can't help.'

Bones nodded. 'That's a bummer, man. I mean, I'm in serious trouble.'

Priest said: 'And don't try to go behind my back and ask Star, because you'll get the same answer.' He put a harsh note into his voice. 'Are you listening to me?'

'Sure, sure,' Bones said, looking scared. 'Be cool, Priest, man, be cool.'

'I'm cool,' Priest said.

*

Priest worried about Melanie all afternoon. She might have changed her mind, and decided to go back to her husband, or simply got scared and taken off in her car. Then he would be finished. There was no way he or anyone else here could interpret the data on Michael Quercus's disc and figure out where to place the seismic vibrator tomorrow.

But she showed up at the end of the afternoon, to his great relief. He told her about Flower being arrested, and warned her that one or two people wanted to put the blame on Melanie and her cute clothes. She said she would get some work clothes from the free shop.

After supper Priest went to Song's cabin and picked up her guitar. 'Are you using this?' he said politely. He would never say 'May I borrow your guitar?' because in theory all property was communal, so the guitar was his as much as hers, even though she had made it. However, in practice everyone always asked.

He sat outside his cabin with Flower and tuned the guitar. Spirit, the dog, watched alertly, as if he, too, was going to learn to play. 'Most songs have three chords,' Priest began. 'If you know three chords you can play nine out of ten of the songs in the whole world.'

He showed her the chord of C. As she struggled to press the strings with her soft fingertips, he studied her face in the evening light: perfect skin, the dark hair, green eyes like Star's, the little frown as she concentrated. *I have to stay alive, to take care of you.*

He thought of himself at that age, already a criminal, experienced, skilled, hardened to violence, with a hatred of cops and a contempt for ordinary citizens who were dumb enough to let themselves get robbed. *At thirteen I had already gone wrong.* He was determined that Flower would not be like that. She had been brought up in a community of love and peace, untouched by the world that had corrupted little Ricky Granger and turned him into a hoodlum before he grew hair on his chin. *You'll be okay, I'll make sure of it.*

She played the chord, and Priest realized that a particular song had been running in his head ever since Bones arrived. It was a folkie number from the early sixties that Star had always liked.

> *Show me the prison*
> *Show me the jail*
> *Show me the prisoner*
> *Whose life has gone stale*

'I'll teach you a song your mommy used to sing to you when you were a baby,' he said. He took the guitar from her. 'Do you remember this?' He sang:

> *I'll show you a young man*
> *With so many reasons why*

In his head he heard Star's unmistakable voice, low and sexy then as now.

> *There, but for fortune*
> *Go you or I*
> *You or I.*

Priest was about the same age as Bones, and Bones was dying. Priest had no doubt about that. Soon the girl and the baby would leave him. He would starve his body and feed his habit. He might overdose, or poison himself with bad drugs, or he might just abuse his system until it gave up and he got pneumonia. One way or another, he was a dead man.

If I lose this place, I'll go the same way as Bones.

As Flower struggled to play the chord of A minor, Priest toyed with the idea of returning to normal society. He fantasized going every day to a job, buying socks and wingtip shoes, owning a TV set and a toaster. The thought made him queasy. He had never lived straight. He had been brought up in a whorehouse, educated on the streets, briefly the owner of a semi-legitimate business, and for most of his life the leader of a hippie commune cut off from the world.

He recalled the one regular job he had ever had. At eighteen he had gone to work for the Jenkinsons, the couple who ran the liquor store down the street. He had thought of them as old, at the time, but now he guessed they had been in their fifties. His intention had been to work just long enough to figure out where they kept their money, then steal it. But then he learned something about himself.

He discovered he had a queer talent for arithmetic. Each morning, Mr Jenkinson put ten dollars' worth of change into the cash register. As customers bought liquor and paid and got change, Priest either served them himself or heard one of the Jenkinsons sing out the total, 'Dollar twenty-nine, please, Mrs Roberto,' or 'Three bucks even, sir.' And the figures seemed to add themselves up in his head. All day long, Priest always knew exactly how much money was in the till, and at the end of the day he could tell Mr Jenkinson the total before he counted it.

He would hear Mr Jenkinson talking to the salesmen who called, and he soon knew the wholesale and retail prices of every item in the store. From then on the automatic register in his brain calculated the profit on every transaction, and he was awestruck by how much the Jenkinsons were making *without stealing from anyone.*

He arranged for them to be robbed four times in a month, then made them an offer for the store. When they turned him down, he arranged a fifth robbery and made sure Mrs Jenkinson got roughed up this time. After that Mr Jenkinson accepted his offer.

Priest borrowed the deposit from the neighbourhood loan shark and paid Mr Jenkinson the instalments out of the store's takings. Although he could not read or write, he always knew his financial position exactly. Nobody could cheat him. One time he employed a respectable-looking middle-aged woman who stole a dollar out of the register every day. At the end of the week he deducted five dollars from her pay, beat her up and told her not to come back.

Within a year he had four stores; two years later he had a wholesale liquor warehouse; after three years he was a millionaire; and at the end of his fourth year he was on the run.

He sometimes wondered what might have happened if he had paid off the loan shark in full, given his accountant honest figures to report to the IRS, and made a plea-bargain deal with the LAPD on the fraud charges. Maybe today he would have a company as big as Coca-Cola and be living in one of those mansions in Beverly Hills with a gardener and a pool boy and a five-car garage.

But as he tried to imagine it, he knew it could never have happened. That was not him. The guy who came down the stairs of the mansion in a white bathrobe, and coolly ordered the maid to squeeze him a glass of orange juice, had someone else's face. Priest could never live in the square world. He had always had a problem with rules: he could never obey other people's. That was why he had to live here.

In Silver River Valley I make the rules, I change the rules, I am the rules.

Flower told him her fingers hurt.

'Then it's time to stop,' Priest said. 'If you like, I'll teach you another song tomorrow.' *If I'm still alive.*

'Does it hurt you?'

'No, but that's only because I'm used to it. When you've practised the guitar a little, your fingertips get hard pads on them, like the skin on your heel.'

'Does Noel Gallagher have hard pads?'

'If Noel Gallagher is a pop guitarist . . .'

'Of course! He's in Oasis!'

'Well, then he has hard pads. Do you think you might like to be a musician?'

'No.'

'That was pretty definite. You have some other ideas?'

She looked guilty, as if she knew he was going to disapprove, but she screwed up her courage and said: 'I want to be a writer.'

He was not sure how he felt about that. *Your Daddy will never be able to read your work.* But he pretended enthusiasm. 'That's good! What kind?'

'For a magazine. Like *Teen*, maybe.'

'Why?'

'You get to meet stars and interview them, and write about fashions and make-up.'

Priest gritted his teeth and tried not to let his revulsion show. 'Well, I like the idea that you might be a writer, anyway. If you wrote poetry and stories, instead of magazine articles, you could still live here in Silver River Valley.'

'Yeah, maybe,' she said doubtfully.

He could see that she was not planning to spend her life here. But she was too young to understand. By the time she was old enough to decide for herself, she would have a different view. *I hope.*

Star came over. 'Time for Truth,' she said.

Priest took the guitar from Flower. 'Go and get ready for bed now,' he said.

He and Star headed for the parking circle, dropping off the guitar at Song's cabin on the way. They found Melanie already there, sitting in the back seat of the 'Cuda, listening to the radio. She had put on a bright yellow T-shirt and blue jeans from the free shop. Both were too big for her, and she had tucked in the T-shirt and pulled the jeans tight with a belt, showing off her tiny waist. She still looked like sex on a stick.

John Truth had a flat nasal twang that could become hypnotic. His specialty was saying aloud the things his listeners believed in their hearts but were ashamed to admit to. It was mostly standard fascist pig stuff: AIDS was a punishment for sin, intelligence was racially inherited, what the world needed was stricter discipline, all politicians were stupid and corrupt, and stuff like that. Priest imagined that his audience was mostly the kind of fat white men who learned everything they knew in bars. 'This guy,' Star said. 'He's everything I hate about America: prejudiced, sanctimonious, hypocritical, self-righteous and really fucking stupid.'

'That's a fact,' Priest said. 'Listen up.'

Truth was saying: 'I'm going to read once more that statement made by the governor's cabinet secretary, Mr Honeymoon.'

Priest's hackles rose, and Star said: 'That son of a bitch!' Honeymoon was the man behind the scheme to flood Silver River Valley, and they hated him.

John Truth went on, speaking slowly and ponderously, as if every syllable was significant. 'Listen to this. "The FBI has investigated the threat which appeared on an Internet bulletin board on the first of May. That investigation has determined that there is no substance to the threat."'

Priest's heart sank. This was what he had expected, but all the same he was dismayed. He had hoped for at least some slight hint of appeasement. But Honeymoon sounded completely intractable.

Truth carried on reading. '"Governor Mike Robson, following the FBI's recommendation, has decided to take no further action." That, my friends, is the statement *in its entirety*.' Truth obviously felt it was outrageously short. 'Are *you* satisfied? The terrorist deadline runs out tomorrow. Do *you* feel reassured?

Call John Truth on this number now to tell the world what *you* think.'

Priest said: 'That means we have to do it.'

Melanie said: 'Well, I never expected the governor to cave in without a demonstration.'

'Nor did I, I guess.' He frowned. 'The statement mentioned the FBI twice. It sounds to me like Mike Robson is getting ready to blame the Feds if things go wrong. And that makes me wonder if in his heart he's not so sure.'

'So, if we give him proof that we really can cause an earthquake . . .'

'Maybe he'll think again.'

Star looked downcast. 'Shit,' she said. 'I guess I've been hoping we wouldn't have to do this.'

Priest was alarmed. He did not want Star to get cold feet at this point. Her support was necessary to carry the rest of the Rice Eaters. 'We can do this without hurting anyone,' he said. 'Melanie has picked the perfect location.' He turned to the back seat. 'Tell Star what we talked about.'

Melanie leaned forward and unfolded a map so that Star and Priest could see it. She did not know that Priest could not read maps. 'Here's the Owens Valley fault,' she said, pointing to a red streak. 'There were major earthquakes in 1790 and 1872, so another one is overdue.'

Star said: 'Surely earthquakes don't happen according to a regular timetable?'

'No. But the history of the fault shows that enough pressure for an earthquake builds up over about a century. Which means we can cause one now if we give a nudge in the right place.'

'Which is where?' Star said.

Melanie pointed to a spot on the map. 'Round about here.'

'You can't be exact?'

'Not until I get there. Michael's data gives us the location within about a mile. When I look at the landscape I should be able to pinpoint the spot.'

'How?'

'Evidence of earlier earthquakes.'

'Okay.'

'Now, the best time, according to Michael's seismic window, will be between one thirty and two twenty.'

'How can you be sure no one will get hurt?'

'Look at the map. Owens Valley is thinly populated, just a few small towns strung along a dried-up river bed. The point I've chosen is miles from any human habitation.'

Priest added: 'We can be sure the earthquake will be minor. The effects will hardly be felt in the nearest town.' He knew this was not certain, and so did Melanie; but he gave her a hard stare and she did not contradict him.

Star said: 'If the effects are hardly felt, no one's going to give a shit, so why do it?'

She was being contrary, but that was just a sign of how tense she was. Priest said: 'We said we would cause an earthquake tomorrow. As soon as we've done it, we'll call John Truth on Melanie's mobile phone and tell him we kept our promise.' *What a moment that will be, what a feeling!*

'Will he believe us?'

Melanie said: 'He'll have to, when he checks the seismograph.'

Priest said: 'Imagine how Governor Robson and his people will feel.' He could hear the exultation in his own voice. 'Especially that asshole Honeymoon. They'll be, like: "Shit! These people really can cause earthquakes, man! What the fuck we gonna do?"'

'And then what?' said Star.

'Then we threaten to do it again. But this time, we don't give them a month. We give them a week.'

'How will we make the threat? Same way we did before?'

Melanie answered. 'I don't think so. I'm sure they have a way of monitoring the bulletin board and tracing the phone call. And if we use a different bulletin board, there's always the chance that no one will notice our message. Remember, it was three weeks before John Truth picked up on our last one.'

'So we call and threaten a second earthquake.'

Priest put in: 'But next time it won't be in a remote wilderness—it'll be someplace where real damage will be done.' He caught an apprehensive look from Star. 'We don't have to mean it,' he added. 'Once we've shown our power, just the threat ought to be enough.'

Star said: '*Inshallah*.' She had picked it up from Poem, who was Algerian. 'If God wills.'

*

It was pitch dark when they left next morning.

The seismic vibrator had not been seen in daylight within a hundred miles of the valley, and Priest wanted to keep it that way. He planned to leave home and return in darkness. The round trip would be about five hundred miles, eleven hours driving in a truck with a top speed of forty-five. They would take the 'Cuda as a back-up car, Priest had decided. Oaktree would come with them to share the driving.

Priest used a flashlight to illuminate the way through the trees to where the truck was concealed. The four of them were silent, anxious. It took them half an hour to remove the branches they had piled over the vehicle.

He was tense when at last he sat behind the wheel, slid the key into the ignition, and turned on the engine. It started first time with a satisfying roar, and he felt exultant.

The commune's houses were more than a mile away, and he was sure no one would hear the engine at such a distance. The dense forest muffled sound. Later, of course, everyone would notice that four commune members were away. Aneth had been briefed to say they had gone to a vineyard in Napa that Paul Beale wanted them to see, where a new hybrid vine had been planted. It was unusual for people to make trips out of the commune; but there would be few questions, for no one liked to challenge Priest.

He turned on the headlights, and Melanie climbed

into the truck beside him. He engaged low gear and steered the heavy vehicle through the trees to the dirt track, then turned uphill and headed for the road. The all-terrain tyres coped easily with stream beds and mud slides.

Jesus, I wonder if this is going to work.

An earthquake? Come on!

But it has to work.

He got on the road and headed east. After twenty minutes they climbed out of Silver River Valley and hit Route 89. Priest turned south. He checked his mirrors and saw that Star and Oaktree were still behind in the 'Cuda.

Beside him, Melanie was very calm. Probing gently, he said: 'Was Dusty okay last night?'

'Fine, he likes visiting his father. Michael could always find time for him, never for me.'

Melanie's bitterness was familiar. What surprised Priest was her lack of fear. Unlike him, she was not agonizing over what would happen to her child if she died today. She seemed completely confident that nothing would go wrong, the earthquake would not harm her. Was it that she knew more than Priest? Or was she the type of person who just ignored uncomfortable facts? Priest was not sure.

As dawn broke they were looping around the north end of Lake Tahoe. The motionless water looked like a disc of polished steel fallen amid the mountains. The seismic vibrator was a conspicuous vehicle on the winding road that followed the pine-fringed shore; but the vacationers were still asleep, and the truck was seen only by a few bleary-eyed workers on their way to jobs in hotels and restaurants.

By sun-up they were on US 395, across the border in Nevada, bowling south through a flat desert landscape. They took a break at a truck stop, parking the seismic vibrator where it could not be seen from the road, and ate a breakfast of oily western omelettes and watery coffee.

When the road swung back into California it climbed into the mountains, and for a couple of hours the scenery was majestic, with steep forested slopes, a grander version of Silver River Valley. They dropped down again beside a silvery sea that Melanie said was Mono Lake.

Soon afterwards they were on a two-lane road that cut a straight line down a long, dusty valley. The valley widened until the mountains on the far side were just a blue haze, then it narrowed again. The ground on either side of the road was tan coloured and stony, with a scattering of low brush. There was no river, but the salt flats looked like a distant sheet of water.

Melanie said: 'This is Owens Valley.'

The landscape gave Priest the feeling that some kind of disaster had blighted it. 'What happened here?' he said.

'The river is dry because the water was diverted to Los Angeles, years ago.'

They passed through a sleepy small town every twenty miles or so. Now there was no way to be inconspicuous. There was little traffic, and the seismic vibrator was stared at every time they waited at a stop light. Plenty of men would remember it. *Yeah, I seen that rig. Look like she might be for layin' blacktop, or somethin'. What was she, anyway?*

Melanie switched on her laptop and unfolded her map. She said musingly: 'Somewhere beneath us, two vast slabs of the earth's crust are wedged together, stuck, straining to spring free.'

The thought made Priest feel cold. He could hardly believe he aimed to release all that pent-up destructive force. *I must be out of my mind.*

'Somewhere in the next five or ten miles,' she said.

'What's the time?'

'Just after one.'

They had cut it fine. The seismic window would open in half an hour and close fifty minutes later.

Melanie directed Priest down a side turning that crossed the flat valley floor. It was not really a road, just a track cleared through the boulders and scrub. Although the ground seemed almost level, the main road disappeared from view behind them, and they could see only the tops of high trucks passing.

'Pull up here,' Melanie said at last.

Priest stopped the truck and they both got out. The sun beat down on them from a merciless sky. The 'Cuda pulled up behind them, and Star and Oaktree got out, stretching their arms and legs after the long drive.

'Look at that,' Melanie said. 'See the dry gulch?'

Priest could see where a stream, long ago dried up, had cut a channel through the rocky ground. But where Melanie was pointing, the gulch came to an abrupt end, as if it had been walled off. 'That's strange,' Priest said.

'Now look a few yards to the right.'

Priest followed her moving finger. The stream bed began again just as abruptly and continued toward the middle of the valley. Priest realized what she was pointing out. 'That's the fault line,' he said. 'Last time there was an earthquake, one whole side of this valley picked up its skirts and shifted five yards, then sat down again.'

'That's about it.'

Oaktree said: 'And we're about to make it happen again, is that right?' There was a note of awe in his voice.

'We're going to try,' Priest said briskly. 'And we don't have much time.' He turned to Melanie. 'Is the truck in exactly the right place?'

'I guess,' she said. 'A few yards one way or another up here on the surface shouldn't make any difference five miles down.'

'Okay.' He hesitated. He almost felt he ought to make a speech. He said: 'Well, I'll get started.'

He got into the cabin of the truck and settled into the driver's seat, then started the engine that ran the vibrator. He threw the switch that lowered the steel plate to the ground. He set the vibrator to shake for thirty seconds in the middle of its frequency range. He looked through the rear window of the cab and checked the gauges. The readouts were normal. He picked up the remote radio controller and got out of the truck.

'All set,' he said.

The four of them got into the 'Cuda. Oaktree took the wheel. They drove back to the road, crossed it, and headed into the scrub on the far side. They went part way up the hillside, then Melanie said: 'This is fine.'

Oaktree stopped the car.

Priest hoped they were not conspicuous from the road. If they were, there was nothing he could do about it. But the muddy colours of the 'Cuda's paint job blended into the brown landscape.

Oaktree said nervously: 'Is this far enough away?'

'I think so,' Melanie said coolly. She was not scared at all. Studying her face, Priest saw a hint of mad excitement in her eyes. It was almost sexual. Was she taking her revenge on the seismologists who had rejected her, or the husband who had let her down, or the whole damn world? Whatever the explanation, she was getting a big charge out of this.

They got out and stood looking across the valley. They could just see the top of the truck.

Star said to Priest: 'It was a mistake for us both to come. If we die, Flower has no one.'

'She has the whole commune,' Priest said. 'You and I are not the only adults she loves and trusts. We're not a nuclear family, and that's one very good reason why.'

Melanie looked annoyed. 'We're a quarter of a mile

from the fault, assuming it runs along the valley floor,' she said in a cut-the-crap tone of voice. 'We'll feel the earth move, but we're not in any danger. People who are hurt in earthquakes generally get hit by parts of buildings: falling ceilings, bridges that collapse, flying glass, stuff like that. We're safe here.'

Star looked over her shoulder. 'The mountain isn't going to fall on us?'

'It might. And we might all be killed in a car wreck driving back to Silver River Valley. But it's so unlikely that we shouldn't waste time worrying about it.'

'That's easy for you to say—your child's father is three hundred miles away in San Francisco.'

Priest said: 'I don't care if I die here. I can't raise my children in suburban America.'

Oaktree muttered: 'This has to work. This just has to work.'

Melanie said: 'For God's sake, Priest, we don't have all day. Just press the damn button.'

Priest looked up and down the road, and waited for a dark green Jeep Grand Cherokee Limited to pass. 'Okay,' he said when the road was clear. 'This is it.'

He pressed the button on the remote control.

He heard the roar of the vibrator immediately, though it was muted by distance. He felt the vibration in the soles of his feet, a faint but definite trembling sensation.

Star said: 'Oh, God.'

A cloud of dust billowed around the truck.

All four of them were taut as guitar strings, their

bodies tensed for the first hint of movement in the earth.

Seconds passed.

Priest's eyes raked the landscape, looking for signs of a tremor, though he guessed he would feel it before he saw it.

Come on, come on!

The seismic exploration crews normally set the vibrator for a seven-second 'sweep'. Priest had set this one for thirty seconds. It seemed like an hour.

At last the noise stopped.

Melanie said: 'God damn it.'

Priest's heart sank. There was no earthquake. It had failed.

Maybe it was just a crazy hippie idea, like levitating the Pentagon.

'Try it again,' said Melanie.

Priest looked at the remote control in his hand. *Why not?*

There was a sixteen-wheel truck approaching along US 395, but this time Priest did not wait. If Melanie was right, the truck would be unaffected by the tremor. If Melanie was wrong, they would all be dead.

He pressed the button.

The distant roar started up, there was a perceptible vibration in the ground, and a cloud of dust engulfed the seismic vibrator.

Priest wondered if the road would open up under the sixteen-wheeler.

Nothing happened.

The thirty seconds passed more quickly this time. Priest was surprised when the noise stopped. *Is that all?*

Despair engulfed him. Perhaps the Silver River Valley commune was a dream that had come to an end. *What am I going to do? Where will I live? How can I avoid ending up like Bones?*

But Melanie was not ready to give up. 'Let's move the truck a ways and try again.'

'But you said the exact position doesn't matter,' Oaktree pointed out. ' "A few yards one way or another up here on the surface shouldn't make any difference five miles down," that's what you said.'

'Then we'll move it more than a few yards,' Melanie said angrily. 'We're running out of time, let's go!'

Priest did not argue with her. She was transformed. Normally she was dominated by Priest. She was a damsel in distress, he had rescued her, and she was so grateful, she had to be eternally submissive to his will. But now she was in charge, impatient and domineering. Priest could put up with that as long as she could do what she had promised. He would bring her back into line later.

They got into the 'Cuda and drove fast across the baked earth to the seismic vibrator. Then Priest and Melanie climbed into the cab of the truck and she directed him as he drove, while Oaktree and Star followed in the car. They were no longer following the track, but cutting straight through the brush. The truck's big wheels crushed the scrubby bushes and rolled easily over the stones, but Priest wondered if the low-slung 'Cuda would suffer damage. He guessed Oaktree would honk if he had trouble.

Melanie scanned the landscape for the tell-tale features that showed where the fault line ran. Priest saw no more displaced stream beds. But after half a mile Melanie pointed at what looked like a miniature cliff about four feet high. 'Fault scarp,' she said. 'About a hundred years old.'

'I see it,' Priest said. There was a dip in the ground, like a bowl; and a break in the rim of the bowl showed where the earth had moved sideways, as if the bowl had cracked and been glued together clumsily.

Melanie said: 'Let's try here.'

Priest stopped the truck and lowered the plate. Swiftly, he rechecked the gauges and set the vibrator. This time he programmed a sixty-second sweep. When all was set he jumped out of the truck.

He checked his watch anxiously. It was two o'clock. They had only twenty minutes left.

Again they drove the 'Cuda across US 395 and up the hill on the far side. The drivers of the few vehicles that passed continued to ignore them. But Priest was nervous. Sooner or later someone would ask what they were doing. He did not want to have to explain himself to a curious cop or a nosey town councilman. He had a plausible story ready, about a university research project on the geology of the dried-up river bed, but he did not want anyone to remember his face.

They all got out of the car and looked across the valley to where the seismic vibrator stood near the scarp. Priest wished with all his heart that this time he would see the earth move and open. *Come on, God—give me this one, okay?*

He pressed the button.

The truck roared, the earth trembled faintly and the dust rose. The vibration went on for a full minute instead of half. But there was no earthquake. They just waited longer for disappointment.

When the noise died away, Star said: 'This isn't going to work, is it?'

Melanie threw her a furious look. Turning to Priest, she said: 'Can you alter the frequency of the vibrations?'

'Yes,' Priest said. 'Right now it's set near the middle, so I can go up or down. Why?'

'There's a theory that pitch may be a crucial factor. See, the earth is constantly resounding with faint vibrations. So why aren't there earthquakes all the time? Maybe because a vibration has to be just the right pitch to dislodge the fault. You know how a musical note can shatter a glass?'

'I never saw it happen, except in a cartoon, but I know what you mean. The answer is yes. When they use the vibrator in seismic exploration, they vary the pitch over a seven-second sweep.'

'They do?' Melanie was curious. 'Why?'

'I don't know, maybe it gives them a better reading on the geophones. Anyway, it didn't seem the right thing for us, so I didn't select that feature, but I can.'

'Let's try it.'

'Okay—but we need to hurry. It's already five after two.'

They jumped into the car. Oaktree drove fast, skidding across the dusty desert. Priest reset the controls of the vibrator for a sweep of gradually increasing pitch over a period of sixty seconds. As they raced back to their observation point, he checked his watch again. 'Two fifteen,' he said. 'This is our last chance.'

'Don't worry,' Melanie said. 'I'm out of ideas. If this doesn't work, I'm giving up.'

Oaktree stopped the car and they got out again.

The thought of driving all the way back to Silver River with nothing to celebrate depressed Priest so profoundly that he felt he would want to crash the truck on the freeway and end it all. Maybe that was his way out. He wondered if Star would like to die with him. *I can see it now: the two of us, an overdose of paracetamol, a bottle of wine to wash down the pills . . .*

'What are you waiting for?' said Melanie. 'It's two twenty. Press the damn button!'

Priest pressed the button.

As before, the truck roared and the ground trembled and a cloud of dust rose from the earth around the pounding steel plate of the vibrator. This time the roar did not stay at the same moderate pitch, but started at a profound bass rumble and began slowly to climb.

Then it happened.

The earth beneath Priest's feet seemed to ripple like a choppy sea. Then he felt as if someone took him by the leg and threw him down. He landed flat on his back, hitting the ground hard. It knocked the wind out of him.

Star and Melanie screamed at the same time, Melanie with a high-pitched shriek and Star with a roar of shock and fright. Priest saw them both fall, Melanie next to him and Star a few steps away. Oaktree staggered, stayed on his feet, and fell last.

Priest was silently terrified. *I've had it, this is it, I'm going to die.*

There was a noise like an express train thundering past close by. Dust rose from the ground, small stones flew through the air, and boulders rolled every which way.

The ground continued to move as if someone had hold of the end of a rug and would not stop shaking it. The feeling was unbelievably disorienting, as if the world had suddenly become a completely strange place. It was terrifying.

I'm not ready to die.

Priest caught his breath and struggled to his knees. Then, as he got one foot flat on the ground, Melanie grabbed his arm and pulled him down again. He screamed at her: 'Let me go, you dumb cunt!' But he could not hear his own words.

The ground heaved up and threw him downhill, away from the 'Cuda. Melanie fell on top of him. He thought the car might turn over and crush both of them, and he tried to roll out of its path. He could not see Star or Oaktree. A flying thorn bush whipped his face, scratching him. Dust got into his eyes and he was momentarily blinded. He lost all sense of direction. He curled up in a ball, covering his face with his arms, and waited for death.

Christ, if I'm going to die, I wish I could die with Star.

The shaking stopped as suddenly as it had started. He had no idea whether it had lasted ten seconds or ten minutes.

A moment later, the noise died away.

Priest rubbed the dust out of his eyes and stood up. His vision cleared slowly. He saw Melanie at his feet. He extended a hand and pulled her up. 'Are you okay?' he said.

'I think so,' she replied shakily.

The dust in the air thinned, and he saw Oaktree unsteadily getting to his feet. Where was Star? Then he saw her a few steps away. She lay on her back with her eyes closed. His heart lurched. *Not dead, please, God, not dead.* He knelt by her side. 'Star!' he said urgently. 'Are you okay?'

She opened her eyes. 'Jesus,' she said. 'That was a blast!'

Priest grinned, fighting back tears of relief.

He helped Star to her feet.

'We're all alive,' he said.

The dust was settling fast. He looked across the valley and saw the truck. It was upright, and seemed undamaged. A few yards from it, there was a great gash in the ground that ran north and south in the middle of the valley as far as he could see.

'Well, I'll be darned,' he said quietly. 'Look at that.'

'It worked,' said Melanie.

'We did it,' Oaktree said. 'God damn it, we caused a motherfucking earthquake!'

217

Priest grinned at them all. 'That's the truth,' he said.

He kissed Star, then Melanie; then Oaktree kissed them both; then Star kissed Melanie. They all laughed. Then Priest started to dance. He did a Red Indian war hop, there in the middle of the broken valley, his boots kicking up the newly settled dust. Star joined in, then Melanie and Oaktree, and the four of them went round and round in a circle, shouting and whooping and laughing until the tears came to their eyes.

PART TWO

SEVEN DAYS

CHAPTER EIGHT

J UDY MADDOX was driving home on Friday at the end of the worst week in her FBI career.

She could not figure out what she had done to deserve this. Okay, she had yelled at her boss, but he had been hostile to her before she blew her cool, so there had to be another reason. She had gone to Sacramento yesterday with every intention of making the Bureau look efficient and competent, and somehow she had ended up giving an impression of muddle and impotence. She felt frustrated and depressed.

Nothing good had happened since her meeting with Al Honeymoon. She had been calling seismology professors and interviewing them by phone. She would ask whether the professor was working on locations of critically stressed points on fault lines. If so, who had access to their data? And did any of those people have connections with terrorist groups?

The seismologists had not been helpful. Most of today's academics had been students in the sixties and seventies, when the FBI had paid every creep on campus to spy on the protest movement. It was a long time ago, but they had not forgotten. To them, the Bureau was the enemy. Judy understood how they felt, but she wished they would not be passive-aggressive with agents who were working in the public interest.

The Hammer of Eden's deadline ran out today, and there had been no earthquake. Judy was deeply relieved, even though it suggested she had been wrong to take the threat seriously. Maybe this would be the end of the whole thing. She told herself she should have a relaxing weekend. The weather was great, sunny and warm. Tonight she would make stir-fried chicken for Bo and open a bottle of wine. Tomorrow she would have to go to the supermarket, but on Sunday she could drive up the coast to Bodega Bay and sit on the beach reading a book like a normal person. On Monday she would probably be given a new assignment. Maybe she could make a fresh start.

She wondered whether to call her girlfriend Virginia and see if she wanted to go to the beach. Ginny was her oldest friend. Also the daughter of a cop, and the same age as Judy, she was sales director of a security firm. But Judy realized it was not feminine company she wanted. It would be nice to lie on the beach beside something with hairy legs and a deep voice. It was a year since she had split up with Don: this was the longest time she had been without a lover since she was a teenager. At college she had been a little wild, almost promiscuous; working at Mutual American Insurance she had had an affair with her boss; then she had lived with Steve Dolen for seven years and almost married him. She often thought about Steve. He was attractive and smart and kind— too kind, maybe, for in the end she came to think of him as weak. Maybe she asked the impossible. Perhaps all considerate, attentive men were weak, and all the strong ones, like Don Riley, ended up shtupping their secretaries.

Her car phone rang. She did not need to pick up the handset: after two rings it connected automatically in hands-free mode. 'Hello,' she said. 'This is Judy Maddox.'

'This is your father.'

'Hi, Bo. Will you be home for supper? We could have—'

He interrupted her. 'Turn on your car radio, quick,' he said. 'Tune to John Truth.'

Christ, what now? She touched the power switch. A rock music station came on. She jabbed at a preset button and got the San Francisco station that broadcast *John Truth Live*. His nasal twang filled the car.

He was speaking in the ponderously dramatic manner he used to suggest that what he had to say was world-shakingly important. 'The California state seismologist has now confirmed that there was an earthquake today—the very day the Hammer of Eden promised it. It took place at twenty minutes after two p.m. in Owens Valley, just as the Hammer of Eden said when they called this show a few minutes ago.'

My God—they did it.

Judy was electrified. She forgot her frustration, and her depression vanished. She felt alive again.

John Truth was saying: 'But the same state seismologist denied that this or any other earthquake could have been caused by a terrorist group.'

Was that true? Judy had to know. What did other seismologists think? She needed to make some calls. Then she heard John Truth say: 'In a moment we will play you a recording of the message left by the Hammer of Eden.'

They're on tape!

That could be a crucial mistake by the terrorists. They would not know it, but a voice on tape would provide a mass of information when analysed by Simon Sparrow.

Truth went on: 'Meanwhile, what do *you* think? Do you believe the state seismologist? Or do you think he's whistling past the graveyard? Maybe *you* are a seismologist and you have an opinion on the technical possibilities here. Or maybe you're just a concerned citizen and you think the authorities ought to be as worried as you are. Call *John Truth Live* on this number now to tell the world what *you* think.'

A commercial for a furniture warehouse came on and Judy muted the volume. 'Are you still there, Bo?'

'Sure.'

'They did it, didn't they?'

'Sure looks like it.'

She wondered whether he was genuinely uncertain or just being cautious. 'What does your instinct say?'

He gave her another ambiguous answer. 'That these people are very dangerous.'

Judy tried to calm her racing heart and turn her mind to what she should do next. 'I'd better call Brian Kincaid—'

'What are you going to tell him?'

'The news ... wait a minute.' Bo was making a point. 'You don't think I should call him.'

'I think you should call your boss when you can give him something he can't get from the radio.'

'You're right.' Judy began to feel calmer as she ran over the possibilities. 'I guess I'm going back to work.' She made a right turn.

'Okay. I'll be home in an hour or so. Call me if you want supper.'

She felt a sudden rush of affection for him. 'Thanks, Bo. You're a great daddy.'

He laughed. 'You're a great kid, too. Later.'

'Later.' She touched the button that terminated the call, then she turned up the volume on the radio.

She heard a low, sexy voice saying: 'This is the Hammer of Eden with a message for Governor Mike Robson.'

The picture that came into her mind was of a mature woman with large breasts and a wide smile, likeable but kind of off-the-wall.

That's my enemy?

The tone changed and the woman muttered: 'Shit, I didn't expect to be talking to a tape recorder.'

She's not the organizational brain behind all this. She's too ditzy. She's taking instructions from someone else.

The woman resumed her formal voice and continued: 'Like we promised, we caused an earthquake today, four weeks after our last message. It happened in Owens Valley a little after two o'clock, you can check it out.'

A faint background noise caused her to hesitate.

What was that?

Simon will find out.

A second later she carried on. 'We do not recognize the jurisdiction of the United States government. Now that you know we can do what we say, you'd better think again about our demand. Announce a freeze on construction of new power plants in California. You have seven days to make up your mind.'

Seven days! Last time they gave us four weeks.

'After that we will trigger another earthquake. But the next one won't be out in the middle of nowhere. If you force us, we'll do real damage.'

A carefully calculated escalation of the threat. Jesus, these people scare me.

'We don't like it, but it's the only way. Please do as we say, so that this nightmare can end.'

John Truth came on. 'There it is, the voice of the Hammer of Eden, the group that claims to have triggered the earthquake that shook Owens Valley today.'

Judy had to have that tape. She turned down the volume again and dialled Raja's home number. He was single, he could give up his Friday evening.

When he answered she said: 'Hi, this is Judy.'

He said immediately: 'I can't, I have tickets for the opera!'

She hesitated, then decided to play along. 'What's on?'

'Uh . . . *Macbeth's Wedding.*'

She suppressed a laugh. 'By Ludwig Sebastian Wagner?'

226

'Right.'

'No such opera, no such composer. You're working tonight.'

'Shit.'

'Why didn't you invent a rock group? I would have believed you.'

'I keep forgetting how old you are.'

She laughed. Raja was twenty-six, Judy was thirty-five. 'I'll take that as a compliment.'

'What's the assignment?' He did not sound too reluctant.

Judy became serious again. 'Okay, here it is. There was an earthquake in the eastern part of the state this afternoon, and the Hammer of Eden claim they triggered it.'

'Wow! Maybe these people are for real after all!' He sounded pleased rather than scared. He was young and keen, and he had not thought through the implications.

'John Truth just played a recorded message from the perpetrators. I need you to go to the radio station and get the tape.'

'I'm on my way.'

'Make sure you get the original, not a copy. If they give you a hard time, tell them we can get a court order in an hour.'

'Nobody gives me a hard time. This is Raja, remember?'

It was true. He was a charmer. 'Take the tape to Simon Sparrow and tell him I need something in the morning.'

'You got it.'

She broke the connection and turned John Truth up again. He was saying: '. . . a minor earthquake, by the way, magnitude five to six.'

How the hell did they do it?

'No one injured, no damage to buildings or other property, but a tremor that was quite definitely felt by the residents of Bishop, Bigpine, Independence, and Lone Pine.'

Some of those people must have seen the perpetrators within the last few hours, Judy realized. She had to get over there and start interviewing them as soon as possible.

Where exactly was the earthquake? She needed to talk to an expert.

The obvious choice was the state seismologist. However, he seemed to have a closed mind. He had already ruled out the possibility of a human-made earthquake. That bothered her. She wanted someone who was willing to entertain all possibilities. She thought of Michael Quercus. He could be a pain in the ass, but he was not afraid to speculate. Plus he was just across the bay in Berkeley, whereas the state seismologist was in Sacramento.

If she showed up without an appointment, he would refuse to see her. She sighed and dialled his number.

For a while there was no answer, and she thought he must be out. He picked up after six rings. 'Quercus.' He sounded annoyed at the interruption.

'This is Judy Maddox from the FBI. I need to talk

to you. It's urgent, and I'd like to come to your place right away.'

'It's out of the question. I'm with someone.'

I might have known you'd be difficult. 'Maybe after your meeting is over?'

'It's not a meeting, and it won't be over till Sunday.'

Yeah, right.

He had a woman there, Judy guessed. But he had told her, at the first meeting, that he was not seeing anyone. For some reason she remembered his exact words: 'I'm separated from my wife, and I don't have a girlfriend.' Perhaps he had lied. Or perhaps this was someone new. It did not sound like a new relationship, if he was expecting her to stay the weekend. On the other hand, he was arrogant enough to assume that a girl would go to bed with him on the first date, and attractive enough that a lot of girls probably would.

I don't know why I'm so interested in his love life.

'Have you been listening to the radio?' she asked him. 'There's been an earthquake, and the terrorist group we talked about claims to have triggered it.'

'Is that so?' He sounded intrigued, despite himself. 'Are they telling the truth?'

'That's what I need to discuss with you.'

'I see.'

Come on, you stubborn son of a gun—give in, for once in your life.

'This is really important, Professor.'

'I'd like to help you . . . but it's really not possible tonight . . . no, wait.' His voice became muffled as he covered the mouthpiece with his hand, but she could still distinguish his words. 'Hey, have you ever met a real live FBI agent?' She could not hear the reply, but after a moment he said to her: 'Okay, my guest would like to meet you. Come on over.'

She did not like the idea of being paraded like some kind of circus freak, but at this point she was not going to say so. 'Thanks, I'll be there in twenty minutes.' She broke the connection.

As she drove over the bridge, she reflected that neither Raja nor Michael had seemed scared. Raja was excited, Michael intrigued. She, too, was electrified by the sudden reanimation of the case; but when she remembered the earthquake of 1989, and the television pictures of rescue workers bringing corpses out of the collapsed double-deck Nimitz freeway right here in Oakland, and she contemplated the possibility of a terrorist group having the power to do that, her heart felt cold and heavy with foreboding.

To clear her mind she tried to guess what Michael Quercus's girlfriend would be like. She had seen a picture of his wife, a striking redhead with a super-model figure and a sulky pout. *He seems to like the exotic.* But they had broken up, so perhaps she was not really his type. Judy could see him with a woman professor, in fashionable thin-framed spectacles, with well-cut short hair but no make-up. On the other hand, that type of woman would not cross the street to meet an FBI agent. Most likely he had picked up a sexy airhead who was easily impressed. Judy visualized a girl in tight clothes, smoking and chewing gum at the same time, looking around his apartment and saying: 'Have you *read* all these books?'

I don't know why I'm obsessing about his girlfriend when I've got so much else to worry about.

She found Euclid Street and parked under the same magnolia tree. She rang his bell and he buzzed her into the building. He came to the apartment door barefoot, looking pleasantly weekendish in blue jeans and a white T-shirt. *A girl could have fun, spending the weekend fooling around with him.* She followed him into his office-cum-living-room.

There, to her astonishment, she saw a little boy of about five, with freckles and fair hair, dressed in pyjamas with dinosaurs all over them. After a moment, she recognized him as the child in the photograph on the desk. Michael's son. This was his weekend guest. She felt embarrassed about the dumb blonde she had imagined. *I was a little unfair to you, Professor.*

Michael said: 'Dusty, meet Special Agent Judy Maddox.'

The boy shook hands politely and said: 'Are you really in the FBI?'

'Yes, I am.'

'Wow.'

'Want to see my badge?' She took her shield from her shoulder bag and gave it to him. He held it reverently.

Michael said: 'Dusty likes to watch *The X-Files.*'

Judy smiled. 'I don't work in the alien spacecraft department, I just catch regular Earth criminals.'

Dusty said: 'Can I see your gun?'

Judy hesitated. She knew that boys were fascinated by weapons, but she did not like to encourage such an interest. She glanced at Michael, who shrugged. She unbuttoned her jacket and took the weapon out of its shoulder holster.

As she did so, she caught Michael looking at her breasts, and she felt a sudden sexual frisson. Now that he was not being curmudgeonly, he was kind of appealing, with his bare feet and his T-shirt untucked.

She said: 'Guns are pretty dangerous, Dusty, so I'm going to hold it, but you can look.'

Dusty's face as he stared at the pistol wore the same expression as Michael's when she opened her jacket. The thought made her grin.

After a minute she holstered the gun.

Dusty said with elaborate politeness: 'We were just going to have some Cap'n Crunch. Would you care to join us?'

Judy was impatient to question Michael, but she sensed he would be more forthcoming if she was patient and played along. 'How nice of you,' she said. 'I'm real hungry, I'd love some Cap'n Crunch.'

'Come into the kitchen.'

The three of them sat at a plastic-topped table in the little kitchen and ate breakfast cereal and milk out of bright blue pottery bowls. Judy realized she was hungry: it was past suppertime. 'My goodness,' she said. 'I'd forgotten how good Cap'n Crunch is.'

Michael laughed. Judy was amazed at the difference in him. He was relaxed and amiable. He seemed a different person from the grouch who had forced her to drive back to the office and phone him for an appointment. She was beginning to like him.

When supper was eaten, Michael got Dusty ready for bed. Dusty said to his father: 'Can Agent Judy tell me a story?'

Judy suppressed her impatience. *I've got seven days, I can wait another five minutes.* She said: 'I think your daddy wants to tell you a story, because he doesn't get to do it as often as he'd like.'

'It's okay,' Michael said with a smile. 'I'll listen in.'

They went into the bedroom. 'I don't know many stories, but I remember one my mommy used to tell me,' Judy said. 'It's the legend of the kindly dragon. Would you like to hear it?'

'Yes, please,' said Dusty.

'Me, too,' said Michael.

'Once upon a time, a long, long, time ago, there was a kindly dragon who lived in China, where all dragons come from. One day the kindly dragon went wandering. He wandered so far that he left China and got lost in the wilderness.

'After many days he came to another land, far to the south. It was the most beautiful country he had ever seen, with forests and mountains and fertile valleys, and rivers for him to splash about in. There were banana palms and mulberry trees laden with ripe fruit. The weather was always warm with a pleasant breeze.

'But there was one thing wrong. It was an empty land. No one lived there: no people, and no dragons. So although the kindly dragon loved the new land, he was terribly lonely.

'However, he didn't know the way home, so he roamed all around, looking for someone to keep him company. At last, one lucky day, he found the one person who lived there—a fairy princess. She was so beautiful that he fell in love with her at once. Now, the princess was lonely too, and although the dragon looked fearsome, he had a kind heart, and so she married him.

'The kindly dragon and the fairy princess loved each other and they had a hundred children. All the children were brave and kindly like their dragon father, and beautiful like their fairy mother.

'The kindly dragon and the fairy princess looked after their children until they were all grown up. Then, suddenly, both parents vanished. They went away to live in love and harmony in the spirit world for all eternity. And their children became the brave, kindly, beautiful people of Vietnam. And that's where my mommy came from.'

Dusty was wide-eyed. 'Is it true?'

Judy smiled. 'I don't know, maybe.'

'It's a beautiful story, anyway,' Michael said. He kissed Dusty goodnight.

As Judy left the room, she heard Dusty whisper: 'She's really nice, isn't she?'

'Yes,' Michael replied.

Back in the living room, Michael said: 'Thank you for that. You were great with him.'

'It wasn't difficult. He's a charmer.'

Michael nodded. 'Gets it from his mother.'

Judy smiled.

Michael grinned and said: 'I notice you don't argue with that.'

'I've never met your wife. In the picture she looks very beautiful.'

'She is. And . . . faithless.'

That was an unexpected confidence, coming so suddenly from a man she took to be proud. She warmed to him. But she did not know what to say in reply.

They were both silent for a moment. Then Michael said: 'You've had enough of the Quercus family. Tell me about the earthquake.'

At last. 'It took place in Owens Valley this afternoon at twenty minutes past two.'

'Let's get the seismograph.' Michael sat at his desk and tapped the keys of his computer. She found herself looking at his bare feet. Some men had ugly feet, but his were well shaped and strong looking, with neatly clipped toenails. The skin was white and there was a small tuft of dark hair on each big toe.

He did not notice her scrutiny. 'When your terrorists made their threat, four weeks ago, did they specify the location?'

'No.'

'Hmm. In the scientific community, we say that a successful earthquake forecast would have to specify date, location, and magnitude. Your people only gave the date. That's not very convincing. There's an earthquake *somewhere* in California more or less every day. Maybe they just claimed responsibility for something that happened naturally.'

'Can you tell me exactly where today's tremor took place?'

'Yes. I can calculate the epicenter by triangulation. Actually, the computer does it automatically. I'll just print out the coordinates.' After a moment his printer whirred.

Judy said: 'Is there any way of knowing how the earthquake was triggered?'

'You mean, can I tell from the graph whether it was caused by human agency? Yes, I should be able to.'

'How?'

He clicked his mouse and turned from the screen to face her. 'A normal earthquake is preceded by a gradual buildup of foreshocks, or lesser tremors, which we can see on the seismograph. By contrast, when the earthquake is triggered by an explosion, there is no buildup—the graph begins with a charac-teristic spike.' He turned back to his computer.

He was probably a good teacher, Judy thought. He explained things clearly. But he would be mercilessly intolerant of student foibles. He would give surprise tests, and refuse to admit latecomers to his lectures.

'That's odd,' he said.

Judy looked over his shoulder at the screen. 'What's odd?'

'The seismograph.'

'I don't see a spike.'

'No. There was no explosion.'

Judy did not know whether to feel relieved or dis-appointed. 'So the earthquake happened naturally?'

He shook his head. 'I'm not sure. There are

foreshocks, yes. But I've never seen foreshocks like this.'

Judy was frustrated. He had promised to tell her whether the Hammer of Eden's claim was plausible. Now he was maddeningly uncertain. 'What's peculiar about the foreshocks?' she asked.

'They're too regular. They look artificial.'

'Artificial?'

He nodded. 'I don't know what caused these vibrations, but they don't look natural. I believe your terrorists did *something*. I just don't know what it is.'

'Can you find out?'

'I hope so. I'll call a few people. Plenty of seismologists will be studying these readings already. Between us we ought to be able to figure out what they mean.'

He didn't sound too sure, but Judy guessed she would have to be content with that for now. She had got all she could out of Michael tonight. Now she needed to get to the scene of the crime. She picked up the sheet that had emerged from the printer. It showed a series of map references.

'Thanks for seeing me,' she said. 'I appreciate it.'

'I enjoyed it.' He smiled at her, a big hundred-watt smile showing two rows of white teeth.

'Have a good weekend with Dusty.'

'Thanks.'

She got in her car and headed back to the city. She would go to the office and look up airline schedules on the Internet, see if there was a flight to somewhere near Owens Valley early tomorrow morning. She would also need to check which FBI field office had jurisdiction over Owens Valley, and talk to them about what she was doing. Then she would call the local sheriff and get him on side.

She reached 450 Golden Gate Avenue, parked in the underground garage, and took the elevator up. As she walked past Brian Kincaid's office, she heard voices. He must be working late.

This was as good a time as any to bring him up to speed. She entered the anteroom and tapped on the open door to the inner office.

'Come in,' he called.

She stepped inside. Her heart sank when she saw that Kincaid was with Marvin Hayes. She and Marvin disliked one another intensely. He was sitting in front of the desk, wearing a tan summer suit with a white button-down shirt and a black-and-gold power tie. He was a good-looking man, with bristly dark hair cut short and a neat moustache. He looked the picture of competence, but in fact he was everything a law enforcement officer should not be: lazy, brutal, slap-dash, and unscrupulous. For his part, he thought Judy was prissy.

Unfortunately, Brian Kincaid liked him, and Brian was now the boss.

The two men looked startled and guilty when Judy walked in, and she realized they must have been talking about her. To make them feel worse, she said: 'Am I interrupting something?'

'We were talking about the earthquake,' Brian said. 'Did you hear the news?'

'Of course. I've been working on it. I just interviewed a seismologist who says the foreshocks are like nothing he's ever seen before, but he's sure they're artificial. He gave me the map coordinates for the exact location of the tremor. I want to go to Owens Valley in the morning to look for witnesses.'

A significant glance passed between the two men. Brian said: 'Judy, no one can cause an earthquake.'

'We don't know that.'

Marvin said: 'I've talked to two seismologists myself, tonight, and they both told me it was impossible.'

'Scientists disagree—'

Brian said: 'We think this group never went near Owens Valley. They found out about the earthquake and claimed credit for it.'

Judy frowned. 'This is my assignment,' she said. 'How come Marvin is calling seismologists?'

'This case is becoming very high profile,' Brian said. Suddenly Judy knew what was coming, and her heart filled with impotent fury. 'Even though we don't believe the Hammer of Eden can do what they claim, they can get a hell of a lot of publicity. I'm not confident you can deal with that.'

Judy struggled to control her rage. 'You can't re-assign me without a reason.'

'Oh, I have a reason,' he said. He picked up a fax from his desk. 'Yesterday you got into an altercation with a California Highway Patrolman. He stopped you for speeding. According to this, you were uncooperative and abusive, and you refused to show him your licence.'

'For Christ's sake, I showed him my badge!'

239

Brian ignored that. Judy realized he was not really interested in the details. The incident with the CHP was just a pretext. 'I'm setting up a special squad to deal with the Hammer of Eden,' he went on. He swallowed nervously, then lifted his chin in an aggressive gesture and said: 'I've asked Marvin to take charge. He won't be needing your help. You're off the case.'

CHAPTER NINE

PRIEST COULD hardly believe he had done it.
I caused an earthquake. I really did. Me.

As he drove the truck north on US 395, heading for home, with Melanie beside him and Star and Oaktree in the 'Cuda behind, he let his imagination run riot. He visualized a white-faced TV reporter giving the news that the Hammer of Eden had done what they promised; riots in the streets as people panicked at the threat of another earthquake; and a distraught Governor Robson, outside the Capitol building, announcing a freeze on the building of new power plants in California.

Maybe that was too optimistic. People might not be ready to panic yet. The governor would not cave in immediately. But he would at least be forced to open negotiations with Priest.

What would the police do? The public would expect them to catch the perpetrators. The governor had called in the FBI. But they had no idea who the Hammer of Eden were, no clues. Their job was next to impossible.

One thing had gone wrong today, and Priest could not help worrying about it. When Star called John

Truth, she had not spoken to an individual, but had left a message on a machine. Priest would have stopped her, but by the time he realized what was happening it was too late.

An unknown voice on a tape was not much use to the cops, he figured. All the same he wished they did not have even such a slender lead.

He found it surprising that the world was carrying on as if nothing had happened. Cars and trucks passed up and down the freeway, people parked at Burger King, the highway patrol stopped a young man in a red Porsche, a maintenance crew trimmed roadside bushes. They should all have been in shock.

He began to wonder if the earthquake had really happened. Had he imagined the whole thing in a dope dream? He had seen it with his own eyes, the gash in the earth that had opened up in Owens Valley —yet the earthquake seemed more far-fetched and impossible now than when it was just an idea. He yearned for public confirmation: a TV news report, a picture on a magazine cover, people talking about it in a bar or the checkout line of a supermarket.

In the late afternoon, while they were on the Nevada side of the border, Priest pulled into a filling station. The 'Cuda followed. Priest and Oaktree filled the tanks, standing in the slanting evening sunlight, while Melanie and Star went to the ladies' room.

'I hope we're on the news,' Oaktree said edgily.

He was thinking the same as Priest. 'How could we not be?' Priest replied. 'We caused an earthquake!'

'The authorities could keep it quiet.'

Like a lot of old hippie types, Oaktree believed that the government controlled the news. Priest thought that might be harder than Oaktree imagined. Priest believed the public were their own censors. They refused to buy newspapers or watch TV shows that challenged their prejudices, so they got fed pap.

However, Oaktree's thought worried him. It might not be too difficult to cover up a small earthquake in a lonely place.

He went inside to pay. The air-conditioning made him shiver. The clerk had a radio playing behind the counter. It occurred to Priest that he might hear the news. He asked the time, and the counterman said it was five to six. After he paid, Priest lingered, pretending to study a rack of magazines while he listened to Billy Jo Spears singing 'Fifty-seven Chevrolet'. Melanie and Star came out of the restrooms together.

At last the news began.

To give them a reason for hanging around, Priest slowly selected some candy bars and took them to the counter while he listened.

The first item was the wedding of two actors who played neighbours in a TV sitcom. Who could give a shit? Priest listened impatiently, tapping his foot. Then came a report on the president's visit to India. Priest hoped he would learn a mantra. The clerk added up the cost of the candy bars and Priest paid. Surely the earthquake would come next? But the third story was about a shooting in a school in Chicago.

Priest walked slowly toward the door, followed by Melanie and Star. Another customer finished filling up his Jeep Wrangler and came in to pay.

Finally the newsreader said: 'The environmental terrorist group the Hammer of Eden has claimed responsibility for a minor earthquake that took place today in Owens Valley, in eastern California.'

Priest whispered: 'Yes!' and smacked his left palm with his right fist in a triumphant gesture.

Star hissed: 'We're not terrorists!'

The newsreader continued: 'The tremor occurred on the day that the group had threatened to trigger one, but state seismologist Matthew Bird denied that this or any other earthquake could be caused by human agency.'

'Liar!' Melanie said under her breath.

'The claim was made in a phone call to this station's premier talk show, *John Truth Live*.'

Just as Priest reached the exit, he was shocked to hear Star's voice. He stopped dead. She was saying: 'We do not recognize the jurisdiction of the United States government. Now that you know we can do what we say, you'd better think again about our demand. Announce a freeze on construction of new power plants in California. You have seven days to make up your mind.'

Star exploded: 'Jesus Christ—that's me!'

'Hush!' Priest said. He looked over his shoulder. The customer with the Jeep Wrangler was talking while the clerk swiped his credit card through a machine. Neither man seemed to have noticed Star's outburst.

'Governor Mike Robson has not responded to this latest threat. In sports today . . .'

They stepped outside.

Star said: 'My God! They broadcast my voice! What am I going to do?'

'Stay calm,' Priest told her. He did not feel calm himself, but he was maintaining. As they walked across the asphalt to the vehicles, he said in a low, reasonable voice: 'Nobody outside our commune knows your voice. You haven't said more than a few words to an outsider for twenty-five years. And people who might remember you from the Haight-Ashbury days don't know where you're living now.'

'I guess you're right,' Star said doubtfully.

'The only exception I can think of is Bones. He might hear the tape and recognize your voice.'

'He would never betray us. Bones is a Rice Eater.'

'I don't know. Junkies will do anything.'

'What about the others—like Dale and Poem?'

'Yeah, they're a worry,' Priest admitted. There were no radios in the cabins, but there was one in the communal pickup truck, which Dale sometimes drove. 'If it happens, we'll just have to level with them.' *Or fall back on the Mario solution.*

No, I couldn't do that—not to Dale or Poem.

Could I?

Oaktree was waiting at the wheel of the 'Cuda. 'Come on, you guys, what's the hold-up?' he said.

Star explained briefly what they had heard. 'Luckily, nobody outside the commune knows my voice—oh,

Christ, I just thought of something!' She turned to Priest. 'The probation officer—in the sheriff's office.'

Priest cursed. Of course. Star had spoken to him only yesterday. Fear gripped his heart. If he heard the radio broadcast and remembered Star's voice, the sheriff and half a dozen deputies might be at the commune right now, just waiting for Star to return.

But maybe he had not heard the news. Priest had to check. But how? 'I'm going to call the sheriff's office,' he told them.

'But what'll you say?' Star said.

'I don't know, I'll think of something. Wait here.'

He went inside, got change from the clerk, and went to the pay phone. He got the Silver City sheriff's number from California information and dialled. The name of the probation officer came back to him. 'I need to speak to Mr Wicks,' he said.

A friendly voice said: 'Billy ain't here.'

'But I saw him yesterday.'

'He caught a plane to Nassau last night. He's lyin' on a beach by now, sippin' a beer and watching the bikinis go by, lucky dog. Back in a couple a weeks. Anyone else help you?'

Priest hung up.

Jesus, what a lucky break.

He went outside. 'God's on our side,' he told the others.

'What?' Star said urgently. 'What happened?'

'The guy went on holiday last night. He's in Nassau for two weeks. I don't think foreign radio stations are likely to broadcast Star's voice. We're safe.'

Star slumped with relief. 'Thank God for that.'

Priest opened the door of the truck. 'Let's get back on the road,' he said.

*

It was approaching midnight when Priest steered the seismic vibrator along the rough winding track that led through the forest to the commune. He returned the truck to its hiding place. Although it was dark and they were all exhausted, Priest made sure they covered every square inch of the vehicle with vegetation, so that it was invisible from all angles and from the air. Then they all got into the 'Cuda to drive the final mile.

Priest turned on the car radio for the midnight bulletin. This time, the earthquake was top of the news. 'Our show *John Truth Live* today played a central role in the continuing drama of the Hammer of Eden, the terrorist environmental group that says it can cause earthquakes,' said an excited voice. 'After a moderate earthquake shook Owens Valley, in the eastern part of California, a woman claiming to represent the group called John Truth and said they had triggered the tremor.'

The station then played Star's message in full.

'Shit,' Star muttered as she listened to her own voice.

Priest could not help feeling dismayed. Although he felt sure this would not help the police, still he hated to hear Star exposed in this way. It made her seem terribly vulnerable, and he yearned to destroy her enemies and make her safe.

After playing the tape, the newsreader said: 'Special Agent Raja Khan tonight took away the recording for analysis by the FBI's experts in psycholinguistics.'

That hit Priest like a punch in the stomach. 'What the fuck is psycholinguistics?' he said.

Melanie answered: 'I never heard the word before, but I guess they study the language you use and draw conclusions about your psychology.'

'I didn't know they were that smart,' Priest said worriedly.

Oaktree said: 'Don't sweat it, man. They can analyse Star's mind as much as they like, it ain't gonna give them her *address*.'

'I guess not.'

The newsreader was saying: 'No comment yet from Governor Mike Robson, but the head of the FBI's field office in San Francisco has promised a press conference tomorrow morning. In other news—'

Priest switched off. Oaktree parked the 'Cuda next to Bones's carnival ride. Bones had covered the truck with a huge tarpaulin, to protect the colourful paintwork. That suggested he was planning to stay a while.

They walked down the hill and through the vineyard to the village. The cookhouse and the children's bunkhouse were in darkness. Candlelight flickered behind Apple's window—she was an insomniac and liked to read into the small hours—and soft guitar chords came from Song's place, but the other cabins were dark and silent. Only Spirit, Priest's dog, came to greet them, wagging a happy tail in the moonlight. They said goodnight quietly and trudged off to their individual homes, too tired to celebrate their triumph.

It was a warm night. Priest lay on his bed naked, thinking. No comment from the governor, but an FBI press conference in the morning. That bothered him. At this point in the game, the governor should be panicking, saying, *The FBI has failed, we can't afford another earthquake, I have to talk to these people*. It made Priest uneasy to be so ignorant of what his enemy was thinking. He always got his way by reading people, figuring out what they really wanted from the way they looked and smiled and folded their arms and scratched their heads. He was trying to manipulate Governor Robson, but it was hard without face-to-face contact. And what was the FBI up to? Was there any significance in this talk of psycholinguistic analysis?

He had to find out more. He could not lie here and wait for the opposition to act.

He wondered whether to call the governor's office and try to speak to him. Would he get through to the man himself? And if he did, would he learn anything? It might be worth a try. However, he disliked the position that put him in. He would be a supplicant, asking for the privilege of a conversation with the great man. His strategy was to impose his will on the governor, not beg for a favour.

Then it occurred to him that he could go to the press conference.

It would be dangerous: if he were found out, all would be lost.

But the idea appealed to him. Posing as a reporter was the kind of thing he used to do in the old days. He had specialized in bold strokes: stealing that white Lincoln and giving it to 'Pigface' Riley; knifing Detective Jack Kassner in the men's room of the Blue Light bar; offering to buy the Fourth Street Liquor Store from the Jenkinsons. He had always managed to get away with stuff like that.

Maybe he would pose as a photographer. He could borrow a fancy camera from Paul Beale. Melanie could be the reporter. She was pretty enough to make any FBI agent take his eye off the ball.

What time was the press conference?

He rolled off the bed, stepped into his sandals, and went outside. In the moonlight he found his way to Melanie's cabin. She was sitting on the edge of her bed, naked, brushing her long red hair. As he walked in, she looked up and smiled. The candlelight outlined her body, throwing an aura behind her neat shoulders, her nipples, the bones of her hips, and the red hair in the fork of her thighs. It took his breath away.

'Hello,' she said.

It took him a moment to remember why he had come. 'I need to use your cellphone,' he said.

She pouted. That was not the reaction she wanted from a man who came upon her naked.

He gave her his bad-boy grin. 'But I may have to throw you to the ground and ravish you, then use your phone.'

She smiled. 'It's okay, you can phone first.'

250

He picked up the phone, then hesitated. Melanie had been assertive all day, and he had put up with it because she was the seismologist; but that was over. He did not like her to give him permission for anything. That was not the relationship they were supposed to have.

He lay on the bed, still holding the phone, and guided Melanie's head to his groin. She hesitated, then did what he wanted.

For a minute or so he lay still, enjoying the sensation.

Then he called information.

Melanie stopped what she was doing, but he grasped a coil of her hair and held her head in place. She hesitated, as if contemplating a protest; but after a moment she resumed.

That's better.

Priest got the number of the FBI in San Francisco and dialled it.

A man's voice answered: 'FBI.'

Inspiration came to Priest, as always. 'This is radio station KCAR in Carson City, Dave Horlock speaking,' he said. 'We want to send a reporter to your press conference tomorrow. Could you give me the address and time?'

'It went out on the wire,' the man said.

Lazy bastard. 'I'm not in the office,' Priest improvised. 'And our reporter may have to leave early tomorrow.'

'It's at twelve noon, here in the Federal Building at 450 Golden Gate Avenue.'

'Do we need an invitation, or can our guy just show up?'

'There are no invitations. All he needs is his regular press accreditation.'

'Thanks for your help.'

'What station did you say you were from?'

Priest hung up.

Accreditation. How am I going to get around that?

Melanie stopped sucking and said: 'I hope they didn't trace that call.'

Priest was surprised. 'Why would they?'

'I don't know. Maybe the FBI routinely trace all incoming calls.'

He frowned. 'Can they do that?'

'With computers, sure.'

'Well, I wasn't on the line long enough.'

'Priest, this isn't the sixties. It doesn't take time, the computer does it in nanoseconds. They just have to check the billing records to find out who owns the number that called at three minutes to one a.m.'

Priest had not heard the word 'nanosecond' before but he could guess what it meant. Now he was worried. 'Shit,' he said. 'Can they figure out where you are?'

'Only while the phone is on.'

Priest hastily switched it off.

He was beginning to feel unnerved. He had been surprised too often today: by the recording of Star's voice, by the concept of psycholinguistic analysis, and now by the notion of computer tracing of phone calls. Was there anything else he had failed to anticipate?

He shook his head. He was thinking negatively.

Caution and worry never got anything done. Imagination and nerve were his strengths. He would show up at the press conference tomorrow, talk his way in, and get a handle on what the enemy was up to.

Melanie lay back on the bed, closed her eyes, and said: 'It's been a long day in the saddle.'

Priest gazed at her body. He loved to look at her breasts. He liked the way they moved when she walked, with a side-to-side rhythm. He enjoyed seeing her pull a sweater off over her head, the reaching gesture making her tits stick up like pointing guns. He loved to watch her put on a brassiere, and adjust her breasts inside the cups to get comfortable. Now, as she lay on her back, they were slightly flattened, bulging out sideways, and the nipples were soft in repose.

He needed to cleanse his mind of worry. The second best way of doing that was meditation. The best was in front of him.

He knelt over her. When he kissed her breasts, she sighed contentedly and stroked his hair, but did not open her eyes.

Priest saw a movement out of the corner of his eye. He glanced at the door and saw Star, wearing a purple silk robe. He smiled. He knew what she had in mind: she had done this sort of thing before. She raised her eyebrows in an expression of enquiry. Priest nodded assent. She came in and closed the door silently.

Priest sucked Melanie's pink nipple, drawing it into his mouth slowly with his lips then teasing it with the tip of his tongue as he let it slide back out, again and again with a steady rhythm. She moaned in pleasure.

Star untied her robe and let it fall to the floor, then she stood watching, gently touching her own breasts. Her body was so different from Melanie's, the skin light tan where Melanie's was white, the hips and shoulders wider, the hair dark and thick where Melanie's was red-gold and fine. After a few moments she leaned over and kissed Priest's ear, then ran her hand down his back, along his spine, and between his legs, stroking and squeezing.

He began to breathe faster.

Slowly, slowly. Savour the moment.

Star knelt beside the bed and began to caress Melanie's breast while Priest sucked it.

Melanie sensed that something was different. She stopped moaning. Her body stiffened, then she opened her eyes. When she saw Star, she let out a stifled scream.

Star smiled and continued to touch her. 'Your body is very beautiful,' she said in a low voice. Priest stared, entranced, as she leaned over and took Melanie's other breast into her mouth.

Melanie shoved them both away and sat upright. 'No!' she said.

'Relax,' Priest told her. 'It's okay, really.' He stroked her hair.

Star caressed the inside of Melanie's thigh. 'You'll like it,' she said. 'A woman can do some things much better than a man. You'll see.'

'No,' Melanie said. She pressed her legs together tightly.

Priest could see that this was not going to work. He felt let down. He loved to see Star go down on another woman, driving her wild with pleasure. But Melanie was too spooked.

Star persisted. Her hand slid up Melanie's thigh, and her fingertips lightly brushed the tuft of red hair.

'No!' Melanie slapped Star's hand away.

It was a hard slap, and Star said: 'Ow! What did you do that for?'

Melanie pushed Star aside and jumped off the bed. 'Because you're fat and old and I don't want to have sex with you!'

Star gasped, and Priest winced.

Melanie stamped to the door and opened it. 'Please!' she said. 'Leave me alone!'

To Priest's surprise, Star began to cry. Indignantly he said: 'Melanie!'

Before Melanie could reply, Star walked out.

Melanie slammed the door.

Priest said to her: 'Wow, baby, that was mean.'

She opened the door again. 'You can go, too, if that's how you feel. Leave me alone!'

Priest was shocked. In twenty-five years, no one had ever told him to leave a house here at the commune. Now he was being ordered out by a beautiful naked girl who was flushed with anger or excitement or both. To add to his humiliation, he had a hard-on like a flagpole.

Am I losing my grip?

The thought disturbed him. He could always get

people to do what he wanted, especially here at the commune. He was so taken aback that he almost obeyed her. He walked to the door without speaking.

Then he realized he could not give in. He might never regain dominance if he let her defeat him now. And he needed Melanie under his control. She was crucial to the plan. He would not be able to trigger another earthquake without her help. He could not let her assert her independence in this way. She was too important.

He turned in the doorway and looked at her, standing naked, hands on her hips. What did she want? She had been in control today, in Owens Valley, because of her expertise, and that had given her the courage for this display of bad temper. But in her heart she did not want to be independent—she would not be here if she did. She preferred to be told what to do by someone with power. That was why she had married her professor. Having left him, she had taken up with another authority figure, the leader of a commune. She had revolted tonight because she did not want to share Priest with another woman. She was probably scared Star would take him away from her. But the last thing she wanted was for Priest to walk away.

He closed the door.

He crossed the little room in three paces and stood in front of her. She was still flushed with anger and breathing hard. 'Lie down,' he commanded.

She looked troubled, but she lay on the bed.

'Open your legs,' he said.

After a moment she obeyed.

He lay on her. As he entered her, she suddenly put her arms around him and held him hard. He moved fast inside her, deliberately rough. She lifted her legs around his waist. He felt her teeth on his shoulder, biting. It hurt, but he liked it. She opened her mouth, breathing hard. 'Ah, fuck,' she said in low, guttural voice. 'Priest, you son of a bitch, I love you.'

*

When Priest woke up, he went to Star's cabin.

She was lying on her side, eyes open, staring at the wall. When he sat on the bed beside her, she began to cry.

He kissed her tears. He was getting a hard-on. 'Talk to me,' he murmured.

'Did you know that Flower puts Dusty to bed?'

He had not been expecting *that*. What did it matter? 'I didn't know,' he said.

'I don't like it.'

'Why not?' He tried not to sound irritated. *Yesterday we triggered an earthquake, and today you're crying about the children?* 'It's a hell of a lot better than stealing movie posters in Silver City.'

'But you have a new family,' she burst out.

'What the heck does that mean?'

'You, and Melanie, and Flower, and Dusty. You're like a family. And there's no place in it for me, I don't fit.'

'Sure you do,' he said. 'You're the mother of my child, and you're the woman I love. How could you not fit?'

'I felt so humiliated last night.'

He stroked her breasts through the cotton of her nightshirt. She covered his hand with her own and pressed his palm hard against her body.

'The group is our family,' he told her. 'It's always been that way. We don't suffer with the hangups of the suburban mom-and-dad-and-two-kids unit.' He was repeating the teachings he had got from her years ago. 'We're one big family. We love the whole group and everyone takes care of everyone else. This way, we don't have to lie to each other, or to ourselves, about sex. You can get it on with Oaktree, or Song, and I'll know you still care for me and our child.'

'But you know something, Priest—no one ever rejected you or me before now.'

There were no rules about who could have sex with whom, but of course no one was obliged to make love if they did not want to. However, now that he thought about it, Priest could not remember an occasion on which a woman had refused him. Obviously it had been the same for Star—until Melanie.

A feeling of panic crept over him. He had felt it several times in the last few weeks. It was the fear that the commune was collapsing, he was losing his grip, and everything he loved was in peril. It was like losing his balance, as if the floor started to move unpredictably and firm ground suddenly became shifting and unreliable, just as it had in Owens Valley yesterday. He fought to suppress his anxiety. He had to stay cool. Only he could keep everyone's loyalty and hold it all together. He had to stay cool.

He lay on the bed beside her and stroked her hair. 'It'll be okay,' he said. 'We scared the shit out of Governor Roberts yesterday. He'll do what we want, you'll see.'

'Are you sure?'

He took both her breasts in his hands. He felt turned on. 'Trust me,' he murmured. He pressed against her so that she could feel his erection.

'Make love to me, Priest,' she said.

He gave her his roguish grin. 'How?'

She smiled back through her tears. 'Any damn way you like.'

*

She went to sleep afterwards. Lying beside her, Priest worried over the problem of accreditation until he thought of the solution. Then he got up.

He went to the kids' bunkhouse and woke Flower. 'I want you to go with me to San Francisco,' he said. 'Get dressed.'

He made toast and orange juice for her in the deserted cookhouse. As she ate, he said: 'You remember we talked about you being a writer? And you told me you'd like to work for a magazine?'

'Yes, *Teen* magazine,' she said.

'Right.'

'But you want me to write poetry so I can live here.'

'And I still do, but today you're going to find out what it's like to be a reporter.'

She looked happy. 'Okay!'

'I'm taking you to an FBI press conference.'

'FBI?'

'This is the kind of thing you have to do if you're a reporter.'

She wrinkled her nose in distaste. She had picked up her mother's dislike of law enforcement people. 'I never read about the FBI in *Teen*.'

'Well, Leonardo DiCaprio isn't giving a press conference today, I checked.'

She grinned sheepishly. 'Too bad.'

'But if you just ask the kind of questions a reporter from *Teen* would think of, you'll be fine.'

She nodded thoughtfully. 'What's the press conference about?'

'A group who claim they caused an earthquake. Now, I don't want you to tell everyone about this. It has to be a secret, okay?'

'Okay.'

He would tell the Rice Eaters about it when he got back, he decided. 'It's all right to talk to Mom and Melanie about it, and Oaktree and Song and Aneth and Paul Beale, but no one else. That's really important.'

'Gotcha.'

He knew he was taking a crazy risk. If things went wrong he could lose everything. He might even be arrested in front of his daughter. This could end up being the worst day of her life. But mad risks had always been his style.

When he had proposed planting the grapevines, Star had pointed out that they held their land on a one-year lease. They could break their backs digging and planting, and never see the fruits of their labour. She had argued that they should negotiate a ten-year lease before starting work. It sounded sensible, but Priest knew it would be fatal. If they postponed the start, they would never do it. He persuaded them to take the risk. At the end of that year, the commune had become a community. And the government had renewed Star's lease—that year and every year, until now.

He thought about putting on the navy blue suit. However, it was so old-fashioned that it would be conspicuous in San Francisco, so he wore his usual blue jeans. Although it was warm, he put on a T-shirt and a checked flannel shirt with a long tail, which he wore untucked. From the tool shed he took a heavy knife with a four-inch blade in a neat leather sheath. He stuck it in the waistband of his jeans, at the back, where it was concealed by the tail of his shirt.

He was high on adrenalin throughout the four-hour drive to San Francisco. He had nightmare visions: the two of them being arrested, himself bundled off to a jail cell, Flower sitting alone in an interrogation room at FBI headquarters being questioned about her parents. But fear gave him a buzz.

They reached the city at 11 a.m. They left the car in a parking lot on Golden Gate. At a drugstore, Priest bought Flower a spiral-bound notebook and two pencils. Then he took her to a coffee shop. While she was drinking her soda, he said: 'I'll be right back,' and stepped outside.

He walked toward Union Square, scanning the faces of passers-by, searching for a man who looked like him. The streets were busy with shoppers, and he had hundreds of faces to pick from. He saw a man with a thin face and dark hair studying the menu outside a restaurant, and for a moment he thought he had found his victim. Feeling wire-taut with tension, he watched for a few seconds; then the guy turned around and Priest saw that his right eye was permanently closed by some kind of injury.

Disappointed, Priest walked on. It was not easy. There were plenty of dark men in their forties, but most of them were twenty or thirty pounds heavier than Priest. He saw another likely candidate but the guy had a camera around his neck. A tourist was no good: Priest needed someone with local credentials. *This is one of the greatest shopping centers in the world and it's Saturday morning: there has to be one man here who looks like me.*

He checked his watch: eleven thirty. He was running out of time.

At last he struck lucky: a thin-faced guy of about fifty, wearing large-framed glasses, walking briskly. He was dressed in navy slacks and a green polo shirt, but carried a worn tan attaché case, and looked miserable: Priest guessed he was going to the office to do some Saturday catching-up. *Now I need his wallet.* Priest followed him around a corner, psyching himself up, waiting for an opportunity.

I'm angry, I'm desperate, I'm a crazy man escaped from the asylum, I've got to have twenty bucks for a fix, I hate everyone, I want to slash and kill, I'm mad, mad, mad . . .

The man walked past the lot where the 'Cuda was parked and turned into a street of old office buildings. For a moment there was no one else in sight. Priest drew the knife, then ran up to him and said: 'Hey!'

The man stopped reflexively and turned.

Priest grabbed the guy by the shirt, shoved the knife in front of his face and screamed: 'GIMME YOUR FUCKIN' WALLET OR I'LL SLIT YOUR FUCKIN' THROAT!'

The guy should have collapsed in terror, but he did not. *Jesus, he's a tough guy.* His face showed anger, not fear.

Staring into his eyes, Priest read the thought: *It's only one guy and he doesn't have a gun.*

Priest hesitated, suddenly fearful. *Shit, I can't afford for this to go wrong.* There was a split-second standoff. *A casually dressed man with a briefcase heading for work on Saturday morning . . . could he be a police detective?*

But it was too late now for second thoughts. Before the guy could move, Priest flicked the blade across his cheek, drawing a thin two-inch line of red blood just below the right lens of his spectacles.

The man's courage evaporated and all thought of resistance left him. His eyes widened in fear and his body seemed to sag. 'Okay! Okay!' he said in a high-pitched, shaky voice.

Not a cop, after all.

Priest screamed: 'NOW! NOW! GIMME IT NOW!'

'It's in my case . . .'

Priest grabbed the briefcase from the man's hand. At the last minute he decided to take the guy's glasses, too. He snatched them off his face, turned around, and ran away.

At the corner he looked back. The guy was throwing up on the sidewalk.

Priest turned right. He dropped his knife into a garbage bin and walked on. At the next corner he stopped by a building site and opened the case. Inside was a file folder, a notebook and some pens, a paper package that looked as if it contained a sandwich, and a leather billfold. Priest took the billfold and threw the case over the fence into a builder's skip.

He returned to the coffee shop and sat down with Flower. His coffee was still warm. *I haven't lost the touch. Thirty years since I last did that but I can still scare the shit out of people. Way to go, Ricky.*

He opened the billfold. It contained money, credit cards, business cards, and some kind of identity card with a photo. Priest pulled out a business card and handed it to Flower. 'My card, ma'am.'

She giggled. 'You're Peter Shoebury, of Watkins, Colefax and Brown.'

'I'm a lawyer?'

'I guess.'

He looked at the photo on the identity card. It was about half an inch square and had been taken in an automatic photo-booth. It was about ten years old, he guessed. It did not look exactly like Priest, but neither did it look much like Peter Shoebury. Photos were like that.

Still, Priest could improve the resemblance. Shoebury had straight dark hair, but it was short. Priest said: 'Can I borrow your hair band?'

'Sure.' Flower took a rubber band out of her hair and shook her locks around her face. Priest did the reverse, pulling his hair back into a ponytail and tying it with the band. Then he put on the glasses.

He showed Flower the photo. 'How do you like my secret identity?'

'Hmm.' She looked at the back of the card. 'This will admit you to the downtown office but not the Oakland branch.'

'I guess I can live with that.'

She grinned. 'Daddy, where did you get this?'

He raised one eyebrow at her and said: 'I borrowed it.'

'Did you pick someone's pocket?'

'Sort of.' He could see she thought that was roguish rather than wicked. He let her believe what she wanted. He looked at the clock on the wall. It was eleven forty-five. 'Are you ready to go?'

'Sure.'

They walked along the street and entered the Federal Building, a forbidding grey granite monolith occupying the entire city block. In the lobby they passed through a metal detector, and Priest was glad he had had the forethought to get rid of the knife. He asked the security guard which floor the FBI was on.

They took the elevator up. Priest felt like he was high on cocaine. The danger made him super-alert. *If this elevator breaks down I could power it with my own psychic energy.* He figured it was okay to be self-confident, maybe even a little arrogant, as he was playing the part of a lawyer.

He led Flower into the FBI office and followed a sign to a conference room off the lobby. There was a table with microphones at the far end of the room. Near the door stood four men, all tall and fit-looking, wearing well-pressed business suits, white shirts, and sober ties. They had to be agents.

If they knew who I was, they'd shoot me down without even thinking about it.

Stay cool, Priest—they ain't mind-readers, they don't know nothing about you.

Priest was six foot, but they were all taller. He sensed immediately that the leader was the older man whose thick white hair was meticulously parted and combed. He was talking to a man with a black moustache. Two younger men were listening, wearing deferential expressions.

A young woman carrying a clipboard approached Priest. 'Hi, can I help you?'

'Well, I sure hope so,' Priest said.

The agents noticed him when he spoke. He read their reactions as they looked at him. When they took in his ponytail and blue jeans they became guarded, then they saw Flower and softened again.

One of the younger men said: 'Everything okay here?'

Priest said: 'My name is Peter Shoebury, I'm an attorney with Watkins, Colefax, and Brown here in the city. My daughter Florence is editor of the school newspaper. She heard on the radio about your press conference and she wanted to cover it for the paper. So I figured hey, it's a public information thing, let's go along. I hope it's okay with you.'

Everyone looked at the white-haired guy, confirming Priest's intuition that he was the boss.

There was an awful moment of hesitation.

Hell, boy, you ain't no lawyer! You're Ricky Granger, used to wholesale amphetamines through a bunch of liquor stores in Los Angeles back in the sixties—are you mixed up in this earthquake shit? Frisk him, boys, and cuff his little girl, too. Let's take 'em in, find out what they know.

The white-haired man held out his hand and said: 'I'm Associate Special Agent in Charge Brian Kincaid, head of the San Francisco field office of the FBI.'

Priest shook hands. 'Good to meet you, Brian.'

'What firm did you say you're with, sir?'

'Watkins, Colefax and Brown.'

Kincaid frowned. 'I thought they were real estate brokers, not lawyers.'

Oh, shit.

Priest nodded and tried for a reassuring smile. 'That's correct, and it's my job to keep them out of trouble.' There was a word for a lawyer who was employed by a corporation. Priest searched his memory and found it. 'I'm in-house counsel.'

'Would you have any kind of ID?'

'Oh, sure.' He opened the stolen wallet and took

out the card with the photo of Peter Shoebury. He held his breath.

Kincaid looked at it, then checked the resemblance to Priest. Priest could tell what he was thinking: *Could be him, I guess.* He handed it back. Priest breathed again.

Kincaid turned to Flower. 'What school are you at, Florence?'

Priest's heart beat faster. *Just make something up, kid.*

'Um . . .' Flower hesitated. Priest was about to answer for her, then she said: 'Eisenhower Junior High.'

Priest felt a surge of pride. She had inherited his nerve. Just in case Kincaid should happen to know the schools in San Francisco, he added: 'That's in Oakland.'

Kincaid seemed satisfied. 'Well, we'd be delighted to have you join us, Florence,' he said.

We did it!

'Thank you, sir,' she said.

'If there are any questions I can answer now, before the press conference starts . . .'

Priest had been careful not to overprepare Flower. If she appeared shy, or fumbled her questions, it would seem only natural, he figured; whereas if she were too poised and seemed well rehearsed she might arouse suspicion. But now he felt a surge of anxiety on her behalf, and he had to suppress the paternal urge to step in and tell her what to do. He bit his lip.

She opened her notebook. 'Are you in charge of this investigation?'

Priest relaxed a little. She would be fine.

'This is only one of many inquiries that I have to keep an eye on,' Kincaid answered. He pointed to the man with the black moustache. 'Special Agent Marvin Hayes has this assignment.'

Flower turned to Hayes. 'I think the school would like to know what kind of person you are, Mr Hayes. Could I ask you some questions about yourself?'

Priest was shocked to observe a hint of coquettishness in the way she tilted her head and smiled at Hayes. *She's too young to flirt with grown men, for God's sake!*

But Hayes bought it. He looked pleased and said: 'Sure, go ahead.'

'Are you married?'

'Yes. I have two children, a boy around your age and a girl a little younger.'

'Do you have any hobbies?'

'I collect boxing memorabilia.'

'That's unusual.'

'I guess it is.'

Priest was both pleased and dismayed by how naturally Flower fell into the role. *She's good at this. Hell, I hope I haven't raised her all these years to become a cheap magazine writer.*

He studied Hayes while the agent answered Flower's innocent questions. This was his opponent. Hayes was carefully dressed in conventional style. His tan lightweight suit, white shirt and dark silk tie had probably come from Brooks Brothers. He wore black oxford shoes, highly shined and tightly laced. His hair and moustache were neatly trimmed.

Yet Priest sensed that the ultra-conservative look was fake. The tie was too striking, there was an overlarge ruby ring on the pinkie of his left hand, and the moustache was a raffish touch. Also, Priest thought that the kind of American Brahmin Hayes was trying to imitate would not be so dressed up on a Saturday morning, even for a press conference.

'What's your favourite restaurant?' Flower asked.

'A lot of us go to Everton's, which is really more of a pub.'

The conference room was filling up with men and women with notebooks and cassette recorders, photographers encumbered with cameras and flashguns, radio reporters with large microphones, and a couple of TV crews with hand-held video cameras. As they came in, the young woman with the clipboard asked them to sign a book. Priest and Flower seemed to have bypassed that. He was thankful. He could not write 'Peter Shoebury' to save his life.

Kincaid, the boss, touched Hayes's elbow. 'We need to prepare for our press conference now, Florence. I hope you'll stay to hear what we have to announce.'

'Yes, thank you,' she said.

Priest said: 'You've really been very kind, Mr Hayes. Florence's teachers will be truly grateful.'

The agents moved to the table at the far end. *My God, we fooled them.* Priest and Flower sat at the back and waited. Priest's tension eased. He really had got away with it.

I knew I would.

He had not gained much hard information yet, but

that would come with the formal press announcement. What he did have was a sense of the people he was dealing with. He was reassured by what he had learned. Neither Kincaid nor Hayes struck him as brilliant. They seemed like ordinary plodding cops, the kind who got by with a mixture of dogged routine and occasional corruption. He had little to fear from them.

Kincaid stood up and introduced himself. He sounded confident but a touch overassertive. Maybe he had not been the boss very long. He said: 'I would like to begin by making one thing very clear. The FBI does not believe that yesterday's earthquake was triggered by a terrorist group.'

The flashguns popped, the tapes whirred, and the reporters scribbled notes. Priest tried not to let his anger show on his face. The bastards were refusing to take him seriously—still!

'This is also the opinion of the state seismologist, who I believe is available for interview in Sacramento this morning.'

What do I have to do to convince you? I threatened an earthquake, then I made it happen, and still you won't believe I did it! Must I kill people before you'll listen?

Kincaid went on: 'Nevertheless, a terrorist threat has been made, and the Bureau intends to catch the people who made it. Our investigation is headed by Special Agent Marvin Hayes. Over to you, Marvin.'

Hayes stood up. He was more nervous than Kincaid, Priest saw at once. He read mechanically from a prepared statement. 'FBI agents have this morning questioned all five paid employees of the Green California Campaign at their homes. The employees are voluntarily cooperating with us.'

Priest was pleased. He had laid a false trail and the Feds were following it.

Hayes went on: 'Agents also visited the headquarters of the campaign, here in San Francisco, and examined documents and computer records.'

They would be combing the organization's mailing list for clues, Priest guessed.

There was more, but it was repetitive. The assembled journalists asked questions that added detail and colour but did not change the basic story. Priest's tension grew again as he sat waiting impatiently for a chance to leave inconspicuously. He was pleased that the FBI investigation was so far off course—they had not yet come upon his *second* false trail—but he felt angry that they still refused to believe in his threat.

At last Kincaid drew the session to a close and the journalists began to get to their feet and pack up their gear.

Priest and Flower made for the door, but they were stopped by the woman with the clipboard, who smiled brightly and said: 'I don't think you two signed in, did you?' She handed Priest a book and a pen. 'Just put your names and the organization you represent.'

Priest froze with fear. *I can't, I can't!*

Don't panic. Relax.

Ley, tor, pur-doy-kor.

'Sir? Would you please sign?'

'Sure.' Priest took the book and the pen. Then he

handed it to Flower. 'I think Florence should sign for us—she's the journalist,' he said, reminding her of her false name. It occurred to him that she might have forgotten the school she was supposed to attend. 'Put your name, and Eisenhower Junior High.'

Flower did not flinch. She wrote in the book and handed it back to the woman.

Now, for Christ's sake, can we go?

'You, too, sir, please,' said the woman, and she gave Priest the book.

He took it reluctantly. Now what? If he just scrawled a squiggle she might ask him to print his name clearly: that had happened to him before. But maybe he could just refuse and walk out. She was only a secretary.

As he hesitated, he heard the voice of Kincaid. 'I hope that was interesting for you, Florence.'

Kincaid is an agent—it's his job to be suspicious.

'Yes, sir, it was,' Flower said politely.

Priest began to sweat under his shirt.

He drew a scrawl where he was supposed to write his name. Then he closed the book before handing it back to the woman.

Kincaid said to Flower: 'Will you remember to send me a copy of your class newspaper when it's printed?'

'Yes, of course.'

Let's go, let's go!

The woman opened the book and said: 'Oh, sir, pardon me, would you mind printing your name here? I'm afraid your signature isn't really clear.'

What am I going to do?

'You'll need an address,' Kincaid said to Flower,

and he took a business card from the breast pocket of his suit coat. 'There you go.'

'Thank you.'

Priest remembered that Peter Shoebury carried business cards. *That's the answer—thank God!* He opened the wallet and gave one to the woman. 'My handwriting is terrible—use this,' he said. 'We have to run.' He shook Kincaid's hand. 'You've been wonderful. I'll make sure Florence remembers to send you the clipping.'

They left the room.

They crossed the lobby and waited for the elevator. Priest imagined Kincaid coming after him, gun drawn, saying: *What kind of attorney can't write his own goddam name, asshole?* But the elevator came and they rode down and walked out of the building into the fresh air.

Flower said: 'I gotta have the craziest dad in the world.'

Priest smiled at her. 'That's the truth.'

'Why did we have false names?'

'Well, I never like the pigs to get my real name,' he said. She would accept that, he thought. She knew how her parents felt about cops.

But she said: 'Well, I'm mad at you about it.'

He frowned. 'Why?'

'I'll never forgive you for calling me Florence,' she said.

Priest stared at her for a moment, then they both burst out laughing.

'Come on, kid,' Priest said fondly. 'Let's go home.'

CHAPTER TEN

JUDY DREAMED she walked along the seashore with Michael Quercus, and his bare feet left neat, shapely prints in the wet sand.

On Saturday morning she helped out at a literacy class for young offenders. They respected her because she carried a gun. She sat in a church hall beside a seventeen-year-old hoodlum, helping him practise writing the date, hoping that somehow this would make it less likely that in ten years' time she would have to arrest him.

In the afternoon she drove the short distance from Bo's house to Gala Foods on Geary Boulevard and shopped.

The familiar Saturday routines failed to soothe her. She was furious with Brian Kincaid for taking her off the Hammer of Eden case, but there was nothing she could do about it, so she stomped up and down the aisles and tried to turn her mind to Chewy Chips Ahoy, Rice A Roni, and Zee 'Decor Collection' kitchen towel printed with yellow patterns. In the breakfast cereal aisle she thought of Michael's son Dusty, and she bought a box of Cap'n Crunch.

But her thoughts kept returning to the case. *Is there*

*really someone out there who can make earthquakes happen?
Or am I nuts?*

Back at home, Bo helped her unload the groceries and asked her about the investigation. 'I hear Marvin Hayes raided the Green California Campaign.'

'It can't have done him much good,' she said. 'They're all clean. Raja interviewed them on Tuesday. Two men and three women, all over fifty. No criminal records—not a speeding ticket between them—and no association with any suspicious persons. If they're terrorists, I'm Kojak.'

'TV news says he's examining their records.'

'Right. That's a list of everyone who ever wrote asking them for information, including Jane Fonda. There are eighteen thousand names and addresses. Now Marvin's team has to run each name through the FBI computer to see who's worth interviewing. It could take a month.'

The doorbell rang. Judy opened the door to Simon Sparrow. She was surprised, but pleased. 'Hey, Simon, come on in!'

He was wearing black cycling shorts and a muscles T-shirt with Nike trainers and wraparound sunglasses. However, he had not come by bicycle: his emerald green Honda Del Sol was parked at the kerb with the roof down. Judy wondered what her mother would have thought of Simon. *Nice boy*, she might have said. *Not very manly, though.*

Bo shook hands with Simon then gave Judy a clandestine look that said, *Who the hell is this fruit?* Judy shocked him by saying: 'Simon is one of the FBI's top linguistic analysts.'

Somewhat bemused, Bo said: 'Well, Simon, I'm sure glad to meet you.'

Simon was carrying a cassette tape and a manila envelope. Holding them up, he said: 'I brought you my report on the Hammer of Eden tape.'

'I'm off the case,' Judy said.

'I know, but I thought you'd still be interested. The voices on the tape don't match any in our acoustic files, unfortunately.'

'No names, then.'

'No, but lots of other interesting stuff.'

Judy's interest was piqued. 'You said "voices". I only heard one.'

'No, there are two.' Simon looked around and saw Bo's radio cassette on the kitchen counter. It was normally used to play *The Greatest Hits of the Everly Brothers*. He slipped his cassette into the player. 'Let me talk you through the tape.'

'I'd love you to, but it's Marvin Hayes's case now.'

'I'd like your opinion anyway.'

Judy shook her head stubbornly. 'You should talk to Marvin first.'

'I know what you're saying. But Marvin is a fucking idiot. Do you know how long it is since he put a bad guy in jail?'

'Simon, if you're trying to get me to work on this case behind Kincaid's back, forget it!'

277

'Hear me out, okay? It can't do any harm.' Simon turned up the volume control and started the tape.

Judy sighed. She was desperately keen to know what Simon had found out about the Hammer of Eden. But if Kincaid learned that Simon had talked to her before Marvin, there would be hell to pay.

The voice of the woman said: 'This is the Hammer of Eden with a message for Governor Mike Robson.'

Simon stopped the tape and looked at Bo. 'What did you visualize when you first heard that?'

Bo grinned. 'I pictured a large woman, about fifty, with a big smile. Kind of sexy. I remember I thought I'd like to...' He glanced at Judy and finished: '... meet her.'

Simon nodded. 'Your instincts are reliable. Untrained people can tell a lot about a speaker just by hearing them. You almost always know if you're listening to a woman or a man, of course. But you can also tell how old they are, and you can generally estimate their height and build pretty accurately. Sometimes you can even guess at their state of health.'

'You're right,' Judy said. She was intrigued despite herself. 'Whenever I hear a voice on the phone, I picture the person, even if I'm listening to a taped announcement.'

'It's because the sound of the voice comes from the body. Pitch, loudness, resonance, huskiness, all vocal characteristics have physical causes. Tall people have a longer vocal tract, old people have stiff tissues and creaky cartilage, sick people have inflamed throats.'

'That makes sense,' Judy said. 'I just never really thought about it before.'

'My computer picks up the same cues as people do, and is more accurate.' Simon took a typed report out of the envelope he had been carrying. 'This woman is between forty-seven and fifty-two. She's tall, within an inch of six foot. She's overweight, but not obese: probably just kind of generously built. She's a drinker and a smoker, but healthy despite that.'

Judy felt anxious but excited. Although she wished she had not let Simon get started, it was fascinating to learn something about the mystery woman behind the voice.

Simon looked at Bo. 'And you're right about the big smile. She has a large mouth cavity, and her speech is under-labialized—she doesn't purse her lips.'

'I like this woman,' Bo said. 'Does the computer say if she's good in bed?'

Simon smiled. 'The reason you think she's sexy is that her voice has a whispery quality. This can be a sign of sexual arousal. But when it's a permanent feature, it doesn't necessarily indicate sexiness.'

'I think you're wrong,' Bo said. 'Sexy women have sexy voices.'

'So do heavy smokers.'

'Okay, that's true.'

Simon wound the tape back to the beginning. 'Now listen to her accent.'

Judy protested. 'Simon, I don't think we should—'

'Just listen. Please!'

'Okay, okay.'

This time he played the first two sentences. 'This is the Hammer of Eden with a message for Governor Mike Robson. Shit, I didn't expect to be talking to a tape recorder.'

He stopped the tape. 'It's a northern California accent, of course. But did you notice anything else?'

Bo said: 'She's middle class.'

Judy frowned. 'She sounded upper class to me.'

'You're both right,' Simon said. 'Her accent changes between the first sentence and the second.'

'Is that unusual?' said Judy.

'No. Most of us get our basic accent from the social group we grew up with, then modify it later in life. Usually, people try to upgrade: blue-collar people try to make themselves sound more affluent, and the nouveaux riches try to talk like old money. Occasionally it goes the other way: a politician from a patrician family might make his accent more down-home, to seem like a man of the people, yuh know what I'm sayin'?'

Judy smiled. 'You betcher ass.'

'The learned accent is used in formal situations,' Simon said as he rewound the tape. 'It comes into play when the speaker is poised. But we revert to our childhood speech patterns when we're under stress. Okay so far?'

Bo said: 'Sure.'

'This woman has downgraded her speech. She makes herself sound more blue-collar than she really is.'

Judy was fascinated. 'You think she's a kind of Patty Hearst figure?'

'In that area, yes. She begins with a rehearsed formal sentence, spoken in her average-person voice. Now, in American speech, the more high-class you are, the more you pronounce the letter *R*. With that in mind, listen to the way she says the word "governor" now.'

Judy was going to stop him, but she was too interested. The woman on the tape said: 'This is the Hammer of Eden with a message for Governor Mike Robson.'

'Hear the way she says "Guvnuh Mike"? This is street talk. But listen to the next bit. The voicemail announcement has put her off guard, and she speaks naturally.'

'Shit, I didn't expect to be talking to a tape recorder.'

'Although she says "Shit," she pronounces the word "recorder" very correctly. A blue-collar type would say "recawduh", pronouncing only the first *R*. The average college graduate says "recorduh", pronouncing the second *R* distinctly. Only very superior people say "recorder" the way she does, carefully pronouncing all three *R*s.'

Bo said: 'Who'd have thought you could find out so much from two sentences?'

Simon smiled, looking pleased. 'But did you notice anything about the vocabulary?'

Bo shook his head. 'Nothing I can put my finger on.'

'What's a tape recorder?'

Bo laughed. 'A machine the size of a small suitcase, with two reels on top. I had one in Vietnam—a Grundig.'

Judy saw what Simon was getting at. The term 'tape recorder' was out of date. The machine they were using today was a cassette player. Voicemail was recorded on the hard disc of a computer. 'She's living in a timewarp,' Judy said. 'It makes me think Patty Hearst again. What happened to her, anyway?'

Bo said: 'She served her time, came out of jail, wrote a book and appeared on *Geraldo*. Welcome to America.'

Judy stood up. 'This has been fascinating, Simon, but I don't feel comfortable with it. I think you should take your report to Marvin now.'

'One more thing I want to show you,' he said. He touched the fast-forward button.

'Really—'

'Just listen to this.'

The woman's voice said: 'It happened in Owens Valley a little after two o'clock, you can check it out.' There was a faint background noise, and she hesitated.

Simon paused the tape. 'I've enhanced that odd little murmur. Here it is, reconstructed.'

He released the pause switch. Judy heard a man's voice, distorted with a lot of background hiss, but clear enough to understand, say: 'We do not recognize the jurisdiction of the United States government.' The background noise returned to normal, and the woman's voice repeated: 'We do not recognize the jurisdiction of the United States government.' She went on: 'Now that you know we can do what we say, you'd better think again about our demand.'

Simon stopped the tape.

Judy said: 'She was speaking words he had given her, and she forgot something, so he reminded her.'

Bo said: 'Didn't you figure the original Internet message had been dictated by a blue-collar guy, maybe illiterate, and typed by an educated woman?'

'Yes,' Simon said. 'But this is a different woman—older.'

'So,' Bo said to Judy, 'now you're beginning to build up profiles of three unknown subjects.'

'No, I'm not,' she said. 'I'm off the case. Come on, Simon, you know this could get me into more trouble.'

'Okay.' He took the tape out of the machine and stood up. 'I've told you all the important stuff, anyway. Let me know if you come up with some brilliant insight that I could pass on to Mogadon Marvin.'

Judy saw him to the door. 'I'll take my report to the office right now—Marvin will probably still be there,' he said. 'Then I'm going to sleep. I was up all night on this.' He got into his sports car and roared off.

When she came back, Bo was making green tea, looking thoughtful. 'So, this streetwise guy has a bunch of classy dames to take dictation from him.'

Judy nodded. 'I believe I know where you're headed.'

'It's a cult.'

'Yes. I was right to think Patty Hearst.' She shivered. The man behind all this must be a charismatic figure with power over women. He was uneducated, but this did not hold him back, for he had others carrying out his orders. 'But something's not right. That demand, for a freeze on new power plants—it's just not wacky enough.'

'I agree,' Bo said. 'It's not showy. I think they have some down-to-earth selfish reason to want this freeze.'

'I wonder,' Judy mused. 'Maybe they have an interest in one particular power plant.'

Bo stared at her. 'Judy, that's brilliant! Like, it's going to pollute their salmon river, or something.'

'In there somewhere,' she said. 'But it hits them really hard.' She felt excited. She was on to something. 'The freeze on *all* plant construction is a cover, then. They're afraid to name the one they're really interested in for fear that would lead us to them.'

'But how many possibilities can there be? Power plants aren't built every day. And these things are controversial. Any proposal has to have been reported.'

'Let's check.'

They went into the den. Judy's laptop was on a side table. She sometimes wrote reports in here while Bo was watching football. The TV did not distract her, and she liked to be near him. She switched the machine on. Waiting for it to boot up, she said: 'If we put together a list of sites where power plants are to be built, the FBI computer would tell us if there's a cult near any of them.'

She accessed the files of the *San Francisco Chronicle*

and searched for references to power plants in the last three years. The search produced 117 articles. Judy scanned the headlines, ignoring stories about Pittsburgh and Cuba. 'Okay, here's a scheme for a nuclear plant in the Mojave Desert . . .' She saved the story. 'A hydroelectric dam in Sierra county . . . an oil-fired plant up near the Oregon border . . .'

Bo said: 'Sierra county? That rings some kind of bell. Got an exact location?'

Judy clicked on the article. 'Yeah . . . the proposal is to dam the Silver River.'

He frowned. 'Silver River Valley . . .'

Judy turned from the computer screen. 'Wait, this is familiar . . . isn't there a vigilante group that has a big spread there?'

'That's right!' said Bo. 'They're called Los Alamos. Run by a speed freak called Poco Latella who originally came from Daly City; that's how I know about them.'

'Right. They're armed to the teeth and they refused to recognize the US government . . . Jesus, they even used that sentence on the tape: "We do not recognize the jurisdiction of the United States government." Bo, I think we've got 'em.'

'What are you going to do?'

Judy's heart sank as she remembered she was off the case. 'If Kincaid finds out I've been working this case, he'll bust a gut.'

'Los Alamos has to be checked out.'

'I'll call Simon.' She picked up the phone and dialled the office. The switchboard operator was a guy she knew. 'Hey, Charlie, this is Judy. Is Simon Sparrow in the office?'

'He came and went,' Charlie said. 'Want me to try his car?'

'Yeah, thanks.'

She waited. Charlie came back on the line and said: 'No answer. I tried his home number, too. Shall I put a message on his pager?'

'Yes, please.' Judy recalled that he had said he was going to sleep. 'I bet he's turned it off, though.'

'I'll send him a message to call you.'

'Thanks.' She hung up and said to Bo: 'I think I have to see Kincaid. I guess if I give him a hot lead, he can't be too mad at me.'

Bo just shrugged. 'You don't have any choice, do you?'

Judy could not risk people getting killed just because she was afraid to confess what she had been doing. 'No, I don't have any choice,' she said.

She was wearing narrow black jeans and a strawberry-pink T-shirt. The T-shirt was too figure-hugging for the office, even on a Saturday. She went up to her room and changed it for a loose white polo shirt. Then she got in her Monte Carlo and drove downtown.

Marvin would have to organize a raid on Los Alamos. There might be trouble: vigilantes were crazy. The raid needed to be heavily manned and meticulously organized. The Bureau was terrified of another Waco. Every agent in the office would be drafted in for it. The Sacramento field office of the FBI would also be involved. They would probably strike at dawn tomorrow.

She went straight to Kincaid's office. His secretary was in the outer room, working at her computer, wearing a Saturday outfit of white jeans and a red shirt. She picked up the phone and said: 'Judy Maddox is here to see you.' After a moment she hung up and said to Judy: 'Go right in.'

Judy hesitated at the door to the inner sanctum. The last two times she had entered this office, she had suffered humiliation and disappointment inside. But she was not superstitious. Maybe this time Kincaid would be understanding and gracious.

It still jarred her to see his beefy figure in the chair that used to belong to the slight, dapper Milton Lestrange. She had not yet visited Milt in hospital, she realized. She made a mental note to go tonight or tomorrow.

Brian's greeting was chilly. 'What can I do for you, Judy?'

'I saw Simon Sparrow earlier,' she began. 'He brought his report to me because he hadn't heard I was off the case. Naturally, I told him to give it to Marvin.'

'Naturally.'

'But he told me a little of what he had found, and I speculated that the Hammer of Eden is a cult that feels somehow threatened by a planned building project for a power plant.'

Brian looked annoyed. 'I'll pass this to Marvin,' he said impatiently.

Judy ploughed on. 'There are several power plant projects in California right now, I checked. And one of them is in Silver River Valley, where there is a right-wing vigilante group called Los Alamos. Brian, I think Los Alamos must be the Hammer of Eden. I think we should raid them.'

'Is that what you think?'

Oh, shit.

'Is there a flaw in my logic?' she said icily.

'You bet there is.' He stood up. 'The flaw is, you're not on the goddam case.'

'I know,' she said. 'But I thought—'

He interrupted her, stretching his arm across the big desk and pointing an accusing finger at her face. 'You've intercepted the psycholinguistic report and you're trying to sneak your way back on the case— and I know why! You think it's a high-profile case and you're trying to get yourself noticed.'

'Who by?' she said indignantly.

'FBI headquarters, the press, Governor Robson.'

'I am not!'

'You just listen up. You are off this case. Do you understand me? O.F.F., off. You don't talk to your friend Simon about it. You don't check power plant schemes. And you don't propose raids on vigilante hangouts.'

'Jesus Christ!'

'This is what you do. You go home. And you leave this case to Marvin and me.'

'Brian—'

'Goodbye, Judy. Have a nice weekend.'

She stared at him. He was red-faced and breathing hard. She felt furious but helpless. She fought back the angry retorts that sprang to her lips. She had been forced to apologize for swearing at him once already, and she did not need that humiliation again. She bit her lip. After a long moment she turned on her heel and walked out of the room.

CHAPTER ELEVEN

P RIEST PARKED the old Plymouth 'Cuda at the side of the road in the faint light of early dawn. He took Melanie's hand and led her into the forest. The mountain air was cool, and they shivered in their T-shirts until the effort of walking warmed their bodies. After a few minutes, they emerged on a bluff that looked over the width of the Silver River Valley.

'This is where they want to build the dam,' Priest said.

At this point the valley narrowed to a bottleneck, so that the far side was no more than four or five hundred yards away. It was still too dark to see the river, but in the morning silence they heard it rushing along below them. As the light strengthened, they could distinguish the dark shapes of cranes and giant earth-moving machines below them, silent and still, like sleeping dinosaurs.

Priest had almost given up hope that Governor Robson would now negotiate. This was the second day since the Owens Valley earthquake, and still there was no word. Priest could not figure out the governor's strategy, but it was not capitulation.

There would have to be another earthquake.

But he was anxious. Melanie and Star might be reluctant, especially as the second tremor would have to do more damage than the first. He had to firm up their commitment. He was starting with Melanie.

'It'll create a lake ten miles long, all the way up the valley,' he told her. He could see her pale oval face become taut with anger. 'Upstream from here, everything you see will be under water.'

Beyond the bottleneck, there was a broad valley floor. As the landscape became visible, they could see a scatter of houses and some neat cultivated fields, all connected by dirt tracks. Melanie said: 'Surely someone tried to stop the dam?'

Priest nodded. 'There was a big legal battle. We took no part. We don't believe in courts and lawyers. And we didn't want reporters and TV crews swarming all over our place—too many of us have secrets to keep. That's why we don't even tell people we're a commune. Most of our neighbours don't know we exist, and the others think the vineyard is run from Napa and staffed by transient workers. So we didn't take part in the protest. But some of the wealthier residents hired lawyers, and the environmental groups sided with the local people. It did no good.'

'How come?'

'Governor Robson backed the dam and put this guy Al Honeymoon on the case.' Priest hated Honeymoon. He had lied and cheated and manipulated the press with total ruthlessness. 'He got the whole thing turned around so that the media made folks here look like a handful of selfish types who wanted to deny electric power to every hospital and school in California.'

'Like it's your fault that people in Los Angeles put underwater lights in their pools and have electric motors to close their drapes.'

'Right. So Coastal Electric got permission to build the dam.'

'And all those people will lose their homes.'

'Plus a pony-trekking centre, a wildlife camp, several summer cabins, and a crazy bunch of armed vigilantes known as Los Alamos. Everyone gets compensation—except us, because we don't own our land, we rent it on a one-year lease. We get nothing—for the best vineyard between Napa and Bordeaux.'

'And the only place I ever felt at peace.'

Priest gave a murmur of sympathy. This was the way he wanted the conversation to go. 'Has Dusty always had these allergies?'

'From birth. He was actually allergic to milk—cow's milk, formula, even breast milk. He survived on goat's milk. That was when I realized. The human race *must* be doing something wrong, if the world is so polluted that my own breast milk is poisonous to my child.'

'But you took him to doctors.'

'Michael insisted. I knew they'd do no good. They gave us drugs that suppressed his immune system in order to inhibit the reaction to allergens. What kind of a way is that to treat his condition? He needed pure water and clean air and a healthy way of life. I guess I've been searching, ever since he was born, for a place like this.'

'It was hard for you.'

'You have no idea. A single woman with a sick kid can't hold down a job, can't get a decent apartment, can't live. You think America's a big place, but it's all the damn same.'

'You were in a bad way when I met you.'

'I was about to kill myself, and Dusty too.' Tears came to her eyes.

'Then you found this place.'

Her face darkened with anger. 'And now they want to take it away from me.'

'The FBI is saying we didn't cause the earthquake, and the governor hasn't said anything.'

'The hell with them, we'll have to do it again! Only this time make sure they *can't* ignore it.'

That was what he wanted her to say. 'It would have to cause real damage, bring down some buildings. People might get hurt.'

'But we have no choice!'

'We could leave the valley, break up the commune, go back to the old way of life: regular jobs, money, poisoned air, greed, jealousy, and hate.'

He had her frightened. 'No!' she cried. 'Don't say that!'

'I guess you're right. We can't go back now.'

'I sure can't.'

He took another look up and down the valley. 'We'll make certain it stays the way God made it.'

She closed her eyes in relief and said: 'Amen.'

He took her hand and led her through the trees back to the car.

Driving along the narrow road up the valley, Priest said: 'Are you going to pick up Dusty from San Francisco today?'

'Yeah, I'll leave after breakfast.'

Priest heard a strange noise over the asthmatic throb of the ancient V8 engine. He glanced up out of the side window and saw a helicopter.

'Shit,' he said, and stamped on the brake.

Melanie was thrown forward. 'What is it?' she said in a frightened voice.

Priest stopped the car and jumped out. The chopper was disappearing northwards.

Melanie got out. 'What's the matter?'

'What's a helicopter doing here?'

'Oh, my God,' she said shakily. 'You think it's looking for us?'

The noise faded then came back. The chopper reappeared suddenly over the trees, flying low.

'I think it's the Feds,' Priest said. 'Damn!' After yesterday's lacklustre press conference, he had felt safe for a few more days. Kincaid and Hayes had seemed a long way from tracking him down. Now they were *here*, in the valley.

Melanie said: 'What are we going to do?'

'Keep calm. They haven't come for us.'

'How do you *know*?'

'I made sure of it.'

She became tearful. 'Priest, why do you keep talking in riddles?'

'I'm sorry.' He remembered that he needed her for what he had to do. That meant he had to explain things to her. He gathered his thoughts. 'They can't be coming for us, because they don't know about us. The commune doesn't appear on any government records—our land is rented by Star. It's not on police or FBI files because we've never come to their attention. There has never been a newspaper article or TV program about us. We're not registered with the IRS. Our vineyard isn't on any map.'

'So why are they here?'

'I think they've come for Los Alamos. Those nutcases must be on file with every law enforcement agency in the continental United States. For God's sake, they stand at their gate holding high-powered rifles, just to make sure that everyone *knows* there's a bunch of dangerous frigging lunatics in there.'

'How can you be sure the FBI are after *them*?'

'I made certain of it. When Star called the John Truth show, I had her say the Los Alamos slogan: "We do not recognize the jurisdiction of the United States government." I laid a false trail.'

'Are we safe, then?'

'Not quite. After they draw a blank at Los Alamos, the Feds may take a look at the other people in the valley. They'll see the vineyard from the chopper and pay us a visit. So we'd better get home to warn the others.'

He jumped into the car. As soon as Melanie was in, he floored the pedal. But the car was twenty-five years old, and had not been designed for speed on winding mountain roads. He cursed its wheezy carburettors and lurching suspension.

As he struggled to maintain speed on the twisting road, he wondered fretfully who at the FBI had ordered this raid. He had not expected Kincaid or Hayes to make the necessary intuitive jump. There had to be someone else on the case. He wondered who.

A black car came up behind, going fast, headlights blazing although it was past daybreak. They were approaching a bend, but the driver honked and pulled out to pass. As it went by, Priest saw the driver and his companion, two burly young men, dressed in casual clothes but clean-shaven and short-haired.

Immediately afterwards, a second car came up behind, honking and flashing.

'Fuck this,' Priest said. When the FBI was in a hurry, it was best to get out of the way. He braked and pulled over. The nearside wheels of the 'Cuda bumped over the roadside grass. The second car flashed by and a third came up. Priest brought his car to a halt.

He and Melanie sat and watched a stream of vehicles race past. As well as cars, there were two armoured trucks and three minivans full of grim-faced men and a few women. 'It's a raid,' Melanie said woefully.

'No fucking kidding,' Priest said, the tension making him sarcastic.

She did not seem to notice.

Then a car peeled off from the convoy and pulled up right behind the 'Cuda.

Priest was suddenly afraid. He stared at the car in his rear-view mirror. It was a dark green Buick Regal. The driver was speaking into a phone. There was another man in the passenger seat. Priest could not make out their faces.

He wished with all his heart that he had not gone to the press conference. One of the guys in the Buick might have been there yesterday. If so, he would be sure to ask what a lawyer from Oakland was doing in Silver River Valley. It could hardly be a coincidence. Any agent with half a brain would immediately put Priest at the top of the suspect list.

The last of the convoy flashed by. In the Buick, the driver put down his phone. Any second now the agents would get out of the car. Priest cast about desperately for a plausible story. *I got so interested in this case, and I remembered a TV show on this vigilante group and their slogan, about not recognizing the government, the same thing the woman said on John Truth's answering machine, so I thought I would, you know, play detective, and check them out myself* . . . But they would not take his word for it. No matter how plausible his story, they would vet him so thoroughly that he could not possibly fool them.

The two agents got out of the car. Priest stared hard at them in his mirror.

He did not recognize either one.

He relaxed a little. There was a film of sweat on his face. He wiped his forehead with the back of his hand.

Melanie said: 'Oh, Jesus, what do they want?'

'Stay cool,' Priest said. 'Don't seem like you want to hurry away. I'm going to pretend I'm real, real interested in them. That'll make them want to get rid of us as fast as they can. Reverse psychology.' He jumped out of the car.

'Hey, are you the police?' he said enthusiastically. 'Is there something big going down?'

The driver, a thin man with black-framed glasses, said: 'We're federal agents. Sir, we checked your plates, and your car is registered to the Napa Bottling Company.'

Paul Beale took care of getting the car insured and smogged and other paperwork. 'That's my employer.'

'May I see your driver's licence?'

'Oh, sure.' Priest took the licence out of his back pocket. 'Was that your chopper I saw?'

'Yes, sir, it was.' The agent checked his licence and handed it back. 'And where are you headed this morning?'

'We work at the wine farm up the valley a way. Hey, I hope you've come after those goddam vigilantes. They got everyone round here scared half to death. They—'

'And where have you been this morning?'

'We were at a party in Silver City last night. It went on kind of late. But I'm sober, don't worry!'

'That's okay.'

'Listen, I write paragraphs for the local paper, you know, the *Silver City Chronicle*? Could I get a quote from you, about this raid? It's going to be the biggest news in Sierra county for years!' As the words came out of his mouth, he realized this was a risky pose for a man who could not read or write. He slapped his pockets. 'Gee, I don't even have a pencil.'

'We can't say anything,' the agent said. 'You'll have

to call the press person at the Sacramento office of the Bureau.'

He pretended disappointment. 'Oh. Oh, sure, I understand.'

'You said you were headed home.'

'Yes. Okay, I guess we'll be on our way. Good luck with those vigilantes!'

'Thank you.'

The agents returned to their car.

They didn't make a note of my name.

Priest jumped back in his car. In his mirror, he watched the agents as they got into their car. Neither one appeared to write anything down.

'Jesus Christ,' he breathed gratefully. 'They bought my story.'

He pulled away, and the Buick followed.

As he approached the entrance to the Los Alamos spread a few minutes later, Priest rolled down his window, listening for gunfire. He heard none. It seemed the FBI had caught Los Alamos sleeping.

He rounded a bend and saw two cars parked near the entrance to the place. The wooden five-bar gate that had blocked the track was smashed to splinters: he guessed the FBI had driven their armoured trucks right through it without stopping. The gate was normally guarded—where was the sentry? Then he saw a man in camouflage pants, face down on the grass, hands cuffed behind his back, guarded by four agents. The Feds were taking no chances.

The agents looked up alertly at the 'Cuda, then relaxed when they saw the green Buick following it.

Priest drove slowly, like a curious passer-by.

Behind him, the Buick pulled over and stopped near the busted gate.

As soon as he was out of sight, Priest stepped on the gas.

*

When he got back to the commune he went straight to Star's cabin, to tell her about the FBI.

He found her in bed with Bones.

He touched her shoulder to wake her, then said: 'We need to talk. I'll wait outside.'

She nodded. Bones did not stir.

Priest stepped outside while she got dressed. He had no objection to Star renewing her relationship with Bones, of course. Priest was sleeping with Melanie regularly, and Star had the right to amuse herself with an old flame. All the same he felt a mixture of curiosity and apprehension. In bed together, were they passionate, hungry for one another—or relaxed and playful? Did Star think of Priest while she was making love to Bones, or did she put all other lovers out of her mind and think only of the one she was with? Did she compare them in her head, and notice that one was more energetic, or more tender, or more skilful? These questions were not new. He recalled having the same thoughts whenever Star had a lover. This was just like the early days, except that they were all so much older.

He knew that his commune was not like others. Paul Beale followed the fortunes of other groups. They had all started with similar ideals, but most had compromised. They generally still worshipped together, following a guru or a religious discipline of some kind, but they had reverted to private property and the use of money, and no longer practised complete sexual freedom. They were weak, Priest figured. They had not had the strength of will to stick to their ideals and make them work. In self-satisfied moments he told himself it was a question of leadership.

Star came out in her jeans and a baggy bright-blue sweatshirt. For someone who had just got up, she looked great. Priest told her so. 'A good fuck does wonders for my complexion,' she said. There was just enough of an edge in her voice to make Priest think that Bones was some kind of revenge for Melanie. Was this going to be a destabilizing factor? He already had too much to worry about.

He put that thought aside for the moment. Walking to the cookhouse, he told Star about the FBI raid on Los Alamos. 'They may decide to check out the other residences in the valley, and if so they'll probably find their way here. They won't be suspicious so long as we don't let them know we're a commune. We just have to maintain our usual pretence. If we're itinerant workers, with no long-term interest in the valley, there's no reason we should care about the dam.'

She nodded. 'You'd better remind everyone at breakfast. The Rice Eaters will know what's really on your mind. The others will think it's just our normal policy of not saying anything that might attract attention. What about the children?'

'They won't question kids. They're the FBI, not the Gestapo.'

'Okay.'

They went into the cookhouse and started coffee.

It was mid-morning when two agents stumbled down the hill with mud on their loafers and weeds clinging to the cuffs of their pants. Priest was watching from the barn. If he recognized anyone from yesterday, he planned to slip away through the cabins and disappear into the woods. But he had never seen these two before. The younger man was tall and broad, with a Nordic look, pale blond hair and fair skin. The older was an Asian man with black hair thinning on top. They were not the two who had questioned him this morning, and he was sure neither had been at the press conference.

Most of the adults were in the vineyard, spraying the vines with diluted hot sauce to stop the deer eating the new shoots. The children were in the temple, having a Sunday school lesson from Star, who was telling them the story of Moses in the bulrushes.

Despite the careful preparations he had made, Priest felt a stab of sheer terror as the agents approached. For twenty-five years, this place had been a secret sanctuary. Until last Thursday, when a cop had come looking for the parents of Flower, no official had ever set foot here: no county surveyor, no mailman, not even a garbage collector. And here was the FBI. If he could have called down a bolt of lightning to strike the agents dead he would have done it without a second thought.

He took a deep breath, then walked across the slope of the hillside to the vineyard. Dale greeted the two agents, as arranged. Priest filled a watering can with the salsa mixture and began to spray, moving toward Dale so that he could hear the conversation.

The Asian man spoke in a friendly tone. 'We're FBI agents, making some routine inquiries in the neighbourhood. I'm Bill Ho and this is John Aldritch.'

That was encouraging, Priest told himself. It sounded like they had no special interest in the vineyard: they were just looking around, hoping to pick up clues. It was a fishing expedition. But the thought did not make him feel much less tense.

Ho looked around appreciatively, taking in the valley. 'What a beautiful spot.'

Dale nodded. 'We're very attached to it.'

Take care, Dale—drop the heavy irony. This is not a frigging game.

Aldritch, the younger agent, said impatiently: 'Are you in charge here?' He had a Southern accent.

'I'm the foreman,' Dale said. 'How can I help you?'

Ho said: 'Do you folks live here?'

Priest pretended to go on working, but his heart was thumping, and he strained to hear.

'Most of us are seasonal workers,' Dale said, following the script agreed with Priest. 'The company provides accommodation because this place is so far from anywhere.'

Aldritch said: 'Strange place for a fruit farm.'

'It's not a fruit farm, it's a winery. Would you like to try a glass of last year's vintage? It's really very good.'

'No, thanks. Unless you have an alcohol-free product.'

'No, sorry. Just the real thing.'

'Who owns the place?'

'The Napa Bottling Company.'

Aldritch made a note.

Ho glanced toward the cluster of buildings on the far side of the vineyard. 'Mind if we take a look around?'

Dale shrugged. 'Sure, go ahead.' He resumed his work.

Priest watched anxiously as the agents headed off. On the surface, it was a plausible story that these people were badly paid workers living in low-grade accommodation provided by a stingy management. But there were clues here that might make a smart agent ask more questions. The temple was the most obvious. Star had folded up the old banner bearing the Five Paradoxes of Baghram. All the same, someone with an enquiring mind might ask why the schoolroom was a round building with no windows and no furniture.

Also, there were marijuana patches in the woods nearby. The FBI agents were not interested in small-time doping, but cultivation did not fit in with the fiction of a transient population. The free shop looked like any other shop until you noticed that there were no prices on anything and no cash register.

There might be a hundred other ways the pretence would fall apart under thorough investigation, but Priest was hoping the FBI was focused on Los Alamos, and just checking out the neighbours as a matter of routine.

He had to fight the temptation to follow the agents. He was desperate to see what they looked at, and hear what they said to each other, as they poked around his home. But he forced himself to keep spraying, glancing up from the vines every minute or two to see where they were and what they were doing.

They went into the cookhouse. Garden and Slow were there, making lasagne for the midday meal. What were the agents saying to them? Was Garden chattering nervously and giving herself away? Had Slow forgotten his instructions and started to jabber enthusiastically about daily meditation?

The agents emerged from the cookhouse. Priest looked hard at them, trying to guess their thoughts; but they were too far away for him to read their faces, and their body language gave nothing away.

They began to wander around the cabins, peeking in. Priest could not guess whether anything they saw would make them suspect that this was anything more than a wine farm.

They checked out the grape press, the barns where the wine was fermented, and the barrels of last year's vintage waiting to be bottled. Had they noticed that nothing was powered by electricity?

They opened the door of the temple. Would they speak to the children, contrary to Priest's prediction? Would Star blow her cool and call them fascist pigs? Priest held his breath.

The agents closed the door without going inside.

They spoke to Oaktree, who was cutting barrel staves in the yard. He looked up at them and answered curtly without stopping in his work. Maybe he figured it would look suspicious if he were friendly.

They came across Aneth hanging diapers out to dry. She refused to use disposable diapers. She was probably explaining this to the agents, saying, *There aren't enough trees in the world for every child to have disposable diapers.*

They walked down to the stream and studied the stones in the shallow brook, seeming to contemplate crossing. The marijuana patches were all on the far side. But the agents apparently did not want to get their feet wet, for they turned around and came back.

At last they returned to the vineyard. Priest tried to study their faces without staring. Were they convinced, or had they seen something that made them suspicious? Aldritch seemed hostile, Ho friendly, but that could just be an act.

Aldritch spoke to Dale. 'Y'all have some of these cabins tricked out kind of nice, for "temporary accommodation", don't you?'

Priest went cold. It was a sceptical question, suggesting that Aldritch did not buy their story. Priest began to wonder if there was any way he could kill both FBI men and get away with it.

'Yeah,' Dale said. 'Some of us come back year after year.' He was improvising: none of this had been scripted. 'And a few of us live here all year round.' Dale was not a practised liar. If this went on too long, he would give himself away.

Aldritch said: 'I want a list of everyone who lives or works here.'

Priest's mind raced. Dale could not use people's communal names, for that would give the game away —and anyway the agents would insist on real names. But some of the communards had police records, including Priest himself. Would Dale think fast enough to realize he had to invent names for everyone? Would he have the nerve to do it?

Ho added: 'We also need ages, and permanent addresses.' His tone was apologetic.

Shit! This is getting worse.

Dale said: 'You could get those from the company's records.'

No, they couldn't.

Ho said: 'I'm sorry, we need them right now.'

Dale looked nonplussed. 'Gee, I guess you'll have to go round asking them all. I sure as heck don't know everyone's birthday. I'm their boss, not their grandad.'

Priest's mind raced. This was dangerous. He could not allow the agents to question everyone. They would give themselves away a dozen times.

He made a snap decision, and stepped forward. 'Mr Arnold?' he said, inventing a name for Dale on the spur of the moment. 'Maybe I could assist the gentlemen.' Without planning it, he had adopted the persona of a friendly dope, eager to help but not very bright. He addressed the agents. 'I've been coming here a few years, I guess I know everybody, and how old they are.'

Dale looked relieved to hand the responsibility back to Priest. 'Okay, go ahead,' he said.

'Why don't you come to the cookhouse?' Priest said to the agents. 'If you won't drink wine, I bet you'd like a cup of coffee.'

Ho smiled and said: 'That'd be real good.'

Priest led them back through the rows of vines and took them into the cookhouse. 'We got some paperwork to do,' he explained to Garden and Slow. 'You two take no notice of us, just go on making that great-smelling pasta.'

Ho offered Priest his notebook. 'Why don't you just write down the names, ages and addresses right here?'

Priest did not take the notebook. 'Oh, my handwriting is the worst in the world,' he said smoothly. 'Now, you sit yourselves down and write the names while I make you coffee.' He put a pot of water on the fire and the agents sat at the long pine table.

'The foreman is Dale Arnold, he's forty-two.' These guys would never be able to check. No one here was in the phone book or on any kind of register.

'Permanent address?'

'He lives here. Everyone does.'

'I thought you were seasonal workers.'

'That's right. Most of them will leave, come November, when the harvest is in and the grapes have been crushed; but they ain't the kind of folks who keep two homes. Why pay rent on a place when you're living somewhere else?'

'So the permanent address for everyone here would be . . . ?'

'Silver River Valley Winery, Silver City, California. But people have their mail sent to the company in Napa, it's safer.'

Aldritch was looking irritated and slightly bemused, as Priest intended. Querulous people did not have the patience to pursue minor inconsistencies.

He poured them coffee as he made up a list of names. To help him remember who was who, he used variations of their commune names: Dale Arnold, Peggy Star, Richard Priestley, Holly Goldman. He left out Melanie and Dusty as they were not there—Dusty was at his father's place, and Melanie had gone to fetch him.

Aldritch interrupted him. 'In my experience, most transient agricultural workers in this state are Mexican, or at least Hispanic.'

'Yeah, and this bunch is everything but,' Priest agreed. 'The company has a few vineyards, and I guess the boss keeps the Hispanics all together in their own gangs, with Spanish-speaking foremen, and puts everyone else on our team. It ain't racism, you understand, just practical.'

They seemed to accept that.

Priest went slowly, dragging out the session as long as possible. The agents could do no harm in the cookhouse. If they got bored and became impatient to leave, so much the better.

While he talked, Garden and Slow carried on cooking. Garden was silent and stone-faced, and somehow managed to stir pots in a haughty manner. Slow was jumpy, and kept darting terrified glances at the agent, but they did not seem to care. Maybe they were used to people being frightened of them. Maybe they liked it.

Priest took fifteen or twenty minutes to give them the names and ages of the commune's twenty-six adults. Ho was closing his notebook when Priest said: 'Now, the children. Let me think. Gee, they grow up so fast, don't they?'

Aldritch gave a grunt of exasperation. 'I don't think we need to know the children's names,' he said.

'Okay,' Priest said equably. 'More coffee for you folks?'

'No, thanks.' Aldritch looked at Ho. 'I think we're done here.'

Ho said: 'So this land is owned by the Napa Bottling Company?'

Priest saw a chance to cover up the slip Dale had made earlier. 'No, that ain't exactly right,' he said. 'The company operates the winery, but I believe the land is owned by the government.'

'So the name on the lease would be Napa Bottling.'

Priest hesitated. Ho, the friendly one, was asking the really dangerous questions. But how was he to reply? It was too risky to lie. They could check this in seconds. Reluctantly he said: 'Matter of fact, I think the name on the lease may be Stella Higgins.' He hated to give Star's real name to the FBI. 'She was the woman who started the vineyard, years ago.' He hoped it would not be of any use to them. He could not see how it gave them any clues.

Ho wrote down the name. 'That's all, I think,' he said.

Priest hid his relief. 'Well, good luck with the rest of your inquiries,' he said as he led them out.

He took them through the vineyard. They stopped to thank Dale for his cooperation. 'Who are you guys after, anyway?' Dale said.

'A terrorist group that's trying to blackmail the Governor of California,' Ho told him.

'Well, I sure hope you catch them,' Dale said sincerely.

No, you don't.

At last the two agents walked away across the field, stumbling occasionally on the uneven ground, and disappeared into the trees.

'Well, that seemed to go pretty well,' Dale said to Priest, looking pleased with himself.

Jesus Christ Almighty, if only you knew.

CHAPTER TWELVE

S UNDAY AFTERNOON, Judy took Bo to see the
new Clint Eastwood movie at the Alexandria
Cinema on the corner of Geary and 18th. To her
surprise, she forgot about earthquakes for a couple of
hours and had a good time. Afterwards they went for
a sandwich and a beer at one of Bo's joints, a cops'
pub with a TV over the bar and a sign on the door
saying *We cheat tourists.*

Bo finished his cheeseburger and took a swig of
Guinness. 'Clint Eastwood should star in the story of
my life,' he said.

'Come on,' Judy said. 'Every detective in the world
thinks that.'

'Yeah, but I even look like Clint.'

Judy grinned. Bo had a round face with a snub
nose. She said: 'I like Mickey Rooney for the part.'

'I think people should be able to divorce their kids,'
Bo said, but he was laughing.

The news came on TV. When Judy saw footage of
the raid on Los Alamos, she smiled sourly. Brian
Kincaid had screamed at her for interfering—then he
had adopted her plan.

However, there was no triumphal interview with

Brian. There was film of a smashed five-bar gate, a sign that read *We do not recognize the jurisdiction of the United States government*, and a SWAT team in their flak jackets returning from the scene. Bo said: 'Looks to me like they didn't find anything.'

That puzzled Judy. 'I'm surprised,' she said. 'Los Alamos seemed like really hot suspects.' She was disappointed. It seemed her instinct had been completely wrong.

The newscaster was saying that no arrests had been made. 'They don't even say they seized evidence,' Bo said. 'I wonder what the story is.'

'If you're about done here, we can go find out,' Judy said.

They left the bar and got into Judy's car. She picked up her car phone and called Simon Sparrow's home number. 'What do you hear about the raid?' she asked him.

'We got zip.'

'That's what I thought.'

'There are no computers on the premises, so it's hard to imagine they could have left a message on the Internet. Nobody there even has a college degree, and I doubt if any one of them could *spell* seismologist. There are four women in the group, but none of them matches either of our two female profiles—these girls are in their late teens and early twenties. And the vigilantes have no beef with the dam. They're happy with the compensation they're getting from Coastal Electric for their land, and they're looking forward to moving to their new place. Oh—and on Friday, at two twenty p.m., six of the seven men were at a store called Frank's Sporting Weapons in Silver City, buying ammunition.'

Judy shook her head. 'Well, whose dumb idea was it to raid them, anyway?'

It had been hers, of course. Simon said: 'This morning at the briefing, Marvin claimed it was his.'

'Serves him right that it was a flop.' Judy frowned. 'I don't get it. It seemed such a good lead.'

'Brian has another meeting with Mr Honeymoon in Sacramento tomorrow afternoon. Looks like he'll go empty-handed.'

'Mr Honeymoon won't like that.'

'I hear he's not a real touchy-feely type guy.'

Judy smiled grimly. She had no sympathy for Kincaid, but she could not take pleasure in the failure of the raid. It meant the Hammer of Eden were still out there somewhere, planning another earthquake. 'Thanks, Simon. See you tomorrow.'

As soon as she hung up, the phone rang. It was the switchboard operator at the office. 'A Professor Quercus called with a message he said was urgent. He has some important news for you.'

Judy debated calling Marvin and passing the message to him. But she was too curious to know what Michael had to say. She dialled his home.

When he answered, she could hear the soundtrack of a TV cartoon in the background. Dusty was still there, she guessed. 'This is Judy Maddox,' she said.

'Hi, how are you?'

She raised her eyebrows. A weekend with Dusty had

mellowed him out. 'I'm fine, but I'm off the case,' she said.

'I know that. I've been trying to reach the guy who's taken over, man with a name like a soul singer . . .'

'Marvin Hayes.'

'Right. Like, "Dancin' in the Grapevine" by Marvin Hayes and the Haystacks.'

Judy laughed.

Michael said: 'But he doesn't return my calls, so I'm stuck with you.'

That was more like Michael. 'Okay, what have you got?'

'Can you come over? I really need to show you.'

She found herself pleased, even a little excited, at the thought of seeing him again. 'Do you have any more Cap'n Crunch?'

'I think there's a little left.'

'Okay, I'll be there in fifteen or twenty minutes.' She hung up. 'I have to go see my seismologist,' she said to Bo. 'Shall I drop you at the bus stop?'

'I can't ride the bus like Jim Rockford. I'm a San Francisco detective!'

'So? You're a human being.'

'Yeah, but the street guys don't know that.'

'They don't know you're human?'

'To them I'm a demigod.'

He was kidding, but there was some truth in it, Judy knew. He had been putting hoodlums behind bars in this city for almost thirty years. Every kid on a street corner with vials of crack in the pockets of his bomber jacket was afraid of Bo Maddox.

'So, you want to ride to Berkeley with me?'

'Sure, why not? I'm curious to meet your handsome seismologist.'

She made a U-turn and headed for the Bay Bridge. 'What makes you think he's handsome?'

He grinned. 'From the way you talked to him,' he said smugly.

'You shouldn't use cop psychology on your own family.'

'Cop, schmop. You're my daughter, I can read your mind.'

'Well, you're right. He's a hunk. But I don't much like him.'

'You don't?' Bo sounded sceptical.

'He's arrogant and difficult. He's better when his kid's around, that softens him.'

'He's married?'

'Separated.'

'Separated is married.'

Judy could sense Bo losing interest in Michael. It felt like a drop in the temperature. She smiled to herself. He was still eager to marry her off, but he had old-fashioned scruples.

They reached Berkeley and drove down Euclid Street. There was an orange Subaru parked in Judy's usual space under the magnolia tree. She found another slot.

When Michael opened the door of his apartment, Judy thought he looked strained. 'Hi, Michael,' she said. 'This is my father, Bo Maddox.'

'Come in,' Michael said abruptly.

His mood seemed to have changed in the short time it had taken to drive here. When they entered the living room, Judy saw why.

Dusty was on the couch, looking terrible. His eyes were red and watering, and his eyeballs seemed swollen. His nose was running and he was breathing noisily. A cartoon was playing on TV, but he was hardly paying attention.

Judy knelt beside him and touched his hair. 'Poor Dusty!' she said. 'What happened?'

'He gets allergy attacks,' Michael explained.

'Did you call the doctor?'

'No need. I've given him the drug he needs to suppress the reaction.'

'How fast does it work?'

'It's already working. He's past the worst. But he may stay like this for days.'

'I wish I could do something for you, little man,' Judy said to Dusty.

A female voice said: 'I'll take care of him, thank you.'

Judy stood up and turned around. The woman who had just walked in looked as if she had stepped off a couturier's catwalk. She had a pale oval face and straight red hair that fell past her shoulders. Although she was tall and thin, her bust was generous and her hips curvy. Her long legs were clad in close-fitting tan jeans and she wore a fashionable lime-green top with a V-neck.

Until this moment Judy had felt smartly dressed, in khaki shorts, tan loafers that showed off her pretty ankles, and a white polo shirt that gleamed against her café-au-lait skin. Now she felt dowdy, middle-aged, and out of date by comparison with this vision of street chic. And Michael was bound to notice that Judy had a big ass and small tits by comparison.

'This is Melanie, Dusty's mom,' Michael said. 'Melanie, meet my friend Judy Maddox.'

Melanie nodded curtly.

So that's his wife.

Michael had not mentioned the FBI. Did he want Melanie to think Judy was a girlfriend?

'This is my father, Bo Maddox,' Judy said.

Melanie did not trouble to make small talk. 'I was just leaving,' she said. She was carrying a small duffel bag with a picture of Donald Duck on the side, obviously Dusty's.

Judy felt put down by Michael's tall, voguish wife. She was annoyed with herself for the reaction. *Why should I give a damn?*

Melanie looked around the room and said: 'Michael, where's the rabbit?'

'Here.' Michael picked up a grubby soft toy from his desk and gave it to her.

She looked at the child on the couch. 'This never happens in the mountains,' she said coldly.

Michael looked anguished. 'What am I going to do, not see him?'

'We'll have to meet somewhere out of town.'

'I want him to *stay* with me. It's not the same if he doesn't sleep over.'

'If he doesn't sleep over, he won't get like this.'

'I know, I know.'

Judy's heart went out to Michael. He was obviously in distress, and his wife was so cold.

Melanie stuffed the rabbit into the Donald Duck bag and closed the zip. 'We have to go.'

'I'll carry him to your car.' Michael picked up Dusty from the couch. 'Come on, tiger, let's go.'

When they had left, Bo looked at Judy and said: 'Wow. Unhappy families.'

She nodded. But she liked Michael better than before. She wanted to put her arms around him and say, *You're doing your best, no one can do more*.

'He's your type, though,' Bo said.

'I have a type?'

'You like a challenge.'

'That's because I grew up with one.'

'Me?' He pretended to be outraged. 'I spoiled you rotten.'

She pecked his cheek. 'You did, too.'

When Michael returned he was grim-faced and preoccupied. He did not offer Judy and Bo a drink or a cup of coffee, and he had forgotten all about Cap'n Crunch. He sat at his computer. 'Look at this,' he said without preamble.

Judy and Bo stood behind him and looked over his shoulder.

He put a chart on the screen. 'Here's the seismograph of the Owens Valley tremor, with the mysterious preliminary vibrations I couldn't understand—remember?'

'I sure do,' Judy said.

'Here's a typical earthquake of about the same magnitude. This has normal foreshocks. See the difference?'

'Yes.' The normal foreshocks were uneven and sporadic, whereas the Owens Valley vibrations followed a pattern that seemed too regular to be natural.

'Now look at this.' He brought a third chart up on the screen. It showed a neat pattern of even vibrations, just like the Owens Valley chart.

'What made those vibrations?' Judy said.

'A seismic vibrator,' Michael announced triumphantly.

Bo said: 'What the hell is that?'

Judy almost said, *I don't know, but I think I want one.* She smothered a grin.

Michael said: 'It's a machine used by the oil industry to explore underground. Basically, it's a huge jackhammer mounted on a truck. It sends vibrations through the earth's crust.'

'And those vibrations triggered the earthquake?'

'I don't think it can be a coincidence.'

Judy nodded solemnly. 'That's it, then. They really can cause earthquakes.' She felt a cold chill descend as the news sank in.

Bo said: 'Jesus, I hope they don't come to San Francisco.'

'Or Berkeley,' said Michael. 'You know, although I told you it was possible, I never really believed it, in my heart, until now.'

Judy said: 'The Owens Valley tremor was quite minor.'

Michael shook his head. 'We can't take comfort from that. The size of the earthquake bears no relation to the strength of the triggering vibration. It depends on the pressure in the fault. The seismic vibrator could trigger anything from a barely perceptible tremor to another Loma Prieta.'

Judy remembered the Loma Prieta earthquake in 1989 as vividly as if it was last night's bad dream. 'Shit,' she said. 'What are we going to do?'

Bo said: 'You're off the case.'

Michael frowned, puzzled. 'You told me that,' he said to Judy. 'But you didn't say why.'

'Office politics,' Judy said. 'We have a new boss who doesn't like me and he reassigned the case to someone he prefers.'

'I don't believe this!' Michael said. 'A terrorist group is causing earthquakes and the FBI is having a family spat about who gets to chase after them!'

'What can I tell you? Do scientists let personal squabbles get in the way of their search for the truth?'

Michael gave one of his sudden unexpected grins. 'You bet your ass they do. But, listen. Surely you can pass on this information to Marvin Whatever?'

'When I told my boss about Los Alamos, he ordered me not to interfere again.'

'This is incredible!' Michael said, becoming angry. 'You can't just *ignore* what I've told you.'

'Don't worry, I won't do that,' Judy said curtly. 'Let's keep cool and think for a moment. What's the first thing we need to do with this information? If we can find out where the seismic vibrator came from, we may have a lead on the Hammer of Eden.'

'Right,' Bo said. 'Either they bought it, or more likely they stole it.'

Judy asked Michael: 'How many of these machines are there in the continental United States? A hundred? A thousand?'

'In there somewhere,' he said.

'Anyhow, not many. So the people who manufacture them probably have a record of every sale. I could track them down tonight, get them to make a list. And if the truck was stolen, it may be listed on the National Crime Information Center.' The NCIC, run by FBI headquarters in Washington DC, could be accessed by any law enforcement agency.

Bo said: 'The NCIC is only as good as the information that's put in. We don't have a licence plate for this, and there's no telling how it might be categorized on the computer. I could have the San Francisco PD put out a multi-state query on the CLETS computer.' CLETS was the California Law Enforcement Telecommunications System. 'And I could get the newspapers to print a picture of one of these trucks, get members of the public looking out for it.'

'Wait a minute,' Judy said. 'If you do that, Kincaid will know I'm behind it.'

Michael rolled up his eyes in an expression of despair.

Bo said: 'Not necessarily. I won't tell the papers that this is connected with the Hammer of Eden. I'll just say we're looking for a stolen seismic vibrator. It's kind of an unusual auto theft, they'll like the story.'

'Great,' Judy said. 'Michael, can I have a printout of the three graphs?'

'Sure.' He touched a key and the printer whirred.

Judy put a hand on his shoulder. His skin was warm through the cotton of his shirt. 'I sure hope Dusty feels better,' she said.

He covered her hand with his own. 'Thanks.' His touch was light, his palm dry. She felt a frisson of pleasure. Then he took his hand away and said: 'Uh, maybe you should give me your pager number, so I can reach you a little faster, if necessary.'

She took out a business card. After a moment's thought, she wrote her home number on it before giving it to him.

Michael said: 'After you two have made these phone calls . . .' He hesitated. 'Would you like to meet for a drink, or maybe dinner? I'd really like to hear how you get on.'

'Not me,' Bo said. 'I have a bowling match.'

'Judy, how about you?'

Is he asking me for a date?

'I was planning to visit someone in hospital,' she said.

Michael looked crestfallen.

Judy realized that there was not a thing she would rather do this evening than have dinner with Michael Quercus.

'But I guess that won't take me all night,' she said.
'Okay, sure.'

*

It was only a week since Milton Lestrange's cancer had
been diagnosed, but already he looked thinner and
older. Perhaps it was the effect of the hospital setting:
the instruments, the bed, the white sheets. Or maybe
it was the baby-blue pyjamas that revealed a triangle of
pale chest below the neck. He had lost all his power
symbols: his big desk, his Mont Blanc fountain pen,
his striped silk tie.

Judy was shocked to see him like this. 'Gee, Milt,
you don't look so great,' she blurted.

He smiled. 'I knew you wouldn't lie to me, Judy.'

She felt embarrassed. 'I'm sorry, it just came out.'

'Don't blush. You're right. I'm in bad shape.'

'What are they doing?'

'They'll operate this week, they haven't said what
day. But that's just to bypass the obstruction in the
bowel. The outlook is poor.'

'What do you mean, poor?'

'Ninety per cent of cases are fatal.'

Judy swallowed. 'Jesus, Milt.'

'I may have a year.'

'I don't know what to say.'

He did not dwell on the grim prognosis. 'Sandy, my
first wife, came to see me yesterday. She told me you
had called her.'

'Yeah. I had no idea whether she'd want to see you,

but I figured at least she'd like to know you were in the hospital.'

He took Judy's hand and squeezed it. 'Thank you. Not many people would have thought of that. I don't know how you got to be so wise, so young.'

'I'm glad she came.'

Milt changed the subject. 'Take my mind off my troubles, tell me about the office.'

'You shouldn't be concerning yourself . . .'

'Hell, I won't. Work doesn't worry you much when you're dying. I'm just curious.'

'Well, I won my case. The Foong brothers are probably going to spend most of the next decade in jail.'

'Well done!'

'You always had faith in me.'

'I knew you could do it.'

'But Brian Kincaid recommended Marvin Hayes as the new supervisor.'

'Marvin? Shit! Brian knows you were supposed to get that job.'

'Tell me about it.'

'Marvin's a tough guy, but slipshod. He cuts corners.'

'I'm baffled,' Judy said. 'Why does Brian rate him so high? What is it with those two—are they *lovers*, or something?'

Milt laughed. 'No, not lovers. But one time, years ago, Marvin saved Brian's life.'

'No kidding?'

'It was a shootout. I was there. We ambushed a boat unloading heroin on Sonoma Beach up in Marin county. It was early one morning in February, and the sea was so cold it hurt. There was no jetty, so the bad guys were stacking kilos of horse on a rubber dinghy to bring them ashore. We let them land the entire cargo, then we moved in.' Milt sighed, and a faraway look came into his blue eyes. It occurred to Judy that he would never see another dawn ambush.

After a moment he went on. 'Brian made a mistake —he let one of them get too close to him. This little Italian grabbed him and pointed a gun at his head. We all had our weapons out, but if we shot the Italian, he would probably have pulled the trigger before he died. Brian was really scared.' Milt lowered his voice. 'He pissed himself, we could see the stain on his suit pants. But Marvin was as cool as the devil himself. He starts walking toward Brian and the Italian. "Shoot me instead," he says. "It won't make any difference." I've never seen anything like it. The Italian fell for it. He swung his gun arm round to aim at Marvin. In that split second, five of our people shot the guy.'

Judy nodded. It was typical of the stories that agents told after a few beers in Everton's. But she did not dismiss it as macho bravado. FBI agents did not often get involved in shootouts. They never forgot the experience. She could imagine that Kincaid felt intensely close to Marvin Hayes after that. 'Well, that explains the trouble I've been having,' she said. 'Brian gave me a bullshit assignment, then, when it turned out to be important, he took it from me and gave it to Marvin.'

Milt sighed. 'I could intervene, I guess. I'm still SAC, technically. But Kincaid is an experienced office politician, and he knows I'm never coming back. He'd fight me. And I'm not sure I have the energy for that.'

Judy shook her head. 'I wouldn't want you to. I can handle this.'

'What's the assignment he gave Marvin?'

'The Hammer of Eden, the people who cause earthquakes.'

'The people who *say* they cause earthquakes.'

'That's what Marvin thinks. But he's wrong.'

Milt frowned. 'Are you serious?'

'Totally.'

'What are you going to do?'

'Work the case behind Brian's back.'

Milt looked troubled. 'That's dangerous.'

'Yeah,' Judy said. 'But not as dangerous as a goddam earthquake.'

*

Michael wore a navy blue cotton suit over a plain white shirt, open at the neck, and no tie. Had he thrown on this ensemble without a moment's thought, Judy wondered, or did he realize it made him look good enough to eat? She had changed into a white silk dress with red polka dots. It was about right for a May evening and she always turned heads when she was wearing it.

Michael took her to a small downtown restaurant that served vegetarian Indian dishes. She had never tasted Indian food, so she let him order for her. She put her mobile phone on the table. 'I know it's bad manners, but Bo promised to call me if he got any information about stolen seismic vibrators.'

'Okay by me,' Michael said. 'Did you call the manufacturers?'

'Yeah. I got a sales director at home watching football. He promised me a list of purchasers tomorrow. I tried for tonight but he said it was impossible.' She frowned in annoyance. *We don't have much time left—five days, now.* 'However, he faxed me a picture.' She took a folded sheet of paper from her purse and showed it to him.

He shrugged. 'It's just a big truck with a piece of machinery on the back.'

'But after Bo puts this picture out on CLETS, every cop in California will be watching for one. And if the newspapers and TV carry the picture tomorrow, half the population will be on the lookout too.'

The food came. It was spicy but delicious. Judy ate with gusto. After a few minutes she caught Michael looking at her with a faint smile. She raised an eyebrow. 'Did I say something witty?'

'I'm pleased you're enjoying the cuisine.'

She grinned. 'Does it show?'

'Yeah.'

'I'll try to be more dainty.'

'Please don't. It's a pleasure to watch you. Besides . . .'

'What?'

'I like your go-for-it attitude. It's one of the things that attracts me to you. You seem to have a big appetite for life. You like Dusty, and you have a good time hanging out with your dad, and you're proud of the FBI, and you obviously love beautiful clothes . . . you even enjoy Cap'n Crunch.'

Judy felt herself flush, but she was pleased. She liked the picture he painted of her. She asked herself what it was about *him* that had attracted *her*. It was his strength, she decided. He could be irritatingly stubborn, but in a crisis he would be a rock. This afternoon, when his wife had been so heartless, most men would have quarrelled, but he had been concerned only for Dusty.

Plus, I'd really love to get my hands inside his jockey shorts.

Judith, behave.

She took a sip of wine and changed the subject. 'We're assuming that the Hammer of Eden have data similar to yours about pressure points along the San Andreas fault.'

'They must have, to pick the locations where the seismic vibrator could trigger an earthquake.'

'Could you go through the same exercise? Study the data and figure out the best place?'

'I guess I could. Probably there would be a cluster of five or six possible sites.' He saw the direction her thoughts were taking. 'Then, I suppose, the FBI could stake out the sites and watch for a seismic vibrator.'

'Yes—if I were in charge.'

'I'll make the list anyway. Maybe I'll fax it to Governor Robson.'

'Don't let too many people see it. You might cause a panic.'

'But if my forecast turned out to be right, it could give my business a shot in the arm.'

'Does it need one?'

'It sure does. I have one big contract, that just about pays the rent and the bill for my ex-wife's mobile phone. I borrowed money from my parents to start the business and I haven't begun to pay it back. I was hoping to land another major client: Mutual American Insurance.'

'I used to work for them, years ago. But go on.'

'I thought the deal was in the bag, but they're delaying the contract. I guess they're having second thoughts. If they back out, I'm in trouble. But if I predicted an earthquake and turned out to be right, I think they'd sign. Then I'd be comfortable.'

'All the same, I hope you'll be discreet. If everyone tries to leave San Francisco at the same time, there'll be riots.'

He gave a devil-may-care grin that was infuriatingly attractive. 'Got you rattled, haven't I?'

She shrugged. 'I'll admit it. My position at the Bureau is vulnerable. If I'm associated with an out-break of mass hysteria, I don't think I could survive there.'

'Is that important to you?'

'Yes and no. Sooner or later I plan to get out and

have children. But I want to quit by my timetable, not someone else's.'

'Do you have anyone in mind to have the children with?'

'No.' She gave him a candid look. 'A good man is hard to find.'

'I imagine there'd be a waiting list.'

'What a nice compliment.' *I wonder if you'd join the line. I wonder if I'd want you to.*

He offered her more wine.

'No, thanks. I'd like a cup of coffee.'

He waved at a waiter. 'Being a parent can be painful, but you never regret it.'

'Tell me about Dusty.'

He sighed. 'I have no pets, no flowers in the apartment, very little dust because of my computers. All the windows are closed tight and the place is air-conditioned. But we walked down to the bookstore and on the way home he petted a cat. An hour later he was the way you saw him.'

'It's too bad. The poor kid.'

'His mother recently moved to a place in the mountains, up near the Oregon border, and since then he's been okay—until today. If he can't visit me without having an attack, I don't know what we'll do. I can't go and live in fucking Oregon, there aren't enough earthquakes there.'

He looked so troubled that she reached across the table and squeezed his hand. 'You'll work something out. You love him, that's obvious.'

331

He smiled. 'Yeah, I do.'

They drank their coffee and he paid. He walked her to her car. 'This evening has gone so fast,' he said.

I think the guy likes me.

Good.

'Do you want to go to a movie some time?'

The dating game. It never changes. 'Yes, I'd like that.'

'Maybe one night this week?'

'Sure.'

'I'll call you.'

'Okay.'

'May I kiss you goodnight?'

'Yes.' She grinned. 'Yes, please.'

He bent his face to hers. It was a soft, tentative kiss. His lips moved gently against hers, but he did not open his mouth. She kissed him back the same way. Her breasts felt sensitive. Without thinking, she pressed her body against his. He squeezed her briefly, then broke away.

'Good night,' he said.

He watched her get into her car, and waved as she drew away from the kerb.

She turned a corner and pulled up at a stop light.

'Wow,' she said.

*

On Monday morning Judy was assigned to a team investigating a militant Muslim group at Stanford University. Her first job was to comb computer records of gun licences looking for Arab names to check out. She found it hard to concentrate on a relatively harmless bunch of religious fanatics when she knew the Hammer of Eden were planning their next earthquake.

Michael called at five past nine. He said: 'How are you, Agent Judy?'

The sound of his voice made her feel happy. 'I'm fine, real good.'

'I enjoyed our date.'

She thought of that kiss, and the corners of her mouth twitched in a private smile. *I'll take another of those, any time.* 'Me too.'

'Are you free tomorrow night?'

'I guess.' That sounded too cool. 'I mean, yes—unless something happens with this case.'

'Do you know Morton's?'

'Sure.'

'Let's meet in the bar at six. Then we can pick a movie together.'

'I'll be there.'

But that was the only bright spot in her morning. By lunchtime she could no longer contain herself, and she called Bo, but he still had nothing. She called the seismic vibrator manufacturers, who said they had almost completed the list and it would be on her fax machine by the end of the business day. *That's another damn day gone! Now we've only got four days to catch these people.*

She was too worried to eat. She went to Simon Sparrow's office. He was wearing a natty English-style shirt, blue with pink stripes. He ignored the unofficial FBI dress code and got away with it, probably because he was so good at his job.

He was talking on the phone and watching the screen of a wave analyser at the same time. 'This may seem like an odd question, Mrs Gorky, but would you tell me what you can see from your front window?' As he listened to the reply, he watched the spectrum of Mrs Gorky's voice, comparing it with a printout he had taped to the side of the monitor. After a few moments he drew a line through a name on a list. 'Thank you for your cooperation, Mrs Gorky. I don't need to trouble you any further. Goodbye.'

Judy said: 'This may seem like an odd question, Mr Sparrow, but why do you need to know what Mrs Gorky sees when she looks out the window?'

'I don't,' Simon said. 'That question generally elicits a response of about the length I need to analyse the voice. By the time she's finished, I know whether she's the woman I'm looking for.'

'And who's that?'

'The one who called the John Truth show, of course.' He tapped the ring-binder on his desk. 'The Bureau, the police, and the radio stations that syndicate the show have so far received a total of one thousand two hundred and twenty-nine calls telling us who she is.'

Judy picked up the file and leafed through it. Could the vital clue be in here somewhere? Simon had got his secretary to collate the tip-off calls. In most cases there was a name, address and phone number for the tipster and the same for the suspect. In some cases there was a quote from the caller:

I've always suspected she had Mob connections.

She's one of those subversive types, I'm not surprised she's involved in something like this.

She seems like a regular mom, but it's her voice—I'd swear on the Bible.

One particularly useless tip gave no name but said:

I know I've heard her voice on the radio, or something. It was so sexy I remembered it. But it was a long time ago. Maybe I heard it on a record album.

It *was* a sexy voice, Judy recalled. She had noticed that at the time. The woman could make a fortune as a telephone salesperson, getting male executives to buy advertising space they did not need.

Simon said: 'So far today I've eliminated one hundred of them. I think I'm going to need some assistance.'

Judy continued leafing through the file. 'I'd help you if I could, but I've been warned off the case.'

'Gee, thanks, that sure makes me feel better.'

'Do you hear how it's going?'

'Marvin's team are calling everyone on the mailing list of the Green California Campaign. He and Brian just left for Sacramento, but I can't imagine what they're going to tell the famous Mr Honeymoon.'

'It's not the goddam Greens, we all know that.'

'He doesn't have any other ideas, though.'

Judy frowned, looking at the file. She had come

across another call that mentioned a record. As before, there was no name for the suspect, but the caller had said:

> *I've heard the voice on an album, I'm darn sure.*
> *Something from way back, like the sixties.*

Judy asked Simon: 'Did you notice that two of the tip-offs mention a record album?'

'They do? I missed that!'

'They think they've heard her voice on an old record.'

'Is that right?' Simon was instantly animated. 'It must be a speech album—bedtime stories, or Shakespeare, or something. A person's speaking voice is quite different from their singing voice.'

Raja Khan passed the door and caught her eye. 'Oh, Judy, your father called, I thought you were at lunch.'

Suddenly Judy felt breathless. She left Simon without a word and rushed back to her desk. Without sitting down, she picked up the phone and dialled Bo's number.

He picked up right away. 'Lieutenant Maddox here.'

'What have you got?'

'A suspect.'

'Jesus—that's great!'

'Get this. A seismic vibrator went missing two weeks ago somewhere between Shiloh, Texas, and Clovis, New Mexico. The regular driver disappeared at the same time, and his burned-out car was found at the local dump, containing what appear to be his ashes.'

'He was *murdered* for his damn truck? These people don't take prisoners, do they?'

'The prime suspect is one Richard Granger, aged forty-eight. They called him Ricky, and they thought he was Hispanic, but with a name like that he could be a Caucasian with a tan. And—wait for it—he has a record.'

'You're a genius, Bo!'

'A copy should be coming out of your fax machine about now. He was a big-time hoodlum in LA around the late sixties, early seventies, in there. Convictions for assault, burglary, grand theft auto. Questioned about three murders, also drug dealing. But he disappeared from the scene in 1972. The LAPD thought he must have been whacked by the Mob—he owed them money—but they never found a body, so they didn't close the file.'

'I get it. Ricky ran from the Mob, got religion, and started a cult.'

'Unfortunately, we don't know where.'

'Except that it's not in Silver River Valley.'

'The LAPD can check out his last known address. It's probably a waste of time, but I'll ask them anyway. Guy in homicide there owes me a favour.'

'Do we have a picture of Ricky?'

'There's one in the file, but it's a photo of a nineteen-year-old. He's pushing fifty now, he probably looks completely different. Luckily, the sheriff in Shiloh prepared an E-fit likeness.' E-fit was the computer program that had replaced the old-style police artist. 'He promised to fax it to me, but it hasn't arrived yet.'

'Refax it to me as soon as you get it, would you?'

'Sure. What'll you do?'

'I'm going to Sacramento.'

*

It was four fifteen when Judy stepped through the door that had GOVERNOR carved over it.

The same secretary sat behind the big desk. She recognized Judy and registered surprise. 'You're one of the FBI people, aren't you? The meeting with Mr Honeymoon started ten minutes ago.'

'That's okay,' Judy said. 'I've brought some important information that came in at the last moment. But before I go into the meeting, did a fax arrive here for me within the last few minutes?' Having left her office before the E-fit picture of Ricky Granger came through, she had called Bo from the car and asked him to fax it to the governor's office.

'I'll check.' She spoke into the phone. 'Yes, your fax is here.' A moment later a young woman appeared from a side door with a sheet of paper.

Judy stared at the face on the fax. This was the man who might kill thousands. Her enemy.

She saw a handsome man who had gone to some trouble to hide the true shape of his face, as if perhaps he had anticipated this moment. His head was covered by a cowboy hat. That suggested that the witnesses who had helped the sheriff create the computer picture had never seen the suspect without a hat. Consequently, there was no indication of what his hair was like. If he was bald, or grizzled, or curly, or long-haired, he would look different from this picture. And the bottom half of his face was equally well concealed by a bushy beard and moustache. There could be any kind of jaw under there. By now, she guessed, he was clean-shaven.

The man had deep-set eyes that stared hypnotically out of the picture. But to the general public, all criminals had staring eyes.

All the same, the picture told her some things. Ricky Granger did not habitually wear spectacles, he was evidently not African-American or Asian, and since his beard was dark and luxuriant he probably had dark hair. From the attached description she learned that he was about six foot tall, slim built, and fit-looking, with no noticeable accent. It was not much, but it was better than nothing.

And nothing was what Brian and Marvin had.

Honeymoon's assistant appeared and ushered Judy into the Horseshoe where the governor and his staff had their offices.

Judy bit her lip. She was about to break the first rule of bureaucracy and make her boss look a fool. It would probably be the end of her career.

Screw it.

All she wanted now was to make her boss get serious about the Hammer of Eden before they killed people. So long as he did that, he could fire her.

They passed the entrance to the governor's personal suite, then the assistant opened the door to Honeymoon's office.

Judy stepped inside.

For a moment she allowed herself to enjoy the shock and dismay on the faces of Brian Kincaid and Marvin Hayes.

Then she looked at Honeymoon.

The cabinet secretary was wearing a pale grey shirt with a subdued black-and-white dotted tie and dark grey patterned suspenders. He looked at Judy with raised eyebrows and said: 'Agent Maddox! Mr Kincaid just got through telling me he took you off the case because you're a ditz.'

Judy was floored. She was supposed to be in control of this scene, she was the one causing consternation. Honeymoon had outdone her. He was not going to be upstaged in his own office.

She recovered fast. *Okay, Mr Honeymoon, if you want to play hardball, I'll go in to bat.*

She said to him: 'Brian's full of shit.'

Kincaid scowled, but Honeymoon just raised his eyebrows slightly.

Judy added: 'I'm the best agent he has, and I just proved it.'

'You did?' Honeymoon said.

'While Marvin has been sitting around with his thumb up his ass pretending there's nothing to worry about, I've solved this case.'

Kincaid stood up, his face flushed. He said angrily:

'Maddox, just what the hell do you think you're doing here?'

She ignored him. 'I know who's sending terrorist threats to Governor Robson,' she said to Honeymoon. 'Marvin and Brian don't. You can make your own decision about who's the ditz.'

Hayes was bright red. He burst out: 'What the hell are you talking about?'

Honeymoon said: 'Let's all sit down. Now that Ms Maddox has interrupted us, we may as well hear what she has to say.' He nodded to his assistant. 'Close the door, John. Now, Agent Maddox, did I hear you say you *know* who's making the threats?'

'Correct.' She put a fax picture on Honeymoon's desk. 'This is Richard Granger, a hoodlum from Los Angeles who was believed, wrongly, to have been killed by the Mob in 1972.'

'And what makes you think he's the culprit?'

'Look at this.' She handed him another piece of paper. 'Here's the seismograph of a typical earthquake. Look at the vibrations that precede the tremor. There's a haphazard series of different magnitudes. These are typical foreshocks.' She showed him a second sheet. 'This is the Owens Valley earthquake. Nothing haphazard here. Instead of a natural-looking mess, there is a neat series of regular vibrations.'

Hayes interrupted. 'No one can figure out what those vibrations are.'

Judy turned to him. '*You* couldn't figure it out, but

I did.' She put another sheet on Honeymoon's desk. 'Look at this chart.'

Honeymoon studied the third chart, comparing it with the second. 'Regular, just like the Owens Valley graph. What makes vibrations like these?'

'A machine called a seismic vibrator.'

Hayes sniggered, but Honeymoon did not crack a smile. 'What's that?'

'One of these.' She handed him the picture sent to her by the manufacturers. 'It's used in oil exploration.'

Honeymoon looked sceptical. 'Are you saying the earthquake *was* man-made?'

'I'm not theorizing, I'm giving you the facts. A seismic vibrator was used in that location immediately before the earthquake. You can make your own judgement about cause and effect.'

He gave her a hard, appraising look. He was asking himself whether she was a bullshitter or not. She stared right back at him. Finally he said: 'Okay. How does that lead you to the guy with the beard?'

'A seismic vibrator was stolen a week ago in Shiloh, Texas.'

She heard Hayes say: 'Oh, shit.'

Honeymoon said: 'And the guy in the picture . . .?'

'Richard Granger is the prime suspect in the theft —and in the murder of the truck's regular driver. Granger was working for the oil exploration team that was using the vibrator. The E-fit picture is based on the recollections of his co-workers.'

Honeymoon nodded. 'Is that it?'

'Isn't it enough?' she expostulated.

Honeymoon did not respond to that. He turned to Kincaid. 'What have you got to say about all this?'

Kincaid gave him a shit-eating grin. 'I don't think we should bother you with internal disciplinary matters—'

'Oh, I want to be bothered,' Honeymoon said. There was a dangerous note in his voice, and the temperature in the room seemed to fall. 'Look at it from my angle. You come here and tell me the earthquake definitely was not man-made.' His voice became louder. 'Now it appears, from this evidence, that it very likely was. So we have a group out there that could cause a major disaster.' Judy felt a surge of triumph as it became clear Honeymoon had bought her story. He was furious with Kincaid. He stood up and pointed a finger at Brian. '*You* tell me you can't find the perpetrators, then in walks Agent Maddox with a name, a police record and a fucking *picture*.'

'I think I should say—'

'I feel like you've been dicking me around, Special Agent Kincaid,' said Honeymoon, overriding Kincaid. His face was dark with anger. 'And when people dick me around I get kind of tetchy.'

Judy sat silent, watching Honeymoon destroy Kincaid. *If this is what you're like when you're tetchy, Al, I'd hate to see you when you're real mad.*

Kincaid tried again. 'I'm sorry if—'

'I also hate people who apologize,' Honeymoon said. 'An apology is designed to make the offender feel okay so that he can do it again. Don't be sorry.'

Kincaid tried to gather the shreds of his dignity. 'What do you want me to say?'

'That you're putting Agent Maddox in charge of this case.'

Judy stared at him. This was even better than she had hoped.

Kincaid looked as if he had been asked to strip naked in Union Square. He swallowed.

Honeymoon said: 'If you have a problem with that, just say so, and I'll have Governor Robson call the Director of the FBI in Washington. The governor could then explain to the director the reasons why we're making this request.'

'That won't be necessary,' Kincaid said.

'So put Maddox in charge.'

'Okay.'

'No, not okay. I want you to say it to her, right here, right now.'

Brian refused to look at Judy, but he said: 'Agent Maddox, you are now in charge of the Hammer of Eden investigation.'

'Thank you,' Judy said.

Saved!

'Now get out of here,' Honeymoon said.

They all got up.

Honeymoon said: 'Maddox.'

She turned at the door. 'Yes.'

'Call me once a day.'

That meant he would continue to support her. She could talk to Honeymoon any time she liked. And Kincaid knew it. 'You got it,' she said.

They went out.

As they were leaving the Horseshoe, Judy gave

Kincaid a sweet smile and repeated the words he had said to her last time they were in this building, four days ago. 'You did just fine in there, Brian. Don't you worry about a thing.'

CHAPTER THIRTEEN

DUSTY WAS sick all day Monday.

Melanie drove into Silver City to pick up more of the allergy drug he needed. She left Dusty being cared for by Flower, who was going through a sudden maternal phase.

She came back in a panic.

Priest was in the barn with Dale. Dale had asked him to taste the blend of last year's wine. It was going to be a nutty vintage, slow to mature but long-lived. Priest suggested using more of the lighter pressing from the lower, shadier slopes of the valley, to make the wine more immediately appealing; but Dale resisted. 'This is a connoisseur's wine now,' he said. 'We don't have to pander to supermarket buyers. Our customers like to keep the wine in their cellars for a few years before drinking it.'

Priest knew this was not the real reason Dale wanted to talk to him, but he argued anyway. 'Don't knock the supermarket buyers—they saved our lives in the early days.'

'Well, they can't save our lives now,' Dale said. 'Priest, why the fuck are we doing this? We have to be off this land by *next Sunday*.'

Priest suppressed a sigh of frustration. *For Christ's sake, give me a chance! I've almost done it—the governor can't ignore earthquakes indefinitely. I just need a little more time. Why can't you have faith?*

He knew that Dale could not be won over by bullying, cajoling, or bullshit. Only logic would work with him. He forced himself to speak calmly, the epitome of sweet reason. 'You could be right,' he said magnanimously. Then he could not resist adding a jibe. 'Pessimists often are.'

'So?'

'All I'm saying to you is, give it those six days. Don't quit *now*. Leave time for a miracle. Maybe it won't happen. But maybe it will.'

'I don't know,' Dale said.

Then Melanie burst in with a newspaper in her hand. 'I have to talk to you,' she said breathlessly.

Priest's heart missed a beat. What had happened? It must be about the earthquakes—and Dale was not in on the secret. Priest gave him a grin that said *Ain't women peculiar?* and led Melanie out of the barn.

'Dale doesn't know!' he said as soon as they were out of earshot. 'What the hell—'

'Look at this!' she said, waving the paper in front of his eyes.

He was shocked to see a photograph of a seismic vibrator.

He hastily scanned the yard and the nearby buildings, but there was no one around. All the same, he did not want to have this conversation with Melanie out in the open. 'Not here!' he said fiercely. 'Put the damn paper under your arm and let's go to my cabin.'

She got a grip on herself.

They walked through the little settlement to his cabin. As soon as they were inside, he took the newspaper from her and looked at the picture again. There was no doubt about it. He could not read the caption or the accompanying story, of course, but the photo was of a truck just like the one he had stolen.

'Shit,' he said, and he threw the newspaper on the table.

'Read it!' Melanie said.

'It's too dim in here,' he replied. 'Tell me what it says.'

'The police are looking for a stolen seismic vibrator.'

'The hell they are.'

'It doesn't say anything about earthquakes,' Melanie went on. "It's just, like, a funny story—who'd want to steal one of these damn things?'

'I don't buy that,' Priest said. 'This can't be a coincidence. The story is about us, even if they don't mention us. They know how we made the earthquake happen, but they haven't told the press yet. They're scared of creating a panic.'

'So why have they released this picture?'

'To make things hard for us. That picture makes it impossible to drive the truck on the open road. Every highway patrol officer in California is on the lookout.' He hit the table with his fist in frustration. 'Fuck it, I can't let them stop me this easily!'

'What if we drive at night?'

He had thought of that. He shook his head. 'Still too risky. There are cops on the road at night.'

'I have to go check on Dusty,' Melanie said. She was close to tears. 'Oh, Priest, he's so sick—we won't have to leave the valley, will we? I'm scared. I'll never find another place where we can be happy, I know it.'

Priest hugged her to give her courage. 'I'm not beaten yet, not by a long way. What else does the report say?'

She picked up the paper. 'There was a demonstration outside the Federal Building in San Francisco.' She smiled through her tears. 'A group of people who say the Hammer of Eden are right, the FBI should leave us alone, and Governor Robson should stop building power plants.'

Priest was pleased. 'Well, what do you know? There are still a few Californians who can think straight!' Then he became solemn again. 'But that doesn't help me figure out how to drive the truck without getting pulled over by the first cop who sees it.'

'I'm going to Dusty,' she said.

Priest went with her. In her cabin, Dusty lay on the bed, eyes streaming, face red, panting for breath. Flower sat beside him, reading aloud from a book with a picture of a giant peach on the cover. Priest touched his daughter's hair. She looked up at him and smiled without pausing in her reading.

Melanie got a glass of water and gave Dusty a pill. Priest felt sorry for Dusty, but he could not help remembering that the boy's illness was a lucky break for the commune. Melanie was caught in a trap. She believed she had to live where the air was pure, but she could not get a job outside the city. The commune was the only answer. If she had to leave here, she might find another, similar commune to take her in— but she might not, and anyway she was too exhausted and discouraged to hit the road again.

And there was more to it than that, he thought. Deep inside her was a terrible rage. He did not know the source of it, but it was strong enough to make her yearn to shake the earth and burn cities and cause people to run screaming from their homes. Most of the time it was hidden beneath the façade of a sexy but disorganized young woman. But sometimes, when her will was thwarted and she felt frustrated and powerless, the anger showed.

He left them and headed for Star's cabin, worrying over the problem of the truck. Star might have some ideas. Maybe there was a way they could disguise the seismic vibrator so that it looked like some other kind of vehicle, a Coke truck or a crane or something.

He stepped into the cabin. Star was putting a band-aid on Ringo's knee, something she had to do about once a day. Priest smiled at his ten-year-old son and said: 'What did you do this time, cowboy?' Then he noticed Bones.

He was lying on the bed, fully clothed but fast asleep—or more likely passed out. There was an empty bottle of Silver River Valley Chardonnay on the rough wooden table. Bones's mouth was open and he was snoring softly.

Ringo began to tell Priest a long story about trying to cross the stream by swinging from a tree, but Priest hardly listened. The sight of Bones had given him inspiration, and his mind was working feverishly.

When Ringo's grazed knee had been attended to, and the boy ran out, Priest told Star about the problem of the seismic vibrator. Then he told her the solution.

*

Priest, Star, and Oaktree helped Bones pull the big tarpaulin off the carnival ride. The vehicle stood revealed in its glorious, gaudy colours: a green dragon breathing red-and-yellow fire over three screaming girls in a spinning seat, and the gaudy lettering which, Bones had told Priest, said *The Dragon's Mouth*.

Priest spoke to Oaktree. 'We drive this vehicle up the track a way and park it next to the seismic vibrator. Then we take off these painted panels and fix them to our truck, covering the machinery. The cops are looking for a seismic vibrator, not a carnival ride.'

Oaktree, who was carrying his toolbox, looked closely at the panels, examining the way they were fixed. 'No problem,' he said after a minute. 'I can do it in a day, with one or two people helping me.'

'And can you put the panels back afterward, so that Bones's ride will look the same?'

'Good as new,' Oaktree promised.

Priest looked at Bones. The great snag with this scheme was that Bones had to be in on it. In the old days, Priest would have trusted Bones with his life. He was a Rice Eater, after all. Perhaps he could not be relied upon to show up for his own wedding, but he could keep a secret. However, since Bones had become a junkie, all bets were off. Heroin lobotomized people. A junkie would steal his mother's wedding ring.

But Priest had to take the risk. He was desperate. He had promised an earthquake four days from now, and he had to carry out his threat. Otherwise all was lost.

Bones had agreed readily to the plan. Priest had half-expected him to demand payment. However, he had been living free at the commune for four days, so it was too late to put his relationship with Priest on a commercial footing. Besides, as a communard Bones knew that the greatest sin imaginable was to value things in money terms.

Bones would be more subtle. In a day or two he would ask Priest for cash to go score some smack. Priest would cross that bridge when he came to it.

'Let's get to it,' he said.

Oaktree and Star climbed into the cab of the carnival ride with Bones. Melanie and Priest took the 'Cuda for the mile-long ride to where the seismic vibrator was hidden.

Priest wondered what else the FBI knew. They had figured out that the earthquake had been triggered using a seismic vibrator. Had they progressed any further? He turned on the car radio, hoping for a bulletin. He got Connie Francis singing 'Breakin' in a Brand New Broken Heart', an oldie even by his standards.

The 'Cuda bumped along the muddy track through the forest behind Bones's truck. Bones handled the big rig confidently, Priest observed, even though he had only just been roused from a drunken sleep. There was a moment when Priest felt sure the carnival ride was going to get stuck in a mud slide, but it pulled through without stopping.

The news came on just as they drew near the hiding place of the seismic vibrator. Priest turned up the volume.

What he heard turned him pale with shock.

'Federal agents investigating the Hammer of Eden terrorist group have issued a photographic likeness of a suspect,' the newsreader said. 'He has been named as Richard or Ricky Granger, aged forty-nine, formerly of Los Angeles.'

Priest said: 'Jesus *Christ*!' and slammed on the brakes.

'Granger is also wanted for a murder in Shiloh, Texas, nine days ago.'

'What?' No one knew he had killed Mario, not even Star.

The Rice Eaters were desperately keen to cause an earthquake that might kill hundreds, but all the same they would be appalled to know he had battered a man to death with a wrench. People were inconsistent.

'That's not true,' Priest said to Melanie. 'I didn't kill anyone.'

Melanie was staring at him. 'Is that your real name?' she said. 'Ricky Granger?'

He had forgotten that she did not know. 'Yeah,' he

said. He racked his brains to think who knew his real name. He had not used it for twenty-five years, except in Shiloh. Suddenly he remembered that he had gone to the sheriff's office in Silver City, to get Flower out of jail, and his heart stopped for a moment; then he recalled that the deputy had assumed he had the same name as Star, and called him Mr Higgins. Thank God.

Melanie said: 'How did they get a photo of you?'

'Not a photo,' he said. 'A *photographic likeness.* That must mean one of those Identikit pictures that they make up.'

'I know what you mean,' she said. 'Only they use a computer program now.'

'There's a computer program for every goddam thing,' Priest muttered. He was now very glad he had changed his appearance before taking the job in Shiloh. It had been worth the time it took to grow a beard, the bother of pinning up his hair every day, and the nuisance of having to wear a hat all the time. With luck, the photograph likeness would not remotely resemble the way he looked now.

But he needed to be sure.

'I need to get to a TV,' he said.

He jumped out of the car. The carnival ride had pulled over near the hiding place of the seismic vibrator, and Oaktree and Star were getting out. In a few words he explained the situation to them. 'You make a start here while I drive into Silver City,' he said. 'I'll take Melanie—I want her opinion, too.'

He got back in the car, drove out of the woods, and headed for Silver City.

On the outskirts of the small town there was an electronics store. Priest parked and they got out.

Priest looked around nervously. It was still light. What if he should meet someone who had seen his face on TV? Everything hung on whether the picture was like him. He had to know. He had to take a chance. He approached the store.

The window displayed several TV sets all showing the same picture. The program was some kind of game show. A silver-haired host in a powder-blue suit was joshing a middle-aged woman wearing too much eyeliner.

Priest glanced up and down the sidewalk. There was no one else about. He looked at his watch: almost seven. The news would be on in a few seconds.

The silver-haired host put his arm around the woman and spoke to camera. There was a shot of an audience applauding with hysterical enthusiasm. Then the news came on. There were two anchors, a man and a woman. They spoke for a few seconds.

Then the multiple screens showed a black-and-white picture of a heavily bearded man in a cowboy hat.

Priest stared at it.

The picture did not look like him at all.

'What do you think?' he said.

'Even I wouldn't know it was supposed to be you,' Melanie said.

Relief washed over him in a tidal wave. His disguise had worked. The beard changed the shape of his face, and the hat hid his most distinctive feature, the long, thick, wavy hair. Even he might not have recognized the picture if he had not known it was supposed to be him.

He relaxed. 'Thank you, god of the hippies,' he said.

The screens all flickered and another picture appeared. Priest was shocked to see, reproduced a dozen times, a police photo of himself at nineteen. He was so thin, his face looked like a skull. He was trim now, but in those days, doping and drinking and never eating a regular meal, he had been a skeleton. His face was drawn, his expression sullen. His hair was lank and dull, with a Beatle haircut that must have been out of date even then.

Priest said: 'Would you recognize me?'

'Yes,' she said. 'By the nose.'

He looked again. She was right, the picture showed his distinctive narrow nose, like a curved knife.

Melanie added: 'But I don't think anyone else would know you, certainly not strangers.'

'That's what I thought.'

She put an arm around his waist and squeezed affectionately. 'You looked such a bad boy when you were young.'

'I guess I was.'

'Where did they get that picture, anyway?'

'From my police record, I'm assuming.'

She looked up at him. 'I didn't know you had a police record. What did you do?'

'You want a list?'

She seemed shocked and disapproving. *Don't get moral on me, baby—remember who told us how to cause an earthquake.* 'I gave up the life of crime when I came to the valley,' he said. 'I didn't do anything wrong for the next twenty-five years—until I met you.'

A frown wrinkled her brow. She did not think of herself as a criminal, he realized. In her own eyes, she was a normally respectable citizen who had been driven to commit a desperate act. She still believed she was of a different race from people who robbed and murdered.

Work it out any way you like, honey—just stay with the plan.

The two anchors reappeared, then the scene shifted to a skyscraper. A line of words appeared at the bottom of the screen. Priest did not need to be able to read them: he recognized the place. It was the Federal Building where the FBI had its San Francisco office. A demonstration was going on, and Priest recalled Melanie reading about it in the newspaper. They were demonstrating in support of the Hammer of Eden, she had said. A bunch of people with placards and bullhorns were haranguing a group entering the building.

The camera focused on a young woman with an Asian cast to her features. She caught Priest's eye because she was beautiful in the exotic way that strongly appealed to him. She was slender, and dressed in an elegant dark pantsuit, but she had a formidable don't-fuck-with-me look on her face, and she elbowed her way through the crowd with a calm ruthlessness.

Melanie said: 'Oh, my God, it's her!'

Priest was startled. 'You know that woman?'

'I met her on Sunday!'

'Where?'

'At Michael's apartment, when I went to get Dusty.'

'Who is she?'

'Michael just introduced her as Judy Maddox, he didn't say anything about her.'

'What's she doing at the Federal Building?'

'It says, right there on the screen: "FBI agent Judy Maddox, in charge of Hammer of Eden case." She's the detective who's after us!'

Priest was fascinated. Was this his enemy? She was gorgeous. Just looking at her on TV made him want to touch her golden skin with his fingertips.

I should be scared, not turned on. She's a hell of a detective. She caught on about the seismic vibrator, found out where it came from, and got my name and picture. She's smart and she works fast.

'And you met her at Michael's place?'

'Yes.'

Priest was spooked. She was too close. She had met Melanie! His intuition told him he was in great danger from this agent. The fact that he was so attracted to her, after seeing her only briefly on TV, made it worse. It was as if she had some kind of power over him.

Melanie went on: 'Michael didn't say she was with the FBI. I thought she was a new girlfriend, so I kind of froze her out. She brought this older guy with her, said he was her father, though he didn't look Asian.'

'Girlfriend or not, I don't like her getting this close to us!' He turned away from the store and walked slowly back to the car. His brain was racing. Maybe it was not so surprising that the agent on the case had consulted a leading seismologist. Agent Maddox had talked to Michael for the same reason Priest had: he knew about earthquakes. Priest guessed it was Michael who had helped her make the link to the seismic vibrator.

What else had he told her?

They sat in the car, but Priest did not start the engine. 'This is bad for us,' he said. 'Very bad.'

'What's bad?' Melanie said defensively. 'It's okay if Michael wants to screw around with an FBI agent. Maybe she sticks her gun up his ass. I don't care.'

It was not like her to talk dirty. *She's really shook.* 'What's bad is, Michael could give her the same information he gave us.'

Melanie frowned. 'I don't get it.'

'Think about it. What's on Agent Maddox's mind? She's asking: "Where will the Hammer of Eden strike next?" Michael can help her with that. He can look at his data, same way you did, and figure out the most likely places for an earthquake. Then the FBI can stake out those locations and watch for a seismic vibrator.'

'I never thought of that.' Melanie stared at him. 'My fucking bastard husband and his FBI floozie are going to screw this up for us, is that what you're telling me?'

Priest glanced at her. She looked about ready to cut his throat. 'Calm down, will you?'

'God *damn.*'

'Wait a minute.' Priest was getting an idea. Melanie was the link. Maybe she could find out what Michael had told the beautiful FBI agent. 'There could be a way around this. Tell me something, how do you feel about Michael now?'

'Like, nothing. It's over, and I'm glad. I just hope we can work out our divorce without too much hostility, is all.'

Priest studied her. He did not believe her. What she felt for Michael was rage. 'We have to know whether the FBI has staked out possible earthquake locations —and if so, which ones. I think he might tell you.'

'Why would he do that?'

'I believe he's still carrying a torch for you, sort of.'

She stared at him. 'Priest, what the hell is this about?'

Priest took a deep breath. 'He'd tell you anything, if you slept with him.'

'Fuck you, Priest, I won't do it. Fuck you!'

'I hate to ask you.' It was true. He did not want her to sleep with Michael. He believed that no one should have sex unless they wanted to. He had learned from Star that the most disgusting thing about marriage was the right it gave one person to have sex with another. So this whole scheme was a betrayal of his beliefs. 'But I have no choice.'

'Forget it,' Melanie said.

'Okay,' he said. 'I'm sorry I asked.' He started the car. 'I just wish I could think of some other way.'

They were silent for a few minutes, driving through the mountains.

'I'm sorry, Priest,' she said eventually. 'I just can't do it.'

'I told you, don't worry about it.'

They turned off the road and drove down the long, rough track toward the commune. The carnival ride was no longer visible from the track: Priest guessed that Oaktree and Star had concealed it for the night.

He parked in the cleared circle at the end of the track. As they walked through the woods to the village in the twilight, he took Melanie's hand. After a moment's hesitation, she moved closer to him and squeezed his hand fondly.

Work in the vineyard was over. Because of the warm weather, the big table had been dragged out of the cookhouse into the yard. Some of the children were putting out plates and cutlery while Slow sliced a long loaf of home-baked bread. There were bottles of the commune's own wine on the table, and a spicy aroma was drifting over the scene.

Priest and Melanie went to Melanie's hut to check on Dusty. They saw immediately that he was better. He was sleeping peacefully. The swelling had gone down, his nose had stopped running, and he was breathing normally. Flower had gone to sleep in the chair beside the bed, with the book open on her lap.

Priest watched as Melanie tucked in the sheet around the sleeping boy and kissed his forehead. She looked up at Priest and whispered: 'This is the only place he's ever been okay.'

'It's the only place *I've* ever been okay,' Priest said quietly. 'It's the only place the *world* has ever been okay. That's why we have to save it.'

'I know,' she said. 'I know.'

CHAPTER FOURTEEN

THE DOMESTIC Terrorism squad of the San Francisco FBI worked in a narrow room along one side of the Federal Building. With its desks and room dividers it looked like a million other offices, except that the shirtsleeved young men and smart-suited women wore guns in holsters on their hips or under their arms.

At seven o'clock on Tuesday morning they were standing, sitting on desk corners, or leaning against the wall, some sipping coffee from styrofoam containers, others holding pens and pads ready to take notes. The whole squad, except for the supervisor, had been put under Judy's orders. There was a low buzz of conversation.

Judy knew what they were talking about. She had gone up against the Acting SAC—and won. It did not happen often. In an hour the entire floor would be alive with rumour and gossip. She would not be surprised to hear by the end of the day that she had prevailed because she was having an affair with Al Honeymoon.

The noise died away when she stood up and said: 'Pay attention, everyone.'

She looked over the group for a moment and experienced a familiar thrill. They were all fit, hard-working, well-dressed, honest and smart, the smartest young people in America. She felt proud to work with them.

She began to speak. 'We're going to divide into two teams. Peter, Jack, Sally and Lee will check out tips based on the pictures we have of Ricky Granger.' She handed out a briefing sheet that she had worked on overnight. A list of questions would enable the agents to eliminate most of the tips and assess which ones merited a visit by an agent or neighbourhood cop. Many of the men identified as 'Ricky Granger' could be ruled out fast: African-Americans, men with foreign accents, twenty-year-olds, short men. On the other hand, the agents would be quick to visit any suspect who fitted the description and had been away from home for the two-week period during which Granger had worked in Shiloh, Texas.

'Dave, Louise, Steve, and Ashok will form the second team. You'll work with Simon Sparrow, checking tip-offs based on the recorded voice of the woman who phoned John Truth. By the way, some of the tip-offs Simon is working on mention a pop record. We asked John Truth to flag that up on his show last night.' She had not done this personally: the office press person had spoken to Truth's producer. 'So we may get calls about it.' She handed out a second briefing sheet with different questions.

'Raja.'

The youngest member of the team grinned

his cocky grin. 'I was afraid you'd forgotten about me.'

'In my dreams,' she said, and they all laughed. 'Raja, I want you to prepare a short briefing to go out to all police departments, and especially the California Highway Patrol, telling them how to recognize a seismic vibrator.' She held up a hand. 'And no vibrator jokes, please.' They laughed again.

'Now I'm going to get us some extra manpower and more work space. Meanwhile, I know you'll do your best. One more thing.'

She paused, choosing her words. She needed to impress them with the importance of their work—but she felt she had to avoid coming right out and saying that the Hammer of Eden could cause earthquakes.

'These people are trying to blackmail the Governor of California. They *say* they can make earthquakes happen.' She shrugged. 'I'm not telling you they can. But it's not as impossible as it sounds, and I'm sure as hell not telling you they *can't*. Either way, you need to understand that this assignment is very, very serious.' She paused again, then finished: 'Let's get to it.'

They all moved to their seats.

Judy left the room and walked briskly along the corridor to the SAC's office. The official start of the working day was 8.15, but she was betting Brian Kincaid had come in early. He would have heard that she had called her team to a seven o'clock briefing, and he would want to know what was happening. She was about to tell him.

His secretary was not yet at her desk. Judy knocked on the inner door and went in.

Kincaid was sitting in the big chair with his suit coat on, looking as if he had nothing to do. The only items on his desk were a bran muffin with one bite taken out of it, and the paper bag it had come in. He was smoking a cigarette. Smoking was not allowed in FBI offices, but Kincaid was the boss, so there was no one to tell him to stop. He gave Judy a hostile glare and said: 'If I asked you to make me a cup of coffee, I guess you'd call me a sexist pig.'

There was no way she was going to make his coffee. He would take it as a sign that he could carry on walking all over her. But she wanted to be conciliatory. 'I'll get you coffee,' she said. She picked up his phone and dialled the DT squad secretary. 'Rosa, would you come to the SAC's office and put on a pot of coffee for Mr Kincaid? Thank you.'

He still looked angry. Her gesture had done nothing to win him round. He probably felt that by getting him coffee without actually making it herself she had in a way outwitted him.

Bottom line, I can't win.

She got down to business. 'I have more than a thousand leads to follow up on the voice of the woman on tape. I'm guessing we'll get even more calls about the picture of Ricky Granger. I can't begin to evaluate them all by Friday with nine people. I need twenty more agents.'

He laughed. 'I'm not putting twenty people on this bullshit assignment.'

She ignored that. 'I've notified the Strategic Information Operations Center.' SIOC was an information clearing house that operated from a bomb-proof office in the Hoover building in Washington, DC. 'I'm assuming that as soon as the news gets around headquarters, they'll send some people here—if only to take the credit for any success we have.'

'I didn't tell you to notify SIOC.'

'I want to convene the Joint Terrorist Task Force, so we'll have delegates here from police departments, Customs, and the US Federal Protective Service, all of whom will need somewhere to sit. And starting from sundown on Thursday, I plan to stake out the likeliest locations for the next earthquake.'

'There isn't going to be one!'

'I'll need extra personnel for that, too.'

'Forget it.'

'There isn't a room big enough here at the office. We're going to have to set up our Emergency Operations Center someplace else. I checked out the Presidio buildings last night.' The Presidio was a disused military base near the Golden Gate bridge. The officers' club was habitable, though a skunk had been living there and the place smelled foul. 'I'm going to use the ballroom of the officers' club.'

Kincaid stood up. 'Are you, hell!' he shouted.

Judy sighed. There was no way to get this done without making a lifetime enemy of Brian Kincaid. 'I have to call Mr Honeymoon soon,' she said. 'Do you want me to tell him you're refusing to give me the manpower I need?'

Kincaid was red with fury. He stared at Judy as if he wanted to pull out his gun and blow her away. At last he said: 'Your FBI career is over, you know that?'

He was probably right, but it hurt to hear him say it. 'I never wanted to fight with you, Brian,' she said, striving to keep her voice low and reasonable. 'But you dicked me around. I deserved a promotion after putting the Foong brothers away. Instead you promoted your buddy and gave me a bullshit assignment. You shouldn't have done that. It was unprofessional.'

'Don't tell me how to—'

She overrode him. 'When the bullshit assignment turned into a big case, you took it away from me then screwed it up. Every bad thing that's happened to you is your own damn fault. Now you're sulking. Well, I know your pride is wounded, and I know your feelings are hurt, and I just want you to understand that I don't give a flying fuck.'

He stared at her with his mouth half open.

She went to the door.

'Now I'm going to talk to Honeymoon at nine thirty,' she said. 'By then I'd like to have a senior logistics person assigned to my team with the authority to organize the manpower I need and set up a command post at the officers' club. If I don't, I'll tell Honeymoon to call Washington. Your move.' She went out and slammed the door.

She felt the exhilaration that comes from a reckless act. She would have to fight every step, so she might as well fight hard. She would never be able to work with Kincaid again. The Bureau's top brass would side with the superior officer in a situation like this. She was almost certainly finished. But this case was more important than her career. Hundreds of lives might be at stake. If she could prevent a catastrophe and capture the terrorists, she would retire proudly, and to hell with them all.

The DT squad secretary was in Kincaid's outer office, filling the coffee machine. 'Thanks, Rosa,' Judy said as she passed through. She returned to the DT office. The phone on her desk was ringing. She picked up. 'Judy Maddox.'

'John Truth here.'

'Hello!' It was weird to hear the familiar radio voice on the other end of a phone. 'You're at work early!'

'I'm at home, but my producer just called me. My voicemail at the radio station was maxed with overnight calls about the Hammer of Eden woman.'

Judy was not supposed to talk to the media herself. All such contacts should go through the office media specialist, Madge Kelly, a young agent with a journalism degree. But Truth was not asking her for a quote, he was giving her information. And she was in too much of a hurry to tell Truth to call Madge. 'Anything good?' she asked.

'You bet. I got two people who remembered the name of the record.'

'No kidding!' Judy was thrilled.

'This woman was reading poetry over a background of psychedelic music.'

'Yuck.'

'Yeah.' He laughed. 'The album was called *Raining*

Fresh Daisies. That also seems to be the name of the band, or "group" as they used to call them then.'

He seemed pleasant and friendly, nothing like the spiteful creep he was on air. Maybe that was just an act. But you could never trust media people. Judy said: 'I never heard of them.'

'Me neither. Before my time, I guess. And we sure don't have the disc at the radio station.'

'Did either of your callers give you a catalogue number, or even the name of the record label?'

'Nope. My producer called both people back, but they don't actually have the record, they just remember it.'

'Damn. I guess we'll just call every record company. I wonder if they keep files that far back . . .'

'The album may have come out on a minor-league label that no longer exists—it sounds like that kind of far-out stuff. Want to know what I'd do?'

'Sure.'

'Haight-Ashbury is full of second-hand record stores with clerks who live in a time warp. I'd check them out.'

'Good idea—thanks.'

'You're welcome. Now, how's the investigation going, otherwise?'

'We're making some progress. Can I get our press officer to call you later with details?'

'Come on! I've just done you a favour, haven't I?'

'You sure have, and I wish I could give you an interview, but agents aren't allowed to talk directly to the media. I'm really sorry.'

His tone turned aggressive. 'Is this the thanks you give to our listeners for calling in with information for you?'

A dreadful thought struck her. 'Are you taping this?'

'You don't mind, do you?'

She hung up. *Shit.* She had been trapped. Talking to the media without authorization was what the FBI called a 'bright-line' issue, meaning you could be fired for it. If John Truth played his tape of their conversation over the air, Judy would be in trouble. She could argue that she had urgently needed the information Truth offered, and a decent boss would probably let her off with a reprimand, but Kincaid would make the most of it.

Heck, Judy, you're already in so much trouble, this won't make any difference.

Raja Khan walked up to her desk with a sheet of paper in his hand. 'Would you like to see this before it goes out? It's the memo to police officers about how to recognize a seismic vibrator.'

That was quick. 'What took you so long?' she said, joshing him.

'I had to look up how to spell "seismic".'

She smiled and glanced over what he had written. It was fine. 'This is great. Send it out.' She handed back the sheet. 'Now I have another job for you. We're looking for an album called *Raining Fresh Daisies.* It's from the sixties.'

'No kidding.'

She grinned. 'Yeah, it does have kind of a hippie feel to it. The voice on the record is the Hammer of Eden woman, and I'm hoping we'll get a name for her. If the label still exists, we might even get a last known address. I want you to contact all the major recording companies, then call stores that sell rare records.'

He looked at his watch. 'It's not yet nine, but I can start with the east coast.'

'Get to it.'

Raja went to his desk. Judy picked up the phone and dialled police headquarters. 'Lieutenant Maddox, please.' A moment later he came on the line. She said: 'Bo, it's me.'

'Hi, Judy.'

'Cast your mind back to the late sixties, when you knew what music was hip.'

'I'd have to go further. Early sixties, late fifties, that's my era.'

'Too bad. I think the Hammer of Eden woman made a record with a band called Raining Fresh Daisies.'

'My favourite groups were called things like Frankie Rock and the Rockabillies. I never liked acts with flowers in their names. Sorry, Jude, I never heard of your outfit.'

'Well, it was worth a try.'

'Listen, I'm glad you called. I've been thinking about your guy, Ricky Granger—he's the man behind the woman, right?'

371

'That's what we think.'

'You know, he's so careful, he's such a planner, he must be dying to know what you're up to.'

'Makes sense.'

'I think the FBI has probably talked to him already.'

'You do?' That was hopeful, if Bo was right. There was a type of perpetrator who insinuated himself into the investigation, approaching the police as a witness, or as a kindly neighbour offering coffee, then tried to befriend officers and chat to them about the progress of the case. 'But Granger also seems ultra-careful.'

'There's probably a war going on inside him, between caution and curiosity. But look at his behaviour—he's daring as all hell. My guess is, curiosity will win out.'

Judy nodded into the phone. Bo's intuitions were worth listening to: they came from thirty years of police experience. 'I'm going to review every interview in the case.'

'Look for something off the wall. This guy never does the normal thing. He'll be a psychic offering to divine where the next earthquake will come, or like that. He's imaginative.'

'Okay. Anything else?'

'What do you want for supper?'

'I probably won't be home.'

'Don't overdo it.'

'Bo, I have three days to catch these people. If I fail, hundreds of people could die! I'm not thinking about supper.'

'If you get tired, you'll miss the crucial clue. Take breaks, eat lunch, get the sleep you need.'

'Like you always did, huh?'

He laughed. 'Good luck.'

'Bye.' She hung up, frowning. She would have to go over every interview Marvin's team had done with the Green California Campaign people, plus all the notes from the raid on Los Alamos, and anything else in the file. It should all be on the office computer network. She touched her keyboard and called up the directory. As she scanned the material, she realized there was far too much for her to review personally. They had interviewed every householder in Silver River Valley, more than a hundred people. When she got her extra personnel, she would put a small team on it. She made a note.

What else? She had to arrange stake-outs on likely earthquake sites. Michael had said he could make a list. She was glad to have a reason to call him. She dialled his number.

He sounded pleased to hear from her. 'I'm looking forward to our date tonight.'

Shit—I forgot all about it. 'I've been put back on the Hammer of Eden case,' she told him.

'Does that mean you can't make it tonight?' He sounded crestfallen.

She certainly could not contemplate dinner and a movie. 'I'd like to see you, but I won't have much time. Could we meet for a drink, maybe?'

'Sure.'

'I'm really sorry, but the case is developing fast. I called you about that list you promised, of likely earthquake sites. Did you make it?'

'No. You got anxious about the information getting out to the public and causing a panic, and that made me think the exercise might be dangerous.'

'Now I need to know.'

'Okay, I'll look at the data.'

'Could you bring the list with you tonight?'

'Sure. Morton's at six?'

'See you there.'

'Listen . . .'

'Still here.'

'I'm really glad you're back on the case. I'm sorry we can't have dinner together, but I feel safer knowing you're after the bad guys. I mean it.'

'Thanks.' As she hung up, she hoped she merited his confidence.

Three days left.

*

By mid-afternoon, the Emergency Operations Center was up and running.

The officers' club looked like a Spanish villa. Inside, it was a gloomy imitation of a country club, with cheap panelling, bad murals, and ugly light fittings. The smell of the skunk had not gone away.

The cavernous ballroom had been fitted out as a command post. In one corner was the Head Shed, a top table with seats for the heads of the principal agencies involved in managing the crisis, including

the San Francisco police, firefighters and medical
people, the mayor's office of emergency services, and
a representative of the governor. The experts from
headquarters, who were even now flying from Washington to San Francisco in an FBI jet, would sit here.

Around the room, groups of tables were set up for
the different teams that would work on the case:
Intelligence & Investigation, the core of the effort;
Negotiation and SWAT teams that would be called in
if hostages were taken; an Administration & Technical
Support team that would grow if the crisis escalated; a
Legal team to expedite search warrants, arrest warrants, or wiretaps; and an Evidence Response Team
that would enter any crime scene after the event and
collect evidence.

Laptop computers on each table were linked in a
local network. The FBI had long used a paper-based
information-control system called Rapid Start, but now
it had developed a computerized version, using Micro-
soft Access software. But paper had not disappeared.
Around two sides of the room, noticeboards covered
the walls: lead status boards, event boards, subject
boards, demand boards, and hostage boards. Key data
and clues would be written up here so that everyone
could see them at a glance. Right now the subject
board had one name—Richard Granger—and two
pictures. The lead status board had a picture of a
seismic vibrator.

The room was big enough for a couple of hundred
people, but so far there were only about forty.
They were mostly grouped around the Intelligence &

Investigation table, speaking into phones, tapping keyboards, and reading files on screen. Judy had divided them into teams, each with a leader who monitored the others, so that she could keep track of progress by talking to three people.

There was an air of subdued urgency. Everyone was calm, but they were concentrating hard and working intensely. No one stopped for coffee or schmoozed over the photocopier or went outside for a cigarette. Later, if the situation developed into a full-blown crisis, the atmosphere would change, Judy knew: people would be yelling into phones, the expletive quotient would multiply, tempers would fray, and it would be her job to keep the lid on the cauldron.

Remembering Bo's tip, she pulled up a chair next to Carl Theobald, a bright young agent in a fashionable dark blue shirt. He was the leader of the team reviewing Marvin Hayes's files. 'Anything?' she said.

He shook his head. 'We don't really know what we're looking for, but whatever it is, we haven't found it yet.'

She nodded. She had given this team a vague task, but she could not help that. They had to look for something out of the ordinary. A lot depended on the intuition of the individual agent. Some people could smell deceit even in a computer.

'Are we sure we have *everything* on file?' she asked.

Carl shrugged. 'We should.'

'Check whether they kept any paper records.'

'They're not supposed to . . .'

'But people do.'

'Okay.'

Rosa called her back to the Head Shed for a phone call. It was Michael. She smiled as she picked up. 'Hi.'

'Hi. I've got a problem tonight. I can't make it.'

She was shocked by his tone. He sounded curt and unfriendly. For the last few days he had been warm and affectionate. But this was the original Michael, the one who had turned her away from his door and told her to make an appointment. 'What is it?' she said.

'Something came up. I'm sorry to cancel on you.'

'Michael, what the hell is wrong?'

'I'm in kind of a rush. I'll call you.'

'Okay,' she said.

He hung up.

She cradled the phone, feeling hurt. 'Now what was all that about?' she said to herself. *Just as I was getting fond of the guy. What is it with him? Why can't he stay the way he was on Sunday night? Or even when he called me this morning?*

Carl Theobald interrupted her thoughts. He looked troubled. 'Marvin Hayes is giving me a hard time,' he said. 'They do have some paper records, but when I said I needed to see them, he pretty much told me to shove it.'

'Don't worry, Carl,' Judy said. 'These things are sent by Heaven to teach us patience and tolerance. I'll just go and tear his balls off.'

The agents nearby heard her and laughed.

'Is that what patience and tolerance means?' Carl said with a grin. 'I must remember that.'

'Come with me, I'll show you,' she said.

They went outside and jumped in her car. It took
fifteen minutes to reach the Federal Building on
Golden Gate Avenue. As they went up in the elevator,
Judy wondered how to deal with Marvin. Should she
tear his balls off, or be conciliatory? The cooperative
approach worked only if the other party was willing.
With Marvin, she had probably gone past that point
for ever.

She hesitated outside the door to the Organized
Crime squad room. *Okay, I'll be Xena, the warrior
princess.*

She went in and Carl followed.

Marvin was on the phone, grinning broadly, telling
a joke. 'So the barman says to the guy, there's a badger
in the back room that gives the best blow job—'

Judy leaned on his desk and said loudly: 'What's
this crap you're giving Carl?'

'Someone's interrupting me, Joe,' he said. 'I'll call
you right back.' He hung up. 'What can I do for you,
Judy?'

She leaned closer, putting herself in his face. 'Stop
dicking around.'

'What is it with you?' he said, sounding aggrieved.
'What do you mean by going over my records as if I
must have made some goddam mistake?'

He had not necessarily made a mistake. When the
perpetrator presented himself to the investigating
team in the guise of a bystander or witness, he generally took care they did not suspect him. It was not the
fault of the investigators, but it was bound to make
them feel foolish.

'I think you may have talked to the perpetrator,' she said. 'Where are these paper records?'

He smoothed his yellow tie. 'All we have are some notes from the press conference that never got keyed into the computer.'

'Show me.'

He pointed to a box file on a side table against the wall. 'Help yourself.'

She opened the file. On top was an invoice for rental of a small public-address system with microphones.

'You won't find a damn thing,' Marvin said.

He might be right, but she had to try, and it was dumb of him to obstruct her. A smarter man would have said, *Hey, if I overlooked something, I sure hope you find it.* Everyone made mistakes. But Marvin was now too defensive to be gracious. He just had to prove Judy wrong.

It would be embarrassing if she *was* wrong.

She riffled through the papers. There were some faxes from newspapers asking for details of the press conference, a note about how many chairs would be needed, and a guest list, a form on which the journalists attending the press conference had been asked to put their names and the publications or broadcasters they represented. Judy ran her eye down the list.

'What the hell is this?' she said suddenly. 'Florence Shoebury, Eisenhower Junior High?'

'She wanted to cover the press conference for the school newspaper,' Marvin said. 'What should we do, tell her to fuck off?'

'Did you check her out?'

'She's a kid!'

'Was she alone?'

'Her father brought her.'

There was a business card stapled to the form. 'Peter Shoebury, from Watkins, Colefax, and Brown. Did you check *him* out?'

Marvin hesitated for a long moment, realizing he had made a mistake. 'No,' he said finally. 'Brian decided to let them into the press conference, and afterward I never followed up.'

Judy handed the form with the business card to Carl. 'Call this guy right away,' she said.

Carl sat at the nearest desk and picked up the phone.

Marvin said: 'Anyway, what makes you so sure we talked to the subject?'

'My father thinks so.' As soon as the words were out of her mouth she realized she had made a mistake.

Marvin sneered. 'Oh, so your *daddy* thinks so. Is that the level we've sunk to? You're checking on me because your *daddy* told you to?'

'Knock it off, Marvin. My father was putting bad guys in jail when you were still wetting your bed.'

'Where are you going with this, anyway? Are you trying to set me up? You looking for someone to blame when you fail?'

'What a great idea,' she said. 'Why didn't I think of it?'

Carl hung up the phone and said: 'Judy.'

'Yeah.'

'Peter Shoebury has never been inside this building, and he has no daughter. But he was mugged on Saturday morning two blocks from here, and his wallet was stolen. It contained his business cards.'

There was a moment's silence, then Marvin said: 'Fuck it.'

Judy ignored his embarrassment. She was too excited by the news. This could be a whole new source of information. 'I guess he didn't look like the E-fit picture we got from Texas.'

'Not a bit,' Marvin said. 'No beard, no hat. He had big glasses and long hair in a ponytail.'

'That's probably another disguise. What about his build, and like that?'

'Tall, slim.'

'Dark hair, dark eyes, about fifty?'

'Yes, yes, and yes.'

Judy almost felt sorry for Marvin. 'It was Ricky Granger, wasn't it?'

Marvin looked at the floor as if he wanted it to open up and swallow him. 'I guess you're right.'

'I would like you to produce a new E-fit, please.'

He nodded, still not looking at her. 'Sure.'

'Now, what about Florence Shoebury?'

'Well, she kind of disarmed us. I mean, what kind of terrorist brings a little girl along with him?'

'One who is completely ruthless. What did the kid look like?'

'White girl about twelve, thirteen. Dark hair, dark eyes, slim build. Pretty.'

'Better do an E-fit of her, too. Do you think she really is his daughter?'

'Oh, sure. That's how they seemed. She showed no signs of being under coercion, if that's what you're thinking.'

'Yes. Okay, I'm going to assume they're father and daughter, for now.' She turned to Carl. 'We're out of here.'

They went out. In the corridor, Carl said: 'Wow. You really did tear off his balls.'

Judy was jubilant. 'But we've got another subject— the kid.'

'Yeah. I just hope you never catch *me* making a mistake.'

She stopped and looked at him. 'It wasn't the mistake, Carl. Anyone can screw up. But he was willing to impede the investigation in order to cover up. That's where he went wrong. And that's why he looks such an asshole now. If you make a mistake, admit it.'

'Yeah,' Carl said. 'But I think I'll keep my legs crossed, too.'

*

Late that evening, Judy got the first edition of the *San Francisco Chronicle* with the two new pictures: the E-fit of Florence Shoebury and the new E-fit of Ricky Granger disguised as Peter Shoebury. Earlier, she had only glanced at the pictures before asking Madge Kelly to get them to the newspapers and TV stations. Now, studying them by the light of her desk lamp, she was struck by the resemblance between Granger and Florence. *They're father and daughter, they have to be. I wonder what will happen to her if I put her daddy in jail?*

She yawned and rubbed her eyes. Bo's advice came back to her. 'Take breaks, eat lunch, get the sleep you need.' It was time to go home. The overnight shift was already here.

Driving home, she reviewed the day and what she had achieved. Sitting at a stop light, looking at twin rows of street lights converging to infinity along Geary Boulevard, she realized that Michael had not faxed her the promised list of likely earthquake sites.

She dialled his number on the car phone, but there was no answer. For some reason that bothered her. She tried again at the next red light and the number was busy. She called the office switchboard and asked them to check with Pacific Bell and find out whether there were voices on the line. The operator called her back and said there were not. The phone had been taken off the hook.

So he was home, but not picking up.

He had sounded odd when he called to cancel their date. He was like that; he could be charming and kind then change abruptly and be difficult and arrogant. But why was his phone off the hook? Judy felt uneasy.

She checked the dashboard clock. It was just before eleven.

Two days left.

I don't have time to screw around.

She turned the car around and headed for Berkeley.

She reached Euclid Street at eleven fifteen. There

were lights on in Michael's apartment. Outside was an old orange Subaru. She had seen the car before, but did not know whose it was. She parked behind it and rang Michael's doorbell.

There was no answer.

Judy was troubled. Michael had crucial information. Today, on the very day she had asked him a key question, he had abruptly cancelled an appointment then had become incommunicado.

It was suspicious.

She wondered what to do. Maybe she should call for police back-up and break in. He could be tied up, or dead in there.

She returned to her car and picked up the two-way radio, but she hesitated. When a man took the phone off the hook at 11 p.m., it might mean a variety of things. He might want to sleep. He might be getting laid, although Michael seemed too interested in Judy to play around—he was not the type to sleep with a different woman every night, she thought.

While she was wavering, a young woman with a briefcase approached the building. She looked like an assistant professor returning home from a late evening at the lab. She stopped at the door and fumbled in her briefcase for keys.

Impulsively, Judy jumped out of her car and walked quickly across the lawn to the entrance. 'Good evening,' she said. She showed her badge. 'FBI Special Agent Judy Maddox. I need access to this building.'

'Something wrong?' the woman said anxiously.

'I hope not. If you go to your apartment and close the door you'll be just fine.'

They went in together. The woman entered a ground-floor apartment and Judy went up the stairs. She rapped on Michael's door with her knuckles.

There was no reply.

What was going on? He was in there. He must have heard her ring and knock. He knew no casual caller would be so persistent at this time of night. Something was wrong, she felt sure.

She knocked again, three times, hard. Then she put her ear to the door and listened.

She heard a scream.

That did it. She took a step back and kicked the door as hard as she could. She was wearing loafers, and she hurt the underside of her right foot, but the wood around the lock splintered: thank God he did not have a steel door. She kicked it again. The lock seemed almost to break. She ran at the door with her shoulder, and it burst open.

She drew her gun. 'FBI!' she shouted. 'Drop your weapons and put up your hands!' There was another scream. It sounded like a woman, she realized in the back of her mind, but there was no time to figure out what that signified. She stepped into the entrance lobby.

Michael's bedroom door was open. She dropped to one knee with her arms extended and aimed into the room.

What she saw stunned her.

Michael was on the bed, naked, perspiring. He was on top of a thin woman with red hair who was breathing hard. It was his wife, Judy realized.

They were making love.

They both stared at Judy in fear and disbelief.

Then Michael recognized her and said: 'Judy? What the hell . . .?'

She closed her eyes. She had never felt such a fool in her life.

'Oh, shit,' she said. 'I'm sorry. Oh, shit.'

CHAPTER FIFTEEN

Early on Wednesday, Priest stood beside the Silver River, looking at the way the morning sky was reflected in the broken planes of the water's shifting surface, marvelling at the luminosity of blue and white in the dawn light. Everyone else was asleep. His dog sat beside him, panting quietly, waiting for something to happen.

It was a tranquil moment, but Priest's soul was not at peace.

His deadline was only two days away, and still Governor Robson had said nothing.

It was maddening. He did not want to trigger another earthquake. This one would have to be more spectacular, destroying roads and bridges, bringing skyscrapers tumbling down. People would die.

Priest was not like Melanie, thirsting for revenge upon the world. He just wanted to be left alone. He was willing to do anything to save the commune, but he knew it would be smarter to avoid killing if he could. After this was all over, and the project to dam the valley had been cancelled, he and the commune wanted to live in peace. That was the whole point. And their chances of staying here undisturbed would be greater if they could win without killing innocent Californian citizens. What had happened so far could be forgotten soon enough. It would drop out of the news and no one would care what became of the nutcases who said they could trigger earthquakes.

As he stood musing, Star appeared. She slipped out of her purple robe and stepped into the cold river to wash. Priest looked hungrily at her voluptuous body, familiar but still desirable. He had shared his bed with no one last night. Star was still spending her nights with Bones, and Melanie was with her husband in Berkeley. *So the great cocksman sleeps alone.*

While she was towelling herself dry, Priest said: 'Let's go get a newspaper. I want to know if Governor Robson said anything last night.'

They got dressed and drove to a gas station. Priest filled the tank of the 'Cuda while Star got the *San Francisco Chronicle*.

She came back white-faced. 'Look,' she said, showing him the front page.

There was a picture of a young girl who looked familiar. After a moment he realized with horror that it was Flower.

Stunned, he picked up the newspaper.

Beside the picture of Flower was one of himself.

Both were computer-generated images. The one of Priest was based on his appearance at the FBI press conference, when he had been disguised as Peter Shoebury, with his hair pulled back and large glasses. He did not think anyone would recognize him from that.

Flower had not been in disguise. Her computer picture was like a poorly drawn portrait—not *her*, but *like* her. Priest felt cold. He was not used to fear. He was a daredevil who enjoyed risk. But this was not about him. He had put his daughter in danger.

Star said angrily: 'Why the hell did you have to go to that press conference?'

'I had to know what they were thinking.'

'It was so dumb!'

'I've always been rash.'

'I know.' Her voice softened, and she touched his cheek. 'If you were timid, you wouldn't be the man I love.'

A month ago it would not have mattered: no one outside the commune knew Flower, and no one inside read newspapers. But she had been going secretly to Silver City to meet boys; she had stolen a poster from a store; she had been arrested; and she had spent a night in custody. Would the people she had met remember her? And if so, would they recognize the picture? The probation officer might remember her, but luckily he was still on vacation in the Bahamas, where he was unlikely to see the *San Francisco Chronicle*. But what about the woman who had guarded her overnight? A schoolteacher who was also the sheriff's sister, Priest recalled. Her name came back: Miss Waterlow. She saw hundreds of little girls, presumably, but she might remember their faces. Maybe she had a bad memory. Maybe she had gone on holiday too. Maybe she had not read today's *Chronicle*.

And maybe Priest was finished.

There was nothing he could do about it. If the schoolteacher saw the picture and recognized Flower and called the FBI, a hundred agents would descend on the commune and it would be all over.

He stared at the paper while Star read the text. 'If you didn't know her, would you recognize her?'

Star shook her head. 'I don't think so.'

'I don't either. But I wish I were sure.'

'I didn't think the Feds were this goddam smart,' Star said.

'Some are, some aren't. It's this Asian girl that worries me. Judy Maddox.' Priest recalled the TV pictures of her, so slender and graceful, pushing through a hostile crowd with a look of bulldog determination on her delicate features. 'I got a bad feeling about her,' he said. 'A real bad feeling. She keeps coming up with leads—first the seismic vibrator, then the picture of me in Shiloh, now Flower. Maybe that's why Governor Robson hasn't said anything. She's got him hoping we'll be caught. Is there a statement from the governor in the paper?'

'No. According to this report, a lot of people are saying Robson should give in and negotiate with the Hammer of Eden, but he refuses to comment.'

'This is no good,' he said. 'I've got to find a way to talk to him.'

*

When Judy woke up she could not remember why she felt so bad. Then the whole ghastly scene came back in a dreadful rush.

Last night she had been paralysed with embarrassment. She had mumbled an apology to Michael and run out of the building, burning with shame. But this morning her mortification had been replaced by a different feeling. Now she just felt sad. She had thought Michael might become part of her life. She had been looking forward to getting to know him, growing more fond of him, making love to him. She had imagined that he cared for her. But the relationship had crashed and burned in no time.

She sat up in bed and looked at the collection of Vietnamese water puppets she had inherited from her mother, arranged on a shelf above the chest of drawers. She had never seen a puppet show—had never been to Vietnam—but her mother had told her how the puppeteers stood waist-deep in a pond, behind a backdrop, and used the surface of the water as their stage. For hundreds of years such painted wooden toys had been used to tell wise and funny tales. They always reminded Judy of her mother's tranquillity. What would she say now? Judy could hear her voice, low and calm. 'A mistake is a mistake. Another mistake is normal. Only the same mistake twice makes you a fool.'

Last night had just been a mistake. Michael had been a mistake. She had to put all that behind her. She had two days to prevent an earthquake. That was *really* important.

On the TV news, people were arguing about whether the Hammer of Eden might really be able to trigger an earthquake. The believers had formed a pressure group to urge Governor Robson to give in. But, as she got dressed, Judy's mind kept returning to Michael. She wished she could speak to her mother about it. She could hear Bo stirring, but this was not the kind of thing to tell your father about. Instead of making breakfast she called her friend Virginia. 'I need someone to talk to,' she told her. 'Have you had breakfast yet?'

They met at a coffee shop near the Presidio. Ginny was a petite blonde, funny and honest. She would always tell Judy exactly what she thought. Judy ordered two chocolate croissants to make herself feel better, then related what had happened last night.

When she came to the part where she burst in with her gun in her hand and found them screwing, Ginny fell about laughing. 'I'm sorry,' she said, and got a piece of toast stuck in her throat.

'I guess it is kind of funny,' Judy said, smiling. 'But it didn't seem that way last night, I can tell you.'

Ginny coughed and swallowed. 'I don't mean to be cruel,' she said when she had recovered. 'I can see it wasn't too hilarious at the time. What he did was really sleazy, dating you and sleeping with his wife.'

'To me, it shows that he's not over her,' Judy said. 'So he's not ready for a new relationship.'

Ginny made a doubtful face. 'I don't necessarily buy that.'

'You think it was like a goodbye, one last embrace for old times' sake?'

'Maybe even simpler. You know, men almost never say no to a fuck if it's offered to them. It sounds as if

THE HAMMER OF EDEN

he's been living the life of a monk since she left him. His hormones are probably giving him hell. She's attractive, you say?'

'Very sexy-looking.'

'So if she walked in wearing a tight sweater and started making moves on him, he probably couldn't help getting a hard-on. And once that happens, a man's brain cuts out and the autopilot in his dick takes control.'

'You think so?'

'Listen, I've never met Michael, but I've known some men, good and bad, and that's my take on the scenario.'

'What would you do?'

'I'd talk to him. Ask him why he did it. See what he says. See if I believed him. If he gave me a line of bullshit, I'd forget him. But if he seemed honest, I'd try to make some kind of sense of the whole incident.'

'I have to call him anyway,' Judy said. 'He still hasn't sent me that list.'

'So call. Get the list. Then ask him what he thinks he's doing. You're feeling embarrassed, but he has something to apologize for, too.'

'I guess you're right.'

It was not yet eight o'clock, but they were both in a hurry to get to work. Judy paid the check and they went out to their cars. 'Boy,' Judy said, 'I'm beginning to feel better about this. Thank you.'

Ginny shrugged. 'What are girlfriends for? Let me know what he says.'

Judy got into her car and dialled Michael's number.

She was afraid he might be asleep, and she would find herself talking to him while he was in bed with his wife. However, his voice sounded alert, as if he had been up for a while. 'I'm sorry about your door,' she said.

'Why did you do it?' He sounded more curious than angry.

'I couldn't understand why you didn't answer. Then I heard a scream. I thought you must be in some kind of trouble.'

'What brought you here so late?'

'You didn't send me that list of earthquake sites.'

'Oh, that's right! It's on my desk. I just forgot. I'll fax it now.'

'Thanks.' She gave him the fax number of the new Emergency Operations Center. 'Michael, there's something I have to ask you.' She took a deep breath. Asking this question was harder than she had anticipated. She was no shrinking violet, but she was not as brash as Ginny. She swallowed and said: 'You gave me the impression you were growing fond of me. Why did you sleep with your wife?' There. It was out.

At the other end of the line there was a long silence. Then he said: 'This is not a good time.'

'Okay.' She tried to keep the disappointment out of her voice.

'I'll send that list right away.'

'Thanks.'

She hung up and started the engine. Ginny's idea had not been so great after all. It took two to talk, and Michael was not willing.

When she reached the officers' club, Michael's fax was waiting for her. She showed it to Carl Theobald. 'We need surveillance teams at each of these locations, watching out for a seismic vibrator,' she said. 'I was hoping to use the police, but I don't think we can. They might talk. And if local people find out that we think they're a target, they'll panic. So we have to use FBI personnel.'

'Okay.' Carl frowned at the sheet. 'You know, these locations are awful big. One team can't really watch an area a mile square. Should we put on multiple teams? Or could your seismologist narrow it down?'

'I'll ask him.' Judy picked up the phone and dialled Michael again. 'Thanks for the fax,' she said. She explained the problem.

'I'd have to visit the sites myself,' he said. 'Signs of earlier earthquake activity, such as dried-up stream beds or fault scarps, would give me a more precise fix.'

'Would you do that today?' she said immediately. 'I can take you to all the locations in an FBI helicopter.'

'Uh . . . sure, I guess,' he said. 'I mean, of course I will.'

'You could be saving lives.'

'Exactly.'

'Can you find your way to the officers' club in the Presidio?'

'Sure.'

'By the time you get here, the chopper will be waiting.'

'Okay.'

'I appreciate this, Michael.'

'You're welcome.'
But I'd still like to know why you slept with your wife.
She hung up.

*

It was a long day. Judy, Michael, and Carl Theobald covered a thousand miles in the helicopter. By nightfall they had set up round-the-clock surveillance at the five locations on Michael's list.

They returned to the Presidio. The helicopter landed on the deserted parade ground. The base was a ghost town, with its mouldering office buildings and rows of vacant houses.

Judy had to go into the Emergency Operations Center and report to a big shot from FBI headquarters in Washington who had shown up at nine o'clock that morning with a take-charge air. But first she walked Michael to his car in the darkened parking lot. 'What if they slip through the surveillance?' she said.

'I thought your people were good.'

'They're the best. But what if? Is there some way I can get notified real fast if there's a tremor anywhere in California?'

'Sure,' he said. 'I could set up on-line seismography right here at your command post. I just need a computer and an ISDN phone line.'

'No problem. Would you do it tomorrow?'

'Okay. That way, you'll know immediately if they start the seismic vibrator someplace that's not on the list.'

'Is that likely?'

'I don't think so. If their seismologist is competent, he'll pick the same places I picked. And if he's incompetent they probably won't be able to trigger an earthquake.'

'Good,' she said. 'Good.' She would remember that. She could tell the Washington big shot that she had the crisis under control.

She looked up at Michael's shadowed face. 'Why did you sleep with your wife?'

'I've been thinking about that all day.'

'Me too.'

'I guess I owe you some kind of explanation.'

'I think so.'

'Until yesterday I was sure it was over. Then, last night, she reminded me of the things that had been good about our marriage. She was beautiful, fun, affectionate, and sexy. More important, she made me forget all the things that were bad.'

'Such as?'

He sighed. 'I think Melanie is drawn to authority figures. I was her professor. She wants the security of being told what to do. I expected an equal partner, someone who would share decisions and take responsibility. She resented that.'

'I get the picture.'

'And there's something else. Deep down, she's mad as hell at the whole world. Most of the time she hides it, but when she's frustrated she can be violent. She would throw things at me, heavy things, like a casserole dish one time. She never hurt me, she's just not strong enough, though if there was a gun in the house I'd be scared. But that level of hostility is hard to live with.'

'And last night . . .?'

'I forgot all that. She seemed to want to try again, and I thought maybe we should, for Dusty's sake. Plus . . .'

She wished she could read his expression, but it was too dark. 'What?'

'I want to tell you the truth, Judy, even though you'll be offended by it. So I have to admit that it wasn't as rational and decent as I'm pretending. Part of it was that she's a beautiful woman and I wanted to fuck her. Now I've said it.'

She smiled in the dark. Ginny had been half right, anyway. 'I knew that,' she said. 'But I'm glad you told me. Goodnight.' She walked away.

'Goodnight,' he said, sounding bewildered.

A few moments later he called after her: 'Are you angry?'

'No,' she said over her shoulder. 'Not any more.'

*

Priest expected Melanie to return to the commune around mid-afternoon. When suppertime came and she still had not arrived, he started to worry.

By nightfall he was frantic. What had happened to her? Had she decided to go back to her husband? Had she confessed everything to him? Was she even now spilling the beans to Agent Judy Maddox in an interrogation room at the Federal Building in San Francisco?

He could not sit still in the cookhouse or lie on his

bed. He took a candle lamp and walked across the vineyard and through the woods to the parking circle and waited there, listening for the engine of her old Subaru—or the throb of the FBI helicopter that would herald the end of everything.

Spirit heard it first. He cocked his ears, tensed, then ran up the mud road, barking. Priest stood up, straining his hearing. It was the Subaru. Relief swamped him. He watched the lights approach through the trees. He had the beginnings of a headache. He had not had a headache for years.

Melanie parked erratically, got out, and slammed the car door.

'I hate you,' she said to Priest. 'I hate you for making me do that.'

'Was I right?' he said. 'Is Michael making a list for the FBI?'

'Fuck you!'

Priest realized he had goofed. He should have been understanding and sympathetic. For a moment he had allowed his anxiety to cloud his judgement. Now he would have to spend time talking her around. 'I asked you to do it because I love you, don't you understand that?'

'No, I don't. I don't understand anything.' She folded her arms across her chest and turned away from him, staring into the darkness of the woods. 'All I know is, I feel like a prostitute.'

Priest was bursting to know what she had found out, but he made himself calm. 'Where have you been?' he said.

'Driving around. I stopped for a drink.'

He was silent for a minute. Then he said: 'A prostitute does it for money—then she spends the money on stupid clothes and drugs. You did it to save your child. I know you feel bad, but you're not bad. You're good.'

At last she turned to him. There were tears in her eyes. 'It's not just that we had sex,' she said. 'It's worse than that. I liked it. That's what makes me feel ashamed. I came. I really did. I screamed.'

Priest felt a hot wave of jealousy and strained to suppress it. He would make Michael Quercus suffer for that, one day. But now was not the time to say so. He needed to cool things down here. 'It's okay,' he murmured. 'Really, it's okay. I understand. Weird things happen.' He put his arms around her and hugged her.

Slowly she relaxed. He could feel the tension leaving her bit by bit. 'You don't mind?' she said. 'You're not mad?'

'Not a bit,' he lied, stroking her long hair. *Come on, come on!*

'You were right about the list,' she said.

At last.

'That FBI woman had asked Michael to work out the best locations for an earthquake, just the way you imagined it.'

Of course she did. I'm so damn smart.

Melanie went on: 'He was sitting at his computer when I got there, just finishing.'

'So what happened?'

'I made him dinner, and stuff like that.'

Priest could imagine. If Melanie decided to be seductive, she was irresistible. And she was at her most alluring when she wanted something. She probably took a bath and put on a robe, then moved around the apartment smelling of soap and flowers, pouring wine or making coffee, letting the robe fall open now and again to show him tantalizing glimpses of her long legs and her soft breasts. She would have asked Michael questions and listened intently to his answers, smiling at him in a way that said, *I like you so much, you can do anything you want with me.*

'When the phone rang I told him not to answer, then I took it off the hook. But the damn woman came over anyway, and when Michael didn't answer the door she broke it down. Boy, did she have a shock.' Priest figured she needed to get all this off her chest, so he did not hurry her. 'She almost died of embarrassment.'

'Did he give her the list?'

'Not then. I guess she was too confused to ask. But she called this morning, and he faxed it to her.'

'And did you get it?'

'While he was in the shower, I got to his computer and printed out another copy.'

So where the hell is it?

She reached into the back pocket of her jeans, pulled out a single sheet of paper folded in four, and gave it to Priest.

Thank God.

He unfolded it and looked at it in the light of the

lamp. The typed letters and numbers meant nothing to him. 'These are the places he's told her to watch?'

'Yes, they're going to stake out each of these locations, looking for a seismic vibrator, just the way you predicted.'

Judy Maddox was clever. The FBI surveillance would make it very difficult for him to operate the seismic vibrator, especially if he had to try several different locations, as he had in Owens Valley.

But he was even cleverer than Judy. He had anticipated this move by her. And he had thought of a way around it. 'You understand how Michael picked these sites?' he said.

'Sure. They're the places where the tension in the fault is highest.'

'So you could do the same thing.'

'I already have. And I picked the same places he did.'

He folded the paper and gave it back to her. 'Now, listen very carefully. This is important. Could you look over the data again and pick the five *next* best locations?'

'Yes.'

'And could we cause an earthquake at one of them?'

'Probably,' she said. 'It's maybe not as sure, but the chances are good.'

'Then that's what we'll do. Tomorrow we'll take a look at the new sites. Right after I talk to Mr Honeymoon.'

CHAPTER SIXTEEN

AT 5 A.M., the guard at the entrance to the Los Alamos place was yawning.

He became alert when Melanie and Priest pulled up in the 'Cuda. Priest got out of the car. 'How are you, buddy?' he said as he walked across to the gate.

The guard hefted his rifle, assumed a mean expression, and said: 'Who are you and what do you want?'

Priest hit him in the face very hard, crushing his nose. Blood spurted. The guard cried out, his hands flying to his face. Priest said: 'Ow!' His fist hurt. It was a long time since he had punched anyone.

His instincts took over. He kicked the guard's legs from under him. The man fell on his back, and his rifle went flying through the air. Priest kicked him in the ribs three or four times, fast and hard, trying to break the bones. Then he kicked his face and head. The man curled up in a ball, sobbing in pain, helpless with fear.

Priest stopped, breathing hard. It all came back to him in a flood of remembered excitement. There had been a time when he had done this sort of thing every day. It was so easy to frighten people when you knew how.

He knelt down and took the handgun from the man's belt. This was what he had come for.

He looked at the weapon in disgust. It was a reproduction of a long-barrelled .44 calibre Remington revolver originally manufactured in the days of the Wild West. It was a stupid, impractical firearm, the kind owned by collectors and kept in a felt-lined display case in the den. It was not for shooting people.

He broke it open. It was loaded.

That was all he really cared about.

He returned to the car and got in. Melanie was at the wheel. She was pale and bright-eyed, breathing fast, as if she had just taken cocaine. Priest guessed she had never witnessed serious violence. 'Will he be okay?' she said in an excited voice.

Priest glanced back at the guard. He was lying on the ground, his hands to his face, rocking slightly. 'Sure he will,' Priest said.

'Wow.'

'Let's go to Sacramento.'

Melanie pulled away.

After a while, she said: 'Do you really think you can talk this Honeymoon guy around?'

'He's got to see sense,' Priest said, sounding more confident than he felt. 'Look at the choice he has. Number one, an earthquake that will do millions of dollars of damage. Or, number two, a sensible proposal to reduce pollution. Plus, if he picks number one, he faces the same choice all over again two days later. He has to take the easy road.'

'I guess,' Melanie said.

They reached Sacramento a few minutes before 7 a.m. The state capital was quiet this early. A few cars and trucks moved unhurriedly along the broad empty boulevards. Melanie parked near the Capitol building. Priest put on a baseball cap and tucked his long hair up inside it. Then he donned sunglasses. 'Wait for me right here,' he said. 'I may be a couple of hours.'

Priest walked around the Capitol block. He had hoped there would be a surface-level parking lot, but he was disappointed. The ground around was all garden, with magnificent trees. On either side of the building, a ramp led down to an underground garage. Both ramps were monitored by security guards in sentry booths.

Priest approached one of the large imposing doors. The building was open, and there was no security check at the entrance. He went into a grand hall with a mosaic-tiled floor.

He took off the sunglasses, which looked conspicuous indoors, and followed a staircase down to the basement. There was a coffee shop where a few early workers were getting a charge of caffeine. He walked past them, looking as if he belonged here, and followed a corridor he thought must lead to the parking garage. As he approached the end of the corridor, a door opened and a fat man in a blue blazer came through. Behind the man, Priest saw cars.

Bingo.

He slipped into the garage and looked around. It was almost empty. There were a few cars, a sport utility, and a sheriff's car parked in the marked spaces. He saw no one.

He slipped behind the back of the sport utility. It was a Dodge Durango. From here, peering through the car windows, he could see the entrance to the garage and the door that led inside the building. Other cars parked either side of the Durango would shield him from the gaze of new arrivals.

He settled to wait. *This is their last chance. There's still time to negotiate and avoid a catastrophe. But if this doesn't work . . . boom.*

Al Honeymoon was a workaholic, Priest figured. He would arrive early. But there was a lot that could go wrong. Honeymoon could be spending the day at the governor's residence. He might call in sick today. Perhaps he had meetings in Washington; maybe he was on a trip to Europe; his wife could be having a baby.

Priest did not think he would have a bodyguard. He was not an elected politician, just a government employee. Would he have a chauffeur? Priest had no idea. That would spoil everything.

A car pulled in every few minutes. Priest studied the drivers from his hiding place. He did not have to wait long. At seven thirty a smart dark blue Lincoln Continental drove in. Behind the wheel was a black man in a white shirt and tie. It was Honeymoon: Priest recognized him from the newspaper photos.

The car pulled into a slot near the Durango. Priest

put on his sunglasses, crossed the garage swiftly, opened the nearside door of the Lincoln, and slid into the passenger seat before Honeymoon could get his seat belt off. He showed him the gun. 'Pull out of the garage,' he said.

Honeymoon stared at him. 'Who the hell are you?'

Arrogant son of a bitch in a chalk-stripe suit with a pin through the collar of your shirt, I'll ask the frigging questions.

Priest cocked the hammer of the revolver. 'I'm the maniac who's going to put a bullet in your guts unless you do as I say. Now drive.'

'Fuck,' Honeymoon said feelingly. 'Fuck.' Then he started the car and pulled out of the garage.

'Smile nicely at the security guard and drive slowly by,' Priest said. 'You say one word to him and I'll kill him.'

Honeymoon did not reply. He slowed the car as it approached the sentry booth. For a moment, Priest thought he was going to try something. Then they saw the guard, a middle-aged black man with white hair. Priest said: 'If you want this brother to die, just go ahead with what's on your mind.'

Honeymoon cursed under his breath and drove on.

'Take Capitol Mall out of town,' Priest told him.

Honeymoon drove around the Capitol building and headed west on the broad avenue that led to the Sacramento River. 'What do you want?' he said. He hardly seemed afraid—more impatient.

Priest would have liked to shoot him. This was the asshole who had made the dam possible. He had done his best to ruin Priest's life. And he was not a bit sorry.

He really did not care. A bullet in the guts was hardly punishment enough.

Controlling his anger, Priest said: 'I want to save people's lives.'

'You're the Hammer of Eden guy, right?'

Priest did not answer. Honeymoon was staring at him. Priest guessed he was trying to memorize his features. *Smartass.* 'Watch the goddam road.'

Honeymoon looked ahead.

They crossed the bridge. Priest said: 'Take I-80 toward San Francisco.'

'Where are we going?'

'You ain't going nowhere.'

Honeymoon pulled on to the freeway.

'Drive at fifty in the slow lane. Why the hell won't you give me what I'm asking for?' Priest had intended to stay cool, but Honeymoon's arrogant calm enraged him. 'Do you *want* a frigging earthquake?'

Honeymoon was deadpan. 'The governor can't give in to blackmail, you must know that.'

'You can get around that problem,' Priest argued. 'Give out that you were planning a freeze anyway.'

'No one would believe us. It would be political suicide for the governor.'

'Would it hell. You can fool the public. What are spin doctors for?'

'I'm the best there is, but I can't do miracles. This is too high profile. You shouldn't have brought John Truth into it.'

Priest said angrily: 'No one listened to us until John Truth got on the case!'

'Well, whatever the reason, this is now a public face-off, and the governor can't back down. If he did, the state of California would be open to blackmail by every idiot with a hunting rifle in his hand and a bug up his ass about some damn cause. But *you* could back off.'

The bastard is trying to talk me around!

Priest said: 'Take the first exit and head back into town.'

Honeymoon indicated right and went on talking: 'Nobody knows who you people are or where to find you. If you drop the whole thing now, you can get away with it. No real harm has been done. But if you set off another earthquake, you'll have every law enforcement agency in the United States after you, and they won't give up until they find you. No one can hide for ever.'

Priest was angered. 'Don't you threaten me!' he yelled. 'I'm the one with the motherfucking gun!'

'I haven't forgotten that. I'm trying to get us both out of this without further damage.'

Honeymoon had somehow taken control of the conversation. Priest felt sick with frustration. 'You listen to me,' he said. 'There's only one way out of this. Make an announcement, today. No more power plant building in California.'

'I can't do that.'

'Pull over.'

'We're on the freeway.'

'Pull the fuck over!'

Honeymoon slowed the car and stopped on the shoulder of the road.

The temptation to shoot was strong, but Priest resisted it. 'Get out of the car.'

Honeymoon put the shift in Park and got out.

Priest slid over behind the wheel. 'You got until midnight to see sense,' he said. He pulled away.

In the rear-view mirror he saw Honeymoon try to wave down a passing car. It drove right by. He tried again. No one would stop.

Seeing the big man in his expensive suit and shiny shoes, standing at the dusty roadside trying to get a ride, gave Priest a small measure of satisfaction, and helped to quell the nagging suspicion that Honeymoon had somehow got the better of the encounter, even though Priest had held the gun.

Honeymoon gave up waving at cars and began to walk.

Priest smiled and drove on into town.

Melanie was waiting where he had left her. He parked the Lincoln, leaving the keys in, and got into the 'Cuda.

'What happened?' Melanie said.

Priest shook his head in disgust. 'Nothing,' he said angrily. 'It was a waste of time. Let's go.'

She started the car and pulled away.

*

Priest rejected the first location Melanie took him to.

It was a small seaside town fifty miles north of San Francisco. They parked on the cliff top, where a stiff breeze rocked the old 'Cuda on its tired springs. Priest

410

rolled down the window to smell the sea. He would have liked to take off his boots and walk barefoot along the beach, feeling the damp sand between his toes, but there was no time.

The location was very exposed. The truck would be too conspicuous here. It was a long distance from the freeway, so there could be no quick getaway. Most important of all, there was not much of value here to be destroyed—just a few houses clustered around a harbour.

Melanie said: 'An earthquake sometimes does the greatest damage many miles from its epicenter.'

'But you can't be sure of that,' Priest said.

'True. You can't be sure of anything.'

'Still, the best way to bring down a skyscraper is to have an earthquake underneath it, am I right?'

'All other things being equal, yes.'

They drove south through the green hills of Marin county and across the Golden Gate bridge. Melanie's second location was in the heart of the city. They followed Route 1 through the Presidio and Golden Gate Park, and pulled up not far from the San Francisco campus of Cal State University.

'This is better,' Priest said immediately. All around him were homes and offices, stores and restaurants.

'A tremor with its epicenter here would cause most damage at the Marina,' Melanie said.

'How come? That's miles away.'

'It's all reclaimed land. The underlying sedimentary deposits are saturated with water. That amplifies the shaking. Whereas the ground here is probably solid. And these buildings look strong. Most buildings survive an earthquake. The ones that fall down are made of unreinforced masonry—typically low-income housing —or concrete-frame structures without bracing.'

This was all quibbling, Priest decided. She was just nervous. *An earthquake is a frigging earthquake, for Christ's sake. No one knows what's going to fall down. I don't care, so long as something does.*

'Let's look at another place,' he said.

Melanie directed him south on Interstate 280. 'Right where the San Andreas fault crosses Route 101, there's a small town called Felicitas,' she said.

They drove for twenty minutes. They almost passed the exit ramp for Felicitas. 'Here, here!' Melanie yelled. 'Didn't you see the sign?'

Priest wrenched the wheel to the right and made the ramp. 'I wasn't looking,' he said.

The exit led to a vantage point overlooking the town. Priest stopped the car and got out. Felicitas was laid out in front of him like a picture. Main Street ran from left to right across his field of vision, lined with low clapboard stores and offices, a few cars parked slantwise in front of the buildings. There was a small wooden church with a bell tower. North and south of the main drag was a neat grid of tree-lined streets. All the houses were one-storey. At either end of the town, the street became a pre-freeway country road and disappeared among fields. The landscape north of the town was split by a meandering river like a jagged crack in a window. In the distance was a railroad track as straight as a draughtsman's line from east to west. Behind Priest, the freeway ran along a viaduct on high concrete arches.

Stepping down the hill was a cluster of six huge bright-blue pipes. They dipped under the freeway, passed the town to the west, and disappeared over the horizon, looking like an infinite xylophone. 'What the hell is that?' Priest said.

Melanie thought for a moment. 'I think it must be a gas pipeline.'

Priest breathed a long sigh of satisfaction. 'This place is perfect,' he said.

*

They made one more stop that day.

After the earthquake, Priest would need to hide the seismic vibrator. His only weapon was the threat of more earthquakes. He had to make Honeymoon and Governor Robson believe he had the power to do this again and again until they gave in. So it was crucial that he kept the truck hidden away.

It was going to become more and more difficult to drive the vibrator on the public roads, so he needed to hide it some place where he could, if necessary, trigger a third earthquake without moving far.

Melanie directed him to 3rd Street, which ran parallel with the shore of the huge natural harbour that was San Francisco Bay. Between 3rd and the waterfront was a rundown industrial neighbourhood. There were disused railroad tracks along the potholed streets; rusting, derelict factories; empty warehouses with smashed windows; and dismal yards full of pallets, tyres, and wrecked cars.

'This is good,' Priest said. 'It's only half an hour from Felicitas, and it's the kind of district where nobody takes much interest in their neighbours.'

Realtors' signs were optimistically fixed to some of the buildings. Melanie, posing as Priest's secretary, called the number on one of the signs and asked if they had a warehouse to rent, real cheap, about fifteen hundred square feet.

An eager young salesman drove out to meet them an hour later. He showed them a crumbling cinder-block ruin with holes in the corrugated roof. There was a broken sign over the door which Melanie read aloud: 'Perpetua Diaries.' There was plenty of room to park the seismic vibrator. The place also had a working bathroom and a small office with a hotplate and a big old Zenith TV left by the previous tenant.

Priest told the salesman he needed a place to store barrels of wine for a month or so. The man did not give a damn what Priest wanted to do with the space. He was delighted to get some rent on a near-valueless property. He promised to have the power and water turned on tomorrow. Priest paid him four weeks' rent in advance, cash, from the secret stash he kept in his old guitar.

The salesman looked like it was his lucky day. He gave Melanie the keys, shook hands, and hurried away before Priest could change his mind.

Priest and Melanie drove back to Silver River Valley.

*

Thursday evening, Judy Maddox took a bath. Lying in the water, she remembered the Santa Rosa earthquake that had so frightened her when she was in first grade. It came back to her as vividly as if it were yesterday. Nothing could be more terrifying than to find that the ground beneath your feet was not fixed and stable but treacherous and deadly. Sometimes, in quiet moments, she saw nightmare visions of multiple car wrecks, bridges collapsing, buildings falling down, fires and floods—but none of these were as dreadful to her as the recollection of her own terror at six years of age.

She washed her hair and thrust the memory to the back of her mind. Then she packed an overnight bag and went back to the officers' club at 10 p.m.

The command post was quiet, but the atmosphere was tense. Still no one knew for certain whether the Hammer of Eden could cause an earthquake. But since Ricky Granger had abducted Al Honeymoon at gunpoint in the garage of the Capitol building and left him stranded on I-80, everyone was sure these terrorists were dead serious.

There were now more than a hundred people in the old ballroom. The on-scene commander was Stuart Cleever, the big shot who had flown in from Washington on Tuesday night. Despite Honeymoon's orders, there was no way the Bureau was going to let a lowly agent take overall charge of something this big. Judy did not want total control and she had not argued about it. However, she had been able to ensure that neither Brian Kincaid nor Marvin Hayes was directly involved.

Judy's title was Investigative Operations Coordinator. That gave her all the control she needed. Alongside her was Charlie Marsh, Emergency Operations Co-ordinator, in command of the SWAT team who were on standby in the next room. Charlie was a man of about forty-five with a grizzled crew-cut. He was ex-army, a fitness freak and a gun collector, not the type Judy normally liked, but he was straightforward and reliable, and she could work with him.

Between the Head Shed and the investigation team table were Michael Quercus and his young seismologists, sitting at their screens, watching for signs of earthquake activity. Michael had gone home for a couple of hours, like Judy. He came back wearing clean khakis and a black polo shirt, carrying a sports duffel, ready for a long spell.

They had talked, during the day, about practical matters, as he set up his equipment and introduced his helpers. At first they had been awkward with one another, but Judy realized he was quickly getting over his feelings of anger and guilt about Tuesday's incident. She felt she ought to sulk about it for a day or two but she was too busy. So the whole thing got shoved to the back of her mind, and she found herself enjoying having Michael around.

She was trying to think of an excuse to talk to him when the phone on her desk rang.

She picked it up. 'Judy Maddox.'

The operator said: 'A call for you from Ricky Granger.'

'Trace it!' she snapped. It would take the operator only seconds to contact Pacific Bell's twenty-four-hour security center. She waved at Cleever and Marsh, indicating that they should listen.

'You got it,' the operator said. 'Shall I connect you or leave him on hold?'

'Put him on. Tape the call.' There was a click. 'Judy Maddox here.'

A male voice said: 'You're smart, Agent Maddox. But are you smart enough to make the governor see sense?'

He sounded irate, frustrated. Judy imagined a man of about fifty, thin, badly dressed, but accustomed to being listened to. He was losing his grip on life and feeling resentful, she speculated.

She said: 'Am I speaking to Ricky Granger?'

'You know who you're speaking to. Why are they forcing me to cause another earthquake?'

'*Forcing* you? Are you kidding yourself that all this is someone *else's* fault?'

This seemed to make him angrier. 'It's not me who's using more and more electric power every year,' he said. 'I don't want more power plants. I don't use electricity.'

'You don't?' *Really?* 'So what's powering your phone—steam?' *A cult that doesn't use electricity. That's a clue.* While she taunted him, she was trying to figure out what this meant. *But where are they?*

'Don't fuck with me, Judy. You're the one that's in trouble.'

Next to her, Charlie's phone rang. He snatched it up and wrote in large letters on his notepad: *Pay phone—Oakland—I-980 & I-580—Texaco.*

'We're all in trouble, Ricky,' she said in a more reasonable voice. Charlie went to the map on the wall. She heard him say the word *roadblocks.*

'Your voice changed,' Granger said suspiciously. 'What happened?'

Judy felt out of her depth. She had no special training in negotiating skills. All she knew was that she had to keep him on the phone. 'I suddenly thought what a catastrophe there will be if you and I don't manage to come to some agreement,' she said.

She could hear Charlie giving urgent orders in a low voice: 'Call the Oakland PD, Alameda county sheriff's office, and the California Highway Patrol.'

'You're bullshitting me,' Granger said. 'Have you traced this call already? Jeeze, that was fast. Are you trying to keep me on the line while your SWAT team comes after me? Forget it! I got a hundred and fifty ways out of here!'

'But only one way out of the jam you're in.'

'It's past midnight,' he said. 'Your time is up. I'm going to cause another earthquake, and there's not one damn thing you can do to stop me.' He hung up.

Judy slammed down the phone. 'Let's go, Charlie!' She ripped the E-fit picture of Granger off the subject board and ran outside. The helicopter was waiting on

418

the parade ground, its rotors turning. She jumped in, with Charlie close behind.

As they took off, he put on headphones and motioned to her to do the same. 'I figure it'll take twenty minutes to get the roadblocks in place,' he said. 'Assume he's driving at sixty, to avoid being stopped for speeding, he could be twenty miles away by the time we're ready for him. So I've ordered the major freeways closed in a twenty-five-mile radius.'

'What about other roads?'

'We have to hope he's going a long way. If he gets off the freeway, we lose him. This is one of the busiest road networks in California. You couldn't seal it off watertight if you had the goddam US army.'

*

Turning on to I-80, Priest heard the throb of a helicopter, and looked up to see it passing overhead, coming from San Francisco across the bay toward Oakland. 'Shit,' he said. 'They can't be after us, can they?'

'I told you,' Melanie said. 'They can trace phone calls, like, instantly.'

'But what are they going to do? They don't even know which way we headed when we left the gas station!'

'They could close the freeway, I guess.'

'Which one? Nine-eighty, eight-eighty, five-eighty, or eighty? North or south?'

'Maybe all of them. You know cops, they do what they like.'

'Shit.' Priest put his foot down.

'Don't get stopped for goddam speeding.'

'Okay, okay!' He slowed down again.

'Can't we get off the freeway?'

He shook his head. 'No other way home. There are side roads, but they don't cross the water. All we could do is hole up in Berkeley. Park somewhere and sleep in the car. But we don't have time, we have to get home to get the seismic vibrator.' He shook his head. 'Nothing to do but run for it.'

The traffic thinned as they left Oakland and Berkeley behind. Priest peered into the darkness ahead, alert for flashing lights. He was relieved to reach the Carquinez Bridge. Once they were across the water, they could use country roads. It might take them half the night to get home but they would be out of danger.

He approached the toll plaza slowly, scanning for signs of police activity. Only one booth was open, but that was not surprising after midnight. No blue lights, no cruisers, no cops. He pulled up and fished in his jeans pocket for change.

When he looked up he saw a highway patrol officer.

Priest's heart seemed to stop.

The cop was in the booth, behind the attendant, staring at Priest with a surprised expression.

The toll attendant took Priest's money but did not turn on the green light.

The officer stepped quickly out of the booth.

Melanie said: 'Shit! What now?'

Priest considered making a run for it, but quickly decided against. That would just start a chase. His old car could not outrun the cops.

'Good evening, sir,' the officer said. He was a fat man of about fifty wearing a bulletproof vest over his uniform. 'Please pull over to the right side of the road.'

Priest did as he said. A highway patrol car was parked beside the road, where it could not be seen from the other side of the toll plaza.

Melanie whispered: 'What are you going to do?'

'Try to stay calm,' Priest said.

There was another officer waiting in the parked car. He got out when he saw Priest pull up. He, too, was wearing a bulletproof vest. The first officer came over from the toll booth.

Priest opened the glove box and took out the revolver he had stolen this morning from Los Alamos.

Then he got out of the car.

*

It took Judy only a few minutes to reach the Texaco gas station from which the phone call had been made. The Oakland police had moved fast. In the parking lot, four cruisers were parked at the corners of a square, facing inward, their blue roof lights flashing, their headlamps illuminating a cleared landing space. The chopper came down.

Judy jumped out. A police sergeant greeted her. 'Take me to the phone,' she said. He led her inside. The pay phone was in a corner next to the rest rooms.

Behind the counter were two clerks, a middle-aged black woman and a young white man with an earring. They looked scared. Judy asked the sergeant: 'Have you questioned them at all?'

'Nope,' he said. 'Just told them it was a routine search.'

They would have to be dumb to believe that, Judy thought, with four police cars and an FBI helicopter outside. She introduced herself and said: 'Did you notice anyone using that phone around—' she checked her watch '—fifteen minutes ago?'

The woman said: 'A lot of people use the phone.' Judy instantly got the sense that she did not like cops.

Judy looked at the young man. 'I'm talking about a tall white man about fifty.'

'There was a guy like that,' he replied. He turned to the woman. 'Didn't you notice him? He looked kind of like an old hippie.'

'I never saw him,' she replied stubbornly.

Judy produced the E-fit picture. 'Could this be him?'

The young man looked dubious. 'He didn't have glasses. And his hair was real long. That's why I thought he must be a hippie.' He looked more closely. 'It could be him, though.'

The woman looked hard at the picture. 'I remember now,' she said. 'I believe that is him. Skinny guy wearing a blue-jean shirt.'

'That's really helpful,' Judy said gratefully. 'Now,

this question is really important. What kind of car was he driving?'

'I didn't look,' the man said. 'You know how many cars come through here every day? And it's dark now.'

Judy looked at the woman, who shook her head sadly. 'Honey, you're asking the wrong person—I can't tell the difference between a Ford and a Cadillac.'

Judy could not hide her disappointment. 'Hell,' she said. She pulled herself together. 'Thanks anyway, folks.'

She stepped outside. 'Any other witnesses?' she said to the sergeant.

'Nope. There may have been other customers in here at the same time, but they're long gone. Only those two work here.'

Charlie Marsh came hurrying up with a mobile phone to his ear. 'Granger's been spotted,' he said to Judy. 'Two CHPs stopped him at the toll plaza at Carquinez Bridge.'

'Incredible!' Judy said. Then something about Charlie's face made her realize the news could not be good. 'We have him in custody?'

'No,' Charlie said. 'He shot them. They were wearing vests, but he shot them both in the head. He got away.'

'Did we get a make on his car?'

'No. Tollbooth attendant didn't notice.'

Judy could not keep the note of despair out of her voice. 'Then he's got clean away?'

'Yeah.'

'And the two highway patrol officers?'

'Both dead.'

The police sergeant paled. 'God rest their souls,' he whispered.

Judy turned away, sick with disgust. 'And God help us catch Ricky Granger,' she said. 'Before he kills anyone else.'

CHAPTER SEVENTEEN

OAKTREE HAD done a great job of making the seismic vibrator look like a carnival ride.

The gaily painted red-and-yellow panels of the Dragon's Mouth completely concealed the massive steel plate, the large vibrating engine, and the complex of tanks and valves that controlled the machine. As Priest drove across the state on Friday afternoon, from the foothills of the Sierra Nevada through the Sacramento Valley to the coastal range, other drivers smiled and honked in a friendly way, and children waved from the rear windows of station wagons.

The highway patrol ignored him.

Priest drove the truck with Melanie beside him. Star and Oaktree followed in the old 'Cuda. They reached Felicitas in the early evening. The seismic window would open a few minutes after 7 p.m. It was a good time: Priest would have twilight for his getaway. Plus, the FBI and the cops had now been on alert for eighteen hours—they should be getting tired, their reactions slow. They might already be starting to believe there would be no earthquake.

He pulled off the freeway and stopped the truck. At the end of the exit ramp there was a gas station and a

Big Ribs restaurant where several families were eating dinner. The kids stared through the windows at the carnival ride. Next to the restaurant was a field with five or six horses grazing, then came a low glass office building. The road leading from here into town was lined with houses, and Priest could also see a school and a small wood-frame building that looked like a Baptist chapel.

Melanie said: 'The fault line runs right across Main Street.'

'How can you tell?'

'Look at the sidewalk trees.' There was a line of mature pines on the far side of the street. 'The trees at the western end stand about five feet further back than those to the east.'

Sure enough, Priest saw that the line was broken about halfway along the street. West of the break, the trees grew in the middle of the sidewalk instead of at the kerb.

Priest turned on the truck's radio. The John Truth show was just beginning. 'Perfect,' he said.

The newsreader said: 'A top aide to Governor Mike Robson was abducted in Sacramento in a bizarre incident yesterday. The kidnapper accosted Cabinet Secretary Al Honeymoon in the parking garage of the Capitol building, forced him to drive out of town, then abandoned him on I-80.'

Priest said: 'You notice they don't mention the Hammer of Eden? They know that was me in Sacramento. But they're trying to pretend it had nothing to do with us. They think they're preventing panic.

426

They're wasting their time. In twenty minutes there's going to be the biggest panic California has ever seen.'

'All right!' Melanie said. She was tense but excited, her face flushed, her eyes bright with hope and fear.

But, secretly, Priest's mind was full of doubt. *Will it work this time?*

Only one way to find out.

He put the truck in gear and drove down the hill.

The link road from the freeway looped around and joined the old country road leading into the town from the east. Priest swung on to Main Street. There was a coffee shop right on the fault line. Priest pulled on to the parking apron in front. The 'Cuda slid in beside the truck. 'Go buy some donuts,' he told Melanie. 'Look natural.'

She jumped out and sauntered across to the coffee shop.

Priest engaged the parking brake and flicked the switch that lowered the hammer of the seismic vibrator to the ground.

A uniformed cop came out of the coffee shop.

Priest said: 'Shit.'

The cop was carrying a paper bag and heading purposefully across the lot. Priest guessed he had stopped off to get coffee for himself and his partner. But where was the patrol car? Priest looked around and spotted the blue-and-white roof light of a car that was mostly concealed by a minivan. He had not noticed it as he drove in. He cursed himself for inattention.

But it was too late for regrets. The cop spotted the

truck, changed direction, and came over to Priest's window.

'Hi, how you doin' today?' the cop said in a friendly tone. He was a tall, thin boy in his early twenties with short fair hair.

'I'm just fine,' Priest said. *Small-town cops, they act like they're everyone's next-door neighbour.* 'How are you?'

'You know you can't operate that ride without a permit, don't you?'

'Same everywhere,' Priest told him. 'But we're aiming to set up in Pismo Beach. We just stopped for coffee, same as you.'

'Okay. Enjoy the rest of your day.'

'You too.'

The cop walked off, and Priest shook his head in amazement. *If you realized who I am, buddy, you'd choke on your chocolate-frosted donut.*

He looked through the rear window and checked the dials of the vibrating mechanism. Everything was green.

Melanie reappeared. 'Go get in the car with the others,' Priest told her. 'I'll be right there.'

He set the machine to vibrate on a signal from the remote control, then jumped out, leaving the engine running.

Melanie and Star were in the back seat of the 'Cuda, sitting as far apart as they could: they were polite but they could not hide their hostility to one another. Oaktree was at the wheel. Priest jumped into the front passenger seat. 'Drive back up the hill to where we stopped before,' he said.

Oaktree pulled away.

Priest turned on the radio and tuned to John Truth.

'Seven twenty-five on Friday evening, and the threat of an earthquake by the terrorist group the Hammer of Eden has failed to materialize, heaven be praised. What's the scariest thing that ever happened to *you*? Call John Truth now and tell us. It could be something dumb, like a mouse in your refrigerator, or maybe you were the victim of a robbery. Share your thoughts with the world, on the John Truth show tonight.'

Priest turned to Melanie. 'Call him on your cellphone.'

'What if they trace the call?'

'It's a radio station, not the goddam FBI, they can't trace calls. Go ahead.'

'Okay.' Melanie tapped out the number John Truth was repeating on the radio. 'It's busy.'

'Keep trying.'

'This phone has automatic redial.'

Oaktree stopped the car at the top of the hill and they looked down on the town. Priest anxiously scanned the parking area in front of the coffee shop. The cops were still there. He did not want to start the vibrator while they were so close—one of them might have the presence of mind to jump into the cab and switch off the engine. 'Those damn cops!' he muttered. 'Why don't they go catch some criminals?'

'Don't say that—they might come after us,' Oaktree joked.

'We're not criminals,' Star said forcefully. 'We're trying to save our country.'

'Damn right,' Priest said with a smile, and he punched the air.

'I mean it,' she said. 'In a hundred years' time, when people look back, they'll say we were the rational ones, and the government were insane for letting America be destroyed by pollution. Like deserters in the First World War—they were hated then, but nowadays everybody says the men who ran away were the only ones who weren't mad.'

Oaktree said: 'That's the truth.'

The police cruiser pulled away from the coffee shop.

'I got through!' Melanie said. 'I got through to—Hello? Yes, I'll hold for John Truth . . . He says to turn off the radio, you guys . . .' Priest snapped off the car radio. 'I want to talk about the earthquake,' Melanie went on, answering questions. 'It's . . . Melinda. Oh! He's gone. Fuck, I nearly told him my name!'

'It wouldn't matter, there must be a million Melanies,' Priest said. 'Give me the phone.'

She handed it over and Priest put it to his ear. He heard a commercial for a Lexus dealership in San Jose. It seemed the station played the show to people waiting on hold. He watched the police cruiser come up the hill toward him. It went past the truck, pulled on to the freeway and disappeared.

Suddenly he heard: 'And Melinda wants to talk about the earthquake threat. Hello, Melinda, you're on John Truth live!'

Priest said: 'Hello, John, this isn't Melinda, it's the Hammer of Eden.'

There was a pause. When Truth spoke again, his voice had taken on the portentous tone he used for announcements of great gravity. 'Buddy, you better not be kidding, because if you are, you could go to jail, you know?'

'I guess I could go to jail if I'm *not* kidding,' Priest said.

Truth did not laugh. 'Why are you calling me?'

'We just want to be sure, this time, that everyone knows the earthquake was caused by us.'

'When will it happen?'

'Within the next few minutes.'

'Where?'

'I can't tell you that, because it might give the FBI the jump on us, but I'll tell you something no one could possibly guess. It will take place right on Route 101.'

*

Raja Khan jumped on a table in the middle of the command post. 'Everyone, shut up and listen!' he yelled. They all heard the shrill note of fear in his voice and the room went dead. 'A guy claiming to be from the Hammer of Eden is on *John Truth Live*.'

There was a burst of noise as everyone asked questions. Judy stood up. 'Quiet, everyone!' she shouted. 'Raja, what did he say?'

Carl Theobald, who was sitting with his ear close to the speaker of a portable radio, answered her question. 'He just said the next earthquake will take place on Route 101 within a few minutes.'

'Well done, Carl! Turn up the volume.' Judy swung around. 'Michael—does that fit any of the locations we have under surveillance?'

'Nope,' he said. 'Shit, I guessed wrong!'

'Then guess again! Try and figure out where these people might be!'

'All right,' he said. 'Stop yelling.' He sat at his computer and put his hand on the mouse.

On Carl Theobald's radio, a voice said: 'Here it comes now.'

An alarm sounded on Michael's computer.

Judy said: 'What's that? Is it a tremor?'

Michael clicked his mouse. 'Wait, it's just coming on screen . . . no, it's not a tremor. It's a seismic vibrator.'

Judy looked over his shoulder. On the screen she saw a pattern just like the one he had shown her on Sunday. 'Where is it?' she said. 'Give me a location!'

'I'm working on it,' he snapped back. 'Shouting at me won't make the computer triangulate faster.'

How could he be so damn touchy at a time like this? 'Why is there no earthquake? Maybe their method isn't working!'

'In Owens Valley it didn't work first time.'

'I didn't know that.'

'Okay, here are the coordinates.'

Judy and Charlie Marsh went to the wall map. Michael sang out coordinates. 'Here!' Judy said triumphantly. 'Right on Route 101, south of San Francisco. A town called Felicitas. Carl, call the local police. Raja,

432

notify the highway patrol. Charlie, I'm coming with you in the chopper.'

'This is not pinpoint accurate,' Michael warned. 'The vibrator could be anywhere within a mile or so of the coordinates.'

'How can we narrow it down?'

'If I look at the landscape I can spot the fault line.'

'You better come in the helicopter. Grab a bullet-proof vest. Let's go!'

*

'It's not working!' Priest said, trying to control his alarm.

Melanie said: 'It didn't work first time in Owens Valley, don't you remember?' She sounded exasperated. 'We had to move the truck and try again.'

'Shit, I hope we have time,' Priest said. 'Drive, Oaktree! Back to the truck!'

Oaktree put the old car in drive and tore down the hill.

Priest turned and shouted to Melanie over the roar of the engine. 'Where do you think we should move it to?'

'There's a side street almost opposite the coffee shop—go down there about four hundred yards. That's where the fault line runs.'

'Okay.'

Oaktree stopped the car in front of the coffee shop. Priest leaped out. A heavy middle-aged woman stood in front of him. 'Did you hear that noise?' she said. 'It seemed to be coming from your truck. It was ear-splitting!'

'Get out of my way or I'll split your fucking head,' Priest said. He jumped into the truck. He raised the plate, put the transmission in drive and pulled away. He shot out on to the street in front of a big old station wagon. The wagon screeched to a halt and the driver honked indignantly. Priest headed down the side street.

He drove four hundred yards and stopped outside a neat one-storey house with a fenced garden. A small white dog barked fiercely at him through the fence. Working with feverish haste, he again lowered the plate of the vibrator and checked its dials. He set it to remote operation, jumped out, and got back into the 'Cuda.

Oaktree screeched around in a U-turn and tore off. As they raced along Main Street, Priest observed that their activities were beginning to attract attention. They were watched by a couple carrying shopping bags, two boys on mountain bikes, and three fat men who came out of a bar to see what was going on.

They came to the end of Main Street and turned up the hill. 'This is far enough,' Priest said. Oaktree stopped the car and Priest activated the remote control.

He could hear the truck vibrating six blocks away.

Star said shakily: 'Are we safe here?'

They were silent, frozen in suspense, waiting for the earthquake.

The truck vibrated for thirty seconds, then stopped.

'Too safe,' Priest said to Star.

Oaktree said: 'It ain't fucking working, Priest!'

'This happened last time,' Priest said desperately. 'It's gonna work!'

Melanie said: 'You know what I think? The earth here is too soft. The town is close to the river. Soft, wet ground soaks up vibrations.'

Priest turned to her accusingly. 'Yesterday you told me earthquakes cause *more* damage on wet ground.'

'I said that buildings on wet soil are more likely to be damaged, because the ground underneath them moves more. But for transmitting shock waves to the fault, rock should be better.'

'Skip the goddam lecture!' Priest said. 'Where do we try next?'

She pointed up the hill. 'Where we came off the freeway. It's not directly on the fault line, but the ground should be rock.'

Oaktree raised an eyebrow at Priest. Priest said: 'Back to the truck, go!'

They raced back along Main Street, watched now by more people. Oaktree screeched into the side street and skidded to a halt next to the seismic vibrator. Priest jumped into the truck, raised the plate, and pulled away, flooring the gas pedal.

The truck moved with painful slowness through the town and crawled up the hill.

When it was halfway up, the police car they had seen earlier came off the freeway ramp, lights flashing and siren sounding, and sped past them, heading into town.

At last the truck arrived at the spot from which Priest had first looked over the town and pronounced it perfect. He stopped across the road from the Big Ribs restaurant. For the third time, he lowered the vibrator's plate.

Behind him he could see the 'Cuda. Coming back up the hill from the town was the police cruiser. Glancing up, he spotted a helicopter in the distant sky.

He had no time to get clear of the truck and use the remote. He would have to activate the vibrator sitting here in the driver's seat.

He put his hand on the control, hesitated, and pulled the lever.

*

From the helicopter, Felicitas looked like a town asleep.

It was a bright, clear evening. Judy could see Main Street and the grid of streets around it, the trees in the gardens and the cars in the driveways, but nothing seemed to be moving. A man watering flowers was so completely motionless he seemed to be a statue; a woman in a big straw hat stood still on the sidewalk; three teenage girls on a street corner were frozen in place; two boys had stopped their bicycles in the middle of the road.

There was movement on the freeway that flew past the town on the elegant arches of a viaduct. As well as the usual mixture of cars and trucks, she spotted two police cruisers a mile or so away, approaching the town at high speed, coming, she assumed, in response to her emergency call.

But in the town no one moved.

After a moment she figured out what was going on.

They were listening.

The roar of the helicopter prevented her from hearing what they were listening to, but she could guess. It had to be the seismic vibrator.

But where was it?

The chopper flew low enough for her to identify the makes of cars parked on Main Street, but she could not see a vehicle big enough to be a seismic vibrator. None of the trees that partly obscured the side streets seemed big enough to hide a full-size truck.

She spoke to Michael over the headset. 'Can you see the fault line?'

'Yes.' He was studying a map and comparing it with the landscape beneath. 'It crosses the railroad, the river, the freeway, and the gas pipeline. Dear God Almighty, there's going to be some damage.'

'But where's the vibrator?'

'What's that on the hillside?'

Judy followed his pointing finger. Above the town, close to the freeway, she saw a small cluster of buildings: a fast-food restaurant of some kind, a glass-walled office building, and a small wooden structure, probably a chapel. On the road near the restaurant were a mud-coloured coupé that looked like an old muscle car from the early seventies, a police cruiser pulling up behind it, and a large truck painted all over with dragons in livid red and acid yellow. She made out the words *The Dragon's Mouth*. 'It's a carnival ride,' she said.

'Or a disguise,' he suggested. 'That's about the right size for a seismic vibrator.'

'My God, I bet you're right!' she said. 'Charlie, are you listening?'

Charlie Marsh was sitting beside the pilot. Six members of his SWAT team were seated behind Judy and Michael, armed with stubby MP-5 sub-machine-guns. The rest of the team were hurtling down the freeway in an armoured truck, their mobile Tactical Operations Center. 'I'm listening,' Charlie said. 'Pilot, can you put us down near that carnival truck on the hill?'

'It's awkward,' the pilot replied. 'The hillside slopes steeply, and the road forms a narrow ledge. I'd rather come down in the parking lot of that restaurant.'

'Do it,' Charlie said.

'There isn't going to be an earthquake, is there?' the pilot said.

Nobody answered him.

As the chopper came down, a figure jumped out of the truck. Judy peered at it. She saw a tall, thin man with long dark hair, and she felt immediately that this had to be her enemy. He stared up at the chopper, and it seemed as if his eyes were on her. She was too far away to see his features clearly, but she felt sure he was Granger.

Stay right there, you son of a bitch, I'm coming to get you.

The helicopter hovered over the parking lot and began to descend.

438

Judy realized that she and everyone with her could die in the next few seconds.

As the helicopter touched the ground, there was a noise like the crack of doom.

*

The bang was a thunderclap so loud it drowned the roar of the seismic vibrator and the thrash of the helicopter rotors.

The ground seemed to rise up and hit Priest like a fist. He was watching the chopper land in the Big Ribs parking lot, thinking that the vibrator was pounding away in vain, his scheme had failed, and he would now be arrested and thrown in jail. Next moment he was flat on his face, feeling as if he had been punched out by Mike Tyson.

He rolled over, gasping for breath, and saw the trees all around him bending and twisting as if a hurricane was blowing.

A moment later he came to his senses and realized —it had worked! He had caused an earthquake.

Yes!

And he was in the middle of it.

Then he was afraid for his life.

The air rang with a terrifying rumbling sound like rocks being shaken in a giant pail. He scrambled to his knees, but the ground would not stay still, and in trying to stand up he fell over again.

Oh, shit, I'm done for.

He rolled over and managed to sit upright.

He heard a sound like a hundred windows breaking. Looking over to his right he saw that was exactly what was happening. The glass walls of the office building were all shattering at the same time. A million shards of glass flowed like a waterfall off the building.

Yes!

The Baptist chapel farther down the road seemed to fall over sideways. It was a flimsy wooden building, and its thin walls went down in a cloud of dust and lay flat on the ground, leaving a massive carved oak lectern standing in the middle of the wreckage.

I did it! I did it!

The windows of Big Ribs smashed, and the screams of terrified children pierced the air. One corner of the roof sagged, then dropped on a group of five or six teenagers, crushing them and their table and their rib dinners. The other patrons rose in a wave and surged toward the now-glassless windows as the rest of the roof started to come down on them.

The air was full of the pungent smell of gasoline. The tremor had ruptured the tanks at the filling station, Priest thought. He looked across and saw a sea of fuel spilling over the forecourt. An out-of-control motorcycle came off the road, weaving from side to side, until the rider fell off and the machine slid across the concrete, striking sparks. The spilling gas caught alight with a *whoosh*, and a second later the entire plaza was ablaze.

Jesus Christ!

The fire was frighteningly close to the 'Cuda. He

could see the car rocking up and down, and the terrified face of Oaktree behind the wheel.

He had never seen Oaktree scared.

The horses from the field next to the restaurant burst through the broken fence and galloped full-tilt along the road toward Priest, eyes staring, mouths open, terrified. Priest had no time to get out of the way. He covered his head with his hands. They raced by either side of him.

Down in the town, the church bell was ringing madly.

*

The helicopter lifted again a second after it had touched down. Judy saw the ground beneath her shimmer like a block of Jell-O. Then it fell away fast as the chopper gained height. She gasped to see the glass walls of the little office building turn to something that looked like surf and fall in a great wave to the ground. She saw a motorcyclist crash into the filling station, and she cried out in grief as the gasoline caught alight and the flames engulfed the fallen rider.

The helicopter swung around and her view changed. Now she saw across the flat plain. In the distance, a freight train was crossing the fields. At first she thought it had escaped damage, then she realized it was slowing harshly. It had come off the rails and, as she watched, horrified, the locomotive ploughed into the field alongside the track. The loaded wagons began to snake as they piled into the back of the loco. Then the chopper swung around again, still rising.

Now Judy could see the town. It was a shocking sight. Desperate, panicky people were running into the street, mouths open in screams of terror that she could not hear, trying to escape as their houses collapsed, walls cracking open and windows exploding and roofs lurching terrifyingly sideways and falling into neat gardens and crushing cars in driveways. Main Street seemed to be on fire and flooded with water at the same time. Cars had crashed in the streets. There was a flash like lightning, then another, and Judy guessed power lines were snapping.

As the helicopter gained height, the freeway came into view, and Judy's hands flew to her mouth in horror as she saw that one of the giant arches supporting the viaduct had twisted and snapped. The roadbed had cracked and a tongue of road now stuck out into midair. At least ten cars had piled up either side of the break, and several were on fire. And the carnage was not over. Even as she watched, a big old Chevrolet with fins hurtled toward the precipice, skidding sideways as the driver tried in vain to stop. Judy heard herself scream as the car flew off the edge. She could see the terrified face of the driver, a young man, as he realized he was about to die. The car tumbled over and over in the air, with ghastly slowness, and finally crashed on the roof of a house below, bursting into flames and setting the building alight.

Judy buried her face in her hands. It was too

dreadful to watch. But then she remembered she was an FBI agent. She forced herself to look again. Cars on the freeway were now slowing early enough to stop before crashing, she saw. But highway patrol vehicles and the SWAT truck that was on its way would not be able to reach Felicitas from the freeway.

A sudden wind blew away the cloud of black smoke over the filling station, and Judy saw the man she thought was Ricky Granger.

You did this. You killed all these people. You piece of shit, I'm going to put you in jail if it's the last thing I do.

Granger struggled to his feet and ran to the brown coupé, shouting and gesticulating to the people inside.

The police cruiser was right behind the coupé, but the cops seemed slow to act.

Judy realized the terrorists were about to flee.

Charlie came to the same conclusion. 'Go down, pilot!' he yelled through the headset.

'Are you out of your mind?' he shouted back.

'Those people did this!' Judy screamed, pointing over the pilot's shoulder. 'They caused all this carnage and now they're getting away!'

'Shit,' the pilot said, and the helicopter swooped toward the ground.

*

Priest yelled at Oaktree through the open window of the 'Cuda. 'Let's get out of here!'

'Okay—which way?'

Priest pointed along the road that led to the town.

'Take this road, but instead of going left into Main Street, turn right along the old country road—it leads back toward San Francisco, I checked.'

'Okay!'

Priest saw the two local cops getting out of their cruiser.

He leaped into the truck, raised the plate, and pulled away, heaving on the steering wheel. Oaktree scorched a U-turn in the 'Cuda and headed down the hill. Priest turned the truck around more slowly.

One of the cops was standing in the middle of the road, pointing his gun at the truck. It was the thin youngster who had told Priest to enjoy the rest of his day. Now he was shouting: 'Police! Stop!'

Priest drove right at him.

The cop let off a wild shot then dived out of the way.

The road ahead skirted the town to the east, avoiding the worst of the damage, which was in the town centre. Priest had to swing around a pair of crashed cars outside the destroyed glass office building, but after that the road looked clear. The truck picked up speed.

We're going to make it!

Then the FBI helicopter landed in the middle of the road a quarter of a mile ahead.

Shit.

Priest saw the 'Cuda screech to a halt.

Okay, assholes, you asked for it.

Priest floored the gas pedal.

Agents in SWAT gear, armed to the teeth, leaped

out of the chopper one by one, and began to take cover at the roadside.

Priest in his truck careered down the hill, gathering speed, and roared past the stopped 'Cuda.

'Now follow me,' Priest muttered, hoping Oaktree would guess what was expected of him.

He saw Judy Maddox jump out of the chopper. A bulletproof vest hid her graceful body and she was holding a shotgun. She knelt behind a telegraph pole. A man tumbled out after her and Priest recognized Melanie's husband, Michael.

Priest glanced in his side mirrors. Oaktree had the 'Cuda tucked in right behind him, making it a difficult target. He had not forgotten everything he had learned in the Marines.

Behind the 'Cuda, a hundred yards back but going like a blue streak and gaining fast, was the police cruiser.

Priest's truck was twenty yards from the agents, heading straight for the chopper.

An FBI agent stood up at the roadside and aimed a stubby machine-gun at the truck.

Jesus, I hope the Feds don't have grenade launchers.

The chopper lifted off the ground.

*

Judy cursed. The helicopter pilot, bad at taking orders, had landed too close to the approaching vehicles. There was hardly time for the SWAT team and the other agents to spill out and take positions before the carnival truck was on them.

Michael staggered to the side of the road. 'Lie flat!' Judy screamed at him. She saw the driver of the truck duck behind the dash as one of the SWAT team opened fire with his sub-machine-gun. The windscreen frosted, and holes appeared in the fenders and the hood, but the truck did not stop. Judy cried out with frustration.

She hastily aimed her M870 five-chamber shotgun and fired at the tyres, but she was off-balance and her shot went wide.

Then the truck was alongside her. All firing stopped: the agents were fearful of hitting one another.

The chopper was lifting out of the way—but then Judy saw, to her horror, that the pilot had been a split-second too slow. The roof of the truck's cab clipped the undercarriage of the helicopter. The aircraft tilted suddenly.

The truck charged on, unaffected. The brown 'Cuda raced by, close behind the truck.

Judy fired wildly at the retreating vehicles.

We let them get by!

The helicopter seemed to wobble in midair as the pilot tried to correct its lurch. Then a rotor blade touched the ground.

'Oh, no!' Judy cried. 'Please, no!'

The tail of the machine swung around and up. Judy could see the frightened expression of the pilot as he fought the controls. Then, suddenly, the helicopter nosedived into the middle of the road. There was a heavy *crump!* of deforming metal and, immediately afterwards, the musical crash of shattering glass. For a moment the chopper stood on its nose. Then it began to fall slowly sideways.

The pursuing police cruiser, travelling at maybe a hundred miles an hour, braked desperately, skidded, and smashed into the crashed helicopter.

There was a deafening bang, and both vehicles burst into flame.

*

Priest saw the crash in his side mirrors and let out a victory whoop. Now the FBI looked stuck: no helicopter, no cars. For the next few minutes they would be desperately trying to rescue the cops and the pilot from the wreckage in case they were still alive. By the time one of them thought of commandeering a car from a nearby house, Priest would be miles away.

He pushed out the frosted glass of his shot-up windshield without slowing the truck.

My God, I think we made it!

Behind him, the 'Cuda was swaying in a peculiar way. After a minute he figured it must have a flat. It was still travelling, so the flat must be a rear tyre. Oaktree could keep going for a mile or two like that.

They reached the crossroads. Three cars had piled up at the junction: a Toyota minivan with a baby seat in the back, a battered Dodge pickup, and an old white Cadillac Coupe de Ville. Priest looked hard at them. None was badly damaged, and the minivan's engine was still running. He could not see the drivers anywhere. They must have gone looking for a phone.

He steered around the pile-up and turned right, away from the town. He pulled up around the first bend. They were now more than a mile from the FBI team and well out of sight. He thought he was safe for a minute or two. He jumped out of the truck.

The 'Cuda pulled up behind and Oaktree jumped out. He was grinning broadly. 'Mission successfully completed, General!' he said. 'I never saw anything like that in the goddam military!'

Priest gave him a high five. 'But we need to get away from the battlefield, and fast,' he said.

Star and Melanie got out of the car. Melanie's cheeks were pink with exhilaration, almost as if she was sexually aroused. 'My God, we did it, we did it!' she said.

Star bent over and threw up at the roadside.

*

Charlie Marsh was talking into a mobile phone. 'The pilot is dead and so are two local cops. There's a hell of a pile-up on Route 101, which needs to be closed. Here in Felicitas we have car wrecks, fires, flooding, a busted gas pipeline and a train wreck. You'll need to call in the Governor's Office of Emergency Management, no question.'

Judy motioned for him to give her the phone.

He nodded to her and said into the mouthpiece: 'Put one of Judy's people on the line.' He handed her the phone.

'This is Judy, who's that?' she said rapidly.

'Carl. How the hell are you?'

'Okay, but mad at myself for losing the suspects. Put out a call for two vehicles. One is a truck painted with red and yellow dragons, looks like a carnival ride. The other is a brown Plymouth 'Cuda twenty-five or thirty years old. Also, send out another chopper to look for the vehicles on the roads leading from Felicitas.' She looked up into the sky. 'It's almost too dark already, but do it anyway. Any vehicle of either description should be stopped and the occupants questioned.'

'And if one of them could conceivably fit the description of Granger . . .?'

'Bring him in and nail him to the floor until I get there.'

'What are you going to do?'

'I guess we'll commandeer some cars and come back to the office. Somehow . . .' She stopped, and fought off a wave of exhaustion and despair. 'Somehow, we've got to stop this happening *again*.'

*

'It's not over yet,' Priest said. 'In an hour or so, every cop in California will be looking for a carnival ride called the Dragon's Mouth.' He turned to Oaktree. 'How fast could we get these panels off?'

'In a few minutes, with a couple of good hammers.'

'The truck has a tool kit.'

Working fast, the two of them took the carnival panels off the truck and tossed them over a wire fence into a field. With luck, in the confusion following the earthquake, it would be a day or two before anyone took a close look at them.

'What the hell you going to tell Bones?' Oaktree said as they worked.

'I'll think of something.'

Melanie helped, but Star stood with her back to them, leaning against the trunk of the 'Cuda. She was crying. She was going to make trouble, Priest knew, but there was no time to gentle her now.

When they had finished with the truck, they stood back, panting with the effort. Oaktree said worriedly: 'Now the damn thing looks like a seismic vibrator again.'

'I know,' Priest said. 'Nothing I can do about that. It's getting dark, I don't have far to go, and every cop within fifty miles is going to be conscripted into rescue work. I'm just hoping to be lucky. Now get out of here. Take Star.'

'First I need to change a wheel—I have a flat.'

'Don't bother,' Priest said. 'We gotta ditch the 'Cuda anyway. The FBI saw it, they'll be looking for it.' He pointed back toward the crossroads. 'I saw three vehicles back there. Grab yourself a new ride.'

Oaktree hurried off.

Star looked at Priest with accusing eyes. 'I can't believe we did this,' she said. 'How many people have we killed?'

'We had no choice,' he said angrily. 'You told me you'd do *anything* to save the commune—don't you remember?'

'But you're so calm about it. All these people killed, more injured, families who have lost their homes—aren't you *heartsick?*'

'Sure.'

'And her.' She nodded at Melanie. 'Look at her face. She's so up. My God, I think she *likes* all this.'

'Star, we'll talk later, okay?'

She shook her head as if amazed. 'I spend twenty-five years with you and never really knew you.'

Oaktree came back driving the Toyota. 'Nothing wrong with this but dents,' he said.

Priest said to Star: 'Go with him.'

She hesitated for a long moment, then she got in the car.

Oaktree pulled away and disappeared fast.

'Get in the truck,' Priest said to Melanie. He got behind the wheel and reversed the seismic vibrator to the crossroads. They both jumped out and looked at the remaining two cars. Priest liked the look of the Cadillac. Its trunk was stove in, but the front end was undamaged, and the keys were in the dash. 'Follow me in the Caddy,' he said to Melanie.

She got in the car and turned the key. It started first time. She said: 'Where are we headed?'

'Perpetua Diaries warehouse.'

'Okay.'

'Give me your phone.'

'Who are you going to call? Not the FBI.'

'No, just the radio station.'

She handed over her phone.

As they were about to leave, there was a huge

explosion in the distance. Priest looked back toward Felicitas and saw a jet of flame shoot high in the sky.

Melanie said: 'Wow, what's that?'

The flame receded and became a bright glow in the evening sky.

'I guess the gas pipeline just caught alight,' Priest said. 'Now that's what I call fireworks.'

*

Michael Quercus was sitting on a patch of grass at the side of the road, looking shocked and helpless.

Judy went over to him. 'Get up,' she said. 'Pull yourself together. People die every day.'

'I know,' he said. 'It's not the killings—although they're enough. It's something else.'

'What?'

'Did you see who was in the car?'

'The 'Cuda? There was a black guy driving it.'

'But in the back?'

'I didn't notice anyone else.'

'I did. A woman.'

'Did you recognize her?'

'I sure did,' he said. 'It was my wife.'

*

It took twenty minutes of redialling on Melanie's cellphone before Priest got through to the John Truth show. By the time he heard the ringing tone, he was on the outskirts of San Francisco.

The show was still on the air. Priest said he was

from the Hammer of Eden and got connected right away.

'You have done a terrible thing,' Truth said. He was using his most portentous voice, but Priest could tell that, underneath the solemn tone, the man was exultant. The earthquake had practically happened on his show. This would make him the most famous radio personality in America. Move over, Howard Stern.

'You're wrong,' Priest told him. 'The people who are turning California into a poison wasteland have done a terrible thing. I'm just trying to stop them.'

'By killing innocent people?'

'Pollution kills innocent people. Automobiles kill innocent people. Call that Lexus dealer that advertises on your show and tell him he did a terrible thing, selling five cars today.'

There was a moment's silence. Priest grinned. Truth was not sure how to answer him. He could not start discussing the ethics of his sponsors. He quickly changed the subject. 'I appeal to you to turn yourself in, right now.'

'I have one thing to say to you and the people of California,' Priest said. 'Governor Robson must announce a statewide freeze on power plant building —otherwise there will be another earthquake.'

'You would do this *again*?' Truth sounded genuinely shocked.

'You bet I would. And—'

Truth tried to interrupt him. 'How can you claim—'

Priest overrode him. '—the next earthquake will be worse than this one.'

'Where will it strike?'

'I can't tell you that.'

'Can you say when?'

'Oh, sure. Unless the governor changes his mind, another earthquake will take place in two days' time.' He paused for dramatic effect. 'Exactly,' he added.

He hung up.

'Now, Mr Governor,' he said aloud. 'Tell the people not to panic.'

PART THREE

FORTY-EIGHT
HOURS

CHAPTER EIGHTEEN

J UDY AND Michael got back to the Emergency Operations Center a few minutes before midnight.

She had been awake for forty hours, but she did not feel sleepy. The horror of the earthquake was still with her. Every few seconds she would see, in her mind's eye, one of the nightmare pictures of those few seconds: the train wreck, the screaming people, the helicopter bursting into flames, or the old Chevy tumbling over and over in the air. She was spooked and jittery as she walked into the old officers' club.

But Michael's revelation had given her new hope. It was a shock to learn that his wife was one of the terrorists, but it was also the most promising lead yet. If Judy could find Melanie, she could find the Hammer of Eden.

And if she could do it in two days, she could prevent another earthquake.

She went into the old ballroom that had become the command post. Stuart Cleever, the big shot from Washington who had taken control, stood at the Head Shed. He was a neat, orderly guy, immaculately dressed in a grey suit with a white shirt and a striped tie.

Beside him stood Brian Kincaid.

The bastard has wormed his way back on to the case. He wants to impress the guy from Washington.

Brian was ready for her. 'What the hell went wrong?' he said as soon as he saw her.

'We were too late, by a few seconds,' she said wearily.

'You told us you had all the sites under surveillance,' he snapped.

'We had the likeliest. But they knew that. So they picked a secondary site. It was a risk for them—more chance of failure—but their gamble paid off.'

Kincaid turned to Cleever with a shrug, as if to say: *Believe that and you'll believe anything.*

Cleever said to Judy: 'As soon as you've made a full report, I want you to go home and get some rest. Brian will take charge of your team.'

I knew it. Kincaid has poisoned Cleever against me.

Time to go for broke.

Judy said: 'I'd like a break, but not just yet. I believe I will have the terrorists under arrest within twelve hours.'

Brian let out an exclamation of surprise.

Cleever said: 'How?'

'I've just developed a new lead. I know who their seismologist is.'

'Who?'

'Her name is Melanie Quercus. She's the estranged wife of Michael, who's been helping us. She got the information about where the fault is under tension from her husband—stole it off his computer. And I suspect she also stole the list of sites we had under surveillance.'

Kincaid said: 'Quercus should be a suspect too! He could be in cahoots with her!'

Judy had anticipated this. 'I'm sure he's not,' she said. 'But he's taking a lie-detector test right now, just to make sure.'

'Good enough,' Cleever said. 'Can you find the wife?'

'She told Michael she was living in a commune in Del Norte county. My team are already searching our databases for communes there. We have a two-man Resident Agency in that neighbourhood, in a town called Eureka, and I've asked them to contact the local police.'

Cleever nodded. He gave Judy an appraising look. 'What do you want to do?'

'I'd like to drive up there now. I'll sleep on the way. By the time I get there the local guys will have the addresses of all communes in the area. I'd like to raid them all at dawn.'

Brian said: 'You don't have enough evidence for search warrants.'

He was right. The mere fact that Melanie had said she was living in a commune in Del Norte county did not constitute probable cause. But Judy knew the law better than Brian. 'After two earthquakes, I think we have exigent circumstances, don't you?' That meant that people's lives were in danger.

Brian looked baffled, but Cleever understood. 'The legal desk can solve that problem, it's what they're here for.' He paused. 'I like this plan,' he said. 'I think we should do it. Brian, do you have any other comment?'

Kincaid looked sulky. 'She better be right, that's all.'

*

Judy rode north in a car driven by a woman agent she did not know, one of several dozen drafted in from FBI offices in Sacramento and Los Angeles to help in the crisis.

Michael sat beside Judy in the back. He had begged to come. He was worried sick about Dusty. If Melanie was part of a terrorist group causing earthquakes, what kind of danger might their son be in? Judy had got Cleever's agreement by arguing that someone had to take care of the boy after Melanie was arrested.

Shortly after they crossed the Golden Gate bridge, Judy took a call from Carl Theobald. Michael had told them which of the five hundred or so American cell-phone companies Melanie used, and Carl had got hold of her call records. The phone company had been able to identify the general area from which each call had been made, because of roaming charges.

Judy was hoping most of them had been made from Del Norte county, but she was disappointed.

'There's really no pattern at all,' Carl said wearily. 'She made calls from the Owens Valley area, from San Francisco, from Felicitas, and from various places in between; but all that tells us is that she's been travelling all over the state, and we knew that already. There are no calls from the part of the state you're headed for.'

'That suggests she has a regular phone there.'

'Or she's cautious.'

'Thanks, Carl. It was worth a try. Now get some sleep.'

'You mean this isn't a dream? Shit.'

Judy laughed and hung up.

The driver tuned the car radio to an easy-listening station, and Nat Cole sang 'Let There Be Love' as they sped through the night. Judy and Michael could talk without being overheard.

'The terrible thing about it is that I'm not surprised,' Michael said after a thoughtful silence. 'I guess I sort of always knew Melanie was crazy. I should never have let her take him away—but she's his mother, you know?'

Judy reached for his hand in the dark. 'You did your best, I guess,' she said.

He squeezed her hand gratefully. 'I just hope he's okay now.'

'Yeah.'

Drifting off to sleep, Judy kept hold of his hand.

*

They all met up at 5 a.m. in the Eureka office of the FBI. As well as the local resident agents, there were representatives from the town's police department and the county sheriff's office. The FBI always liked to involve local law enforcement personnel in a raid—it was a way of maintaining good relations with people whose help they often needed.

There were four residential communes in Del Norte county listed in *Communities Directory: A Guide to Co-operative Living*. The FBI database had revealed a fifth, and local knowledge had added two more.

One of the local FBI agents pointed out that the commune known as Phoenix Village was only eight miles from the site of a proposed nuclear power plant. Judy's pulse accelerated when she heard that, and she led the group that raided Phoenix.

As she approached the location, in a Del Norte county sheriff's cruiser at the head of a convoy of four cars, her tiredness fell away. She felt keen and energetic again. She had failed to prevent the Felicitas earthquake but she could make sure there was not another.

The entrance to Phoenix was a side turning off a country road, marked by a neat painted sign showing a bird rising from flames. There was no gate or guard. The cars roared into the settlement on a well-made road and pulled up around a traffic circle. The agents leaped out of the cars and fanned out through the houses. Each had a copy of the picture of Melanie and Dusty that Michael kept on his desk.

She's here, somewhere, probably in bed with Ricky Granger, sleeping after the exertions of yesterday. I hope they're having bad dreams.

The village looked peaceful in the early light. There were several barnlike buildings plus a geodesic dome.

The agents covered front and back entrances before knocking on the doors. Near the traffic circle, Judy found a map of the village painted on a board, listing the houses and other buildings. There was a shop, a massage centre, a mail room, and an auto repair shop. As well as fifteen houses, the map showed pasture, orchards, playgrounds, and a sports field.

It was cool in the morning, this far north, and Judy shivered, wishing she had worn something heavier than her linen pantsuit.

She waited for the shout of triumph that would tell her an agent had identified Melanie. Michael paced around the traffic circle, his whole body stiff with tension. *What a shock, to learn that your wife has become a terrorist, the kind of person a cop would shoot and everyone would cheer. No wonder he's tense. It's a miracle he isn't banging his head against the wall.*

Next to the map was a village notice board. Judy read about a folk dance workshop that was being organized to raise funds for the Expanding Light Fireplace fund. These people had an air of harmlessness that was remarkably plausible.

The agents entered every building and looked in every room, moving rapidly from house to house. After a few minutes, a man came out of one of the larger houses and walked across to the traffic circle. He was about fifty, with dishevelled hair and beard, wearing home-made leather sandals and a rough blanket around his shoulders. He said to Michael: 'Are you in charge here?'

Judy said: 'I'm in charge.'

He turned to her. 'Would you please tell me what the hell is going on?'

'I'd be glad to,' she said crisply. 'We're looking for this woman.' She held out the photo.

The man did not take it from her. 'I've already seen that,' he said. 'She's not one of us.'

Judy had a depressing feeling that he was telling the truth.

'This is a religious community,' he said with mounting indignation. 'We're law-abiding citizens. We don't use drugs. We pay our taxes and obey local ordinances. We don't deserve to be treated like criminals.'

'We just have to be sure this woman is not hiding out here.'

'Who is she, and why do you think she's here? Or is it just that you assume people who live in communes are suspect?'

'No, we don't make that assumption,' Judy said. She was tempted to snap at the guy, but she reminded herself that *she* had woken *him* up at six o'clock in the morning. 'This woman is part of a terrorist group. She told her estranged husband she was living in a commune in Del Norte county. We're sorry we have to wake up everyone in every commune in the county, but I hope you can understand that it is very important. If it wasn't, we wouldn't have disturbed you, and, frankly, we wouldn't have put ourselves to so much trouble.'

He looked at her keenly then nodded, his attitude changing. 'Okay,' he said. 'I believe you. Is there anything I can do to make your job easier?'

She thought for a moment. 'Is every building in your community marked on this map?'

'No,' he said. 'There are three new houses on the west side just beyond the orchard. But please try to be quiet—there's a new baby in one of them.'

'Okay.'

Sally Dobro, a middle-aged woman agent, came up. 'I think we've checked every building here,' she said. 'There's no sign of any of our suspects.'

Judy said: 'There are three houses west of the orchard—did you find those?'

'No,' Sally said. 'Sorry. I'll do it right away.'

'Go quietly,' Judy said. 'There's a new baby in one.'

'You got it.'

Sally went off, and the man in the blanket nodded his appreciation.

Judy's mobile phone rang. She answered and heard the voice of Agent Frederick Tan. 'We've just checked out every building in the Magic Hill commune. Zilch.'

'Thanks, Freddie.'

In the next ten minutes the other raid leaders called her.

They all had the same message.

Melanie Quercus was not to be found.

Judy sank into a pit of despair. 'Hell,' she said. 'I screwed it up.'

Michael was equally dismayed. He said fretfully: 'Do you think we've missed a commune?'

'Either that, or she lied about the location.'

He looked thoughtful. 'I'm just remembering the

conversation,' he said. 'I asked *her* where she was living, but *he* answered the question.'

Judy nodded. 'I think he lied. He's smart like that.'

'I've just remembered his name,' Michael said. 'She called him Priest.'

CHAPTER NINETEEN

O N SATURDAY morning at breakfast, Dale and Poem stood up in the cookhouse in front of everyone and asked for quiet. 'We have an announcement,' Poem said.

Priest thought she must be pregnant again. He got ready to cheer and clap and make the short congratulatory speech that would be expected of him. He felt full of exuberance. Although he had not yet saved the commune, he was close. His opponent might not be out for the count, but he was down on the canvas, struggling to stay in the fight.

Poem hesitated, then looked at Dale. His face was solemn. 'We're leaving the commune today,' he said.

There was a shocked silence. Priest was dumbstruck. People did not leave, not unless he wanted them to. These folk were under his spell. And Dale was the oenologist, the key man in winemaking. They could not afford to lose him.

And today of all days! If Dale had heard the news— as Priest had, an hour ago, sitting in a stationary car listening to the radio—he would know that California was in a panic. The airports were mobbed and the freeways were jammed with people fleeing the cities and all neighbourhoods close to the San Andreas fault. Governor Robson had called out the national guard. The vice-president was on a plane, coming to inspect the damage at Felicitas. More and more people—state senators and congressmen, city mayors, community leaders, and journalists—were urging the governor to give in to the demand made by the Hammer of Eden. But Dale knew nothing of all this.

Priest was not the only one to be shocked by the announcement. Apple burst into tears, and at that Poem started crying too. Melanie was the first to speak. She said: 'But Dale—why?'

'You know why,' he said. 'This valley is going to be flooded.'

'But where will you go?'

'Rutherford. It's in Napa Valley.'

'You have a regular job?'

Dale nodded. 'In a winery.'

It was no surprise that Dale had been able to get a job, Priest thought. His expertise was priceless. He would probably make big money. The surprise was that he wanted to go back to the straight world.

Several of the women were crying now. Song said: 'Can't you wait and hope, like the rest of us?'

Poem answered her tearfully. 'We have three children. We have no right to take risks with their lives. We can't stay here, hoping for a miracle, until the waters start rising around our homes.'

Priest spoke for the first time. 'This valley is not going to be flooded.'

'You don't know that,' Dale said.

The room went quiet. It was unusual for someone to contradict Priest so directly.

'This valley is not going to be flooded,' Priest repeated.

Dale said: 'We all know that something's been going on, Priest. In the last six weeks you've been away more than you've been home. Yesterday four of you were out until midnight, and this morning there's a dented Cadillac up there in the parking circle. But whatever you're up to, you haven't shared it with us. And I can't risk the future of my children on your faith. Shirley feels the same.'

Poem's real name was Shirley, Priest recalled. For Dale to use it meant he was already detaching himself from the commune.

'I'll tell you what will save this valley,' Priest said. *Why not tell them about the earthquake—why not? They should be pleased—proud!* 'The power of prayer. Prayer will save us.'

'I'll pray for you,' Dale said. 'So will Shirley. We'll pray for all of you. But we're not staying.'

Poem wiped her tears on her sleeve. 'I guess that's it. We're sorry. We packed last night, not that we have much. I hope Slow will drive us to the bus station in Silver City.'

Priest stood up and went to them. He put one arm around Dale's shoulders and the other around Poem's. Hugging them to him, he said in a low, persuasive voice: 'I understand your pain. Let's all go to the temple and meditate together. After that, whatever you decide to do will be the right thing.'

Dale moved away, detaching himself from Priest's embrace. 'No,' he said. 'Those days are gone.'

Priest was shocked. He was using his full persuasive power and it was not working. Fury rose inside him, dangerously uncontrollable. He wanted to scream at Dale's faithlessness and ingratitude. He would have killed them both if he could. But he knew that showing his anger would be a mistake. He had to maintain the façade of calm control.

However, he could not summon up the grit to bid them a gracious farewell. Torn between rage and the need for restraint, he walked silently, with as much dignity as he could muster, out of the cookhouse.

He returned to his cabin.

Two more days and it would have been okay. One day!

He sat on the bed and lit a cigarette. Spirit lay on the floor, watching him mournfully. They were both silent and still, brooding. Melanie would follow him in a minute or two.

But it was Star who came in.

She had not spoken to him since she and Oaktree had driven away from Felicitas last night in the Toyota minivan. He knew she was angered and distressed by the earthquake. He had not yet had time to talk her down.

She said: 'I'm going to the police.'

Priest was astonished. Star loathed cops passionately. For her to enter a precinct house would be like Billy Graham going to a gay club. 'You're out of your mind,' he said.

'We killed people yesterday,' she said. 'I listened to

470

the radio on the drive back. At least twelve people died and more than a hundred were hospitalized. There were babies and children hurt. People lost their homes, everything they had—poor people, not just rich. And we did that to them.'

Everything is falling apart—just when I'm about to win!

He reached for her hand. 'Do you think I *wanted* to kill people?'

She backed away, refusing to take his hand. 'You sure as hell didn't look sad when it happened.'

I've got to hold it together for just a little longer. I must.

He made himself look penitent. 'I was happy the vibrator worked, yes. I was glad we were able to carry out our threat. But I didn't intend to hurt anyone. I knew there was a risk, and I decided to take it, because what was at stake was so important. I thought you made the same decision.'

'I did, and it was a bad decision, a wicked decision.' Tears came to her eyes. 'For Christ's sake, can't you see what's happened to us? We were the kids who believed in love and peace—now we're killing people! You're just like Lyndon Johnson. He bombed the Vietnamese and justified it. We said he was full of shit, and he was. I've dedicated my whole life to *not* being like that!'

'So you feel you made a mistake,' Priest said. 'I can understand that. What's hard for me to dig is that you want to redeem yourself by punishing me and the whole commune. You want to betray us to the cops.'

She was taken aback. 'I hadn't looked at it that way,' she said. 'I don't want to punish anyone.'

He had her now. 'So what do you really want?' He did not give her time to answer for herself. 'I think you need to be sure it's over.'

'I guess so, yeah.'

He reached out to her, and this time she let him hold her hands. 'It's over,' he said softly.

'I don't know,' she said.

'There will be no more earthquakes. The governor will give in. You'll see.'

*

Speeding back to San Francisco, Judy was diverted to Sacramento for a meeting at the governor's office. She grabbed another three or four hours' sleep in the car, and when she arrived at the Capitol building she felt ready to bite the world.

Stuart Cleever and Charlie Marsh had flown there from San Francisco. The head of the FBI's Sacramento office joined them. They met at noon in the conference room of the Horseshoe, the governor's suite. Al Honeymoon was in the chair.

'There's a twelve-mile traffic jam on I-80 with people trying to get away from the San Andreas fault,' Honeymoon said. 'The other major freeways are almost as bad.'

Cleever said: 'The president called the Director of the FBI and asked him about public order.' He looked at Judy as if all this was her fault.

'He called Governor Robson, too,' Honeymoon said.

'As of this moment, we do not have a serious public

order problem,' Cleever said. 'There are reports of looting in three neighbourhoods in San Francisco and one in Oakland, but it's sporadic. The governor has called out the national guard and stationed them in the armouries, although we don't need them yet. However, if there should be another earthquake . . .'

The thought made Judy feel ill. 'There can't be another earthquake,' she said.

They all looked at her. Honeymoon made a sardonic face. 'You have a suggestion?'

She did. It was a poor one, but they were desperate. 'There's only one thing I can think of,' she said. 'Set a trap for him.'

'How?'

'Tell him Governor Robson wants to negotiate with him personally.'

Cleever said: 'I don't believe he'd fall for it.'

'I don't know.' Judy frowned. 'He's smart, and any smart person would suspect a trap. But he's a psychopath, and they just love controlling others, calling attention to themselves and their actions, manipulating people and circumstances. The idea of personally negotiating with the Governor of California is going to tempt him mightily.'

Honeymoon said: 'I guess I'm the only person here who's met him.'

'That's right,' Judy said. 'I've seen him, and spoken to him on the phone, but you spent several minutes in a car with him. What was your impression?'

'You've summed him up about right—a smart psychopath. I believe he was angry with me for not being more impressed by him. Like I should have been, I don't know, more deferential.'

Judy suppressed a grin. Honeymoon did not defer to many people.

Honeymoon went on: 'He understood the political difficulties of what he was asking for. I told him the governor could not give in to blackmail. He'd thought of that already, and he had his answer prepared.'

'What was it?'

'He said we could deny what really happened. Announce a freeze on power plant building and say it had nothing to do with the earthquake threat.'

'Is that a possibility?' Judy said.

'Yes. I wouldn't recommend it, but if the governor put it to me as a plan, I'd have to say it could be made to work. However, the question is academic. I know Mike Robson, and he won't do it.'

'But he could pretend,' Judy said.

'What do you mean?'

'We could tell Granger the governor is willing to announce the freeze, but only under the right conditions, as he has to protect his political future. He wants to talk personally with Granger to agree those conditions.'

Stuart Cleever put in: 'The Supreme Court has ruled that law enforcement personnel may use trickery, ruse, and deceit. The only thing we're not permitted to do is threaten to take away the suspect's children. And if we promise immunity from prosecution, it sticks—we can't prosecute. But we can certainly do what Judy suggests without violating any laws.'

'Okay,' Honeymoon said. 'I don't know if this is going to work, but I guess we have to try. Let's do it.'

*

Priest and Melanie drove into Sacramento in the dented Cadillac. It was a sunny Saturday afternoon, and the town was thronged with people.

Listening to the car radio soon after midday, Priest had heard the voice of John Truth, although it was not time for his show. 'Here is a special message for Peter Shoebury of Eisenhower High School,' Truth had said. Shoebury was the man whose identity Priest had borrowed for the FBI press conference, and Eisenhower was the imaginary school attended by Flower. Priest realized the message was for him. 'Would Peter Shoebury please call me at the following number,' Truth had said.

'They want to make a deal,' he had said to Melanie. 'That's it—we've won!'

While Melanie drove around downtown, surrounded by hundreds of cars and thousands of people, Priest made the call from her mobile. Even if the FBI was tracing the call, he figured, they would not be able to pick one car out of the traffic.

His heart was in his mouth as he listened to the ringing tone. *I won the lottery and I'm here to pick up my cheque.*

The call was answered by a woman. 'Hello?' She

sounded guarded. Maybe she had received a lot of crank calls in response to the radio spot.

'This is Peter Shoebury from Eisenhower High.'

The response was instant. 'I'm going to connect you with Al Honeymoon, the governor's cabinet secretary.'

Yes!

'I just need to verify your identity first.'

It's a trick. 'How do you propose to do that?'

'Would you mind giving me the name of the student reporter who was with you a week ago?'

Priest remembered Flower saying, *I'll never forgive you for calling me Florence.*

Warily, he said: 'It was Florence.'

'Connecting you now.'

No trick—just a precaution.

Priest scanned the streets anxiously, alert for a police car, or a bunch of FBI men bearing down on his car. He saw nothing but shoppers and tourists. A moment later the deep voice of Honeymoon said: 'Mr Granger?'

Priest got right to the point. 'Are you ready to do the sensible thing?'

'We're ready to talk.'

'What does that mean?'

'The governor wants to meet with you today, with the object of negotiating a resolution to this crisis.'

Priest said: 'Is the governor willing to announce the freeze we want?'

Honeymoon hesitated. 'Yes,' he said reluctantly. 'But there must be conditions.'

'What kind?'

'When you and I spoke, in my car, and I told you that the governor could not give in to blackmail, you mentioned spin doctors.'

'Yes.'

'You're a sophisticated individual, you understand that the governor's political future is at risk here. The announcement of this freeze will have to be handled very delicately.'

Honeymoon had changed his tune, Priest thought with satisfaction. The arrogance had gone. He had developed respect for his opponent. That was gratifying. 'In other words, the governor has to cover his ass and he wants to make sure I won't blow it for him.'

'You might look at it that way.'

'Where do we meet?'

'In the governor's office here at the Capitol building.'

You're out of your frigging mind.

Honeymoon went on: 'No police, no FBI. You would be guaranteed freedom to leave the meeting without hindrance, regardless of the outcome.'

Yeah, right.

Priest said: 'Do you believe in fairies?'

'What?'

'You know, little flying people that can do magic? You believe they exist?'

'No, I guess I don't.'

'Me neither. So I'm not going to fall into your trap.'

'I give you my word—'

'Forget it. Just forget it, okay?'

There was silence at the other end.

Melanie turned a corner and they drove past the grand classical façade of the Capitol building. Honeymoon was in there somewhere, talking on the phone, surrounded by FBI men. Looking at the white columns and the dome, Priest said: 'I'll tell you where we'll meet, and you'd better make notes. Are you ready?'

'Don't worry, I'm taking notes.'

'Set up a little round table and a couple of garden chairs in front of the Capitol building, on the lawn there, right in the middle. It'll be like a photo-opportunity. Have the governor sitting there at three o'clock.'

'Out in the open?'

'Hey, if I was going to shoot him, I could do it easier than this.'

'I guess so . . .'

'In his pocket the governor must have a signed letter guaranteeing me immunity from prosecution.'

'I can't agree to all this—'

'Talk to your boss. He'll agree.'

'I'll talk to him.'

'Have a photographer there with one of them instant cameras. I want a picture of him handing me the letter of immunity, for proof. Got that?'

'Got it.'

'You better play this straight. No tricks. My seismic vibrator is already in place, ready to trigger another earthquake. This one will strike a major city, I'm not saying which one, but I'm talking thousands of deaths.'

'I understand.'

'If the governor doesn't appear today at three o'clock . . . *bang*.'

He broke the connection.

'Wow,' said Melanie. 'A meeting with the governor. Do you think it's a trap?'

Priest frowned. 'It might be,' he said. 'I don't know. I just don't know.'

*

Judy could not fault the set-up. Charlie Marsh had worked on it with the Sacramento FBI. There were at least thirty agents within sight of the white garden table with the umbrella that sat prettily on the lawn, but she could not see any of them. Some stood behind the windows of the surrounding government offices, others crouched in cars and vans on the street and in the parking lot, more lurked in the pillared cupola of the Capitol building. All were heavily armed.

Judy herself was playing the part of the photographer, with cameras and lenses around her neck. Her gun was in a camera bag slung from her shoulder. While she waited for the governor to appear, she looked through her viewfinder at the table and chairs, pretending to frame a shot.

In case Granger should recognize her, she wore a blonde wig. It was one she kept permanently in her car. She used it a lot on surveillance work, especially if she spent several days following the same targets, to reduce the risk that she might be noticed and recognized. She had to put up with a certain amount of teasing when she wore it. *Hey, Maddox, send the cute blonde over to my car, but you can stay where you are.*

Granger was watching, she knew. No one had spotted him, but he had called, an hour ago, to protest against the erection of crowd barriers around the block. He wanted the public using the street, and visitors touring the building, just as normal.

The barriers had been taken away.

There was no other fence around the grounds, so tourists were wandering freely across the lawns, and tour parties were following their prescribed routes around the Capitol, its gardens and the elegant government buildings on adjacent streets. Judy surreptitiously studied everyone through her lens. She ignored superficial appearances and concentrated on features that could not easily be disguised. She scrutinized every tall, thin man of middle age, regardless of hair, face or dress.

At one minute to three, she still had not seen Ricky Granger.

Michael Quercus, who had met Granger face to face, was also watching. He was in a surveillance van with blacked-out windows parked around the corner. He had to stay out of sight, for fear Granger would recognize him and be spooked.

Judy spoke into a little microphone under her shirt, clipped to her bra. 'My guess is that Granger won't show until after the governor appears.'

A tiny speaker behind her ear crackled, and she heard Charlie Marsh reply. 'We were just saying the same thing. I wish we could have got this done without exposing the governor.'

They had talked about using a body double, but Governor Robson himself had nixed that plan, saying he would not allow someone else to risk dying in his place.

Now Judy said: 'But if we can't . . .'

'So be it,' said Charlie.

A moment later the governor emerged from the grand front entrance of the building.

Judy was surprised that he was a little below average height. Seeing him on television, she had imagined him a tall man. He looked bulkier than usual on account of the bulletproof vest under his suit coat. He walked across the lawn with a relaxed, confident stride, and sat at the little table under the sunshade.

Judy took a few pictures of him. She kept her camera bag slung from her shoulder so that she could get to her weapon quickly.

Then, out of the corner of her eye, she saw movement.

An old Chevrolet Impala was approaching slowly on 10th Street.

It had a faded two-tone paint job, sky blue and cream, rusting around the wheel arches. The face of the driver was in shade.

She darted a glance around. Not a single agent was in sight, but every one would be watching the car.

It stopped at the kerb right opposite Governor Robson.

Judy's heart beat faster.

'I guess this is him,' said the governor in a remarkably calm voice.

The door of the car opened.

The figure that stepped out wore blue jeans, a checked work shirt open over a white T-shirt, and sandals. When he stood upright, Judy saw that he was about six foot tall, maybe a little more, and thin, with long, dark hair.

He wore large-framed sunglasses and a colourful cotton scarf as a headband.

Judy stared at him, wishing she could see his eyes.

Her earpiece crackled. 'Judy? Is it him?'

'I can't tell!' she said. 'It could be.'

He looked around. It was a big lawn, and the table had been placed twenty or thirty yards back from the kerb. He started toward the governor.

Judy could feel everyone's eyes on her, waiting for her sign.

She moved, placing herself between him and the governor. The man noticed her move, hesitated, then came on.

Charlie spoke again. 'Well?'

'I don't know!' she whispered, trying not to move her lips. 'Give me a few more seconds!'

'Don't leave it too long.'

'I don't think it's him,' Judy said. All the pictures had shown a nose like the blade of a knife. This man had a broad, flat nose.

'Sure?'

'It's not him.'

The man was within touching distance of Judy. He

stepped around her and approached the governor. Without pausing in his stride, he put his hand inside his shirt.

In her earpiece, Charlie said: 'He's reaching for something!'

Judy dropped to one knee and fumbled for the pistol in her camera bag.

The man began to pull something out of his shirt. Judy saw a dark-coloured cylinder, like the barrel of a gun. She yelled: 'Freeze! FBI!'

Agents burst out of cars and vans and came running from the Capitol building.

The man froze.

Judy pointed her gun at his head and said: 'Pull it out real slow and pass it to me.'

'Okay, okay, don't shoot me!' The man drew the object out of his shirt. It was a magazine, rolled up into a cylinder, with a rubber band around it.

Judy took it from him. Still pointing her gun at him, she examined the magazine. It was this week's *Time*. There was nothing inside the cylinder.

The man said in a frightened voice: 'Some guy gave me a hundred dollars to hand it to the governor!'

Agents surrounded Mike Robson and bundled him back into the Capitol building.

Judy looked around, scanning the grounds and the streets. Granger was watching this, he had to be. Where the hell is he? People had stopped to stare at the running agents. A tour group was coming down the steps of the grand entrance, led by a guide. As Judy watched, a man in a Hawaiian shirt peeled off from the group and walked away, and something about him caught Judy's eye.

She frowned. He was tall. Because the shirt was baggy, and hung loose around his hips, she could not tell whether he was thin or fat. His hair was covered by a baseball cap.

She went after him, walking fast.

He did not seem to be in a hurry. Judy did not raise the alarm. If she got every agent here chasing some innocent tourist, that might permit the real Granger to get away. But instinct made her quicken her pace. She had to see this man's face.

He turned the corner of the building. Judy broke into a run.

She heard Charlie's voice in her earpiece. 'Judy? What's up?'

'Just checking someone out,' she said, panting a little. 'Probably a tourist, but get a couple of guys to follow me in case I need back-up.'

'You got it.'

She reached the corner and saw the Hawaiian shirt pass through a pair of tall wood doors and disappear into the Capitol building. It seemed to her that he was walking more briskly. She looked back over her shoulder. Charlie was talking to a couple of youngsters and pointing at her.

On the side street across the garden, Michael jumped out of a parked van and came running toward her. She pointed into the building. 'Did you see that guy?' she yelled.

'Yes, that was him!' he called back.

'You stay here,' she shouted. He was a civilian, she did not want him involved. 'Keep the hell out of this!' She ran into the Capitol building.

She found herself in a grand lobby with an elaborate mosaic floor. It was cool and quiet. Ahead of her was a broad carpeted staircase with an ornately carved balustrade. Did he go left or right, up or down? She chose left. The corridor dog-legged right. She raced past an elevator bank and found herself in the rotunda, a circular room with some kind of sculpture in the middle. The room extended up two floors to a richly decorated dome. Here she faced another choice: had he gone straight ahead, turned right toward the Horseshoe, or gone up the stairs on her left? She looked around. A tour group stared fearfully at her gun. She glanced up to the circular gallery at second-floor level and caught a glimpse of a brightly coloured shirt.

She bounded up one of the paired grand staircases.

At the top of the stairs she looked across the gallery. On the far side was an open doorway leading to a different world, a modern corridor with strip lighting and a plastic-tiled floor. The Hawaiian shirt was in the corridor.

He was running now.

Judy went after him. As she ran, she spoke into her bra mike, panting. 'It is him, Charlie! What the hell happened to my back-up?'

'They lost you, where are you?'

'On the second floor in the office section.'

'Okay.'

The office doors were shut and there was no one in the corridors: it was Saturday. She followed the shirt around a corner, then another, and a third. She was keeping him in view but not gaining on him.

The bastard is very fit.

Coming full circle, he returned to the gallery. She lost sight of him momentarily, and guessed he had gone up again.

Breathing hard, she went up another ornate staircase to the third floor.

Helpful signs told her that the Senate gallery was to her right, the Assembly to her left. She turned left, came to the door of the gallery, and found it locked. No doubt the other would be the same. She returned to the head of the staircase. Where had he gone?

In a corner she noticed a sign that read *North Stair —no roof access*. She opened it and found herself in a narrow functional stairwell with plain floor tiles and an iron balustrade. She could hear her quarry clattering down the stairs but she could not see him.

She hurtled down.

She emerged at ground level in the rotunda. She could not see Granger, but she spotted Michael, looking around distractedly. He caught her eye. 'Did you see him?' she called.

'No.'

'Stay back!'

From the rotunda, a marble corridor led to the governor's quarters. Her view was obscured by a tour party being shown the door to the Horseshoe. Was that a Hawaiian shirt beyond them? She was not sure.

She hared after it, along the marble hall, past framed displays featuring each county in the state. To her left, another corridor led to an exit with a plate-glass automatic door. She saw the shirt going out.

She followed. Granger was darting across L Street, dodging perilously through the impatient traffic. Drivers swerved to avoid him and honked indignantly. He jumped on the hood of a yellow coupé, denting it. The driver opened the door and leaped out in a rage, then saw Judy with her gun and hastily got back in his car.

She sprinted across the street, taking the same mad risks with the traffic. She darted in front of a bus that pulled up with a screech of brakes, ran across the hood of the same yellow coupé, and forced a stretch limousine to swerve across three lanes. She was almost at the sidewalk when a motorcycle came speeding up the inside lane straight at her. She stepped back and he missed her by an inch.

Granger sped along 11th Street then dodged into an entrance. Judy flew after him. He had gone into a parking garage. She turned into the garage, going as fast as she could, and something hit her a mighty blow in the face.

Pain exploded in her nose and forehead. She was blinded. She fell on her back, hitting the concrete with a crash. She lay still, paralysed by shock and pain, unable even to think. A few seconds later she felt a strong hand behind her head and heard, as if from a great distance, the voice of Michael saying: 'Judy, for God's sake, are you alive?'

Her head began to clear and her vision came back. Michael's face swam into focus.

'Speak to me, say something!' Michael said.

She opened her mouth. 'It hurts,' she mumbled.

'Thank God!' He pulled a handkerchief from the pocket of his khakis and wiped her mouth with surprising gentleness. 'Your nose is bleeding.'

She sat upright. 'What happened?'

'I saw you turning inside, going like greased lightning, then next minute you were flat on the ground. I think he was waiting for you and hit you as you came around the corner. If I get my hands on him . . .'

Judy realized she had dropped her weapon. 'My gun . . .'

He looked around, picked it up, and handed it to her.

'Help me up.'

He pulled her to her feet.

Her face hurt like hell, but she could see clearly and her legs felt steady. She tried to think straight.

Maybe I haven't lost him yet.

There was an elevator, but he could not have had time to take it. He must have gone up the ramp. She knew this garage—she parked here herself when she came to see Honeymoon—and she recalled that it spanned the width of the block, with entrances on 10th and 11th Streets. Maybe Granger knew that too, and was already getting away by the 10th Street door.

There was nothing for it but to follow.

'I'm going after him,' she said.

She ran up the ramp. Michael followed. She let

him. She had twice ordered him to stay back, and she could not spare the breath to tell him again.

They reached the first parking level. Judy's head started throbbing and her legs suddenly felt weak. She knew she could not go much farther. They started across the floor.

Suddenly a black car shot out of its parking slot straight at them.

Judy leaped sideways, fell to the ground, and rolled, frantically fast, until she was underneath a parked car.

She saw the wheels of the black car as it turned with a squeal of tyres and accelerated down the ramp like a shot from a gun.

Judy stood up, searching frantically for Michael. She had heard him shout with surprise and fear. Had the car hit him?

She saw him a few yards from her, on his hands and knees, white with shock.

'Are you all right?' she said.

He got to his feet. 'I'm fine, just shook up.'

Judy looked to see the make of the black car but it had disappeared.

'Shit,' she said. 'I lost him.'

CHAPTER TWENTY

As Judy was entering the officers' club at 7 p.m., Raja Khan came running out.

He stopped when he saw her. 'What happened to you?'

What happened to me? I failed to prevent the earthquake, I made a wrong guess about where Melanie Quercus was hiding out, and I let Ricky Granger slip through my fingers. I blew it, and tomorrow there will be another earthquake, and more people will die, and it will be my fault.

'Ricky Granger punched me on the nose,' she said. She had a bandage across her face. The pills they had given her at the hospital in Sacramento had eased the pain, but she felt battered and dispirited. 'Where are you going in such a hurry?'

'We were looking for a record album called *Raining Fresh Daisies*, remember?'

'Sure. We hoped it might give us a lead on the woman that called the John Truth show.'

'I've located a copy—and it's right here in town. A store called Vinyl Vic's.'

'Give that agent a gold star!' Judy felt her energy returning. This could be the lead she needed. It wasn't much, but it filled her with hope again. Perhaps there was still a chance she could prevent another earth-quake. 'I'm coming with you.'

They jumped into Raja's dirty Dodge Colt. The floor was littered with sweet wrappers. Raja tore out of the parking lot and headed for Haight-Ashbury. 'The guy who owns the store is called Vic Plumstead,' he said as he drove. 'When I called, a couple of days ago, he wasn't there, and I got a part-time kid who said he didn't think they had the record but he would ask the boss. I left a card, and Vic called me five minutes ago.'

'At last, a piece of luck!'

'The record was released in 1969 on a San Francisco label, Transcendental Tracks. It got some publicity and sold a few copies in the Bay area, but the label never had another success and went out of business after a few months.'

Judy's elation cooled. 'That means there are no files we can search for clues to where she might be now.'

'Maybe the album itself will give us something.'

Vinyl Vic's was a small store stuffed to bursting with old records. A few conventional sales racks in the middle of the floor had been swamped by cardboard boxes and fruit crates stacked to the ceiling. The place smelled like a dusty old library. There was one cus-tomer, a tattooed man in leather shorts studying an early David Bowie album. At the back, a small, thin man in tight blue jeans and a tie-dyed T-shirt stood beside a cash register sipping coffee from a mug that said: 'Legalize it!'

Raja introduced himself. 'You must be Vic. I spoke to you on the phone a few minutes ago.'

Vic stared at them. He seemed surprised. He said: 'Finally, the FBI hits my place, and it's two Asians? What happened?'

Raja said: 'I'm the token non-white and she's the token woman. Every FBI office has to have one of each, it's a rule. All the other agents are white men with short haircuts.'

'Oh, right.' Vic looked baffled. He did not know whether Raja was kidding or not.

Judy said impatiently: 'What about this record?'

'Here it is.' Vic turned to one side, and Judy saw he had a turntable behind the cash register. He swung the arm over the disc and lowered the stylus. A burst of manic guitar introduced a surprisingly laid-back jazz-funk track with piano chords over a complex drum beat. Then the woman's voice came in:

> I am melting
> Feel me melting
> Liquefaction
> Turning softer

'I think it's quite meaningful, actually,' Vic said.

Judy thought it was crap, but she did not care. It was the voice on the John Truth tape, without question. Younger, clearer, gentler, but with that same unmistakable low, sexy tone. 'Do you have the sleeve?' she said urgently.

'Sure.' He handed it to her.

It was curling at the corners, and the transparent plastic coating was peeling off the glossy paper. The front had a swirling multicoloured design that induced eyestrain. The words *Raining Fresh Daisies* could just be discerned. Judy turned it over. The back was grubby and there was a coffee ring in the top right-hand corner.

The sleeve notes began: 'Music opens the doors that lead to parallel universes . . .'

Judy skipped over the words. At the bottom was a row of five monochrome photographs, just head and shoulders, four men and a woman. She read the captions:

> *Dave Rolands, keyboards*
> *Ian Kerry, guitar*
> *Ross Muller, bass*
> *Jerry Jones, drums*
> *Stella Higgins, poetry*

Judy frowned. 'Stella Higgins,' she said excitedly. 'I believe I've heard that name before!' She felt sure, but she could not remember where. Maybe it was wishful thinking. She stared at the small black-and-white mug-shot. She saw a girl of about twenty with a smiling sensual face framed by wavy dark hair and the wide, generous mouth Simon Sparrow had predicted. 'She was beautiful,' Judy murmured, almost to herself. She searched the face for the craziness that would make a person threaten an earthquake, but she could see no sign of it. All she saw was a young woman full of vitality and hope. *What went wrong with your life?*

'Can we borrow this?' Judy said.

Vic looked sulky. 'I'm here to sell records, not lend them,' he said.

She was not going to argue. 'How much?'

'Fifty bucks.'

'Okay.'

He stopped the turntable, picked up the disc, and slipped it into its paper cover. Judy paid him. 'Thank you, Vic. We appreciate your help.'

Driving back in Raja's car, she said: 'Stella Higgins. Where have I seen that name?'

Raja shook his head. 'It doesn't ring any bells with me.'

As they got out of the car, she gave him the album. 'Make blow-ups of her photo and circulate them to police departments,' she said. 'Give the record to Simon Sparrow. You never know what he might come up with.'

They entered the command post. The big ballroom now looked crowded. The Head Shed had been augmented by another table. Among the people crowded around would be several more suits from FBI headquarters in Washington, Judy assumed, plus people from the city, state, and federal emergency management agencies.

She went to the Investigation team table. Most of her people were working the phones, running down leads. Judy spoke to Carl Theobald. 'What are you on?'

'Sightings of tan Plymouth 'Cudas.'

'I've got something better for you. We have the

California phone book on CD-ROM here somewhere. Look up the name Stella Higgins.'

'And if I find her?'

'Call her and see if she sounds like the woman on the John Truth tape.'

She sat at a computer and initiated a search of criminal records. There was a Stella Higgins in the files, she found. The woman had been fined for possession of marijuana and been given a suspended sentence for assaulting a police officer at a demonstration. Her date of birth was about right, and her address was on Haight Street. There was no picture in the database, but it sounded like the right woman.

Both convictions were dated 1968, and there was nothing since.

Stella's record was like that of Ricky Granger, who had dropped off the radar in the early seventies. Judy printed the file and pinned it to the suspect board. She sent an agent to check out the Haight Street address, though she felt sure Higgins would not be there thirty years later.

She felt a hand on her shoulder. It was Bo. His eyes were full of concern. 'My baby, what happened to your face?' He touched the bandage on her nose with gentle fingertips.

'I guess I was careless,' she said.

He kissed the top of her head. 'I'm on duty tonight, but I had to stop by and see how you are.'

'Who told you I was hurt?'

'That married guy, Michael.'

That married guy. She grinned. *Reminding me that Michael belongs to someone else.* 'There's no real damage, but I guess I'm going to have two beautiful black eyes.'

'You got to get some rest. When are you going home?'

'I don't know. I just made a breakthrough. Take a seat.' She told him about *Raining Fresh Daisies.* 'The way I see it, she's a beautiful girl living in San Francisco in the sixties, going on demos, smoking dope and hanging out with rock bands. The sixties turn into the seventies, she becomes disillusioned or maybe just bored, and she hooks up with a charismatic guy who is on the run from the Mob. The two of them start a cult. Somehow the group survives, making jewellery or whatever, for three decades. Then something goes wrong. Somehow, their existence is threatened by a plan to build a power plant. As they face the ruin of everything they've worked for and built up over the years, they cast about for some way, any way, to block this power plant. Then a seismologist joins the group and comes up with a crazy idea.'

Bo nodded. 'It makes sense, or a kind of sense, the kind that appeals to wackos.'

'Granger has the criminal experience to steal the seismic vibrator, and the personal magnetism to persuade other cult members to go along with the scheme.'

Bo looked thoughtful. 'They probably don't own their home,' he said.

'Why?'

'Well, imagine they live someplace close to where this nuclear plant is going, so they have to move away. If they owned their house, or farm, or whatever, they'd get compensation, and they could start again somewhere else. So I'm guessing they have a short lease, or maybe they're squatters.'

'You're probably right, but it doesn't help. There's no statewide database of land leases.'

Carl Theobald came up with a notebook in his hand. 'Three hits in the phone book. Stella Higgins in Los Angeles is a woman of about seventy with a quavery voice. Mrs Higgins in Stockton has a strong accent from some African country, maybe Nigeria. And S. J. Higgins in Diamond Heights is a man called Sidney.'

'Damn,' Judy said. She explained to Bo: 'Stella Higgins is the voice on the John Truth tape—and I'm sure I've seen the name before.'

Bo said: 'Try your own files.'

'What?'

'If the name seems familiar, that could be because it has already come up during this investigation. Search the case files.'

'Good idea.'

'I gotta go,' he said. 'With all these people getting out of the city and leaving their homes empty, the San Francisco PD is going to have a busy night. Good luck —and get some rest.'

'Thanks, Bo.' Judy activated the Find function on the computer and had it search the entire Hammer of Eden directory for 'Stella Higgins'.

Carl watched over her shoulder. It was a big directory and the search took a while.

Finally the screen flickered and said:

1 file(s) found

Judy felt a burst of elation.

Carl shouted: 'Christ! The name is already in the computer!'

Oh, my God, I think I've found her.

Two more agents looked over Judy's shoulder as she opened the file.

It was a large document containing all the notes made by agents during the abortive raid on Los Alamos six days ago.

'What the hell?' Judy was mystified. 'Was she at Los Alamos and we missed her?'

Start Cleever appeared at her side. 'What's all the fuss about?'

'We've found the woman who called John Truth!' Judy said.

'Where?'

'Silver River Valley.'

'How did she slip through your fingers?'

It was Marvin Hayes, not me, who organized that raid. 'I don't know, I'm working on it, give me a minute!' She used the Find function to locate the name in the notes.

Stella Higgins had not been at Los Alamos. That was why they had missed her.

Two agents had visited a winery a few miles up the

valley. The site was rented from the federal government, and the name of the tenant was Stella Higgins.

'Damn, we were so close!' Judy cried in exasperation. 'We almost had her a week ago!'

'Print this so everyone can see it,' Cleever said.

Judy hit the print button and read on.

The agents had conscientiously noted the name
and age of every adult at the winery. Some were
couples with children, Judy saw, and most gave
their address as that of the winery. So they were living
there.

Maybe it was a cult, and the agents simply had not
realized that.

Or the people had been careful to conceal the true
nature of their community.

'We've got them!' Judy said. 'We were sidetracked,
the first time, by Los Alamos, who seemed perfect
suspects. Then, when they turned out to be clean, we
thought we must be barking up the wrong tree. That
made us careless about checking for *other* communes
in that valley. So we overlooked the real perpetrators.
But we've found them now.'

Stuart Cleever said: 'I think you're right.' He turned
to the SWAT team table. 'Charlie, call the Sacramento
office and organize a joint raid. Judy has the location.
We'll hit them at first light.'

Judy said: 'We should raid them now. If we wait
until morning, they may be gone.'

'Why would they leave now?' Cleever shook his
head. 'Night time is too risky. The suspects can slip
away in the darkness, especially in the countryside.'

He had a point, but instinct told Judy not to wait. 'I'd rather take that risk,' she said. 'Now that we know where they are, let's go get 'em.'

'No,' he said decisively. 'No further discussion, please, Judy. We raid at dawn.'

She hesitated. She was sure it was the wrong decision. But she was too tired to argue any more. 'So be it,' she said. 'What time do we head out, Charlie?'

Marsh looked at his watch. 'Leaving here at 2 a.m.'

'I may grab a couple of hours' rest.'

She seemed to remember parking her car outside on the parade ground. It felt like months ago, but in fact it had been Thursday night, only forty-eight hours ago.

On the way out she met Michael. 'You look exhausted,' he said. 'Let me drive you home.'

'Then how will I get back here?'

'I'll nap on your couch and drive you back.'

She stopped and looked at him. 'I have to tell you, my face is so sore I don't think I could kiss, let alone anything else.'

'I'll settle for holding your hand,' he said with a smile.

I'm beginning to think this guy cares for me.

He raised a questioning eyebrow. 'Well, what do you say?'

'Will you tuck me into bed, and bring me hot milk and aspirins?'

'Yes. Will you let me watch you sleep?'

Oh, boy, I'd like that better than anything in the world.

He read her expression. 'I think I'm hearing yes,' he said.

She smiled. 'Yes.'

*

Priest was mad as hell when he got back from Sacramento. He had been sure the governor was going to make a deal. He felt he was on the very brink of victory. He had been congratulating himself already. And it had all been a sham. Governor Robson had had no thought of making a deal. The whole thing had been a set-up. The FBI had imagined they could catch him in a dumbass trap like some two-bit crook. It was the disrespect that really got to him. They thought he was some dope.

They would learn the truth. And the lesson would be dear.

It would cost them another earthquake.

Everyone at the commune was still stunned by the departure of Dale and Poem. It had reminded them of something they had been pretending to forget: that tomorrow they were all supposed to leave the valley.

Priest told the Rice Eaters how much pressure they had put on the governor. The freeways were still jammed with minivans full of kids and suitcases escaping from the earthquake to come. In the semi-deserted neighbourhoods they had left behind, looters were walking out of suburban homes loaded with microwave ovens and CD players and computers.

But they also knew the governor showed no signs of giving in.

Although it was Saturday night, nobody wanted to party. After supper and evening worship, most of them retired to their cabins. Melanie went to the bunkhouse to read to the children. Priest sat outside his cabin, watching the moon go down over the valley, and slowly calmed down. He opened a five-year-old bottle of his own wine, a vintage with the smoky flavour he loved.

It was a battle of nerves, he told himself when he was able to think calmly. Who could tough it out longest, him or the governor? Which of them could best keep their people under control? Would the earthquakes bring the state government to its knees before the FBI could track Priest down to his mountain lair?

Star came into view, backlit by moonlight, walking barefoot and smoking a joint. She took a deep pull on her spliff, bent over Priest, and kissed him, opening her mouth. He inhaled the intoxicating smoke from her lungs. He breathed out, smiled, and said: 'I remember the first time you did that. It was the sexiest thing that ever happened to me.'

'Really?' she said. 'Sexier than a blow job?'

'A lot. Remember, when I was seven years old I saw my mother giving a blow job to a john. She never kissed them, though. I was the only person she kissed. She told me that.'

'Priest, what a hell of a life you've had.'

He frowned. 'You make it sound as if it's over.'

'This part of it is over, though, isn't it?'

'No!'

'It's almost midnight. Your deadline is about to run out. The governor isn't going to give in.'

'He has to,' Priest said. 'It's only a matter of time.' He stood up. 'I have to listen to the radio news.'

She walked with him as he crossed the vineyard in the moonlight and climbed the track to the cars. 'Let's go away,' she said suddenly. 'Just you and me and Flower. Let's get in a car, right now, and leave. We won't say goodbye, or pack a case, or even take spare clothes or anything. We'll just take off, the way I did when I left San Francisco in 1969. We'll go where the mood takes us—Oregon, or Las Vegas, or even New York. What about Charleston? I've always wanted to see the South.'

Without answering, he got in the Cadillac and turned on the radio. Star sat beside him. Brenda Lee was singing 'Let's Jump the Broomstick'.

'Come on, Priest, what do you say?'

The news came on and he turned up the volume.

'Suspected Hammer of Eden terrorist leader Richard Granger slipped through the fingers of the FBI in Sacramento today. Meanwhile, residents fleeing neighbourhoods near the San Andreas fault have brought traffic to a standstill on many freeways within the San Francisco Bay area, with miles of cars blocking long sections of Interstate Routes 280, 580, 680 and 880. And a Haight-Ashbury rare record dealer claims FBI agents bought from him an album with a photograph of another terrorist suspect.'

'Album?' Star said. 'What the fuck . . .?'

'Store owner Vic Plumstead told reporters the FBI

called him in to help track down a sixties album, which they believed featured the voice of one of the Hammer of Eden suspects. After days of effort, he said, he found the album, by an obscure rock band, *Raining Fresh Daisies.*'

'Jesus Christ! I'd almost forgotten them myself!'

'The FBI would not confirm or deny they are seeking the vocalist, Stella Higgins.'

'Shit!' Star burst out. 'They know my name!'

Priest's mind was racing. How dangerous was this? The name was not much use to them. Star had not used it for almost thirty years. No one knew where Stella Higgins lived.

Yes, they did.

He suppressed a groan of despair. The name Stella Higgins was on the lease for this land. And he had said that to the two FBI agents who had come here on the day they raided Los Alamos.

This changed everything. Sooner or later, someone at the FBI would make the connection.

And if by some mischance the FBI failed to figure it out, there was a Silver City sheriff's deputy, currently on holiday in the Bahamas, who had written the name Stella Higgins on a file that was due to come up in court in a couple of weeks' time.

Silver River Valley was a secret no more.

The thought made him unbearably sad.

What could he do?

Maybe he should run away with Star now. The keys were in the car. They could be in Nevada in a couple of hours. By midday tomorrow they would be five hundred miles away.

Hell, no. I'm not beat yet.

He could still hold things together.

His original plan had been that the authorities would never know who the Hammer of Eden were or why they had demanded a ban on new power plants. Now the FBI were about to find out—but maybe they could be forced to keep it secret. That could become part of Priest's demand. If they could bring themselves to agree to the freeze, they could swallow this too.

Yes, it was outrageous—but this whole thing was outrageous. He could do it.

But he would have to stay out of the clutches of the FBI.

He opened the car door and got out. 'Let's go,' he said to Star. 'I've got a lot to do.'

She got out slowly. 'You won't run away with me?' she said sadly.

'Hell, no.' He slammed the door and walked away.

She followed him across the vineyard and back to the settlement. She went to her cabin without saying goodnight.

Priest went to Melanie's cabin. She was asleep. He shook her roughly to wake her. 'Get up,' he said. 'We have to go. Quickly.'

*

Judy watched and waited while Stella Higgins cried her heart out.

She was a big woman, and though she might have been attractive in different circumstances, she now looked destroyed. Her face was contorted with grief, her old-fashioned eye make-up was running down her cheeks, and her heavy shoulders shook with sobs.

They sat in the tiny cabin that was her home. All around were medical supplies: boxes of bandages, cartons of aspirin and Rol-aids, Tylenol and Trojans, bottles of gripe water, cough linctus, and iodine. The walls were decorated with kids' drawings of Star taking care of sick children. It was a primitive building, without electric power or running water, but it had a happy feel.

Judy went to the door and looked out, giving Star a minute to recover her composure. The place was beautiful in the pale sunlight of early morning. The last ribbons of a light mist were vanishing from the trees on the steep hillsides, and the river flashed and glittered in the fork of the valley. On the lower slopes was a neat vineyard, the ordered rows of vines with their shoots tied to wooden trellises. For a moment, Judy was taken by a sense of spiritual peace, a feeling that here in this place things were as they should be, and it was the rest of the world that was weird. She shook herself to get rid of the spooky sensation.

Michael appeared. Once again he had wanted to be here to take care of Dusty, and Judy had told Stuart Cleever that he should be indulged because his expertise was so important to the investigation. He was leading Dusty by the hand. 'How is he?' Judy asked.

'He's just fine,' Michael said.

'Have you found Melanie?'

'She's not here. Dusty says there's a big girl called Flower who's been looking after him.'

'Any idea where Melanie went?'

'No.' He nodded toward Star. 'What does she say?'

'Nothing, yet.' Judy went back inside and sat on the edge of the bed. 'Tell me about Ricky Granger,' she said.

'There's good in him as well as bad,' Star said as her weeping subsided. 'He was a hoodlum before, I know, he's even killed people, but in all the time we were together, twenty-five years, he didn't once hurt anyone, until now, until someone thought up the idea of this stupid fucking dam.'

'All I want to do,' Judy said gently, 'is find him before he hurts any more people.'

Star nodded. 'I know.'

Judy made Star look at her. 'Where did he go?'

'I'd tell you if I knew,' Star said. 'But I don't.'

CHAPTER TWENTY-ONE

Priest and Melanie drove to San Francisco in the commune's pickup truck. Priest figured the dented Cadillac was too conspicuous and the police might be looking for Melanie's orange Subaru.

All the traffic was heading in the opposite direction, so they were not much delayed. They reached the city a little after five on Sunday morning. There were a few people on the streets: a teenage couple embracing at a bus stop, two nervy crackheads buying one last rock from a dealer in a long coat, a helpless drunk zigzagging across the road. However, the waterfront district was deserted. The derelict industrial landscape looked bleak and eerie in the early morning light. They found the Perpetua Diaries warehouse and Priest unlocked the door. The realtor had kept his promise: the electric power was on and there was water in the restroom.

Melanie drove the pickup inside and Priest checked the seismic vibrator. He started the engine, then lowered and raised the plate. Everything worked.

They lay down to sleep on the couch in the small office, close together. Priest stayed awake, running over his position again and again. No matter how he looked at it, the only smart thing for Governor Robson to do was give in. Priest found himself making imaginary speeches on the John Truth show, pointing out how dumb the governor was being. *He could stop the earthquakes with one word!* After an hour of this he realized it was pointless. Lying on his back, he went through the relaxation ritual he used for meditation. His body became still, his heartbeat calmed, his mind emptied, and he went to sleep.

When he woke it was ten o'clock in the morning.

He put a pan of water on the hotplate. He had brought from the commune a can of organic ground coffee and some cups.

Melanie turned on the TV. 'I miss the news, living at the commune,' she said. 'I used to watch it all the time.'

'I hate the news, normally,' Priest said. 'It gets you worried about a million things you can't do nothing about.' But he watched with her, to see if there was anything about him.

It was *all* about him.

'Authorities in California are taking seriously the threat of an earthquake today as the terrorist deadline looms closer,' said the anchor, and there was film of city employees erecting a tent hospital in Golden Gate Park.

The sight made Priest angry. 'Why don't you just give us what we want?' he said to the TV.

The next clip showed FBI agents raiding log cabins in the mountains. After a moment Melanie said: 'My God, it's our commune!'

They saw Star, wrapped in her old purple silk robe, her face a picture of grief, being walked out of her cabin by two men in bulletproof vests.

Priest cursed. He was not surprised—it was the possibility of a raid that had led him to leave so hastily last night—but all the same he found himself plunged into rage and despair by the sight. His home had been violated by these self-righteous bastards.

You should have left us alone. Now it's too late.

He saw Judy Maddox, looking grim. *You were hoping to catch me in your net, weren't you?* She was not so pretty today. She had two black eyes and a large band-aid across her nose. *You lied to me and tried to trap me, and you got a bloody nose for it.*

But in his heart he was daunted. All along, he had underestimated the FBI. When he started out he had never dreamed that he would see agents invade the sanctuary of the valley that had been a secret place for so many years. Judy Maddox was smarter than he had imagined.

Melanie gasped. There was a shot of her husband, Michael, carrying Dusty. 'Oh, no!' she said.

'They're not arresting Dusty,' Priest said impatiently.

'But where will Michael take him?'

'Does it matter?'

'It does if there's going to be an earthquake!'

'Michael knows better than anyone where the fault lines are! He won't be anywhere dangerous.'

'Oh, God, I hope not, especially if he has Dusty with him.'

Priest had watched enough TV. 'Let's go out,' he said. 'Bring your phone.'

Melanie drove the pickup out and Priest locked the warehouse behind them. 'Head for the airport,' he told her as he got in.

Avoiding the freeways, they got close to the airport before they were stuck in traffic. Priest figured there had to be thousands of people using phones in the vicinity—trying to get flights, calling their families, checking how big the traffic jam was. He called the John Truth show.

John Truth himself answered. Priest figured he was hoping for this call. 'I have a new demand, so listen carefully,' Priest said.

'Don't worry, I'm taping this,' Truth said.

'I guess I'll be on your show tonight, huh, John?' Priest said with a smile.

'I hope you'll be in goddam jail,' Truth said nastily.

'Well, fuck you, too.' There was no need for the guy to get pissy. 'My new demand is a presidential pardon for everyone in the Hammer of Eden.'

'I'll let the President know.'

Now it was like he was being sarcastic. Didn't he understand how important this was? 'That's as well as the freeze on new power plants.'

'Wait a minute,' Truth said. 'Now that everyone knows where your commune is, you don't need a statewide freeze. You just want to stop your valley being flooded, don't you?'

Priest considered. He had not thought of this, but Truth was right. Still, he decided not to agree. 'Hell, no,' he said. 'I've got principles. California needs less electric power, not more, if it's going to be a decent place for my grandchildren to live in. Our original demand stands. There will be another earthquake if the governor doesn't agree.'

'How can you do this?'

The question took Priest by surprise. 'What?'

'How can you do this? How can you bring such suffering and misery to so many people—killing, wounding, damaging property, making people flee their homes in fear . . . How will you ever sleep?'

The question angered Priest. 'Don't make like *you're* the ethical one,' he said. 'I'm trying to save California.'

'By killing people.'

Priest lost patience. 'Shut the fuck up and listen,' he said. 'I'm going to tell you about the next earthquake.' According to Melanie, the seismic window would open at 6.40 p.m. 'Seven o'clock,' Priest said. 'It will hit at seven tonight.'

'Can you tell me—'

Priest broke the connection.

He was silent for a while. The conversation left him with an uneasy feeling. Truth should have been scared to death, but he had almost bantered with Priest. He had treated Priest like a loser, that was it.

They came to a junction. 'We could turn here and head back,' Melanie said. 'No traffic the other way.'

'Okay.'

She made the turn. She was thoughtful. 'Will we ever go back to the valley?' she said. 'Now the FBI and everyone knows about it?'

'Yes!' he said.

'Don't shout!'

'Yes, we will,' he said more quietly. 'I know it looks bad, and we may have to stay away for a while. I'm sure we'll lose this year's vintage. The media will crawl all over the place for weeks. But they will forget about us, eventually. There'll be a war, or an election, or a sex scandal, and we'll be old news. Then we can slip quietly back, and move into our homes, and get the vines back in shape, and grow a new crop.'

Melanie smiled. 'Yeah,' she said.

She believes it. I'm not sure I do. But I'm not going to think about it any more. Fretting will sap my will. No doubts, now. Just action.

Melanie said: 'You want to go back to the warehouse?'

'No. I'll go crazy shut up in that hole all day. Head for the city and see if we can find a restaurant that's serving brunch. I'm starving.'

*

Judy and Michael took Dusty to Stockton, where Michael's parents lived. They went in a helicopter. Dusty was thrilled. It landed on the football field of a high school in the suburbs.

Michael's father was a retired accountant, and they had a neat suburban house that backed on to a golf course. Judy drank coffee in the kitchen while Michael settled Dusty in. Mrs Quercus said worriedly: 'Maybe this dreadful affair will give the business a boost, anyway—it's an ill wind that blows nobody any good.'

Judy recalled that they had put money into Michael's consultancy, and he was worried about paying them back. But Mrs Quercus was right—his being the FBI's earthquake expert might help.

Judy's mind was on the seismic vibrator. It was not in Silver River Valley. It had not been sighted since Friday evening, though the panels that made it look like a carnival ride had been found at the roadside by one of the hundreds of rescue workers still clearing up the mess at Felicitas.

She knew what Granger was driving. She had found out by asking the commune members what cars they had and checking which was missing. He was using a pickup truck, and she had put out an all-points bulletin on it. In theory, every cop in California should be looking for it, although most of them would be too busy coping with the emergency.

She was tantalized unbearably by the thought that she might have caught Granger at the commune if she had fought harder, and persuaded Cleever to raid the place last night instead of this morning. But she had just been too tired. She felt better today—the raid had pumped adrenalin into her system and given her energy. But she was bruised physically and mentally, running on empty.

A small TV set on the kitchen counter was on with the sound muted. The news came on and Judy asked Mrs Quercus to turn up the volume. There was an interview with John Truth, who had spoken on the phone to Granger. He played an extract from his tape of the conversation. 'Seven o'clock,' Granger said on the tape. 'The next earthquake will be at seven tonight.'

Judy shivered. He meant it. There was no regret or remorse in his voice, no sign that he hesitated to risk the lives of so many people. He sounded rational, but there was a flaw in his humanity. He did not really care about the sufferings of others. It was the characteristic of psychopaths.

She wondered what Simon Sparrow would make of the voice. But it was too late now for psycholinguistics. She went to the kitchen door and called: 'Michael! We have to go!'

She would have liked to leave Michael here with Dusty, where they would both be safe. But she needed him at the command post. His expertise might be crucial.

He came in with Dusty. 'I'm about ready,' he said. The phone rang and Mrs Quercus picked it up. After a moment she held the receiver out to Dusty. 'Someone for you,' she said.

Dusty took the phone and said tentatively: 'Hello?' Then his face brightened. 'Hi, Mom!'

Judy froze.

It was Melanie.

Dusty said: 'I woke up this morning and you were gone! Then Daddy came to get me!'

Melanie was with Priest and the seismic vibrator, almost certainly. Judy grabbed her mobile and dialled the command post. She got Raja and said quietly: 'Trace a call. Melanie Quercus is calling a number in Stockton.' She read the number off the instrument

Dusty was using. 'Call started a minute ago, still in progress.'

'I'm on it,' Raja said.

Judy broke the connection.

Dusty was listening, nodding and shaking his head occasionally, forgetting that his mother could not see his movements.

Then he abruptly offered the phone to his father. 'She wants you.'

Judy whispered to Michael: 'For God's sake find out where she is!'

He took the phone from Dusty and held it against his chest, muffling it. 'Pick up the bedroom extension.'

'Where?'

Mrs Quercus said: 'Just across the hall, dear.'

Judy darted into the bedroom, threw herself across the flowered counterpane, and grabbed the phone from the bedside table, covering the mouthpiece with her hand.

She heard Michael say: 'Melanie—where the hell are you?'

'Never mind,' Melanie replied. 'I saw you and Dusty on TV. Is he okay?'

So she's been watching TV, wherever she is.

'Dusty's fine,' Michael said. 'We just got here.'

'I was hoping you'd be there.'

Her voice was low, and Michael said: 'Can you speak up?'

'No, I can't, so just listen harder, okay?'

She doesn't want Granger to hear her. That's good—it may be a sign that they're beginning to disagree.

'Okay, okay,' Michael said.

'You're going to stay there with Dusty, right?'

'No,' Michael said. 'I'm going into the city.'

'What? For God's sake, Michael, it's dangerous!'

'Is that where the earthquake will be—in San Francisco?'

'I can't tell you.'

'Will it be on the peninsula?'

'Yes, on the peninsula, so keep Dusty away!'

Judy's cellphone beeped. Keeping the mouthpiece of the bedroom phone tightly covered, she put the cellphone to her other ear and said: 'Yeah.'

It was Raja. 'She's calling on her mobile. It's in downtown San Francisco. They can't do better than that for a digital phone.'

'Get some people out in the streets looking for that pickup!'

'You got it.'

Judy broke the connection.

Michael was saying: 'If you're so worried, why don't you just tell me where the seismic vibrator is?'

'I can't do that!' Melanie hissed. 'You're out of your mind!'

'Come on. *I'm* out of my mind? You're the one who's causing earthquakes!'

'I can't talk any more.' There was a click.

Judy replaced the handset on the bedside phone and rolled over onto her back, her mind racing.

Melanie had given away a great deal of information. She was somewhere in downtown San Francisco, and although that did not make her easy to find, it was a smaller haystack than California. She had said the earthquake would be triggered somewhere on the San Francisco peninsula, the broad neck of land between the Pacific Ocean and the San Francisco Bay. The seismic vibrator had to be somewhere in that area. But most intriguing, to Judy, had been the hint of some division between Melanie and Granger. She had obviously been making the call without telling him, and she had seemed to be afraid he might overhear. That was hopeful. There might be a way Judy could take advantage of a split.

She closed her eyes, concentrating. Melanie was worried about Dusty. That was her weakness. How could it be used against her?

She heard footsteps and opened her eyes. Michael came into the room. He gave her a strange look.

'What?' she said.

'This may seem inappropriate, but you look great lying on a bed.'

She remembered she was in his parents' house. She stood up.

He wrapped his arms around her. It felt good. 'How's your face?' he said.

She looked up at him. 'If you're very gentle . . .'

He kissed her lips softly.

If he wants to kiss me when I look this bad, he must really like me.

'Mm,' she said. 'When this is all over . . .'

'Yes.'

She closed her eyes for a moment.

Then she started thinking about Melanie again. 'Michael . . .'

'Still here.'

She detached herself from his embrace. 'Melanie is worried that Dusty might be in the earthquake zone.'

'He's going to be here.'

'But you didn't confirm that. She asked you, but you said if she was worried, she should tell you where the seismic vibrator is, and you never answered her question properly.'

'Still, the implication . . . I mean, why would I take him into danger?'

'I'm just saying, she may have a nagging doubt. And, wherever she is, there's a TV.'

'She leaves the news on all day sometimes—it relaxes her.'

Judy felt a stab of jealousy. *He knows her so well.* 'What if we had a reporter interview you, at the Emergency Operations Center in San Francisco, about what you're doing to help the Bureau . . . and Dusty was, like, just in the background somewhere?'

'Then she'd know he was in San Francisco.'

'And what would she do?'

'Call me and scream at me, I guess.'

'And if she couldn't reach you . . .'

'She'd be real scared.'

'But would she stop Granger operating the seismic vibrator?'

'Maybe. If she could.'

'Is it worth a try?'

'Is there another choice?'

*

Priest had a do-or-die feeling. Maybe the governor and the president would not give in to him, even after Felicitas. But tonight there would be a third earthquake. Then he would call John Truth and say: *I'll do it again! Next time it could be Los Angeles, or San Bernadino, or San Jose. I can do this as often as I like. I'm going to keep on until you give in. The choice is yours!*

Downtown San Francisco was a ghost town. Few people wanted to shop or do sightseeing, though plenty were going to church. The restaurant was half empty. Priest ordered eggs and drank three Bloody Marys. Melanie was subdued, worrying about Dusty. Priest thought the kid would be fine, he was with his father.

'Did I ever tell you why I'm called Granger?' he said to Melanie.

'It's not your parents' name?'

'My mother called herself Veronica Nightingale. She told me my father's name was Stewart Granger. He had gone on a long trip, she said, but one day he would come back, in a big limousine loaded with presents—perfume and chocolates for her, and a bicycle for me. On rainy days, when I couldn't play in the streets, I used to sit at the window watching for him, hour after hour.'

For a moment Melanie seemed to forget her own problems. 'Poor kid,' she said.

'I was about twelve when I realized that Stewart Granger had been a big movie star. He played Allan Quatermain in *King Solomon's Mines* just about the time I was born. I guess he was my mother's fantasy. Broke my heart, I can tell you. All those hours looking out the damn window.' Priest smiled, but the memory hurt.

'Who knows?' Melanie said. 'Maybe he *was* your father. Movie stars go to hookers.'

'I guess I should ask him.'

'He's dead.'

'Is he? I didn't know that.'

'Yeah, I read it in *People* magazine, a few years ago.'

Priest felt a pang of loss. Stewart Granger was the nearest thing to a father he had ever had. 'Well, now I'll never know.' He shrugged and called for the check.

When they left the restaurant, Priest did not want to return to the warehouse. He could easily sit doing nothing when he was at the commune, but in a dingy room in an industrial wasteland he would get cabin fever. Twenty-five years of living in Silver River Valley had spoiled him for the city. So he and Melanie walked around Fisherman's Wharf, making like tourists, enjoying the salty breeze off the bay.

They had altered their appearance, as a precaution. She had put up her distinctive long red hair and concealed it under a hat, and she wore sunglasses. Priest had greased his dark hair and plastered it to his head, and he had three days' growth of dark stubble on his cheeks, giving him a Latin lover air that was quite different from his usual ageing-hippie look. No one gave them a second glance.

Priest listened in to the conversations of the few people walking around. Everyone had an excuse for not leaving town.

'I'm not worried, our building is earthquake-proof . . .'

'So's mine, but at seven o'clock I'm going to be in the middle of the park . . .'

'I'm a fatalist, either this earthquake has my name on it or it doesn't . . .'

'Exactly, you could drive to Vegas and get killed in a car wreck . . .'

'I've had my house retrofitted . . .'

'No one can cause earthquakes, it was a coincidence . . .'

They got back to the car a few minutes after four.

Priest did not see the cop until it was almost too late.

The Bloody Marys had made him strangely calm, and he felt almost invulnerable, so he was not looking out for the police. He was only eight or ten feet from the pickup truck when he noticed a uniformed San Francisco cop staring at the licence plate and speaking into a walkie-talkie.

Priest stopped dead and grabbed Melanie's arm.

A moment later he realized that the smart thing to do was walk right by; but by then it was too late.

The cop glanced up from the licence plate and caught Priest's eye.

Priest looked at Melanie. She had not seen the cop.

He almost said *Don't look at the car*, but just in time he realized that would be sure to make her look. Instead he said the next thing that came into his head. 'Look at my hand.' He turned his palm up.

She stared at it then looked at him again. 'What am I supposed to see?'

'Keep looking at my hand while I explain.'

She did as he said.

'We're going to walk right past the car. There's a cop taking the number. He's noticed us, I can see him out of the corner of my eye.'

She looked up from his hand to his face. Then, to his astonishment, she slapped him.

It hurt. He gasped.

Melanie cried: 'And now you can just go back to your dumb blonde!'

'What?' he said angrily.

She walked on.

He watched her in astonishment. She strode past the pickup truck.

The cop looked at Priest with a faint grin.

Priest walked after Melanie, saying: 'Now just wait a minute!'

The cop returned his attention to the licence plate.

Priest caught up with Melanie and they turned a corner.

'Very cute,' he said. 'But you didn't have to hit me so hard.'

*

523

A powerful portable spotlight shone on Michael, and a miniature microphone was clipped to the front of his dark green polo shirt. A small television camera on a tripod was aimed at him. Behind him, the young seismologists he had brought in worked at their screens. In front of him sat Alex Day, a twenty-something television reporter with a fashionably short haircut. He was wearing a camouflage jacket, which Judy thought was overly dramatic.

Dusty stood beside Judy, holding her hand trustingly, watching his daddy being interviewed.

Michael was saying: 'Yes, we can identify locations where an earthquake could most easily be triggered—but, unfortunately, we can't tell which one the terrorists have chosen until they start up their seismic vibrator.'

'And what's your advice to citizens?' Alex Day asked. 'How can they protect themselves if there is an earthquake?'

'The motto is "Duck, cover, and hold," and that's the best counsel,' he replied. 'Duck under a table or desk, cover your face to protect yourself from flying glass, and hold your position until the shaking stops.'

Judy whispered to Dusty: 'Okay, go to Daddy.'

Dusty walked into shot. Michael lifted the boy onto his knee. On cue, Alex Day said: 'Anything special we can do to protect youngsters?'

'Well, you could practise the "Duck, cover, and hold" drill with them right now, so they'll know what to do if they feel a tremor. Make sure they're wearing sturdy shoes, not thongs or sandals, because there will be a lot of broken glass around. And keep them close, so you don't have to go searching for them afterwards.'

'Anything people should avoid?'

'Don't run out of the house. Most injuries in earth-quakes are caused by falling bricks and other debris from damaged buildings.'

'Professor Quercus, thank you for being with us today.'

Alex Day smiled at Michael and Dusty for a long frozen moment, then the cameraman said: 'Great.'

Everyone relaxed. The crew started rapidly packing up their equipment.

Dusty said: 'When can I go to Grandma's in the helicopter?'

'Right now,' Michael told him.

Judy said: 'How soon will that be on the air, Alex?'

'It hardly needs editing, so it will go right out. Within half an hour, I'd say.'

Judy looked at the clock. It was five fifteen.

*

Priest and Melanie walked for half an hour without seeing a taxi. Then Melanie called a cab service on her mobile phone. They waited, but no car came.

Priest felt as if he was going mad. After all he had done, his great scheme was in jeopardy because he could not find a goddam taxi!

But at last a dusty Chevrolet pulled up at Pier 39. The driver had an unreadable Central European name, and he seemed stoned. He understood no English except 'left' and 'right', and he was probably the only person in San Francisco who had not heard about the earthquake.

They got back to the warehouse at six twenty.

*

At the Emergency Operations Center, Judy slumped in her chair, staring at the phone.

It was six twenty-five. In thirty-five minutes, Granger would start up his seismic vibrator. If it worked as well as it had the last two times, there would be an earthquake. But this one would be the worst. Assuming Melanie had told the truth, and the vibrator was somewhere in the San Francisco peninsula, the quake would almost certainly hit the city.

Around two million people had fled the metropolitan area since Friday night, when Granger had announced on the John Truth show that the next earthquake would hit San Francisco. But that left more than a million men, women, and children who were unable or unwilling to leave their homes: the poor, the old, and the sick, plus all the cops, firefighters, nurses, and city employees waiting to begin rescue work. And that included Bo.

On the TV screen, Alex Day was speaking from a temporary studio set up at the mayor's Emergency Command Center on Turk Street, a few blocks away. The mayor was wearing a hard hat and a purple vest, and telling citizens to duck, cover, and hold.

The interview with Michael ran every few minutes on all channels: the television editors had been told its real purpose.

But it seemed Melanie was not watching.

Priest's pickup had been found parked at Fisherman's Wharf at four o'clock. It was under surveillance, but he had not returned to it. Right now, every garage and parking lot in the neighbourhood was being searched for a seismic vibrator.

The ballroom of the officers' club was full of people. There were at least forty suits around the Head Shed. Michael and his helpers were clustered around their computers, waiting for the inappropriately cheerful musical warning sound that would be the first sign of the seismic tremor they all feared. Judy's team were still working the phones, following up sightings of people who looked like Granger or Melanie, but there was an increasingly desperate tone to their voices. Using Dusty in the TV interview with Michael had been their last shot, and it seemed to have failed.

Most of the agents working in the EOC had homes in the Bay area. The Admin desk had organized the evacuation of all their families. The building they were in was considered as safe as any: it had been retrofitted by the military to make it earthquake-resistant. But they could not flee. Like soldiers, like firefighters, like cops, they had to go where the danger was. It was their job. Outside, on the parade ground, a fleet of helicopters stood ready, with their rotors turning, waiting to take Judy and her colleagues into the earthquake zone.

*

Priest went to the bathroom. While he was washing his hands, he heard Melanie scream.

He ran to the office with wet hands. He found her staring at the TV. 'What is it?' he said.

Her face was white and her hand covered her mouth. 'Dusty!' she said, pointing at the screen.

Priest saw Melanie's husband being interviewed. He had their son on his knee. A moment later the picture changed, and a female anchor said: 'That was Alex Day, interviewing one of the world's leading seismologists, Professor Michael Quercus, at the FBI's Emergency Operations Center in the Presidio.'

'Dusty's in San Francisco!' Melanie said hysterically.

'No, he's not,' Priest said. 'Maybe he *was*, when the interview was filmed. By now he's miles away.'

'You don't know that!'

'Of course I do. So do you. Michael's going to take care of his kid.'

'I wish I could be sure,' Melanie said in a shaky voice.

'Make a cup of coffee,' Priest said, just to give her something to do.

'Okay.' She took the pan from the hotplate and went to fill it with water in the restroom.

*

Judy looked at the clock. It was six thirty.

Her phone rang.

The room fell silent.

She snatched up the handset, dropped it, cursed, picked it up again, and held it to her ear. 'Yes?'

The switchboard operator said: 'Melanie Quercus asking for her husband.'

Thank God! Melanie pointed at Raja. 'Trace the call.'

He was already speaking into his phone.

Judy said to the operator: 'Put her on.'

All the suits from the Head Shed gathered around Judy's chair. They stood silent, straining to hear.

This could be the most important phone call of my life.

There was a click on the line. Judy tried to make her voice calm and said: 'Agent Maddox here.'

'Where's Michael?'

Melanie sounded so frightened and lost that Judy felt a surge of compassion for her. She seemed no more than a foolish mother worried about her child.

Get real, Judy. This woman is a killer.

Judy hardened her heart. 'Where are *you*, Melanie?'

'Please,' Melanie whispered. 'Just tell me where he's taken Dusty.'

'Let's do a deal,' Judy said. 'I'll make sure Dusty's okay—if you tell me where the seismic vibrator is.'

'Can I speak to my husband?'

'Are you with Ricky Granger? I mean Priest?'

'Yes.'

'And you have the seismic vibrator, wherever you are?'

'Yes.'

Then we've almost got you.

'Melanie—do you really want to kill all those people?'

'No, but we have to . . .'

'You won't be able to take care of Dusty while you're in jail. You'll miss watching him grow up.' Judy heard a sob at the other end of the line. 'You'll only ever see him through a glass partition. By the time they let you out, he'll be a grown man who doesn't know you.'

Melanie was crying.

'Tell me where you are, Melanie.'

In the big ballroom, the silence was total. No one moved.

Melanie whispered something, but Judy could not hear it.

'Speak up!'

At the other end of the line, in the background, a man shouted: 'Who the fuck are you calling?'

Judy said: 'Quickly, quickly! Tell me where you are!'

The man roared: 'Give me that goddam cellphone!'

Melanie said: 'Perpetua—' Then she screamed.

A moment later, the connection was broken.

Raja said: 'She's somewhere on the Bay Shore, south of the city.'

'That's not good enough!' Judy cried.

'They can't be more precise!'

'Shit!'

Stuart Cleever said: 'Quiet, everybody. We'll play the tape back in a moment. First, Judy, did she give you any clues?'

'She said something at the end. It sounded like "Perpetual". Carl, check for a street called Perpetual.'

Raja said: 'We should check for a company, too. They could be in the garage of an office building.'

'Do that.'

Cleever pounded the table in frustration. 'What made her hang up?'

'I think Granger found her calling and took the phone away.'

'What do you want to do now?'

'I'd like to get in the air,' Judy said. 'We can fly down the shoreline. Michael can come with me and point out where fault lines run. Maybe we'll spot the seismic vibrator.'

'Do it,' Cleever said.

*

Priest stared at Melanie in fury as she cowered up against the grimy washbasin. She had tried to betray him. He would have shot her right there and then if he had had a gun. But the revolver he had taken from the guard at Los Alamos was in the seismic vibrator, under the driving seat.

He switched off Melanie's phone, dropped it into his shirt pocket, and tried to make himself calm. This was something Star had taught him. As a young man he had given way to his rages, knowing that they frightened others, because people were easier to deal with when they were scared. But Star had taught him to breathe right and relax and *think*, which was better in the long run.

Now he considered the damage Melanie had done. Had the FBI been able to trace her phone? Could they find out where a mobile was calling from? He had to assume they could. If so, they would soon be cruising the neighbourhood, looking for a seismic vibrator.

He had run out of time. The seismic window opened at six forty. He looked at his watch: it was six thirty-five. To hell with his seven o'clock deadline—he had to trigger the earthquake right now.

He ran out of the restroom. The seismic vibrator stood in the middle of the empty warehouse, facing the high entrance doors. He jumped up into the driver's cabin and started the engine.

It took a minute or two for pressure to build up in the vibrating mechanism. He watched the gauges impatiently. *Come on, come on!* At last the readings went green.

The passenger door of the truck opened and Melanie climbed in. 'Don't do it!' she yelled. 'I don't know where Dusty is!'

Priest reached out to the lever that lowered the plate of the vibrator to the ground.

Melanie knocked his hand aside. 'Please, don't!'

Priest hit her backhanded across the face. She screamed, and blood came from her lip. 'Stay out of the damn way!' he yelled. He pulled the lever, and the plate descended.

Melanie reached across and threw the lever back to its start position.

Priest saw red. He hit her again.

She cried out and covered her face with her hands, but she did not flee.

Priest returned the lever to the down position.

'Please,' she said. 'Don't.'

What am I going to do with this stupid bitch? He remembered the gun. It was under his seat. He reached down and snatched it up. It was too big, a clumsy weapon in such a small space. He pointed it at Melanie. 'Get out of the truck,' he said.

To his surprise she reached across him again, pressing her body against the barrel of the gun, and threw the lever.

He pulled the trigger.

The bang was deafening in the little cabin of the truck.

For a split second, a small part of his mind felt a shock of grief that he had ruined her beautiful body; but he dismissed the feeling.

She was thrown back across the cab. The door was still open, and she fell out and tumbled down, hitting the floor of the warehouse with a sickening thud.

Priest did not stop to see if she was dead.

For the third time, he pulled the lever.

Slowly, the plate descended to the ground.

When it made contact, Priest started the machine.

*

The helicopter was a four-seater. Judy sat next to the pilot, Michael behind. As they flew south along the shore of the San Francisco Bay, Judy heard in her headphones the voice of one of Michael's student assistants, calling from the command post. 'Michael! This is Paula! It's started up—a seismic vibrator!'

Judy went cold with fear. *I thought I had more time!* She checked her watch: it was six forty-five. Granger's deadline was still fifteen minutes away. Melanie's phone call must have made him start early.

Michael was saying: 'Any tremors on the seismograph?'

'No—just the seismic vibrator, so far.'

No earthquake yet. Thank God.

Judy shouted into her microphone: 'Give us the location, quickly!'

'Wait a minute, the coordinates are coming up now.'

Judy grabbed a map.

Hurry, hurry!

A long moment later, Paula read the numbers off her screen. Judy found the location on her map. She said to the pilot: 'Due south two miles, then about five hundred yards inland.'

Her stomach lurched as the chopper dived and picked up speed.

They were flying over the old waterfront neighbourhood, full of derelict factories and car dumps. It would have been quiet on a normal Sunday: today it was empty. Judy scanned the horizon, looking for a truck that could be the seismic vibrator.

To the south, she saw two police patrol cars speeding toward the same location. Looking west, she spotted the FBI SWAT wagon approaching. Back at the Presidio, the other helicopters would be lifting off, full of armed agents. Soon half the law enforcement vehicles in northern California would be heading for the map coordinates Paula had given out.

Michael said into his microphone: 'Paula! What's happening on your screens?'

'Nothing—the vibrator is operating, but it's not having any effect.'

'Thank God!' Judy said.

Michael said: 'If he follows his previous pattern, he'll move the truck a quarter of a mile and try again.'

The pilot said: 'This is it. We've arrived at the coordinates.' The helicopter began to circle.

Judy and Michael stared out, searching frantically for the seismic vibrator.

On the ground, nothing moved.

*

Priest cursed.

The vibrating machinery was operating, but there was no earthquake.

This had happened before, both times. Melanie had said she did not really understand why it worked in some locations but not others. It probably had something to do with different kinds of subsoil. Both times, the vibrator had triggered an earthquake on the third try. But today Priest really needed to be lucky first time.

He was not.

Boiling with frustration, he turned off the mechanism and raised the plate.

He had to move the truck.

He jumped out. Stepping over Melanie, who was crumpled up against the wall, bleeding onto the concrete floor, he ran to the entrance. There was a pair of old-fashioned high doors that folded back to admit big vehicles. Inset into one panel was a small, people-sized door. Priest threw it open.

*

Over the entrance to a small warehouse Judy saw a sign that read: *Perpetua Diaries.*

She had thought Melanie was saying 'Perpetual'.

'That's the place!' she yelled. 'Go down!'

The helicopter descended rapidly, avoiding a power line that ran from pole to pole along the side of the road, and touched down in the middle of the deserted street.

As soon as she felt the bump of contact with the ground, Judy opened the door.

*

Priest looked out.

A helicopter had landed in the road. As he watched, someone jumped out. It was a woman with a wound dressing on her face. He recognized Judy Maddox.

He screamed a curse that was lost in the noise of the chopper.

There was no time to open the big doors.

He dashed back to the truck, got in, and rammed the shift into reverse. He backed as far as he could into the warehouse, stopping when the rear bumper hit the wall. Then he engaged first gear. He revved the engine high, then let out the clutch with a jerk. The truck lurched forward.

Priest pressed the pedal to the floor. Engine

screaming, the big truck gathered speed the length of the warehouse then crashed into the old wooden door.

Judy Maddox was standing right in front of the door, gun in hand. Shock and fear showed on her face as the truck burst through the door. Priest grinned savagely as he bore down on her. She dived sideways, and the truck missed her by an inch.

The helicopter was in the middle of the road. A man was getting out. Priest recognized Michael Quercus.

He steered toward the helicopter, changed up a gear, and accelerated.

*

Judy rolled over, aimed at the driver's door, and squeezed off two shots. She thought she might have hit something, but she failed to stop the truck.

The chopper lifted quickly.

Michael ran to the side of the road.

Judy guessed that Granger was hoping to clip the helicopter's undercarriage, as he had in Felicitas, but this time the pilot was too quick for him, and lifted high as the truck charged the space where the aircraft had been.

But, in his haste, the pilot forgot the roadside power lines.

There were five or six cables stretched between tall poles. The rotor blade caught in the lines, slicing through some. The helicopter's engine faltered. One of the poles tilted under the strain and fell. The rotor blade began to spin freely again, but the chopper had lost lift, and it fell to the ground with a mighty crash.

*

Priest had one hope left.

If he could drive a quarter of a mile, then get the plate down and the vibrator operating, he might yet trigger an earthquake before the FBI could get to him. And in the chaos of an earthquake, he might escape, as he had before.

He wrenched the wheel around and headed down the road.

*

Judy fired again as the truck swung away from the downed helicopter. She was hoping to hit either Granger or some essential part of the engine, but she was unlucky. The truck lumbered down the potholed road.

She looked at the crashed helicopter. The pilot was not moving. She looked back to the seismic vibrator as it gradually gathered speed.

I wish I had a rifle.

Michael ran up to her. 'Are you okay?'

'Yes,' she said. She made a decision. 'You see if you can help the pilot—I'll go after Granger.'

He hesitated, then said: 'Okay.'

Judy holstered her pistol and ran after the truck.

It was a sluggish vehicle, taking long moments to accelerate. At first she closed the distance rapidly. Then Granger changed gear and the truck picked up speed. Judy ran as fast as she could, heart pounding, chest aching. The tail of the truck carried a huge spare wheel. She was still gaining on it, but not so rapidly. Just when she thought she would never catch it, Granger shifted gear again, and, in the momentary slowdown, Judy put on a burst of speed and leaped for the tailgate.

She got one foot on the bumper and grabbed the spare wheel. For a frightening moment she thought she would slip and fall; and she looked down to see the road speeding beneath her. But she managed to hold on. She clambered on to the flatbed among the tanks and valves of the machinery. She staggered to keep her balance, almost fell, and righted herself.

She did not know whether Granger had seen her.

He could not operate the vibrator while the truck was in motion, so she remained where she was, heart thumping, waiting for him to stop.

But he had seen her.

She heard glass shatter and saw the barrel of a gun poke through the rear window of the driver's cabin. She ducked instinctively. Next moment she heard a slug ricochet off a tank beside her. She leaned to the left, so that she was directly behind Granger, and crouched low, heart in her mouth. She heard another shot, and cringed, but it missed her. Then he seemed to give up.

But he had not.

The truck braked fiercely. Judy was thrown forward, banging her head painfully against a pipe. Then Granger swerved violently to the right. Judy swung sideways and thought for a terrifying moment that she would be hurled to her death on the hard surface of the road, but she managed to hang on. She saw that Granger was heading suicidally straight for the brick front of a disused factory. She clung to a tank.

At the last moment, he braked hard and swerved, but he was a fraction of a second too late. He averted a head-on smash, but the offside fender ploughed into the brickwork with a crash of crumpling metal and breaking glass. Judy felt an agonizing pain in her ribs as she was crushed against the tank she was holding. Then she was thrown into the air.

For a dizzy moment she was totally disoriented. Then she hit the ground, landing on her left side. All the breath was knocked out of her body so that she could not even yell with pain. Her head banged against the road, her left arm went numb, and panic filled her mind.

Her head cleared a second or two later. She hurt, but she could move. Her bulletproof jacket had helped to protect her. Her black corduroys were ripped and one knee was bleeding, but not badly. Her nose was bleeding, too: she had reopened the wound Granger had given her yesterday.

She had fallen near the rear corner of the truck, close to its enormous double wheels. If Granger reversed a yard he would kill her. She rolled sideways, staying behind the truck but getting away from its giant tyres. The effort sent sharp pain through her ribs, and she cursed.

The truck did not reverse. Granger was not trying

to run her over. Perhaps he had not seen where she had fallen.

She looked up and down the street. She could see Michael struggling to get the pilot out of the crashed helicopter, four hundred yards away. In the other direction, there was no sign of the SWAT wagon or the police cars she had spotted from the air, nor of the other FBI helicopters. They were probably seconds away—but she did not have seconds to spare.

She got to her knees and drew her weapon. She expected Granger to jump out of the cabin and shoot at her, but he did not.

She struggled painfully to her feet.

If she approached on the driver's side of the truck, he would surely see her in his door mirror. She went to the other side and risked a peek around the rear corner. There was a big mirror on this side, too.

She dropped to her knees, lay flat on her belly, and crawled under the truck.

She wriggled forward until she was almost beneath the driver's cab.

She heard a new noise above her, and wondered what it was. Glancing up, she saw a huge steel plate above her.

It was being lowered on to her.

Frantically she rolled sideways. Her foot caught on one of the rear wheels. For a few horrendous seconds she struggled to free herself as the massive plate moved inexorably down. It would crush her leg like a plastic toy. At the last moment she pulled her foot out of her shoe and rolled clear.

She was out in the open. Granger would see her at any second. If he leaned out of the passenger door now, gun in hand, he could shoot her easily.

There was a blast like a bomb in her ears and the ground beneath her shook violently. He had started the vibrator.

She had to stop it. She thought momentarily of Bo's house. In her mind she saw it crumble and fall, then the whole street collapse.

Pressing her left hand to her side to ease the pain, she forced herself to her feet.

Two paces took her to the nearside door. She needed to open it with her right hand, so she shifted the gun to her left—she could shoot with either—and pointed it up to the sky.

Now.

She jumped on to the step, grabbed the door handle, and flung it open.

She came face to face with Richard Granger.

He looked as scared as she felt.

She pointed the gun at him with her left hand. 'Turn it off!' she screamed. 'Turn it off!'

'Okay,' he said, and he grinned and reached beneath his seat.

The grin alerted her. She knew he was not going to turn off the vibrator. She got ready to shoot him.

She had never shot anyone before.

His hand came up holding a revolver like something out of the Wild West.

As the long barrel swung toward her, she aimed her pistol at his head and squeezed the trigger.

The bullet hit him in the face, beside the nose.

He shot her a split second later. The flash and noise of the double gunshot was terrific. She felt a burning pain across her right temple.

Years of training came into play. She had been taught always to fire twice, and her muscles remembered. Automatically, she pulled the trigger again. This time she hit his shoulder. Blood spurted immediately. He spun sideways and fell back against the door, dropping the gun from limp fingers.

Oh, Jesus, is that what it's like when you kill someone?

Judy felt her own blood course down her right cheek. She fought a wave of faintness and nausea. She held the gun pointed at Granger.

The machine was still vibrating.

She stared at the mass of switches and dials. She had just shot the one person who knew how to turn the thing off. Panic swept over her. She fought it down. *There must be a key.*

There was.

She reached over the inert body of Ricky Granger and turned it.

Suddenly there was quiet.

She glanced along the street. Outside the Perpetua Diaries warehouse, the helicopter was on fire.

Michael!

She opened the door of the truck, fighting to stay conscious. She knew there was something she ought to do, something important, before she went to help Michael, but she could not think what it was. She gave up trying to remember and climbed out of the truck.

A distant police siren came closer and she saw a patrol car approaching. She waved it down. 'FBI,' she said weakly. 'Take me to that chopper.' She opened the door and fell into the car.

The cop drove the four hundred yards to the warehouse and pulled up a safe distance from the burning aircraft. Judy got out. She could not see anyone inside the helicopter. 'Michael!' she yelled. 'Where are you?'

'Over here!' He was behind the busted doors of the warehouse, bending over the pilot. Judy ran to him. 'This guy needs help,' Michael said. He looked at her face. 'Jesus, so do you!'

'I'm all right,' she said. 'Help is on the way.' She pulled out her cellphone and called the command post. She got Raja. He said: 'Judy, what's happening?'

'You tell me, for Christ's sake!'

'The vibrator stopped.'

'I know, I stopped it. Any tremors?'

'No. Nothing at all.'

Judy slumped with relief. She had stopped the machine in time. There would be no earthquake.

She leaned against the wall. She felt faint. She struggled to stay upright.

She felt no triumph, no sense of victory. Perhaps that would come later, with Raja and Carl and the others, in Everton's bar. For now, she was drained empty.

Another patrol car pulled up, and an officer got out. 'Lieutenant Forbes,' he said. 'What the hell went on here? Where's the perpetrator?'

Judy pointed along the street to the seismic vibrator. 'He's in the front of that truck,' she said. 'Dead.'

'We'll take a look.' The lieutenant got back in his car and tore off down the street.

Michael had disappeared. Looking for him, Judy stepped inside the warehouse.

She saw him sitting on the concrete floor in a pool of blood. But he was unhurt. In his arms he held Melanie. Her face was even paler than usual, and her skimpy T-shirt was soaked with blood from a grisly wound in her chest.

Michael's face was contorted with grief.

Judy went to him and knelt beside him. She felt for a pulse in Melanie's neck. There was none.

'I'm sorry, Michael,' she said. 'I'm so sorry.'

He swallowed. 'Poor Dusty,' he said.

Judy touched his face. 'It will be all right,' she said.

*

A few moments later, Lieutenant Forbes reappeared. 'Pardon me, ma'am,' he said politely. 'Did you say there was a dead man in that truck?'

'Yes,' she said. 'I shot him.'

'Well,' the cop said, 'he ain't there now.'

CHAPTER TWENTY-TWO

S TAR WAS jailed for ten years.

At first, prison was torture. The regimented existence was hell for someone whose whole life had been about freedom. Then a pretty wardress called Jane fell in love with her, and brought her make-up and books and marijuana, and things began to look up.

Flower was placed with foster parents, a Methodist minister and his wife. They were kind-hearted people who could not begin to understand where Flower was coming from. She missed her parents, did poorly at school, and got in more trouble with the police. Then, a couple of years later, she found her grandma. Veronica Nightingale had been thirteen when she gave birth to Priest, so she was only in her mid-sixties when Flower found her. She was running a store in Los Angeles selling sex toys, lingerie and porno videos. She had an apartment in Beverly Hills and drove a red sports car, and she told Flower stories about her daddy when he was a little boy. Flower ran away from the minister and his wife, and moved in with her grandma.

Oaktree disappeared. Judy knew there had been a fourth person in the 'Cuda at Felicitas, and she had been able to piece together his role in the affair. She even got a full set of fingerprints from his woodwork shop at the commune. But no one knew where he had gone. However, his prints showed up a couple of years later, on a stolen car that had been used in an armed robbery in Seattle. The police did not suspect him, because he had a solid alibi, but Judy was automatically notified. When she reviewed the file with the US attorney—her old friend Don Riley, now married to an insurance saleswoman—they realized they had only a weak case against Oaktree for his part in the Hammer of Eden, and they decided to let him be.

Milton Lestrange died of cancer. Brian Kincaid retired. Marvin Hayes resigned and became security director for a supermarket chain.

Michael Quercus became moderately famous. Because he was nice-looking and good at explaining seismology, TV shows always called him first when they wanted a quote about earthquakes. His business prospered.

Judy was promoted to supervisor. She moved in with Michael and Dusty. When Michael's business started to make real money, they bought a house together and decided to have a baby. A month later she was pregnant, so they got married. Bo cried at the wedding.

Judy figured out how Granger had got away.

The wound to his face was nasty but not serious. The bullet to his shoulder had nicked a vein, and the sudden loss of blood caused him to lose consciousness. Judy should have checked his pulse before going to help Michael, but she was weakened by her injuries and confused because of loss of blood, and she failed to follow routine.

Granger's slumped position caused his blood pressure to rise again, and he came round a few seconds after she left. He crawled around the corner to 3rd Street, where he was lucky enough to find a car waiting at a stop light. He got in, pointed his gun at the driver, and demanded to be taken to the city. En route he used Melanie's mobile to call Paul Beale, the wine bottler who was a criminal associate of Granger's from the old days. Beale gave him the address of a crooked doctor.

Granger made the driver drop him at a corner in a grungy neighbourhood. (The traumatized citizen drove home, called the local police precinct house, got a busy signal, and did not get around to reporting the incident until the next day.) The doctor, a disbarred surgeon who was a diamorphine addict, patched Granger up. Granger stayed at the doctor's apartment overnight then left.

Judy never found out where he went after that.

*

The water is rising fast. It has flooded all the little wooden houses. Behind the closed doors, the home-made beds and chairs are floating. The cookhouse and the temple are also awash.

He has waited weeks for the water to reach the vineyard. Now it has, and the precious plants are drowning.

He had been hoping he might find Spirit here, but his dog is long gone.

He has drunk a bottle of his favourite wine. It is difficult for him to drink or eat, because of the wound to his face, which has been sewn up badly by a doctor who was stoned. But he has succeeded in pouring enough down his throat to make himself drunk.

He throws the bottle away and takes from his pocket a big joint of marijuana laced with enough heroin to knock him out. He lights the spliff, takes a puff, and walks down the hill.

When the water is up to his thighs, he sits down.

He takes a last look around his valley. It is almost unrecognizable. There is no tumbling stream. Only the roofs of the buildings are visible, and they look like upturned ship-wrecks floating on the surface of a lagoon. The vines he planted twenty-five years ago are now submerged.

It is not a valley any more. It has become a lake, and everything that was here has been killed.

He takes a long pull on the joint between his fingers. He draws the deadly smoke deep into his lungs. He feels the rush of pleasure as the drug enters his bloodstream and the chemicals flood his brain. Little Ricky, happy at last, he thinks.

He rolls over and falls in the water. He lies face down, helpless, stoned out of his mind. Slowly, his consciousness fades, like a distant lamp becoming dimmer, until, at last, the light goes out.

ACKNOWLEDGEMENTS

I am grateful to the following people for help with this book:

Governor Pete Wilson of California; Jonathan R. Wilcox, Deputy Director, Office of Public Affairs, Office of Governor Pete Wilson; Andrew Poat, Chief Deputy Director, Department of Transportation;

Mark D. Zoback, Prof. of Geophysics, Chairman, Dept of Geophysics, Stanford University.

In the San Francisco Field Office of the FBI: Special Agent George E. Grotz, Director of Press Relations & Public Affairs, who opened many doors; Special Agent Candice DeLong, Profiling Coordinator, who generously spent much time helping me with the details of an agent's life and work; Bob Walsh, Special Agent in Charge; George Vinson, Assistant Special Agent in Charge; Charles W. Matthews, III, Associate Special Agent in Charge; Supervising Special Agent John Gray, Crisis Management Coordinator; Supervising Special Agent Don Whaley, Chief Division Counsel; Supervising Special Agent Larry Long, Tech Squad; Special

ACKNOWLEDGEMENTS

Agent Tony Maxwell, Evidence Response Team Co-ordinator; Dominic Gizzi, Administrative Officer.

In the Sacramento Field Office of the FBI: Special Agent Carole Micozzi; Special Agent Mike Ernst;

Pearle Greaves, Computer Specialist, Information Resources Division, FBI headquarters;

Sierra County Sheriff Lee Adams;

Lucien G. Canton, Director, Mayor's Office of Emergency Services, San Francisco;

James F. Davis, PhD, California State Geologist; Sherry Reser, Information Officer, Dept of Conservation;

Charles Yanez, Manager, South Texas, Western Geophysical; Janet Loveday, Western Geophysical; Donnie McLendon, Western Geophysical, Freer, Texas; Mr Jesse Rosas, bulldozer driver;

Seth Rosing DeLong;

Dr Keith J. Rosing, Director of Emergency Services, Irvine Medical Center;

Brian Butterworth, Professor of Cognitive Neuropsychology, University College, London.

Most of the above were found for me by Dan Starer, of Research for Writers, New York City.

As always my outlines and drafts were read and criticized constructively by my agent, Al Zuckerman; my editors, Ann Patty in New York and Suzanne Baboneau in London; and numerous friends and relatives including George Brennan, Barbara Follett, Angus James, Jann Turner and Kim Turner.

Permissions Acknowledgements

'SMOKE ON THE WATER' Words and music by
Jon Lord, Ritchie Blackmore, Ian Gillan, Roger Glover and
Ian Paice (Deep Purple) © 1972, reproduced by permission of
B. Feldman & Co. trading as Hec Music, London WC2H 0EA

'THERE BUT FOR FORTUNE' by Phil Ochs
© 1963 Barricade Music ASCAP, quoted by kind permission of
Barricade Music, a division of Rondor Music International

TRIPLE

It must be appreciated that the only difficult part of making a fission bomb of some sort is the preparation of a supply of fissionable material of adequate purity; the design of the bomb itself is relatively easy . . .

— *Encyclopedia Americana*

To Al Zuckerman

TRIPLE

PROLOGUE

T HERE WAS a time, just once, when they were all
together.

They met many years ago, when they were young,
before all *this* happened; but the meeting cast shadows
far across the decades.

It was the first Sunday in November, 1947, to be exact;
and each of them met all the others – indeed, for a few
minutes they were all in one room. Some of them
immediately forgot the faces they saw and the names
they heard spoken in formal introductions. Some of
them actually forgot the whole day; and when it became
so important, twenty-one years later, they had to pretend
to remember; to stare at blurred photographs and
murmur 'Ah, yes, of course,' in a knowing way.

This early meeting is a coincidence, but not a very
startling one. They were mostly young and able; they
were destined to have power, to take decisions, and to
make changes, each in their different ways, in their
different countries; and those people often meet in
their youth at places like Oxford University. Furthermore, when all this happened, those who were not
involved initially were sucked into it just because they
had met the others at Oxford.

3

However, it did not seem like an historic meeting at the time. It was just another sherry party in a place where there were too many sherry parties (and, undergraduates would add, not enough sherry). It was an uneventful occasion. Well, almost.

Al Cortone knocked and waited in the hall for a dead man to open the door.

The suspicion that his friend was dead had grown to a conviction in the past three years. First, Cortone had heard that Nat Dickstein had been taken prisoner. Towards the end of the war, stories began to circulate about what was happening to Jews in the Nazi camps. Then, at the end, the grim truth came out.

On the other side of the door, a ghost scraped a chair on the floor and padded across the room.

Cortone felt suddenly nervous. What if Dickstein were disabled, deformed? Suppose he had become unhinged? Cortone had never known how to deal with cripples or crazy men. He and Dickstein had become very close, just for a few days back in 1943; but what was Dickstein like now?

The door opened, and Cortone said, 'Hi, Nat.'

Dickstein stared at him, then his face split in a wide grin and he came out with one of his ridiculous Cockney phrases: 'Gawd, stone the crows!'

Cortone grinned back, relieved. They shook hands, and slapped each other on the back, and let rip some soldierly language just for the hell of it; then they went inside.

Dickstein's home was one high-ceilinged room of an old house in a run-down part of the city. There was a single bed, neatly made up in army fashion; a heavy old wardrobe of dark wood with a matching dresser; and a table piled with books in front of a small window. Cortone thought the room looked bare. If he had to live here he would put some personal stuff all around to make the place look like his own: photographs of his family, souvenirs of Niagara and Miami Beach, his high school football trophy.

Dickstein said, 'What I want to know is, how did you find me?'

'I'll tell you, it wasn't easy.' Cortone took off his uniform jacket and laid it on the narrow bed. 'It took me most of yesterday.' He eyed the only easy chair in the room. Both arms tilted sideways at odd angles, a spring poked through the faded chrysanthemums of the fabric, and one missing foot had been replaced with a copy of Plato's *Theaetetus*. 'Can human beings sit on that?'

'Not above the rank of sergeant. But—'

'They aren't human anyway.'

They both laughed: it was an old joke. Dickstein brought a bentwood chair from the table and straddled it. He looked his friend up and down for a moment and said, 'You're getting fat.'

Cortone patted the slight swell of his stomach. 'We live well in Frankfurt – you really missed out, getting demobilized.' He leaned forward and lowered his voice, as if what he was saying was somewhat confidential. 'I have made a *fortune*. Jewellery, china, antiques all bought for cigarettes and soap. The Germans are starving. And – best of all – the girls will do anything for a Tootsie Roll.' He sat back, waiting for a laugh, but Dickstein just stared at him straight-faced. Disconcerted, Cortone changed the subject. 'One thing you ain't, is fat.'

At first he had been so relieved to see Dickstein still in one piece and grinning the same grin that he had not looked at him closely. Now he realized that his friend was worse than thin: he looked wasted. Nat Dickstein had always been short and slight, but now he seemed all bones. The dead-white skin, and the large brown eyes behind the plastic-rimmed spectacles, accentuated the effect. Between the top of his sock and the cuff of his trouser-leg a few inches of pale shin showed like matchwood. Four years ago Dickstein had been brown, stringy, as hard as the leather soles of his British Army boots. When Cortone talked about his English buddy, as he often did, he would say, 'The toughest, meanest bastard fighting soldier that ever saved my goddamn life, and I ain't shittin' you.'

'Fat? No,' Dickstein said. 'This country is still on iron rations, mate. But we manage.'

'You've known worse.'

Dickstein smiled. 'And eaten it.'

'You got took prisoner.'

'At La Molina.'

'How the hell did they tie you down?'

'Easy.' Dickstein shrugged. 'A bullet broke my leg and I passed out. When I came round I was in a German truck.'

Cortone looked at Dickstein's legs. 'It mended okay?'

'I was lucky. There was a medic in my truck on the POW train – he set the bone.'

Cortone nodded. 'And then the camp...' He thought maybe he should not ask, but he wanted to know.

Dickstein looked away. 'It was all right until they found out I'm Jewish. Do you want a cup of tea? I can't afford whisky.'

'No.' Cortone wished he had kept his mouth shut. 'Anyway, I don't drink whisky in the morning anymore. Life doesn't seem as short as it used to.'

Dickstein's eyes swivelled back toward Cortone. 'They decided to find out how many times they could break a leg in the same place and mend it again.'

'Jesus.' Cortone's voice was a whisper.

'That was the best part,' Dickstein said in a flat monotone. He looked away again.

Cortone said, 'Bastards.' He could not think of anything else to say. There was a strange expression on Dickstein's face; something Cortone had not seen before, something – he realized after a moment – that was very like fear. It was odd. After all, it was over now, wasn't it? 'Well, hell, at least we won, didn't we?' He punched Dickstein's shoulder.

Dickstein grinned. 'We did. Now, what are you doing in England? And how did you find me?'

'I managed to get a stopover in London on my way back to Buffalo. I went to the War Office ...' Cortone hesitated. He had gone to the War Office to find out how and when Dickstein died. 'They gave me an address in Stepney,' he continued. 'When I got there,

there was only one house left standing in the whole street. In this house, underneath an inch of dust, I find this old man.'

'Tommy Coster.'

'Right. Well, after I drink nineteen cups of weak tea and listen to the story of his life, he sends me to another house around the corner, where I find your mother, drink more weak tea and hear the story of her life. By the time I get your address it's too late to catch the last train to Oxford, so I wait until the morning, and here I am. I only have a few hours – my ship sails tomorrow.'

'You've got your discharge?'

'In three weeks, two days and ninety-four minutes.'

'What are you going to do, back home?'

'Run the family business. I've discovered, in the last couple of years, that I am a terrific businessman.'

'What business is your family in? You never told me.'

'Trucking,' Cortone said shortly. 'And you? What is this with Oxford University, for Christ's sake? What are you studying?'

'Hebrew Literature.'

'You're kidding.'

'I could write Hebrew before I went to school, didn't I ever tell you? My grandfather was a real scholar. He lived in one smelly room over a pie shop in the Mile End Road. I went there every Saturday and Sunday, since before I can remember. I never complained – I loved it. Anyway, what else would I study?'

Cortone shrugged. 'I don't know, atomic physics maybe, or business management. Why study at all?'

'To become happy, clever and rich.'

Cortone shook his head. 'Weird as ever. Lots of girls here?'

'Very few. Besides, I'm busy.'

He thought Dickstein was blushing. 'Liar. You're in love, you fool. I can tell. Who is she?'

'Well, to be honest . . .' Dickstein was embarrassed. 'She's out of reach. A professor's wife. Exotic, intelligent, the most beautiful woman I've ever seen.'

Cortone made a dubious face. 'It's not promising, Nat.'

'I know, but still . . .' Dickstein stood up. 'You'll see what I mean.'

'I get to meet her?'

'Professor Ashford is giving a sherry party. I'm invited. I was just leaving when you got here.' Dickstein put on his jacket.

'A sherry party in Oxford,' Cortone said. 'Wait till they hear about this in Buffalo!'

It was a cold, bright morning. Pale sunshine washed the cream-coloured stone of the city's old buildings. They walked in comfortable silence, hands in pockets, shoulders hunched against the biting November wind which whistled through the streets. Cortone kept muttering, 'Dreaming spires. Fuck.'

There were very few people about, but after they had walked a mile or so Dickstein pointed across the road to a tall man with a college scarf wound around his neck. 'There's the Russian,' he said. He called, 'Hey, Rostov!'

The Russian looked up, waved, and crossed to their side of the street. He had an army haircut, and was too long and thin for his mass-produced suit. Cortone was beginning to think everyone was thin in this country.

Dickstein said, 'Rostov's at Balliol, same college as me. David Rostov, meet Alan Cortone. Al and I were together in Italy for a while. Going to Ashford's house, Rostov?'

The Russian nodded solemnly. 'Anything for a free drink.'

Cortone said, 'You interested in Hebrew Literature too?'

Rostov said, 'No, I'm here to study bourgeois economics.'

Dickstein laughed loudly. Cortone did not see the joke. Dickstein explained, 'Rostov is from Smolensk. He's a member of the CPSU – the Communist Party of the Soviet Union.' Cortone still did not see the joke.

'I thought nobody was allowed to leave Russia,' Cortone said.

Rostov went into a long and involved explanation which had to do with his father's having been a diplomat in Japan when the war broke out. He had an earnest expression which occasionally gave way to a sly smile. Although his English was imperfect, he managed to give Cortone the impression that he was condescending. Cortone turned off, and began to think about how you could love a man as if he was your own brother, fighting side by side with him, and then he could go off and study Hebrew Literature and you would realize you never really knew him at all.

Eventually Rostov said to Dickstein, 'Have you decided yet, about going to Palestine?'

Cortone said, 'Palestine? What for?'

Dickstein looked troubled. 'I haven't decided.'

'You should go,' said Rostov. 'The Jewish National Home will help to break up the last remnants of the British Empire in the Middle East.'

'Is that the Party line?' Dickstein asked with a faint smile.

'Yes,' Rostov said seriously. 'You're a socialist—'

'Of sorts.'

'—and it is important that the new State should be socialist.'

Cortone was incredulous. 'The Arabs are murdering you people out there. Jeez, Nat, you only just escaped from the Germans!'

'I haven't decided,' Dickstein repeated. He shook his head irritably. 'I don't know what to do.' It seemed he did not want to talk about it.

They were walking briskly. Cortone's face was freezing, but he was perspiring beneath his winter uniform. The other two began to discuss a scandal: a man called Mosley – the name meant nothing to Cortone – had been persuaded to enter Oxford in a van and make a speech at the Martyr's Memorial. Mosley was a Fascist, he gathered a moment later. Rostov was arguing that the incident proved how social democracy was closer to Fascism than Communism. Dickstein claimed the undergraduates who organized the event were just trying to be 'shocking'.

Cortone listened and watched the two men. They

11

were an odd couple: tall Rostov, his scarf like a striped bandage, taking long strides, his too-short trousers flapping like flags; and diminutive Dickstein with big eyes and round spectacles, wearing a demob suit, looking like a skeleton in a hurry. Cortone was no academic, but he figured he could smell out bullshit in any language, and he knew that neither of them was saying what he believed: Rostov was parroting some kind of official dogma, and Dickstein's brittle unconcern masked a different, deeper attitude. When Dickstein laughed about Mosley, he sounded like a child laughing after a nightmare. They both argued cleverly but without emotion: it was like a fencing match with blunted swords.

Eventually Dickstein seemed to realize that Cortone was being left out of the discussion and began to talk about their host. 'Stephen Ashford is a bit eccentric, but a remarkable man,' he said. 'He spent most of his life in the Middle East. Made a small fortune and lost it, by all accounts. He used to do crazy things, like crossing the Arabian Desert on a camel.'

'That might be the least crazy way to cross it,' Cortone said.

Rostov said, 'Ashford has a Lebanese wife.'

Cortone looked at Dickstein. 'She's—'

'She's younger than he is,' Dickstein said hastily. 'He brought her back to England just before the war and became Professor of Semitic Literature here. If he gives you Marsala instead of sherry it means you've overstayed your welcome.'

'People know the difference?' Cortone said.

12

'This is his house.'

Cortone was half expecting a Moorish villa, but the Ashford home was imitation Tudor, painted white with green woodwork. The garden in front was a jungle of shrubs. The three young men walked up a brick pathway to the house. The front door was open. They entered a small, square hall. Somewhere in the house several people laughed: the party had started. A pair of double doors opened and the most beautiful woman in the world came out.

Cortone was transfixed. He stood and stared as she came across the carpet to welcome them. He heard Dickstein say, 'This is my friend Alan Cortone,' and suddenly he was touching her long brown hand, warm and dry and fine-boned, and he never wanted to let go.

She turned away and led them into the drawing room. Dickstein touched Cortone's arm and grinned: he had known what was going on in his friend's mind.

Cortone recovered his composure sufficiently to say, 'Wow.'

Small glasses of sherry were lined up with military precision on a little table. She handed one to Cortone, smiled, and said, 'I'm Eila Ashford, by the way.'

Cortone took in the details as she handed out the drinks. She was completely unadorned: there was no make-up on her astonishing face, her black hair was straight, and she wore a white dress and sandals – yet the effect was almost like nakedness, and Cortone was embarrassed at the animal thoughts that rushed through his mind as he looked at her.

He forced himself to turn away and study his

surroundings. The room had the unfinished elegance of a place where people are living slightly beyond their means. The rich Persian carpet was bordered by a strip of peeling grey linoleum; someone had been mending the radio, and its innards were all over a kidney table; there were a couple of bright rectangles on the wall-paper where pictures had been taken down; and some of the sherry glasses did not quite match the set. There were about a dozen people in the room.

An Arab wearing a beautiful pearl-grey Western suit was standing at the fireplace, looking at a wooden carving on the mantelpiece. Eila Ashford called him over. 'I want you to meet Yasif Hassan, a friend of my family from home,' she said. 'He's at Worcester College.'

Hassan said, 'I know Dickstein.' He shook hands all around.

Cortone thought he was fairly handsome, for a nigger, and haughty, the way they were when they made some money and got invited to white homes.

Rostov asked him, 'You're from Lebanon?'

'Palestine.'

'Ah!' Rostov became animated. 'And what do you think of the United Nations partition plan?'

'Irrelevant,' the Arab said languidly. 'The British must leave, and my country will have a democratic government.'

'But then the Jews will be in a minority,' Rostov argued.

'They are in a minority in England. Should they be given Surrey as a national home?'

'Surrey has never been theirs. Palestine was, once.'

Hassan shrugged elegantly. 'It was – when the Welsh had England, the English had Germany, and the Norman French lived in Scandinavia.' He turned to Dickstein. 'You have a sense of justice – what do you think?'

Dickstein took off his glasses. 'Never mind justice. I want a place to call my own.'

'Even if you have to steal mine?' Hassan said.

'You can have the rest of the Middle East.'

'I don't want it.'

Rostov said, 'This discussion proves the necessity for partition.'

Eila Ashford offered a box of cigarettes. Cortone took one, and lit hers. While the others argued about Palestine, Eila asked Cortone, 'Have you known Dickstein long?'

'We met in 1943,' Cortone said. He watched her brown lips close around the cigarette. She even smoked beautifully. Delicately, she picked a fragment of tobacco from the tip of her tongue.

'I'm terribly curious about him,' she said.

'Why?'

'Everyone is. He's only a boy, and yet he seems so old. Then again, he's obviously a Cockney, but he's not in the least intimidated by all these upper-class Englishmen. But he'll talk about anything except himself.'

Cortone nodded. 'I'm finding out that I don't really know him, either.'

'My husband says he's a brilliant student.'

'He saved my life.'

'Good Lord.' She looked at him more closely, as if she were wondering whether he was just being melodramatic. She seemed to decide in his favour. 'I'd like to hear about it.'

A middle-aged man in baggy corduroy trousers touched her shoulder and said, 'How is everything, my dear?'

'Fine,' she said. 'Mr Cortone, this is my husband, Professor Ashford.'

Cortone said, 'How are you.' Ashford was a balding man in ill-fitting clothes. Cortone had been expecting Lawrence of Arabia. He thought: Maybe Nat has a chance after all.

Eila said, 'Mr Cortone was telling me how Nat Dickstein saved his life.'

'Really!' Ashford said.

'It's not a long story,' Cortone said. He glanced over at Dickstein, now deep in conversation with Hassan and Rostov; and noted how the three men displayed their attitudes by the way they stood: Rostov with his feet apart, wagging a finger like a teacher, sure in his dogma; Hassan leaning against a bookcase, one hand in his pocket, smoking, pretending that the international debate about the future of his country was of merely academic interest; Dickstein with arms folded tightly, shoulders hunched, head bowed in concentration, his stance giving the lie to the dispassionate character of his remarks. Cortone heard *The British promised Palestine to the Jews*, and the reply, *Beware the gifts of a thief.* He turned back to the Ashfords and began to tell them the story.

'It was in Sicily, near a place called Ragusa, a hill town,' he said. 'I'd taken a T-force around the outskirts. To the north of the town we came on a German tank in a little hollow, on the edge of a clump of trees. The tank looked abandoned but I put a grenade into it to make sure. As we drove past there was a shot – only one – and a German with a machine gun fell out of a tree. He'd been hiding up there, ready to pick us off as we passed. It was Nat Dickstein who shot him.'

Eila's eyes sparkled with something like excitement, but her husband had gone white. Obviously the professor had no stomach for tales of life and death. Cortone thought: If that upsets you, pop, I hope Dickstein never tells you any of *his* stories.

'The British had come around the town from the other side,' Cortone went on. 'Nat had seen the tank, like I did, and smelled a trap. He had spotted the sniper and was waiting to see if there were any more when we turned up. If he hadn't been so damn smart I'd be dead.'

The other two were silent for a moment. Ashford said, 'It's not long ago, but we forget so fast.'

Eila remembered her other guests. 'I want to talk to you some more before you go,' she said to Cortone. She went across the room to where Hassan was trying to open a pair of doors that gave on to the garden.

Ashford brushed nervously at the wispy hair behind his ears. 'The public hears about the big battles, but I suppose the soldier remembers those little personal incidents.'

Cortone nodded, thinking that Ashford clearly had

no conception of what war was like, and wondering if the professor's youth had really been as adventurous as Dickstein claimed. 'Later, I took him to meet my cousins – the family comes from Sicily. We had pasta and wine, and they made a hero of Nat. We were together only for a few days, but we were like brothers, you know?'

'Indeed.'

'When I heard he was taken prisoner, I figured I'd never see him again.'

'Do you know what happened to him?' Ashford said. 'He doesn't say much . . .'

Cortone shrugged. 'He survived the camps.'

'He was fortunate.'

'Was he?'

Ashford looked at Cortone for a moment, confused, then turned away and looked around the room. After a moment he said, 'This is not a very typical Oxford gathering, you know. Dickstein, Rostov and Hassan are somewhat unusual students. You should meet Toby – he's the archetypal undergraduate.' He caught the eye of a red-faced youth in a tweed suit and a very wide paisley tie. 'Toby, come and meet Dickstein's comrade-in-arms – Mr Cortone.'

Toby shook hands and said abruptly, 'Any chance of a tip from the stable? Will Dickstein win?'

'Win what?' Cortone said.

Ashford explained, 'Dickstein and Rostov are to play a chess match – they're both supposed to be terribly good. Toby thinks you might have inside information – he probably wants to bet on the outcome.'

Cortone said, 'I thought chess was an old man's game.'

Toby said, 'Ah!' rather loudly, and emptied his glass. He and Ashford seemed nonplussed by Cortone's remark. A little girl, four or five years old, came in from the garden carrying an elderly grey cat. Ashford introduced her with the coy pride of a man who has become a father in middle age.

'This is Suza,' he said.

The girl said, 'And this is Hezekiah.'

She had her mother's skin and hair; she too would be beautiful. Cortone wondered whether she was really Ashford's daughter. There was nothing of him in her looks. She held out the cat's paw, and Cortone obligingly shook it and said, 'How are you, Hezekiah?'

Suza went over to Dickstein. 'Good morning, Nat. Would you like to stroke Hezekiah?'

'She's very cute,' Cortone said to Ashford. 'I have to talk to Nat. Would you excuse me?' He went over to Dickstein, who was kneeling down and stroking the cat.

Nat and Suza seemed to be pals. He told her, 'This is my friend Alan.'

'We've met,' she said, and fluttered her eyelashes. Cortone thought: She learned that from her mother.

'We were in the war together,' Dickstein continued.

Suza looked directly at Cortone. 'Did you kill people?'

He hesitated. 'Sure.'

'Do you feel bad about it?'

'Not too bad. They were wicked people.'

'Nat feels bad about it. That's why he doesn't like to talk about it too much.'

The kid had got more out of Dickstein than all the grown-ups put together.

The cat jumped out of Suza's arms with surprising agility. She chased after it. Dickstein stood up.

'I wouldn't say Mrs Ashford is out of reach,' Cortone said quietly.

'Wouldn't you?' Dickstein said.

'She can't be more than twenty-five. He's at least twenty years older, and I'll bet he's no pistol. If they got married before the war, she must have been around seventeen at the time. And they don't seem affectionate.'

'I wish I could believe you,' Dickstein said. He was not as interested as he should have been. 'Come and see the garden.'

They went through the French doors. The sun was stronger, and the bitter cold had gone from the air. The garden stretched in a green-and-brown wilderness down to the edge of the river. They walked away from the house.

Dickstein said, 'You don't much like this crowd.'

'The war's over,' Cortone said. 'You and me, we live in different worlds now. All this – professors, chess matches, sherry parties . . . I might as well be on Mars. My life is doing deals, fighting off the competition, making a few bucks. I was fixing to offer you a job in my business, but I guess I'd be wasting my time.'

'Alan . . .'

'Listen, what the hell. We'll probably lose touch now

20

– I'm not much of a letter writer. But I won't forget that I owe you my life. One of these days you might want to call in the debt. You know where to find me.'

Dickstein opened his mouth to speak, then they heard the voices.

'Oh . . . no, not here, not now . . .' It was a woman.

'Yes!' A man.

Dickstein and Cortone were standing beside a thick box hedge which cut off a corner of the garden: someone had begun to plant a maze and never finished the job. A few steps from where they were a gap opened, then the hedge turned a right angle and ran along the river bank. The voices came clearly from the other side of the foliage.

The woman spoke again, low and throaty. 'Don't, damn you, or I'll scream.'

Dickstein and Cortone stepped through the gap.

Cortone would never forget what he saw there. He stared at the two people and then, appalled, he glanced at Dickstein. Dickstein's face was grey with shock, and he looked ill; his mouth dropped open as he gazed in horror and despair. Cortone looked back at the couple.

The woman was Eila Ashford. The skirt of her dress was around her waist, her face was flushed with pleasure, and she was kissing Yasif Hassan.

CHAPTER ONE

THE PUBLIC-ADDRESS system at Cairo airport made a noise like a doorbell, and then the arrival of the Alitalia flight from Milan was announced in Arabic, Italian, French and English. Towfik el-Masiri left his table in the buffet and made his way out to the observation deck. He put on his sunglasses to look over the shimmering concrete apron. The Caravelle was already down and taxiing.

Towfik was there because of a cable. It had come that morning from his 'uncle' in Rome, and it had been in code. Any business could use a code for international telegrams, provided it first lodged the key to the code with the post office. Such codes were used more and more to save money – by reducing common phrases to single words – than to keep secrets. Towfik's uncle's cable, transcribed according to the registered code book, gave details of his late aunt's will. However, Towfik had another key, and the message he read was:

OBSERVE AND FOLLOW PROFESSOR FRIEDRICH SCHULZ ARRIVING CAIRO FROM MILAN WEDNESDAY 28 FEBRUARY 1968 FOR SEVERAL DAYS. AGE 51 HEIGHT 180 CM WEIGHT 150

POUNDS HAIR WHITE EYES BLUE NATIONALITY
AUSTRIAN COMPANIONS WIFE ONLY.

The passengers began to file out of the aircraft, and
Towfik spotted his man almost immediately. There was
only one tall, lean white-haired man on the flight. He
was wearing a light blue suit, a white shirt and a tie,
and carrying a plastic shopping bag from a duty-free
store and a camera. His wife was much shorter, and
wore a fashionable mini-dress and a blonde wig. As they
crossed the airfield they looked about them and sniffed
the warm, dry desert air the way most people did the
first time they landed in North Africa.

The passengers disappeared into the arrivals hall.
Towfik waited on the observation deck until the baggage came off the plane, then he went inside and
mingled with the small crowd of people waiting just
beyond the customs barrier.

He did a lot of waiting. That was something they did
not teach you – how to wait. You learned to handle
guns, memorize maps, break open safes and kill people
with your bare hands, all in the first six months of the
training course; but there were no lectures in patience,
no exercises for sore feet, no seminars on tedium. And
it was beginning to seem like *There is something wrong
here* beginning to seem *Lookout lookout* beginning to—

There was another agent in the crowd.

Towfik's subconscious hit the fire alarm while he was
thinking about patience. The people in the little crowd,
waiting for relatives and friends and business acquaint-

ances off the Milan plane, were impatient. They smoked, shifted their weight from one foot to the other, craned their necks and fidgeted. There was a middle-class family with four children, two men in the traditional striped cotton *galabiya* robes, a businessman in a dark suit, a young white woman, a chauffeur with a sign saying FORD MOTOR COMPANY, and—

And a patient man.

Like Towfik, he had dark skin and short hair and wore a European-style suit. At first glance he seemed to be with the middle-class family – just as Towfik would seem, to a casual observer, to be with the businessman in the dark suit. The other agent stood nonchalantly, with his hands behind his back, facing the exit from the baggage hall, looking unobtrusive. There was a streak of paler skin alongside his nose, like an old scar. He touched it, once, in what might have been a nervous gesture, then put his hand behind his back again.

The question was, had he spotted Towfik?

Towfik turned to the businessman beside him and said, 'I never understand why this has to take so long.' He smiled, and spoke quietly, so that the businessman leaned closer to hear him and smiled back; and the pair of them looked like acquaintances having a casual conversation.

The businessman said, 'The formalities take longer than the flight.'

Towfik stole another glance at the other agent. The man stood in the same position, watching the exit. He had not attempted any camouflage. Did that mean that he had not spotted Towfik? Or was it just that he had second-guessed Towfik, by deciding that a piece of camouflage would give him away?

The passengers began to emerge, and Towfik realized there was nothing he could do, either way. He hoped the people the agent was meeting would come out before Professor Schulz.

It was not to be. Schulz and his wife were among the first little knot of passengers to come through.

The other agent approached them and shook hands.

Of course, of course.

The agent was there to meet Schulz.

Towfik watched while the agent summoned porters and ushered the Schulzes away; then he went out by a different exit to his car. Before getting in he took off his jacket and tie and put on sunglasses and a white cotton cap. Now he would not be easily recognizable as the man who had been waiting at the meeting point.

He figured the agent would have parked in a no-waiting zone right outside the main entrance, so he drove that way. He was right. He saw the porters loading the Schulz baggage into the boot of a five-year-old grey Mercedes. He drove on.

He steered his dirty Renault on to the main highway which ran from Heliopolis, where the airport was, to Cairo. He drove at 60 kph and kept to the slow lane. The grey Mercedes passed him two or three minutes later, and he accelerated to keep it within sight. He memorized its number, as it was always useful to be able to recognize the opposition's cars.

The sky began to cloud over. As he sped down the straight, palm-lined highway, Towfik considered what he had found out so far. The cable had told him nothing about Schulz except what the man looked like and the fact that he was an Austrian professor. The meeting at the airport meant a great deal, though. It had been a kind of clandestine VIP treatment. Towfik had the agent figured for a local: everything pointed to that – his clothes, his car, his style of waiting. That meant Schulz was probably here by invitation of the government, but either he or the people he had come to see wanted the visit kept secret.

It was not much. What was Schulz professor *of?* He could be a banker, arms manufacturer, rocketry expert or cotton buyer. He might even be with Al Fatah, but Towfik could not quite see the man as a resurrected Nazi. Still, anything was possible.

Certainly Tel Aviv did not think Schulz was important: if they had, they would not have used Towfik, who was young and inexperienced, for this surveillance. It was even possible that the whole thing was yet another training exercise.

They entered Cairo on the Shari Ramses, and Towfik closed the gap between his car and the Mercedes until there was only one vehicle between them. The grey car turned right on to the Corniche al-Nil, then crossed the river by the 26 July Bridge and entered the Zamalek district of Gezira island.

There was less traffic in the wealthy, dull suburb, and Towfik became edgy about being spotted by the agent at the wheel of the Mercedes. However, two minutes later the other car turned into a residential street near the Officers' Club and stopped outside an apartment block with a jacaranda tree in the garden. Towfik immediately took a right turn and was out of sight before the doors of the other car could open. He parked, jumped out, and walked back to the corner. He was in time to see the agent and the Schulzes disappear into the building followed by a caretaker in *galabiya* struggling with their luggage.

Towfik looked up and down the street. There was nowhere a man could convincingly idle. He returned to his car, backed it around the corner and parked between two other cars on the same side of the road as the Mercedes.

Half an hour later the agent came out alone, got into his car, and drove off.

Towfik settled down to wait.

It went on for two days, then it broke.

Until then the Schulzes behaved like tourists, and seemed to enjoy it. On the first evening they had dinner in a nightclub and watched a troupe of belly-dancers. Next day they did the Pyramids and the Sphinx, with lunch at Groppi's and dinner at the Nile Hilton. In the morning on the third day they got up early and took a taxi to the mosque of Ibn Tulun.

Towfik left his car near the Gayer-Anderson Museum and followed them. They took a perfunctory look around the mosque and headed east on the Shari al-Salibah. They were dawdling, looking at fountains and buildings, peering into dark tiny shops, watching *baladi* women buy onions and peppers and camel's feet at street stalls.

They stopped at a crossroads and went into a tea-shop. Towfik crossed the street to the *sebeel*, a domed fountain behind windows of iron lace, and studied the baroque relief around its walls. He moved on up the street, still within sight of the tea-shop, and spent some time buying four misshapen giant tomatoes from a white-capped stallholder whose feet were bare.

The Schulzes came out of the tea-shop and turned north, following Towfik, into the street market. Here it was easier for Towfik to idle, sometimes ahead of them and sometimes behind. Frau Schulz bought slippers and a gold bangle, and paid too much for a sprig of mint from a half-naked child. Towfik got far enough in front of them to drink a small cup of strong, un-sweetened Turkish coffee under the awning of a café called Nasif's.

They left the street market and entered a covered *souq* specializing in saddlery. Schulz glanced at his wristwatch and spoke to his wife – giving Towfik the first faint tremor of anxiety – and then they walked a little faster until they emerged at Bab Zuweyla, the gateway to the original walled city.

For a few moments the Schulzes were obscured from Towfik's view by a donkey pulling a cart loaded with Ali-Baba jars, their mouths stoppered with crumpled paper. When the cart passed, Towfik saw that Schulz was saying goodbye to his wife and getting into an oldish grey Mercedes.

Towfik cursed under his breath.

The car door slammed and it pulled away. Frau Schulz waved. Towfik read the licence plate – it was the car he had followed from Heliopolis – and saw it go west, then turn left into the Shari Port Said.

Forgetting Frau Schulz, he turned around and broke into a run.

They had been walking for about an hour, but they had covered only a mile. Towfik sprinted through the saddlery *souq* and the street market, dodging around the stalls and bumping into robed men and women in black, dropping his bag of tomatoes in a collision with a Nubian sweeper, until he reached the museum and his car.

He dropped into the driver's seat, breathing hard and grimacing at the pain in his side. He started the engine and pulled away on an interception course for the Shari Port Said.

The traffic was light, so when he hit the main road he guessed he must be behind the Mercedes. He continued southwest, over the island of Roda and the Giza Bridge onto the Giza Road.

Schulz had not been deliberately trying to shake a tail, Towfik decided. Had the professor been a pro he would have lost Towfik decisively and finally. No, he had simply been taking a morning walk through the market before meeting someone at a landmark. But Towfik was sure that the meeting place, and the walk beforehand, had been suggested by the agent.

They might have gone anywhere, but it seemed likely they were leaving the city – otherwise Schulz could simply have taken a taxi at Bab Zuweyla – and this was the major road westward. Towfik drove very fast. Soon there was nothing in front of him but the arrow-straight grey road, and nothing either side but yellow sand and blue sky.

He reached the Pyramids without catching the Mercedes. Here the road forked, leading north to Alexandria or south to Faiyum. From where the Mercedes had picked up Schulz, this would have been an unlikely, roundabout route to Alexandria; so Towfik plumped for Faiyum.

When at last he saw the other car it was behind him, coming up very fast. Before it reached him it turned right off the main road. Towfik braked to a halt and reversed the Renault to the turnoff. The other car was already a mile ahead on the side road. He followed.

This was dangerous, now. The road probably went deep into the Western Desert, perhaps all the way to the oil field at Qattara. It seemed little used, and a strong wind might obscure it under a layer of sand. The agent in the Mercedes was sure to realize he was being followed. If he were a good agent, the sight of the Renault might even trigger memories of the journey from Heliopolis.

This was where the training broke down, and all the careful camouflage and tricks of the trade became useless; and you had to simply get on someone's tail and stick with him whether he saw you or not, because the whole point was to find out where he was going, and if you could not manage that you were no use at all.

So he threw caution to the desert wind and followed; and still he lost them.

The Mercedes was a faster car, and better designed for the narrow, bumpy road, and within a few minutes it was out of sight. Towfik followed the road, hoping he might catch them when they stopped or at least come across something that might be their destination.

Sixty kilometres on, deep in the desert and beginning to worry about getting petrol, he reached a tiny oasis village at a crossroads. A few scrawny animals grazed in sparse vegetation around a muddy pool. A jar of fava beans and three Fanta cans on a makeshift table outside a hut signified the local café. Towfik got out of the car and spoke to an old man watering a bony buffalo.

'Have you seen a grey Mercedes?'

The peasant stared at him blankly, as if he were speaking a foreign language.

'Have you seen a grey car?'

The old man brushed a large black fly off his forehead and nodded, once.

'When?'

'Today.'

That was probably as precise an answer as he could hope for. 'Which way did it go?'

The old man pointed west, into the desert.

Towfik said, 'Where can I get petrol?'

The man pointed east, toward Cairo.

Towfik gave him a coin and returned to the car. He started the engine and looked again at the petrol gauge. He had enough fuel to get back to Cairo, just; if he went farther west he would run out on the return journey.

He had done all he could, he decided. Wearily, he turned the Renault around and headed back toward the city.

Towfik did not like his work. When it was dull he was bored, and when it was exciting he was frightened. But they had told him that there was important, dangerous work to be done in Cairo, and that he had the qualities necessary to be a good spy, and that there were not enough Egyptian Jews in Israel for them to be able just to go out and find another one with all the qualities if he said no; so, of course, he had agreed. It was not out of idealism that he risked his life for his country. It was more like self-interest: the destruction of Israel would mean his own destruction; in fighting for Israel he was fighting for himself; he risked his life to save his life. It was the logical thing to do. Still, he looked forward to the time – in five years? Ten? Twenty? – when he would be too old for field work, and they would bring him home and sit him behind a desk, and he could find a nice Jewish girl and marry her and settle down to enjoy the land he had fought for.

Meanwhile, having lost Professor Schulz, he was following the wife.

She continued to see the sights, escorted now by a young Arab who had presumably been laid on by the Egyptians to take care of her while her husband was away. In the evening the Arab took her to an Egyptian restaurant for dinner, brought her home, and kissed her cheek under the jacaranda tree in the garden.

The next morning Towfik went to the main post office and sent a coded cable to his uncle in Rome:

SCHULZ MET AT AIRPORT BY SUSPECTED LOCAL AGENT. SPENT TWO DAYS SIGHTSEEING. PICKED UP BY AFORESAID AGENT AND DRIVEN DIRECTION QATTARA. SURVEILLANCE ABORTED. NOW WATCHING WIFE.

He was back in Zamalek at nine A.M. At eleven-thirty he saw Frau Schulz on a balcony, drinking coffee, and was able to figure out which of the apartments was the Schulzes'.

By lunchtime the interior of the Renault had become very hot. Towfik ate an apple and drank tepid beer from a bottle.

Professor Schulz arrived late in the afternoon, in the same grey Mercedes. He looked tired and a little rumpled, like a middle-aged man who had travelled too far. He left the car and went into the building without looking back. After dropping him, the agent drove past the Renault and looked straight at Towfik for an instant. There was nothing Towfik could do about it.

Where had Schulz been? It had taken him most of a day to get there, Towfik speculated; he had spent a night, a full day and a second night there; and it had taken most of today to get back. Qattara was only one of several possibilities: the desert road went all the way to Matruh on the Mediterranean coast; there was a turnoff to Karkur Tohl in the far south; with a change of car and a desert guide they could even have gone to a rendezvous on the border with Libya.

At nine P.M. the Schulzes came out again. The professor looked refreshed. They were dressed for dinner. They walked a short distance and hailed a taxi.

Towfik made a decision. He did not follow them.

He got out of the car and entered the garden of the building. He stepped on to the dusty lawn and found a vantage point behind a bush from where he could see into the hall through the open front door. The Nubian caretaker was sitting on a low wooden bench, picking his nose.

Towfik waited.

Twenty minutes later the man left his bench and disappeared into the back of the building.

Towfik hurried through the hall and ran, soft-footed, up the staircase.

He had three Yale-type skeleton keys, but none of them fitted the lock of apartment three. In the end he got the door open with a piece of bendy plastic broken off a college set-square.

He entered the apartment and closed the door behind him.

It was now quite dark outside. A little light from a streetlamp came through the unshaded windows. Towfik drew a small flashlight from his trousers pocket, but he did not switch it on yet.

The apartment was large and airy, with white-painted walls and English-colonial furniture. It had the sparse, chilly look of a place where nobody actually lived.

There was a big drawing room, a dining room, three bedrooms and a kitchen. After a quick general survey Towfik started snooping in earnest.

The two smaller bedrooms were bare. In the larger one, Towfik went rapidly through all the drawers and cupboards. A wardrobe held the rather gaudy dresses of a woman past her prime: bright prints, sequinned gowns, turquoise and orange and pink. The labels were American. Schulz was an Austrian national, the cable had said, but perhaps he lived in the USA. Towfik had never heard him speak.

On the bedside table were a guide to Cairo in English, a copy of *Vogue* and a reprinted lecture on isotopes.

So Schulz was a scientist.

Towfik glanced through the lecture. Most of it was over his head. Schulz must be a top chemist or physicist, he thought. If he was here to work on weaponry, Tel Aviv would want to know.

There were no personal papers – Schulz evidently had his passport and wallet in his pocket. The airline labels had been removed from the matching set of tan suitcases.

On a low table in the drawing room, two empty glasses smelled of gin: they had had a cocktail before going out.

In the bathroom Towfik found the clothes Schulz had worn into the desert. There was a lot of sand in the shoes, and on the trouser cuffs he found small dusty grey smears which might have been cement. In the breast pocket of the rumpled jacket was a blue plastic container, about one-and-a-half inches square, very slender. It contained a light-tight envelope of the kind used to protect photographic film.

Towfik pocketed the plastic box.

The airline labels from the luggage were in a waste basket in the little hall. The Schulzes' address was in Boston, Massachusetts, which probably meant that the professor taught at Harvard, MIT or one of the many lesser universities in the area. Towfik did some rapid arithmetic. Schulz would have been in his twenties during World War Two: he could easily be one of the German rocketry experts who went to the USA after the war.

Or not. You did not have to be a Nazi to work for the Arabs.

Nazi or not, Schulz was a cheapskate: his soap, toothpaste and after-shave were all taken from airlines and hotels.

On the floor beside a rattan chair, near the table with the empty cocktail glasses, lay a lined foolscap notepad, its top sheet blank. There was a pencil lying on the pad. Perhaps Schulz had been making notes on his trip while he sipped his gin sling. Towfik searched the apartment for sheets torn from the pad.

He found them on the balcony, burned to cinders in a large glass ashtray.

The night was cool. Later in the year the air would be warm and fragrant with the blossom of the jacaranda tree in the garden below. The city traffic snored in the distance. It reminded Towfik of his father's apartment in Jerusalem. He wondered how long it would be before he saw Jerusalem again.

He had done all he could here. He would look again at that foolscap pad, to see whether Schulz's pencil had pressed hard enough to leave an impression on the next page. He turned away from the parapet and crossed the balcony to the French windows leading back into the drawing room.

He had his hand on the door when he heard the voices.

Towfik froze.

'I'm sorry, honey, I just couldn't face another over-done steak.'

'We could have eaten something, for God's sake.'

The Schulzes were back.

Towfik rapidly reviewed his progress through the rooms: bedrooms, bathroom, drawing room, kitchen . . . he had replaced everything he had touched, except the little plastic box. He had to keep that anyway. Schulz would have to assume he had lost it.

If Towfik could get away unseen now, they might never know he had been there.

He bellied over the parapet and hung at full length by his fingertips. It was too dark for him to see the ground. He dropped, landed lightly and strolled away.

It had been his first burglary, and he felt pleased. It had gone as smoothly as a training exercise, even to the early return of the occupant and sudden exit of spy by prearranged emergency route. He grinned in the dark. He might yet live to see that desk job.

He got into his car, started the engine and switched on the lights.

Two men emerged from the shadows and stood on either side of the Renault.

Who . . . ?

He did not pause to figure out what was going on. He rammed the gearshift into first and pulled away. The two men hastily stepped aside.

They had made no attempt to stop him. So why had they been there? To make sure he stayed in the car . . . ?

He jammed on the brakes and looked into the back seat, and then he knew, with unbearable sadness, that he would never see Jerusalem again.

A tall Arab in a dark suit was smiling at him over the snout of a small handgun.

'Drive on,' the man said in Arabic, 'but not quite so fast, please.'

Q: What is your name?
A: Towfik el-Masiri.
Q: Describe yourself.
A: Age twenty-six, five-foot-nine, one hundred and eighty pounds, brown eyes, black hair, Semitic features, light brown skin.
Q: Who do you work for?
A: I am a student.
Q: What day is today?
A: Saturday.
Q: What is your nationality?
A: Egyptian.

Q: What is twenty minus seven?

A: Thirteen.

The above questions are designed to facilitate fine calibration of the lie detector.

Q: You work for the CIA.

A: No. (TRUE)

Q: The Germans?

A: No. (TRUE)

Q: Israel, then.

A: No. (FALSE)

Q: You really are a student?

A: Yes. (FALSE)

Q: Tell me about your studies.

A: I'm doing chemistry at Cairo University. (TRUE) I'm interested in polymers. (TRUE) I want to be a petrochemical engineer. (FALSE)

Q: What are polymers?

A: Complex organic compounds with long-chain molecules – the commonest is polythene. (TRUE)

Q: What is your name?

A: I told you, Towfik el-Masiri. (FALSE)

Q: The pads attached to your head and chest measure your pulse, heartbeat, breathing and perspiration. When you tell untruths, your metabolism betrays you – you breathe faster, sweat more, and so on. This machine, which was given to us by our Russian friends, tells me when you are lying. Besides, I happen to know that Towfik el-Masiri is dead. Who are you?

A: (no reply)

Q: The wire taped to the tip of your penis is part of a

different machine. It is connected to this button here. When I press the button—

A: (scream)

Q: —an electric current passes through the wire and gives you a shock. We have put your feet in a bucket of water to improve the efficiency of the apparatus. What is your name?

A: Avram Ambache.

The electrical apparatus interferes with the functioning of the lie detector.

Q: Have a cigarette.

A: Thank you.

Q: Believe it or not, I hate this work. The trouble is, people who like it are never any good at it – you need sensitivity, you know. I'm a sensitive person . . . I hate to see people suffer. Don't you?

A: (no reply)

Q: You're now trying to think of ways to resist me. Please don't bother. There is no defence against modern techniques of . . . interviewing. What is your name?

A: Avram Ambache. (TRUE)

Q: Who is your control?

A: I don't know what you mean. (FALSE)

Q: Is it Bosch?

A: No, Friedman. (READING INDETERMINATE)

Q: It is Bosch.

A: Yes. (FALSE)

Q: No, it's not Bosch. It's Krantz.

A: Okay, it's Krantz – whatever you say. (TRUE)

Q: How do you make contact?

A: I have a radio. (FALSE)

Q: You're not telling me the truth.

A: (scream)

Q: How do you make contact?

A: A dead-letter box in the *faubourg*.

Q: You are thinking that when you are in pain, the lie detector will not function properly, and that there is therefore safety in torture. You are only partly right. This is a very sophisticated machine, and I spent many months learning to use it properly. After I have given you a shock, it takes only a few moments to readjust the machine to your faster metabolism; and then I can once more tell when you are lying. How do you make contact?

A: A dead-letter – (scream)

Q: Ali! He's kicked his feet free – these convulsions are very strong. Tie him again, before he comes round. Pick up that bucket and put more water in it.

      (pause)

      Right, he's waking, get out. Can you hear me, Towfik?

A: (indistinct)

Q: What is your name?

A: (no reply)

Q: A little jab to help you—

A: (scream)

Q: —to think.

A: Avram Ambache.

Q: What day is today?

A: Saturday.

Q: What did we give you for breakfast?

A: Fava beans.

Q: What is twenty minus seven?

A: Thirteen.

Q: What is your profession?

A: I'm a student. No don't please and a spy yes I'm a spy don't touch the button please oh god oh god—

Q: How do you make contact?

A: Coded cables.

Q: Have a cigarette. Here ... oh, you don't seem to be able to hold it between your lips – let me help ... there.

A: Thank you.

Q: Just try to be calm. Remember, as long as you're telling the truth, there will be no pain.
(pause)
Are you feeling better?

A: Yes.

Q: So am I. Now then, tell me about Professor Schulz. Why were you following him?

A: I was ordered to. (TRUE)

Q: By Tel Aviv?

A: Yes. (TRUE)

Q: Who in Tel Aviv?

A: I don't know. (READING INDETERMINATE)

Q: But you can guess.

A: Bosch. (READING INDETERMINATE)

Q: Or Krantz?

A: Perhaps. (TRUE)

Q: Krantz is a good man. Dependable. How's his wife?

A: Very well, I—(scream)

Q: His wife died in 1958. Why do you make me hurt you? What did Schulz do?

A: Went sightseeing for two days, then disappeared into the desert in a grey Mercedes.

Q: And you burglarized his apartment.

A: Yes. (TRUE)

Q: What did you learn?

A: He is a scientist. (TRUE)

Q: Anything else?

A: American. (TRUE) That's all. (TRUE)

Q: Who was your instructor in training?

A: Ertl. (READING INDETERMINATE)

Q: That wasn't his real name, though.

A: I don't know. (FALSE) No! Not the button let me think it was just a minute I think somebody said his real name was Manner. (TRUE)

Q: Oh, Manner. Shame. He's the old-fashioned type. He still believes you can train agents to resist interrogation. It's his fault you're suffering so much, you know. What about your colleagues? Who trained with you?

A: I never knew their real names. (FALSE)

Q: Didn't you?

A: (scream)

Q: Real names.

A: Not all of them—

Q: Tell me the ones you did know.

A: (no reply)
   (scream)

The prisoner fainted.

   (pause)

Q: What is your name?

A: Uh ... Towfik. (scream)

Q: What did you have for breakfast?

A: Don't know.

Q: What is twenty minus seven?

A: Twenty-seven.

Q: What did you tell Krantz about Professor Schulz?

A: Sightseeing ... Western Desert ... surveillance aborted ...

Q: Who did you train with?

A: (no reply)

Q: Who did you train with?

A: (scream)

Q: Who did you train with?

A: Yea, though I walk through the valley of the shadow of death—

Q: Who did you train with?

A: (scream)

The prisoner died.

When Kawash asked for a meeting, Pierre Borg went. There was no discussion about times and places: Kawash sent a message giving the rendezvous, and Borg made sure to be there. Kawash was the best double agent Borg had ever had, and that was that.

The head of the Mossad stood at one end of the northbound Bakerloo Line platform in Oxford Circus underground station, reading an advertisement for a course of lectures in Theosophy, waiting for Kawash. He had no idea why the Arab had chosen London for this meeting; no idea what he told his masters he was doing in the city; no idea, even, why Kawash was a traitor. But this man had helped the Israelis win two wars and avoid a third, and Borg needed him.

Borg glanced along the platform, looking for a high brown head with a large, thin nose. He had an idea he knew what Kawash wanted to talk about. He hoped his idea was right.

Borg was very worried about the Schulz affair. It had started out as a piece of routine surveillance, just the right kind of assignment for his newest, rawest agent in Cairo: a high-powered American physicist on vacation in Europe decides to take a trip to Egypt. The first warning sign came when Towfik lost Schulz. At that point Borg had stepped up activity on the project. A freelance journalist in Milan who occasionally made inquiries for German Intelligence had established that Schulz's air ticket to Cairo had been paid for by the wife of an Egyptian diplomat in Rome. Then the CIA had routinely passed to the Mossad a set of satellite photographs of the area around Qattara which seemed to show signs of construction work – and Borg had remembered that Schulz had been heading in the direction of Qattara when Towfik lost him.

Something was going on, and he did not know what, and that worried him.

He was always worried. If it was not the Egyptians, it was the Syrians; if it was not the Syrians it was the Fedayeen; if it was not his enemies it was his friends and the question of how long they would continue to be his friends. He had a worrying job. His mother had once said, 'Job, *nothing* – you were *born* worrying, like your poor father – if you were a *gardener* you would worry about your job.' She might have been right, but all the same, paranoia was the only rational frame of mind for a spymaster.

Now Towfik had broken contact, and that was the most worrying sign of all.

Maybe Kawash would have some answers.

A train thundered in. Borg was not waiting for a train. He began to read the credits on a movie poster. Half the names were Jewish. Maybe I should have been a movie producer, he thought.

The train pulled out, and a shadow fell over Borg. He looked up into the calm face of Kawash.

The Arab said, 'Thank you for coming.' He always said that.

Borg ignored it: he never knew how to respond to thanks. He said, 'What's new?'

'I had to pick up one of your youngsters in Cairo on Friday.'

'You *had* to?'

'Military Intelligence were bodyguarding a VIP, and they spotted the kid tailing them. Military don't have operational personnel in the city, so they asked my department to pick him up. It was an official request.'

'God *damn*,' Borg said feelingly. 'What happened to him?'

'I had to do it by the book,' Kawash said. He looked very sad. 'The boy was interrogated and killed. His name was Avram Ambache, but he worked as Towfik el-Masiri.'

Borg frowned. 'He told you his real name?'

'He's dead, Pierre.'

Borg shook his head irritably: Kawash always wanted to linger over personal aspects. 'Why did he tell you his name?'

'We're using the Russian equipment – the electric shock and the lie detector together. You're not training them to cope with it.'

Borg gave a short laugh. 'If we told them about it, we'd never get any fucking recruits. What else did he give away?'

'Nothing we didn't know. He would have, but I killed him first.'

'*You* killed him?'

'I conducted the interrogation, in order to make sure he did not say anything important. All these interviews are taped now, and the transcripts filed. We're learning from the Russians.' The sadness deepened in the brown eyes. 'Why – would you prefer that I should have someone else kill your boys?'

Borg stared at him, then looked away. Once again he had to steer the conversation away from the sentimental. 'What did the boy discover about Schulz?'

'An agent took the professor into the Western Desert.'

'Sure, but what for?'

'I don't know.'

'You must know, you're in Egyptian Intelligence!' Borg controlled his irritation. Let the man do things at his own pace, he told himself; whatever information he's got, he'll tell.

'I don't know what they're doing out there, because they've set up a special group to handle it,' Kawash said. 'My department isn't informed.'

'Any idea why?'

The Arab shrugged. 'I'd say they don't want the Russians to know about it. These days Moscow gets everything that goes through us.'

Borg let his disappointment show. 'Is that all Towfik could manage?'

Suddenly there was anger in the soft voice of the Arab. 'The kid died for you,' he said.

'I'll thank him in heaven. Did he die in vain?'

'He took this from Schulz's apartment.' Kawash drew a hand from inside his coat and showed Borg a small, square box of blue plastic.

Borg took the box. 'How do you know where he got it?'

'It has Schulz's fingerprints on it. And we arrested Towfik right after he broke into the apartment.'

Borg opened the box and fingered the light-proof envelope. It was unsealed. He took out the photographic negative.

The Arab said, 'We opened the envelope and developed the film. It's blank.'

With a deep sense of satisfaction, Borg reassembled the box and put it into his pocket. Now it all made sense; now he understood; now he knew what he had to do. A train came in. 'You want to catch this one?' he said.

Kawash frowned slightly, nodded assent, and moved to the edge of the platform as the train stopped and the doors opened. He boarded, and stood just inside. He said, 'I don't know what on earth the box is.'

Borg thought, You don't like me, but I think you're just great. He smiled thinly at the Arab as the doors of the underground train began to slide shut. 'I do,' he said.

CHAPTER TWO

THE AMERICAN girl was quite taken with Nat Dickstein.

They worked side by side in a dusty vineyard, weeding and hoeing, with a light breeze blowing over them from the Sea of Galilee. Dickstein had taken off his shirt and worked in shorts and sandals, with the contempt for the sun which only the city-born possess.

He was a thin man, small-boned, with narrow shoulders, a shallow chest, and knobby elbows and knees. Karen would watch him when she stopped for a break – which she did often, although he never seemed to need a rest. Stringy muscles moved like knotted rope under his brown, scarred skin. She was a sensual woman, and she wanted to touch those scars with her fingers and ask him how he got them.

Sometimes he would look up and catch her staring, and he would grin, unembarrassed, and carry on working. His face was regular and anonymous in repose. He had dark eyes behind cheap round spectacles of the kind which Karen's generation liked because John Lennon wore them. His hair was dark, too, and short: Karen would have liked him to grow it. When he grinned that lopsided grin, he looked younger; though at any time it was hard to say just how old he might be. He had the strength and energy of a young man, but she had seen the concentration camp tattoo under his wristwatch, so he could not be much less than forty, she thought.

He had arrived at the kibbutz shortly after Karen, in the summer of 1967. She had come, with her deodorants and her contraceptive pills, looking for a place where she could live out hippy ideals without getting stoned twenty-four hours a day. He had been brought here in an ambulance. She assumed he had been wounded in the Six-Day War, and the other kibbutzniks agreed, vaguely, that it was something like that.

His welcome had been very different from hers. Karen's reception had been friendly but wary: in her philosophy they saw their own, with dangerous additions. Nat Dickstein returned like a long-lost son. They clustered around him, fed him soup and came away from his wounds with tears in their eyes.

If Dickstein was their son, Esther was their mother. She was the oldest member of the kibbutz. Karen had said, 'She looks like Golda Meir's mother,' and one of the others had said, 'I think she's Golda's *father*,' and they all laughed affectionately. She used a walking stick, and stomped about the village giving unsolicited advice, most of it very wise. She had stood guard outside Dickstein's sickroom chasing away noisy children, waving her stick and threatening beatings which even the children knew would never be administered.

Dickstein had recovered very quickly. Within a few days he was sitting out in the sun, peeling vegetables for the kitchen and telling vulgar jokes to the older children. Two weeks later he was working in the fields, and soon he was labouring harder than all but the youngest men.

His past was vague, but Esther had told Karen the story of his arrival in Israel in 1948, during the War of Independence.

Nineteen forty-eight was part of the recent past for Esther. She had been a young woman in London in the first two decades of the century, and had been an activist in half a dozen radical left-wing causes from suffragism to pacifism before emigrating to Palestine; but her memory went back further, to pogroms in Russia which she recalled vaguely in monstrous nightmare images. She had sat under a fig tree in the heat of the day, varnishing a chair she had made with her own gnarled hands, and talked about Dickstein like a clever but mischievous schoolboy.

'There were eight or nine of them, some from the university, some working men from the East End. If they ever had any money, they'd spent it before they got to France. They hitched a ride on a truck to Paris, then jumped a freight train to Marseilles. From there, it seems, they walked most of the way to Italy. Then they stole a huge car, a German Army staff car, a Mercedes, and drove all the way to the toe of Italy.' Esther's face was creased in smiles, and Karen thought: She would love to have been there with them.

'Dickstein had been to Sicily in the war, and it seems he knew the Mafia there. They had all the guns left over from the war. Dickstein wanted guns for Israel, but he had no money. He persuaded the Sicilians to sell a boatload of submachine guns to an Arab purchaser, and then to tell the Jews where the pickup would take place. They knew what he was up to, and they loved it. The deal was done, the Sicilians got their money, and then Dickstein and his friend stole the boat with its cargo and sailed to Israel!'

Karen had laughed aloud, there under the fig tree, and a grazing goat looked up at her balefully.

'Wait,' said Esther, 'you haven't heard the end of it. Some of the university boys had done a bit of rowing, and one of the other lot was a docker, but that was all the experience they had of the sea, and here they were sailing a five-thousand-ton cargo vessel on their own. They figured out a little navigation from first principles: the ship had charts and a compass. Dickstein had looked up in a book how to start the ship, but he says the book did not tell how to stop it. So they steamed into Haifa, yelling and waving and throwing their hats into the air, just like it was a varsity rag – and ploughed straight into the dock.

'They were forgiven instantly, of course – the guns were more precious than gold, literally. And that's when they started to call Dickstein "The Pirate".'

He did not look much like a pirate, working in the vineyard in his baggy shorts and his spectacles, Karen thought. All the same, he was attractive. She wanted to seduce him, but she could not figure out how. He obviously liked her, and she had taken care to let him know she was available. But he never made a move.

Perhaps he felt she was too young and innocent. Or maybe he was not interested in women.

His voice broke into her thoughts. 'I think we've finished.'

She looked at the sun: it was time to go. 'You've done twice as much as me.'

'I'm used to the work. I've been here, on and off, for twenty years. The body gets into the habit.'

They walked back toward the village as the sky turned purple and yellow. Karen said, 'What else do you do – when you're not here?'

'Oh . . . poison wells, kidnap Christian children.'

Karen laughed.

Dickstein said, 'How does this life compare with California?'

'This is a wonderful place,' she told him. 'I think there's a lot of work still to be done before the women are genuinely equal.'

'That seems to be the big topic at the moment.'

'You never have much to say about it.'

'Listen, I think you're right; but it's better for people to take their freedom rather than be given it.'

Karen said, 'That sounds like a good excuse for doing nothing.'

Dickstein laughed.

As they entered the village they passed a young man on a pony, carrying a rifle, on his way to patrol the borders of the settlement. Dickstein called out, 'Be careful, Yisrael.' The shelling from the Golan Heights had stopped, of course, and the children no longer had to sleep underground; but the kibbutz kept up the patrols. Dickstein had been one of those in favour of maintaining vigilance.

'I'm going to read to Mottie,' Dickstein said.

'Can I come?'

'Why not?' Dickstein looked at his watch. 'We've just got time to wash. Come to my room in five minutes.'

They parted, and Karen went into the showers. A kibbutz was the best place to be an orphan, she thought as she took off her clothes. Mottie's parents were both dead – the father blown up in the attack on the Golan Heights during the last war, the mother killed a year earlier in a shootout with Fedayeen. Both had been close friends of Dickstein. It was a tragedy for the child, of course; but he still slept in the same bed, ate in the same room, and had almost one hundred other adults to love and care for him – he was not foisted on to unwilling aunts or ageing grandparents or, worst of all, an orphanage. And he had Dickstein.

When she had washed off the dust Karen put on clean clothes and went to Dickstein's room. Mottie was already there, sitting on Dickstein's lap, sucking his thumb and listening to *Treasure Island* in Hebrew. Dickstein was the only person Karen had ever met who spoke Hebrew with a Cockney accent. His speech was even more strange now, because he was doing different voices for the characters in the story: a high-pitched boy's voice for Jim, a deep snarl for Long John Silver, and a half whisper for the mad Ben Gunn. Karen sat and watched the two of them in the yellow electric light, thinking how boyish Dickstein appeared, and how grown-up the child was.

When the chapter was finished they took Mottie to his dormitory, kissed him goodnight, and went into the dining room. Karen thought: If we continue to go about together like this, everyone will think we're lovers already.

They sat with Esther. After dinner she told them a story, and there was a young woman's twinkle in her eye. 'When I first went to Jerusalem, they used to say that if you owned a feather pillow, you could buy a house.'

Dickstein willingly took the bait. 'How was that?'

'You could sell a good feather pillow for a pound. With that pound you could join a loan society, which entitled you to borrow ten pounds. Then you found a plot of land. The owner of the land would take ten pounds deposit and the rest in promissory notes. Now you were a landowner. You went to a builder and said, "Build a house for yourself on this plot of land. All I want is a small flat for myself and my family."'

They all laughed. Dickstein looked toward the door. Karen followed his glance and saw a stranger, a stocky man in his forties with a coarse, fleshy face. Dickstein got up and went to him.

Esther said to Karen, 'Don't break your heart, child. That one is not made to be a husband.'

Karen looked at Esther, then back at the doorway. Dickstein had gone. A few moments later she heard the sound of a car starting up and driving away.

Esther put her old hand on Karen's young one, and squeezed.

Karen never saw Dickstein again.

Nat Dickstein and Pierre Borg sat in the back seat of a big black Citroën. Borg's bodyguard was driving, with his machine pistol lying on the front seat beside him. They travelled through the darkness with nothing ahead but the cone of light from the headlamps. Nat Dickstein was afraid.

He had never come to see himself the way others did, as a competent, indeed brilliant, agent who had proved his ability to survive just about anything. Later, when the game was on and he was living by his wits, grappling at close quarters with strategy and problems and personalities, there would be no room in his mind for fear; but now, when Borg was about to brief him, he had no plans to make, no forecasts to refine, no characters to assess. He knew only that he had to turn his back on peace and simple hard work, the land and the sunshine and caring for growing things; and that ahead of him there were terrible risks and great danger, lies and pain and bloodshed and, perhaps, his death. So he sat in the corner of the seat, his arms and legs crossed tightly, watching Borg's dimly lit face, while fear of the unknown knotted and writhed in his stomach and made him nauseous.

In the faint, shifting light, Borg looked like the giant in a fairy story. He had heavy features: thick lips, broad cheeks, and protruding eyes shadowed by thick brows.

As a child he had been told he was ugly, and so he had grown into an ugly man. When he was uneasy – like now – his hands went continually to his face, covering his mouth, rubbing his nose, scratching his forehead, in a subconscious attempt to hide his unsightliness. Once, in a relaxed moment, Dickstein had asked him, 'Why do you yell at everybody?' and he had replied, 'Because they're all so fucking handsome.'

They never knew what language to use when they spoke. Borg was French-Canadian originally, and found Hebrew a struggle. Dickstein's Hebrew was good and his French only passable. Usually they settled for English.

Dickstein had worked under Borg for ten years, and still he did not like the man. He felt he understood Borg's troubled, unhappy nature; and he respected his professionalism and his obsessional devotion to Israeli Intelligence; but in Dickstein's book this was not enough cause to like a person. When Borg lied to him, there were always good sound reasons, but Dickstein resented the lie no less.

He retaliated by playing Borg's tactics back against him. He would refuse to say where he was going, or he would lie about it. He never checked in on schedule while he was in the field: he simply called or sent messages with peremptory demands. And he would sometimes conceal from Borg part or all of his game plan. This prevented Borg from interfering with schemes of his own, and it was also more secure – for what Borg knew, he might be obliged to tell to politicians, and what they knew might find its way to the opposition. Dickstein knew the strength of his position – he was responsible for many of the triumphs which had distinguished Borg's career – and he played it for all it was worth.

The Citroën roared through the Arab town of Nazareth – deserted now, presumably under curfew – and went on into the night, heading for Tel Aviv. Borg lit a thin cigar and began to speak.

'After the Six-Day War, one of the bright boys in the Ministry of Defence wrote a paper entitled "The Inevitable Destruction of Israel." The argument went like this. During the War of Independence, we bought arms from Czechoslovakia. When the Soviet bloc began to take the Arab side, we turned to France, and later West Germany. Germany called off all deals as soon as the Arabs found out. France imposed an embargo after the Six-Day War. Both Britain and the United States have consistently refused to supply us with arms. We are losing our sources one by one.

'Suppose we are able to make up those losses, by continually finding new suppliers and by building our own munitions industry: even then, the fact remains that Israel must be the loser in a Middle East arms race. The oil countries will be richer than us throughout the foreseeable future. Our defence budget is already a terrible burden on the national economy whereas our enemies have nothing better to spend their billions on. When they have ten thousand tanks, we'll need six thousand; when they have twenty thousand tanks, we'll need twelve thousand; and so on. Simply by doubling their arms expenditure every year, they will be able to cripple our national economy without firing a shot.

'Finally, the recent history of the Middle East shows a pattern of limited wars about once a decade. The logic of this pattern is against us. The Arabs can afford to lose a war from time to time. We can't: our first defeat will be our last war.

'Conclusion: the survival of Israel depends on our breaking out of the vicious spiral our enemies have prescribed for us.'

Dickstein nodded. 'It's not a novel line of thought. It's the usual argument for "peace at any price." I should think the bright boy got fired from the Ministry of Defence for that paper.'

'Wrong both times. He went on to say, "We must inflict, or have the power to inflict, permanent and crippling damage to the next Arab army that crosses our borders. We must have nuclear weapons."'

Dickstein was very still for a moment; then he let out his breath in a long whistle. It was one of those devastating ideas that seems completely obvious as soon as it has been said. It would change everything. He was silent for a while, digesting the implications. His mind teemed with questions. Was it technically feasible? Would the Americans help? Would the Israeli Cabinet approve it? Would the Arabs retaliate with their own bomb? What he said was, 'Bright boy in the Ministry, hell. That was Moshe Dayan's paper.'

'No comment,' said Borg.

'Did the Cabinet adopt it?'

'There has been a long debate. Certain elder states-men argued that they had not come this far to see the Middle East wiped out in a nuclear holocaust. But the opposition faction relied mainly on the argument that if we have a bomb, the Arabs will get one too, and we will be back at square one. As it turned out, that was their big mistake.' Borg reached into his pocket and took out a small plastic box. He handed it to Dickstein.

Dickstein switched on the interior light and exam-ined the box. It was about an inch and a half square, thin, and blue in colour. It opened to reveal a small envelope made of heavy light-proof paper. 'What's this?' he said.

Borg said, 'A physicist named Friedrich Schulz vis-ited Cairo in February. He is Austrian but he works in the United States. He was apparently on holiday in Europe, but his plane ticket to Egypt was paid for by the Egyptian government.

'I had him followed, but he gave our boy the slip and disappeared into the Western Desert for forty-eight hours. We know from CIA satellite pictures that there is a major construction project going on in that part of the desert. When Schulz came back, he had that in his pocket. It's a personnel dosimeter. The envelope, which is light-tight, contains a piece of ordinary photographic film. You carry the box in your pocket, or pinned to your lapel or trouser belt. If you're exposed to radia-tion, the film will show fogging when it's developed. Dosimeters are carried, as a matter of routine, by everyone who visits or works in a nuclear power station.'

Dickstein switched off the light and gave the box back to Borg. 'You're telling me the Arabs are already making atom bombs,' he said softly.

'That's right.' Borg spoke unnecessarily loudly.

'So the Cabinet gave Dayan the go-ahead to make a bomb of his own.'

'In principle, yes.'

'How so?'

'There are some practical difficulties. The mechanics of the business are simple – the actual clockwork of the bomb, so to speak. Anyone who can make a conventional bomb can make a nuclear bomb. The problem is getting hold of the explosive material, plutonium. You get plutonium out of an atomic reactor. It's a by-product. Now, we have a reactor, at Dimona in the Negev Desert. Did you know that?'

'Yes.'

'It's our worst-kept secret. However, we don't have the equipment for extracting the plutonium from the spent fuel. We could build a reprocessing plant, but the problem is that we have no uranium *of our own* to put through the reactor.'

'Wait a minute.' Dickstein frowned. 'We must have uranium, to fuel the reactor for normal use.'

'Correct. We get it from France, and it's supplied to us on condition we return the spent fuel to them for reprocessing, so they get the plutonium.'

'Other suppliers?'

'Would impose the same condition – it's part of all the nuclear non-proliferation treaties.'

Dickstein said, 'But the people at Dimona could siphon off some of the spent fuel without anyone noticing.'

'No. Given the quantity of uranium originally supplied, it's possible to calculate precisely how much plutonium comes out the other end. And they weigh it very carefully – it's expensive stuff.'

'So the problem is to get hold of some uranium.'

'Right.'

'And the solution?'

'The solution is, you're going to steal it.'

Dickstein looked out of the window. The moon came out, revealing a flock of sheep huddled in a corner of a field, watched by an Arab shepherd with a staff: a Biblical scene. So this was the game: stolen uranium for the land of milk and honey. Last time it had been the murder of a terrorist leader in Damascus; the time before, blackmailing a wealthy Arab in Monte Carlo to stop him funding the Fedayeen.

Dickstein's feelings had been pushed into the background while Borg talked about politics and Schulz and nuclear reactors. Now he was reminded that this involved *him*; and the fear came back, and with it a memory. After his father died the family had been desperately poor, and when creditors called, Nat had been sent to the door to say mummy was out. At the age of thirteen, he had found it unbearably humiliating, because the creditors knew he was lying, and he knew they knew, and they would look at him with a mixture of contempt and pity which pierced him to the quick.

He would never forget that feeling – and it came back, like a reminder from his unconscious, when somebody like Borg said something like, 'Little Nathaniel, go steal some uranium for your motherland.'

To his mother he had always said, 'Do I have to?' And now he said to Pierre Borg, 'If we're going to steal it anyway, why not buy it and simply refuse to send it back for reprocessing?'

'Because that way, everyone would know what we're up to.'

'So?'

'Reprocessing takes time – many months. During that time two things could happen: one, the Egyptians would hurry their programme; and two, the Americans would pressure us not to build the bomb.'

'Oh!' It was worse. 'So you want me to steal this stuff without anyone knowing that it's us.'

'More than that.' Borg's voice was harsh and throaty. 'Nobody must even know it's been stolen. It must look as if the stuff has just been lost. I want the owners, and the international agencies, to be so embarrassed about the stuff disappearing that they will hush it up. Then, when they discover they've been robbed, they will be compromised by their own cover-up.'

'It's bound to come out eventually.'

'Not before we've got our bomb.'

They had reached the coast road from Haifa to Tel Aviv, and as the car butted through the night Dickstein could see, over to the right, occasional glimpses of the Mediterranean, glinting like jewellery in the moonlight.

When he spoke he was surprised at the note of weary resignation in his voice. 'How much uranium do we need?'

'They want twelve bombs. In the yellowcake form – that's the uranium ore – it would mean about a hundred tons.'

'I won't be able to slip it into my pocket, then.' Dickstein frowned. 'What would all that cost if we bought it?'

'Something over one million US dollars.'

'And you think the losers will just hush it up?'

'If it's done right.'

'How?'

'That's your job, Pirate.'

'I'm not so sure it's possible,' Dickstein said.

'It's got to be. I told the Prime Minister we could pull it off. I laid my career on the line, Nat.'

'Don't talk to me about your bleeding career.'

Borg lit another cigar – a nervous reaction to Dickstein's scorn. Dickstein opened his window an inch to let the smoke out. His sudden hostility had nothing to do with Borg's clumsy personal appeal: that was typical of the man's inability to understand how people felt toward him. What had unnerved Dickstein was a sudden vision of mushroom clouds over Jerusalem and Cairo, of cotton fields by the Nile and vineyards beside the Sea of Galilee blighted by fallout, the Middle East wasted by fire, its children deformed for generations.

He said, 'I still think peace is an alternative.'

Borg shrugged. 'I wouldn't know. I don't get involved in politics.'

'Bullshit.'

Borg sighed. 'Look, if they have a bomb, we have to have one too, don't we?'

'If that was all there was to it, we could just hold a press conference, announce that the Egyptians are making a bomb, and let the rest of the world stop them. I think our people want the bomb anyway. I think they're glad of the excuse.'

'And maybe they're right!' Borg said. 'We can't go on fighting a war every few years – one of these days we might lose one.'

'We could make peace.'

Borg snorted. 'You're so fucking naive.'

'If we gave way on a few things – the Occupied Territories, the Law of Return, equal rights for Arabs in Israel—'

'The Arabs have equal rights.'

Dickstein smiled mirthlessly. 'You're so fucking naive.'

'Listen!' Borg made an effort at self-control. Dick-stein understood his anger: it was a reaction he had in common with many Israelis. They thought that if these liberal ideas should ever take hold, they would be the thin edge of the wedge, and concession would follow concession until the land was handed back to the Arabs on a plate – and that prospect struck at the very roots of their identity. 'Listen,' Borg said again. 'Maybe we should sell our birthright for a mess of potage. But this is the real world, and the people of this country won't vote for peace-at-any-price; and in your heart you know that the Arabs aren't in any great hurry for peace either. So, in the real world, we still have to fight them; and if we're going to fight them we'd better win; and if we're to be sure of winning, you'd better steal us some uranium.'

Dickstein said, 'The thing I dislike most about you is, you're usually right.'

Borg wound down his window and threw away the stub of his cigar. It made a trail of sparks on the road, like a firecracker. The lights of Tel Aviv became visible ahead: they were almost there.

Borg said, 'You know, with most of my people I don't feel obliged to argue politics every time I give them an assignment. They just take orders, like operatives are supposed to.'

'I don't believe you,' Dickstein said. 'This is a nation of idealists, or it's nothing.'

'Maybe.'

'I once knew a man called Wolfgang. He used to say, "I just take orders." Then he used to break my leg.'

'Yeah,' Borg said. 'You told me.'

When a company hires an accountant to keep the books, the first thing he does is announce that he has so much work to do on the overall direction of the company's financial policy that he needs to hire a junior accountant to keep the books. Something similar happens with spies. A country sets up an intelligence service to find out how many tanks its neighbour has and where they are kept, and before you can say MI5 the intelligence service announces that it is so busy spying on subversive elements at home that a separate service is needed to deal with military intelligence.

So it was in Egypt in 1955. The country's fledgling intelligence service was divided into two directorates. Military Intelligence had the job of counting Israel's tanks; General Investigations had all the glamour.

The man in charge of both these directorates was called the Director of General Intelligence, just to be confusing; and he was supposed – in theory – to report to the Minister of the Interior. But another thing that always happens to spy departments is that the Head of State tries to take them over. There are two reasons for this. One is that the spies are continually hatching lunatic schemes of murder, blackmail and invasion which can be terribly embarrassing if they ever get off the ground, so Presidents and Prime Ministers like to keep a personal eye on such departments. The other reason is that intelligence services are a source of power, especially in unstable countries, and the Head of State wants that power for himself.

So the Director of General Intelligence in Cairo always, in practice, reported either to the President or to the Minister of State at the Presidency.

Kawash, the tall Arab who interrogated and killed Towfik and subsequently gave the personnel dosimeter to Pierre Borg, worked in the Directorate of General Investigations, the glamorous civilian half of the service. He was an intelligent and dignified man of great integrity, but he was also deeply religious – to the point of mysticism. His was the solid, powerful kind of mysticism which could support the most unlikely – not to say bizarre – beliefs about the real world. He adhered to a brand of Christianity which held that the return of the Jews to the Promised Land was ordained in the Bible, and was a portent of the end of the world. To work against the return was therefore a sin; to work for it, a holy task. This was why Kawash was a double agent.

The work was all he had. His faith had led him into the secret life, and there he had gradually cut himself off from friends, neighbors, and – with exceptions – family. He had no personal ambitions except to go to heaven. He lived ascetically, his only earthly pleasure being to score points in the espionage game. He was a lot like Pierre Borg, with this difference: Kawash was happy.

At present, though, he was troubled. So far he was losing points in the affair which had begun with Professor Schulz, and this depressed him. The problem was that the Qattara project was being run not by General Investigations but by the other half of the intelligence effort – Military Intelligence. However, Kawash had fasted and meditated, and in the long watches of the night he had developed a scheme for penetrating the secret project.

He had a second cousin, Assam, who worked in the office of the Director of General Intelligence – the body which coordinated Military Intelligence and General Investigations. Assam was more senior than Kawash, but Kawash was smarter.

The two cousins sat in the back room of a small, dirty coffee house near the Sherif Pasha in the heat of the day, drinking lukewarm lime cordial and blowing tobacco smoke at the flies. They looked alike in their lightweight suits and Nasser moustaches. Kawash wanted to use Assam to find out about Qattara. He had devised a plausible line of approach which he thought Assam would go for, but he knew he had to put the matter very delicately in order to win Assam's support. He appeared his usual imperturbable self, despite the anxiety he felt inside.

He began by seeming to be very direct. 'My cousin, do you know what is happening at Qattara?'

A rather furtive look came over Assam's handsome face. 'If you don't know, I can't tell you.'

Kawash shook his head, as if Assam had misunderstood him. 'I don't want you to reveal secrets. Besides, I can guess what the project is.' This was a lie. 'What bothers me is that Maraji has control of it.'

'Why?'

'For your sake. I'm thinking of your career.'

'I'm not worried—'

'Then you should be. Maraji wants your job, you must know that.'

The café proprietor brought a dish of olives and two flat loaves of pita bread. Kawash was silent until he went out. He watched Assam as the man's natural insecurity fed on the lie about Maraji.

Kawash continued, 'Maraji is reporting directly to the Minister, I gather.'

'I see all the documents, though,' Assam said defensively.

'You don't know what he is saying privately to the Minister. He is in a very strong position.'

71

Assam frowned. 'How did you find out about the project, anyway?'

Kawash leaned back against the cool concrete wall. 'One of Maraji's men was doing a bodyguarding job in Cairo and realized he was being followed. The tail was an Israeli agent called Towfik. Maraji doesn't have any field men in the city, so the bodyguard's request for action was passed to me. I picked Towfik up.'

Assam snorted with disgust. 'Bad enough to let himself be followed. Worse to call the wrong department for help. This is terrible.'

'Perhaps we can do something about it, my cousin.'

Assam scratched his nose with a hand heavy with rings. 'Go on.'

'Tell the Director about Towfik. Say that Maraji, for all his considerable talents, makes mistakes in picking his men, because he is young and inexperienced by comparison with someone such as yourself. Insist that you should have charge of personnel for the Qattara project. Then put a man loyal to us into a job there.'

Assam nodded slowly. 'I see.'

The taste of success was in Kawash's mouth. He leaned forward. 'The Director will be grateful to you for having discovered this area of slackness in a top-security matter. And you will be able to keep track of everything Maraji does.'

'This is a very good plan,' Assam said. 'I will speak to the Director today. I'm grateful to you, cousin.'

Kawash had one more thing to say – the most important thing – and he wanted to say it at the best possible moment. It would wait a few minutes, he decided. He stood up and said, 'Haven't you always been my patron?'

They went arm-in-arm out into the heat of the city. Assam said, 'And I will find a suitable man immediately.'

'Ah, yes,' Kawash said, as if that reminded him of another small detail. 'I have a man who would be ideal. He is intelligent, resourceful, and very discreet – and the son of my late wife's brother.'

Assam's eyes narrowed. 'So he would report to you, too.'

Kawash looked hurt. 'If this is too much for me to ask . . .' He spread his hands in a gesture of resignation.

'No,' Assam said. 'We have always helped one another.'

They reached the corner where they parted company. Kawash struggled to keep his feeling of triumph from showing in his face. 'I will send the man to see you. You will find him completely reliable.'

'So be it,' said Assam.

Pierre Borg had known Nat Dickstein for twenty years. Back in 1948 Borg had been sure the boy was not agent material, despite that stroke with the boatload of rifles. He had been thin, pale, awkward, unprepossessing. But it had not been Borg's decision, and they had given Dickstein a trial. Borg had rapidly come to acknowledge that the kid might not look much but he was smart as shit. He also had an odd charm that Borg never understood. Some of the women in the Mossad were crazy about him – while others, like Borg, failed to see the attraction. Dickstein showed no interest either way – his dossier said, 'Sex life: none.'

Over the years Dickstein had grown in skill and confidence, and now Borg would rely on him more than any other agent. Indeed, if Dickstein had been more personally ambitious he could have had the job Borg now held.

Nevertheless, Borg did not see how Dickstein could fulfil his brief. The result of the policy debate over nuclear weapons had been one of those asinine political compromises which bedevilled the work of all civil servants: they had agreed to steal the uranium only if it could be done in such a way that nobody would know, at least for many years, that Israel had been the thief. Borg had fought the decision – he had been all for a sudden, swift piece of buccaneering and to hell with the consequences. A more judicious view had prevailed in the Cabinet; but it was Borg and his team who had to put the decision into effect.

There were other men in the Mossad who could carry out a prescribed scheme as well as Dickstein – Mike, the head of Special Operations, was one, and Borg himself was another. But there was nobody else to whom Borg could say, as he had said to Dickstein: This is the problem – go solve it.

The two men spent a day in a Mossad safe house in the town of Ramat Gan, just outside Tel Aviv. Security-vetted Mossad employees made coffee, served meals, and patrolled the garden with revolvers under their jackets. In the morning Dickstein saw a young physics teacher from the Weizmann Institute at Rehovot. The scientist had long hair and a flowered tie, and he explained the chemistry of uranium, the nature of radioactivity and the working of an atomic pile with limpid clarity and endless patience. After lunch Dickstein talked to an administrator from Dimona about uranium mines, enrichment plants, fuel fabrication works, storage and transport; about safety rules and international regulations; and about the International Atomic Energy Agency, the US Atomic Energy Commission, the United Kingdom Atomic Energy Authority and Euratom.

In the evening Borg and Dickstein had dinner together. Borg was on a halfhearted diet, as usual: he ate no bread with his skewered lamb and salad, but he drank most of the bottle of red Israeli wine. His excuse was that he was calming his nerves so that he would not reveal his anxiety to Dickstein.

After dinner he gave Dickstein three keys. 'There are spare identities for you in safety-deposit boxes in London, Brussels and Zurich,' he said. 'Passports, driving licences, cash and a weapon in each. If you have to switch, leave the old documents in the box.'

Dickstein nodded. 'Do I report to you or Mike?'

Borg thought: You never report anyway, you bastard. He said, 'To me, please. Whenever possible, call me direct and use the jargon. If you can't reach me, contact any embassy and use the code for a meeting – I'll try to get to you, wherever you are. As a last resort, send coded letters via the diplomatic bags.'

Dickstein nodded expressionlessly: all this was routine. Borg stared at him, trying to read his mind. How did *he* feel? Did he think he could do it? Did he have any ideas? Did he plan to go through the motions of trying it and then report that it was impossible? Was he really convinced the bomb was the right thing for Israel?

Borg could have asked, but he would have got no answers.

Dickstein said, 'Presumably there's a deadline.'

'Yes, but we don't know what it is.' Borg began to pick onions out of the remains of the salad. 'We must have our bomb before the Egyptians get theirs. That means your uranium has to go on stream in the reactor before the Egyptian reactor goes operational. After that point, everything is chemistry – there's nothing either side can do to hurry subatomic particles. The first to start will be the first to finish.'

'We need an agent in Qattara,' Dickstein said.

'I'm working on it.'

Dickstein nodded. 'We must have a very good man in Cairo.'

This was not what Borg wanted to talk about. 'What are you trying to do, pump me for information?' he said crossly.

'Thinking aloud.'

There was silence for a few moments. Borg crunched some more onions. At last he said, 'I've told you what I want, but I've left to you all the decisions about how to get it.'

'Yes, you have, haven't you.' Dickstein stood up. 'I think I'll go to bed.'

'Have you got any idea where you're going to start?'

Dickstein said, 'Yes, I have. Goodnight.'

CHAPTER THREE

N AT DICKSTEIN never got used to being a
secret agent. It was the continual deceit that
bothered him. He was always lying to people, hiding,
pretending to be someone he was not, surreptitiously
following people and showing false documents to
officials at airports. He never ceased to worry about
being found out. He had a daytime nightmare in which
he was surrounded suddenly by policemen who
shouted, 'You're a spy! You're a spy!' and took him off
to prison where they broke his leg.

He was uneasy now. He was at the Jean-Monnet
building in Luxembourg, on the Kirchberg Plateau
across a narrow river valley from the hilltop city. He sat
in the entrance to the offices of the Euratom Safeguards
Directorate, memorizing the faces of the employees as
they arrived at work. He was waiting to see a press
officer called Pfaffer but he had intentionally come
much too early. He was looking for weakness. The
disadvantage of this ploy was that all the staff got to see
his face, too; but he had no time for subtle precautions.

Pfaffer turned out to be an untidy young man with
an expression of disapproval and a battered brown
briefcase. Dickstein followed him into an equally untidy

office and accepted his offer of coffee. They spoke French. Dickstein was accredited to the Paris office of an obscure journal called *Science International.* He told Pfaffer that it was his ambition to get a job on *Scientific American.*

Pfaffer asked him, 'Exactly what are you writing about at the moment?'

'The article is called "MUF".' Dickstein explained in English, 'Material Unaccounted For.' He went on, 'In the United States radioactive fuel is continually getting lost. Here in Europe, I'm told, there's an international system for keeping track of all such material.'

'Correct,' Pfaffer said. 'The member countries hand over control of fissile substances to Euratom. We have, first of all, a complete list of civilian establishments where stocks are held – from mines through prep- aration and fabrication plants, stores, and reactors, to reprocessing plants.'

'You said civilian establishments.'

'Yes. The military are outside our scope.'

'Go on.' Dickstein was relieved to get Pfaffer talking before the press officer had a chance to realize how limited was Dickstein's knowledge of these subjects.

'As an example,' Pfaffer continued, 'take a factory making fuel elements from ordinary yellowcake. The raw material coming into the factory is weighed and analyzed by Euratom inspectors. Their findings are programmed into the Euratom computer and checked against the information from the inspectors at the dispatching installation – in this case, probably a ura- nium mine. If there is a discrepancy between the quantity that left the dispatching installation and the quantity that arrived at the factory, the computer will say so. Similar measurements are made of the material leaving the factory – quantity and quality. These figures will in turn be checked against information supplied by inspectors at the premises where the fuel is to be used – a nuclear power station, probably. In addition, all waste at the factory is weighed and analyzed.

'This process of inspection and double-checking is carried on up to and including the final disposal of radioactive wastes. Finally, stocktaking is done at least twice a year at the factory.'

'I see.' Dickstein looked impressed and felt desperately discouraged. No doubt Pfaffer was exaggerating the efficiency of the system – but even if they made half the checks they were supposed to, how could anyone spirit away one hundred tons of yellowcake without their computer noticing? To keep Pfaffer talking, he said, 'So, at any given moment, your computer knows the location of every scrap of uranium in Europe.'

'Within the member countries – France, Germany, Italy, Belgium, the Netherlands and Luxembourg. And it's not just uranium, it's all radioactive material.'

'What about details of transportation?'

'All have to be approved by us.'

Dickstein closed his notebook. 'It sounds like a good system. Can I see it in operation?'

'That wouldn't be up to us. You'd have to contact the atomic energy authority in the member country and ask permission to visit an installation. Some of them do guided tours.'

'Can you let me have a list of phone numbers?'

'Certainly.' Pfaffer stood up and opened a filing cabinet.

Dickstein had solved one problem only to be confronted with another. He had wanted to know where he could go to find out the location of stockpiles of radioactive material, and he now had the answer: Euratom's computer. But all the uranium the computer knew about was subject to the rigorous monitoring system, and therefore extremely difficult to steal. Sitting in the untidy little office, watching the smug Herr Pfaffer rummage through his old press releases, Dickstein thought: If only you knew what's in my mind, little bureaucrat, you'd have a blue fit; and he suppressed a grin and felt a little more cheerful.

Pfaffer handed him a cyclostyled leaflet. Dickstein folded it and put it in his pocket. He said, 'Thank you for your help.'

Pfaffer said, 'Where are you staying?'

'The Alfa, opposite the railway station.'

Pfaffer saw him to the door. 'Enjoy Luxembourg.'

'I'll do my best,' Dickstein said, and shook his hand.

The memory thing was a trick. Dickstein had picked it up as a small child, sitting with his grandfather in a smelly room over a pie shop in the Mile End Road, struggling to recognize the strange characters of the Hebrew alphabet. The idea was to isolate one unique feature of the shape to be remembered and ignore everything else. Dickstein had done that with the faces of the Euratom staff.

He waited outside the Jean-Monnet building in the late afternoon, watching people leave for home. Some of them interested him more than others. Secretaries, messengers and coffee-makers were no use to him, nor were senior administrators. He wanted the people in between: computer programmers, office managers, heads of small departments, personal assistants and assistant chiefs. He had given names to the likeliest ones, names which reminded him of their memorable feature: Diamante, Stiffcollar, Tony Curtis, No-nose, Snowhead, Zapata, Fatbum.

Diamante was a plump woman in her late thirties without a wedding ring. Her name came from the crystal glitter on the rims of her spectacles. Dickstein followed her to the car park, where she squeezed herself into the driving seat of a white Fiat 500. Dickstein's rented Peugeot was parked nearby.

She cross the Pont-Adolphe, driving badly but slowly, and went about fifteen kilometers southeast, finishing up at a small village called Mondorf-les-Bains. She parked in the cobbled yard of a square Luxembourgeois house with a nail-studded door. She let herself in with a key.

The village was a tourist attraction, with thermal springs. Dickstein slung a camera around his neck and wandered about, passing Diamante's house several times. On one pass he saw, through a window, Diamante serving a meal to an old woman.

The baby Fiat stayed outside the house until after midnight, when Dickstein left.

She had been a poor choice. She was a spinster living with her elderly mother, neither rich nor poor – the house was probably the mother's – and apparently without vices. If Dickstein had been a different kind of man he might have seduced her, but otherwise there was no way to get at her.

He went back to his hotel disappointed and frustrated – unreasonably so, for he had made the best guess he could on the information he had. Nevertheless he felt he had spent a day skirting the problem and he was impatient to get to grips with it so he could stop worrying vaguely and start worrying specifically.

He spent three more days getting nowhere. He drew blanks with Zapata, Fatbum and Tony Curtis.

But Stiffcollar was perfect.

He was about Dickstein's age, a slim, elegant man in a dark blue suit, plain blue tie, and white shirt with starched collar. His dark hair, a little longer than was usual for a man of his age, was greying over the ears. He wore handmade shoes.

He walked from the office across the Alzette River and uphill into the old town. He went down a narrow cobbled street and entered an old terraced house. Two minutes later a light went on in an attic window.

Dickstein hung around for two hours.

When Stiffcollar came out he was wearing close-fitting light trousers and an orange scarf around his neck. His hair was combed forward, making him look younger, and his walk was jaunty.

Dickstein followed him to the Rue Dicks, where he ducked into an unlit doorway and disappeared. Dickstein stopped outside. The door was open but there was nothing to indicate what might be inside. A bare flight of stairs went down. After a moment, Dickstein heard faint music.

Two young men in matching yellow jeans passed him and went in. One of them grinned back at him and said, 'Yes, this is the place.' Dickstein followed them down the stairs.

It was an ordinary-looking nightclub with tables and chairs, a few booths, a small dance floor and a jazz trio in a corner. Dickstein paid an entrance fee and sat at a booth, within sight of Stiffcollar. He ordered beer.

He had already guessed why the place had such a discreet air, and now, as he looked around, his theory was confirmed: it was a homosexual club. It was the first club of this kind he had been to, and he was mildly surprised to find it so unexceptional. A few of the men wore light make-up, there were a couple of outrageous queens camping it up by the bar, and a very pretty girl was holding hands with an older woman in trousers; but most of the customers were dressed normally by the standards of peacock Europe, and there was no one in drag.

Stiffcollar was sitting close to a fair-haired man in a maroon double-breasted jacket. Dickstein had no feelings about homosexuals as such. He was not offended when people supposed, wrongly, that he might be homosexual because he was a bachelor in his early forties. To him, Stiffcollar was just a man who worked at Euratom and had a guilty secret.

He listened to the music and drank his beer. A waiter came across and said, 'Are you on your own, dear?'

Dickstein shook his head. 'I'm waiting for my friend.'

A guitarist replaced the trio and began to sing vulgar folk songs in German. Dickstein missed most of the jokes, but the rest of the audience roared with laughter. After that several couples danced.

Dickstein saw Stiffcollar put his hand on his companion's knee. He got up and walked across to their booth.

'Hello,' he said cheerfully, 'didn't I see you at the Euratom office the other day?'

Stiffcollar went white. 'I don't know . . .'

Dickstein stuck out his hand. 'Ed Rodgers,' he said, giving the name he had used with Pfaffer. 'I'm a journalist.'

Stiffcollar muttered, 'How do you do.' He was shaken, but he had the presence of mind not to give his name.

'I've got to rush away,' Dickstein said. 'It was nice to see you.'

'Goodbye, then.'

Dickstein turned away and went out of the club. He had done all that was necessary, for now: Stiffcollar knew that his secret was out, and he was frightened.

Dickstein walked towards his hotel, feeling grubby and ashamed.

He was followed from the Rue Dicks.

The tail was not a professional, and made no attempt at camouflage. He stayed fifteen or twenty steps behind, his leather shoes making a regular slap-slap on the pavement. Dickstein pretended not to notice. Crossing the road, he got a look at the tail: a large youth, long hair, worn brown leather jacket.

Moments later another youth stepped out of the shadows and stood squarely in front of Dickstein, blocking the pavement. Dickstein stood still and waited, thinking: What the hell is this? He could not imagine who could be tailing him already, nor why anyone who wanted him tailed would use clumsy amateurs from off the streets.

The blade of a knife glinted in the street light. The tail came up behind.

The youth in front said, 'All right, nancy-boy, give us your wallet.'

Dickstein was deeply relieved. They were just thieves who assumed that anyone coming out of that nightclub would be easy game.

'Don't hit me,' Dickstein said, 'I'll give you my money.' He took out his wallet.

'The wallet,' the youth said.

Dickstein did not want to fight them; but, while he could get more cash easily, he would be greatly inconvenienced if he lost all his papers and credit cards. He removed the notes from the wallet and offered them. 'I need my papers. Just take the money, and I won't report this.'

The boy in front snatched the notes.

The one behind said, 'Get the credit cards.'

The one in front was the weaker. Dickstein looked squarely at him and said, 'Why don't you quit while you're ahead, sonny?' Then he walked forward, passing the youth on the outside of the pavement.

Leather shoes beat a brief tattoo as the other rushed Dickstein, and then there was only one way for the encounter to end.

Dickstein spun about, grabbed the boy's foot as he aimed a kick, pulled and twisted, and broke the boy's ankle. The kid shouted with pain and fell down.

The one with the knife came at Dickstein then. He danced back, kicked the boy's shin, danced back, and kicked again. The boy lunged with the knife. Dickstein dodged and kicked him a third time in exactly the same place. There was a noise like a bone snapping, and the boy fell down.

Dickstein stood for a moment looking at the two injured muggers. He felt like a parent whose children had pushed him until he was obliged to strike them. He thought: Why did you make me do it? They *were* children: about seventeen, he guessed. They were vicious – they preyed on homosexuals; but that was exactly what Dickstein had been doing this night.

He walked away. It was an evening to forget. He decided to leave town in the morning.

When Dickstein was working he stayed in his hotel room as much as possible to avoid being seen. He might have been a heavy drinker, except it was unwise to drink during an operation – alcohol blunted the sharp edge of his vigilance – and at other times he felt no need of it. He spent a lot of time looking out of windows or sitting in front of a flickering television screen. He did not walk around the streets, did not sit in hotel bars, did not even eat in hotel restaurants – he always used room service. But there were limits to the precautions a man could take: he could not be invisible. In the lobby of the Alfa Hotel in Luxembourg he bumped into someone who knew him.

He was standing at the desk, checking out. He had looked over the bill and presented a credit card in the name of Ed Rodgers, and he was waiting to sign the American Express slip when a voice behind him said in English, 'My God! It's Nat Dickstein, isn't it?'

It was the moment he dreaded. Like every agent who used cover identities, he lived in constant fear of accidentally coming up against someone from his distant past who could unmask him. It was the nightmare of the policemen who shouted. 'You're a spy!' and it was the debt-collector saying, 'But your mother *is* in, I just saw her, through the window, hiding under the kitchen table.'

Like every agent he had been trained for this moment. The rule was simple: *Whoever it is, you don't know him.* They made you practise in the school. They would say, 'Today you are Chaim Meyerson, engineering student,' and so on; and you would have to walk around and do your work and be Chaim Meyerson; and then, late in the afternoon, they would arrange for you to bump into your cousin, or your old college professor, or a rabbi who knew your whole family. The first time, you always smiled and said 'Hello,' and talked about old times for a while, and then that evening your tutor told you that you were dead. Eventually you learned to look old friends straight in the eye and say, 'Who the hell are you?'

Dickstein's training came into play now. He looked first at the desk clerk, who was at that moment checking him out in the name of Ed Rodgers. The clerk did not react: presumably either he did not understand, or he had not heard, or he did not care.

A hand tapped Dickstein's shoulder. He started an apologetic smile and turned around, saying in French, 'I'm afraid you've got the wrong—'

The skirt of her dress was around her waist, her face was flushed with pleasure, and she was kissing Yasif Hassan.

'It *is* you!' said Yasif Hassan.

And then, because of the dreadful impact of the memory of that morning in Oxford twenty years ago, Dickstein lost control for an instant, and his training deserted him, and he made the biggest mistake of his career. He stared in shock, and he said, 'Christ. Hassan.'

Hassan smiled, and stuck out his hand, and said, 'How long . . . it must be . . . more than twenty years!'

Dickstein shook the proffered hand mechanically, conscious that he had blundered, and tried to pull himself together. 'It must be,' he muttered. 'What are you doing here?'

'I live here. You?'

'I'm just leaving.' Dickstein decided the only thing to do was get out, fast, before he did himself any more harm. The clerk handed him the credit-card form and he scribbled 'Ed Rodgers' on it. He looked at his wristwatch. 'Damn, I've got to catch this plane.'

'My car's outside,' Hassan said. 'I'll take you to the airport. We *must* talk.'

'I've ordered a taxi . . .'

Hassan spoke to the desk clerk. 'Cancel that cab – give this to the driver for his trouble.' He handed over some coins.

Dickstein said, 'I really am in a rush.'

'Come on, then!' Hassan picked up Dickstein's case and went outside.

Feeling helpless, foolish and incompetent, Dickstein followed.

They got into a battered two-seater English sports car. Dickstein studied Hassan as he steered the car out of a no-waiting zone and into the traffic. The Arab had changed, and it was not just age. The grey streaks in his moustache, the thickening of his waist, his deeper voice – these were to be expected. But something else was different. Hassan had always seemed to Dickstein to be the archetypal aristocrat. He had been slow-moving, dispassionate and faintly bored when everyone else was young and excitable. Now his hauteur seemed to have gone. He was like his car: somewhat the worse for wear, with a rather hurried air. Still, Dickstein had sometimes wondered how much of his upper-class appearance was cultivated.

Resigning himself to the consequences of his error, Dickstein tried to find out the extent of the damage. He asked Hassan, 'You live here now?'

'My bank has its European headquarters here.'

So, maybe he's still rich, Dickstein thought. 'Which bank is that?'

'The Cedar Bank of Lebanon.'

'Why Luxembourg?'

'It's a considerable financial centre,' Hassan replied. 'The European Investment Bank is here, and they have an international stock exchange. But what about you?'

'I live in Israel. My kibbutz makes wine – I'm sniffing at the possibilities of European distribution.'

'Taking coals to Newcastle.'

'I'm beginning to think so.'

'Perhaps I can help you, if you're coming back. I have a lot of contacts here. I could set up some appointments for you.'

'Thank you. I'm going to take you up on that offer.' If the worst came to the worst, Dickstein thought, he could always keep the appointments and sell some wine.

Hassan said, 'So, now your home is in Palestine and

my home is in Europe.' His smile was forced, Dickstein thought.

'How is the bank doing?' Dickstein asked, wondering whether 'my bank' had meant 'the bank I own' or 'the bank I manage' or 'the bank I work for'.

'Oh, remarkably well.'

They seemed not to have much more to say to each other. Dickstein would have liked to ask what had happened to Hassan's family in Palestine, how his affair with Eila Ashford had ended, and why he was driving a sports car; but he was afraid the answers might be painful, either for Hassan or for himself.

Hassan asked, 'Are you married?'

'No. You?'

'No.'

'How odd,' Dickstein said.

Hassan smiled. 'We're not the type to take on responsibilities, you and I.'

'Oh, I've got responsibilities,' Dickstein said, thinking of the orphan Mottie who had not yet finished *Treasure Island*.

'But you have a roving eye, eh?' Hassan said with a wink.

'As I recall, you were the ladies' man,' Dickstein said uncomfortably.

'Ah, those were the days.'

Dickstein tried not to think about Eila. They reached the airport, and Hassan stopped the car.

Dickstein said, 'Thank you for the lift.'

Hassan swivelled around in the bucket seat. He

stared at Dickstein. 'I can't get over this,' he said. 'You actually look younger than you did in 1947.'

Dickstein shook his hand. 'I'm sorry to be in such a rush.' He got out of the car.

'Don't forget – call me next time you're here,' Hassan said.

'Goodbye.' Dickstein closed the car door and walked into the airport.

Then, at last, he allowed himself to remember.

The four people in the chilly garden were still for one long heartbeat. Then Hassan's hands moved on Eila's body. Instantly Dickstein and Cortone moved away, through the gap in the hedge and out of sight. The lovers never saw them.

They walked toward the house. When they were well out of earshot Cortone said, 'Jesus, that was hot stuff.'

'Let's not talk about it,' Dickstein said. He felt like a man who, looking backward over his shoulder, has walked into a lamp-post: there was pain and rage, and nobody to blame but himself.

Fortunately the party was breaking up. They left without speaking to the cuckold, Professor Ashford, who was in a corner deep in conversation with a graduate student. They went to the George for lunch. Dickstein ate very little but drank some beer.

Cortone said, 'Listen, Nat, I don't know why you're getting so down in the mouth about it. I mean, it just goes to show she's available, right?'

'Yes,' Dickstein said, but he did not mean it.

The bill came to more than ten shillings. Cortone paid it. Dickstein walked him to the railway station. They shook hands solemnly, and Cortone got on the train.

Dickstein walked in the park for several hours, hardly noticing the cold, trying to sort out his feelings. He failed. He knew he was not envious of Hassan, or disillusioned with Eila, nor disappointed in his hopes, for he had never been hopeful. He was shattered, and he had no words to say why. He wished he had somebody to whom he could talk about it.

Soon after this he went to Palestine, although not just because of Eila.

In the next twenty-one years he never had a woman; but that, too, was not entirely because of Eila.

Yasif Hassan drove away from Luxembourg airport in a black rage. He could picture, as clearly as if it were yesterday, the young Dickstein: a pale Jew in a cheap suit, thin as a girl, always standing slightly hunched as if he expected to be flogged, staring with adolescent longing at the ripe body of Eila Ashford, arguing doggedly that his people would have Palestine whether the Arabs consented or not. Hassan had thought him ridiculous, a child. Now Dickstein lived in Israel, and grew grapes to make wine: he had found a home, and Hassan had lost one.

Hassan was no longer rich. He had never been fabulously wealthy, even by Levantine standards, but he had always had fine food, expensive clothes and the best education, and he had consciously adopted the manners of Arab aristocracy. His grandfather had been a successful doctor who set up his elder son in medicine and his younger son in business. The younger, Hassan's father, bought and sold textiles in Palestine, Lebanon and Transjordan. The business prospered under British rule, and Zionist immigration swelled the market. By 1947 the family had shops all over the Levant and owned their native village near Nazareth.

The 1948 war ruined them.

When the State of Israel was declared and the Arab armies attacked, the Hassan family made the fatal mistake of packing their bags and fleeing to Syria. They never came back. The warehouse in Jerusalem burned down; the shops were destroyed or taken over by Jews; and the family lands became 'administered' by the Israeli government. Hassan had heard that the village was now a kibbutz.

Hassan's father had lived ever since in a United Nations refugee camp. The last positive thing he had done was to write a letter of introduction for Yasif to his Lebanese bankers. Yasif had a university degree and spoke excellent English: the bank gave him a job.

He applied to the Israeli government for compensation under the 1953 Land Acquisition Act, and was refused.

He visited his family in the camp only once, but what he saw there stayed with him for the rest of his life. They lived in a hut made of boards and shared the communal toilets. They got no special treatment: they were just one among thousands of families without a home, a purpose or a hope. To see his father who had been a clever, decisive man ruling a large business with a firm hand, reduced now to queuing for food and wasting his life playing backgammon, made Yasif want to throw bombs at school buses.

The women fetched water and cleaned house much as always, but the men shuffled around in secondhand clothes, waiting for nothing, their bodies getting flabby while their minds grew dull. Teenagers strutted and squabbled and fought with knives, for there was nothing ahead of them but the prospect of their lives shrivelling to nothing in the baking heat of the sun.

The camp smelled of sewage and despair. Hassan never returned to visit, although he continued to write to his mother. He had escaped the trap, and if he was deserting his father, well, his father had helped him do it, so it must have been what he wanted.

He was a modest success as a bank clerk. He had intelligence and integrity, but his upbringing did not fit him for careful, calculating work involving much shuffling of memoranda and keeping of records in triplicate. Besides, his heart was elsewhere.

He never ceased bitterly to resent what had been taken from him. He carried his hatred through life like a secret burden. Whatever his logical mind might tell him, his soul said he had abandoned his father in time of need, and the guilt fed his hatred of Israel. Each year he expected the Arab armies to destroy the Zionist invaders, and each time they failed he grew more wretched and more angry.

In 1957 he began to work for Egyptian Intelligence.

He was not a very important agent, but as the bank expanded its European business he began to pick up the occasional titbit, both in the office and from general banking gossip. Sometimes Cairo would ask him for specific information about the finances of an arms manufacturer, a Jewish philanthropist, or an Arab millionaire; and if Hassan did not have the details in his bank's files he could often get them from friends and business contacts. He also had a general brief to keep an eye on Israeli businessmen in Europe, in case they were agents; and that was why he had approached Nat Dickstein and pretended to be friendly.

Hassan thought Dickstein's story was probably true. In his shabby suit, with the same round spectacles and the same inconspicuous air, he looked exactly like an underpaid salesman with a product he could not promote. However, there was that odd business in the Rue Dicks the previous night: two youths, known to the police as petty thieves, had been found in the gutter savagely disabled. Hassan had got all the details from a contact on the city police force. Clearly they had picked on the wrong sort of victim. Their injuries were professional: the man who had inflicted them had to be a soldier, a policeman, a bodyguard . . . or an agent. After an incident like that, any Israeli who flew out in a hurry the next morning was worth checking up on.

Hassan drove back to the Alfa Hotel and spoke to the desk clerk. 'I was here an hour ago when one of your guests was checking out,' he said. 'Do you remember?'

'I think so, sir.'

Hassan gave him two hundred Luxembourg francs. 'Would you tell me what name he was registered under?'

'Certainly, sir.' The clerk consulted a file. 'Edward Rodgers, from *Science International* magazine.'

'Not Nathaniel Dickstein?'

The clerk shook his head patiently.

'Would you just see whether you had a Nathaniel Dickstein, from Israel, registered at all?'

'Certainly.' The clerk took several minutes to look through a wad of papers. Hassan's excitement rose. If Dickstein had registered under a false name, then he was not a wine salesman – so what else could he be but an Israeli agent? Finally the clerk closed his file and looked up. 'Definitely not, sir.'

'Thank you.' Hassan left. He was jubilant as he drove back to his office: he had used his wits and discovered something important. As soon as he got to his desk he composed a message.

SUSPECTED ISRAELI AGENT SEEN HERE. NAT DICKSTEIN ALIAS ED RODGERS. FIVE FOOT SIX, SMALL BUILD, DARK HAIR, BROWN EYES, AGE ABOUT 40.

He encoded the message, added an extra code word at its top and sent it by telex to the bank's Egyptian headquarters. It would never get there: the extra code word instructed the Cairo post office to reroute the telex to the Directorate of General Investigations.

97

Sending the message was an anticlimax, of course. There would be no reaction, no thanks from the other end. Hassan had nothing to do but get on with his bank work, and try not to daydream.

Then Cairo called him on the phone.

It had never happened before. Sometimes they sent him cables, telexes, and even letters, all in code, of course. Once or twice he had met with people from Arab embassies and been given verbal instructions. But they had never phoned. His report must have caused more of a stir than he had anticipated.

The caller wanted to know more about Dickstein. 'I want to confirm the identity of the customer referred to in your message,' he said. 'Did he wear round spectacles?'

'Yes.'

'Did he speak English with a Cockney accent? Would you recognize such an accent?'

'Yes, and yes.'

'Did he have a number tattooed on his forearm?'

'I didn't see it today, but I know he has it . . . I was at Oxford University with him, years ago. I'm quite sure it is him.'

'You *know* him?' There was astonishment in the voice from Cairo. 'Is this information on your file?'

'No, I've never—'

'Then it should be,' the man said angrily. 'How long have you been with us?'

'Since 1957.'

'That explains it . . . those were the old days. Okay, now listen. This man is a very important . . . client. We

98

want you to stay with him twenty-four hours a day, do you understand?'

'I can't,' Hassan said miserably. 'He left town.'

'Where did he go?'

'I dropped him at the airport, I don't know where he went.'

'Then find out. Phone the airlines, ask which flight he was on, and call me back in fifteen minutes.'

'I'll do my best—'

'I'm not interested in your best,' said the voice from Cairo. 'I want his destination, and I want it before he gets there. Just be sure you call me in fifteen minutes. Now that we've contacted him, *we must not lose him again.*'

'I'll get on to it right away,' said Hassan, but the line was dead before he could finish the sentence.

He cradled the phone. True, he had got no thanks from Cairo; but this was better. Suddenly he was important, his work was urgent, they were depending on him. He had a chance to do something for the Arab cause, a chance to strike back at last.

He picked up the phone again and started calling the airlines.

CHAPTER FOUR

N AT DICKSTEIN chose to visit a nuclear power station in France simply because French was the only European language he spoke passably well, except for English, but England was not part of Euratom. He travelled to the power station in a bus with an assorted party of students and tourists. The countryside slipping past the windows was a dusty southern green, more like Galilee than Essex, which had been 'the country' to Dickstein as a boy. He had travelled the world since, getting on planes as casually as any jetsetter, but he could remember the time when his horizons had been Park Lane in the west and Southend-on-Sea in the east. He could also remember how suddenly those horizons had receded, when he began to try to think of himself as a man, after his bar mitzvah and the death of his father. Other boys of his age saw themselves getting jobs on the docks or in printing plants, marrying local girls, finding houses within a quarter of a mile of their parents' homes and settling down; their ambitions were to breed a champion greyhound, to see West Ham win the Cup Final, to buy a motor car. Young Nat thought he might go to California or Rhodesia or Hong Kong and become a brain surgeon or an archaeologist or a millionaire. It was partly that he was cleverer than most of his contemporaries; partly that to them foreign languages were alien, mysterious, a school subject like algebra rather than a way of talking; but mainly the difference had to do with being Jewish. Dickstein's boyhood chess partner, Harry Chieseman, was brainy and forceful and quick-witted, but he saw himself as a working-class Londoner and believed he would always be one. Dickstein knew – although he could not remember anyone actually telling him this – that wherever they were born, Jews were able to find their way into the greatest universities, to start new industries like motion pictures, to become the most successful bankers and lawyers and manufacturers; and if they could not do it in the country where they were born, they would move somewhere else and try again. It was curious, Dickstein thought as he recollected his boyhood, that a people who had been persecuted for centuries should be so convinced of their ability to achieve anything they set their minds to. Like, when they needed nuclear bombs, they went out and got them.

The tradition was a comfort, but it gave him no help with the ways and means.

The power station loomed in the distance. As the bus got closer, Dickstein realized that the reactor was going to be bigger than he had imagined. It occupied a ten-storey building. Somehow he had imagined the thing fitting into a small room.

The external security was on an industrial, rather than military, level. The premises were surrounded by one high fence, not electrified. Dickstein looked into the gatehouse while the tour guide went through the formalities: the guards had only two closed-circuit television screens. Dickstein thought: I could get fifty men inside the compound in broad daylight without the guards noticing anything amiss. It was a bad sign, he decided glumly: it meant they had other reasons to be confident.

He left the bus with the rest of the party and walked across the tar-macadamed parking lot to the reception building. The place had been laid out with a view to the public image of nuclear energy: there were well-kept lawns and flower beds and lots of newly planted trees; everything was clean and natural, white-painted and smokeless. Looking back toward the gatehouse, Dickstein saw a grey Opel pull up on the road. One of the two men in it got out and spoke to the security guards, who appeared to give directions. Inside the car, something glinted briefly in the sun.

Dickstein followed the tour party into the lounge. There in a glass case was a rugby football trophy won by the power station's team. An aerial photograph of the establishment hung on the wall. Dickstein stood in front of it, imprinting its details on his mind, idly figuring out how he would raid the place while the back of his mind worried about the grey Opel.

They were led around the power station by four hostesses in smart uniforms. Dickstein was not interested in the massive turbines, the space-age control room with its banks of dials and switches, or the water-intake system designed to save the fish and return them to the river. He wondered if the men in the Opel had been following him, and if so, why.

He was enormously interested in the delivery bay. He asked the hostess, 'How does the fuel arrive?'

'On trucks,' she said archly. Some of the party giggled nervously at the thought of uranium running around the countryside on trucks. 'It's not dangerous,' she went on as soon as she had got the expected laugh. 'It isn't even radioactive until it is fed into the atomic pile. It is taken off the truck straight into the elevator and up to the fuel store on the seventh floor. From there, everything is automatic.'

'What about checking the quantity and quality of the consignment?' Dickstein said.

'This is done at the fuel fabrication plant. The consignment is sealed there, and only the seals are checked here.'

'Thank you.' Dickstein nodded, pleased. The system was not quite as rigorous as Mr Pfaffer of Euratom had claimed. One or two schemes began to take vague shape in Dickstein's mind.

They saw the reactor loading machine in operation. Worked entirely by remote control, it took the fuel element from the store to the reactor, lifted the concrete lid of a fuel channel, removed the spent element, inserted the new one, closed the lid and dumped the used element into a water-filled shaft which led to the cooling ponds.

The hostess, speaking perfect Parisian French in an oddly seductive voice, said, 'The reactor has three thousand fuel channels, each channel containing eight fuel rods. The rods last four to seven years. The loading machine renews five channels in each operation.'

They went on to see the cooling ponds. Under twenty feet of water the spent fuel elements were loaded into pannets, then – cool, but still highly radioactive – they were locked into fifty-ton lead flasks, two hundred elements to a flask, for transport by road and rail to a reprocessing plant.

As the hostesses served coffee and pastries in the lounge Dickstein considered what he had learned. It had occurred to him that, since plutonium was ultimately what was wanted, he might steal used fuel. Now he knew why nobody had suggested it. It would be easy enough to hijack the truck – he could do it single-handed – but how would he sneak a fifty-ton lead flask out of the country and take it to Israel without anyone noticing?

Stealing uranium from inside the power station was no more promising an idea. Sure, the security was flimsy – the very fact that he had been permitted to make this reconnaissance, and had even been given a guided tour, showed that. But fuel inside the station was locked into an automatic, remote-controlled system. The only way it could come out was by going right through the nuclear process and emerging in the cooling ponds; and then he was back with the problem of sneaking a huge flask of radioactive material through some European port.

There had to be a way of breaking into the fuel store, Dickstein supposed; then you could manhandle the stuff into the elevator, take it down, put it on a truck and drive away; but that would involve holding some or all of the station personnel at gunpoint for some time, and his brief was to do this thing surreptitiously.

A hostess offered to refill his cup, and he accepted. Trust the French to give you good coffee. A young engineer began a talk on nuclear safety. He wore unpressed trousers and a baggy sweater. Scientists and technicians all had a look about them, Dickstein had observed: their clothes were old, mismatched and comfortable, and if many of them wore beards, it was usually a sign of indifference rather than vanity. He thought it was because in their work, force of personality generally counted for nothing, brains for everything, so there was no point in trying to make a good visual impression. But perhaps that was a romantic view of science.

He did not pay attention to the lecture. The physicist from the Weizmann Institute had been much more concise. 'There is no such thing as a safe level of radiation,' he had said. 'Such talk makes you think of radiation like water in a pool: if it's four feet high you're safe, if it's eight feet high you drown. But in fact radiation levels are much more like speed limits on the highway – thirty miles per hour is safer than eighty, but not as safe as twenty, and the only way to be completely safe is not to get in the car.'

Dickstein turned his mind back to the problem of stealing uranium. It was the requirement of *secrecy* that defeated every plan he dreamed. Maybe the whole thing was doomed to failure. After all, impossible is impossible, he thought. No, it was too soon to say that. He went back to first principles.

He would have to take a consignment in transit: that much was clear from what he had seen today. Now, the fuel elements were not checked at this end, they were fed straight into the system. He could hijack a truck, take the uranium out of the fuel elements, close them up again, reseal the consignment and bribe or frighten the truck driver to deliver the empty shells. The dud elements would gradually find their way into the reactor, five at a time, over a period of months. Eventually the reactor's output would fall marginally. There would be an investigation. Tests would be done. Perhaps no conclusions would be reached before the empty elements ran out and new, genuine fuel elements went in, causing output to rise again. Maybe no one would understand what had happened until the duds were reprocessed and the plutonium recovered was too little, by which time – four to seven years later – the trail to Tel Aviv would have gone cold.

But they might find out sooner. And there was still the problem of getting the stuff out of the country.

Still, he had the outline of one possible scheme, and he felt a bit more cheerful.

The lecture ended. There were a few desultory questions, then the party trooped back to the bus. Dickstein sat at the back. A middle-aged woman said to him, 'That was my seat,' and he stared at her stonily until she went away.

Driving back from the power station, Dickstein kept looking out of the rear window. After about a mile the grey Opel pulled out of a turnoff and followed the bus. Dickstein's cheerfulness vanished.

He had been spotted. It had happened either here or in Luxembourg, probably Luxembourg. The spotter might have been Yasif Hassan – no reason why he should not be an agent – or someone else. They must be following him out of general curiosity because there was no way – was there? – that they could know what he was up to. All he had to do was lose them.

He spent a day in and around the town near the nuclear power station, travelling by bus and taxi, driving a rented car, and walking. By the end of the day he had identified the three vehicles – the grey Opel, a dirty little flatbed truck, and a German Ford – and five of the men in the surveillance team. The men looked vaguely Arabic, but in this part of France many of the criminals were North African: somebody might have hired local help. The size of the team explained why he had not sniffed the surveillance earlier. They had been able continually to switch cars and personnel. The trip to the power station, a long there-and-back journey on a country road with very little traffic, explained why the team had finally blown themselves.

The next day he drove out of town and on to the autoroute. The Ford followed him for a few miles, then the grey Opel took over. There were two men in each car. There would be two more in the flatbed truck, plus one at his hotel.

The Opel was still with him when he found a

pedestrian bridge over the road in a place where there were no turnoffs from the highway for four or five miles in either direction. Dickstein pulled over to the shoulder, stopped the car, got out and lifted the hood. He looked inside for a few minutes. The grey Opel disappeared up ahead, and the Ford went by a minute later. The Ford would wait at the next turnoff, and the Opel would come back on the opposite side of the road to see what he was doing. That was what the textbook prescribed for this situation.

Dickstein hoped these people would follow the book, otherwise his scheme would not work.

He took a collapsible warning triangle from the trunk of the car and stood it behind the offside rear wheel.

The Opel went by on the opposite side of the highway.

They were following the book.

Dickstein began to walk.

When he got off the highway he caught the first bus he saw and rode it until it came to a town. On the journey he spotted each of the three surveillance vehicles at different times. He allowed himself to feel a little premature triumph: they were going for it.

He took a taxi from the town and got out close to his car but on the wrong side of the highway. The Opel went by, then the Ford pulled off the road a couple of hundred yards behind him.

Dickstein began to run.

He was in good condition after his months of out-door work in the kibbutz. He sprinted to the pedestrian bridge, ran across it and raced along the shoulder on the other side of the road. Breathing hard and sweating, he reached his abandoned car in under three minutes.

One of the men from the Ford had got out and started to follow him. The man now realized he had been taken in. The Ford moved off. The man ran back and jumped into it as it gathered speed and swung into the slow lane.

Dickstein got into his car. The surveillance vehicles were now on the wrong side of the highway and would have to go all the way to the next junction before they could cross over and come after him. At sixty miles per hour the round trip would take them ten minutes, which meant he had at least five minutes start on them. They would not catch him.

He pulled away, heading for Paris, humming a musical chant that came from the football terraces of West Ham: 'Easy, easy, eeeezeee.'

There was a godalmighty panic in Moscow when they heard about the Arab atom bomb.

The Foreign Ministry panicked because they had not heard of it earlier, the KGB panicked because they had not heard about it first, and the Party Secretary's office panicked because the last thing they wanted was another who's-to-blame row between the Foreign Ministry and the KGB; the previous one had made life hell in the Kremlin for eleven months.

Fortunately, the way the Egyptians chose to make

their revelation allowed for a certain amount of covering of rears. The Egyptians wanted to make the point that they were not diplomatically obliged to tell their allies about this secret project, and the technical help they were asking for was not crucial to its success. Their attitude was 'Oh, by the way, we're building this nuclear reactor in order to get some plutonium to make atom bombs to blow Israel off the face of the earth, so would you like to give us a hand, or not?' The message, trimmed and decorated with ambassadorial niceties, was delivered, in the manner of an afterthought, at the end of a routine meeting between the Egyptian Ambassador in Moscow and the deputy chief of the Middle East desk at the Foreign Ministry.

The deputy chief who received the message considered very carefully what he should do with the information. His first duty, naturally, was to pass the news to his chief, who would then tell the Secretary. However, the credit for the news would go to his chief, who would also not miss the opportunity for scoring points off the KGB. Was there a way for the deputy chief to gain some advantage to himself out of the affair?

He knew that the best way to get on in the Kremlin was to put the KGB under some obligation to yourself. He was now in a position to do the boys a big favour. If he warned them of the Egyptian Ambassador's message, they would have a little time to get ready to pretend they knew all about the Arab atom bomb and were about to reveal the news themselves.

He put on his coat, thinking to go out and phone

his acquaintance in the KGB from a phone booth in case his own phone were tapped – then he realized how silly that would be, for he was going to call the KGB, and it was they who tapped people's phones anyway; so he took off his coat and used his office phone.

The KGB desk man he talked to was equally expert at working the system. In the new KGB building on the Moscow ring road, he kicked up a huge fuss. First he called his boss's secretary and asked for an urgent meeting in fifteen minutes. He carefully avoided speaking to the boss himself. He fired off half a dozen more noisy phone calls, and sent secretaries and messengers scurrying about the building to take memos and collect files. But his master stroke was the agenda. It so happened that the agenda for the next meeting of the Middle East political committee had been typed the previous day and was at this moment being run off on a duplicating machine. He got the agenda back and at the top of the list added a new item: 'Recent Developments in Egyptian Armaments – Special Report,' followed by his own name in brackets. Next he ordered the new agenda to be duplicated, still bearing the previous day's date, and sent around to the interested departments that afternoon by hand.

Then when he had made certain that half Moscow would associate his name and no one else's with the news, he went to see his boss.

The same day a much less striking piece of news came in. As part of the routine exchange of information between Egyptian Intelligence and the KGB, Cairo sent notice that an Israeli agent named Nat Dickstein had been spotted in Luxembourg and was now under surveillance. Because of the circumstances, the report got less attention than it deserved. There was only one man in the KGB who entertained the mildest suspicion that the two items might be connected.

His name was David Rostov.

David Rostov's father had been a minor diplomat whose career was stunted by a lack of connections, particularly secret service connections. Knowing this, the son, with the remorseless logic which was to characterize his decisions all his life, joined what was then called the NKVD, later to become the KGB.

He had already been an agent when he went to Oxford. In those idealistic times, when Russia had just won the war and the extent of the Stalin purge was not comprehended, the great English universities had been ripe recruiting-grounds for Soviet Intelligence. Rostov had picked a couple of winners, one of whom was still sending secrets from London in 1968. Nat Dickstein had been one of his failures.

Young Dickstein had been some kind of socialist, Rostov remembered, and his personality was suited to espionage: he was withdrawn, intense and mistrustful. He had brains, too. Rostov recalled debating the Middle East with him, and with Professor Ashford and Yasif Hassan, in the green-and-white house by the river. And the Rostov–Dickstein chess match had been a hard-fought affair.

But Dickstein did not have the light of idealism in

his eyes. He had no evangelical spirit. He was secure in his convictions, but he had no wish to convert the rest of the world. Most of the war veterans had been like that. Rostov would lay the bait – 'Of course, if you *really* want to join the struggle for world socialism, you have to work for the Soviet Union' – and the veterans would say 'Bullshit.'

After Oxford Rostov had worked in Russian embassies in a series of European capitals – Rome, Amsterdam, Paris. He never got out of the KGB and into the diplomatic service. Over the years he came to realize that he did not have the breadth of political vision to become the great statesman his father wanted him to be. The earnestness of his youth disappeared. He still thought, on balance, that socialism was probably the political system of the future; but this credo no longer burned inside him like a passion. He believed in Communism the way most people believed in God: he would not be greatly surprised or disappointed if he turned out to be wrong, and meanwhile it made little difference to the way he lived.

In his maturity he pursued narrower ambitions with, if anything, greater energy. He became a superb technician, a master of the devious and cruel skills of the intelligence game; and – equally important in the USSR as well as the West – he learned how to manipulate the bureaucracy so as to gain maximum kudos for his triumphs.

The First Chief Directorate of the KGB was a kind of Head Office, responsible for collection and analysis of information. Most of the field agents were attached to the Second Chief Directorate, the largest department of the KGB, which was involved in subversion, sabotage, treason, economic espionage and any internal police work considered politically sensitive. The Third Chief Directorate, which had been called Smersh until that name got a lot of embarrassing publicity in the West, did counter-espionage and special operations, and it employed some of the bravest, cleverest, nastiest agents in the world.

Rostov worked in the Third, and he was one of its stars.

He held the rank of colonel. He had gained a medal for liberating a convicted agent from a British jail called Wormwood Scrubs. Over the years he had also acquired a wife, two children and a mistress. The mistress was Olga, twenty years his junior, a blonde Viking goddess from Murmansk and the most exciting woman he had ever met. He knew she would not have been his lover without the KGB privileges that came with him; all the same he thought she loved him. They were alike, and each knew the other to be coldly ambitious, and somehow that had made their passion all the more frantic. There was no passion in his marriage any more, but there were other things: affection, companionship, stability and the fact that Mariya was still the only person in the world who could make him laugh helplessly, convulsively, until he fell down. And the boys: Yuri Davidovitch, studying at Moscow State University and listening to smuggled Beatles records; and Vladimir Davidovitch, the young genius, already considered a potential world champion chess player. Vladimir had applied for a place at the prestigious Phys-Mat School No. 2, and Rostov was sure he would succeed: he deserved the place on merit, and a colonel in the KGB had a little influence too.

Rostov had risen high in the Soviet meritocracy, but he reckoned he could go a little higher. His wife no longer had to queue up in markets with the hoi polloi – she shopped at the Beryozka stores with the elite – and they had a big apartment in Moscow and a little dacha on the Baltic; but Rostov wanted a chauffeur-driven Volga limousine, a second dacha at a Black Sea resort where he could keep Olga, invitations to private showings of decadent Western movies, and treatment in the Kremlin Clinic when old age began to creep up on him.

His career was at a crossroads. He was fifty this year. He spent about half his time behind a desk in Moscow, the other half in the field with his own small team of operatives. He was already older than any other agent still working abroad. From here he would go in one of two directions. If he slowed up, and allowed his past victories to be forgotten, he would end his career lecturing to would-be agents at KGB school No. 311 in Novosibirsk, Siberia. If he continued to score spectacular points in the intelligence game, he would be promoted to a totally administrative job, get appointed to one or two committees, and begin a challenging – but safe – career in the organization of the Soviet Union's intelligence effort – and *then* he would get the Volga limousine and the Black Sea dacha.

Sometime in the next two or three years he would

need to pull off another great coup. When the news about Nat Dickstein came in, he wondered for a while whether this might be his chance.

He had watched Dickstein's career with the nostalgic fascination of a mathematics teacher whose brightest pupil has decided to go to art school. While still at Oxford he had heard stories about the stolen boatload of guns, and as a result had himself initiated Dickstein's KGB file. Over the years additions had been made to the file by himself and others, based on occasional sightings, rumours, guesswork and good old-fashioned espionage. The file made it clear that Dickstein was now one of the most formidable agents in the Mossad. If Rostov could bring home his head on a platter, the future would be assured.

But Rostov was a careful operator. When he was able to pick his targets, he picked easy ones. He was no death-or-glory man: quite the reverse. One of his more important talents was the ability to become invisible when chancy assignments were being handed out. A contest between himself and Dickstein would be uncomfortably even.

He would read with interest any further reports from Cairo on what Nat Dickstein was doing in Luxembourg; but he would take care not to get involved.

He had not come this far by sticking his neck out.

The forum for discussion of the Arab bomb was the Middle East political committee. It could have been any one of eleven or twelve Kremlin committees, for the same factions were represented on all the interested committees, and they would have said the same things; and the result would have been the same, because this issue was big enough to override factional considerations.

The committee had nineteen members, but two were abroad, one was ill and one had been run over by a truck on the day of the meeting. It made no difference. Only three people counted: one from the Foreign Ministry, one KGB man and one man who represented the Party Secretary. Among the supernumeraries were David Rostov's boss, who collected all the committee memberships he could just on general principles, and Rostov himself, acting as aide. (It was by signs such as this that Rostov knew he was being considered for the next promotion.)

The KGB was against the Arab bomb, because the KGB's power was clandestine and the bomb would shift decisions into the overt sphere and out of the range of KGB activity. For that very reason the Foreign Ministry was in favour – the bomb would give them more work and more influence. The Party Secretary was against, because if the Arabs were to win decisively in the Middle East, how then would the USSR retain a foothold there?

The discussion opened with the reading of the KGB report 'Recent Developments in Egyptian Armaments'. Rostov could imagine exactly how the one fact in the report had been spun out with a little background gleaned from a phone call to Cairo, a good deal of guesswork and much bullshit, into a screed which took twenty minutes to read. He had done that kind of thing himself more than once.

A Foreign Ministry underling then stated, at some length, his interpretation of Soviet policy in the Middle East. Whatever the motives of the Zionist settlers, he said, it was clear that Israel had survived only because of the support it had received from Western capitalism; and capitalism's purpose had been to build a Middle East outpost from which to keep an eye on its oil interests. Any doubts about this analysis had been swept away by the Anglo-Franco-Israeli attack on Egypt in 1956. Soviet policy was to support the Arabs in their natural hostility to this rump of colonialism. Now, he said, although it might have been imprudent – in terms of global politics – for the USSR to *initiate* Arab nuclear armament, nevertheless once such armament had commenced it was a straightforward extension of Soviet policy to *support* it. The man talked for ever.

Everyone was so bored by this interminable statement of the obvious that the discussion thereafter became quite informal: so much so, in fact, that Rostov's boss said, 'Yes, but, shit, we can't give atom bombs to those fucking lunatics.'

'I agree,' said the Party Secretary's man, who was also chairman of the committee. 'If they have the bomb, they'll use it. That will force the Americans to attack the Arabs, with or without nukes – I'd say with. Then the Soviet Union has only two options: let down its allies, or start World War Three.'

'Another Cuba,' someone muttered.

The man from the Foreign Ministry said, 'The answer to that might be a treaty with the Americans under which both sides agree that in no circumstances will they use nuclear weapons in the Middle East.' If he could get started on a project like that, his job would be safe for twenty-five years.

The KGB man said, 'Then if the Arabs dropped the bomb, would that count as our breaking the treaty?'

A woman in a white apron entered, pulling a trolley of tea, and the committee took a break. In the interval the Party Secretary's man stood by the trolley with a cup in his hand and a mouth full of fruitcake and told a joke. 'It seems there was a captain in the KGB whose stupid son had great difficulty understanding the concepts of the Party, the Motherland, the Unions and the People. The captain told the boy to think of his father as the Party, his mother as the Motherland, his grandmother as the Unions and himself as the People. Still the boy did not understand. In a rage the father locked the boy in a wardrobe in the parental bedroom. That night the boy was still in the wardrobe when the father began to make love to the mother. The boy, watching through the wardrobe keyhole, said, "Now I understand! The Party rapes the Motherland while the Unions sleep and the People have to stand and suffer!"'

Everybody roared with laughter. The tea-lady shook her head in mock disgust. Rostov had heard the joke before.

When the committee went reluctantly back to work, it was the Party Secretary's man who asked the crucial question. 'If we refuse to give the Egyptians the technical help they're asking for, will they still be able to build the bomb?'

The KGB man who had presented the report said, 'There is not enough information to give a definite answer, sir. However, I have taken background briefing from one of our scientists on this point, and it seems that to build a crude nuclear bomb is actually no more difficult, technically, than to build a conventional bomb.'

The Foreign Ministry man said, 'I think we must assume that they will be able to build it without our help, if perhaps more slowly.'

'I can do my own guessing,' the chairman said sharply.

'Of course,' said the Foreign Ministry man, chastened.

The KGB man continued, 'Their only serious problem would be to obtain a supply of plutonium. Whether they have one or not, we simply do not know.'

David Rostov took in all this with great interest. In his opinion there was only one decision the committee could possibly take. The chairman now confirmed his view.

'My reading of the situation is as follows,' he began. 'If we help the Egyptians build their bomb, we continue and strengthen our existing Middle East policy, we improve our influence in Cairo, and we are in a position to exert some control over the bomb. If we refuse to help, we estrange ourselves from the Arabs, and we possibly leave a situation in which they still have a bomb but we have no control over it.'

The Foreign Ministry man said, 'In other words, if they're going to have a bomb anyway, there had better be a Russian finger on the trigger.'

The chairman threw him a look of irritation, and continued, 'We might, then, recommend to the Secretariat as follows: the Egyptians should be given technical help with their nuclear reactor project, such help always to be structured with a view to Soviet personnel gaining ultimate control of the weaponry.'

Rostov permitted himself the ghost of a satisfied smile: it was the conclusion he had expected.

The Foreign Ministry man said, 'So move.'

The KGB man said, 'Seconded.'

'All in favour?'

They were all in favour.

The committee proceeded to the next item on the agenda.

It was not until after the meeting that Rostov was struck by this thought: if the Egyptians were in fact *not* able to build their bomb unaided – for lack of uranium, for instance – then they had done a very expert job of bluffing the Russians into giving them the help they needed.

Rostov liked his family, in small doses. The advantage of his kind of job was that by the time he got bored with them – and it *was* boring, living with children – he was off on another trip abroad, and by the time he came back he was missing them enough to put up with them for a few more months. He was fond of Yuri, the elder boy, despite his cheap music and contentious views about dissident poets; but Vladimir, the younger, was the apple of his eye. As a baby Vladimir had been so pretty that people thought he was a girl. From the start Rostov had taught the boy games of logic, spoken to him in complex sentences, discussed with him the geography of distant countries, the mechanics of engines, and the workings of radios, flowers, water taps and political parties. He had come to the top of every class he was put into – although now, Rostov thought, he might find his equals at Phys-Mat No. 2.

Rostov knew he was trying to instil in his son some of the ambitions he himself had failed to fulfil. Fortunately this meshed with the boy's own inclinations: he knew he was clever, he liked being clever, and he wanted to be a Great Man. The only thing he balked at was the work he had to do for the Young Communist League: he thought this was a waste of time. Rostov had often said, 'Perhaps it is a waste of time, but you will never get anywhere in any field of endeavour unless you also make progress in the Party. If you want to change the system, you'll have to get to the top and change it from within.' Vladimir accepted this and went to the Young Communist League meetings: he had inherited his father's unbending logic.

Driving home through the rush-hour traffic, Rostov looked forward to a dull, pleasant evening at home. The four of them would have dinner together, then watch a television serial about heroic Russian spies outwitting the CIA. He would have a glass of vodka before bed.

Rostov parked in the road outside his home. His building was occupied by senior bureaucrats, about half of whom had small Russian-built cars like his, but there were no garages. The apartments were spacious by Moscow standards: Yuri and Vladimir had a bedroom each, and nobody had to sleep in the living room.

There was a row going on when he entered his home. He heard Mariya's voice raised in anger, the sound of something breaking, and a shout; then he heard Yuri call his mother a foul name. Rostov flung open the kitchen door and stood there, briefcase still in hand, face as black as thunder.

Mariya and Yuri confronted one another across the kitchen table: she was in a rare rage and close to hysterical tears, he was full of ugly adolescent resentment. Between them was Yuri's guitar, broken at the neck. Mariya has smashed it, Rostov thought instantly; then, a moment later: but this is not what the row is about.

They both appealed to him immediately.

'She broke my guitar!' Yuri said.

Mariya said, 'He has brought disgrace upon the family with this decadent music.'

Then Yuri again called his mother the same foul name.

Rostov dropped his briefcase, stepped forward and slapped the boy's face.

Yuri rocked backward with the force of the blow, and his cheeks reddened with pain and humiliation. The son was as tall as his father, and broader: Rostov had not struck him like this since the boy became a

123

man. Yuri struck back immediately, his fist shooting out: if the blow had connected it would have knocked Rostov cold. Rostov moved quickly aside with the instincts of many years' training and, as gently as possible, threw Yuri to the floor.

'Leave the house,' he said quietly. 'Come back when you're ready to apologize to your mother.'

Yuri scrambled to his feet. 'Never!' he shouted. He went out, slamming the door.

Rostov took off his hat and coat and sat down at the kitchen table. He removed the broken guitar and set it carefully on the floor. Mariya poured tea and gave it to him: his hand was shaking as he took the cup. Finally he said, 'What was that all about?'

'Vladimir failed the exam.'

'Vladimir? What has that to do with Yuri's guitar? What exam did he fail?'

'For the Phys-Mat. He was rejected.'

Rostov stared at her dumbly.

Mariya said, 'I was so upset, and Yuri laughed – he is a little jealous, you know, of his younger brother – and then Yuri started playing this Western music, and I thought it could not be that Vladimir is not clever enough, it must be that his family has not enough influence, perhaps we are considered unreliable because of Yuri and his opinions and his music; I know this is foolish, but I broke his guitar in the heat of the moment.'

Rostov was no longer listening. Vladimir rejected? Impossible. The boy was smarter than his teachers, much too smart for ordinary schools, they could not handle him. The school for exceptionally gifted children was the Phys-Mat. Besides, the boy had said the examination was not difficult, he thought he had scored one hundred per cent, and he *always* knew how he had done in examinations.

'Where's Vladimir?' Rostov asked his wife.

'In his room.'

Rostov went along the corridor and knocked at the bedroom door. There was no answer. He went in. Vladimir was sitting on the bed, staring at the wall, his face red and streaked with tears.

Rostov said, 'What did you score in that exam?'

Vladimir looked up at his father, his face a mask of childish incomprehension. 'One hundred per cent,' he said. He handed over a sheaf of papers. 'I remember the questions. I remember my answers. I've checked them all twice: no mistakes. And I left the examination room five minutes before the time was up.'

Rostov turned to leave.

'Don't you *believe* me?'

'Yes, of course I do,' Rostov told him. He went into the living room, where the phone was. He called the school. The head teacher was still at work.

'Vladimir got full marks in that test,' Rostov said.

The head teacher spoke soothingly. 'I'm sorry, Comrade Colonel. Many very talented youngsters apply for places here—'

'Did they all get one hundred per cent in the exam?'

'I'm afraid I can't divulge—'

'You know who I am,' Rostov said bluntly. 'You know I can find out.'

'Comrade Colonel, I like you and I want to have your son in my school. Please don't make trouble for yourself by creating a storm about this. If your son would apply again in one year's time, he would have an excellent chance of gaining a place.'

People did not warn KGB officers against making trouble for themselves. Rostov began to understand. 'But he *did* score full marks.'

'Several applicants scored full marks in the written paper—'

'Thank you,' Rostov said. He hung up.

The living room was dark, but he did not put the lights on. He sat in his armchair, thinking. The head teacher could easily have told him that all the applicants had scored full marks; but lies did not come easily to people on the spur of the moment, evasions were easier. However, to question the results would create trouble for Rostov.

So. Strings had been pulled. Less talented youngsters had gained places because their fathers had used more influence. Rostov refused to be angry. Don't get mad at the system, he told himself: use it.

He had some strings of his own to pull.

He picked up the phone and called his boss, Feliks Vorontsov, at home. Feliks sounded a little odd, but Rostov ignored it. 'Listen, Feliks, my son has been turned down for the Phys-Mat.'

'I'm sorry to hear that,' Vorontsov said. 'Still, not everybody can get in.'

It was not the expected response. Now Rostov paid

attention to Vorontsov's tone of voice. 'What makes you say that?'

'My son was accepted.'

Rostov was silent for a moment. He had not known that Feliks's son had even applied. The boy was smart, but not half as clever as Vladimir. Rostov pulled himself together. 'Then let me be the first to congratulate you.'

'Thank you,' Feliks said awkwardly. 'What did you call about, though?'

'Oh ... look, I won't interrupt your celebration. It will keep until morning.'

'All right. Goodbye.'

Rostov hung up and put the phone gently down on the floor. If the son of some bureaucrat or politico had got into the school because of string-pulling, Rostov could have fought it: everyone's file had something nasty in it. The only kind of person he could not fight was a more senior KGB man. There was no way he could overturn this year's awards of places.

So, Vladimir would apply again next year. But the same thing could happen again. Somehow, by this time next year, he had to get into a position where the Vorontsovs of this world could not nudge him aside. Next year he would handle the whole thing differently. He would call on the head teacher's KGB file, for a start. He would get the complete list of applicants and work on any who might be a threat. He would have phones tapped and mail opened to find out who was putting on the pressure.

But first he had to get into a position of strength.

And now he realized that his complacency about his career so far had been erroneous. If they could do this to him, his star must be fading fast.

That coup which he was so casually scheduling for some time in the next two or three years had to be brought forward.

He sat in the dark living room, planning his first moves.

Mariya came in after a while and sat beside him, not speaking. She brought him food on a tray and asked him if he wanted to watch TV. He shook his head and put the food aside. A little later, she went quietly to bed.

Yuri came in at midnight, a little drunk. He entered the living room and switched on the light. He was surprised to see his father sitting there. He took a frightened step back.

Rostov stood up and looked at his elder son, remembering the growing pains of his own teenage years, the misdirected anger, the clear, narrow vision of right and wrong, the quick humiliations and the slow acquisition of knowledge. 'Yuri,' he said, 'I want to apologize for hitting you.'

Yuri burst into tears.

Rostov put an arm around his broad shoulders and led him toward his room. 'We were both wrong, you and I,' he continued. 'Your mother, too. I'm going away again soon, I'll try to bring back a new guitar.'

He wanted to kiss his son, but they had got like Westerners, afraid to kiss. Gently, he pushed him into the bedroom and closed the door on him.

Going back to the living room, he realized that in the last few minutes his plans had hardened into shape in his mind. He sat in the armchair again, this time with a soft pencil and a sheet of paper, and began to draft a memorandum.

To: Chairman, Committee for State Security
From: Acting Chief, European Desk
Copy: Chief, European Desk
Date: 24 May 1968

Comrade Andropov:

My department chief, Feliks Vorontsov, is absent today and I feel that the following matters are too urgent to await his return.

An agent in Luxembourg has reported the sighting there of the Israeli operative Nathaniel ('Nat') David Jonathan Dickstein, alias Edward ('Ed') Rodgers, known as The Pirate.

Dickstein was born in Stepney, East London, in 1925, the son of a shopkeeper. The father died in 1938, the mother in 1951. Dickstein joined the British Army in 1943, fought in Italy, was promoted sergeant and taken prisoner at La Molina. After the war he went to Oxford University to read Semitic Languages. In 1948 he left Oxford without graduating and emigrated to Palestine, where he began almost immediately to work for the Mossad.

At first he was involved in stealing and secretly buying arms for the Zionist state. In the Fifties he mounted an operation against an Egyptian-supported group of Palestinian freedom fighters based in the Gaza Strip, and was personally responsible for the booby-trap bomb which killed Commander Aly. In the late Fifties and early Sixties he was a leading member of the assassination team which hunted escaped Nazis. He directed the terrorist effort against German rocket scientists working for Egypt in 1963–4.

On his file the entry under 'Weaknesses' reads: 'None known.' He appears to have no family, either in Palestine or elsewhere. He is not interested in alcohol, narcotics or gambling. He has no known romantic liaisons, and there is on his file a speculation that he may be sexually frozen as a result of being the subject of medical experiments conducted by Nazi scientists.

I, personally, knew Dickstein intimately in the formative years 1947–8, when we were both at Oxford University. I played chess with him. I initiated his file. I have followed his subsequent career with special interest. He now appears to be operating in the territory which has been my speciality for twenty years. I doubt if there is anyone among the 110,000 employees of your committee who is as well qualified as I am to oppose this formidable Zionist operative.

I therefore recommend that you assign me to discover what Dickstein's mission is and, if appropriate, to stop him.

(Signed)
David Rostov.

To: Acting Chief, European Desk
From: Chairman, Committee for State Security
Copy: Chief, European Desk
Date: 24 May 1968

Comrade Rostov:
    Your recommendation is approved.
                    (Signed)
                Yuri Andropov.

To: Chairman, Committee for State Security
From: Chief, European Desk
Copy: Deputy Chief, European Desk
Date: 26 May 1968

Comrade Andropov:
    I refer to the exchange of memoranda which
took place between yourself and my deputy, David
Rostov, during my recent short absence on State
business in Novosibirsk.
    Naturally I agree wholeheartedly with Comrade
Rostov's concern and your approval thereof,
although I feel there was no good reason for his
haste.
    As a field agent Rostov does not, of course, see
things in quite the same broad perspective as his
superiors, and there is one aspect of the situation
which he failed to bring to your attention.
    The current investigation of Dickstein was
initiated by our Egyptian allies, and indeed at this
moment remains exclusively their undertaking. For

political reasons I would not recommend that we brush them aside without a second thought, as Rostov seems to think we can. At most, we should offer them our cooperation.

Needless to say, this latter undertaking, involving as it would international liaison between intelligence services, ought to be handled at chief-of-desk level rather than deputy-chief level.

(Signed)

Feliks Vorontsov.

To:	Chief, European Desk
From:	Office of the Chairman, Committee for State Security
Copy:	Deputy Chief, European Desk
Date:	28 May 1968

Comrade Vorontsov:

Comrade Andropov has asked me to deal with your memorandum of 26 May.

He agrees that the political implications of Rostov's scheme must be taken into account, but he is unwilling to leave the initiative in Egyptian hands while we merely 'cooperate'. I have now spoken with our allies in Cairo and they have agreed that Rostov should command the team investigating Dickstein on condition that one of their agents serves as a full member of the team.

(Signed)

Maksim Bykov, personal assistant to the Chairman.

(pencilled addendum)

Feliks: Don't bother me with this again until you've got a result. And keep an eye on Rostov – he wants your job, and unless you shape up I'm going to give it to him. Yuri.

To:	Deputy Chief, European Desk
From:	Office of the Chairman, Committee for State Security
Copy:	Chief, European Desk
Date:	29 May 1968

Comrade Rostov:

Cairo has now nominated the agent to serve with your team in the Dickstein investigation. He is in fact the agent who first spotted Dickstein in Luxembourg. His name is Yasif Hassan.

(Signed)

Maksim Bykov, personal assistant to the Chairman.

When he gave lectures at the training school, Pierre Borg would say, 'Call in. Always call in. Not just when you need something, but every day if possible. We need to know what you're doing – and we may have vital information for you.' Then the trainees went into the bar and heard that Nat Dickstein's motto was: 'Never call in for less than $100,000.'

Borg was angry with Dickstein. Anger came easily to him, especially when he did not know what was happening. Fortunately anger rarely interfered with his judgment. He was angry with Kawash, too. He could understand why Kawash had wanted to meet in Rome – the Egyptians had a big team here, so it was easy for Kawash to find an excuse to visit – but there was no reason why they should meet in a goddamn bathhouse.

Borg got angry by sitting in his office in Tel Aviv, wondering and worrying about Dickstein and Kawash and the others, waiting for messages, until he began to think they would not call because they did not like him; and so he got mad and broke pencils and fired his secretary.

A bathhouse in Rome, for God's sake – the place was bound to be full of queers. Also, Borg did not like his body. He slept in pyjamas, never went swimming, never tried on clothes in shops, never went naked except to take a quick shower in the morning. Now he stood in the steam-room, wearing around his waist the largest towel he could find, conscious that he was white except for his face and hands, his flesh softly plump, with a pelt of greying hair across his shoulders.

He saw Kawash. The Arab's body was lean and dark brown, with very little hair. Their eyes met across the steamroom and, like secret lovers, they went side by side, not looking at one another, into a private room with a bed.

Borg was relieved to get out of public view and impatient to hear Kawash's news. The Arab switched on the machine that made the bed vibrate: its hum would swamp a listening device, if there were one. The two men stood close together and spoke in low voices.

Embarrassed, Borg turned his body so that he was facing away from Kawash and had to speak over his shoulder.

'I've got a man into Qattara,' Kawash said.

'*Formidable*,' Borg said, pronouncing it the French way in his great relief. 'Your department isn't even involved in the project.'

'I have a cousin in Military Intelligence.'

'Well done. Who is the man in Qattara?'

'Saman Hussein, one of yours.'

'Good, good, *good*. What did he find?'

'The construction work is finished. They've built the reactor housing, plus an administration block, staff quarters, and an airstrip. They're much farther ahead than anyone imagined.'

'What about the reactor itself? That's what counts.'

'They're working on it now. It's hard to say how long it will take – there's a certain amount of precision work.'

'Are they going to be able to manage that?' Borg wondered. 'I mean, all those complex control systems . . .'

'The controls don't need to be sophisticated, I understand. You slow the speed of the nuclear reaction simply by pushing metal rods into the atomic pile. Anyway, there's been another development. Saman found the place crawling with Russians.'

Borg said, 'Oh, fuck.'

'So now I guess they'll have all the fancy electronics they need.'

Borg sat on the chair, forgetting the bathhouse and the vibrating bed and his soft white body. 'This is bad news,' he said.

'There's worse. Dickstein is blown.'

Borg stared at Kawash, thunderstruck. 'Blown?' he said as if he did not know what the word meant. 'Blown?'

'Yes.'

Borg felt furious and despairing by turns. After a moment he said, 'How did he manage that ... the prick?'

'He was recognized by an agent of ours in Luxembourg.'

'What was he doing there?'

'*You* should know.'

'Skip it.'

'Apparently it was just a chance meeting. The agent is called Yasif Hassan. He's small fry – works for a Lebanese bank and keeps an eye on visiting Israelis. Of course, our people recognized the name Dickstein—'

'He's using his real name?' Borg said incredulously. It got worse and worse.

'I don't think so,' Kawash said. 'This Hassan knew him from way back.'

Borg shook his head slowly. 'You wouldn't think we were the Chosen People, with our luck.'

'We put Dickstein under surveillance and informed Moscow,' Kawash continued. 'He lost the surveillance team quite quickly, of course, but Moscow is putting together a big effort to find him again.'

Borg put his chin in his hand and stared without

seeing at the erotic frieze on the tiled wall. It was as if there were a world-wide conspiracy to frustrate Israeli policy in general and his plans in particular. He wanted to give it all up and go back to Quebec; he wanted to hit Dickstein over the head with a blunt instrument; he wanted to wipe that imperturbable look off Kawash's handsome face.

He made a gesture of throwing something away. 'Great,' he said. 'The Egyptians are well ahead with their reactor; the Russians are helping them; Dickstein is blown; and the KGB has put a team on him. We could lose this race, do you realize that? Then they'll have a nuclear bomb and we won't. And do you think they will use it?' He had Kawash by the shoulders now, shaking him. 'They're your people, you tell me, will they drop the bomb on Israel? You bet your ass they will!'

'Stop shouting,' Kawash said calmly. He detached Borg's hands from his shoulders. 'There's a long road ahead before one side or the other has won.'

'Yeah.' Borg turned away.

'You'll have to contact Dickstein and warn him,' Kawash said. 'Where is he now?'

'Fucked if I know,' said Pierre Borg.

CHAPTER FIVE

THE ONLY completely innocent person whose life was ruined by the spies during the affair of the yellowcake was the Euratom official whom Dickstein named Stiffcollar.

After losing the surveillance team in France Dickstein returned to Luxembourg by road, guessing they would have set a twenty-four-hours-a-day watch for him at Luxembourg airport. And, since they had the number of his rented car, he stopped off in Paris to turn it in and hire another from a different company.

On his first evening in Luxembourg he went to the discreet nightclub in the Rue Dicks and sat alone, sipping beer, waiting for Stiffcollar to come in. But it was the fair-haired friend who arrived first. He was a younger man, perhaps twenty-five or thirty, broad-shouldered and in good shape underneath his maroon double-breasted jacket. He walked across to the booth they had occupied last time. He was graceful, like a dancer: Dickstein thought he might be the goalkeeper on a soccer team. The booth was vacant. If the couple met here every night it was probably kept for them.

The fair-haired man ordered a drink and looked at his watch. He did not see Dickstein observing him.

Stiffcollar entered a few minutes later. He wore a red V-necked sweater and a white shirt with a button-down collar. As before, he went straight to the table where his friend sat waiting. They greeted each other with a double handshake. They seemed happy. Dickstein prepared to shatter their world.

He called a waiter. 'Please take a bottle of champagne to that table, for the man in the red sweater. And bring me another beer.'

The waiter brought his beer first, then took the champagne in a bucket of ice to Stiffcollar's table. Dickstein saw the waiter point him out to the couple as the donor of the champagne. When they looked at him, he raised his beer glass in a toast, and smiled. Stiffcollar recognized him and looked worried.

Dickstein left his table and went to the cloakroom. He washed his face, killing time. After a couple of minutes Stiffcollar's friend came in. The young man combed his hair, waiting for a third man to leave the room. Then he spoke to Dickstein.

'My friend wants you to leave him alone.'

Dickstein gave a nasty smile. 'Let him tell me so himself.'

'You're a journalist, aren't you? What if your editor were to hear that you come to places like this?'

'I'm freelance.'

The young man came closer. He was five inches taller than Dickstein and at least thirty pounds heavier. 'You're to leave us alone,' he said.

'No.'

'Why are you doing this? What do you want?'

'I'm not interested in you, pretty boy. You'd better go home while I talk to your friend.'

'Damn you,' the young man said, and he grabbed the lapels of Dickstein's jacket in one large hand. He drew back his other arm and made a fist. He never landed the punch.

With his fingers Dickstein poked the young man in the eyes. The blond head jerked back and to the side reflexively. Dickstein stepped inside the swinging arm and hit him in the belly, very hard. The breath rattled out of him and he doubled over, turning away. Dickstein punched him once again, very precisely, on the bridge of the nose. Something snapped, and blood spurted. The young man collapsed on the tiled floor.

It was enough.

Dickstein went out quickly, straightening his tie and smoothing his hair on the way. In the club the cabaret had begun and the German guitarist was singing a song about a gay policeman. Dickstein paid his bill and left. As he went he saw Stiffcollar, looking worried, making his way to the cloakroom.

On the street it was a mild summer night, but Dickstein was shivering. He walked a little way, then went into a bar and ordered brandy. It was a noisy, smoky place with a television set on the counter. Dickstein carried his drink to a corner table and sat facing the wall.

The fight in the cloakroom would not be reported to the police. It would look like a quarrel over a lover, and neither Stiffcollar nor the club management would want to bring that sort of thing to official notice.

Stiffcollar would take his friend to a doctor, saying he had walked into a door.

Dickstein drank the brandy and stopped shivering. There was, he thought, no way to be a spy without doing things like this. And there was no way to be a nation, in this world, without having spies. And without a nation Nat Dickstein could not feel safe.

It did not seem possible to live honourably. Even if he gave up this profession, others would become spies and do evil on his behalf, and that was almost as bad. You had to be bad to live. Dickstein recalled that a Nazi camp doctor called Wolfgang had said much the same.

He had long ago decided that life was not about right and wrong, but about winning and losing. Still there were times when that philosophy gave him no consolation.

He left the bar and went into the street, heading for Stiffcollar's home. He had to press his advantage while the man was demoralized. He reached the narrow cobbled street within a few minutes and stood guard opposite the old terraced house. There was no light in the attic window.

The night became cooler as he waited. He began to pace up and down. European weather was dismal. At this time of year Israel would be glorious: long sunny days and warm nights, hard physical work by day and companionship and laughter in the evenings. Dickstein wished he could go home.

At last Stiffcollar and his friend returned. The friend's head was wrapped in bandages, and he was obviously having trouble seeing: he walked with one hand on Stiffcollar's arm, like a blind man. They stopped outside the house while Stiffcollar fumbled for a key. Dickstein crossed the road and approached them. They had their backs to him, and his shoes made no noise.

Stiffcollar opened the door, turned to help his friend, and saw Dickstein. He jumped with shock. 'Oh, God!'

The friend said, 'What is it? What is it?'

'It's him.'

Dickstein said, 'I have to talk to you.'

'Call the police,' said the friend.

Stiffcollar took his friend's arm and began to lead him through the door. Dickstein put out a hand and stopped them. 'You'll have to let me in,' he said. 'Otherwise I'll create a scene in the street.'

Stiffcollar said, 'He'll make our lives miserable until he gets what he wants.'

'But what does he want?'

'I'll tell you in a minute,' Dickstein said. He walked into the house ahead of them and started up the stairs.

After a moment's hesitation, they followed.

The three men climbed the stairs to the top. Stiffcollar unlocked the door of the attic flat, and they went in. Dickstein looked around. It was bigger than he imagined, and very elegantly decorated with period furniture, striped wallpaper, and many plants and pictures. Stiffcollar put his friend in a chair, then took a cigarette from a box, lit it with a table lighter and put it in his friend's mouth. They sat close together, waiting for Dickstein to speak.

'I'm a journalist,' Dickstein began.

Stiffcollar interrupted, 'Journalists interview people, they don't beat them up.'

'I didn't beat him up. I hit him twice.'

'Why?'

'He attacked me, didn't he tell you?'

'I don't believe you,' said Stiffcollar.

'How much time would you like to spend arguing about it?'

'None.'

'Good. I want a story about Euratom. A good story – my career needs it. Now then, one possibility is the prevalence of homosexuals in positions of responsibility within the organization.'

'You're a lousy bastard,' said Stiffcollar's friend.

'Quite so,' Dickstein said. 'However, I'll drop the story if I get a better one.'

Stiffcollar ran a hand across his grey-tipped hair, and Dickstein noticed that he wore clear nail polish. 'I think I understand this,' he said.

'What? What do you understand?' said his friend.

'He wants information.'

'That's right,' said Dickstein. Stiffcollar was looking relieved. Now was the time to be a little friendly, to come across as a human being, to let them think that things might not be so bad after all. Dickstein got up. There was whisky in a decanter on a highly polished side table. He poured small shots into three glasses as he said, 'Look, you're vulnerable and I've picked on you, and I expect you to hate me for that; but I'm not going to pretend that I hate you. I'm a bastard and I'm using you, and that's all there is to it. Except that I'm drinking your booze as well.' He handed them drinks and sat down again.

There was a pause, then Stiffcollar said, 'What is it that you want to know?'

'Well, now.' Dickstein took the tiniest sip of whisky: he hated the taste. 'Euratom keeps records of all movements of fissionable materials into, out of and within the member countries, right?'

'Yes.'

'To be more precise: before anyone can move an ounce of uranium from A to B he has to ask your permission.'

'Yes.'

'Complete records are kept of all permits given.'

'The records are on a computer.'

'I know. If asked, the computer would print out a list of all future uranium shipments for which permission has been given.'

'It does, regularly. A list is circulated once a month within the office.'

'Splendid,' said Dickstein. 'All I want is that list.'

There was a long silence. Stiffcollar drank some whisky. Dickstein left his alone: the two beers and one large brandy he had already drunk this evening were more than he normally took in a fortnight.

The friend said, 'What do you want the list *for*?'

'I'm going to check all the shipments in a given month. I expect to be able to prove that what people do in reality bears little or no relation to what they tell Euratom.'

Stiffcollar said, 'I don't believe you.'

The man was not stupid, Dickstein thought. He shrugged. 'What do you think I want it for?'

'I don't know. You're not a journalist. Nothing you've said has been true.'

'It makes no difference, does it?' Dickstein said. 'Believe what you like. You've no choice but to give me the list.'

'I have,' Stiffcollar said. 'I'm going to resign the job.'

'If you do,' Dickstein said slowly, 'I will beat your friend to a pulp.'

'We'll go to the police!' the friend said.

'I would go away,' Dickstein said. 'Perhaps for a year. But I would come back. And I'd find you. And I will very nearly kill you. Your face will be unrecognizable.'

Stiffcollar stared at Dickstein. 'What *are* you?'

'It really doesn't matter what I am, does it? You know I can do what I threaten.'

'Yes,' Stiffcollar said. He buried his face in his hands.

Dickstein let the silence build. Stiffcollar was cornered, helpless. There was only one thing he could do, and he was now realizing this. Dickstein let him take his time. It was several moments before Dickstein spoke.

'The printout will be bulky,' he said gently.

Stiffcollar nodded without looking up.

'Is your briefcase checked as you leave the office?'

He shook his head.

'Are the printouts supposed to be kept under lock and key?'

'No. 'Stiffcollar gathered his wits with a visible effort. 'No,' he said wearily, 'this information is not classified. It's merely confidential, not to be made public.'

'Good. Now, you'll need tomorrow to think about the details – which copy of the printout to take, exactly what you'll tell your secretary, and so on. The day after tomorrow you will bring the printout home. You'll find a note from me waiting for you. The note will tell you how to deliver the document to me.' Dickstein smiled. 'After that, you'll probably never see me again. '

Stiffcollar said, 'By God, I hope so.'

Dickstein stood up. 'You'd rather not be bothered by phone calls for a while,' he said. He found the telephone and pulled the cord out of the wall. He went to the door and opened it.

The friend looked at the disconnected wire. His eyes seemed to be recovering. He said, 'Are you afraid he'll change his mind?'

Dickstein said, 'You're the one who should be afraid of that.' He went out, closing the door softly behind him.

Life is not a popularity contest, especially in the KGB. David Rostov was now very unpopular with his boss and with all those in the section who were loyal to his boss. Feliks Vorontsov was boiling with anger at the way he had been bypassed: from now on he would do anything he could to destroy Rostov.

Rostov had anticipated this. He did not regret his decision to go for broke on the Dickstein affair. On the contrary, he was rather glad. He was already planning the finely stitched, stylishly cut dark blue English suit he would buy when he got his pass for Section 100 on the third floor of the GUM department store in Moscow.

What he did regret was leaving a loophole for Vorontsov. He should have thought of the Egyptians and their reaction. That was the trouble with the Arabs, they were so clumsy and useless that you tended to ignore them as a force in the intelligence world. Fortunately Yuri Andropov, head of the KGB and confidant of Leonid Brezhnev, had seen what Feliks Vorontsov was trying to do, namely win back control of the Dickstein project; and he had not permitted it.

So the only consequence of Rostov's error was that he would be forced to work with the wretched Arabs.

That was bad enough. Rostov had his own little team, Nik Bunin and Pyotr Tyrin, and they worked well together. And Cairo was as leaky as a sieve: half the stuff that went through them got back to Tel Aviv.

The fact that the Arab in question was Yasif Hassan might or might not help.

Rostov remembered Hassan very clearly: a rich kid, indolent and haughty, smart enough but with no drive, shallow politics, and too many clothes. His wealthy father had got him into Oxford, not his brains; and

Rostov resented that more now than he had then. Still, knowing the man should make it easier to control him. Rostov planned to start by making it clear Hassan was essentially superfluous, and was on the team for purely political reasons. He would need to be very clever about what he told Hassan and what he kept secret: say too little, and Cairo would bitch to Moscow; too much, and Tel Aviv would be able to frustrate his every move.

It was damned awkward, and he had only himself to blame for it.

He was uneasy about the whole affair by the time he reached Luxembourg. He had flown in from Athens, having changed identities twice and planes three times since Moscow. He took this little precaution because, if you came direct from Russia, the local intelligence people sometimes made a note of your arrival and kept an eye on you, and that could be a nuisance.

There was nobody to meet him at the airport, of course. He took a taxi to his hotel.

He had told Cairo he would be using the name David Roberts. When he checked into the hotel under that name, the desk clerk gave him a message. He opened the envelope as he went up in the lift with the porter. It said simply 'Room 179.'

He tipped the porter, picked up the room phone and dialled 179. A voice said, 'Hello?'

'I'm in 142. Give me ten minutes, then come here for a conference.'

'Fine. Listen, is that—'

'Shut up!' Rostov snapped. 'No names. Ten minutes.'

'Of course, I'm sorry, I—'

Rostov hung up. What kind of idiots was Cairo hiring now? The kind that used your real name over the hotel phone system, obviously. It was going to be even worse than he had feared.

There was a time when he would have been over-professional, and turned out the lights and sat watching the doorway with a gun in his hand until the other man arrived, in case of a trap. Nowadays he considered that sort of behaviour to be obsessive and left it to the actors in the television shows. Elaborate personal precautions were not his style, not any more. He did not even carry a gun, in case customs officials searched his luggage at airports. But there were precautions and precautions, weapons and weapons: he did have one or two KGB gadgets subtly concealed – including an electric tooth-brush that gave out a hum calculated to jam listening devices, a miniature Polaroid camera, and a bootlace garrotte.

He unpacked his small case quickly. There was very little in it: a safety razor, the toothbrush, two American-made wash-and-wear shirts and a change of underwear. He made himself a drink from the room bar – Scotch whisky was one of the perks of working abroad. After exactly ten minutes there was a knock on the door. Rostov opened it, and Yasif Hassan came in.

Hassan smiled broadly. 'How are you?'

'How do you do,' said Rostov, and shook his hand.

'It's twenty years . . . how have you been?'

'Busy.'

'That we should meet again, after so long, and because of Dickstein!'

'Yes. Sit down. Let's talk about Dickstein.' Rostov sat, and Hassan followed suit. 'Bring me up to date,' Rostov continued. 'You spotted Dickstein, then your people picked him up again at Nice airport. What happened next?'

'He went on a guided tour of a nuclear power station, then shook off the tail,' Hassan said. 'So we've lost him again.'

Rostov gave a grunt of disgust. 'We'll have to do better than that.'

Hassan smiled – a salesman's smile, Rostov thought – and said, 'If he wasn't the sort of agent who is bound to spot a tail and lose it, we wouldn't be so concerned about him, would we?'

Rostov ignored that. 'Was he using a car?'

'Yes. He hired a Peugeot.'

'Okay. What do you know about his movements before that, when he was here in Luxembourg?'

Hassan spoke briskly, adopting Rostov's businesslike air. 'He stayed at the Alfa Hotel for a week under the name Ed Rodgers. He gave as his address the Paris bureau of a magazine called *Science International*. There is such a magazine; they do have a Paris address, but it's only a forwarding address for mail; they do use a freelance called Ed Rodgers, but they haven't heard from him for over a year.'

Rostov nodded. 'As you may know, that is a typical Mossad cover story. Nice and tight. Anything else?'

'Yes. The night before he left there was an incident in the Rue Dicks. Two men were found quite savagely beaten. It had the look of a professional job – neatly broken bones, you know the kind of thing. The police aren't doing anything about it: the men were known thieves, thought to have been lying in wait close to a homosexual nightclub.'

'Robbing the queers as they come out?'

'That's the general idea. Anyway, there's nothing to connect Dickstein with the incident, except that he is capable of it and he was here at the time.'

'That's enough for a strong presumption,' Rostov said. 'Do you think Dickstein is a homosexual?'

'It's possible, but Cairo says there's nothing like that in his file, so he must have been very discreet about it all these years.'

'And therefore too discreet to go to queer clubs while he's on assignment. Your argument is self-defeating, isn't it?'

A trace of anger showed in Hassan's face. 'So what do you think?' he said defensively.

'My guess is that he had an informant who is queer.' He stood up and began to pace the room. He felt he had made the right start with Hassan, but enough was enough: no point in making the man surly. It was time to ease up a little. 'Let's speculate for a moment. Why would he want to look around a nuclear power station?'

Hassan said, 'The Israelis have been on bad terms

with the French since the Six-Day War. De Gaulle cut off the supply of arms. Maybe the Mossad plans some retaliation: like blowing up the reactor?'

Rostov shook his head. 'Even the Israelis aren't that irresponsible. Besides, why then would Dickstein be in Luxembourg?'

'Who knows?'

Rostov sat down again. 'What is there, here in Luxembourg? What makes it an important place? Why is your bank here, for example?'

'It's an important European capital. My bank is here because the European Investment Bank is here. But there are also several Common Market institutions – in fact, there's a European Centre over on the Ritchberg.'

'Which institutions?'

'The Secretariat of the European Parliament, the Council of Ministers, and the Court of Justice. Oh, and Euratom.'

Rostov stared at Hassan. 'Euratom?'

'It's short for the European Atomic Energy Community, but everybody—'

'I know what it is,' Rostov said. 'Don't you see the connection? He comes to Luxembourg, where Euratom has its headquarters, then he goes to visit a nuclear reactor.'

Hassan shrugged. 'An interesting hypothesis. What's that you're drinking?'

'Whisky. Help yourself. As I recall, the French helped the Israelis build their nuclear reactor. Now they've probably cut off their aid. Dickstein may be after scientific secrets.'

Hassan poured himself a drink and sat down again. 'How shall we operate, you and I? My orders are to cooperate with you.'

'My team is arriving this evening,' Rostov said. He was thinking: Cooperate, hell – you'll follow my orders. He said, 'I always use the same two men – Nik Bunin and Pyotr Tyrin. We operate very well together. They know how I like things done. I want you to work with them, do what they say – you'll learn a lot, they're very good agents.'

'And my people . . .'

'We won't need them much longer,' Rostov said briskly. 'A small team is best. Now, our first job is to make sure we see Dickstein if and when he comes back to Luxembourg.'

'I've got a man at the airport twenty-four hours a day.'

'He'll have thought of that, he won't fly in. We must cover some other spots. He might go to Euratom . . .'

'The Jean-Monnet building, yes.'

'We can cover the Alfa Hotel by bribing the desk clerk, but he won't go back there. And the nightclub in the Rue Dicks. Now, then, you said he hired a car.'

'Yes, in France.'

'He'll have dumped it by now – he knows that you know the number. I want you to call the rental company and find out where it was left – that may tell us what direction he's travelling in.'

'Very well.'

'Moscow has put his photograph on the wire, so our people will be looking out for him in every capital city in the world.' Rostov finished his drink. 'We'll catch him. One way or another.'

'Do you really think so?' Hassan asked.

'I've played chess with him, I know how his mind works. His opening moves are routine, predictable; then suddenly he does something completely un-expected, usually something highly risky. You just have to wait for him to stick out his neck – then you chop his head off.'

Hassan said, 'As I recall, you lost that chess match.'

Rostov gave a wolfish grin. 'Yes, but this is real life,' he said.

There are two kinds of shadow: pavement artists and bulldogs. Pavement artists regard the business of shadowing people as a skill of the highest order, comparable with acting or cellular biophysics or poetry. They are perfectionists, capable of being almost invis-ible. They have wardrobes of unobtrusive clothes, they practise blank expressions in front of their mirrors, they know dozens of tricks with shop doorways and bus queues, policemen and children, spectacles and shop-ping bags and hedges. They despise the bulldogs, who think that shadowing someone is the same as following him, and trail the mark the way a dog follows its master.

Nik Bunin was a bulldog. He was a young thug, the type of man who always becomes either a policeman or a criminal, depending on his luck. Luck had brought Nik into the KGB: his brother, back in Georgia, was a dope dealer, running hashish from Tbilisi to Moscow

University (where it was consumed by – among others – Rostov's son Yuri). Nik was officially a chauffeur, unofficially a bodyguard, and even more unofficially a full-time professional ruffian.

It was Nik who spotted The Pirate.

Nik was a little under six feet tall, and very broad. He wore a leather jacket across his wide shoulders. He had short blond hair and watery green eyes, and he was embarrassed about the fact that at the age of twenty-five he still did not need to shave every day.

At the nightclub in the Rue Dicks they thought he was cute as hell.

He came in at seven-thirty, soon after the club opened, and sat in the same corner all night, drinking iced vodka with lugubrious relish, just watching. Somebody asked him to dance, and he told the man to piss off in bad French. When he turned up the second night they wondered if he was a jilted lover lying in wait for a showdown with his ex. He had about him the air of what the gays called rough trade, what with those shoulders and the leather jacket and his dour expression.

Nik knew nothing of these undercurrents. He had been shown a photograph of a man and told to go to a club and look out for the man; so he memorized the face, then went to the club and looked. It made little difference to him whether the place was a whorehouse or a cathedral. He liked occasionally to get the chance to beat people up, but otherwise all he asked was regular pay and two days off every week to devote to his enthusiasms, which were vodka and colouring books.

When Nat Dickstein came into the nightclub, Nik felt no sense of excitement. When he did well, Rostov always assumed it was because he had scrupulously obeyed precise orders, and he was generally right. Nik watched the mark sit down alone, order a drink, get served and sip his beer. It looked like he, too, was waiting.

Nik went to the phone in the lobby and called the hotel. Rostov answered.

'This is Nik. The mark just came in.'

'Good!' said Rostov. 'What's he doing?'

'Waiting.'

'Good. Alone?'

'Yes.'

'Stay with him and call me if he does anything.'

'Sure.'

'I'm sending Pyotr down. He'll wait outside. If the mark leaves the club you follow him, doubling with Pyotr. The Arab will be with you in a car, well back. It's a ... wait a minute ... it's a green Volkswagen hatchback.'

'Okay.'

'Get back to him now.'

Nik hung up and returned to his table, not looking at Dickstein as he crossed the club.

A few minutes later a well-dressed, good-looking man of about forty came into the club. He looked around, then walked past Dickstein's table and went to the bar. Nik saw Dickstein pick up a piece of paper from the table and put it in his pocket. It was all very discreet:

only someone who was carefully observing Dickstein would know anything had happened.

Nik went to the phone again.

'A queer came in and gave him something – it looked like a ticket,' he told Rostov.

'Like a theatre ticket, maybe?'

'Don't know.'

'Did they speak?'

'No, the queer just dropped the ticket on the table as he went by. They didn't even look at each other.'

'All right. Stay with it. Pyotr should be outside by now.'

'Wait,' Nik said. 'The mark just came into the lobby. Hold on ... he's going to the desk ... he's handed over the ticket, that's what it was, it was a cloakroom ticket.'

'Stay on the line, tell me what happens.' Rostov's voice was deadly calm.

'The guy behind the counter is giving him a brief-case. He leaves a tip ...'

'It's a delivery. Good.'

'The mark is leaving the club.'

'Follow him.'

'Shall I snatch the briefcase?'

'No, I don't want us to show ourselves until we know what he's doing, just find out where he goes, and stay low. Go!'

Nik hung up. He gave the cloakroom attendant some notes, saying: 'I have to rush, this will cover my bill.' Then he went up the staircase after Nat Dickstein.

Out on the street it was a bright summer evening, and there were plenty of people making their way to restaurants and cinemas or just strolling. Nik looked left and right, then saw the mark on the opposite side of the road, fifty yards away. He crossed over and followed.

Dickstein was walking quickly, looking straight ahead, carrying the briefcase under his arm. Nik plodded after him for a couple of blocks. During this time, if Dickstein looked back he would see some distance behind him a man who had also been in the nightclub, and he would begin to wonder if he were being shadowed. Then Pyotr came alongside Nik, touched his arm, and went on ahead. Nik dropped back to a position from which he could see Pyotr but not Dickstein. If Dickstein looked again now, he would not see Nik and he would not recognize Pyotr. It was very difficult for the mark to sniff this kind of surveillance; but of course, the longer the distance for which the mark was shadowed, the more men were needed to keep up the regular switches.

After another half mile the green Volkswagen pulled to the kerb beside Nik. Yasif Hassan leaned across from the driving seat and opened the door. 'New orders,' he said. 'Jump in.'

Nik got into the car and Hassan steered back toward the nightclub in the Rue Dicks.

'You did very well,' Hassan said.

Nik ignored this.

'We want you to go back to the club, pick out the delivery man and follow him home,' Hassan said.

'Colonel Rostov said this?'

'Yes.'

'Okay.'

Hassan stopped the car close to the club. Nik went in. He stood in the doorway, looking carefully all about the club.

The delivery man had gone.

The computer printout ran to more than one hundred pages. Dickstein's heart sank as he flicked through the prized sheets of paper he had worked so hard to get. None of it made sense.

He returned to the first page and looked again. There were a lot of jumbled numbers and letters. Could it be in code? No – this printout was used every day by the ordinary office workers of Euratom, so it had to be fairly easily comprehensible.

Dickstein concentrated. He saw 'U234'. He knew that to be an isotope of uranium. Another group of letters and numbers was 'I80KG' – one hundred and eighty kilograms. 'I7F68' would be a date, the seventeenth of February this year. Gradually the lines of computer-alphabet letters and numbers began to yield up their meanings: he found place-names from various European countries, words such as TRAIN and TRUCK with distances affixed next to them, and names with suffixes 'SA' or 'INC', indicating companies. Eventually the layout of the entries became clear: the first line gave the quantity and type of material, the second line the name and address of the sender, and so on.

His spirits lifted. He read on with growing comprehension and a sense of achievement. About sixty consignments were listed in the printout. There seemed to be three main types: large quantities of crude uranium ore coming from mines in South Africa, Canada and France to European refineries; fuel elements – oxides, uranium metal or enriched mixtures – moving from fabrication plants to reactors; and spent fuel from reactors going for reprocessing and disposal. There were a few non-standard shipments, mostly of plutonium and transuranium elements extracted from spent fuel and sent to laboratories in universities and research institutes.

Dickstein's head ached and his eyes were bleary by the time he found what he was looking for. On the very last page there was one shipment headed 'NON-NUCLEAR.'

He had been briefly told, by the Rehovot physicist with the flowered tie, about the non-nuclear uses of uranium and its compounds in photography, in dyeing, as colouring agents for glass and ceramics and as industrial catalysts. Of course the stuff always had the potential for fission no matter how mundane and innocent its use, so the Euratom regulations still applied. However, Dickstein thought it likely that in ordinary industrial chemistry the security would be less strict.

The entry on the last page referred to two hundred tons of yellowcake, or crude uranium oxide. It was in Belgium, at a metal refinery in the countryside near the Dutch border, a site licenced for storage of fissionable material. The refinery was owned by the Société Générale de la Chimie, a mining conglomerate with head-quarters in Brussels. SGC had sold the yellowcake to a German concern called F.A. Pedler of Wiesbaden. Pedler planned to use it for 'manufacture of uranium compounds, especially uranium carbide, in commercial quantities.' Dickstein recalled that the carbide was a catalyst for the production of synthetic ammonia.

However, it seemed that Pedler were not going to work the uranium themselves, at least not initially. Dickstein's interest sharpened as he read that they had not applied for their own works in Wiesbaden to be licenced, but instead for permission to ship the yellow-cake to Genoa by sea. There it was to undergo 'non-nuclear processing' by a company called Angeluzzi e Bianco.

By sea! The implications struck Dickstein instantly: the load would be passed through a European port by someone else.

He read on. Transport would be by railway from SGC's refinery to the docks at Antwerp. There the yellowcake would be loaded on to the motor vessel *Coparelli* for shipment to Genoa. The short journey from the Italian port to the Angeluzzi e Bianco works would be made by road.

For the trip the yellowcake – looking like sand but yellower – would be packed into five hundred and sixty 200-litre oil drums with heavily sealed lids. The train would require eleven cars, the ship would carry no other cargo for this voyage, and the Italians would use six trucks for the last leg of the journey.

It was the sea journey that excited Dickstein: through

the English Channel, across the Bay of Biscay, down the Atlantic coast of Spain, through the Strait of Gibraltar and across one thousand miles of the Mediterranean.

A lot could go wrong in that distance.

Journeys on land were straightforward, controlled: a train left at noon one day and arrived at eight-thirty the following morning; a truck travelled on roads that always carried other traffic including police cars; a plane was continually in contact with someone or other on the ground. But the sea was unpredictable, with its own laws – a trip could take ten days or twenty, there might be storms and collisions and engine trouble, unscheduled ports of call and sudden changes of direction. Hijack a plane and the whole world would see it on television an hour later; hijack a ship and no one would know about it for days, weeks, perhaps for ever.

The sea was the inevitable choice for The Pirate.

Dickstein thought on, with growing enthusiasm and a sense that the solution to his problem was within his reach. Hijack the *Coparelli* ... then what? Transfer the cargo to the hold of the pirate ship. The *Coparelli* would probably have its own derricks. But transferring a cargo at sea could be chancy. Dickstein looked on the print-out for the proposed date of the voyage. November. That was bad. There might be storms – even the Mediterranean could blow up a gale in November. What, then? Take over the *Coparelli* and sail her to Haifa? It would be hard to dock a stolen ship secretly, even in top-security Israel.

Dickstein glanced at his wristwatch. It was past midnight. He began to undress for bed. He needed to know more about the *Coparelli*: her tonnage, how many crew, present whereabouts, who owned her, and if possible her layout. Tomorrow he would go to London. You could find out anything about ships at Lloyd's of London.

There was something else he needed to know: who was following him around Europe? There had been a big team in France. Tonight as he left the nightclub in the Rue Dicks a thuggish face had been behind him. He had suspected a tail, but the face had disappeared – coincidence, or another big team? It rather depended on whether Hassan was in the game. He could make inquiries about that, too, in England.

He wondered how to travel. If somebody had picked up his scent tonight he ought to take some precautions tomorrow. Even if the thuggish face were nobody, Dickstein had to make sure he was not spotted at Luxembourg airport.

He picked up the phone and dialled the desk. When the clerk answered, he said, 'Wake me at six-thirty, please.'

'Very good, sir.'

He hung up and got into bed. At last he had a definite target: the *Coparelli*. He did not yet have a plan, but he knew in outline what had to be done. Whatever other difficulties came up, the combination of a non-nuclear consignment and a sea journey was irresistible.

He turned out the light and closed his eyes, thinking: What a good day.

*

David Rostov had always been a condescending bastard, and he had not improved with age, thought Yasif Hassan. 'What you probably don't realize . . .' he would say with a patronizing smile; and, 'We won't need your people much longer – a small team is better;' and, 'You can tag along in the car and keep out of sight;' and now, 'Man the phone while I go to the Embassy.'

Hassan had been prepared to work under Rostov's orders as one of the team, but it seemed his status was lower than that. It was, to say the least, insulting to be considered inferior to a man like Nik Bunin.

The trouble was, Rostov had some justification. It was not that the Russians were smarter than the Arabs; but the KGB was undoubtedly a larger, richer, more powerful and more professional organization than Egyptian Intelligence.

Hassan had no choice but to suffer Rostov's attitude, justified or not. Cairo was delighted to have the KGB hunting one of the Arab world's greatest enemies. If Hassan were to complain, he rather than Rostov would be taken off the case.

Rostov might remember, thought Hassan, that it was the Arabs who had first spotted Dickstein; there would be no investigation at all had it not been for my original discovery.

All the same, he wanted to win Rostov's respect; to have the Russian confide in him, discuss developments, ask his opinion. He would have to prove to Rostov that he was a competent and professional agent, easily the equal of Nik Bunin and Pyotr Tyrin.

The phone rang. Hassan picked it up hastily. 'Hello?'

'Is the other one there?' It was Tyrin's voice.

'He's out. What's happening?'

Tyrin hesitated. 'When will he be back?'

'I don't know,' Hassan lied. 'Give me your report.'

'Okay. The client got off the train at Zurich.'

'Zurich? Go on.'

'He took a taxi to a bank, entered and went down into the vault. This particular bank has safe-deposit boxes. He came out carrying a briefcase.'

'And then?'

'He went to a car dealer on the outskirts of the city and bought a used E-type Jaguar, paying with cash he had in the case.'

'I see.' Hassan thought he knew what was coming next.

'He drove out of Zurich in the car, got onto the El7 autobahn and increased his speed to one hundred and forty miles per hour.'

'And you lost him,' said Hassan, feeling gratification and anxiety in equal parts.

'We had a taxi and an embassy Mercedes.'

Hassan was visualizing the road map of Europe. 'He could be headed for anywhere in France, Spain, Germany, Scandinavia ... unless he doubles back, in which case Italy, Austria ... He's vanished, then. All right – come back to base.' He hung up before Tyrin could question his authority.

So, he thought, the great KGB is not invincible after

all. Much as he liked to see them fall on their collective face, his malicious pleasure was overshadowed by the fear that they had lost Dickstein permanently.

He was still thinking about what they ought to do next when Rostov came back.

'Anything?' the Russian asked.

'Your people lost Dickstein,' Hassan said, suppressing a smile.

Rostov's face darkened. 'How?'

Hassan told him.

Rostov asked, 'So what are they doing now?'

'I suggested they might come back here. I guess they're on their way.'

Rostov grunted.

Hassan said, 'I've been thinking about what we should do next.'

'We've got to find Dickstein again.' Rostov was fiddling with something in his suitcase, and his replies were distracted.

'Yes, but apart from that.'

Rostov turned around. 'Get to the point.'

'I think we should pick up the delivery man and ask him what he passed to Dickstein.'

Rostov stood still, considering. 'Yes,' he said thoughtfully. Hassan was delighted.

'We'll have to find him . . .'

'That shouldn't be impossible,' Rostov said. 'If we keep watch on the nightclub, the airport, the Alfa Hotel and the Jean-Monnet building for a few days . . .'

Hassan watched Rostov, studying his tall thin figure, and his impassive, unreadable face with its high forehead and close-cropped greying hair. I'm right, Hassan thought, and he's got to admit it.

'You're right,' Rostov said. 'I should have thought of that.'

Hassan felt a glow of pride, and thought: maybe he's not such a bastard after all.

CHAPTER SIX

THE CITY of Oxford had not changed as much as the people. The city was predictably different: it was bigger, the cars and shops were more numerous and more garish, and the streets were more crowded. But the predominant characteristic of the place was still the cream-coloured stone of the college buildings, with the occasional glimpse, through an arch, of the startling green turf of a deserted quadrangle. Dickstein noticed also the curious pale English light, such a contrast with the brassy glare of Israeli sunshine: of course it had always been there, but as a native he had never seen it. However, the students seemed a totally new breed. In the Middle East and all over Europe Dickstein had seen men with hair growing over their ears, with orange and pink neckerchiefs, with bell-bottom trousers and high-heeled shoes; and he had not been expecting people to be dressed as they were in 1948, in tweed jackets and corduroy trousers, with Oxford shirts and Paisley ties from Hall's. All the same he was not prepared for this. Many of them were barefoot in the streets, or wore peculiar open sandals without socks. Men and women had trousers which seemed to Dickstein to be vulgarly tight-fitting. After observing several women whose breasts wobbled freely inside loose, colourful shirts, he concluded that brassieres were out of fashion. There was a great deal of blue denim – not just jeans but shirts, jackets, skirts and even coats. And the hair! It was this that really shocked him. The men grew it not just over their ears but sometimes halfway down their backs. He saw two chaps with pigtails. Others, male and female, grew it upward and outward in great masses of curls so that they always looked as if they were peering through a hole in a hedge. This apparently being insufficiently outrageous for some, they had added Jesus beards, Mexican moustaches, or swooping side-whiskers. They might have been men from Mars.

He walked through the city centre, marvelling, and headed out. It was twenty years since he had followed this route, but he remembered the way. Little things about his college days came back to him: the discovery of Louis Armstrong's astonishing cornet-playing; the way he had been secretly self-conscious about his Cockney accent; wondering why everyone but he liked so much to get drunk; borrowing books faster than he could read them so that the pile on the table in his room always grew higher.

He wondered whether the years had changed him. Not much, he thought. Then he had been a frightened man looking for a fortress: now he had Israel for a fortress, but instead of hiding there he had to come out and fight to defend it. Then as now he had been a lukewarm socialist, knowing that society was unjust, not sure how it might be changed for the better. Growing older, he had gained skills but not wisdom. In fact, it seemed to him that he knew more and understood less.

He was somewhat happier now, he decided. He knew who he was and what he had to do; he had figured out what life was about and discovered that he could cope with it; although his attitudes were much the same as they had been in 1948, he was now more sure of them. However, the young Dickstein had hoped for certain other kinds of happiness which, in the event, had not come his way; indeed, the possibility had receded as the years passed. This place reminded him uncomfortably of all that. This house, especially.

He stood outside, looking at it. It had not changed at all: the paintwork was still green and white, the garden still a jungle in the front. He opened the gate, walked up the path to the door, and knocked.

This was not the efficient way to do it. Ashford might have moved away, or died, or simply gone on holiday. Dickstein should perhaps have called the university to check. However, if the inquiry was to be casual and discreet it was necessary to risk wasting a little time. Besides, he had rather liked the idea of seeing the old place again after so many years.

The door opened and the woman said, 'Yes?'

Dickstein went cold with shock. His mouth dropped open. He staggered slightly, and put a hand against the wall to steady himself. His face creased into a frown of astonishment.

It was she, and she was still twenty-five years old.

In a voice full of incredulity, Dickstein said,
'Elia . . . ?'

She stared at the odd little man on the doorstep. He
looked like a don, with his round spectacles and his old
grey suit and his bristly short hair. There had been
nothing wrong with him when she opened the door,
but as soon as he set eyes on her he had turned quite
grey.

This kind of thing had happened to her once before,
walking down the High Street. A delightful old gentle-
man had stared at her, doffed his hat, stopped her and
said, 'I say, I know we haven't been introduced but . . .'

This was obviously the same phenomenon, so she
said, 'I'm not Eila. I'm Suza.'

'Suza!' said the stranger.

'They say I look exactly like my mother did when she
was my age. You obviously knew her. Will you come in?'

The man stayed where he was. He seemed to be
recovering from the surprise, although he was still pale.
'I'm Nat Dickstein,' he said with a little smile.

'How do you do,' Suza said. 'Won't you—' Then she
realized what he had said. It was her turn to be
surprised. 'Mister Dickstein!' she said, her voice rising
almost to a squeal. She threw her arms around his neck
and kissed him.

'You remembered,' he said when she let go. He
looked pleased and embarrassed.

'Of course!' she said. 'You used to pet Hezekiah. You

were the only one who could understand what he was saying.'

He gave that little smile again. 'Hezekiah the cat . . . I'd forgotten.'

'Well, come in!'

He stepped past her into the house, and she closed the door. Taking his arm, she led him across the square hall. 'This is wonderful,' she said. 'Come into the kitchen, I've been messing about trying to make a cake.'

She gave him a stool. He sat down and looked about slowly, giving little nods of recognition at the old kitchen table, the fireplace, the view through the window.

'Let's have some coffee,' Suza said. 'Or would you prefer tea?'

'Coffee, please. Thank you.'

'I expect you want to see daddy. He's teaching this morning, but he'll be back soon for lunch.' She poured coffee beans into a hand-operated grinder.

'And your mother?'

'She died fourteen years ago. Cancer.' Suza looked at him, expecting the automatic 'I'm sorry.' The words did not come, but the thought showed on his face. Somehow she liked him more for that. She ground the beans. The noise filled the silence.

When she had finished, Dickstein said, 'Professor Ashford is still teaching . . . I was just trying to work out his age.'

'Sixty-five,' she said. 'He doesn't do a lot.' Sixty-five sounded ancient but daddy didn't seem old, she thought fondly: his mind was still sharp as a knife. She wondered what Dickstein did for a living. 'Didn't you emigrate to Palestine?' she asked him.

'Israel. I live on a kibbutz. I grow grapes and make wine.'

Israel. In this house it was always called Palestine. How would daddy react to this old friend who now stood for everything daddy stood against? She knew the answer: it would make no difference, for daddy's politics were theoretical, not practical. She wondered why Dickstein had come. 'Are you on holiday?'

'Business. We now think the wine is good enough to export to Europe.'

'That's very good. And you're selling it?'

'Looking out the possibilities. Tell me about yourself. I'll bet you're not a university professor.'

The remark annoyed her a little, and she knew she was blushing faintly just below her ears: she did not want this man to think she was not clever enough to be a don. 'What makes you say that?' she said coolly.

'You're so . . . warm.' Dickstein looked away, as if he immediately regretted the choice of word. 'Anyway, too young.'

She had misjudged him. He had not been condescending. 'I have my father's ear for languages, but not his academic turn of mind, so I'm an air hostess,' she said, and wondered if it were true that she did not have an academic mind, whether she really was not clever enough to be a don. She poured boiling water into a filter, and the smell of coffee filled the room. She did not know what to say next. She glanced up at Dickstein and discovered that he was openly gazing at her, deep in thought. His eyes were large and dark brown. Suddenly she felt shy – which was most unusual. She told him so.

'Shy?' he said. 'That's because I've been staring at you as if you were a painting, or something. I'm trying to get used to the fact that you're not Eila, you're the little girl with the old grey cat.'

'Hezekiah died, it must have been soon after you left.'

'There's a lot that's changed.'

'Were you great friends with my parents?'

'I was one of your father's students. I admired your mother from a distance. Eila . . .' Again he looked away, as if to pretend that it was someone else speaking. 'She wasn't just beautiful – she was *striking*.'

Suza looked into his face. She thought: You loved her. The thought came unbidden; it was intuitive; she immediately suspected it might be wrong. However, it would explain the severity of his reaction on the doorstep when he saw her. She said, 'My mother was the original hippy – did you know that?'

'I don't know what you mean.'

'She wanted to be free. She rebelled against the restrictions put on Arab women, even though she came from an affluent, liberal home. She married my father to get out of the Middle East. Of course she found that Western society had its own ways of repressing women – so she proceeded to break most of the rules.' As she spoke Suza remembered how she had realized, while she was becoming a woman and beginning to under-

174

stand passion, that her mother was promiscuous. She had been shocked, she was sure, but somehow she could not recall the feeling.

'That makes her a hippy?' Dickstein said.

'Hippies believe in free love.'

'I see.'

And from his reaction to *that* she knew that her mother had not loved Nat Dickstein. For no reason at all this made her sad. 'Tell me about your parents,' she said. She was talking to him as if they were the same age.

'Only if you pour the coffee.'

She laughed. 'I was forgetting.'

'My father was a cobbler,' Dickstein began. 'He was good at mending boots but he wasn't much of a businessman. Still, the Thirties were good years for cobblers in the East End of London. People couldn't afford new boots, so they had their old ones mended year after year. We were never rich, but we had a little more money than most of the people around us. And, of course, there was some pressure on my father from his family to expand the business, open a second shop, employ other men.'

Suza passed him his coffee. 'Milk, sugar?'

'Sugar, no milk. Thank you.'

'Do go on.' It was a different world, one she knew nothing about: it had never occurred to her that a shoe repairer would do well in a depression.

'The leather dealers thought my father was a tartar – they could never sell him anything but the best. If there was a second-rate hide they would say, "Don't bother giving that to Dickstein, he'll send it straight back." So I was told, anyway.' He gave that little smile again.

'Is he still alive?' Suza asked.

'He died before the war.'

'What happened?'

'Well. The Thirties were the Fascist years in London. They used to hold open-air meetings every night. The speakers would tell them how Jews the world over were sucking the blood of working people. The speakers, the organizers, were respectable middle-class men, but the crowds were unemployed ruffians. After the meetings they would march through the streets, breaking windows and roughing-up passersby. Our house was a perfect target for them. We were Jews; my father was a shopkeeper and therefore a bloodsucker; and, true to their propaganda, we were slightly better off than the people around us.'

He stopped, staring into space. Suza waited for him to go on. As he told this story, he seemed to huddle – crossing his legs tightly, wrapping his arms around his body, hunching his back. Sitting there on the kitchen stool, in his ill-fitting suit of clerical grey, with his elbows and knees and shoulders pointing at all angles, he looked like a bundle of sticks in a bag.

'We lived over the shop. Every damn night I used to lie awake, waiting for them to go past. I was blind terrified, mainly because I knew my father was so frightened. Sometimes they did nothing, just went by. Usually they shouted out slogans. Often, often they broke the windows. A couple of times they got into the shop and smashed it up. I thought they were going to come up the stairs. I put my head under the pillow, crying, and cursed God for making me Jewish.'

'Didn't the police do anything?'

'What they could. If they were around they stopped it. But they had a lot to do in those days. The Communists were the only people who would help us fight back, and my father didn't want their help. All the political parties were against the Fascists, of course – but it was the Reds who gave out pickaxe handles and crowbars and built barricades. I tried to join the Party but they wouldn't have me – too young.'

'And your father?'

'He just sort of lost heart. After the shop was wrecked the second time there was no money to fix it. It seemed he didn't have the energy to start again somewhere else. He went on the dole, and just kind of wasted. He died in 1938.'

'And you?'

'Grew up fast. Joined the army as soon as I looked old enough. Got taken prisoner early. Came to Oxford after the war, then dropped out and went to Israel.'

'Have you got a family out there?'

'The whole kibbutz is my family ... but I never married.'

'Because of my mother?'

'Perhaps. Partly. You're very direct.'

She felt the glow of a faint blush below her ears again: it had been a very intimate question to ask someone who was practically a stranger. Yet it had come quite naturally. She said, 'I'm sorry.'

'Don't apologize,' Dickstein said. 'I rarely talk like this. Actually, this whole trip is, I don't know, full of the past. There's a word for it. Redolent.'

'That means smelling of death.'

Dickstein shrugged.

There was a silence. I like this man at lot, Suza thought. I like his conversation and his silences, his big eyes and his old suit and his memories. I hope he'll stay a while.

She picked up the coffee cups and opened the dishwasher. A spoon slid off a saucer and bounced under the large old freezer. She said, 'Damn.'

Dickstein got down on his knees and peered underneath.

'It's there for ever, now,' Suza said. 'That thing is too heavy to move.'

Dickstein lifted one end of the freezer with his right hand and reached underneath it with his left. He lowered the end of the freezer, stood up and handed the spoon to Suza.

She stared at him. 'What are you – Captain America? That thing is *heavy*.'

'I work in the fields. How do you know about Captain America? He was the rage in my boyhood.'

'He's the rage now. The art in those comics is fantastic.'

'Well, stone the crows,' he said. 'We had to read them in secret because they were trash. Now they're art. Quite right, too.'

She smiled. 'Do you really work in the fields?' He looked like a clerk, not a field hand.

'Of course.'

'A wine salesman who actually gets dirt under his fingernails in the vineyard. That's unusual.'

'Not in Israel. We're a little ... obsessive, I suppose ... about the soil.'

Suza looked at her watch and was surprised to see how late it was. 'Daddy should be home any minute. You'll eat with us, won't you? I'm afraid it's only a sandwich.'

'That would be lovely.'

She sliced a French loaf and began to make salad. Dickstein offered to wash lettuce, and she gave him an apron. After a while she caught him watching her again, smiling. 'What are you thinking?'

'I was remembering something that would embarrass you,' he said.

'Tell me anyway.'

'I was here one evening, around six,' he began. 'Your mother was out. I had come to borrow a book from your father. You were in your bath. Your father got a phone call from France, I can't remember why. While he was talking you began to cry. I went upstairs, took you out of the bath, dried you and put you into your nightdress. You must have been four or five years old.'

Suza laughed. She had a sudden vision of Dickstein in a steamy bathroom, reaching down and effortlessly lifting her out of a hot bath full of soap bubbles. In the vision she was not a child but a grown woman with wet breasts and foam between her thighs, and his hands were strong and sure as he drew her against his chest. Then the kitchen door opened and her father came in, and the dream vanished, leaving only a sense of intrigue and a trace of guilt.

Nat Dickstein thought Professor Ashford had aged well. He was now bald except for a monkish fringe of white hair. He had put on a little weight and his movements were slower, but he still had the spark of intellectual curiosity in his eyes.

Suza said, 'A surprise guest, daddy.'

Ashford looked at him and, without hesitation, said, 'Young Dickstein! Well, I'm blessed! My dear fellow.'

Dickstein shook his hand. The grip was firm. 'How are you, professor?'

'In the pink, dear boy, especially when my daughter's here to look after me. You remember Suza?'

'We've spent the morning reminiscing,' Dickstein said.

'I see she's put you in an apron already. That's fast, even for her. I've told her she'll never get a husband this way. Take it off, dear boy, and come and have a drink.'

With a rueful grin at Suza, Dickstein did as he was told and followed Ashford into the drawing room.

'Sherry?' Ashford asked.

'Thank you, a small one.' Dickstein suddenly remembered he was here for a purpose. He had to get information out of Ashford without the old man realizing it. He had been, as it were, off-duty, for a couple of hours, and now he had to turn his mind back to work. But softly, softly, he thought.

Ashford handed him a small glass of pale sherry. 'Now tell me, what have you been up to all these years?'

Dickstein sipped the sherry. It was very dry, the way they liked it at Oxford. He told the professor the story he had given to Hassan and to Suza, about finding export markets for Israeli wine. Ashford asked informed questions. Were young people leaving the kibbutzim for the cities? Had time and prosperity eroded the communalist ideas of the kibbutzniks? Did European Jews mix and intermarry with African and Levantine Jews? Dickstein's answers were yes, no, and not much. Ashford courteously avoided the question of their opposing views on the political morality of Israel, but nevertheless there was, underlying his detached inquiries about Israeli problems, a detectable trace of eagerness for bad news.

Suza called them to the kitchen for lunch before Dickstein had an opportunity to ask his own questions. Her French sandwiches were vast and delicious. She had opened a bottle of red wine to go with them. Dickstein could see why Ashford had put on weight.

Over coffee Dickstein said, 'I ran into a contemporary of mine a couple of weeks ago – in Luxembourg, of all places.'

Ashford said, 'Yasif Hassan?'

'How did you know?'

'We've kept in touch. I know he lives in Luxembourg.'

'Have you seen him much?' Dickstein asked, thinking: Softly, softly.

'Several times, over the years.' Ashford paused. 'It

needs to be said, Dickstein, that the wars which have given you everything took everything away from him. His family lost all their money and went into a refugee camp. He's understandably bitter about Israel.'

Dickstein nodded. He was now almost certain that Hassan was in the game. 'I had very little time with him – I was on my way to catch a plane. How is he otherwise?'

Ashford frowned. 'I find him a bit ... *distrait*,' he finished, unable to find the right English word. 'Sudden errands he has to run, cancelled appointments, odd phone calls at all times, mysterious absences. Perhaps it's the behaviour of a dispossessed aristocrat.'

'Perhaps,' Dickstein said. In fact it was the typical behaviour of an agent, and he was now one hundred per cent sure that the meeting with Hassan had blown him. He said, 'Do you see anyone else from my year?'

'Only old Toby. He's on the Conservative Front Bench now.'

'Perfect!' Dickstein said delightedly. 'He always did talk like an Opposition spokesman – pompous and defensive at the same time. I'm glad he's found his niche.'

Suza said, 'More coffee, Nat?'

'No, thank you.' He stood up. 'I'll help you clear away, then I must get back to London. I'm so glad I dropped in on you.'

'Daddy will clear up,' Suza said. She grinned. 'We have an agreement.'

'I'm afraid it is so,' Ashford confessed. 'She won't be anybody's drudge, least of all mine.' The remark surprised Dickstein because it was so obviously untrue. Perhaps Suza didn't wait on him hand and foot, but she seemed to look after him the way a working wife would.

'I'll walk into town with you,' Suza said. 'Let me get my coat.'

Ashford shook Dickstein's hand. 'A real pleasure to see you, dear boy, a real pleasure.'

Suza came back wearing a velvet jacket. Ashford saw them to the door and waved, smiling.

As they walked along the street Dickstein talked just to have an excuse to keep looking at her. The jacket matched her black velvet trousers, and she wore a loose cream-coloured shirt that looked like silk. Like her mother, she knew how to dress to make the most of her shining dark hair and perfect tan skin. Dickstein gave her his arm, feeling rather old-fashioned, just to have her touching him. There was no doubt that she had the same physical magnetism as her mother: there was that something about her which filled men with the desire to possess her, a desire not so much like lust as greed; the need to *own* such a beautiful object, so that it would never be taken away. Dickstein was old enough now to know how false such desires were, and to know that Eila Ashford would not have made him happy. But the daughter seemed to have something the mother had lacked, and that was warmth. Dickstein was sorry he would never see Suza again. Given time, he might . . .

Well. It was not to be.

When they reached the station he asked her, 'Do you ever go to London?'

'Of course,' she said. 'I'm going tomorrow.'

'What for?'

'To have dinner with you,' she said.

When Suza's mother died, her father was wonderful.

She was eleven years of age: old enough to understand death, but too young to cope with it. Daddy had been calm and comforting. He had known when to leave her to weep alone and when to make her dress up and go out to lunch. Quite unembarrassed, he had talked to her about menstruation and gone with her cheerfully to buy new brassieres. He gave her a new role in life: she became the woman of the house, giving instructions to the cleaner, writing the laundry list, handing out sherry on Sunday mornings. At the age of fourteen she was in charge of the household finances. She took care of her father better than Eila ever had. She would throw away worn shirts and replace them with identical new ones without daddy ever knowing. She learned that it was possible to be alive and secure and loved even without a mother.

Daddy gave her a role, just as he had her mother; and, like her mother, she had rebelled against the role while continuing to play it.

He wanted her to stay at Oxford, to be first an undergraduate, then a graduate student, then a teacher. It would have meant that she was always around to take care of him. She said she was not smart enough, with an uneasy feeling that this was an excuse for something else, and took a job that obliged her to be away from home and unable to look after daddy for weeks at a time. High in the air and thousands of miles from Oxford, she served drinks and meals to middle-aged men, and wondered if she really had changed anything.

Walking home from the railway station. she thought about the groove she was in and whether she would ever get out of it.

She was at the end of a love affair which, like the rest of her life, had wearily followed a familiar pattern. Julian was in his late thirties, a philosophy lecturer specializing in the pre-Socratic Greeks: brilliant, dedicated and helpless. He took drugs for everything – cannabis to make love, amphetamine to work, Mogadon to sleep. He was divorced, without children. At first she had found him interesting, charming and sexy. When they were in bed he liked her to get on top. He took her to fringe theatres in London and bizarre student parties. But it all wore off: she realized that he wasn't really very interested in sex, that he took her out because she looked good on his arm, that he liked her company just because she was so impressed by his intellect. One day she found herself ironing his clothes while he took a tutorial; and then it was as good as over.

Sometimes she went to bed with men her own age or younger, mostly because she was consumed with lust for their bodies. She was usually disappointed and they all bored her eventually.

She was already regretting the impulse which had led her to make a date with Nat Dickstein. He was depressingly true to type: a generation older than she and patently in need of care and attention. Worst of all, he had been in love with her mother. At first sight he was a father-figure like all the rest.

But he was different in some ways, she told herself. He was a farmer, not an academic – he would probably be the least well-read person she had ever dated. He had gone to Palestine instead of sitting in Oxford coffee shops talking about it. He could pick up one end of the freezer with his right hand. In the time they had spent together he had more than once surprised her by not conforming to her expectations.

Maybe Nat Dickstein will break the pattern, she thought.

And maybe I'm kidding myself, again.

Nat Dickstein called the Israeli Embassy from a phone booth at Paddington Station. When he got through he asked for the Commercial Credit Office. There was no such department: this was a code for the Mossad message centre. He was answered by a young man with a Hebrew accent. This pleased Dickstein, for it was good to know there were people for whom Hebrew was a native tongue and not a dead language. He knew the conversation would automatically be tape-recorded, so he went straight into his message: 'Rush to Bill. Sale jeopardized by presence of opposition team. Henry.' He hung up without waiting for an acknowledgment.

He walked to his hotel from the station, thinking about Suza Ashford. He was to meet her at Paddington tomorrow evening. She would spend the night at the flat of a friend. Dickstein did not really know where to begin – he could not remember ever taking a woman out to dinner just for pleasure. As a teenager he had been too poor; after the war he had been too nervous and awkward; as he grew older he somehow never got into the habit. There had been dinners with colleagues, of course, and with kibbutzniks after shopping expeditions in Nazareth; but to take a woman, just the two of you, for nothing more than the pleasure of each other's company . . .

What did you do? You were supposed to pick her up in your car, wearing your dinner jacket, and give her a box of chocolates tied with a big ribbon. Dickstein was meeting Suza at the railway station, and he had neither car nor dinner jacket. Where would he take her? He did not know any posh restaurants in Israel, let alone England.

Walking alone through Hyde Park, he smiled broadly. This was a laughable situation for a man of forty-three to be in. She knew he was no sophisticate, and obviously she did not care, for she had invited herself to dinner. She would also know the restaurants and what to order. It was hardly a matter of life and death. Whatever happened, he was going to enjoy it.

There was now a hiatus in his work. Having discovered that he was blown, he could do nothing until he had talked to Pierre Borg and Borg had decided whether or not to abort. That evening he went to see a French film called *Un Homme et Une Femme*. It was a simple love story, beautifully told, with an insistent

Latin-American tune on the soundtrack. He left before the movie was halfway through, because the story made him want to cry; but the tune ran through his mind all night.

In the morning he went to a phone booth in the street near his hotel and phoned the Embassy again. When he got through to the message centre he said, 'This is Henry. Any reply?'

The voice said, 'Go to ninety-three thousand and confer tomorrow.'

Dickstein said, 'Reply: conference agenda at airport information.'

Pierre Borg would be flying in at nine-thirty tomorrow.

The four men sat in the car with the patience of spies, silent and watchful, as the day darkened.

Pyotr Tyrin was at the wheel, a stocky middle-aged man in a raincoat, drumming his fingernails on the dashboard, making a noise like pigeons' feet on a roof. Yasif Hassan sat beside him. David Rostov and Nik Bunin were in the back.

Nik had found the delivery man on the third day, the day he spent watching the Jean-Monnet building on the Kirchberg. He had reported a positive identification. 'He doesn't look quite so much of a nancy-boy in his office suit, but I'm quite sure it's him. I should say he must work here.'

'I should have guessed,' Rostov had said. 'If Dickstein is after secrets his informants won't be from the airport or the Alfa Hotel. I should have sent Nik to Euratom first.'

He was addressing Pyotr Tyrin, but Hassan heard and said, 'You can't think of everything.'

'Yes, I can,' Rostov told him.

He had instructed Hassan to get hold of a large dark car. The American Buick they now sat in was a little conspicuous, but it was black and roomy. Nik had followed the Euratom man home, and now the four spies waited in the cobbled street close to the old terraced house.

Rostov hated this cloak-and-dagger stuff. It was so old-fashioned. It belonged to the Twenties and Thirties, to places like Vienna and Istanbul and Beirut, not to western Europe in 1968. It was just *dangerous* to snatch a civilian off the street, bundle him into a car, and beat him until he gave you information. You might be seen by passersby who were not afraid to go to the police and tell what they had observed. Rostov liked things to be straightforward and clear-cut and predictable, and he preferred to use his brains rather than his fists. But this delivery man had gained in importance with each day that Dickstein failed to surface. Rostov had to know what he had delivered to Dickstein, and he had to know today.

Pyotr Tyrin said, 'I wish he would come out.'

'We're in no hurry,' Rostov said. It was not true, but he did not want the team to get edgy and impatient and make mistakes. To relieve the tension he continued speaking. 'Dickstein did this, of course. He did what we've done and what we're doing. He watched the

Jean-Monnet building, he followed this man home, and he waited here in the street. The man came out and went to the homosexual club, and then Dickstein knew the man's weakness and used it to turn him into an informant.'

Nik said, 'He hasn't been at the club the past two nights.'

Rostov said, 'He's discovered that everything has its price, especially love.'

'Love?' Nik said with scorn in his voice.

Rostov did not reply.

The darkness thickened and the street lights came on. The air coming through the open car window tasted faintly damp: Rostov saw a swirl or two of mist around the lights. The vapour came from the river. A fog would be too much to hope for in June.

Tyrin said, 'What's this?'

A fair-haired man in a double-breasted jacket was walking briskly along the street toward them.

'Quiet, now,' Rostov said.

The man stopped at the house they were watching. He rang a doorbell.

Hassan put a hand on the door handle.

Rostov hissed: 'Not yet.'

A net curtain was briefly drawn aside in the attic window.

The fair-haired man waited, tapping his foot.

Hassan said, 'The lover, perhaps?'

'For God's sake shut up,' Rostov told him.

After a minute the front door opened and the fair-haired man stepped inside. Rostov got a glimpse of the person who had opened up: it was the delivery man. The door closed and their chance was gone.

'Too quick,' Rostov said. 'Damn it.'

Tyrin began to drum his fingers again, and Nik scratched himself. Hassan gave an exasperated sigh, as if he had known all along that it was foolish to wait. Rostov decided that it was time to bring him down a peg or two.

Nothing happened for an hour.

Tyrin said, 'They're spending an evening indoors.'

'If they've had a brush with Dickstein they're probably afraid to go out at night,' Rostov said.

Nik asked, 'Do we go in?'

'There's a problem,' Rostov answered. 'From the window they can see who's at the door. I guess they won't open up for strangers.'

'The lover might stay the night,' Tyrin said.

'Quite.'

Nik said, 'We'll just have to bust in.'

Rostov ignored him. Nik always wanted to bust in, but he would not start any rough stuff until he was told to. Rostov was thinking that they might now have to snatch two people, which was more tricky and more dangerous. 'Have we got any firearms?' he said.

Tyrin opened the glove box in front of him and drew out a pistol.

'Good,' Rostov said. 'So long as you don't fire it.'

'It's not loaded,' Tyrin said. He stuffed the gun into his raincoat pocket.

Hassan said, 'If the lover stays the night do we take them in the morning?'

'Certainly not,' Rostov said. 'We can't do this sort of thing in broad daylight.'

'What, then?'

'I haven't decided.'

He thought about it until midnight, and then the problem solved itself.

Rostov was watching the doorway through half-closed eyes. He saw the first movement of the door as it began to open. He said: 'Now.'

Nik was first out of the car. Tyrin was next. Hassan took a moment to realize what was happening, then he followed suit.

The two men were saying goodnight, the younger one on the pavement, the older just inside the door wearing a robe. The older one, the delivery man, reached out and gave his lover's arm a farewell squeeze. They both looked up, alarmed, as Nik and Tyrin burst out of the car and came at them.

'Don't move, be silent,' Tyrin said softly in French, showing them the gun.

Rostov noticed that Nik's sound tactical instinct had led him to stand beside and slightly behind the younger man.

The older one said, 'Oh, my God, no, no more please.'

'Get in the car,' Tyrin said.

The younger man said, 'Why can't you fuckers leave us alone?'

Watching and listening from the back seat of the car, Rostov thought: This is the moment they decide whether to come quietly or make trouble. He glanced quickly up and down the darkened street. It was empty.

Nik, sensing that the younger man was thinking of disobedience, seized both his arms just below the shoulders and held him tightly.

'Don't hurt him, I'll go,' said the older man. He stepped out of the house.

His friend said, 'The hell you will!'

Rostov thought: *Damn.*

The younger man struggled in Nik's grip, then tried to stamp on Nik's foot. Nik stepped back a pace and hit the boy in the kidney with his right fist.

'No, Pierre!' the older one said, too loud.

Tyrin jumped him and put a big hand over the man's mouth. He struggled, got his head free, and shouted 'Help!' before Tyrin gagged him again.

Pierre had fallen to one knee and was groaning.

Rostov leaned across the back seat of the car and called through the open window, 'Let's *go!*'

Tyrin lifted the older man off his feet and carried him bodily across the pavement toward the car. Pierre suddenly recovered from Nik's punch and sprinted away. Hassan stuck out a leg and tripped him. The boy went sprawling on to the cobbled road.

Rostov saw a light go on in an upstairs window at a neighbouring house. If the fracas continued much longer they would all get arrested.

Tyrin bundled the delivery man into the back of the car. Rostov grabbed hold of him and said to Tyrin: 'I've got him. Start the car. Quick.'

Nik had picked up the younger one and was carrying him to the car. Tyrin got into the driver's seat and Hassan opened the other door. Rostov said, 'Hassan, shut the door of the house, idiot!'

Nik pushed the young man into the car next to his friend, then got into the back seat so that the two captives were between Rostov and himself. Hassan closed the door of the house and jumped into the front passenger seat of the car. Tyrin gunned the car away from the kerb.

Rostov said in English, 'Jesus Christ almighty, what a fuck-up.'

Pierre was still groaning. The older prisoner said, 'We haven't done anything to hurt you.'

'Haven't you?' Rostov replied. 'Three nights ago, at the club in the Rue Dicks, you delivered a briefcase to an Englishman.'

'Ed Rodgers?'

'That's not his name,' Rostov said.

'Are you the police?'

'Not exactly.' Rostov would let the man believe what he wanted to. 'I'm not interested in collecting evidence, building a case, and bringing you to a trial. I'm interested in what was in that briefcase.'

There was a silence. Tyrin spoke over his shoulder. 'Want me to head out of town, look for a quiet spot?'

'Wait,' Rostov said.

The older man said, 'I'll tell you.'

'Just drive around town,' Rostov told Tyrin. He looked at the Euratom man. 'So tell me.'

'It was a Euratom computer printout.'

'And the information on it?'

'Details of licenced shipments of fissionable materials.'

'Fissionable? You mean nuclear stuff?'

'Yellowcake, uranium metal, nuclear waste, plutonium . . .'

Rostov sat back in the seat and looked out of the window at the lights of the city going by. His blood raced with excitement: Dickstein's operation was becoming visible. Licenced shipments of fissionable materials . . . the Israelis wanted nuclear fuel. Dickstein would be looking for one of two things on that list – either a holder of uranium who might be prepared to sell some on the black market, or a consignment of uranium he might be able to steal.

As for what they would *do* with the stuff once they got it . . .

The Euratom man interrupted his thoughts. 'Will you let us go home now?'

Rostov said, 'I'll have to have a copy of that printout.'

'I can't take another one, the disappearance of the first was suspicious enough!'

'I'm afraid you'll have to,' Rostov said. 'But if you like, you can take it back to the office after we've photographed it.'

'Oh, God,' the man groaned.

'You've got no choice.'

'All right.'

'Head back to the house,' Rostov told Tyrin. To the

Euratom man he said, 'Bring the printout home tomorrow night. Someone will come to your house during the evening to photograph it.'

The big car moved through the streets of the city. Rostov felt the snatch had not been such a disaster after all. Nik Bunin said to Pierre, 'Stop looking at me.'

They reached the cobbled street. Tyrin stopped the car. 'Okay,' Rostov said. 'Let the older man out. His friend stays with us.'

The Euratom man yelped as if hurt. 'Why?'

'In case you're tempted to break down and confess everything to your bosses tomorrow. Young Pierre will be our hostage. Get out.' Nik opened the door and let the man out. He stood on the pavement for a moment. Nik got back in and Tyrin drove off.

Hassan said, 'Will he be all right? Will he do it?'

'He'll work for us until he gets his friend back,' Rostov said.

'And then?'

Rostov said nothing. He was thinking that it would probably be prudent to kill them both.

This is Suza's nightmare.

It is evening at the green-and-white house by the river. She is alone. She takes a bath, lying for a long time in the hot scented water. Afterwards she goes into the master bedroom, sits in front of the three-sided mirror, and dusts herself with powder from an onyx box that belonged to her mother.

She opens the wardrobe, expecting to find her

mother's clothes moth-eaten, falling away from the hangers in dun-coloured tatters, transparent with age; but it is not so: they are all clean and new and perfect, except for a faint odour of mothballs. She chooses a nightgown, white as a shroud, and puts it on. She gets into the bed.

She lies still for a long time, waiting for Nat Dickstein to come to his Eila. The evening becomes night. The river whispers. The door opens. The man stands at the foot of the bed and takes off his clothes. He lies on top of her, and her panic begins like the first small spark of a conflagration as she realizes that it is not Nat Dickstein but her father; and that she is, of course, long dead: and as the nightgown crumbles to dust and her hair falls out and her flesh withers and the skin of her face dries and shrinks baring the teeth and the skull and she becomes, even as the man thrusts at her, a skeleton, so she screams and screams and screams and wakes up, and she lies perspiring and shivering and frightened, wondering why nobody comes rushing in to ask what is wrong, until she realizes with relief that even the screams were dreamed; and consoled, she wonders vaguely about the meaning of the dream while she drifts back into sleep.

In the morning she is her usual cheerful self, except perhaps for a small imprecise darkness, like a smudge of cloud in the sky of her mood, not remembering the dream at all, only aware that there was once something that troubled her, not worrying any more, though, because, after all, dreaming is instead of worrying.

CHAPTER SEVEN

'NAT DICKSTEIN is going to steal some uranium,' said Yasif Hassan.

David Rostov nodded agreement. His mind was elsewhere. He was trying to figure out how to get rid of Yasif Hassan.

They were walking through the valley at the foot of the crag which was the old city of Luxembourg. Here, on the banks of the Petrusse River, were lawns and ornamental trees and footpaths. Hassan was saying, 'They've got a nuclear reactor at a place called Dimona in the Negev Desert. The French helped them build it, and presumably supplied them with fuel for it. Since the Six-Day War, de Gaulle has cut off their supplies of guns, so perhaps he's cut off the uranium as well.'

This much was obvious, Rostov thought, so it was best to allay Hassan's suspicions by agreeing vehemently. 'It would be a completely characteristic Mossad move to just go out and steal the uranium they need,' he said. 'That's exactly how those people think. They have this backs-to-the-wall mentality which enables them to ignore the niceties of international diplomacy.'

Rostov was able to guess a little farther than Hassan – which was why he was at once so elated and so anxious to get the Arab out of the way for a while. Rostov knew about the Egyptian nuclear project at Qattara: Hassan almost certainly did not – why should they tell such secrets to an agent in Luxembourg?

However, because Cairo was so leaky it was likely the Israelis also knew about the Egyptian bomb. And what would they do about it? Build their own – for which they needed, in the Euratom man's phrase, 'fissionable material'. Rostov thought Dickstein was going to try to get some uranium for an Israeli atom bomb. But Hassan would not be able to reach that conclusion, not yet; and Rostov was not going to help him, for he did not want Tel Aviv to discover how close he was.

When the printout arrived that night it would take him farther still. For it was the list from which Dickstein would probably choose his target. Rostov did not want Hassan to have that information, either.

David Rostov's blood was up. He felt the way he did in a chess game at the moment when three or four of the opponent's moves began to form a pattern and he could see from where the attack would come and how he would have to turn it into a rout. He had not forgotten the reasons why he had entered into battle with Dickstein – that other conflict inside the KGB between himself and Feliks Vorontsov, with Yuri Andropov as umpire and a place at the Phys-Mat School as the prize – but that receded to the back of his mind. What moved him now, what kept him tense and alert and sharpened the edge of his ruthlessness, was the thrill of the chase and the scent of the quarry in his nostrils.

Hassan stood in his way. Eager, amateur, touchy, bungling Hassan, reporting back to Cairo, was at this moment a more dangerous enemy than Dickstein himself. For all his faults, he was not stupid – indeed, Rostov thought, he had a sly intelligence that was typically Levantine, inherited no doubt from his capitalist father. He would know that Rostov wanted him out of the way. Therefore Rostov would have to give him a real job to do.

They passed beneath the Pont Adolphe, and Rostov stopped to look back, admiring the view through the arch of the bridge. It reminded him of Oxford, and then, suddenly, he knew what to do about Hassan.

Rostov said, 'Dickstein knows someone has been following him, and presumably he's connected that fact with his meeting with you.'

'You think so?' Hassan said.

'Well, look. He goes on an assignment, he bumps into an Arab who knows his real name and suddenly he's tailed.'

'He's sure to speculate, but he doesn't *know*.'

'You're right.' Looking at Hassan's face, Rostov realized that the Arab just loved him to say *You're right*. Rostov thought: He doesn't like me, but he wants my approval – wants it badly. He's a proud man – I can use that. 'Dickstein has to check,' Rostov went on. 'Now, are you on file in Tel Aviv?'

Hassan shrugged, with a hint of his old aristocratic nonchalance. 'Who knows?'

'How often have you had face-to-face contacts with other agents – Americans, British, Israelis?'

'Never,' Hassan said. 'I'm too careful.'

Rostov almost laughed out loud. The truth was that Hassan was too insignificant an agent to have come to the notice of the major intelligence services, and had never done anything important enough to have met other spies. 'If you're not on file,' Rostov said, 'Dickstein has to talk to your friends. Have you any acquaintances in common?'

'No. I haven't seen him since college. Anyway, he could learn nothing from my friends. They know nothing of my secret life. I don't go around telling people—'

'No, no,' Rostov said, suppressing his impatience. 'But all Dickstein would have to do is ask casual questions about your general behaviour to see whether it conforms to the pattern of clandestine work – for example, do you have mysterious phone calls, sudden absences, friends whom you don't introduce around . . . Now, is there anybody from Oxford whom you still see?'

'None of the students.' Hassan's tone had become defensive, and Rostov knew he was about to get what he wanted 'I've kept in touch with some of the faculty, on and off: Professor Ashford, in particular – once or twice he has put me in touch with people who are prepared to give money to our cause.'

'Dickstein knew Ashford, if I remember rightly.'

'Of course. Ashford had the chair of Semitic Languages, which was what both Dickstein and I read.'

'There. All Dickstein has to do is call on Ashford and mention your name in passing. Ashford will tell him what you're doing and how you behave. Then Dickstein will know you're an agent.'

'It's a bit hit-and-miss,' Hassan said dubiously.

'Not at all,' Rostov said brightly, although Hassan was right. 'It's a standard technique. I've done it myself. It works.'

'And if he has contacted Ashford . . .'

'We have a chance of picking up his trail again. So I want you to go to Oxford.'

'Oh!' Hassan had not seen where the conversation was leading, and now was boxed in. 'Dickstein might have just called on the phone . . .'

'He might, but that kind of inquiry is easier to make in person. Then you can say you were in town and just dropped by to talk about old times . . . It's hard to be that casual on the international telephone. For the same reasons, you must go there rather than call.'

'I suppose you're right,' Hassan said reluctantly. 'I was planning to make a report to Cairo as soon as we've read the printout . . .'

That was exactly what Rostov was trying to avoid. 'Good idea,' he said. 'But the report will look so much better if you can also say that you have picked up Dickstein's trail again.'

Hassan stood staring at the view, peering into the distance as if he was trying to see Oxford. 'Let's go back,' he said abruptly. 'I've walked far enough.'

It was time to be chummy. Rostov put an arm around Hassan's shoulders. 'You Europeans are soft.'

'Don't try to tell me the KGB have a tough life in Moscow.'

'Want to hear a Russian joke?' Rostov said as they climbed the side of the valley toward the road. 'Brezhnev was telling his old mother how well he had done. He showed her his apartment – huge, with Western furniture, dishwasher, freezer, servants, everything. She didn't say a word. He took her to his dacha on the Black Sea – a big villa with a swimming pool, private beach, more servants. Still she wasn't impressed. He took her to his hunting lodge in his Zil limousine, showed off the beautiful grounds, the guns, the dogs. Finally he said, "Mother, mother, why don't you say something? Aren't you proud?" So she said, "It's wonderful, Leonid. But what will you do if the Communists come back?"'

Rostov roared with laughter at his own story, but Hassan only smiled.

'You don't think it's funny?' Rostov said.

'Not very,' Hassan told him. 'It's guilt that makes you laugh at that joke. I don't feel guilty, so I don't find it funny.'

Rostov shrugged, thinking: Thank you Yasif Hassan, Islam's answer to Sigmund Freud. They reached the road and stood there for a while, watching the cars speed by as Hassan caught his breath. Rostov said, 'Oh, listen, there's something I've always wanted to ask you. Did you really screw Ashford's wife?'

'Only four or five times a week,' Hassan said, and he laughed, loudly.

Rostov said, 'Who feels guilty now?'

*

He arrived at the station early, and the train was late, so he had to wait for a whole hour. It was the only time in his life he read *Newsweek* from cover to cover. She came through the ticket barrier at a half-run, smiling broadly. Just like yesterday, she threw her arms around him and kissed him; but this time the kiss was longer. He had vaguely expected to see her in a long dress and a mink wrap, like a banker's wife on a night out at the 61 Club in Tel Aviv; but of course Suza belonged to another country and another generation, and she wore high boots which disappeared under the hem of her below-the-knee skirt, with a silk shirt under an embroidered waistcoat such as a matador might wear. Her face was not made up. Her hands were empty: no coat, no handbag, no overnight case. They stood still, smiling at each other, for a moment. Dickstein, not quite sure what to do, gave her his arm as he had the day before, and that seemed to please her. They walked to the taxi stand.

As they got into the cab Dickstein said, 'Where do you want to go?'

'You haven't booked?'

I should have reserved a table, he thought. He said, 'I don't know London restaurants.'

'Kings Road,' Suza said to the driver.

As the cab pulled away she looked at Dickstein and said, 'Hello, Nathaniel.'

Nobody ever called him Nathaniel. He liked it.

The Chelsea restaurant she chose was small, dim and trendy. As they walked to a table Dickstein thought he

saw one or two familiar faces, and his stomach tightened as he strove to place them; then he realized they
were pop singers he had seen in magazines, and he
relaxed again. He was glad his reflexes still worked like
this in spite of the atypical way he was spending his
time this evening. He was also pleased that the other
diners in the place were of all ages, for he had been a
little afraid he might be the oldest man in sight.

They sat down, and Dickstein said, 'Do you bring all
your young men here?'

Suza gave him a cold smile. 'That's the first witless
thing you've said.'

'I stand corrected.' He wanted to kick himself.

She said, 'What do you like to eat?' and the moment
passed.

'At home I eat a lot of plain, wholesome, communal
food. When I'm away I live in hotels, where I get junk
tricked out as haute cuisine. What I like is the kind of
food you don't get in either sort of place: roast leg of
lamb, steak and kidney pudding, Lancashire hot-pot.'

'What I like about you,' she grinned, 'is that you
have no idea whatsoever about what is trendy and what
isn't; and furthermore you don't give a damn.'

He touched his lapels. 'You don't like the suit?'

'I love it,' she said. 'It must have been out-of-date
when you bought it.'

He decided on roast beef from the trolley, and she
had some kind of sautéed liver which she ate with
enormous relish. He ordered a bottle of Burgundy: a
more delicate wine would not have gone well with the

liver. His knowledge of wine was the only polite accomplishment he possessed. Still, he let her drink most of it: his appetites were small.

She told him about the time she took LSD. 'It was quite unforgettable. I could feel my whole body, inside and out. I could hear my heart. My skin felt wonderful when I touched it. And the colours, of everything . . . Still, the question is, did the drug show me amazing things, or did it just make me amazed? Is it a new way of seeing the world, or does it merely synthesize the sensations you would have if you really saw the world in a new way?'

'You didn't need more of it, afterwards?' he asked.

She shook her head. 'I don't relish losing control of myself to that extent. But I'm glad I know what it's like.'

'That's what I hate about getting drunk – the loss of self-possession. Although I'm sure it's not in the same league. At any rate, the couple of times I've been drunk I haven't felt I've found the key to the universe.'

She made a dismissing gesture with her hand. It was a long, slender hand, just like Eila's; and suddenly Dickstein remembered Eila making exactly the same graceful gesture. Suza said, 'I don't believe in drugs as the solution to the world's problems.'

'What do you believe in, Suza?'

She hesitated, looking at him, smiling faintly. 'I believe that all you need is love.' Her tone was a little defensive, as if she anticipated scorn.

'That philosophy is more likely to appeal to a swinging Londoner than an embattled Israeli.'

'I guess there's no point in trying to convert you.'

'I should be so lucky.'

She looked into his eyes. 'You never know your luck.'

He looked down at the menu and said, 'It's got to be strawberries.'

Suddenly, she said, 'Tell me who you love, Nathaniel.'

'An old woman, a child and a ghost,' he said immediately, for he had been asking himself the same question. 'The old woman is called Esther, and she remembers the pogroms in Czarist Russia. The child is a boy called Mottie. He likes *Treasure Island*. His father died in the Six-Day War.'

'And the ghost?'

'You will have some strawberries?'

'Yes, please.'

'Cream?'

'No, thanks. You're not going to tell me about the ghost, are you?'

'As soon as I know, you'll know.'

It was June, and the strawberries were perfect. Dickstein said, 'Now tell me who you love.'

'Well,' she said, and then she thought for a minute. 'Well . . .' She put down her spoon. 'Oh, shit, Nathaniel, I think I love you.'

Her first thought was: What the *hell* has got into me? Why did I say that?

Then she thought: I don't care, it's true.

And finally: But *why* do I love him?

She did not know why, but she knew when. There

had been two occasions when she had been able to look inside him and see the real Dickstein: once when he spoke about the London Fascists in the Thirties, and once when he mentioned the boy whose father had been killed in the Six-Day War. Both times he had dropped his mask. She had expected to see a small, frightened man, cowering in a corner. In fact, he had appeared to be strong, confident and determined. At those moments she could sense his strength as if it were a powerful scent. It made her feel a little dizzy.

The man was weird, intriguing and powerful. She wanted to get close to him, to understand his mind, to know his secret thoughts. She wanted to touch his bony body, and feel his strong hands grasping her, and look into his sad brown eyes when he cried out in passion. She wanted his love.

It had never been like this for her before.

Nat Dickstein knew it was all wrong.

Suza had formed an attachment to him when she was five years old and he was a kind grown-up who knew how to talk to children and cats. Now he was exploiting that childhood affection.

He had loved Eila, who had died. There was something unhealthy about his relationship with her look-alike daughter.

He was not just a Jew, but an Israeli; not just an Israeli, but a Mossad agent. He of all people could not love a girl who was half Arab.

Whenever a beautiful girl falls in love with a spy, the

spy is obliged to ask himself which enemy intelligence service she might be working for.

Over the years, each time a woman had become fond of Dickstein, he had found reasons like these for being cool to her, and sooner or later she had understood and gone away disappointed; and the fact that Suza had outmanoeuvred his subconscious by being too quick for his defences was just another reason to be suspicious.

It was all wrong.

But Dickstein did not care.

They took a taxi to the flat where she planned to stay the night. She invited him in – her friends, the owners of the flat, were away on holiday – and they went to bed together; and that was when their problems began.

At first Suza thought he was going to be too eagerly passionate when, standing in the little hallway, he gripped her arms and kissed her roughly, and when he groaned, 'Oh, God,' as she took his hands and placed them on her breasts. There flashed through her mind the cynical thought: I've seen this act before, he is so overcome by my beauty that he practically rapes me, and five minutes after getting into bed he is fast asleep and snoring. Then she pulled away from his kiss and looked into his soft, big, brown eyes, and she thought: Whatever happens, it won't be an act.

She led him into the little single bedroom at the back of the flat, overlooking the courtyard. She stayed here so often that it was regarded as her room; indeed some of her clothes were in the wardrobe and the drawers. She sat on the edge of the single bed and took off her shoes. Dickstein stood in the doorway, watching. She looked up at him and smiled. 'Undress,' she said.

He turned out the light.

She was intrigued: it ran through her like the first tingle of a cannabis high. What was he really like? He was a Cockney, but an Israeli; he was a middle-aged schoolboy; a thin man as strong as a horse; a little gauche and nervous superficially, but confident and oddly powerful underneath. What did a man like *that* do in bed?

She got in beneath the sheet, curiously touched that he wanted to make love in the dark. He got in beside her and kissed her, gently this time. She ran her hands over his hard, bony body, and opened her mouth to his kisses. After a momentary hesitation, he responded; and she guessed he had not kissed like that before, or at least not for a long time.

He touched her tenderly now, with his fingertips, exploring, and he said 'Oh!' with a sense of wonder in his voice when he found her nipple taut. His caresses had none of the facile expertise so familiar to her from previous affairs: he was like . . . well, he was like a virgin. The thought made her smile in the darkness.

'Your breasts are beautiful,' he said.

'So are yours,' she said, touching them.

The magic began to work, and she became immersed in sensation: the roughness of his skin, the hair on his legs, the faint masculine smell of him. Then, suddenly, she sensed a change in him. There was no apparent reason for it, and for a moment she wondered if she might be imagining it, for he continued to caress her; but she knew that now it was mechanical, he was thinking of something else, she had lost him.

She was about to speak of it when he withdrew his hands and said, 'It's not working. I can't do it.'

She felt panic, and fought it down. She was frightened, not for herself – *You've known enough stiff pricks in your time, girl, not to mention a few limp ones* – but for him, for his reaction, in case he should be defeated or ashamed and—

She put both arms around him and held him tightly, saying, 'Whatever you do, please don't go away.'

'I won't.'

She wanted to put the light on, to see his face, but it seemed like the wrong thing to do right now. She pressed her cheek against his chest. 'Have you got a wife somewhere?'

'No.'

She put out her tongue and tasted his skin. 'I just think you might feel guilty about something. Like, me being half an Arab?'

'I don't think so.'

'Or, me being Eila Ashford's daughter? You loved her, didn't you?'

'How did you know?'

'From the way you talked about her.'

'Oh. Well, I don't think I feel guilty about that, but I could be wrong, doctor.'

'Mmm.' He was coming out of his shell. She kissed his chest. 'Will you tell me something?'

'I expect so.'

'When did you last have sex?'

'Nineteen forty-four.'

'You're kidding!' she said, genuinely astonished.

'That's the first witless thing you've said.'

'I ... you're right, I'm sorry.' She hesitated. 'But why?'

He sighed. 'I can't ... I'm not able to talk about it.'

'But you *must*.' She reached out to the bedside lamp and turned on the light. Dickstein closed his eyes against the glare. Suza propped herself up on one elbow. 'Listen,' she said, 'there are no rules. We're grown-ups, we're naked in bed, and this is nineteen sixty-eight: nothing is wrong, it's whatever turns you on.'

'There isn't anything.' His eyes were still closed.

'And there are no secrets. If you're frightened or disgusted or inflamed, you can say so, and you must. I've never said "I love you" before tonight, Nat. Speak to me, please.'

There was a long silence. He lay still, impassive, eyes closed. At last he began to talk.

'I didn't know where I was – still don't. I was taken there in a cattle truck, and in those days I couldn't tell one country from another by the landscape. It was a special camp, a medical research centre. The prisoners were selected from other camps. We were all young, healthy and Jewish.

'Conditions were better than in the first camp I was at. We had food, blankets, cigarettes; there was no thieving, no fighting. At first I thought I had struck

212

lucky. There were lots of tests – blood, urine, blow into this tube, catch this ball, read the letters on the card. It was like being in a hospital. Then the experiments began.

'To this day I don't know whether there was any real scientific curiosity behind it. I mean, if somebody did those things with animals, I could see that it might be, you know, quite interesting, quite revealing. On the other hand, the doctors must have been insane. I don't know.'

He stopped, and swallowed. It was becoming more difficult for him to speak calmly. Suza whispered, 'You must tell me what happened – everything.'

He was pale, and his voice was very low. Still he kept his eyes shut. 'They took me to this laboratory. The guards who escorted me kept winking and nudging and telling me I was *glücklich* – lucky. It was a big room with a low ceiling and very bright lights. There were six or seven of them there, with a movie camera. In the middle of the room was a low bed with a mattress on it, no sheets. There was a woman on the mattress. They told me to fuck her. She was naked, and shivering – she was a prisoner too. She whispered to me, "You save my life and I'll save yours." And then we did it. But that was only the beginning.'

Suza ran her hand over his loins and found his penis taut. *Now* she understood. She stroked him, gently at first, and waited for him to go on – for she knew that now he would tell all of the story.

'After that they did variations on the experiment. Every day for months, there was something. Drugs, sometimes. An old woman. A man, once. Intercourse in different positions – standing up, sitting, everything. Oral sex, anal sex, masturbation, group sex. If you didn't perform, you were flogged or shot. That's why the story never came out after the war, do you see? Because all the survivors were guilty.'

Suza stroked him harder. She was certain, without knowing why, that this was the right thing to do. 'Tell me. All of it.'

He was breathing faster. His eyes opened and he stared up at the blank white ceiling, seeing another place and another time. 'At the end ... the most shameful of all ... she was a nun. At first I thought they were lying to me, they had just dressed her up, but then she started praying, in French. She had no legs ... they had amputated her, just to observe the effect on me ... it was horrible, and I ... and I ...'

Then he jerked, and Suza bent and closed her mouth over his penis, and he said, 'Oh, no, no, no!' in rhythm with his spasms, and then it was all over and he wept.

She kissed his tears, and told him it was all right, over and over again. Slowly he calmed down, and eventually he seemed to sleep for a few minutes. She lay there watching his face as the tension seeped away and he became peaceful. Then he opened his eyes and said, 'Why did you do that?'

'Well.' At the time she had not understood exactly why, but now she thought she did. 'I could have given

you a lecture,' she said. 'I could have told you that
there is nothing to be ashamed of; that everybody has
grisly fantasies, that women dream of being flogged
and men have visions of flogging them; that you can
buy, here in London, pornographic books about sex
with amputees, including full-colour pictures. I could
have told you that many men would have been able to
summon up enough bestiality to perform in that Nazi
laboratory. I could have argued with you, but it
wouldn't have made any difference. I had to show you.
Besides—' She smiled ruefully. 'Besides, I have a dark
side, too.'

He touched her cheek, then leaned forward and
kissed her lips. 'Where did you get this wisdom, child?'

'It isn't wisdom, it's love.'

Then he held her very tightly and kissed her and
called her darling and after a while they made love,
very simply, hardly speaking, without confessions or
dark fantasies or bizarre lusts, giving and taking
pleasure with the familiarity of an old couple who know
each other very well; and afterwards they went to sleep
full of peace and joy.

David Rostov was bitterly disappointed with the Euratom printout. After he and Pyotr Tyrin had spent hours
getting it doped out, it became clear that the list of
consignments was very long. They could not possibly
cover every target. The only way they could discover
which one would be hit was to pick up Dickstein's trail
again.

Yasif Hassan's mission to Oxford thereupon assumed much greater importance.

They waited for the Arab to call. At ten o'clock Nik Bunin, who enjoyed sleep the way other people enjoy sunbathing, went to bed. Tyrin stuck it out until midnight, then he too retired. Rostov's phone finally rang at one A.M. He jumped as if frightened, grabbed the phone, then waited a few moments before speaking in order to compose himself.

'Yes?'

Hassan's voice came three hundred miles along the international telephone cables. 'I did it. The man was here. Two days ago.'

Rostov clenched a fist in suppressed excitement. 'Jesus. What a piece of luck.'

'What now?'

Rostov considered. 'Now, he knows that we know.'

'Yes. Shall I come back to base?'

'I don't think so. Did the professor say how long the man plans to be in England?'

'No. I asked the question directly. The professor didn't know: the man didn't tell him.'

'He wouldn't.' Rostov frowned, calculating. 'First thing the man has to do now is report that he's blown. That means he has to contact his London office.'

'Perhaps he already has.'

'Yes, but he may want a meeting. This man takes precautions, and precautions take time. All right, leave it with me. I'll be in London later today. Where are you now?'

'I'm still in Oxford. I came straight here off the plane. I can't get back to London until the morning.'

'All right. Check into the Hilton and I'll contact you there around lunchtime.'

'Check. *A bientôt.*'

'Wait.'

'Still here.'

'Don't do anything on your own initiative, now. Wait until I get there. You've done well, don't screw it up.'

Hassan hung up.

Rostov sat still for a moment, wondering whether Hassan was planning some piece of foolishness or simply resented being told to be a good boy. The latter, he decided. Anyway, there was no damage he could do over the next few hours.

Rostov turned his mind back to Dickstein. The man would not give them a second chance to pick up his trail. Rostov had to move fast and he had to move now. He put on his jacket, left the hotel and took a taxi to the Russian Embassy.

He had to wait some time, and identify himself to four different people, before they would let him in in the middle of the night. The duty operator stood at attention when Rostov entered the communications room. Rostov said, 'Sit down. There's work to do. Get the London office first.'

The operator picked up the scrambler phone and began to call the Russian Embassy in London. Rostov took off his jacket and rolled up his sleeves.

The operator said, 'Comrade Colonel David Rostov

will speak to the most senior security officer there.' He motioned Rostov to pick up the extension.

'Colonel Petrov.' It was the voice of a middle-aged soldier.

'Petrov, I need some help,' Rostov said without preamble. 'An Israeli agent named Nat Dickstein is believed to be in England.'

'Yes, we've had his picture sent to us in the diplomatic pouch – but we weren't notified he was thought to be here.'

'Listen. I think he may contact his embassy. I want you to put all known Israeli legals in London under surveillance from dawn today.'

'Hang on, Rostov,' said Petrov with a half laugh. 'That's a lot of manpower.'

'Don't be stupid. You've got hundreds of men, the Israelis only have a dozen or two.'

'Sorry, Rostov, I can't mount an operation like that on your say-so.'

Rostov wanted to get the man by the throat. 'This is urgent!'

'Let me have the proper documentation, and I'm at your disposal.'

'By then he'll be somewhere else!'

'Not my fault, comrade.'

Rostov slammed the phone down, furious, and said, 'Bloody Russians! Never do anything without six sets of authorization. Get Moscow, tell them to find Feliks Vorontsov and patch him through to me wherever he is.'

The operator got busy. Rostov drummed his fingers

on the desk impatiently. Petrov was probably an old
soldier close to retirement, with no ambition for anything but his pension. There were too many men like
that in the KGB.

A few minutes later the sleepy voice of Rostov's boss,
Feliks, came on the line. 'Yes, who is it?'

'David Rostov. I'm in Luxembourg. I need some
backing. I think The Pirate is about to contact the
Israeli Embassy in London and I want their legals
watched.'

'So call London.'

'I did. They want authorization.'

'Then apply for it.'

'For God's sake, Feliks, I'm applying for it now!'

'There's nothing I can do at this time of night. Call
me in the morning.'

'What is this? Surely you can—' Suddenly Rostov
realized what was happening. He controlled himself
with an effort. 'All right, Feliks. In the morning.'

'Goodbye.'

'Feliks—'

'Yes?'

'I'll remember this.'

The line went dead.

'Where next?' the operator asked.

Rostov frowned. 'Keep the Moscow line open. Give
me a minute to think.' He might have guessed he would
get no help from Feliks. The old fool wanted him to
fail on this mission, to prove that he, Feliks, should
have been given control of it in the first place. It was
even possible that Feliks was pally with Petrov in

London and had unofficially told Petrov not to cooperate.

There was only one thing for Rostov to do. It was a dangerous course of action and might well get him pulled off the case – in fact it could even be what Feliks was hoping for. But he could not complain if the stakes were high, for it was he who had raised them.

He thought for a minute or two about exactly how he should do it. Then he said, 'Tell Moscow to put me through to Yuri Andropov's apartment at number twenty-six Kutuzov Prospekt.' The operator raised his eyebrows – it was probably the first and last time he would be instructed to get the head of the KGB on the phone – but he said nothing. Rostov waited, fidgeting. 'I bet it isn't like this working for the CIA,' he muttered.

The operator gave him the sign, and he picked up the phone. A voice said, 'Yes?'

Rostov raised his voice and barked: 'Your name and rank!'

'Major Pyotr Eduardovitch Scherbitsky.'

'This is Colonel Rostov. I want to speak to Andropov. It's an emergency, and if he isn't on this phone within one hundred and twenty seconds you'll spend the rest of your life building dams in Bratsk, do I make myself clear?'

'Yes, colonel. Please hold the line.'

A moment later Rostov heard the deep, confident voice of Yuri Andropov, one of the most powerful men in the world. 'You certainly managed to panic young Eduardovitch, David.'

'I had no alternative, sir.'

'All right, let's have it. It had better be good.'

'The Mossad are after uranium.'

'Good God.'

'I think The Pirate is in England. He may contact his embassy. I want surveillance on the Israelis there, but an old fool called Petrov in London is giving me the runaround.'

'I'll talk to him now, before I go back to bed.'

'Thank you, sir.'

'And, David?'

'Yes?'

'It was worth waking me up – but only just.'

There was a click as Andropov hung up. Rostov laughed as the tension drained out of him, and he thought: Let them do their worst – Dickstein, Hassan, Feliks – I can handle them.

'Success?' the operator asked with a smile.

'Yes,' Rostov said. 'Our system is inefficient and cumbersome and corrupt, but in the end, you know, we get what we want.'

CHAPTER EIGHT

I T WAS quite a wrench for Dickstein to leave Suza in the morning and go back to work.

He was still ... well, stunned ... at eleven A.M., sitting in the window of a restaurant in the Fulham Road waiting for Pierre Borg to show. He had left a message with airport information at Heathrow telling Borg to go to a café opposite the one where Dickstein now sat. He thought he was likely to stay stunned for a long time, maybe permanently.

He had awakened at six o'clock, and suffered a moment of panic wondering where he was. Then he saw Suza's long brown hand lying on the pillow beside his head, curled up like a small animal sleeping, and the night had come flooding back, and he could hardly believe his good fortune. He thought he should not wake her, but suddenly he could not keep his hands off her body. She opened her eyes at his touch, and they made love playfully, smiling at one another, laughing sometimes, and looking into each other's eyes at the moment of climax. Then they fooled around in the kitchen, half-dressed, making the coffee too weak and burning the toast.

Dickstein wanted to stay there for ever.

Suza had picked up his undershirt with a cry of horror. 'What's this?'

'My undershirt.'

'Undershirt? I forbid you to wear undershirts. They're old-fashioned and unhygienic and they'll get in the way when I want to feel your nipples.'

Her expression was so lecherous that he burst out laughing. 'All right,' he said. 'I won't wear them.'

'Good.' She opened the window and threw the undershirt out into the street, and he laughed all over again.

He said, 'But you mustn't wear trousers.'

'Why not?'

It was his turn to leer.

'But all my trousers have flies.'

'No good,' he said. 'No room to manoeuvre.'

And like that.

They acted as if they had just invented sex. The only faintly unhappy moment came when she looked at his scars and asked how he got them. 'We've had three wars since I went to Israel,' he said. It was the truth, but not the whole truth.

'What made you go to Israel?'

'Safety.'

'But it's just the opposite of *safe* there.'

'It's a different kind of safety.' He said this dismissively, not wanting to explain it, then he changed his mind, for he wanted her to know all about him. 'There had to be a place where nobody could say, "You're different, you're not a human being, you're a Jew," where nobody could break my windows or experiment on my body just because I'm Jewish. You see . . .' She had been looking at him with that clear-eyed, frank gaze of hers, and he had struggled to tell her the whole truth, without evasions, without trying to make it look better than it was. 'It didn't matter to me whether we chose Palestine or Uganda or Manhattan Island – wherever it was, I would have said, "That place is *mine*," and I would have fought tooth and nail to keep it. That's why I never try to argue the moral rights and wrongs of the establishment of Israel. Justice and fair play never entered into it. After the war . . . well, the suggestion that the concept of fair play had any role in international politics seemed like a sick joke to me. I'm not pretending this is an admirable attitude, I'm just telling you how it is for me. Any other place Jews live – New York, Paris, Toronto – no matter how good it is, how assimilated they are, they never know how long it's going to last, how soon will come the next crisis that can conveniently be blamed on them. In Israel I know that whatever happens, I won't be a victim of *that*. So, with that problem out of the way, we can get on and deal with the realities that are part of everyone's life: planting and reaping, buying and selling, fighting and dying. That's why I went, I think . . . Maybe I didn't see it all so clearly back then – in fact, I've never put it into words like this – but that's how I felt, anyway.'

After a moment Suza said, 'My father holds the opinion that Israel itself is now a racist society.'

'That's what the youngsters say. They've got a point. If . . .'

She looked at him, waiting.

'If you and I had a child, they would refuse to classify him as Jewish. He would be a second-class citizen. But I don't think that sort of thing will last for ever. At the moment the religious zealots are powerful in the government: it's inevitable, Zionism was a religious movement. As the nation matures that will fade away. The race laws are already controversial. We're fighting them, and we'll win in the end.'

She came to him and put her head on his shoulder, and they held each other in silence. He knew that she did not care about Israeli politics: it was the mention of a son that had moved her.

Sitting in the restaurant window, remembering, he knew that he wanted Suza in his life always, and he wondered what he would do if she refused to go to his country. Which would he give up, Israel or Suza? He did not know.

He watched the street. It was typical June weather: raining steadily and quite cold. The familiar red buses and black cabs swished up and down, butting through the rain, splashing in the puddles on the road. A country of his own, a woman of his own: maybe he could have both.

I should be so lucky.

A cab drew up outside the café opposite, and Dickstein tensed, leaning closer to his window and peering through the rain. He recognized the bulky figure of Pierre Borg, in a dark short raincoat and a trilby hat, climbing out of the cab. He did not recognize the second man, who got out and paid the driver. The two men went into the café. Dickstein looked up and down the road.

A grey Mark II Jaguar had stopped on a double yellow line fifty yards from the café. Now it reversed and backed into a side street, parking on the corner within sight of the café. The passenger got out and walked toward the café.

Dickstein left his table and went to the phone booth in the restaurant entrance. He could still see the café opposite. He dialled its number.

'Yes?'

'Let me speak to Bill, please.'

'Bill? Don't know him.'

'Would you just ask, please?'

'Sure. Hey, anybody here called Bill?' A pause. 'Yes, he's coming.'

After a moment Dickstein heard Borg's voice. 'Yes?'

'Who's the face with you?'

'Head of London Station. Do you think we can trust him?'

Dickstein ignored the sarcasm. 'One of you picked up a shadow. Two men in a grey Jaguar.'

'We saw them.'

'Lose them.'

'Of course. Listen, you know this town – what's the best way?'

'Send the Head of Station back to the Embassy in a cab. That should lose the Jaguar. Wait ten minutes, then take a taxi to . . .'

Dickstein hesitated, trying to think of a quiet street not too far away. 'To Redcliffe Street. I'll meet you there.'

'Okay.'

Dickstein looked across the road. 'Your tail is just going into your café.' He hung up.

He went back to his window seat and watched. The other man came out of the café, opened an umbrella, and stood at the kerb looking for a cab. The tail had either recognized Borg at the airport or had been following the Head of Station for some other reason. It did not make any difference. A taxi pulled up. When it left, the grey Jaguar came out of the side street and followed. Dickstein left the restaurant and hailed a cab for himself. Taxi drivers do well out of spies, he thought.

He told the cabbie to go to Redcliffe Street and wait. After eleven minutes another taxi entered the street and Borg got out. 'Flash your lights,' Dickstein said. 'That's the man I'm meeting.' Borg saw the lights and waved acknowledgment. As he was paying, a third taxi entered the street and stopped. Borg spotted it.

The shadow in the third taxi was waiting to see what happened. Borg realized this, and began to walk away from his cab. Dickstein told his driver not to flash his lights again.

Borg walked past them. The tail got out of his taxi, paid the driver and walked after Borg. When the tail's cab had gone Borg turned, came back to Dickstein's cab, and got in. Dickstein said, 'Okay, let's go.' They pulled away, leaving the tail on the pavement looking for another taxi. It was a quiet street: he would not find one for five or ten minutes.

Borg said, 'Slick.'

'Easy,' Dickstein replied.

The driver said, 'What was all that about, then?'

'Don't worry,' Dickstein told him. 'We're secret agents.'

The cabbie laughed. 'Where to now – Ml5?'

'The Science Museum.'

Dickstein sat back in his seat. He smiled at Borg. 'Well, Bill, you old fart, how the hell are you?'

Borg frowned at him. 'What have you got to be so fucking cheerful about?'

They did not speak again in the cab, and Dickstein realized he had not prepared himself sufficiently for this meeting. He should have decided in advance what he wanted from Borg and how he was going to get it.

He thought: What *do* I want? The answer came up out of the back of his mind and hit him like a slap. I want to give Israel the bomb – and then I want to go home.

He turned away from Borg. Rain streaked the cab window like tears. He was suddenly glad they could not speak because of the driver. On the pavement were three coatless hippies, soaking wet, their faces and hands upturned to enjoy the rain. *If I could do this, if I could finish this assignment, I could rest.*

The thought made him unaccountably happy. He looked at Borg and smiled. Borg turned his face to the window.

They reached the museum and went inside. They stood in front of a reconstructed dinosaur. Borg said, 'I'm thinking of taking you off this assignment.'

Dickstein nodded, suppressing his alarm, thinking fast. Hassan must be reporting to Cairo, and Borg's man in Cairo must be getting the reports and passing them to Tel Aviv. 'I've discovered I'm blown,' he told Borg.

'I knew that weeks ago,' Borg said. 'If you'd keep in touch you'd be up-to-date on these things.'

'If I kept in touch I'd be blown more often.'

Borg grunted and walked on. He took out a cigar, and Dickstein said, 'No smoking in here.' Borg put the cigar away.

'Blown is nothing,' Dickstein said. 'It's happened to me half a dozen times. What counts is how much they know.'

'You were fingered by this Hassan, who knows you from years back. He's working with the Russians now.'

'But what do they *know*?'

'You've been in Luxembourg and France.'

'That's not much.'

'I realize it's not much. I know you've been in Luxembourg and France too, and *I* have no idea what you did there.'

'So you'll leave me in,' Dickstein said, and looked hard at Borg.

'That depends. What *have* you been doing?'

'Well.' Dickstein continued looking at Borg. The man had become fidgety, not knowing what to do with his hands now that he could not smoke. The bright lights on the displays illuminated his bad complexion: his troubled face was like a gravel parking lot. Dickstein needed to judge very carefully how much he told Borg: enough to give the impression that a great deal had been achieved; not so much that Borg would think he could get another man to operate Dickstein's plan . . . 'I've picked a consignment of uranium for us to steal,' he began. 'It's going by ship from Antwerp to Genoa in November. I'm going to hijack the ship.'

'Shit!' Borg seemed both pleased and afraid at the audacity of the idea. He said, 'How the hell will you keep that secret?'

'I'm working on that.' Dickstein decided to tell Borg just a tantalizing little bit more. 'I have to visit Lloyd's, here in London. I'm hoping the ship will turn out to be one of a series of identical vessels – I'm told most ships are built that way. If I can buy an identical vessel, I can switch the two somewhere in the Mediterranean.'

Borg rubbed his hand across his close-cropped hair twice, then pulled at his ear. 'I don't see . . .'

'I haven't figured out the details yet, but I'm sure this is the only way to do the thing clandestinely.'

'So get on and figure out the details.'

'But you're thinking of pulling me out.'

'Yeah . . .' Borg tilted his head from one side to the other, a gesture of indecision. 'If I put an experienced man in to replace you, he may be spotted too.'

'And if you put in an unknown he won't be experienced.'

'Plus, I'm really not sure there is anyone, experienced or otherwise, who can pull this off apart from you. And there is something else you don't know.'

They stopped in front of a model of a nuclear reactor.

'Well?' Dickstein said.

'We've had a report from Qattara. The Russians are helping them now. We're in a hurry, Dickstein. I can't afford delay, and changes of plan cause delay.'

'Will November be soon enough?'

Borg considered. 'Just,' he said. He seemed to come to a decision. 'All right, I'm leaving you in. You'll have to take evasive action.'

Dickstein grinned broadly and slapped Borg on the back. 'You're a pal, Pierre. Don't you worry now. I'll run rings around them.'

Borg frowned. 'Just what is it with you? You can't stop grinning.'

'It's seeing you that does it. Your face is like a tonic. Your sunny disposition is infectious. When you smile, Pierre, the whole world smiles with you.'

'You're crazy, you prick,' said Borg.

Pierre Borg was vulgar, insensitive, malicious, and boring, but he was not stupid. 'He may be a bastard,' people would say, 'but he's a clever bastard.' By the time they parted company he knew that something important had changed in Nat Dickstein's life.

He thought about it, walking back to the Israeli Embassy at No. 2 Palace Green in Kensington. In the twenty years since they had first met, Dickstein had hardly changed. It was still only rarely that the force of the man showed through. He had always been quiet and withdrawn; he continued to look like an out-of-work bank clerk; and, except for occasional flashes of rather cynical wit, he was still dour.

Until today.

At first he had been his usual self – brief to the point of rudeness. But toward the end he had come on like the stereotyped chirpy Cockney sparrow in a Hollywood movie.

Borg had to know why.

He would tolerate a lot from his agents. Provided they were efficient, they could be neurotic, or aggressive, or sadistic, or insubordinate – so long as he knew about it. He could make allowances for faults: but he could not allow for unknown factors. He would be unsure of his hold over Dickstein until he had figured out the cause of the change. That was all. He had no objection in principle to one of his agents acquiring a sunny disposition.

He came within sight of the embassy. He would put Dickstein under surveillance, he decided. It would take two cars and three teams of men working in eight-hour shifts. The Head of London Station would complain. The hell with *him*.

The need to know why Dickstein's disposition had changed was only one reason Borg had decided not to pull him out. The other reason was more important. Dickstein had half a plan; another man might not be able to complete it. Dickstein had a mind for this sort of thing. Once Dickstein had figured it all out, *then* somebody else could take over. Borg had decided to take him off the assignment at the first opportunity. Dickstein would be furious: he would consider he had been shafted.

The hell with him, too.

Major Pyotr Alekseivitch Tyrin did not actually like Rostov. He did not like any of his superiors: in his view, you had to be a rat to get promoted above the rank of major in the KGB. Still, he had a sort of awestruck affection for his clever, helpful boss. Tyrin had considerable skills, particularly with electronics, but he could not manipulate people. He was a major only because he was on Rostov's incredibly successful team.

Abba Allon. High Street exit. Fifty-two, or nine? Where are you, fifty-two?

Fifty-two. We're close. We'll take him. What does he look like?

Plastic raincoat, green hat, moustache.

As a friend Rostov was not much; but he was a lot worse as an enemy. This Colonel Petrov in London had discovered that. He had tried to mess around with Rostov and had been surprised by a middle-of-the-night phone call from the head of the KGB, Yuri Andropov himself. The people in the London Embassy said Petrov had looked like a ghost when he hung up. Since then Rostov could have anything he wanted: if he sneezed five agents rushed out to buy handkerchiefs.

Okay, this is Ruth Davisson, and she's going . . . north . . .

Nineteen, we can take her—

Relax, nineteen. False alarm. It's a secretary who looks like her.

Rostov had commandeered all Petrov's best pavement artists and most of his cars. The area around the Israeli Embassy in London was crawling with agents – someone had said, 'There are more Reds here than in the Kremlin Clinic' – but it was hard to spot them. They were in cars, vans, minicabs, trucks and one vehicle that looked remarkably like an unmarked Metropolitan Police bus. There were more on foot, some in public buildings and others walking the streets and the footpaths of the park. There was even one inside the Embassy, asking in dreadfully broken English what he had to do to emigrate to Israel.

The Embassy was ideally suited for this kind of exercise. It was in a little diplomatic ghetto on the edge of Kensington Gardens. So many of the lovely old houses belonged to foreign legations that it was known as Embassy Row. Indeed, the Soviet Embassy was close by in Kensington Palace Gardens. The little group of streets formed a private estate, and you had to tell a policeman your business before you could get in.

Nineteen, this time it is Ruth Davisson ... nineteen, do you hear me?

Nineteen here, yes.

Are you still on the north side?

Yes. And we know what she looks like.

None of the agents was actually in sight of the Israeli Embassy. Only one member of the team could see the door – Rostov, who was a half mile away, on the twentieth floor of a hotel, watching through a powerful Zeiss telescope mounted on a tripod. Several high buildings in the West End of London had clear views across the park to Embassy Row. Indeed, certain suites in certain hotels fetched inordinately high prices because of rumours that from them you could see into Princess Margaret's backyard at the neighbouring palace, which gave its name to Palace Green and Kensington Palace Gardens.

Rostov was in one of those suites, and he had a radio transmitter as well as the telescope. Each of his sidewalk squads had a walkie-talkie. Petrov spoke to his men in fast Russian, using confusing codewords, and the wavelength on which he transmitted and on which the men replied was changed every five minutes according to a computer program built into all the sets. The system was working very well, Tyrin thought – he had invented it – except that somewhere in the cycle everyone was subjected to five minutes of BBC Radio One.

Eight, move up to the north side.

Understood.

If the Israelis had been in Belgravia, the home of the more senior embassies, Rostov's job would have been more difficult. There were almost no shops, cafés or public offices in Belgravia – nowhere for agents to make themselves unobtrusive; and because the whole district was quiet, wealthy and stuffed with ambassadors it was easy for the police to keep an eye open for suspicious activities. Any of the standard surveillance ploys – telephone repair van, road crew with striped tent – would have drawn a crowd of bobbies in minutes.

By contrast the area around the little oasis of Embassy Row was Kensington, a major shopping area with several colleges and four museums.

Tyrin himself was in a pub in Kensington Church Street. The resident KGB men had told him that the pub was frequented by detectives from 'Special Branch' – the rather coy name for Scotland Yard's political police. The four youngish men in rather sharp suits drinking whisky at the bar were probably detectives. They did not know Tyrin, and would not have been much interested in him if they had. Indeed, if Tyrin were to approach them and say, 'By the way, the KGB is tailing every Israeli legal in London at the moment,' they would probably say, 'What, again?' and order another round of drinks.

In any event Tyrin knew he was not a man to attract second glances. He was small and rather rotund, with a big nose and a drinker's veined face. He wore a grey raincoat over a green sweater. The rain had removed the last memory of a crease from his charcoal flannel trousers. He sat in a corner with a glass of English beer and a small bag of potato chips. The radio in his shirt pocket was connected by a fine, flesh-coloured wire to the plug – it looked like a hearing aid – in his left ear. His left side was to the wall. He could talk to Rostov by pretending to fumble in the inside pocket of his raincoat, turning his face away from the room and muttering into the perforated metal disc on the top edge of the radio.

He was watching the detectives drink whisky and thinking that the Special Branch must have better expense accounts than its Russian equivalent: he was allowed one pint of beer per hour, the potato crisps he had to buy himself. At one time agents in England had even been obliged to buy beer in half pints, until the accounts department had been told that in many pubs a man who drank halves was as peculiar as a Russian who took his vodka in sips instead of gulps.

Thirteen, pick up a green Volvo, two men, High Street.

Understood.

And one on foot . . . I think that's Yigael Meier . . . Twenty?

Tyrin was 'Twenty.' He turned his face into his shoulder and said, 'Yes. Describe him.'

Tall, grey hair, umbrella, belted coat. High Street gate.

Tyrin said, 'I'm on my way.' He drained his glass and left the pub.

It was raining. Tyrin took a collapsible umbrella from his raincoat pocket and opened it. The wet pavements were crowded with shoppers. At the traffic lights he spotted the green Volvo and, three cars behind it, 'Thirteen' in an Austin.

Another car. Five, this one's yours. Blue Volkswagen Beetle.

Understood.

Tyrin reached Palace Gate, looked up Palace Avenue, saw a man fitting the description heading toward him, and walked on without pausing. When he had calculated that the man had had time to reach the street he stood at the kerb, as if about to cross, and looked up and down. The mark emerged from Palace Avenue and turned west, away from Tyrin.

Tyrin followed.

Along High Street tailing was made easier by the crowds. Then they turned south into a maze of side streets, and Tyrin became a bit nervous; but the Israeli did not seem to be watching for a shadow. He simply butted ahead through the rain, a tall, bent figure under an umbrella, walking fast, intent on his destination.

He did not go far. He turned into a small modern hotel just off the Cromwell Road. Tyrin walked past the entrance and, glancing through the glass door, saw the mark step into a phone booth in the lobby. A little farther along the road Tyrin passed the green Volvo, and concluded that the Israeli and his colleagues in the Volvo were staking out the hotel.

He crossed the road and came back on the opposite side, just in case the mark were to come out again immediately. He looked for the blue Volkswagen Beetle and did not see it, but he was quite sure it would be close by.

He spoke into his shirt pocket. 'This is Twenty. Meier and the green Volvo have staked out the Jacobean Hotel.'

Confirmed, Twenty. Five and Thirteen have the Israeli cars covered. Where is Meier?

'In the lobby.' Tyrin looked up and down and saw the Austin which was following the green Volvo.

Stay with him.

'Understood.' Tyrin now had a difficult decision to make. If he went straight into the hotel Meier might spot him, but if he took the time to find the back entrance Meier might go away in the meanwhile.

He decided to chance the back entrance, on the

grounds that he was supported by two cars which could cover for a few minutes if the worst happened. Beside the hotel there was a narrow alley for delivery vans. Tyrin walked along it and came to an unlocked fire exit in the blank side wall of the building. He went in and found himself in a concrete stairwell, obviously built to be used only as a fire escape. As he climbed the stairs he collapsed his umbrella, put it in his raincoat pocket and took off the raincoat. He folded it and left it in a little bundle on the first half landing, where he could quickly pick it up if he needed to make a fast exit. He went to the second floor and took the elevator down to the lobby. When he emerged in his sweater and trousers he looked like a guest at the hotel.

The Israeli was still in the phone booth.

Tyrin went up to the glass door at the front of the lobby, looked out, checked his wristwatch and returned to the waiting area to sit down as if he were meeting someone. It did not seem to be his lucky day. The object of the whole exercise was to find Nat Dickstein. He was known to be in England, and it was hoped that he would have a meeting with one of the legals. The Russians were following the legals in order to witness that meeting and pick up Dickstein's trail. The Israeli team at this hotel was clearly not involved in a meeting. They were staking out someone, presumably with a view to tailing him as soon as he showed, and that someone was not likely to be one of their own agents. Tyrin could only hope that what they *were* doing would at least turn out to be of some interest.

He watched the mark come out of the phone booth

and walk off in the direction of the bar. He wondered if the lobby could be observed from the bar. Apparently not, because the mark came back a few minutes later with a drink in his hand, then sat down across from Tyrin and picked up a newspaper.

The mark did not have time to drink his beer.

The elevator doors hissed open, and out walked Nat Dickstein.

Tyrin was so surprised that he made the mistake of staring straight at Dickstein for several seconds. Dickstein caught his eye, and nodded politely. Tyrin smiled weakly and looked at his watch. It occurred to him – more in hope than conviction – that staring was such a bad mistake that Dickstein might take it as proof that Tyrin was *not* an agent.

There was no time for reflection. Moving quickly with – Tyrin thought – something of a spring in his step, Dickstein crossed to the counter and dropped a room key, then proceeded quickly out into the street. The Israeli tail, Meier, put his newspaper on the table and followed. When the plate-glass door closed behind Meier, Tyrin got up, thinking: I'm an agent following an agent following an agent. Well, at least we keep each other in employment.

He went into the elevator and pressed the button for the first floor. He spoke into his radio. 'This is Twenty. I have Pirate.' There was no reply – the walls of the building were blocking his transmission. He got out of the elevator at the first floor and ran down the fire stairs, picking up his raincoat at the half landing. As soon as he was outside he tried the radio again. 'This is Twenty, I have the Pirate.'

All right, Twenty. Thirteen has him too.

Tyrin saw the mark crossing Cromwell Road. 'I'm following Meier,' he said into his radio.

Five and Twenty, both of you listen to me. Do not follow. Have you got that – Five?

Yes.

Twenty?

Tyrin said, 'Understood.' He stopped walking and stood on the corner watching Meier and Dickstein disappear in the direction of Chelsea.

Twenty, go back into the hotel. Get his room number. Book a room close to his. Call me on the telephone as soon as it's done.

'Understood.' Tyrin turned back, rehearsing his dialogue: Excuse me, the fellow that just walked out of here, short man with glasses, I think I know him but he got into a cab before I could catch up with him . . . his name is John but we all used to call him Jack, what room . . . ? As it turned out, none of that was necessary. Dickstein's key was still on the desk. Tyrin memorized the number.

The desk clerk came over. 'Can I help you?'

'I'd like a room,' Tyrin said.

He kissed her, and he was like a man who has been thirsty all day. He savoured the smell of her skin and the soft motions of her lips. He touched her face and said, 'This, this, this is what I need.' They stared into each other's eyes, and the truth between them was like nakedness. He thought: I can do anything I want. The idea ran through his mind again and again like an incantation, a magic spell. He touched her body greedily. He stood face to face with her in the little blue-and-yellow kitchen, looking into her eyes while he fingered the secret places of her body. Her red mouth opened a fraction and he felt her breath coming faster and hot on his face; he inhaled deeply so as to breathe the air from her. He thought: If I can do anything I want, so can she; and, as if she had read his mind, she opened his shirt, and bent to his chest, and took his nipple between her teeth, and sucked. The sudden, astonishing pleasure of it made him gasp aloud. He held her head gently in his hands and rocked to and fro a little to intensify the sensation. He thought: Anything I want! He reached behind her, lifted her skirt, and feasted his eyes on the white panties clinging to her curves and contrasting with the brown skin of her long legs. His right hand stroked her face and gripped her shoulder and weighed her breasts; his left hand moved over her hips and inside her panties and between her legs; and everything felt so good, so good, that he wished he had four hands to feel her with, six. Then, suddenly, he wanted to see her face, so he gripped her shoulders and made her stand upright, saying, 'I want to look at you.' Her eyes filled with tears, and he knew that these were signs not of sadness but of intense pleasure. Again they stared into each other's eyes, and this time it was not just truth between them but raw emotion gushing from one to another in rivers, in torrents. Then he knelt at her feet like a supplicant. First he laid his head on her thighs, feeling the heat of her body through her clothing. Then he reached beneath her skirt with both hands, found the waist of her panties, and drew them down slowly, holding the shoes on her feet as she stepped out. He got up from the floor. They were still standing on the spot where they had kissed when he had first come into the room. Just there, standing up, they began to make love. He watched her face. She looked peaceful, and her eyes were half closed. He wanted to do this, moving slowly, for a long time: but his body would not wait. He was compelled to thrust harder and faster. He felt himself losing his balance, so he put both arms around her, lifted her an inch off the floor, and without withdrawing from her body moved two paces so that her back was against the wall. She pulled his shirt out of his waistband and dug her fingers into the hard muscles of his back. He linked his hands beneath her buttocks and took her weight. She lifted her legs high, her thighs gripping his hips, her ankles crossed behind his back, and, incredibly, he seemed to penetrate even deeper inside her. He felt he was being wound up like a clockwork motor, and everything she did, every look on her face, tightened the spring. He watched her through a haze of lust. There came into her eyes an expression of something like panic; a wild, wide-eyed animal emotion; and it pushed him over the edge, so that he knew that it was coming, the beautiful thing was going to happen now, and he wanted to tell her, so he said, 'Suza, here it comes,' and she said, 'Oh, and me,' and she dug her nails into the skin of his back and drew them down his spine in a long sharp tear which went through him like an electric shock and he felt the earthquake in her body just as his own erupted and he was still looking at her and he saw her mouth open wide, wide as she drew breath and the peak of delight overtook them both and she *screamed*.

'We follow the Israelis and the Israelis follow Dickstein. All it needs is for Dickstein to start following us and we can all go around in a circle for the rest of the day,' Rostov said. He strode down the hotel corridor. Tyrin hurried beside him, his short plump legs almost running to keep up.

Tyrin said, 'I was wondering what, exactly, was your thinking in abandoning the surveillance as soon as we saw him?'

'It's obvious,' Rostov said irritably; then he reminded himself that Tyrin's loyalty was valuable, and he decided to explain. 'Dickstein has been under surveillance a great deal during the last few weeks. Each time he has eventually spotted us and thrown us off. Now a certain amount of surveillance is inevitable for someone who has been in the game as long as Dickstein. But on a particular operation, the more he is followed the more likely he is to abandon what he's doing and hand it over to someone else – and we might not know who. All too often the information we gain by following someone is cancelled out because they discover that we're following them and therefore they know that we've got the information in question. This way – by abandoning the surveillance as we have done today – we know where he is but he doesn't know we know.'

'I see,' said Tyrin.

'He'll spot those Israelis in no time at all,' Rostov added. 'He must be hypersensitive by now.'

'Why do you suppose they're following their own man?'

'I really can't understand that.' Rostov frowned, thinking aloud. 'I'm sure Dickstein met Borg this morning – which would explain why Borg threw off his tail with that taxi manoeuvre. It's possible Borg pulled Dickstein out and now he's simply checking that Dickstein really does come out, and doesn't try to carry on unofficially.' He shook his head, a gesture of frustration. 'That doesn't convince me. But the alternative is that Borg doesn't trust Dickstein any more, and I find that unlikely, too. Careful, now.'

They were at the door to Dickstein's hotel room. Tyrin took out a small, powerful flashlight and shone it around the edges of the door. 'No telltales,' he said.

Rostov nodded, waiting. This was Tyrin's province. The little round man was the best general technician in the KGB, in Rostov's opinion. He watched as Tyrin took from his pocket a skeleton key, one of a large collection of such keys that he had. By trying several on the door of his own room here, he had already established which one fitted the locks of the Jacobean Hotel. He opened Dickstein's door slowly and stayed outside, looking in.

'No booby traps,' he said after a minute.

He stepped inside and Rostov followed, closing the door. This part of the game gave Rostov no pleasure at all. He liked to watch, to speculate, to plot: burglary was not his style. He felt exposed and vulnerable. If a maid should come in now, or the hotel manager, or even Dickstein who might evade the sentry in the lobby ... it would be so undignified, so humiliating. 'Let's make it fast,' he said.

The room was laid out according to the standard plan: the door opened into a little passage with the bathroom on one side and the wardrobe opposite. Beyond the bathroom the room was square, with the single bed against one wall and the television set against the other. There was a large window in the exterior wall opposite the door.

Tyrin picked up the phone and began to unscrew the mouthpiece. Rostov stood at the foot of the bed, looking around, trying to get an impression of the man who was staying in this room. There was not much to go on. The room had been cleaned and the bed made. On the bedside table were a book of chess problems and an evening newspaper. There were no signs of tobacco or alcohol. The wastepaper basket was empty. A small black vinyl suitcase on a stool contained clean underwear and one clean shirt. Rostov muttered, 'The man travels with one spare shirt!' The drawers of the dresser were empty. Rostov looked into the bathroom. He saw a toothbrush, a rechargeable electric shaver with spare plugs for different kinds of electrical outlets, and – the only personal touch – a pack of indigestion tablets.

Rostov went back into the bedroom, where Tyrin was reassembling the telephone. 'It's done.'

'Put one behind the headboard,' Rostov said.

Tyrin was taping a bug to the wall behind the bed when the phone rang.

If Dickstein returned the sentry in the lobby was to call Dickstein's room on the house phone, let it ring twice, then hang up.

It rang a second time. Rostov and Tyrin stood still, silent, waiting.

It rang again.

They relaxed.

It stopped after the seventh ring.

Rostov said, 'I wish he had a car for us to bug.'

'I've got a shirt button.'

'What?'

'A bug like a shirt button.'

'I didn't know such things existed.'

'It's new.'

'Got a needle? And thread?'

'Of course.'

'Then go ahead.'

Tyrin went to Dickstein's case and without taking the shirt out snipped off the second button, carefully removing all the loose thread. With a few swift strokes he sewed on the new button. His pudgy hands were surprisingly dexterous.

Rostov watched but his thoughts were elsewhere. He wanted desperately to do more to ensure that he would hear what Dickstein said and did. The Israeli might find the bugs in the phone and the headboard; he would not wear the bugged shirt all the time. Rostov liked to be sure of things, and Dickstein was maddeningly slippery: there was nowhere you could hook on to him. Rostov had harboured a faint hope that somewhere in this room there would be a photograph of someone Dickstein loved.

'There.' Tyrin showed him his handiwork. The shirt was plain white nylon with the commonest sort of white button. The new one was indistinguishable from the others.

'Good,' Rostov said. 'Close the case.'

Tyrin did so. 'Anything else?'

'Take another quick look around for telltales. I can't believe Dickstein would go out without taking any precautions at all.'

They searched again, quickly, silently, their movements practised and economical, showing no signs of the haste they both felt. There were dozens of ways of planting telltales. A hair lightly stuck across the crack of the door was the most simple; a scrap of paper jammed against the back of a drawer would fall out when the drawer was opened; a lump of sugar under a thick carpet would be silently crushed by a footstep; a penny behind the lining of a suitcase lid would slide from front to back if the case were opened . . .

They found nothing.

Rostov said, 'All Israelis are paranoid. Why should he be different?'

'Maybe he's been pulled out.'

Rostov grunted. 'Why else would he suddenly get careless?'

'He could have fallen in love,' Tyrin suggested.

Rostov laughed. 'Sure,' he said. 'And Joe Stalin could have been canonized by the Vatican. Let's get out of here.'

He went out, and Tyrin followed, closing the door softly behind him.

So it was a woman.

Pierre Borg was shocked, amazed, mystified, intrigued and deeply worried.

Dickstein *never* had women.

Borg sat on a park bench under an umbrella. He had been unable to think in the Embassy, with phones ringing and people asking him questions all the time, so he had come out here, despite the weather. The rain blew across the empty park in sheets, and every now and then a drop would land on the tip of his cigar and he would have to relight it.

It was the tension in Dickstein that made the man so fierce. The last thing Borg wanted was for him to learn how to relax.

The pavement artists had followed Dickstein to a small apartment house in Chelsea where he had met a woman. 'It's a sexual relationship,' one of them had said. 'I heard her orgasm.' The caretaker of the building had been interviewed, but he knew nothing about the woman except that she was a close friend of the people who owned the apartment.

The obvious conclusion was that Dickstein owned the flat (and had bribed the caretaker to lie); that he used it as a rendezvous; that he met someone from the opposition, a woman; that they made love and he told her secrets.

Borg might have bought that idea if he had found out about the woman some other way. But if Dickstein had suddenly become a traitor he would not have allowed Borg to become suspicious. He was too clever. He would have covered his tracks. He would not have led the pavement artists straight to the flat without once looking over his shoulder. His behaviour had innocence written all over it. He had met with Borg, looking like the cat that got at the cream, either not knowing or not caring that his mood was all over his face. When Borg asked what was going on, Dickstein made jokes. Borg was bound to have him tailed. Hours later Dickstein was screwing some girl who liked it so much you could hear her out in the fucking *street*. The whole thing was so damn naïve it had to be true.

All right, then. Some woman had found a way to get past Dickstein's defences and seduce him. Dickstein was reacting like a teenager because he never had a teenage. The important question was, who was she?

The Russians had files, too, and they ought to have assumed, like Borg, that Dickstein was invulnerable to a sexual approach. But maybe they thought it was worth a try. And maybe they were right.

Once again, Borg's instinct was to pull Dickstein out immediately. And once again, he hesitated. If it had been any project other than this one, any agent other than Dickstein, he would have known what to do. But Dickstein was the only man who could solve this problem. Borg had no option but to stick to his original scheme: wait until Dickstein had fully conceived his plan, then pull him out.

He could at least have the London Station investigate the woman and find out all they could about her.

Meanwhile he would just have to hope that if she were an agent Dickstein would have the sense not to tell her anything.

It would be a dangerous time, but there was no more Borg could do.

His cigar went out, but he hardly noticed. The park was completely deserted now. Borg sat on his bench, his body uncharacteristically still, holding the umbrella over his head, looking like a statue, worrying himself to death.

The fun was over, Dickstein told himself: it was time to get back to work.

Entering his hotel room at ten o'clock in the morning, he realized that – incredibly – he had left no telltales. For the first time in twenty years as an agent, he had simply forgotten to take elementary precautions. He stood in the doorway, looking around, thinking about the shattering effect that she had had on him. Leaving her and going back to work was like climbing into a familiar car which has been garaged for a year: he had to let the old habits, the old instincts, the old paranoia seep back into his mind.

He went into the bathroom and ran a tub. He now had a kind of emotional breathing-space. Suza was going back to work today. She was with BOAC, and this tour of duty would take her all the way around the world. She expected to be back in twenty-one days, but it might be longer. He had no idea where he might be in three weeks' time; which meant he did not know when he would see her again. But see her again he would, if he lived.

Everything looked different now, past and future. The last twenty years of his life seemed dull, despite the fact that he had shot people and been shot at, travelled all over the world, disguised himself and deceived people and pulled off outrageous, clandestine coups. It all seemed trivial.

Sitting in the tub he wondered what he would do with the rest of his life. He had decided he would not be a spy any more – but what would he be? It seemed all possibilities were open to him. He could stand for election to the Knesset, or start his own business, or simply stay on the kibbutz and make the best wine in Israel. Would he marry Suza? If he did, would they live in Israel? He found the uncertainty delicious, like wondering what you would be given for your birthday.

If I live, he thought. Suddenly there was even more at stake. He was afraid to die. Until now death had been something to avoid with all skill only because it constituted, so to speak, a losing move in the game. Now he wanted desperately to live: to sleep with Suza again, to make a home with her, to learn all about her, her idiosyncrasies and her habits and her secrets, the books she liked and what she thought about Beethoven and whether she snored.

It would be terrible to lose his life so soon after she had saved it.

He got out of the bath, rubbed himself dry and dressed. The way to keep his life was to win this fight.

His next move was a phone call. He considered the hotel phone, decided to start being extra careful here and now, and went out to find a call box.

The weather had changed. Yesterday had emptied the sky of rain, and now it was pleasantly sunny and warm. He passed the phone booth nearest to the hotel and went on to the next one: extra careful. He looked up Lloyd's of London in the directory and dialled their number.

'Lloyd's, good morning.'

'I need some information about a ship.'

'That's Lloyd's of London Press – I'll put you through.'

While he waited Dickstein looked out of the windows of the phone booth at the London traffic, and wondered whether Lloyd's would give him what he wanted. He hoped so – he could not think where else to go for the information. He tapped his foot nervously.

'Lloyd's of London Press.'

'Good morning, I'd like some information about a ship.'

'What sort of information?' the voice said, with – Dickstein thought – a trace of suspicion.

'I want to know whether she was built as part of a series; and if so, the names of her sister ships, who owns them, and their present locations. Plus plans, if possible.'

'I'm afraid I can't help you there.'

Dickstein's heart sank. 'Why not?'

'We don't keep plans, that's Lloyd's Register, and they only give them out to owners.'

'But the other information? The sister ships?'

'Can't help you there either.'

Dickstein wanted to get the man by the throat. 'Then who can?'

'We're the only people who have such information.'

'And you keep it secret?'

'We don't give it out over the phone.'

'Wait a minute, you mean you can't help me *over the phone*.'

'That's right.'

'But you can if I write or call personally.'

'Um ... yes, this inquiry shouldn't take too long, so you could call personally.'

'Give me the address.' He wrote it down. 'And you could get these details while I wait?'

'I think so.'

'All right. I'll give you the name of the ship now, and you should have all the information ready by the time I get there. Her name is *Coparelli*.' He spelled it.

'And your name?'

'Ed Rodgers.'

'The company?'

'*Science International.*'

'Will you want us to bill the company?'

'No, I'll pay by personal cheque.'

'So long as you have some identification.'

'Of course. I'll be there in an hour. Goodbye.'

Dickstein hung up and left the phone booth, thinking: Thank God for that. He crossed the road to a café and ordered coffee and a sandwich.

He had lied to Borg, of course: he knew exactly how he would hijack the *Coparelli*. He would buy one of the sister ships – if there were such – and take his team on to meet the *Coparelli* at sea. After the hijack, instead of the dicey business of transferring the cargo from one ship to another offshore, he would sink his own ship and transfer its papers to the *Coparelli*. He would also paint out the *Coparelli*'s name and over it put the name of the sunken sister ship. And then he would sail what would appear to be his own ship into Haifa.

This was good, but it was still only the rudiments of a plan. What would he do about the crew of the *Coparelli*? How would the apparent loss of the *Coparelli* be explained? How would he avoid an international inquiry into the loss at sea of tons of uranium ore?

The more he thought about it, the bigger this last problem seemed. There would be a major search for any large ship which was thought to have sunk. With uranium aboard, the search would attract publicity and consequently be even more thorough. And what if the searchers found not the *Coparelli* but the sister ship which was supposed to belong to Dickstein?

He chewed over the problem for a while without coming up with any answers. There were still too many unknowns in the equation. Either the sandwich or the problem had stuck in his stomach: he took an indigestion tablet.

He turned his mind to evading the opposition. Had

he covered his tracks well enough? Only Borg could know of his plans. Even if his hotel room were bugged – even if the phone booth nearest the hotel were bugged – still nobody else could know of his interest in the *Coparelli*. He had been extra careful.

He sipped his coffee; then another customer, on his way out of the café, jogged Dickstein's elbow and made him spill coffee all down the front of his clean shirt.

'*Coparelli*,' said David Rostov excitedly. 'Where have I heard of a ship called the *Coparelli*?'

Yasif Hassan said, 'It's familiar to me, too.'

'Let me see that computer printout.'

They were in the back of a listening van parked near the Jacobean Hotel. The van, which belonged to the KGB, was dark blue, without markings, and very dirty. Powerful radio equipment occupied most of the space inside, but there was a small compartment behind the front seats where Rostov and Hassan could squeeze in. Pyotr Tyrin was at the wheel. Large speakers above their heads were giving out an undertone of distant conversation and the occasional clink of crockery. A moment ago there had been an incomprehensible exchange, with someone apologizing for something and Dickstein saying it was all right, it had been an accident. Nothing distinct had been said since then.

Rostov's pleasure at being able to listen to Dickstein's conversation was marred only by the fact that Hassan was listening too. Hassan had become self-confident since his triumph in discovering that Dickstein was in

England: now he thought he was a professional spy like everyone else. He had insisted on being in on every detail of the London operation, threatening to complain to Cairo if he were excluded. Rostov had considered calling his bluff, but that would have meant another head-on collision with Feliks Vorontsov, and Rostov did not want to go over Feliks's head to Andropov again so soon after the last time. So he had settled on an alternative: he would allow Hassan to come along, and caution him against reporting anything to Cairo.

Hassan, who had been reading the printout, passed it across to Rostov. While the Russian was looking through the sheets, the sound from the speakers changed to street noises for a minute or two, followed by more dialogue.

Where to, guv?

Dickstein's voice: *Lime Street.*

Rostov looked up and spoke to Tyrin. 'That'll be Lloyd's, the address he was given over the phone. Let's go there.'

Tyrin started the van and moved off, heading east toward the City district. Rostov returned to the printout.

Hassan said pessimistically, 'Lloyd's will probably give him a written report.'

Tyrin said, 'The bug is working very well . . . so far.' He was driving with one hand and biting the fingernails of the other.

Rostov found what he was looking for. 'Here it is!' he said. 'The *Coparelli*. Good, good, good!' He thumped his knee in enthusiasm.

Hassan said, 'Show me.'

Rostov hesitated momentarily, realized there was no way he could get out of it, and smiled at Hassan as he pointed to the last page. 'Under NON-NUCLEAR. Two hundred tons of yellowcake to go from Antwerp to Genoa aboard the motor vessel *Coparelli*.'

'That's *it*, then,' said Hassan. 'That's Dickstein's target.'

'But if you report this to Cairo, Dickstein will probably switch to a different target. Hassan—'

Hassan's colour deepened with anger. 'You've said all that once,' he said coldly.

'Okay,' Rostov said. He thought: Damn it, you have to be a diplomat too. He said, 'Now we know what he's going to steal, and who he's going to steal it from. I call that some progress.'

'We don't know when, where, or how,' Hassan said.

Rostov nodded. 'All this business about sister ships must have something to do with it.' He pulled his nose. 'But I don't see how.'

Two and sixpence, please, guv.

Keep the change.

'Find somewhere to park, Tyrin,' said Rostov.

'That's not so easy around here,' Tyrin complained.

'If you can't find a space, just stop. Nobody cares if you get a parking ticket,' Rostov said impatiently.

Good morning. My name's Ed Rodgers.

Ah, yes. Just a moment, please . . .

Your report has just been typed, Mr Rodgers. And here's the bill.

You're very efficient.

Hassan said, 'It *is* a written report.'

Thank you very much.

Goodbye, Mr Rodgers.

'He's not very chatty, is he?' said Tyrin.

Rostov said, 'Good agents never are. You might bear that in mind.'

'Yes, sir.'

Hassan said, 'Damn. Now we won't know the answers to his questions.'

'Makes no difference,' Rostov told him. 'It's just occurred to me.' He smiled. 'We know the questions. All we have to do is ask the same questions ourselves and we get the answers he got. Listen, he's on the street again. Go around the block, Tyrin, let's try to spot him.'

The van moved off, but before it had completed a circuit of the block the street noises faded again.

Can I help you, sir?

'He's gone into a shop,' Hassan said.

Rostov looked at Hassan. When he forgot about his pride, the Arab was as thrilled as a schoolboy about all this – the van, the bugs, the tailing. Maybe he would keep his mouth shut, if only so that he could continue to play spies with the Russians.

I need a new shirt.

'Oh, no!' said Tyrin.

I can see that, sir. What is it?

Coffee.

It should have been sponged right away, sir. It will be very difficult to get the stain out now. Did you want a similar shirt?

Yes. Plain white nylon, button cuffs, collar size fourteen and a half.

Here we are. This one is thirty-two and sixpence.

That's fine.

Tyrin said, 'I'll bet he charges it to expenses.'

Thank you. Would you like to put it on now, perhaps?

Yes, please.

The fitting room is just through here.

Footsteps, then a brief silence.

Would you like a bag for the old one, sir?

Perhaps you'd throw it away for me.

'That button cost two thousand roubles!' Tyrin said.

Certainly, sir.

'That's it,' Hassan said. 'We won't get any more now.'

'Two thousand rubles!' Tyrin said again.

Rostov said, 'I think we got our money's worth.'

'Where are we heading?' Tyrin asked.

'Back to the Embassy,' Rostov told him. 'I want to stretch my legs. I can't feel the left one at all. Damn, but we've done a good morning's work.'

As Tyrin drove west, Hassan said thoughtfully, 'We need to find out where the *Coparelli* is right now.'

'The squirrels can do that,' Rostov said.

'Squirrels?'

'Desk workers in Moscow Centre. They sit on their behinds all day, never doing anything more risky than crossing Granovsky Street in the rush hour, and get paid more than agents in the field.' Rostov decided to use the opportunity to further Hassan's education. 'Remember, an agent should never spend time acquiring information that is public knowledge. Anything in books, reports and files can be found by the squirrels. Since a squirrel is cheaper to run than an agent – not because of salaries but because of support work – the Committee always prefers a squirrel to do a given job of work if he can. Always use the squirrels. Nobody will think you're being lazy.'

Hassan smiled nonchalantly, an echo of his old, languid self. 'Dickstein doesn't work that way.'

'The Israelis have a completely different approach. Besides, I suspect Dickstein isn't a team man.'

'How long will the squirrels take to get us the *Coparelli*'s location?'

'Maybe a day. I'll put in the inquiry as soon as we get to the Embassy.'

Tyrin spoke over his shoulder. 'Can you put through a fast requisition at the same time?'

'What do you need?'

'Six more shirt buttons.'

'Six?'

'If they're like the last lot, five won't work.'

Hassan laughed. 'Is this Communist efficiency?'

'There's nothing wrong with Communist efficiency,' Rostov told him. 'It's Russian efficiency we suffer from.'

The van entered Embassy Row and was waved on by the duty policeman. Hassan asked, 'What do we do when we've located the *Coparelli*?'

'Obviously,' said Rostov, 'we put a man aboard.'

CHAPTER NINE

T HE DON had had a bad day.

It had started at breakfast with the news that some of his people had been busted in the night. The police had stopped and searched a truck containing two thousand five hundred pairs of fur-lined bedroom slippers and five kilos of adulterated heroin. The load, on its way from Canada to New York City, had been hit at Albany. The smack was confiscated and the driver and co-driver jailed.

The stuff did not belong to the don. However, the team that did the run paid dues to him, and in return expected protection. They would want him to get the men out of jail and get the heroin back. It was close to impossible. He might have been able to do it if the bust had involved only the state police; but if only the state police had been involved, the bust would not have happened.

And that was just the start. His eldest son had wired from Harvard for more money, having gambled away the whole of his next semester's allowance weeks before classes started. He had spent the morning finding out why his chain of restaurants was losing money, and the afternoon explaining to his mistress why he could not take her to Europe this year. Finally his doctor told him he had gonorrhoea, again.

He looked in his dressing-room mirror, adjusting his bow tie, and said to himself, 'What a shitty day.'

It had turned out that the New York City police had been behind the bust: they had passed the tip to the state police in order to avoid trouble with the city Mafia. The city police could have ignored the tip, of course: the fact that they did not was a sign that the tip had originated with someone important, perhaps the Drug Enforcement Agency of the Treasury Department. The don had assigned lawyers to the jailed drivers, sent people to visit their families, and opened negotiations to buy back the heroin from the police.

He put on his jacket. He liked to change for dinner; he always had. He did not know what to do about his son Johnny. Why wasn't he home for the summer? College boys were supposed to come home for the summer. The don had thought of sending somebody to see Johnny; but then the boy would think his father was only worried about the money. It looked like he would have to go himself.

The phone rang, and the don picked it up. 'Yes.'

'Gate here, sir. I got an Englishman asking for you, won't give his name.'

'So send him anyway,' said the don, still thinking about Johnny.

'He said to tell you he's a friend from Oxford University.'

'I don't know anybody ... wait a minute. What's he look like?'

'Little guy with glasses, looks like a bum.'

'No kidding!' The don's face broke into a smile. 'Bring him in – and put out the red carpet!'

It had been a year for seeing old friends and observing how they had changed; but Al Cortone's appearance was the most startling yet. The increase in weight which had just begun when he returned from Frankfurt seemed to have continued steadily through the years, and now he weighed at least two hundred and fifty pounds. There was a look of sensuality about his puffy face that had been only hinted at in 1947 and totally absent during the war. And he was completely bald. Dickstein thought this was unusual among Italians.

Dickstein could remember, as clearly as if it were yesterday, the occasion when he had put Cortone under an obligation. In those days he had been learning about the psychology of a cornered animal. When there is no longer any possibility of running away, you realize how fiercely you can fight. Landed in a strange country, separated from his unit, advancing across unknown terrain with his rifle in his hand, Dickstein had drawn on reserves of patience, cunning and ruthlessness he did not know he had. He had lain for half an hour in that thicket, watching the abandoned tank which he *knew* – without understanding how – was the bait in a trap. He had spotted the one sniper and was looking for another when the Americans came roaring up. That made it safe for Dickstein to shoot – if there were another sniper, he would fire at the obvious target, the

Americans, rather than search the bushes for the source of the shot.

So, with no thought for anything but his own survival, Dickstein had saved Al Cortone's life.

Cortone had been even more new to the war than Dickstein, and learning just as fast. They were both streetwise kids applying old principles to new terrain. For a while they fought together, and cursed and laughed and talked about women together. When the island was taken, they had sneaked off during the buildup for the next push and visited Cortone's Sicilian cousins.

Those cousins were the focus of Dickstein's interest now.

They had helped him once before, in 1948. There had been profit for them in that deal, so Dickstein had gone straight to them with the plan. This project was different: he wanted a favour and he could offer no percentage. Consequently he had to go to Al and call in the twenty-four-year-old debt.

He was not at all sure it would work. Cortone was rich now. The house was large – in England it would have been called a mansion – with beautiful grounds inside a high wall and guards at the gate. There were three cars in the gravel drive, and Dickstein had lost count of the servants. A rich and comfortable middle-aged American might not be in a hurry to get involved in Mediterranean political shenanigans, even for the sake of a man who had saved his life.

Cortone seemed very pleased to see him, which was a good start. They slapped each other on the back, just as they had on that November Sunday in 1947, and kept saying, 'How the hell are you?' to each other.

Cortone looked Dickstein up and down. 'You're the same! I lost all my hair and gained a hundred pounds, and you haven't even turned grey. What have you been up to?'

'I went to Israel. I'm sort of a farmer. You?'

'Doing business, you know? Come on, let's eat and talk.'

The meal was a strange affair. Mrs Cortone sat at the foot of the table without speaking or being spoken to throughout. Two ill-mannered boys wolfed their food and left early with a roar of sports-car exhaust. Cortone ate large quantities of the heavy Italian food and drank several glasses of California red wine. But the most intriguing character was a well-dressed, shark-faced man who behaved sometimes like a friend, sometimes like an adviser and sometimes like a servant: once Cortone called him a counsellor. No business was talked about during dinner. Instead they told war stories – Cortone told most of them. He also told the story of Dickstein's 1948 coup against the Arabs: he had heard it from his cousins and had been as delighted as they. The tale had become embroidered in the retelling.

Dickstein decided that Cortone was genuinely glad to see him. Maybe the man was bored. He should be, if he ate dinner every night with a silent wife, two surly boys and a shark-faced counsellor. Dickstein did all he could to keep the bonhomie going: he wanted Cortone in a good mood when he asked his favour.

Afterwards Cortone and Dickstein sat in leather

armchairs in a den and a butler brought brandy and cigars. Dickstein refused both.

'You used to be a hell of a drinker,' Cortone said.

'It was a hell of a war,' Dickstein replied. The butler left the room. Dickstein watched Cortone sip brandy and pull on the cigar, and thought that the man ate, drank and smoked joylessly, as though he thought that if he did these things long enough he would eventually acquire the taste. Recalling the sheer fun the two of them had had with the Sicilian cousins, Dickstein wondered whether there were any real people left in Cortone's life.

Suddenly Cortone laughed out loud. 'I remember every minute of that day in Oxford. Hey, did you ever make it with that professor's wife, the Ay-rab?'

'No.' Dickstein barely smiled. 'She's dead, now.'

'I'm sorry.'

'A strange thing happened. I went back there, to that house by the river, and met her daughter . . . She looks just like Eila used to.'

'No kidding. And . . .' Cortone leered. 'And you made it with the daughter – I don't believe it!'

Dickstein nodded. 'We made it in more ways than one. I want to marry her. I plan to ask her next time I see her.'

'Will she say yes?'

'I'm not sure. I think so. I'm older than she is.'

'Age doesn't matter. You could put on a little weight, though. A woman likes to have something to get hold of.'

The conversation was annoying Dickstein, and now

he realized why: Cortone was set on keeping it trivial. It might have been the habit of years of being close-mouthed; it might have been that so much of his 'family business' was criminal business and he did not want Dickstein to know it (but Dickstein had already guessed); or there might have been something else he was afraid of revealing, some secret disappointment he could not share: anyhow, the open, garrulous, excitable young man had long since disappeared inside this fat man. Dickstein longed to say, Tell me what gives you joy, and who you love, and how your life runs on.

Instead he said, 'Do you remember what you said to me in Oxford?'

'Sure. I told you I owe you a debt, you saved my life.' Cortone inhaled on his cigar.

At least that had not changed. 'I'm here to ask for your help.'

'Go ahead and ask.'

'Mind if I put the radio on?'

Cortone smiled. 'This place is swept for bugs about once a week.'

'Good,' said Dickstein, but he put the radio on all the same. 'Cards on the table, Al. I work for Israeli Intelligence.'

Cortone's eyes widened. 'I should have guessed.'

'I'm running an operation in the Mediterranean in November. It's . . .' Dickstein wondered how much he needed to tell, and decided very little. 'It's something that could mean the end of the wars in the Middle

East.' He paused, remembering a phrase Cortone had used habitually. 'And I ain't shittin' you.'

Cortone laughed. 'If you were going to shit me, I figure you would have been here sooner than twenty years.'

'It's important that the operation should not be traceable back to Israel. I need a base from which to work. I need a big house on the coast with a landing for small boats and an anchorage not too far offshore for a big ship. While I'm there – a couple of weeks, maybe more – I need to be protected from inquiring police and other nosy officials. I can think of only one place where I could get all that, and only one person who could get it for me.'

Cortone nodded. 'I know a place – a derelict house in Sicily. It's not exactly plush, kid ... no heat, no phone – but it could fill the bill.'

Dickstein smiled broadly. 'That's terrific,' he said. 'That's what I came to ask for.'

'You're kidding,' said Cortone. 'That's *all*?'

To: Head of Mossad
From: Head of London Station
Date: 29 July 1968

Suza Ashford is almost certainly an agent of an Arab intelligence service.

She was born in Oxford, England, 17 June 1944, the only child of Mr (now Professor) Stephen Ashford (born Guildford, England, 1908) and Eila

Zuabi (born Tripoli, Lebanon, 1925). The mother, who died in 1954, was a full-blooded Arab. The father is what is known in England as an 'Arabist'; he spent most of the first forty years of his life in the Middle East and was an explorer, entrepreneur and linguist. He now teaches Semitic Languages at Oxford University, where he is well known for his moderately pro-Arab views.

Therefore, although Suza Ashford is strictly speaking a U.K. national, her loyalties may be assumed to lie with the Arab cause.

She works as an air hostess for BOAC on intercontinental routes, travelling frequently to Tehran, Singapore and Zurich, among other places. Consequently, she has numerous opportunities to make clandestine contacts with Arab diplomatic staff.

She is a strikingly beautiful young woman (see attached photograph – which, however, does not do her justice, according to the field agent on this case). She is promiscuous, but not unusually so by the standards of her profession nor by those of her generation in London. To be specific: for her to have sexual relations with a man for the purpose of obtaining information might be an unpleasant experience but not a traumatic one.

Finally – and this is the clincher – Yasif Hassan, the agent who spotted Dickstein in Luxembourg, studied under her father, Professor Ashford, at the same time as Dickstein, and has remained in occasional contact with Ashford in the intervening years. He may have visited Ashford – a man answering his description certainly *did* visit – about the time Dickstein's affair with Suza Ashford began.

I recommend that surveillance be continued.

(Signed)
Robert Jakes

To: Head of London Station
From: Head of Mossad
Date: 30 July 1968

With all that against her, I cannot understand why you do not recommend we kill her.

(Signed)
Pierre Borg

To: Head of Mossad
From: Head of London Station
Date: 31 July 1968

I do not recommend eliminating Suza Ashford for the following reasons:

1. The evidence against her is strong but circumstantial.

2. From what I know of Dickstein, I doubt very much that he has given her any information, even if he is romantically involved.

3. If we eliminate her the other side will begin looking for another way to get at Dickstein. Better the devil we know.

4. We may be able to use her to feed false information to the other side.

5. I do not like to kill on the basis of circumstantial evidence. We are not barbarians. We are Jews.

6. If we kill a woman Dickstein loves, I think he will kill you, me and everyone else involved.

(Signed)
Robert Jakes

To: Head of London Station
From: Head of Mossad
Date: 1 August 1968
Do it your way.

(Signed)
Pierre Borg

POSTSCRIPT (marked Personal):

Your point 5 is very noble and touching, but remarks like that won't get you promoted in this man's army. – P.B.

She was a small, old, ugly, dirty, cantankerous bitch.

Rust bloomed like a skin rash in great orange blotches all over her hull. If there had ever been any paint on her upperworks it had long ago been peeled away and blasted off and dissolved by the wind and the rain and the sea. Her starboard gunwale had been badly buckled just aft of the prow in an old collision, and nobody had ever bothered to straighten it out. Her funnel bore a layer of grime ten years thick. Her deck was scored and dented and stained; and although it was swabbed often, it was never swabbed thoroughly, so that there were traces of past cargoes – grains of corn, splinters of timber, bits of rotting vegetation and fragments of sacking – hidden behind lifeboats and under coils of rope and inside cracks and joints and holes. On a warm day she smelled foul.

She was some 2,500 tons, 200 feet long and a little over 30 feet broad. There was a tall radio mast in her blunt prow. Most of her deck was taken up by two large hatches opening into the main cargo holds. There were three cranes on deck: one forward of the hatches, one aft and one in between. The wheelhouse, officers' cabins, galley and crew's quarters were in the stern, clustered around the funnel. She had a single screw driven by a six-cylinder diesel engine theoretically capable of developing 2,450 b.h.p. and maintaining a service speed of thirteen knots.

Fully loaded, she would pitch badly. In ballast she would yaw like the very devil. Either way she would troll through seventy degrees of arc at the slightest provocation. The quarters were cramped and poorly ventilated, the galley was often flooded and the engine room had been designed by Hieronymus Bosch.

She was crewed by thirty-one officers and men, not one of whom had a good word to say for her.

The only passengers were a colony of cockroaches in the galley, a few mice and several hundred rats.

Nobody loved her, and her name was *Coparelli*.

CHAPTER TEN

NAT DICKENSTEIN went to New York to become a shipping tycoon. It took him all morning.

He looked in the Manhattan phone book and selected a lawyer with an address on the lower East Side. Instead of calling on the phone he went there personally, and was satisfied when he saw that the lawyer's office was one room over a Chinese restaurant. The lawyer's name was Mr Chung.

Dickstein and Chung took a cab to the Park Avenue offices of Liberian Corporation Services Inc., a company set up to assist people who wanted to register a Liberian corporation but had no intention of ever going within three thousand miles of Liberia. Dickstein was not asked for references, and he did not have to establish that he was honest or solvent or sane. For a fee of five hundred dollars – which Dickstein paid in cash – they registered the Savile Shipping Corporation of Liberia. The fact that at this stage Dickstein did not own so much as a rowboat was of no interest to anyone.

The company's headquarters was listed as No. 80 Broad Street, Monrovia, Liberia; and its directors were P. Satia, E.K. Nugba and J.D. Boyd, all residents of

Liberia. This was also the headquarters address of most Liberian corporations, and the address of the Liberian Trust Company. Satia, Nugba and Boyd were founding directors of many such corporations; indeed this was the way they made their living. They were also employees of the Liberian Trust Company.

Mr Chung asked for fifty dollars and cab fare. Dickstein paid him in cash and told him to take the bus.

So, without so much as giving an address, Dickstein had created a fully legitimate shipping company which could not be traced back either to him or to the Mossad.

Satia, Nugba and Boyd resigned twenty-four hours later, as was the custom; and that same day the notary public of Montserrado County, Liberia, stamped an affidavit which said that total control of the Savile Shipping Corporation now lay in the hands of one Andre Papagopolous.

By that time Dickstein was riding the bus from Zurich airport into town, on his way to meet Papagopolous for lunch.

When he had time to reflect on it, even he was shaken by the complexity of his plan, the number of pieces that had to be made to fit into the jigsaw puzzle, the number of people who had to be persuaded, bribed or coerced into performing their parts. He had been successful so far, first with Stiffcollar and then with Al Cortone, not to mention Lloyd's of London and Liberian Corporation Services, Inc., but how long could it go on?

Papagopolous was in some ways the greatest challenge: a man as elusive, as powerful, and as free of weakness as Dickstein himself.

He had been born in 1912 in a village that during his boyhood was variously Turkish, Bulgarian and Greek. His father was a fisherman. In his teenage he graduated from fishing to other kinds of maritime work, mostly smuggling. After World War Two he turned up in Ethiopia, buying for knock-down prices the piles of surplus military supplies which had suddenly become worthless when the war ended. He bought rifles, handguns, machine guns, anti-tank guns, and ammunition for all of these. He then contacted the Jewish Agency in Cairo and sold the arms at an enormous profit to the underground Israeli Army. He arranged shipping – and here his smuggling background was invaluable – and delivered the goods to Palestine. Then he asked if they wanted more.

This was how he had met Nat Dickstein.

He soon moved on, to Farouk's Cairo and then to Switzerland. His Israeli deals had marked a transition from totally illegal business to dealings which were at worst shady and at best pristine. Now he called himself a ship broker and that was most, though by no means all, of his business.

He had no address. He could be reached via half a dozen telephone numbers all over the world, but he was never *there* – always, somebody took a message and Papagopolous called you back. Many people knew him and trusted him, especially in the shipping business, for he never let anyone down; but this trust was based on reputation, not personal contact. He lived well but quietly, and Nat Dickstein was one of the few people in the world who knew of his single vice, which was that he liked to go to bed with lots of girls – but *lots*: like, ten or twelve. He had no sense of humour.

Dickstein got off the bus at the railway station, where Papagopolous was waiting for him on the pavement. He was a big man, olive-skinned with thin dark hair combed over a growing bald patch. On a bright summer day in Zurich he wore a navy-blue suit, pale blue shirt and dark blue striped tie. He had small dark eyes.

They shook hands. Dickstein said, 'How's business?'

'Up and down.' Papagopolous smiled. 'Mostly up.'

They walked through the clean, tidy streets, looking like a managing director and his accountant. Dickstein inhaled the cold air. 'I like this town,' he said.

'I've booked a table at the Veltliner Keller in the old city,' Papagopolous said. 'I know you don't care about food, but I do.'

Dickstein said, 'You've been to the Pelikanstrasse?'

'Yes.'

'Good.' The Zurich office of Liberian Corporation Services, Inc., was in the Pelikanstrasse. Dickstein had asked Papagopolous to go there to register himself as president and chief executive of Savile Shipping. For this he would receive ten thousand U.S. dollars, paid out of Mossad's account in a Swiss bank to Papagopolous's account in the same branch of the same bank – a transaction very difficult for anyone to uncover.

Papagopolous said, 'But I didn't promise to do anything else. You may have wasted your money.'

'I'm sure I didn't.'

They reached the restaurant. Dickstein had expected that Papagopolous would be known there, but there was no sign of recognition from the head waiter, and Dickstein thought: Of course, he's not known anywhere.

They ordered food and wine. Dickstein noted with regret that the domestic Swiss white wine was still better than the Israeli.

While they ate, Dickstein explained Papagopolous's duties as president of Savile Shipping.

'One: buy a small, fast ship, a thousand or fifteen hundred tons, small crew. Register her in Liberia.' This would involve another visit to the Pelikanstrasse and a fee of about a dollar per ton. 'For the purchase, take your percentage as a broker. Do some business with the ship, and take your broker's percentage on that. I don't care what the ship does so long as she completes a voyage by docking in Haifa on or before October 7. Dismiss the crew at Haifa. Do you want to take notes?'

Papagopolous smiled. 'I think not.'

The implication was not lost on Dickstein. Papagopolous was listening, but he had not yet agreed to do the job. Dickstein continued. 'Two: buy any one of the ships on this list.' He handed over a single sheet of paper bearing the names of the four sister ships of the *Coparelli*, with their owners and last known locations – the information he had got from Lloyd's. 'Offer whatever price is necessary: I must have one of them. Take your broker's percentage. Deliver her to Haifa by October 7. Dismiss the crew.'

Papagopolous was eating chocolate mousse, his smooth face imperturbable. He put down his spoon and put on gold-rimmed glasses to read the list. He folded the sheet of paper in half and set it on the table without comment.

Dickstein handed him another sheet of paper. 'Three: buy this ship – the *Coparelli*. But you must buy her at exactly the right time. She sails from Antwerp on Sunday, November 17. We must buy her *after* she sails but *before* she passes through the Strait of Gibraltar.'

Papapopolous looked dubious. 'Well . . .'

'Wait, let me give you the rest of it. Four: early in 1969 you sell ship No. 1, the little one, and ship No. 3, the *Coparelli*. You get from me a certificate showing that ship No. 2 has been sold for scrap. You send that certificate to Lloyd's. You wind up Savile Shipping.' Dickstein smiled and sipped his coffee.

'What you want to do is make a ship disappear without a trace.'

Dickstein nodded. Papagopolous was as sharp as a knife.

'As you must realize,' Papagopolous went on, 'all this is straightforward except for the purchase of the *Coparelli* while she is at sea. The normal procedure for the sale of a ship is as follows: negotiations take place, a price is agreed, and the documents are drawn up. The ship goes into dry dock for inspection. When she has been pronounced satisfactory the documents are signed, the money is paid and the new owner takes her out of dry dock. Buying a ship while she is sailing is most irregular.'

'But not impossible.'

'No, not impossible.'

Dickstein watched him. He became thoughtful, his gaze distant: he was grappling with the problem. It was a good sign.

Papagopolous said, 'We would have to open negotiations, agree on the price and have the inspection arranged for a date after her November voyage. Then, when she has sailed, we say that the purchaser needs to spend the money immediately, perhaps for tax reasons. The buyer would then take out insurance against any major repairs which might prove necessary after the inspection, but this is not the seller's concern. He is concerned about his reputation as a shipper. He will want cast-iron guarantees that his cargo will be delivered by the new owner of the *Coparelli.*'

'Would he accept a guarantee based on your personal reputation?'

'Of course. But why would I give such a guarantee?'

Dickstein looked him in the eye. 'I can promise you that the owner of the cargo will not complain.'

Papagopolous made an open-handed gesture. 'It is obvious that you are perpetrating some kind of a swindle here. You need me as a respectable front. That I can do. But you also want me to lay my reputation on the line and take your word that it will not suffer?'

'Yes. Listen. Let me ask you one thing. You trusted the Israelis once before, remember?'

'Of course.'

'Did you ever regret it?'

Papagopolous smiled, remembering the old days. 'It was the best decision I ever made.'

'So, will you trust us again?' Dickstein held his breath.

'I had less to lose in those days. I was . . . thirty-five. We used to have a lot of fun. This is the most intriguing offer I've had in twenty years. What the hell, I'll do it.'

Dickstein extended his hand across the restaurant table. Papagopolous shook it.

A waitress brought a little bowl of Swiss chocolates for them to eat with their coffee. Papagopolous took one, Dickstein refused.

'Details,' Dickstein said. 'Open an account for Savile Shipping at your bank here. The Embassy will put funds in as they are required. You report to me simply by leaving a written message at the bank. The note will be picked up by someone from the Embassy. If we need to meet and talk, we use the usual phone numbers.'

'Agreed.'

'I'm glad we're doing business together again.'

Papagopolous was thoughtful. 'Ship No. 2 is a sister ship of the *Coparelli*,' he mused. 'I think I can guess what you're up to. There's one thing I'd like to know, although I'm sure you won't tell me. What the hell kind of cargo will the *Coparelli* be carrying – uranium?'

Pyotr Tyrin looked gloomily at the *Coparelli* and said, 'She's a grubby old ship.'

Rostov did not reply. They were sitting in a rented

Ford on a quay at Cardiff docks. The squirrels at Moscow Centre had informed them that the *Coparelli* would make port there today, and they were now watching her tie up. She was to unload a cargo of Swedish timber and take on a mixture of small machinery and cotton goods: it would take her some days.

'At least the mess decks aren't in the foc'sle,' Tyrin muttered, more or less to himself.

'She's not *that* old,' Rostov said.

Tyrin was surprised Rostov knew what he was talking about. Rostov continually surprised him with odd bits of knowledge.

From the rear seat of the car Nik Bunin said, 'Is that the front or the back of the boat?'

Rostov and Tyrin looked at one another and grinned at Nik's ignorance. 'The back,' Tyrin said. 'We call it the stern.'

It was raining. The Welsh rain was even more persistent and monotonous than the English, and colder. Pyotr Tyrin was unhappy. It so happened that he had done two years in the Soviet Navy. That, plus the fact that he was the radio and electronics expert, made him the obvious choice as the man to be planted aboard the *Coparelli*. He did not want to go back to sea. In truth, the main reason he had applied to join the KGB was to get out of the navy. He hated the damp and the cold and the food and the discipline. Besides, he had a warm, comfortable wife in an apartment in Moscow, and he missed her.

Of course, there was no question of his saying no to Rostov.

'We'll get you on as radio operator, but you must take your own equipment as a fallback,' Rostov said.

Tyrin wondered how this was to be managed. His approach would have been to find the ship's radio man, knock him on the head, throw him in the water, and board the ship to say, 'I hear you need a new radio operator.' No doubt Rostov would be able to come up with something a little more subtle: that was why he was a colonel.

The activity on deck had died down, and the *Coparelli*'s engines were quiet. Five or six sailors came across the gangplank in a bunch, laughing and shouting, and headed for the town. Rostov said, 'See which pub they go to, Nik.' Bunin got out of the car and followed the sailors.

Tyrin watched him go. He was depressed by the scene: the figures crossing the wet concrete quay with their raincoat collars turned up; the sounds of tugs hooting and men shouting nautical instructions and chains winding and unwinding; the stacks of pallets; the bare cranes like sentries; the smell of engine oil and the ship's ropes and salt spray. It all made him think of the Moscow flat, the chair in front of the paraffin heater, salt fish and black bread, beer and vodka in the refrigerator, and an evening of television.

He was unable to share Rostov's irrepressible cheerfulness about the way the operation was going. Once again they had no idea where Dickstein was – even though they had not exactly lost him, they had deliberately let him go. It had been Rostov's decision: he was afraid of getting too close to Dickstein, of scaring the man off. 'We'll follow the *Coparelli*, and Dickstein will come to us,' Rostov had said. Yasif Hassan had argued with him, but Rostov had won. Tyrin, who had no contribution to make to such strategic discussions, thought Rostov was correct, but also thought he had no reason to be so confident.

'Your first job is to befriend the crew,' Rostov said. interrupting Tyrin's thoughts. 'You're a radio operator. You suffered a minor accident aboard your last ship, the *Christmas Rose* – you broke your arm – and you were discharged here in Cardiff to convalesce. You got an excellent compensation payment from the owners. You are spending the money and having a good time while it lasts. You say vaguely that you'll look for another job when your money runs out. You must discover two things: the identity of the radio man, and the anticipated date and time of departure of the ship.'

'Fine,' said Tyrin, though it was far from fine. Just *how* was he to 'befriend' these people? He was not much of an actor, in his view. Would he have to play the part of a hearty hail-fellow-well-met? Suppose the crew of this ship thought him a bore, a lonely man trying to attach himself to a jolly group? What if they just plain did not like him?

Unconsciously he squared his broad shoulders. Either he would do it, or there would be some reason why it could not be done. All he could promise was to try his best.

Bunin came back across the quay. Rostov said, 'Get in the back, let Nik drive.' Tyrin got out and held the door for Nik. The young man's face was streaming with rain. He started the car. Tyrin got in.

As the car pulled away Rostov turned around to speak to Tyrin in the back seat. 'Here's a hundred pounds,' he said, and handed over a roll of banknotes. 'Don't spend it too carefully.'

Bunin stopped the car opposite a small dockland pub on a corner. A sign outside, flapping gently in the wind, read, 'Brains Beers'. A smoky yellow light glowed behind the frosted-glass windows. There were worse places to be on a day like this, Tyrin thought.

'What nationality are the crew?' he said suddenly.

'Swedish,' Bunin said.

Tyrin's false papers made him out to be Austrian. 'What language should I use with them?'

'All Swedes speak English,' Rostov told him. There was a moment of silence. Rostov said, 'Any more questions? I want to go back to Hassan before he gets up to any mischief.'

'No more questions.' Tyrin opened the car door.

Rostov said, 'Speak to me when you get back to the hotel tonight – no matter how late.'

'Sure.'

'Good luck.'

Tyrin slammed the car door and crossed the road to the pub. As he reached the entrance someone came out, and the warm smell of beer and tobacco engulfed Tyrin for a moment. He went inside.

It was a poky little place, with hard wooden benches around the walls and plastic tables nailed to the floor.

Four of the sailors were playing darts in the corner and a fifth was at the bar calling out encouragement to them.

The barman nodded to Tyrin. 'Good morning,' Tyrin said. 'A pint of lager, a large whisky and a ham sandwich.'

The sailor at the bar turned around and nodded pleasantly. Tyrin smiled. 'Have you just made port?'

'Yes. The *Coparelli*,' the sailor replied.

'*Christmas Rose*,' Tyrin said. 'She left me behind.'

'You're lucky.'

'I broke my arm.'

'So?' said the Swedish sailor with a grin. 'You can drink with the other one.'

'I like that,' Tyrin said. 'Let me buy you a drink. What will it be?'

Two days later they were still drinking. There were changes in the composition of the group as some sailors went on duty and others came ashore; and there was a short period between four A.M. and opening time when there was nowhere in the city, legal or illegal, where one could buy a drink; but otherwise life was one long pub crawl. Tyrin had forgotten how sailors could drink. He was dreading the hangover. He was glad, however, that he had not got into a situation where he felt obliged to go with prostitutes: the Swedes were interested in women, but not in whores. Tyrin would never have been able to convince his wife that he had caught venereal disease in the service of Mother Russia. The Swedes' other vice was gambling. Tyrin had lost about fifty pounds of KGB money at poker. He was so well in with the crew of the *Coparelli* that the previous night he had been invited aboard at two A.M. He had fallen asleep on the mess deck and they had left him there until eight bells.

Tonight would not be like that. The *Coparelli* was to sail on the morning tide, and all officers and men had to be aboard by midnight. It was now ten past eleven. The landlord of the pub was moving about the room collecting glasses and emptying ashtrays. Tyrin was playing dominoes with Lars, the radio operator. They had abandoned the proper game and were now competing to see who could stand the most blocks in a line without knocking the lot down. Lars was very drunk, but Tyrin was pretending. He was also very frightened about what he had to do in a few minutes' time.

The landlord called out, 'Time, gentlemen, please! Thank you very much.'

Tyrin knocked his dominoes down, and laughed. Lars said, 'You see – I am smaller alcoholic than you.'

The other crew were leaving. Tyrin and Lars stood up. Tyrin put his arm around Lars' shoulders and together they staggered out into the street.

The night air was cool and damp. Tyrin shivered. From now on he had to stay very close to Lars. I hope Nik gets his timing right, he thought. I hope the car doesn't break down. And then: I hope to Christ Lars doesn't get killed.

He began talking, asking questions about Lars' home and family. He kept the two of them a few yards behind the main group of sailors.

They passed a blonde woman in a microskirt. She touched her left breast. 'Hello, boys, fancy a cuddle?'

Not tonight, sweetheart, Tyrin thought, and kept walking. He must not let Lars stop and chat. Timing, it was the timing. Nik, where are you?

There. They approached a dark blue Ford Capri 2000 parked at the roadside with its lights out. As the interior light flashed on and off Tyrin glimpsed the face of the man at the wheel: it was Nik Bunin. Tyrin took a flat white cap from his pocket and put it on, the signal that Bunin was to go ahead. When the sailors had passed on the car started up and moved away in the opposite direction.

Not long now.

Lars said, 'I have a fiancée.'

Oh, no, don't start that.

Lars giggled. 'She has . . . hot pants.'

'Are you going to marry her?' Tyrin was peering ahead intently, listening, talking only to keep Lars close.

Lars leered. 'What for?'

'Is she faithful?'

'Better be or I slit her throat.'

'I thought Swedish people believed in free love.' Tyrin was saying anything that came into his head.

'Free love, yes. But she better be faithful.'

'I see.'

'I can explain . . .'

Come on, Nik. Get it over with . . .

One of the sailors in the group stopped to urinate in the gutter. The others stood around making ribald remarks and laughing. Tyrin wished the man would hurry up – the timing, the timing – but he seemed as if he would go on for ever.

At last he finished, and they all walked on.

Tyrin heard a car.

He tensed. Lars said, 'What's matter?'

'Nothing.' Tyrin saw the headlights. The car was moving steadily toward them in the middle of the road. The sailors moved on to the pavement to get out of its way. It wasn't right, it shouldn't be like this, it wouldn't work this way! Suddenly Tyrin was confused and panic-stricken – then he saw the outline of the car more clearly as it passed beneath a street light, and he realized it was not the one he was waiting for, it was a patrolling police car. It went harmlessly by.

The end of the street opened into a wide, empty square, badly paved. There was no traffic about. The sailors headed straight across the middle of the square.

Now.

Come on.

They were halfway across.

Come *on*!

A car came tearing around a corner and into the square, headlights blazing. Tyrin tightened his grip on Lars' shoulder. The car was veering wildly.

'Drunk driver,' Lars said thickly.

It was a Ford Capri. It swung toward the bunch of sailors in front. They stopped laughing and scattered out of its way, shouting curses. The car turned away, then screeched around and accelerated straight for Tyrin and Lars.

'Look out!' Tyrin yelled.

When the car was almost on top of them he pulled Lars to one side, jerking the man off balance, and threw himself sideways. There was a stomach-turning thud, followed by a scream and crash of breaking glass. The car went by.

It's done, Tyrin thought.

He scrambled to his feet and looked for Lars.

The sailor lay on the road a few feet away. Blood glistened in the lamplight.

Lars groaned.

He's alive, Tyrin thought; thank God.

The car braked. One of its headlights had gone out – the one that had hit Lars, he presumed. It coasted, as if the driver were hesitating. Then it gathered speed and, one-eyed, it disappeared into the night.

Tyrin bent over Lars. The other sailors gathered around, speaking Swedish. Tyrin touched Lars' leg. He yelled out in pain.

'I think his leg is broken,' Tyrin said. *Thank God that's all.*

Lights were going on in some of the buildings around the square. One of the officers said something, and a rating ran off toward a house presumably to call for an ambulance. There was more rapid dialogue and another went off in the direction of the dock.

Lars was bleeding, but not too heavily. The officer bent over him. He would not allow anyone to touch his leg.

The ambulance arrived within minutes, but it seemed forever to Tyrin: he had never killed a man, and he did not want to.

They put Lars on a stretcher. The officer got into the ambulance, and turned to speak to Tyrin. 'You had better come.'

'Yes.'

'You saved his life, I think.'

'Oh.'

He got into the ambulance with the officer.

They sped through the wet streets. the flashing blue light on the roof casting an unpleasant glow over the buildings. Tyrin sat in the back, unable to look at Lars or the officer, unwilling to look out of the windows like a tourist, not knowing where to direct his eyes. He had done many unkind things in the service of his country and Colonel Rostov – he had taped the conversations of lovers for blackmail, he had shown terrorists how to make bombs, he had helped capture people who would later be tortured – but he had never been forced to ride in the ambulance with his victim. He did not like it.

They arrived at the hospital. The ambulance men carried the stretcher inside. Tyrin and the officer were shown where to wait. And, suddenly, the rush was over. They had nothing to do but worry. Tyrin was astonished to look at the plain electric clock on the hospital wall and see that it was not yet midnight. It seemed hours since they had left the pub.

After a long wait a doctor came out. 'He's broken his leg and lost some blood,' he said. He seemed very tired. 'He's got a lot of alcohol in him, which doesn't help. But he's young, strong and healthy. His leg will mend and he should be fit again in a few weeks.'

Relief flooded Tyrin. He realized he was shaking.

The officer said, 'Our ship sails in the morning.'

'He won't be on it,' the doctor said. 'Is your captain on his way here?'

'I sent for him.'

'Fine.' The doctor turned and left.

The captain arrived at the same time as the police. He spoke to the officer in Swedish while a young sergeant took down Tyrin's vague description of the car.

Afterwards the captain approached Tyrin. 'I believe you saved Lars from a much worse accident.'

Tyrin wished people would stop saying that. 'I tried to pull him out of the way, but he fell. He was very drunk.'

'Horst here says you are between ships.'

'Yes, sir.'

'You are a fully qualified radio operator?'

'Yes, sir.'

'I need a replacement for poor Lars. Would you like to sail with us in the morning?'

Pierre Borg said, 'I'm pulling you out.'

Dickstein whitened. He stared at his boss.

Borg said, 'I want you to come back to Tel Aviv and run the operation from the office.'

Dickstein said, 'You go and fuck yourself.'

They stood beside the lake at Zurich. It was crowded with boats, their multicoloured sails flapping prettily in the Swiss sunshine. Borg said, 'No arguments, Nat.'

'No arguments, *Pierre*. I won't be pulled out. Finish.'

'I'm ordering you.'

'And I'm telling you to fuck yourself.'

'Look.' Borg took a deep breath. 'Your plan is complete. The only flaw in it is that you've been compromised: the opposition knows you're working, and they're trying to find you and screw up whatever it is you're doing. You can still run the project – all you have to do is hide your face.'

'No,' Dickstein said. 'This isn't the kind of project where you can sit in an office and push all the buttons to make it go. It's too complex, there are too many variables. I have to be in the field myself to make instant decisions.' Dickstein stopped himself talking and began to think: *Why* do I want to do it myself? Am I really the only man in Israel who can pull this off? Is it just that I want the glory?

Borg voiced his thoughts. 'Don't try to be a hero, Nat. You're too smart for that. You're a professional: you follow orders.'

Dickstein shook his head. 'You should know better than to take that line with me. Remember how Jews feel about people who always follow orders?'

'All right, so you were in a concentration camp – that doesn't give you the right to do whatever the hell you like for the rest of your life!'

Dickstein made a deprecatory gesture. 'You can stop me. You can withdraw support. But you also won't get your uranium, because I'm not going to tell anyone else how it can be done.'

Borg stared at him. 'You bastard, you mean it.'

Dickstein watched Borg's expression. He had once had the embarrassing experience of seeing Borg have a row with his teenage son Dan. The boy had stood there, sullenly confident, while Borg tried to explain that going on peace marches was disloyal to father, mother, country and God, until Borg had strangled himself with his own inarticulate rage. Dan, like Dickstein, had learned how to refuse to be bullied, and Borg would never quite know how to handle people who could not be bullied.

The script now called for Borg to go red in the face and begin to yell. Suddenly Dickstein realized that this was not going to happen. Borg was remaining calm.

Borg smiled slyly and said, 'I believe you're fucking one of the other side's agents.'

Dickstein stopped breathing. He felt as if he had been hit from behind with a sledgehammer. This was the last thing he had been expecting. He was filled with irrational guilt, like a boy caught masturbating: shame, embarrassment, and the sense of something spoiled. Suza was private, in a compartment separate from the rest of his life, and now Borg was dragging her out and holding her up to public view: Just *look* at what Nat was doing!

'No,' Dickstein said tonelessly.

'I'll give you the headlines,' Borg said. 'She's Arab, her father's politics are pro-Arab, she travels all over the world in her cover job to have opportunity for contacts, and the agent Yasif Hassan, who spotted you in Luxembourg, is a friend of the family.'

Dickstein turned to face Borg, standing too close, gazing fiercely into Borg's eyes, his guilt turning to resentment. 'That's all?'

'All? What the fuck do you mean, *all*? You'd shoot people on that much evidence!'

'Not people I know.'

'Has she got any information out of you?'

Dickstein shouted, 'No!'

'You're getting angry because you know you've made a mistake.'

Dickstein turned away and looked across the lake, struggling to make himself calm: rage was Borg's act, not his. After a long pause he said, 'Yes, I'm angry because I've made a mistake. I should have told you about her; not the other way around. I understand how it must seem to you—'

'Seem? You mean you don't believe she's an agent?'

'Have you checked through Cairo?'

Borg gave a false little laugh. 'You talk as if Cairo was my intelligence service. I can't just call and ask them to look her up in their files while I hold the line.'

'But you've got a very good double agent in Egyptian Intelligence.'

'How can he be good? Everybody seems to know about him.'

'Stop playing games. Since the Six-Day War even the newspapers say you have good doubles in Egypt. The point is, you haven't checked her.'

Borg held up both hands, palms outward, in a

gesture of appeasement. 'Okay, I'm going to check her with Cairo. It will take a little time. Meanwhile, you're going to write a report giving all details of your scheme and I'm going to put other agents on the job.'

Dickstein thought of Al Cortone and Andre Papagopolous: neither of them would do what he had agreed to do for anyone other than Dickstein. 'It won't work, Pierre,' he said quietly. 'You've got to have the uranium, and I'm the only one who can get it for you.'

'And if Cairo confirms her to be an agent?'

'I'm confident the answer will be negative.'

'But if it's not?'

'You'll kill her, I suppose.'

'Oh, no.' Borg pointed a finger at Dickstein's nose, and when he spoke there was real, deep-down malice in his voice. 'Oh, no, I won't, Dickstein. If she's an agent, *you* will kill her.'

With deliberate slowness, Dickstein took hold of Borg's wrist and removed the pointing finger from in front of his face. There was only the faintest perceptible tremor in his voice as he said, 'Yes, Pierre. I will kill her.'

CHAPTER ELEVEN

IN THE bar at Heathrow Airport David Rostov ordered another round of drinks and decided to take a gamble on Yasif Hassan. The problem, still, was how to stop Hassan telling all he knew to an Israeli double agent in Cairo. Rostov and Hassan were both going back for interim debriefing so a decision had to be made now. Rostov was going to let Hassan know everything, then appeal to his professionalism – such as it was. The alternative was to provoke him, and just now he needed him as an ally, not a suspicious antagonist.

'Look at this,' Rostov said, and he showed Hassan a decoded message.

To: Colonel David Rostov *via* London Residency
From: Moscow Centre
Date: 3 September 1968

Comrade Colonel:
    We refer to your signal g/35–21a, requesting further information concerning each of four ships named in our signal r/35–21.
    The motor vessel *Stromberg*, 2500 tons, Dutch

ownership and registration, has recently changed hands. She was purchased for DM 1,500,000 by one Andre Papagopolous, a ship broker, on behalf of the Savile Shipping Corporation of Liberia.

Savile Shipping was incorporated on 6 August this year at the New York office of Liberian Corporation Services Inc., with a share capital of five hundred dollars. The shareholders are Mr Lee Chung, a New York lawyer, and a Mr Robert Roberts, whose address is care of Mr Chung's office. The three directors were provided in the usual way by Liberian Corporation Services, and they resigned the day after the company was set up, again in the usual way. The aforementioned Papagopolous took over as president and chief executive.

Savile Shipping has also bought the motor vessel *Gil Hamilton*, 1500 tons, for £80,000.

Our people in New York have interviewed Chung. He says that 'Mr Roberts' came into his office from the street, gave no address and paid his fee in cash. He appeared to be an Englishman. The detailed description is on file here, but it is not very helpful.

Papagopolous is known to us. He is a wealthy international businessman of indeterminate nationality. Shipbroking is his principal activity. He is believed to operate close to the fringes of the law. We have no address for him. There is considerable material in his file, but much of it is speculative. He is believed to have done business with Israeli

Intelligence in 1948. Nevertheless, he has no known
political affiliation.

We continue to gather information on all the
ships in the list.

– Moscow Centre.

Hassan gave the sheet of paper back to Rostov. 'How
do they get hold of all this stuff?'

Rostov began tearing the signal into shreds. 'It's all
on file somewhere or other. The sale of the *Stromberg*
would have been notified to Lloyd's of London. Someone from our consulate in Liberia would have got the
details on Savile Shipping from public records in Monrovia. Our New York people got Chung's address out of
the phone book, and Papagopolous was on file in
Moscow. None of it is secret, except the Papagopolous
file. The trick is knowing where to go to ask the
questions. The squirrels specialize in that trick. It's all
they do.'

Rostov put the shreds of paper into a large glass
ashtray and set fire to them. 'Your people should have
squirrels,' he added.

'I expect we're working on it.'

'Suggest it yourself. It won't do you any harm. You
might even get the job of setting it up. That could help
your career.'

Hassan nodded. 'Perhaps I will.'

Fresh drinks arrived: vodka for Rostov, gin for
Hassan. Rostov was pleased that Hassan was responding
well to his friendly overtures. He examined the cinders

in the ashtray to make sure the signal had burned completely.

Hassan said, 'You're assuming Dickstein is behind the Savile Shipping Corporation.'

'Yes.'

'So what will we do about the *Stromberg*?'

'Well . . .' Rostov emptied his glass and set it on the table. 'My guess is he wants the *Stromberg* so he can get an exact layout of the sister ship *Coparelli*.'

'It will be an expensive blueprint.'

'He can sell the ship again. However, he may also use the *Stromberg* in the hijack of the *Coparelli* – I don't quite see how, just yet.'

'Will you put a man aboard the *Stromberg*, like Tyrin on the *Coparelli*?'

'No point. Dickstein is sure to get rid of the old crew and fill the ship with Israeli sailors. I'll have to think of something else.'

'Do we know where the *Stromberg* is now?'

'I've asked the squirrels. They'll have an answer by the time I get to Moscow.'

Hassan's flight was called. He stood up. 'We meet in Luxembourg?'

'I'm not sure. I'll let you know. Listen, there's something I've got to say. Sit down again.'

Hassan sat down.

'When we started to work together on Dickstein I was very hostile to you. I regret that now, I'm apologizing; but I must tell you there was a reason for it. You see, Cairo isn't secure. It's certain there are double agents in the Egyptian Intelligence apparatus. What I was concerned about – and still am – is that everything you report to your superiors will get back, via a double agent, to Tel Aviv; and then Dickstein will know how close we are and will take evasive action.'

'I appreciate your frankness.'

Appreciate, Rostov thought: He loves it. 'However, you are now completely in the picture, and what we must discuss is how to prevent the information you have in your possession getting back to Tel Aviv.'

Hassan nodded. 'What do you suggest?'

'Well. You'll have to tell what we've found out, of course, but I want you to be as vague as possible about the details. Don't give names, times, places. When you're pushed, complain about me, say I've refused to let you share all the information. Don't talk to anyone except the people you're obliged to report to. In particular, tell nobody about Savile Shipping, the *Stromberg*, or the *Coparelli*. As for Pyotr Tyrin being aboard the *Coparelli* – try to forget it.'

Hassan looked worried. 'What's left to tell?'

'Plenty. Dickstein, Euratom, uranium, the meeting with Pierre Borg . . . you'll be a hero in Cairo if you tell half the story.'

Hassan was not convinced. 'I'll be as frank as you. If I do this your way, my report will not be as impressive as yours.'

Rostov gave a wry smile. 'Is that unfair?'

'No,' Hassan conceded, 'you deserve most of the credit.'

'Besides, nobody but the two of us will know how different the reports are. And you're going to get all the credit you need in the end.'

'All right,' Hassan said. 'I'll be vague.'

'Good.' Rostov waved his hand for a waiter. 'You've got a little time, have a quick one before you go.' He settled back in his chair and crossed his legs. He was satisfied: Hassan would do as he had been told. 'I'm looking forward to getting home.'

'Any plans?'

'I'll try to take a few days on the coast with Mariya and the boys. We've a dacha in the Riga Bay.'

'Sounds nice.'

'It's pleasant there – but not as warm as where you're going, of course. Where will you head for – Alexandria?'

The last call for Hassan's flight came over the public address system, and the Arab stood up. 'No such luck,' he said. 'I expect to spend the whole time stuck in filthy Cairo.'

And Rostov had the peculiar feeling that Yasif Hassan was lying.

Franz Albrecht Pedler's life was ruined when Germany lost the war. At the age of fifty, a career officer in the Wehrmacht, he was suddenly homeless, penniless and unemployed. And, like millions of other Germans, he started again.

He became a salesman for a French dye manufacturer: small commission, no salary. In 1946 there were few customers, but by 1951 German industry was rebuilding and when at last things began to look up Pedler was in a good position to take advantage of the new opportunities. He opened an office in Wiesbaden, a rail junction on the right bank of the Rhine that promised to develop into an industrial centre. His product list grew, and so did his tally of customers: soon he was selling soaps as well as dyes, and he gained entry to the U.S. bases, which at the time administered that part of occupied Germany. He had learned, during the hard years, to be an opportunist: if a U.S. Army procurement officer wanted disinfectant in pint bottles, Pedler would buy disinfectant in ten-gallon drums, pour the stuff from the drums into secondhand bottles in a rented barn, put on a label saying 'F. A. Pedler's Special Disinfectant' and resell at a fat profit.

From buying in bulk and repackaging it was not a very big step to buying ingredients and manufacturing. The first barrel of F. A. Pedler's Special Industrial Cleanser – never called simply 'soap' – was mixed in the same rented barn and sold to the U.S. Air Force for use by aircraft maintenance engineers. The company never looked back.

In the late Fifties Pedler read a book about chemical warfare and went on to win a big defence contract to supply a range of solutions designed to neutralize various kinds of chemical weapon.

F. A. Pedler had become a military supplier, small but secure and profitable. The rented barn had grown into a small complex of single-storey buildings. Franz married again – his first wife had been killed in the

1944 bombing – and fathered a child. But he was still an opportunist at heart, and when he heard about a small mountain of uranium ore going cheap, he smelled a profit.

The uranium belonged to a Belgian company called Société Générale de la Chimie. Chimie was one of the corporations which ran Belgium's African colony, the Belgian Congo, a country rich in minerals. After the 1960 pullout Chimie stayed on; but, knowing that those who did not walk out would eventually be thrown out, the company expended all its efforts to ship home as much raw material as it could before the gates slammed shut. Between 1960 and 1965 it accumulated a large stockpile of yellowcake at its refinery near the Dutch border. Sadly for Chimie, a nuclear test ban treaty was ratified in the meantime, and when Chimie was finally thrown out of the Congo there were few buyers for uranium. The yellowcake sat in a silo, tying up scarce capital.

F. A. Pedler did not actually use very much uranium in the manufacture of their dyes. However, Franz loved a gamble of this sort: the price was low, he could make a little money by having the stuff refined, and if the uranium market improved – as it was likely to sooner or later – he would make a big capital profit. So he bought some.

Nat Dickstein liked Pedler right away. The German was a sprightly seventy-three-year-old who still had all his hair and the twinkle in his eye. They met on a Saturday. Pedler wore a loud sports jacket and fawn trousers, spoke good English with an American accent and gave Dickstein a glass of Sekt, the local champagne.

They were wary of each other at first. After all, they had fought on opposite sides in a war which had been cruel to them both. But Dickstein had always believed that the enemy was not Germany but Fascism, and he was nervous only that Pedler might be uneasy. It seemed the same was true of Pedler.

Dickstein had called from his hotel in Wiesbaden to make an appointment. His call had been awaited eagerly. The local Israeli consul had alerted Pedler that Mr Dickstein, a senior army procurement officer with a large shopping list, was on his way. Pedler had suggested a short tour of the factory on Saturday morning, when it would be empty, followed by lunch at his home.

If Dickstein had been genuine he would have been put off by the tour: the factory was no gleaming model of German efficiency, but a straggling collection of old huts and cluttered yards with a pervasive bad smell.

After sitting up half the night with a textbook on chemical engineering Dickstein was ready with a handful of intelligent questions about agitators and baffles, materials-handling and quality-control and packaging. He relied upon the language problem to camouflage any errors. It seemed to be working.

The situation was peculiar. Dickstein had to play the role of a buyer and be dubious and noncommittal while the seller wooed him, whereas in reality he was hoping to seduce Pedler into a relationship the German would be unable or unwilling to sever. It was Pedler's uranium he wanted, but he was not going to ask for it, now or ever. Instead he would try to manoeuvre Pedler into a position where he was dependent upon Dickstein for his livelihood.

After the factory tour Pedler drove him in a new Mercedes from the works to a wide chalet-style house on a hillside. They sat in front of a big window and sipped their Sekt while Frau Pedler – a pretty, cheerful woman in her forties – busied herself in the kitchen. Bringing a potential customer home to lunch on the weekend was a somewhat Jewish way of doing business, Dickstein mused, and he wondered if Pedler had thought of that.

The window overlooked the valley. Down below, the river was wide and slow, with a narrow road running alongside it. Small grey houses with white shutters clustered in small groups along the banks, and the vineyards sloped upward to the Pedlers' house and beyond it to the treeline. If I were going to live in a cold country, Dickstein thought, this would do nicely.

'Well, what do you think?' said Pedler.

'About the view, or the factory?''

Pedler smiled and shrugged. 'Both.'

'The view is magnificent. The factory is smaller than I expected.'

Pedler lit a cigarette. He was a heavy smoker – he was lucky to have lived so long. 'Small?'

'Perhaps I should explain what I'm looking for.'

'Please.'

Dickstein launched into his story. 'Right now the Army buys cleaning materials from a variety of suppliers: detergents from one, ordinary soap from another, solvents for machinery from someone else and so on. We're trying to cut costs, and perhaps we can do this by taking our entire business in this area to one manufacturer.'

Pedler's eyes widened. 'That is . . .' He fumbled for a phrase '. . . a tall order.'

'I'm afraid it may be too tall for you,' Dickstein said, thinking: Don't say yes!

'Not necessarily. The only reason we haven't got that kind of bulk manufacturing capacity is simply that we've never had this scale of business. We certainly have the managerial and technical knowhow, and with a large firm order we could get finance to expand . . . it all depends on the figures, really.'

Dickstein picked up his briefcase from beside his chair and opened it. 'Here are the specifications for the products,' he said, handing Pedler a list. 'Plus the quantities required and the time scale. You'll want time to consult with your directors and do your sums—'

'I'm the boss,' Pedler said with a smile. 'I don't have to consult anybody. Give me tomorrow to work on the figures, and Monday to see the bank. On Tuesday I'll call and give you prices.'

'I was told you were a good man to work with,' Dickstein said.

'There are some advantages to being a small company.'

Frau Pedler came in from the kitchen and said, 'Lunch is ready.'

My darling Suza.

I have never written a love letter before. I don't think I ever called anyone darling until now. I must tell you, it feels very good.

I am alone in a strange town on a cold Sunday afternoon. The town is quite pretty, with lots of parks, in fact I'm sitting in one of them now, writing to you with a leaky ballpoint pen and some vile green stationery, the only kind I could get. My bench is beneath a curious kind of pagoda with a circular dome and Greek columns all around in a circle – like a folly, or the kind of summer house you might find in an English country garden designed by a Victorian eccentric. In front of me is a flat lawn dotted with poplar trees, and in the distance I can hear a brass band playing something by Edward Elgar. The park is full of people with children and footballs and dogs.

I don't know why I'm telling you all this. What I really want to say is I love you and I want to spend the rest of my life with you. I knew that a couple of days after we met. I hesitated to tell you, not because I wasn't sure, but . . .

Well, if you want to know the truth, I thought it might scare you off. I know you love me, but I also know that you are twenty-five, that love comes easily to you (I'm the opposite way), and that love which comes easily may go easily. So I thought: Softly,

softly, give her a chance to get to like you before
you ask her to say 'For ever.' Now that we've been
apart for so many weeks I'm no longer capable of
such deviousness, I just have to tell you how it is
with me. For ever is what I want, and you might as
well know it now.

I'm a changed man. I know that sounds trite, but
when it happens to you it isn't trite at all, it's just
the opposite. Life looks different to me now, in
several ways – some of which you know about,
others I'll tell you one day. Even this is different,
this being alone in a strange place with nothing to
do until Monday. Not that I mind it, particularly.
But before, I wouldn't even have thought of it as
something I might like or dislike. Before, there was
nothing I'd prefer to do. Now there is always
something I'd rather do, and you're the person I'd
rather do it to. I mean *with*, not to. Well, either, or
both. I'm going to have to get off that subject, it's
making me fidget.

I'll be gone from here in a couple of days, don't
know where I'm going next, don't know – and this
is the worst part – don't even know when I'll see you
again. But when I do, believe me, I'm not going to
let you out of my sight for ten or fifteen years.

None of this sounds how it's supposed to sound.
I want to tell you how I feel, and I can't put it into
words. I want you to know what it's like for me to
picture your face many times every day, to see a
slender girl with black hair and hope, against all
reason, that somehow she might be you, to imagine

all the time what you might say about a view, a
newspaper article, a small man with a large dog, a
pretty dress; I want you to know how, when I get
into bed alone, I just ache with the need to touch
you.

I love you so much.

N.

Franz Pedler's secretary phoned Nat Dickstein at his
hotel on Tuesday morning and made a date for lunch.

They went to a modest restaurant in the Wilhelm-
strasse and ordered beer instead of wine: this was to be
a working session. Dickstein controlled his impatience
– Pedler, not he, was supposed to do the wooing.

Pedler said, 'Well, I think we can accommodate you.'

Dickstein wanted to shout 'Hooray!' but he kept his
face impassive.

Pedler continued: 'The prices, which I'll give you in
a moment, are conditional. We need a five-year contract. We will guarantee prices for the first twelve
months; after that they may be varied in accordance
with an index of world prices of certain raw materials.
And there's a cancellation penalty amounting to ten
per cent of the value of one year's supply.'

Dickstein wanted to say, 'Done!' and shake hands on
the deal, but he reminded himself to continue to play
his part. 'Ten per cent is stiff.'

'It's not excessive,' Pedler argued. 'It certainly would
not recompense us for our losses if you did cancel. But
it must be large enough to deter you from cancelling
except under very compelling circumstances.'

'I see that. But we may suggest a smaller percentage.'

Pedler shrugged. 'Everything is negotiable. Here are the prices.'

Dickstein studied the list, then said, 'This is close to what we're looking for.'

'Does that mean we have a deal?'

Dickstein thought: Yes, yes! But he said, 'No, it means that I think we can do business.'

Pedler beamed. 'In that case,' he said, 'let's have a real drink. Waiter!'

When the drinks came Pedler raised his glass in a toast. 'To many years of business together.'

'I'll drink to that,' Dickstein said. As he raised his glass he was thinking: How about that – I did it again!

Life at sea was uncomfortable, but it was not as bad as Pyotr Tyrin had expected. In the Soviet Navy, ships had been run on the principles of unremitting hard work, harsh discipline and bad food. The *Coparelli* was very different. The captain, Eriksen, asked only for safety and good seamanship, and even there his standards were not remarkably high. The deck was swabbed occasionally, but nothing was ever polished or painted. The food was quite good, and Tyrin had the advantage of sharing a cabin with the cook. In theory Tyrin could be called upon at any hour of the day or night to send radio signals, but in practice all the traffic occurred during the normal working day so he even got his eight hours sleep every night. It was a comfortable regimen, and Pyotr Tyrin was concerned about comfort.

Sadly, the ship was the opposite of comfortable. She was a bitch. As soon as they rounded Cape Wrath and left The Minch and the North Sea she began to pitch and roll like a toy yacht in a gale. Tyrin felt terribly seasick, and had to conceal it since he was supposed to be a sailor. Fortunately this occurred while the cook was busy in the galley and Tyrin was not needed in the radio room, so he was able to lie flat on his back in his bunk until the worst was over.

The quarters were poorly ventilated and inadequately heated, so immediately it got a little damp above, the mess decks were full of wet clothing hanging up to dry and making the atmosphere worse.

Tyrin's radio gear was in his sea-bag, well protected by polythene and canvas and some sweaters. However, he could not set it up and operate it in his cabin, where the cook or anyone else might walk in. He had already made routine radio contact with Moscow on the ship's radio, during a quiet – but nonetheless tense – moment when nobody was listening; but he needed something safer and more reliable.

Tyrin was a nest-building man. Whereas Rostov would move from embassy to hotel room to safe house without noticing his environment, Tyrin liked to have a base, a place where he could feel comfortable and familiar and secure. On static surveillance, the kind of assignment he preferred, he would always find a large easy chair to place in front of the window, and would sit at the telescope for hours, perfectly content with his bag of sandwiches, his bottle of soda and his thoughts. Here on the *Coparelli*, he had found a place to nest.

Exploring the ship in daylight, he had discovered a little labyrinth of stores up in the bow beyond the for'ard hatch. The naval architect had put them there merely to fill a space between the hold and the prow. The main store was entered by a semiconcealed door down a flight of steps. It contained some tools, several drums of grease for the cranes and – inexplicably – a rusty old lawnmower. Several smaller rooms opened off the main one: some containing ropes, bits of machinery and decaying cardboard boxes of nuts and bolts; others empty but for insects. Tyrin had never seen anyone enter the area – stuff that was used was stored aft, where it was needed.

He chose a moment when darkness was falling and most of the crew and officers were at supper. He went to his cabin, picked up his sea-bag and climbed the companionway to the deck. He took a flashlight from a locker below the bridge but did not yet switch it on.

The almanac said there was a moon, but it did not show through the thick clouds. Tyrin made his way stealthily for'ard holding on to the gunwale, where his silhouette would be less likely to show against the off-white deck. There was some light from the bridge and the wheelhouse, but the duty officers would be watching the surrounding sea, not the deck.

Cold spray fell on him, and as the *Coparelli* executed her notorious roll he had to grab the rail with both hands to avoid being swept overboard. At times she shipped water – not much, but enough to soak into Tyrin's sea boots and freeze his feet. He hoped fervently

that he would never find out what she was like in a real
gale.

He was miserably wet and shivering when he reached
the bow and entered the little disused store. He closed
the door behind him, switched on his flashlight and
made his way through the assorted junk to one of the
small rooms off the main store. He closed that door
behind him too. He took off his oilskin, rubbed his
hands on his sweater to dry and warm them some, then
opened his bag. He put the transmitter in a corner,
lashed it to the bulkhead with a wire tied through rings
in the deck, and wedged it with a cardboard box.

He was wearing rubber soles, but he put on rubber
gloves as an additional precaution for the next task.
The cables to the ship's radio mast ran through a pipe
along the deckhead above him. With a small hacksaw
pilfered from the engine room Tyrin cut away a six-
inch section of the pipe, exposing the cables. He took
a tap from the power cable to the power input of the
transmitter, then connected the aerial socket of his
radio with the signal wire from the mast.

He switched on the radio and called Moscow.

His outgoing signals would not interfere with the
ship's radio because he was the radio operator and it
was unlikely that anyone else would attempt to send on
the ship's equipment. However, while he was using his
own radio, incoming signals would not reach the ship's
radio room; and he would not hear them either since
his set would be tuned to another frequency. He could
have wired everything so that both radios would receive
at the same time, but then Moscow's replies to him

would be received by the ship's radio, and somebody might notice . . . Well, there was nothing very suspicious about a small ship taking a few minutes to pick up signals. Tyrin would take care to use his radio only at times when no traffic was expected for the ship.

When he reached Moscow he made: *Checking secondary transmitter.*

They acknowledged, then made: *Stand by for signal from Rostov.* All this was in a standard KGB code.

Tyrin made: *Standing by, but hurry.*

The message came: *Keep your head down until something happens. Rostov.*

Tyrin made: *Understood. Over and out.* Without waiting for their sign-off he disconnected his wires and restored the ship's cables to normal. The business of twisting and untwisting bare wires, even with insulated pliers, was time-consuming and not very safe. He had some quick-release connectors amongst his equipment in the ship's radio room: he would pocket a few and bring them here next time to speed up the process.

He was well satisfied with his evening's work. He had made his nest, he had opened his lines of communication, and he had remained undiscovered. All he had to do now was sit tight: and sitting tight was what he liked to do.

He decided to drag in another cardboard box to put in front of the radio and conceal it from a casual glance. He opened the door and shone his flashlight into the main store – and got a shock.

He had company.

The overhead light was on, casting restless shadows

with its yellow glow. In the centre of the storeroom, sitting against a grease drum with his legs stretched out before him, was a young sailor. He looked up, just as startled as Tyrin and – Tyrin realized from his face – just as guilty.

Tyrin recognized him. His name was Ravlo. He was about nineteen years old, with pale blond hair and a thin white face. He had not joined in the pub-crawls in Cardiff, yet he often looked hung over, with dark discs under his eyes and a distracted air.

Tyrin said, 'What are you doing here?' And then he saw.

Ravlo had rolled up his left sleeve past the elbow. On the deck between his legs was a phial, a watch-glass and a small waterproof bag. In his right hand was a hypodermic syringe, with which he was about to inject himself.

Tyrin frowned. 'Are you diabetic?'

Ravlo's face twisted and he gave a dry, humourless laugh.

'An addict,' Tyrin said, understanding. He did not know much about drugs, but he knew that what Ravlo was doing could get him discharged at the next port of call. He began to relax a little. This could be handled.

Ravlo was looking past him, into the smaller store. Tyrin looked back and saw that the radio was clearly visible. The two men stared at one another, each understanding that the other was doing something he needed to hide.

Tyrin said, 'I will keep your secret, and you will keep mine.'

Ravlo gave the twisted smile and the dry, humourless laugh again: then he looked away from Tyrin, down at his arm, and he stuck the needle into his flesh.

The exchange between the *Coparelli* and Moscow was picked up and recorded by a U.S. Naval Intelligence listening station. Since it was in standard KGB code, they were able to decipher it. But all it told them was that someone aboard a ship – they did not know which ship – was checking his secondary transmitter, and somebody called Rostov – the name was not on any of their files – wanted him to keep his head down. Nobody could make any sense of it, so they opened a file titled 'Rostov' and put the signal in the file and forgot about it.

CHAPTER TWELVE

W HEN HE had finished his interim debriefing in Cairo, Hassan asked permission to go to Syria to visit his parents in the refugee camp. He was given four days. He took a plane to Damascus and a taxi to the camp.

He did not visit his parents.

He made certain inquiries at the camp, and one of the refugees took him, by means of a series of buses, to Dara, across the Jordanian border, and all the way to Amman. From there another man took him on another bus to the Jordan River.

On the night of the second day he crossed the river, guided by two men who carried submachine guns. By now Hassan was wearing Arab robes and a headdress like them, but he did not ask for a gun. They were young men, their soft adolescent faces just taking on lines of weariness and cruelty, like recruits in a new army. They moved across the Jordan valley in confident silence, directing Hassan with a touch or a whisper: they seemed to have made the journey many times. At one point all three of them lay flat behind a stand of cactus while lights and soldiers' voices passed a quarter of a mile away.

Hassan felt helpless – and something more. At first he thought that the feeling was due to his being so completely in the hands of these boys, his life dependent on their knowledge and courage. But later, when they had left him and he was alone on a country road trying to get a lift, he realized that this journey was a kind of regression. For years now he had been a European banker, living in Luxembourg with his car and his refrigerator and his television set. Now, suddenly, he was walking in sandals along the dusty Palestine roads of his youth: no car, no jet; an Arab again, a peasant, a second-class citizen in the country of his birth. None of his reflexes would work here – it was not possible to solve a problem by picking up a phone or pulling out a credit card or calling a cab. He felt like a child, a pauper and a fugitive all at the same time.

He walked five miles without seeing a vehicle, then a fruit truck passed him, its engine coughing unhealthily and pouring smoke, and pulled up a few yards ahead. Hassan ran after it.

'To Nablus?' he shouted.

'Jump in.'

The driver was a heavy man whose forearms bulged with muscle as he heaved the truck around bends at top speed. He smoked all the time. He must have been certain there would not be another vehicle in the way all night, driving as he did on the crown of the road and never using the brake. Hassan could have used some sleep, but the driver wanted to talk. He told Hassan that the Jews were good rulers, business had prospered since they occupied Jordan, but of course the land must be free one day. Half of what he said was insincere, no doubt; but Hassan could not tell which half.

They entered Nablus in the cool Samaritan dawn, with a red sun rising behind the hillside and the town still asleep. The truck roared into the market square and stopped. Hassan said goodbye to the driver.

He walked slowly through the empty streets as the sun began to take away the chill of the night. He savoured the clean air and the low white buildings, enjoying every detail, basking in the glow of nostalgia for his boyhood: he was in Palestine, he was home.

He had precise directions to a house with no number in a street with no name. It was in a poor quarter, where the little stone houses were crowded too close together and nobody swept the streets. A goat was tethered outside, and he wondered briefly what it ate, for there was no grass. The door was unlocked.

He hesitated a moment outside, fighting down the excitement in his belly. He had been away too long – now he was back in the Land. He had waited too many years for this opportunity to strike a blow in revenge for what they had done to his father. He had suffered exile, he had endured with patience, he had nursed his hatred enough, perhaps too much.

He went in.

There were four or five people asleep on the floor. One of them, a woman, opened her eyes, saw him and sat up instantly, her hand under the pillow reaching for what might have been a gun.

'What do you want?'

Hassan spoke the name of the man who commanded the Fedayeen.

Mahmoud had lived not far from Yasif Hassan when they were both boys in the late Thirties, but they had never met, or if they had neither remembered it. After the European war, when Yasif went to England to study, Mahmoud tended sheep with his brothers, his father, his uncles and his grandfather. Their lives would have continued to go in quite different directions but for the 1948 war. Mahmoud's father, like Yasif's, made the decision to pack up and flee. The two sons – Yasif was a few years older than Mahmoud – met at the refugee camp. Mahmoud's reaction to the ceasefire was even stronger than Yasif's, which was paradoxical, for Yasif had lost more. But Mahmoud was possessed by a great rage that would allow him to do nothing other than fight for the liberation of his homeland. Until then he had been oblivious of politics, thinking it had nothing to do with shepherds; now he set out to understand it. Before he could do that, he had to teach himself to read.

They met again in the Fifties, in Gaza. By then Mahmoud had blossomed, if that was the right word for something so fierce. He had read Clausewitz on war and Plato's *Republic*, *Das Kapital* and *Mein Kampf*, Keynes and Mao and Galbraith and Gandhi, history and biography, classical novels and modern plays. He spoke good English and bad Russian and a smattering of Cantonese. He was directing a small cadre of terrorists

on forays into Israel, bombing and shooting and stealing and then returning to disappear into the Gaza
camps like rats into a garbage dump. The terrorists
were getting money, weapons and intelligence from
Cairo: Hassan was, briefly, part of the intelligence
backup, and when they met again Yasif told Mahmoud
where his ultimate loyalty lay – not with Cairo, not even
with the pan-Arab cause, but with Palestine.

Yasif had been ready to abandon everything there
and then – his job at the bank, his home in Luxembourg, his role in Egyptian Intelligence – and join the
freedom fighters. But Mahmoud had said no, and the
habit of command was already fitting him like a tailored
coat. In a few years, he said – for he took a long view –
they would have all the guerrillas they wanted, but they
would still need friends in high places, European
connections, and secret intelligence.

They had met once more, in Cairo, and set up lines
of communication which bypassed the Egyptians. With
the Intelligence Establishment Hassan had cultivated a
deceptive image: he pretended to be a little less percep-
tive than he was. At first Yasif sent over much the same
kind of stuff he was giving to Cairo, principally the
names of loyal Arabs who were stashing away fortunes
in Europe and could therefore be touched for funds.
Recently he had been of more immediate practical
value as the Palestinian movement began to operate
in Europe. He had booked hotels and flights, rented
cars and houses, stockpiled weapons and transferred
funds.

He was not the kind of man to use a gun. He knew this and was faintly ashamed of it, so he was all the more proud to be so useful in other, non-violent but nonetheless practical, ways.

The results of his work had begun to explode in Rome that year. Yasif believed in Mahmoud's programme of European terrorism. He was convinced that the Arab armies, even with Russian support, could never defeat the Jews, for this allowed the Jews to think of themselves as a beleaguered people defending their homes against foreign soldiers, and that gave them strength. The truth was, in Yasif's view, that the Palestine Arabs were defending their home against invading Zionists. There were still more Arab Palestinians than Jewish Israelis. counting the exiles in the camps; and it was *they*, not a rabble of soldiers from Cairo and Damascus, who would liberate the homeland. But first they had to believe in the Fedayeen. Acts such as the Rome airport affair would convince them that the Fedayeen had international resources. And when the people believed in the Fedayeen, the people would be the Fedayeen, and then they would be unstoppable.

The Rome airport affair was trivial, a peccadillo, by comparison with what Hassan had in mind.

It was an outrageous, mind-boggling scheme that would put the Fedayeen on the front pages of the world's newspapers for weeks and prove that they were a powerful international force, not a bunch of ragged refugees. Hassan hoped desperately that Mahmoud would accept it.

Yasif Hassan had come to propose that the Fedayeen should hijack a holocaust.

They embraced like brothers, kissing cheeks, then stood back to look at one another.

'You smell like a whore,' said Mahmoud.

'You smell like a goatherd,' said Hassan. They laughed and embraced again.

Mahmoud was a big man, a fraction taller than Hassan and much broader; and he *looked* big, the way he held his head and walked and spoke. He did smell, too: a sour familiar smell that came from living very close to many people in a place that lacked the modern inventions of hot baths and sanitation and garbage disposal. It was three days since Hassan had used aftershave and talcum powder, but he still smelled like a scented woman to Mahmoud.

The house had two rooms: the one Hassan had entered, and behind that another, where Mahmoud slept on the floor with two other men. There was no upper storey. Cooking was done in a yard at the back, and the nearest water supply was one hundred yards away. The woman lit a fire and began to make a porridge of crushed beans. While they waited for it, Hassan told Mahmoud his story.

'Three months ago in Luxembourg I met a man I had known at Oxford, a Jew called Dickstein. It turns out he is a big Mossad operative. Since then I have been watching him, with the help of the Russians, in particular a KGB man named Rostov. We have discovered that Dickstein plans to steal a shipload of uranium so the Zionists will be able to make atom bombs.'

At first Mahmoud refused to believe this. He cross-questioned Hassan: how good was the information, what exactly was the evidence, who might be lying, what mistakes might have been made? Then, as Hassan's answers made more and more sense, the truth began to sink in, and Mahmoud became very grave.

'This is not only a threat to the Palestinian cause. These bombs could ravage the whole of the Middle East.'

It was like him, Hassan thought, to see the big picture.

'What do you and this Russian propose to do?' Mahmoud asked.

'The plan is to stop Dickstein and expose the Israeli plot, showing the Zionists to be lawless adventurers. We haven't worked out the details yet. But I have an alternative proposal.' He paused, trying to form the right phrases, then blurted it out. 'I think the Fedayeen should hijack the ship before Dickstein gets there.'

Mahmoud stared blankly at him for a long moment.

Hassan thought: Say something, for God's sake! Mahmoud began to shake his head from side to side slowly, then his mouth widened in a smile, and at last he began to laugh, beginning with a small chuckle and finishing up giving a huge, body-shaking bellow that brought the rest of the household around to see what was happening.

Hassan ventured, 'But what do you think?'

Mahmoud sighed. 'It's wonderful,' he said. 'I don't see how we can do it, but it's a wonderful idea.'

Then he started asking questions.

He asked questions all through breakfast and for most of the morning: the quantity of uranium, the names of the ships involved, how the yellowcake was converted into nuclear explosive, places and dates and people. They talked in the back room, just the two of them for most of the time, but occasionally Mahmoud would call someone in and tell him to listen while Hassan repeated some particular point.

About midday he summoned two men who seemed to be his lieutenants. With them listening, he again went over the points he thought crucial.

'The *Coparelli* is an ordinary merchant ship with a regular crew?'

'Yes.'

'She will be sailing through the Mediterranean to Genoa.'

'Yes.'

'What does this yellowcake weigh?'

'Two hundred tons.'

'And it is packed in drums.'

'Five hundred and sixty of them.'

'Its market price?'

'Two million American dollars.'

'And it is used to make nuclear bombs.'

'Yes. Well, it is the raw material.'

'Is the conversion to the explosive form an expensive or difficult process?'

'Not if you've got a nuclear reactor. Otherwise, yes.'

Mahmoud nodded to the two lieutenants. 'Go and tell this to the others.'

In the afternoon, when the sun was past its zenith and it was cool enough to go out, Mahmoud and Yasif walked over the hills outside the town. Yasif was desperate to know what Mahmoud really thought of his plan, but Mahmoud refused to talk about uranium. So Yasif spoke about David Rostov and said that he admired the Russian's professionalism despite the difficulties he had made for him.

'It is well to admire the Russians,' Mahmoud said, 'so long as we do not trust them. Their heart is not in our cause. There are three reasons why they take our side. The least important is that we cause trouble for the West, and anything that is bad for the West is good for the Russians. Then there is their image. The underdeveloped nations identify with us rather than with the Zionists, so by supporting us the Russians gain credit with the Third World – and remember, in the contest between the United States and the Soviet Union the Third World has all the floating voters. But the most important reason – the only *really* important reason – is oil. The Arabs have oil.'

They passed a boy tending a small flock of bony sheep. The boy was playing a flute. Yasif remembered that Mahmoud had once been a shepherd boy who could neither read nor write.

'Do you understand how important oil is?' Mahmoud said. 'Hitler lost the European war because of oil.'

'No.'

'Listen. The Russians defeated Hitler. They were bound to. Hitler knew this: he knew about Napoleon, he knew nobody could conquer Russia. So why did he try? He was running out of oil. There is oil in Georgia, in the Caucasian oilfields. Hitler had to have the Caucasus. But you cannot hold the Caucasus secure unless you have Volgograd, which was then called Stalingrad, the place where the tide turned against Hitler. Oil. That's what our struggle is about, whether we like it or not, do you realize that? If it were not for oil, nobody but us would care about a few Arabs and Jews fighting over a dusty little country like ours.'

Mahmoud was magnetic when he talked. His strong, clear voice rolled out short phrases, simple explanations, statements that sounded like devastating basic truths: Hassan suspected he said these same things often to his troops. In the back of his mind he remembered the sophisticated ways in which politics were discussed in places like Luxembourg and Oxford, and it seemed to him now that for all their mountains of information those people knew less than Mahmoud. He knew, too, that international politics were complicated: that there was more than oil behind these things, yet at bottom he believed Mahmoud was right.

They sat in the shade of a fig tree. The smooth, dun-coloured landscape stretched all around them, empty. The sky glared hot and blue, cloudless from one horizon to the other. Mahmoud uncorked a water bottle and gave it to Hassan, who drank the tepid liquid and handed it back. Then he asked Mahmoud whether he wanted to rule Palestine after the Zionists were beaten back.

'I have killed many people,' Mahmoud said. 'At first I did it with my own hands, with a knife or a gun or a bomb. Now I kill by devising plans and giving orders, but I kill them still. We know this is a sin, but I cannot repent. I have no remorse, Yasif. Even if we make a mistake, and we kill children and Arabs instead of soldiers and Zionists, still I think only, "This is bad for our reputation," not, "This is bad for my soul." There is blood on my hands, and I will not wash it off. I will not try. There is a story called *The Picture of Dorian Gray*. It is about a man who leads an evil and debilitating life, the kind of life that should make him look old, give him lines on his face and bags under his eyes, a destroyed liver and venereal disease. Still, he does not suffer. Indeed, as the years go by he seems to stay young, as if he had found the elixir of life. But in a locked room in his house there is a painting of him, and it is the picture that ages, and takes on the ravages of evil living and terrible disease. Do you know the story? It is English.'

'I saw the movie,' said Yasif.

'I read it when I was in Moscow. I would like to see that film. Do you remember how it ended?'

'Oh, yes. Dorian Gray destroyed the painting, and then all the disease and damage fell on him in an instant, and he died.'

'Yes.' Mahmoud put the stopper back in the bottle,

329

and looked out over the brown hillsides with unseeing eyes. Then he said, 'When Palestine is free, my picture will be destroyed.'

After that they sat in silence for a while. Eventually, without speaking, they stood up and began to walk back to the town.

Several men came to the little house in Nablus that evening at dusk, just before curfew. Hassan did not know who they were exactly: they might have been the local leaders of the movement, or an assorted group of people whose judgment Mahmoud respected, or a permanent council of war that stayed close to Mahmoud but did not actually live with him. Hassan could see the logic in the last alternative, for if they all lived together, they could all be destroyed together.

The woman gave them bread and fish and watery wine, and Mahmoud told them of Hassan's scheme. Mahmoud had thought it through more thoroughly than Hassan. He proposed that they hijack the *Coparelli* before Dickstein got there, then ambush the Israelis as they came aboard. Expecting only an ordinary crew and halfhearted resistance, Dickstein's group would be wiped out. Then the Fedayeen would take the *Coparelli* to a North African port and invite the world to come aboard and see the bodies of the Zionist criminals. The cargo would be offered to its owners for a ransom of half its market price – one million U.S. dollars.

There was a long debate. Clearly a faction of the

movement was already nervous about Mahmoud's policy of taking the war into Europe, and saw the proposed hijack as a further extension of the same strategy. They suggested that the Fedayeen could achieve most of what they wanted simply by calling a press conference in Beirut or Damascus and revealing the Israeli plot to the international press. Hassan was convinced that was not enough: accusations were cheap, and it was not the lawlessness of Israel that had to be demonstrated, it was the power of the Fedayeen.

They spoke as equals, and Mahmoud seemed to listen to each with the same attention. Hassan sat quietly, hearing the low, calm voices of these people who looked like peasants and spoke like senators. He was at once hopeful and fearful that they would adopt his plan: hopeful because it would be the fulfilment of twenty years of vengeful dreams; fearful because it would mean he would have to do things more difficult, violent and risky than the work he had been involved in so far.

In the end he could not stand it any longer and he went outside and squatted in the mean yard, smelling the night and the dying fire. A little later there was a chorus of quiet voices from inside, like voting.

Mahmoud came out and sat beside Hassan. 'I have sent for a car.'

'Oh?'

'We must go to Damascus. Tonight. There is a lot to do. It will be our biggest operation. We must start work immediately.'

'It is decided, then.'

'Yes. The Fedayeen will hijack the ship and steal the uranium.'

'So be it,' said Yasif Hassan.

David Rostov had always liked his family in small doses, and as he got older the doses got smaller. The first day of his holiday was fine. He made breakfast, they walked along the beach, and in the afternoon Vladimir, the young genius, played chess against Rostov, Mariya, and Yuri simultaneously, and won all three games. They took hours over supper, catching up on all the news and drinking a little wine. The second day was similar, but they enjoyed it less; and by the third day the novelty of each other's company had worn off. Vladimir remembered he was supposed to be a prodigy and stuck his nose back into his books; Yuri began to play degenerate Western music on the record player and argued with his father about dissident poets; and Mariya fled into the kitchen of the dacha and stopped putting make-up on her face.

So when the message came to say that Nik Bunin was back from Rotterdam and had successfully bugged the *Stromberg*, Rostov used that as an excuse to return to Moscow.

Nik reported that the *Stromberg* had been in dry dock for the usual inspection prior to completion of the sale to Savile Shipping. A number of small repairs were in progress, and without difficulty Nik had got on board, posing as an electrician, and planted a powerful radio beacon in the prow of the ship. On leaving he had been questioned by the dock foreman, who did not have any electrical work on his schedule for that day; and Nik had pointed out that if the work had not been requested, no doubt it would not have to be paid for.

From that moment, whenever the ship's power was on – which was all the time she was at sea and most of the time she was in dock – the beacon would send out a signal every thirty minutes until the ship sank or was broken up for scrap. For the rest of her life, wherever in the world she was, Moscow would be able to locate her within an hour.

Rostov listened to Nik, then sent him home. He had plans for the evening. It was a long time since he had seen Olga, and he was impatient to see what she would do with the battery-operated vibrator he had brought her as a present from London.

In Israeli Naval Intelligence there was a young captain named Dieter Koch who had trained as a ship's engineer. When the *Coparelli* sailed from Antwerp with her cargo of yellowcake Koch had to be aboard.

Nat Dickstein reached Antwerp with only the vaguest idea of how this was to be achieved. From his hotel room he phoned the local representative of the company that owned the *Coparelli*.

When I die, he thought as he waited for the connection, they will bury me from a hotel room.

A girl answered the phone. Dickstein said briskly, 'This is Pierre Beaudaire, give me the director.'

'Hold on, please.'

A man's voice, 'Yes?'

'Good morning, this is Pierre Beaudaire from the Beaudaire Crew List.' Dickstein was making it up as he went along.

'Never heard of you.'

'That's why I'm calling you. You see, we're contemplating opening an office in Antwerp, and I'm wondering whether you would be willing to try us.'

'I doubt it, but you can write to me and—'

'Are you completely satisfied with your present crew agency?'

'They could be worse. Look here—'

'One more question and I won't trouble you further. May I ask whom you use at the moment?'

'Cohen's. Now, I haven't any more time—'

'I understand. Thank you for your patience. Goodbye.'

Cohen's! That was a piece of luck. Perhaps I will be able to do this bit without brutality, Dickstein thought as he put down the phone. Cohen! It was unexpected – docks and shipping were not typical Jewish business. Well, sometimes you got lucky.

He looked up Cohen's crew agency in the phone book, memorized the address, put on his coat, left the hotel and hailed a cab. Cohen had a little two-room office above a sailor's bar in the red-light district of the city. It was not yet midday, and the night people were still asleep – the whores and thieves, musicians and strippers and waiters and bouncers, the people who made the place come to life in the evening. Now it might have been any run-down business district, grey and cold in the morning, and none too clean.

Dickstein went up a staircase to a first-floor door, knocked and went in. A middle-aged secretary presided over a small reception room furnished with filing cabinets and orange plastic chairs.

'I'd like to see Mr Cohen,' Dickstein told her.

She looked him over and seemed to think he did not appear to be a sailor. 'Are you wanting a ship?' she said doubtfully.

'No,' he said. 'I'm from Israel.'

'Oh.' She hesitated. She had dark hair and deep-set, shadowed eyes, and she wore a wedding ring. Dickstein wondered if she might be Mrs Cohen. She got up and went through a door behind her desk into the inner office. She was wearing a pants suit, and from behind she looked her age.

A minute later she reappeared and ushered him into Cohen's office. Cohen stood up, shook hands and said without preamble, 'I give to the cause every year. In the war I gave twenty thousand guilders, I can show you the cheque. This is some new appeal? There is another war?'

'I'm not here to raise money, Mr Cohen,' Dickstein said with a smile. Mrs Cohen had left the door open: Dickstein closed it. 'Can I sit down?'

'If you don't want money, sit down, have some coffee, stay all day,' said Cohen, and he laughed.

Dickstein sat. Cohen was a short man in spectacles, bald and clean-shaven, and looked to be about fifty years old. He wore a brown check suit that was not very new. He had a good little business here, Dickstein guessed, but he was no millionaire.

Dickstein said, 'Were you here in World War II?'

Cohen nodded. 'I was a young man. I went into the country and worked on a farm where nobody knew me, nobody knew I was Jewish. I was lucky.'

'Do you think it will happen again?'

'Yes. It's happened all through history, why should it stop now? It will happen again – but not in my lifetime. It's all right here. I don't want to go to Israel.'

'Okay. I work for the government of Israel. We would like you to do something for us.'

Cohen shrugged. 'So?'

'In a few weeks' time, one of your clients will call you with an urgent request. They will want an engineer officer for a ship called *Coparelli*. We would like you to send them a man supplied by us. His name is Koch, and he is an Israeli, but he will be using a different name and false papers. However, he *is* a ship's engineer – your clients will not be dissatisfied.'

Dickstein waited for Cohen to say something. You're a nice man, he thought; a decent Jewish businessman, smart and hardworking and a little frayed at the edges; don't make me get tough with you.

Cohen said, 'You're not going to tell me why the government of Israel wants this man Koch aboard the *Coparelli*?'

'No.'

There was a silence.

'You carry any identification?'

'No.'

The secretary came in without knocking and gave them coffee. Dickstein got hostile vibrations from her. Cohen used the interruption to gather his thoughts. When she had gone out he said, 'I would have to be *meshugenah* to do this.'

'Why?'

'You come in off the street saying you represent the government of Israel, yet you have no identification, you don't even tell me your name. You ask me to take part in something that is obviously underhanded and probably criminal; you will not tell me what it is that you're trying to do. Even if I believe your story, I don't know that I would approve of the Israelis doing what you want to do.'

Dickstein sighed, thinking of the alternatives: blackmail him, kidnap his wife, take over his office on the crucial day . . . He said, 'Is there anything I can do to convince you?'

'I would need a personal request from the Prime Minister of Israel before I would do this thing.'

Dickstein stood up to leave, then he thought: Why not? Why the hell not? It was a wild idea, they would think he was crazy . . . but it would work, it would serve the purpose . . . He grinned as he thought it through. Pierre Borg would have apoplexy.

He said to Cohen, 'All right.'

'What do you mean, "all right"?'

'Put on your coat. We'll go to Jerusalem.'

'Now?'

'Are you busy?'

'Are you serious?'

'I told you it's important.' Dickstein pointed to the phone on the desk. 'Call your wife.'

'She's just outside.'

Dickstein went to the door and opened it. 'Mrs Cohen?'

'Yes.'

'Would you come in here, please?'

She hurried in, looking worried. 'What is it, Josef?' she asked her husband.

'This man wants me to go to Jerusalem with him.'

'When?'

'Now.'

'You mean this week?'

Dickstein said, 'I mean this morning, Mrs Cohen. I must tell you that all this is highly confidential. I've asked your husband to do something for the Israeli government. Naturally he wants to be certain that it is the government that is asking this favour and not some criminal. So I'm going to take him there to convince him.'

She said, 'Don't get involved, Josef—'

Cohen shrugged. 'I'm Jewish, I'm involved already. Mind the shop.'

'You don't know anything about this man!'

'So I'm going to find out.'

'I don't like it.'

'There's no danger,' Cohen told her. 'We'll take a scheduled flight, we'll go to Jerusalem. I'll see the Prime Minister and we'll come back.'

'The Prime Minister!' Dickstein realized how proud

she would be if her husband met the Prime Minister of Israel. He said, 'This has to be secret. Mrs Cohen. Please tell people your husband has gone to Rotterdam on business. He will be back tomorrow.'

She stared at the two of them. 'My Josef meets the Prime Minister, and I can't tell Rachel Rothstein?'

Then Dickstein knew it was going to be all right.

Cohen took his coat from a hook and put it on. Mrs Cohen kissed him, then put her arms around him.

'It's all right,' he told her. 'This is very sudden and strange, but it's all right.'

She nodded dumbly and let him go.

They took a cab to the airport. Dickstein's sense of delight grew as they travelled. The scheme had an air of mischief about it, he felt a bit like a schoolboy, this was a terrific prank. He kept grinning, and had to turn his face away so that Cohen would not see.

Pierre Borg would go through the *roof*.

Dickstein bought two round-trip tickets to Tel Aviv, paying with his credit card. They had to take a connecting flight to Paris. Before they took off he called the embassy in Paris and arranged for someone to meet them in the transit lounge.

In Paris he gave the man from the embassy a message to send to Borg, explaining what was required. The diplomat was a Mossad man, and treated Dickstein with deference. Cohen was allowed to listen to the conversation, and when the man had gone back to the embassy he said, 'We could go back. I'm convinced already.'

'Oh, no,' Dickstein said. 'Now that we've come this far I want to be sure of you.'

On the plane Cohen said, 'You must be an important man in Israel.'

'No. But what I'm doing is important.'

Cohen wanted to know how to behave, how to address the Prime Minister. Dickstein told him, 'I don't know, I've never met him. Shake hands and call him by his name.'

Cohen smiled. He was beginning to share Dickstein's feeling of mischievousness.

Pierre Borg met them at Lod Airport with a car to take them to Jerusalem. He smiled and shook hands with Cohen, but he was seething underneath. As they walked to the car he muttered to Dickstein, 'You better have a fucking good reason for all this.'

'I have.'

They were with Cohen all the while, so Borg did not have an opportunity to cross-examine Dickstein. They went straight to the Prime Minister's residence in Jerusalem. Dickstein and Cohen waited in an anteroom while Borg explained to the Prime Minister what was required and why.

A couple of minutes later they were admitted. 'This is Nat Dickstein, sir,' Borg said.

They shook hands, and the Prime Minister said, 'We haven't met before, but I've heard of you, Mr Dickstein.'

Borg said, 'And this is Mr Josef Cohen of Antwerp.'

'Mr Cohen.' The Prime Minister smiled. 'You're a very cautious man. You should be a politician. Well, now . . . please do this thing for us. It is very important, and you will come to no harm from it.'

Cohen was bedazzled. 'Yes, sir, of course I will do this, I'm sorry to have caused so much trouble . . .'

'Not at all. You did the right thing.' He shook Cohen's hand again. 'Thank you for coming. Goodbye.'

Borg was less polite on the way back to the airport. He sat silent in the front seat of the car, smoking a cigar and fidgeting. At the airport he managed to get Dickstein alone for a minute. 'If you ever pull a stunt like this again . . .'

'It was necessary,' Dickstein said. 'It took less than a minute. Why not?'

'Why not, is because half my fucking department has been working all day to fix that minute. Why didn't you just point a gun at the man's head or something?'

'Because we're not barbarians,' Dickstein said.

'So people keep telling me.'

'They do? That's a bad sign.'

'Why?'

'Because you shouldn't need to be told.'

Then their flight was called. Boarding the plane with Cohen, Dickstein reflected that his relationship with Borg was in ruins. They had always talked like this, with bantering insults, but until now there had been an undertone of . . . perhaps not affection, but at least respect. Now that had vanished. Borg was genuinely hostile. Dickstein's refusal to be pulled out was a piece of basic defiance which could not be tolerated. If Dickstein had wanted to continue in the Mossad, he would have had to fight Borg for the job of director –

there was no longer sufficient room for both men in the organization. But there would be no contest now, for Dickstein was going to resign.

Flying back to Europe through the night, Cohen drank some gin and went to sleep. Dickstein ran over in his mind the work he had done in the past five months. Back in May he had started out with no real idea of how he was going to steal the uranium Israel needed. He had taken the problems as they came up, and found a solution to each one: how to locate uranium, which uranium to steal, how to hijack a ship, how to camouflage the Israeli involvement in the theft, how to prevent the disappearance of the uranium being reported to the authorities, how to placate the owners of the stuff. If he had sat down at the beginning and tried to dream up the whole scheme he could never have foreseen all the complications.

He had had some good luck and some bad. The fact that the owners of the *Coparelli* used a Jewish crew agency in Antwerp was a piece of luck; so was the existence of a consignment of uranium for non-nuclear purposes, and one going by sea. The bad luck mainly consisted of the accidental meeting with Yasif Hassan.

Hassan, the fly in the ointment. Dickstein was reasonably certain he had shaken off the opposition when he flew to Buffalo to see Cortone, and that they had not picked up his trail again since. But that did not mean they had dropped the case.

It would be useful to know how much they had found out before they lost him.

Dickstein could not see Suza again until the whole

affair was over, and Hassan was to blame for that too. If he were to go to Oxford, Hassan was sure to pick up the trail somehow.

The plane began its descent. Dickstein fastened his seat belt. It was all done now, the scheme in place, the preparations made. The cards had been dealt. He knew what was in his hand, and he knew some of his opponents' cards, and they knew some of his. All that remained was to play out the game, and no one could foretell the outcome. He wished he could see the future more clearly, he wished his plan were less complicated, he wished he did not have to risk his life once more, and he wished the game would start so that he could stop wishing and start doing things.

Cohen was awake. 'Did I dream all that?' he said.

'No.' Dickstein smiled. There was one more unpleasant duty he had to perform: he had to scare Cohen half to death. 'I told you this was important, and secret.'

'Of course, I understand.'

'You don't understand. If you talk about this to anyone other than your wife, we will take drastic action.'

'Is that a threat? What are you saying?'

'I'm saying, if you don't keep your mouth shut, we will kill your wife.'

Cohen stared, and went pale. After a moment he turned away and looked out of the window at the airport coming up to meet them.

CHAPTER THIRTEEN

Moscow's Hotel Rossiya was the largest hotel in Europe. It had 5,738 beds, ten miles of corridors, and no air-conditioning.

Yasif Hassan slept very badly there.

It was simple to say, 'The Fedayeen should hijack the ship before Dickstein gets there,' but the more he thought about it, the more terrified he was.

The Palestine Liberation Organization in 1968 was not the tightly-knit political entity it pretended to be. It was not even a loose federation of individual groups working together. It was more like a club for people with a common interest: it represented its members, but it did not control them. The individual guerrilla groups could speak with one voice through the PLO, but they did not and could not act as one. So when Mahmoud said the Fedayeen would do something, he spoke only for his own group. Furthermore, in this case it would be unwise even to ask for PLO cooperation. The organization was given money, facilities and a home by the Egyptians, but it had also been infiltrated by them: if you wanted to keep something secret from the Arab establishment, you had to keep it secret from the PLO. Of course, after the coup, when the world's press came to look over the captured ship with its atomic cargo, the Egyptians would know and would probably suspect that the Fedayeen had deliberately thwarted them, but Mahmoud would play innocent and the Egyptians would be obliged to join in the general acclamation of the Fedayeen for frustrating an Israeli act of aggression.

Anyway, Mahmoud believed he did not need the help of the others. His group had the best connections outside Palestine, the best European set-up, and plenty of money. He was now in Benghazi arranging to borrow a ship while his international team was gathered up from various parts of the world.

But the most crucial task devolved on Hassan: if the Fedayeen were to get to the *Coparelli* before the Israelis, he would have to establish exactly when and where Dickstein's hijack was to take place. For that, he needed the KGB.

He felt terribly uneasy around Rostov now. Until his visit to Mahmoud he had been able to tell himself he was working for two organizations with a common objective. Now he was indisputably a double agent, merely pretending to work with the Egyptians and the KGB while he sabotaged their plans. He felt different – he felt a traitor, in a way – and he was afraid that Rostov would observe the difference in him.

When Hassan had flown in to Moscow Rostov himself had been uneasy. He had said there was not enough room in his apartment for Hassan to stay, although Hassan knew the rest of the family were away on holiday. It seemed Rostov was hiding something.

Hassan suspected he was seeing some woman and did not want his colleague getting in the way.

After his restless night at the Hotel Rossiya, Hassan met Rostov at the KGB building on the Moscow ring road, in the office of Rostov's boss, Feliks Vorontsov. There were undercurrents there too. The two men were having an argument when Hassan entered the room, and although they broke it off immediately the air was stiff with unspoken hostility. Hassan, however, was too busy with his own clandestine moves to pay much attention to theirs.

He sat down. 'Have there been any developments?'

Rostov and Vorontsov looked at one another. Rostov shrugged. Vorontsov said, 'The *Stromberg* has been fitted with a very powerful radio beacon. She's out of dry dock now and heading south across the Bay of Biscay. The assumption would be that she is going to Haifa to take on a crew of Mossad agents. I think we can all be quite satisfied with our intelligence-gathering work. The project now falls into the sphere of positive action. Our task becomes prescriptive rather than descriptive, as it were.'

'They all talk like this in Moscow Centre,' Rostov said irreverently. Vorontsov glared at him.

Hassan said, 'What action?'

'Rostov here is going to Odessa to board a Polish merchant ship called the *Karla*,' Vorontsov said. 'She's an ordinary cargo vessel superficially, but she's very fast and has certain extra equipment – we use her quite often.'

Rostov was staring up at the ceiling, an expression of

mild distaste on his face. Hassan guessed that Rostov wanted to keep some of these details from the Egyptians: perhaps that was what he and Vorontsov had been arguing about.

Vorontsov went on, 'Your job is to get an Egyptian vessel and make contact with the *Karla* in the Mediterranean.'

'And then?' Hassan said.

'We wait for Tyrin, aboard the *Coparelli*, to tell us when the Israeli hijack takes place. He will also tell us whether the uranium is transferred from the *Coparelli* to the *Stromberg*, or simply left aboard the *Coparelli* to be taken to Haifa and unloaded.'

'And then?' Hassan persisted.

Vorontsov began to speak, but Rostov forestalled him. 'I want you to tell Cairo a cover story,' he said to Hassan. 'I want your people to think that we don't know about the *Coparelli*, we just know the Israelis are planning something in the Mediterranean and we are still trying to discover what.'

Hassan nodded, keeping his face impassive. He had to know what the plan was, and Rostov did not want to tell him! He said, 'Yes, I'll tell them that – if you tell me the actual plan.'

Rostov looked at Voronstov and shrugged. Vorontsov said, 'After the hijack the *Karla* will set a course for Dickstein's ship, whichever one carries the uranium. The *Karla* will collide with that ship.'

'Collide!'

'Your ship will witness the collision, report it, and observe that the crew of the vessel are Israelis and their

347

cargo is uranium. You will report these facts too. There will be an international inquiry into the collision. The presence of both Israelis and stolen uranium on the ship will be established beyond doubt. Meanwhile the uranium will be returned to its rightful owners and the Israelis will be covered with opprobrium.'

'The Israelis will fight,' Hassan said.

Rostov said, 'So much the better, with your ship there to see them attack us and help us beat them off.'

'It's a good plan,' said Vorontsov. 'It's simple. All they have to do is crash – the rest follows automatically.'

'Yes, it's a good plan,' Hassan said. It fitted in perfectly with the Fedayeen plan. Unlike Dickstein, Hassan knew that Tyrin was aboard the *Coparelli*. After the Fedayeen had hijacked the *Coparelli* and ambushed the Israelis, they could throw Tyrin and his radio into the sea, then Rostov would have no way of locating them.

But Hassan needed to know when and where Dickstein intended to carry out his hijack so that the Fedayeen could be sure of getting there first.

Vorontsov's office was hot. Hassan went to the window and looked down at the traffic on the Moscow ring road. 'We need to know exactly when and where Dickstein will hijack the *Coparelli*,' he said.

'Why?' Rostov asked, making a gesture with both arms spread, palms upward. 'We have Tyrin aboard the *Coparelli* and a beacon on the *Stromberg*. We know where both of them are at all times. We need only to stay close and move in when the time comes.'

'My ship has to be in the right area at the crucial time.'

'Then follow the *Stromberg*, staying just over the horizon – you can pick up her radio signal. Or keep in touch with me on the *Karla*. Or both.'

'Suppose the beacon fails, or Tyrin is discovered?'

Rostov said, 'The risk of that must be weighed against the danger of tipping our hand if we start following Dickstein around again – assuming we could find him.'

'He has a point, though,' Vorontsov said.

It was Rostov's turn to glare.

Hassan unbuttoned his collar. 'May I open a window?'

'They don't open,' said Vorontsov.

'Haven't you people heard of air-conditioning?'

'In Moscow?'

Hassan turned and spoke to Rostov. 'Think about it. I want to be perfectly sure we nail these people.'

'I've thought about it,' Rostov said. 'We're as sure as we can be. Go back to Cairo, organize that ship and stay in touch with me.'

You patronizing bastard, Hassan thought. He turned to Vorontsov. 'I cannot, in all honesty, tell my people I'm happy with the plan unless we can eliminate that remaining uncertainty.'

Vorontsov said, 'I agree with Hassan.'

'Well, I don't,' said Rostov. 'And the plan as it stands has already been approved by Andropov.'

Until now Hassan had thought he was going to have his way, since Vorontsov was on his side and Vorontsov was Rostov's boss. But the mention of the Chairman of the KGB seemed to constitute a winning move in this game: Vorontsov was almost cowed by it, and once again Hassan had to conceal his desperation.

Vorontsov said, 'The plan can be changed.'

'Only with Andropov's approval,' Rostov said. 'And you won't get my support for the change.'

Vorontsov's lips were compressed into a thin line. He hates Rostov, thought Hassan; and so do I.

Vorontsov said, 'Very well, then.'

In all his time in the intelligence business Hassan had been part of a professional team – Egyptian Intelligence, the KGB, even the Fedayeen. There had been other people, experienced and decisive people, to give him orders and guidance and to take ultimate responsibility. Now, as he left the KGB building to return to his hotel, he realized he was on his own.

Alone, he had to find a remarkably elusive and clever man and discover his most closely guarded secret.

For several days he was in a panic. He returned to Cairo, told them Rostov's cover story, and organized the Egyptian ship Rostov had requested. The problem stayed in front of his mind like a sheer cliff he could not begin to climb until he saw at least part of the route to the top. Unconsciously he searched back in his personal history for attitudes and approaches which would enable him to tackle such a task, to act independently.

He had to go a long way back.

Once upon a time Yasif Hassan had been a different

kind of man. He had been a wealthy, almost aristocratic young Arab with the world at his feet. He had gone about with the attitude that he could do more or less anything – and thinking had made it so. He had gone to study in England, an alien country, without a qualm; and he had entered its society without caring or even wondering what people thought of him.

There had been times, even then, when he had to learn; but he did that easily too. Once a fellow under-graduate, a Viscount something-or-other, had invited him down to the country to play polo. Hassan had never played polo. He had asked the rules and watched the others play for a while, noticing how they held the mallets, how they hit the ball, how they passed it and why; then he had joined in. He was clumsy with the mallet but he could ride like the wind: he played passably well, he thoroughly enjoyed the game, and his team won.

Now, in 1968, he said to himself: I can do anything, but whom shall I emulate?

The answer, of course, was David Rostov.

Rostov was independent, confident, capable. brilliant. He could find Dickstein, even when it seemed he was stumped, clueless, up a blind alley. He had done it twice. Hassan recalled:

Question: Why is Dickstein in Luxembourg?

Well, what do we know about Luxembourg? What is there here?

There is the stock exchange, the banks, the Council of Europe, Euratom –

Euratom!

Question: Dickstein has disappeared – where might he have gone?

Don't know.

But who do we know that he knows?

Only Professor Ashford in Oxford—

Oxford!

Rostov's approach was to search out bits of information – *any* information, no matter how trivial – in order to get on the target. The trouble was, they seemed to have used all the bits of information they had.

So I'll get some more, Hassan thought; I can do anything.

He racked his brains for all that he could remember from the time they had been at Oxford together. Dickstein had been in the war, he played chess, his clothes were shabby –

He had a mother.

But she had died.

Hassan had never met any brothers or sisters, no relatives of any sort. It was all such a long time ago, and they had not been very close even then.

There was, however, someone else who might know a little more about Dickstein: Professor Ashford.

So, in desperation, Yasif Hassan went back to Oxford.

All the way – in the plane from Cairo, the taxi from London airport to Paddington Station, the train to Oxford and the taxi to the little green-and-white house by the river – he wondered about Ashford. The truth

was, he despised the professor. In his youth perhaps he
had been an adventurer, but he had become a weak
old man, a political dilettante, an academic who could
not even hold his wife. One could not respect an old
cuckold – and the fact that the English did not think
like that only increased Hassan's contempt.

He worried that Ashford's weakness, together with
some kind of loyalty to Dickstein as one who had been
a friend and a student, might make him balk at getting
involved.

He wondered whether to play up to the fact that
Dickstein was Jewish. He knew from his time at Oxford
that the most enduring anti-Semitism in England was
that of the upper classes: the London clubs that still
blackballed Jews were in the West End, not the East
End. But Ashford was an exception there. He loved the
Middle East, and his pro-Arab stance was ethical, not
racial, in motivation. No: that approach would be a
mistake.

In the end he decided to play it straight; to tell
Ashford why he wanted to find Dickstein, and hope
that Ashford would agree to help for the same reasons.

When they had shaken hands and poured sherry, they
sat down in the garden and Ashford said, 'What brings
you back to England so soon?'

Hassan told the truth. 'I'm chasing Nat Dickstein.'

They were sitting by the river in the little corner of
the garden that was cut off by the hedge, where Hassan

had kissed the beautiful Eila so many years ago. The corner was sheltered from the October wind, and there was a little autumn sunshine to warm them.

Ashford was guarded, wary, his face expressionless. 'I think you'd better tell me what's going on.'

Hassan observed that during the summer the professor had actually yielded a little to fashion. He had cultivated side-whiskers and allowed his monkish fringe of hair to grow long, and was wearing denim jeans with a wide leather belt beneath his old tweed jacket.

'I'll tell you,' Hassan said, with an awful feeling that Rostov would have been more subtle than this, 'but I must have your word that it will go no farther.'

'Agreed.'

'Dickstein is an Israeli spy.'

Ashford's eyes narrowed, but he said nothing.

Hassan plunged on. 'The Zionists are planning to make nuclear bombs but they have no plutonium. They need a secret supply of uranium to feed to their reactor to make plutonium. Dickstein's job is to steal that uranium – and my job is to find him and stop him. I want you to help me.'

Ashford stared into his sherry, then drained the glass at a gulp. 'There are two questions at issue here,' he said, and Hassan realized that Ashford was going to treat this as an intellectual problem, the characteristic defence of the frightened academic. 'One is whether or not I *can* help; the other, whether or not I *should*. The latter is prior, I think; morally, anyway.'

Hassan thought: I'd like to pick you up by the scruff

of the neck and shake you. Maybe I can do that, at least figuratively. He said, 'Of course you *should*. You believe in our cause.'

'It's not so simple. I'm asked to interfere in a contest between two people, both of whom are my friends.'

'But only one of them is in the right.'

'So I should help the one who is in the right – and betray the one who is in the wrong?'

'Of course.'

'There isn't any "of course" about it . . . What will you do, if and when you find Dickstein?'

'I'm with Egyptian Intelligence, professor. But my loyalty – and, I believe, yours – lies with Palestine.'

Ashford refused to take the bait. 'Go on,' he said noncommittally.

'I have to find out exactly when and where Dickstein plans to steal this uranium.' Hassan hesitated. 'The Fedayeen will get there before Dickstein and steal it for themselves.'

Ashford's eyes glittered. 'My God,' he said. 'How marvellous.'

He's almost there, Hassan thought. He's frightened, but he's excited too. 'It's easy for you to be loyal to Palestine, here in Oxford, giving lectures, going to meetings. Things are a little more difficult for those of us who are out there fighting for the country. I'm here to ask you to do something concrete about your politics, to decide whether your ideals mean anything or not. This is where you and I find out whether the Arab cause is anything more to you than a romantic concept. This is the test, professor.'

Ashford said, 'Perhaps you're right.'

And Hassan thought: I've got you.

Suza had decided to tell her father that she was in love with Nat Dickstein.

At first she had not been sure of it herself, not really. The few days they had spent together in London had been wild and happy and loving, but afterwards she had realized that those feelings could be transient. She had resolved to make no resolutions. She would carry on normally and see how things turned out.

Something had happened in Singapore to change her mind. Two of the cabin stewards on the trip were gay, and used only one of the two hotel rooms allotted to them; so the crew could use the other room for a party. At the party the pilot had made a pass at Suza. He was a quiet, smiling blond man with delicate bones and a delightfully wacky sense of humour. The steward-esses all agreed he was a piece of ass. Normally Suza would have got into bed with him without thinking twice. But she had said no, astonishing the whole crew. Thinking about it later, she decided that she no longer wanted to get laid. She had just gone off the whole idea. All she wanted was Nathaniel. It was like . . . it was a bit like five years ago when the second Beatles album came out, and she had gone through her pile of records by Elvis and Roy Orbison and the Everly Brothers and realized that she did not want to play them, they held no more enchantment for her, the old familiar tunes had been heard once too often, and now she wanted music of a higher order. Well, it was a bit like that, but more so.

Dickstein's letter had been the clincher. It had been written God knew where and posted at Orly Airport, Paris. In his small neat handwriting with its incongruously curly loops on the g and y he had poured out his heart in a manner that was all the more devastating because it came from a normally taciturn man. She had cried over that letter.

She wished she could think of a way to explain all that to her father.

She knew that he disapproved of Israelis. Dickstein was an old student, and her father had been genuinely pleased to see him and prepared to overlook the fact that the old student was on the enemy side. But now she planned to make Dickstein a permanent part of her life, a member of the family. His letter said, 'For ever is what I want,' and Suza could hardly wait to tell him, 'Oh, yes; me, too.'

She thought both sides were in the wrong in the Middle East. The plight of the refugees was unjust and pitiful, but she thought they ought to set about making themselves new homes – it was not easy, but it was easier than war, and she despised the theatrical heroics which so many Arab men found irresistible. On the other hand, it was clear that the whole damn mess was originally the fault of the Zionists, who had taken over a country that belonged to other people. Such a cynical view had no appeal for her father, who saw Right on one side and Wrong on the other, and the beautiful ghost of his wife on the side of Right.

It would be hard for him. She had long ago scotched his dreams of walking up the aisle with his daughter beside him in a white wedding dress; but he still talked occasionally of her settling down and giving him a granddaughter. The idea that this grandchild might be Israeli would come as a terrible blow.

Still, that was the price of being a parent, Suza thought as she entered the house. She called, 'Daddy, I'm home,' as she took off her coat and put down her airline bag. There was no reply, but his briefcase was in the hall: he must be in the garden. She put the kettle on and walked out of the kitchen and down toward the river, still searching in her mind for the right words with which to tell him her news. Maybe she should begin by talking about her trip, and gradually work around—

She heard voices as she approached the hedge.

'And what will you do with him?' It was her father's voice.

Suza stopped, wondering whether she ought to interrupt or not.

'Just follow him,' said another voice, a strange one. 'Dickstein must not be killed until afterwards, of course.'

She put her hand over her mouth to stifle a gasp of horror. Then, terrified, she turned around and ran, soft-footed, back to the house.

'Well, now,' said Professor Ashford, 'following what we might call the Rostov Method, let us recall everything we know about Nat Dickstein.'

Do it any way you want, Hassan thought, but for God's sake come up with *something*.

Ashford went on: 'He was born in the East End of London. His father died when he was a boy. What about the mother?'

'She's dead, too, according to our files.'

'Ah. Well, he went into the army midway through the war – 1943, I think it was. Anyway he was in time to be part of the attack on Sicily. He was taken prisoner soon afterwards, about halfway up the leg of Italy, I can't remember the place. It was rumoured – you'll remember this, I'm sure – that he had a particularly bad time in the concentration camps, being Jewish. After the war he came here. He—'

'Sicily,' Hassan interrupted.

'Yes?'

'Sicily is mentioned in his file. He is supposed to have been involved in the theft of a boatload of guns. Our people had bought the guns from a gang of criminals in Sicily.'

'If we are to believe what we read in the newspapers,' said Ashford, 'there is only one gang of criminals in Sicily.'

Hassan added, 'Our people suspected that the hijackers had bribed the Sicilians for a tip-off.'

'Wasn't it Sicily where he saved that man's life?'

Hassan wondered what Ashford was talking about. He controlled his impatience, thinking: Let him ramble – that's the whole idea. 'He saved someone's life?'

'The American. Don't you remember? I've never forgotten it. Dickstein brought the man here. A rather brutish G.I. He told me the whole story, right here at this house. Now we're getting somewhere. You must have met the man, you were here that day, don't you remember?'

'I can't say I do,' Hassan muttered. He was embarrassed ... he had probably been in the kitchen feeling Eila up.

'It was ... unsettling,' Ashford said. He stared at the slowly moving water as his mind went back twenty years, and his face was shadowed by sadness for a moment, as if he were remembering his wife. Then he said, 'Here we all were, a gathering of academics and students, probably discussing atonal music or existentialism while we sipped our sherry, when in came a big soldier and started talking about snipers and tanks and blood and death. It cast a real chill: that's why I recall it so clearly. He said his family originated in Sicily, and his cousins had fêted Dickstein after the life-saving incident. Did you say a Sicilian gang had tipped off Dickstein about the boatload of guns?'

'It's possible, that's all.'

'Perhaps he didn't have to bribe them.'

Hassan shook his head. This was information, the kind of trivial information Rostov always seemed to make something of – but how was he going to use it? 'I don't see what use all this is going to be to us,' he said. 'How could Dickstein's ancient hijack be connected with the Mafia?'

'The Mafia,' said Ashford. 'That's the word I was looking for. And the man's name was Cortone – Tony Cortone – no, Al Cortone, from Buffalo. I told you, I remember every detail.'

'But the connection?' Hassan said impatiently.

Ashford shrugged. 'Simply this. Once before Dickstein used his connection with Cortone to call on the Sicilian Mafia for help with an act of piracy in the Mediterranean. People repeat their youth, you know: he may do the same thing again.'

Hassan began to see: and, as enlightenment dawned, so did hope. It was a long shot, a guess, but it made sense, the chance was real, maybe he could catch up with Dickstein again.

Ashford looked pleased with himself. 'It's a nice piece of speculative reasoning – I wish I could publish it, with footnotes.'

'I wonder,' said Hassan longingly. 'I wonder.'

'It's getting cool, let's go into the house.'

As they walked up the garden Hassan thought fleetingly that he had not learned to be like Rostov; he had merely found in Ashford a substitute. Perhaps his former proud independence had gone for ever. There was something unmanly about it. He wondered if the other Fedayeen felt the same way, and if that was why they were so bloodthirsty.

Ashford said, 'The trouble is, I don't suppose Cortone will tell you anything, whatever he knows.'

'Would he tell you?'

'Why should he? He'll hardly remember me. Now, if Eila were alive, she could have gone to see him and told him some story . . .'

'Well . . .' Hassan wished Eila would stay out of the conversation. 'I'll have to try myself.'

They entered the house. Stepping into the kitchen,

they saw Suza; and then they looked at each other and knew they had found the answer.

By the time the two men came into the house Suza had almost convinced herself that she had been mistaken when, in the garden, she thought she heard them talk about killing Nat Dickstein. It was simply unreal: the garden, the river, the autumn sunshine, a professor and his guest ... murder had no place there, the whole idea was fantastic, like a polar bear in the Sahara Desert. Besides, there was a very good psychological explanation for her mistake: she had been planning to tell her father that she loved Dickstein, and she had been afraid of his reaction – Freud could probably have predicted that at that point she might well imagine her father plotting to kill her lover.

Because she nearly believed this reasoning, she was able to smile brightly at them and say, 'Who wants coffee? I've just made some.'

Her father kissed her cheek. 'I didn't realize you were back, my dear.'

'I just arrived, I was thinking of coming out to look for you.' Why am I telling these lies?

'You don't know Yasif Hassan – he was one of my students when you were very small.'

Hassan kissed her hand and stared at her the way people always did when they had known Eila. 'You're every bit as beautiful as your mother,' he said, and his voice was not flirtatious at all, not even flattering: it sounded amazed.

Her father said, 'Yasif was here a few months ago, shortly after a contemporary of his visited us – Nat Dickstein. You met Dickstein, I think, but you were away by the time Yasif came.'

'Was there any connec-connection?' she asked, and silently cursed her voice for cracking on the last word.

The two men looked at one another, and her father said, 'Matter of fact, there was.'

And then she knew it was true, she had not misheard, they really were going to kill the only man she had ever loved. She felt dangerously close to tears, and turned away from them to fiddle with cups and saucers.

'I want to ask you to do something, my dear,' said her father. 'Something very important, for the sake of your mother's memory. Sit down.'

No more, she thought; this can't get worse, please.

She took a deep breath, turned around, and sat down facing him.

He said, 'I want you to help Yasif here to find Nat Dickstein.'

From that moment she hated her father. She knew then suddenly, instantly, that his love for her was fraudulent, that he had never seen her as a person, that he used her as he had used her mother. Never again would she take care of him, serve him; never again would she worry about how he felt, whether he was lonely, what he needed . . . She realized, in the same flash of insight and hatred, that her mother had reached this same point with him, at some time; and that she would now do what Eila had done, and despise him.

Ashford continued, 'There is a man in America who may know where Dickstein is. I want you to go there with Yasif and ask this man.'

She said nothing. Hassan took her blankness for incomprehension, and began to explain. 'You see, this Dickstein is an Israeli agent, working against our people. We must stop him. Cortone – the man in Buffalo – may be helping him, and if he is he will not help us. But he will remember your mother, and so he may cooperate with you. You could tell him that you and Dickstein are lovers.'

'Ha-hah!' Suza's laugh was faintly hysterical, and she hoped they would assume the wrong reasons for it. She controlled herself, and managed to become numb, to keep her body still and her face expressionless, while they told her about the yellowcake, and the man aboard the *Coparelli*, and the radio beacon on the *Stromberg*, and about Mahmoud and his hijack plan, and how much it would all mean for the Palestine liberation movement; and at the end she was numb, she no longer had to pretend.

Finally her father said, 'So, my dear, will you help? Will you do it?'

With an effort of self-control that astonished her, she gave them a bright air-hostess smile, got up from her stool, and said, 'It's a lot to take in in one go, isn't it? I'll think about it while I'm in the bath.'

And she went out.

*

It all sank in, gradually, as she lay in the hot water with a locked door between her and them.

So this was the thing that Nathaniel had to do before he could see her again: steal a ship. And then, he had said, he would not let her out of his sight for ten or fifteen years . . . Perhaps that meant he could give up this work.

But, of course, none of his plans was going to succeed, because his enemies knew all about them. This Russian planned to ram Nat's ship, and Hassan planned to steal the ship first and ambush Nat. Either way Dickstein was in danger; either way they wanted to destroy him. Suza could warn him.

If only she knew where he was.

How little those men downstairs knew about her! Hassan simply assumed, just like an Arab male chauvinist pig, that she would do as she was told. Her father assumed she would take the Palestinian side, because he did and he was the brains of the family. He had never known what was in his daughter's mind: for that matter, he had been the same with his wife. Eila had always been able to deceive him: he never suspected that she might not be what she seemed.

When Suza realized what she had to do, she was terrified all over again.

There was, after all, a way she might find Nathaniel and warn him.

'Find Nat' was what *they* wanted her to do.

She knew she could deceive them, for they already assumed she was on their side, when she was not.

So she could do what they wanted. She could find Nat – and then she could warn him.

Would she be making things worse? To find him herself, she had to lead them to him.

But even if Hassan did not find him, Nat was in danger from the Russian.

And if he was forewarned, he could escape both dangers.

Perhaps, too, she could get rid of Hassan somehow, before she actually reached Nat.

What was the alternative? To wait, to go on as if nothing had happened, to hope for a phone call that might never come . . . It was, she realized, partly her need to see Dickstein again that made her think like this, partly the thought that after the hijack he might be dead, that this might be her last chance. But there were good reasons, too: by doing nothing she might help frustrate Hassan's scheme, but that still left the Russians and their scheme.

Her decision was made. She would pretend to work with Hassan so that she could find Nathaniel.

She was peculiarly happy. She was trapped, but she felt free; she was obeying her father, yet she felt that at last she was defying him; for better or worse, she was committed to Nathaniel.

She was also very, very frightened.

She got out of the bath, dried herself, dressed, and went downstairs to tell them the good news.

*

At four A.M. on November 16, 1968, the *Coparelli* hove to at Vlissingen, on the Dutch coast, and took on board a port pilot to guide her through the channel of the Westerschelde to Antwerp. Four hours later, at the entrance to the harbour, she took on another pilot to negotiate her passage through the docks. From the main harbour she went through Royers Lock, along the Suez Canal, under the Siberia Bridge and into Kattendijk Dock, where she tied up at her berth.

Nat Dickstein was watching.

When he saw her sweep slowly in, and read the name *Coparelli* on her side, and thought of the drums of yellowcake that would soon fill her belly, he was overcome by a most peculiar feeling, like the one he had when he looked at Suza's naked body . . . yes, almost like lust.

He looked away from berth No. 42 to the railway line, which ran almost to the edge of the quay. There was a train on the line now, consisting of eleven cars and an engine. Ten of the cars carried fifty-one 200-litre drums with sealed lids and the word PLUMBAT stencilled on the side; the eleventh car had only fifty drums. He was so close to those drums, to that uranium; he could stroll over and touch the railway cars – he already had done this once, earlier in the morning, and had thought: Wouldn't it be terrific just to raid this place with choppers and a bunch of Israeli commandos and simply *steal* the stuff.

The *Coparelli* was scheduled for a fast turnaround. The port authorities had been convinced that the yellowcake could be handled safely, but all the same they did not want the stuff hanging about their harbour one minute longer than necessary. There was a crane standing by ready to load the drums on to the ship.

Nevertheless, there were formalities to be completed before loading could begin.

The first person Dickstein saw boarding the ship was an official from the shipping company. He had to give the pilots their *pourboire* and secure from the captain a crew list for the harbour police.

The second person aboard was Josef Cohen. He was here for the sake of customer relations: he would give the captain a bottle of whisky and sit down for a drink with him and the shipping company official. He also had a wad of tickets for free entry and one drink at the best nightclub in town, which he would give to the captain for the officers. And he would discover the name of the ship's engineer. Dickstein had suggested he do this by asking to see the crew list, then counting out one ticket for each officer on the list.

Whatever way he had decided to do it, he had been successful: as he left the ship and crossed the quay to return to his office he passed Dickstein and muttered, 'The engineer's name is Sarne,' without breaking stride.

It was not until afternoon that the crane went into action and the dockers began loading the drums into the three holds of the *Coparelli*. The drums had to be moved one at a time, and inside the ship each drum had to be secured with wedges of wood. As expected, the loading was not completed that day.

In the evening Dickstein went to the best nightclub in town. Sitting at the bar, close to the telephone, was a quite astonishing woman of about thirty, with black hair and a long, aristocratic face possessed of a faintly haughty expression. She wore an elegant black dress which made the most of her sensational legs and her high, round breasts. Dickstein gave her an almost imperceptible nod but did not speak to her.

He sat in a corner, nursing a glass of beer, hoping the sailors would come. Surely they would. Did sailors ever refuse a free drink?

Yes.

The club began to fill up. The woman in the black dress was propositioned a couple of times but refused both men, thereby establishing that she was not a hooker. At nine o'clock Dickstein went out to the lobby and phoned Cohen. By previous arrangement, Cohen had called the captain of the *Coparelli* on a pretext. He now told Dickstein what he had discovered: that all but two of the officers were using their free tickets. The exceptions were the captain himself, who was busy with paperwork, and the radio operator – a new man they had taken on in Cardiff after Lars broke his leg – who had a head cold.

Dickstein then dialled the number of the club he was in. He asked to speak to Mr Sarne, who, he understood, would be found in the bar. While he waited he could hear a barman calling out Sarne's name: it came to him two ways, one directly from the bar, the other through several miles of telephone cable. Eventually he heard, over the phone, a voice say, 'Yes? Hello? This is Sarne. Is anybody there? Hello?'

Dickstein hung up and walked quickly back into the bar. He looked over to where the bar phone was. The woman in the black dress was speaking to a tall, suntanned blond man in his thirties whom Dickstein had seen on the quay earlier that day. So this was Sarne.

The woman smiled at Sarne. It was a nice smile, a smile to make any man look twice: it was warm and red-lipped, showing even, white teeth, and it was accompanied by a certain languid half-closing of the eyes, which was very sexy and looked not at all as though it had been rehearsed a thousand times in front of a mirror.

Dickstein watched, spellbound. He had very little idea how this sort of thing worked, how men picked up women and women picked up men, and he understood even less how a woman could pick up a man while letting the man believe *he* was doing the picking up.

Sarne had his own charm, it seemed. He gave her his smile, a grin with something wickedly boyish in it that made him look ten years younger. He said something to her, and she smiled again. He hesitated, like a man who wants to talk some more but cannot think of anything to say; then, to Dickstein's horror, he turned away to go.

The woman was equal to this: Dickstein need not have worried. She touched the sleeve of Sarne's blazer, and he turned back to her. A cigarette had suddenly appeared in her hand. Sarne slapped his pockets for matches. Apparently he did not smoke. Dickstein groaned inwardly. The woman took a lighter from the evening bag on the bar in front of her and handed it to him. He lit her cigarette.

Dickstein could not go away, or watch from a distance; he would have a nervous breakdown. He had to listen. He pushed his way through the bar and stood behind Sarne, who was facing the woman. Dickstein ordered another beer.

The woman's voice was warm and inviting, Dickstein knew already, but now she was really using it. Some women had bedroom eyes, she had a bedroom voice.

Sarne was saying, 'This kind of thing is always happening to me.'

'The phone call?' the woman said.

Sarne nodded. 'Woman trouble. I hate women. All my life, women have caused me pain and suffering. I wish I were a homosexual.'

Dickstein was astonished. What was he saying? Did he mean it? Was he trying to give her the brush-off?

She said, 'Why don't you become one?'

'I don't fancy men.'

'Be a monk.'

'Well, you see, I have this other problem, this insatiable sexual appetite. I have to get laid, all the time, often several times a night. It's a great problem to me. Would you like a fresh drink?'

Ah. It was a line of chat. How did he think it up? Dickstein supposed that sailors did this sort of thing all the time, they had it down to a fine art.

It went on that way. Dickstein had to admire the way the woman led Sarne by the nose while letting him think he was making the running. She told him she was stopping over in Antwerp just for the night, and let him know she had a room in a good hotel. Before long he said they should have champagne, but the champagne sold in the club was very poor stuff, not like they might be able to get somewhere else; at a hotel, say; her hotel, for example.

They left when the floor show started. Dickstein was pleased: so far, so good. He watched a line of girls kicking their legs for ten minutes, then he went out.

He took a cab to the hotel and went up to the room. He stood close to the communicating door which led through to the next room. He heard the woman giggle and Sarne say something in a low voice.

Dickstein sat on the bed and checked the cylinder of gas. He turned the tap on and off quickly, and got a sharp whiff of sweetness from the face mask. It had no effect on him. He wondered how much you had to breathe before it worked. He had not had time to try out the stuff properly.

The noises from the next room became louder, and Dickstein began to feel embarrassed. He wondered how conscientious Sarne was. Would he want to go back to his ship as soon as he had finished with the woman? That would be awkward. It would mean a fight in the hotel corridor – unprofessional, risky.

Dickstein waited – tense, embarrassed. anxious. The woman was good at her trade. She knew Dickstein wanted Sarne to sleep afterwards, and she was trying to tire him. It seemed to take for ever.

It was past two A.M. when she knocked on the

communicating door. The code was three slow knocks
to say he was asleep, six fast knocks to say he was
leaving.

She knocked three times, slowly.

Dickstein opened the door. Carrying the gas cylinder
in one hand and the face mask in the other, he walked
softly into the next room.

Sarne lay flat on his back, naked, his blond hair
mussed, his mouth wide open, his eyes closed. His body
looked fit and strong. Dickstein went close and listened
to his breathing. He breathed in, then all the way out –
then, just as he began to inhale again, Dickstein turned
on the tap and clapped the mask over the sleeping
man's nose and mouth.

Sarne's eyes opened wide. Dickstein held the mask on
more firmly. Half a breath: incomprehension in Sarne's
eyes. The breath turned into a gasp, and Sarne moved
his head, failed to weaken Dickstein's grip, and began
to thrash about. Dickstein leaned on the sailor's chest
with an elbow, thinking: For God's sake, this is too slow!

Sarne breathed out. The confusion in his eyes had
turned to fear and panic. He gasped again, about to
increase his struggles. Dickstein thought of calling the
woman to help hold him down. But the second inhala-
tion defeated its purpose: the struggles were perceptibly
weaker; the eyelids fluttered and closed; and by the time
he exhaled the second breath, he was asleep.

It had taken about three seconds. Dickstein relaxed.
Sarne would probably never remember it. He gave him
a little more of the gas to make sure, then he stood up.

He looked at the woman. She was wearing shoes.

stockings, and garters; nothing else. She looked ravishing. She caught his gaze, and opened her arms, offering herself: at your service, sir. Dickstein shook his head with a regretful smile that was only partly disingenuous.

He sat in the chair beside the bed and watched her dress: skimpy panties, soft brassiere, jewellery, dress, coat, bag. She came to him, and he gave her eight thousand Dutch guilders. She kissed his cheek, then she kissed the banknotes. She went out without speaking.

Dickstein went to the window. A few minutes later he saw the headlights of her sports car as it went past the front of the hotel, heading back to Amsterdam.

He sat down to wait, again. After a while he began to feel sleepy. He went into the next room and ordered coffee from room service.

In the morning Cohen phoned to say the first officer of the *Coparelli* was searching the bars, brothels and flophouses of Antwerp for his engineer.

At twelve-thirty Cohen phoned again. The captain had called him to say that all the cargo was now loaded and he was without an engineer officer. Cohen had said, 'Captain, it's your lucky day.'

At two-thirty Cohen called to say he had seen Dieter Koch aboard the *Coparelli* with his kitbag over his shoulder.

Dickstein gave Sarne a little more gas each time he showed signs of waking. He administered the last dose at six A.M. the following day, then he paid the bill for the two rooms and left.

*

When Sarne finally woke up he found that the woman he had slept with had gone without saying goodbye. He also found he was massively, ravenously hungry.

During the course of the morning he discovered that he had been asleep not for one night, as he had imagined, but for two nights and the day in between.

He had an insistent feeling in the back of his mind that there was something remarkable he had forgotten, but he never found out what had happened to him during that lost twenty-four hours.

Meanwhile, on Sunday, November 17, 1968, the *Coparelli* had sailed.

CHAPTER FOURTEEN

WHAT SUZA should have done was phone any Israeli embassy and give them a message for Nat Dickstein.

This thought occurred to her an hour after she had told her father that she would help Hassan. She was packing a case at the time, and she immediately picked up the phone in her bedroom to call Inquiries for the number. But her father came in and asked her whom she was calling. She said the airport, and he said he would take care of that.

Thereafter she constantly looked for an opportunity to make a clandestine call, but there was none. Hassan was with her every minute. They drove to the airport, caught the plane, changed at Kennedy for a flight to Buffalo, and went straight to Cortone's house.

During the journey she came to loathe Yasif Hassan. He made endless vague boasts about his work for the Fedayeen; he smiled oilily and put his hand on her knee; he hinted that he and Eila had been more than friends, and that he would like to be more than friends with Suza. She told him that Palestine would not be free until its women were free; and that Arab men had to learn the difference between being manly and being porcine. That shut him up.

They had some trouble discovering Cortone's address – Suza half hoped they would fail – but in the end they found a taxi driver who knew the house. Suza was dropped off; Hassan would wait for her half a mile down the road.

The house was large, surrounded by a high wall, with guards at the gate. Suza said she wanted to see Cortone, that she was a friend of Nat Dickstein.

She had given a lot of thought to what she should say to Cortone: should she tell him all or only part of the truth? Suppose he knew, or could find out, where Dickstein was: why should he tell her? She would say Dickstein was in danger, she had to find him and warn him. What reason did Cortone have to believe her? She would charm him – she knew how to do that with men his age – but he would still be suspicious.

She wanted to explain to Cortone the complete picture: that she was looking for Nat to warn him, but she was also being used by his enemies to lead them to him, that Hassan was half a mile down the road in a taxi waiting for her. But then he would certainly never tell her anything.

She found it very difficult to think clearly about all this. There were so many deceits and double deceits involved. And she wanted so badly to see Nathaniel's face and speak to him herself.

She still had not decided what to say when the guard opened the gate for her, then led her up the gravel drive to the house. It was a beautiful place, but rather overripe, as if a decorator had furnished it lavishly then the owners had added a lot of expensive junk of their own choosing. There seemed to be a lot of servants. One of them led Suza upstairs, telling her that Mr Cortone was having late breakfast in his bedroom.

When she walked in Cortone was sitting at a small table, digging into eggs and homefries. He was a fat man, completely bald. Suza had no memory of him from the time he had visited Oxford, but he must have looked very different then.

He glanced at her, then stood upright with a look of terror on his face and shouted: 'You should be old!' and then his breakfast went down the wrong way and he began to cough and splutter.

The servant grabbed Suza from behind, pinning her arms in a painful grip; then let her go and went to pound Cortone on the back. 'What did you do?' he yelled at her. 'What did you do, for Christ's sake?'

In a peculiar way this farce helped calm her a little. She could not be terrified of a man who had been so terrified of her. She rode the wave of confidence, sat down at his table and poured herself coffee. When Cortone stopped coughing she said, 'She was my mother.'

'My God,' Cortone said. He gave a last cough, then waved the servant away and sat down again 'You're so like her, hell, you scared me half to death.' He screwed up his eyes, remembering. 'Would you have been about four or five years old, back in, um, 1947?'

'That's right.'

378

'Hell, I remember you, you had a ribbon in your hair. And now you and Nat are an item.'

She said, 'So he has been here.' Her heart leaped with joy.

'Maybe,' Cortone said. His friendliness vanished. She realized he would not be easy to manipulate.

She said, 'I want to know where he is.'

'And I want to know who sent you here.'

'Nobody sent me.' Suza collected her thoughts, struggling to hide her tension. 'I guessed he might have come to you for help with this . . . project he's working on. The thing is, the Arabs know about it, and they'll kill him, and I have to warn him . . . Please, if you know where he is, please help me.'

She was suddenly close to tears, but Cortone was unmoved. 'Helping you is easy,' he said. 'Trusting you is the hard part.' He unwrapped a cigar and lit it, taking his time. Suza watched in an agony of impatience. He looked away from her and spoke almost to himself. 'You know, there was a time when I'd just see something I wanted and I'd grab it. It's not so simple any more. Now I've got all these complications. I got to make choices, and none of them are what I really want. I don't know whether it's the way things are now or if it's me.'

He turned again and faced her. 'I owe Dickstein my life. Now I have a chance to save his, if you're telling the truth. This is a debt of honour. I have to pay it myself, in person. So what do I do?' He paused.

Suza held her breath.

'Dickstein is in a wreck of a house somewhere on the Mediterranean. It's a ruin, hasn't been lived in for years, so there's no phone there. I could send a message, but I couldn't be sure it would get there, and like I said, I have to do this myself, in person.'

He drew on the cigar. 'I could tell you where to go look for him, but you just might pass the information on to the wrong people. I won't take that risk.'

'What, then?' Suza said in a high-pitched voice. 'We have to help him!'

'I know that,' Cortone said imperturbably. 'So I'm going there myself.'

'Oh!' Suza was taken by surprise: it was a possibility she had never considered.

'And what about you?' he went on. 'I'm not going to tell you where I'm headed, but you could still have people follow me. I need to keep you real close from now on. Let's face it, you could be playing it both ways. So I'm taking you with me.'

She stared at him. Tension drained out of her in a flood, she slumped in her chair. 'Oh, thank you,' she said. Then, at last, she cried.

They flew first class. Cortone always did. After the meal Suza left him to go to the toilet. She looked through the curtain into economy, hoping against hope, but she was disappointed: there was Hassan's wary brown face staring at her over the rows of headrests.

She looked into the galley and spoke to the chief

steward in a confiding voice. She had a problem, she said. She needed to contact her boyfriend but she couldn't get away from her Italian father, who wanted her to wear iron knickers until she was twenty-one. Would he phone the Israeli consulate in Rome and leave a message for a Nathaniel Dickstein? Just say, Hassan has told me everything, and he and I are coming to see you. She gave him money for the phone call, far too much, it was a way of tipping him. He wrote the message down and promised.

She went back to Cortone. Bad news, she said. One of the Arabs was back there in economy. He must be following us.

Cortone cursed, then told her never mind, the man would just have to be taken care of later.

Suza thought: Oh, God, what have I done?

From the big house on the clifftop Dickstein went down a long zigzag flight of steps cut into the rock to the beach. He splashed through the shallows to a waiting motorboat, jumped in and nodded to the man at the wheel.

The engine roared and the boat surged through the waves out to sea. The sun had just set. In the last faint light the clouds were massing above, obscuring the stars as soon as they appeared. Dickstein was deep in thought, racking his brains for things he had not done, precautions he might yet take, loopholes he still had time to close. He went over his plan again and again in his mind, like a man who has learned by heart an important speech he must make but still wishes it were better.

The high shadow of the *Stromberg* loomed ahead, and the boatman brought the little vessel around in a foamy arc to stop alongside, where a rope ladder dangled in the water. Dickstein scrambled up the ladder and on to the deck.

The ship's master shook his hand and introduced himself. Like all the officers aboard the *Stromberg*, he was borrowed from the Israeli Navy.

They took a turn around the deck. Dickstein said, 'Any problems, captain?'

'She's not a good ship,' the captain said. 'She's slow, clumsy and old. But we've got her in good shape.'

From what Dickstein could see in the twilight the *Stromberg* was in better condition than her sister ship the *Coparelli* had been in Antwerp. She was clean, and everything on deck looked squared away, shipshape.

They went up to the bridge, looked over the powerful equipment in the radio room, then went down to the mess, where the crew were finishing dinner. Unlike the officers, the ordinary seamen were all Mossad agents, most with a little experience of the sea. Dickstein had worked with some of them before. They were all, he observed, at least ten years younger than he. They were bright-eyed, well-built, dressed in a peculiar assortment of denims and homemade sweaters: all tough, humorous, well-trained men.

Dickstein took a cup of coffee and sat at one of the tables. He outranked all these men by a long way, but there was not much bull in the Israeli armed forces, and even less in the Mossad. The four men at the table nodded and said hello. Ish, a gloomy Palestine-born Israeli with a dark complexion, said, 'The weather's changing.'

'Don't say that. I was planning to get a tan on this cruise.' The speaker was a lanky ash-blond New Yorker named Feinberg, a deceptively pretty-faced man with eyelashes women envied. Calling this assignment a 'cruise' was already a standing joke. In his briefing earlier in the day Dickstein had said the *Coparelli* would be almost deserted when they hijacked it. 'Soon after she passes through the Strait of Gibraltar,' he had told them, 'her engines will break down. The damage will be such that it can't be repaired at sea. The captain cables the owners to that effect – and we are now the owners. By an apparently lucky coincidence, another of our ships will be close by. She's the *Gil Hamilton*, now moored across the bay here. She will go to the *Coparelli* and take off the whole crew except for the engineer. Then she's out of the picture: she'll go to her next port of call, where the crew of the *Coparelli* will be let off and given their train fares home.'

They had had the day to think about the briefing, and Dickstein was expecting questions. Now Levi Abbas, a short, solid man 'built like a tank and about as handsome,' Feinberg had said, asked Dickstein, 'You didn't tell us how come you're so sure the *Coparelli* will break down when you want her to.'

'Ah.' Dickstein sipped his coffee. 'Do you know Dieter Koch, in naval intelligence?'

Feinberg knew him.

'He's the *Coparelli*'s engineer.'

Abbas nodded. 'Which is also how come we know we'll be able to repair the *Coparelli*. We know what's going to go wrong.'

'Right.'

Abbas went on. 'We paint out the name *Coparelli*, rename her *Stromberg*, switch log books, scuttle the old *Stromberg* and sail the *Coparelli*, now called the *Stromberg*, to Haifa with the cargo. But why not transfer the cargo from one ship to the other at sea? We have cranes.'

'That was my original idea,' Dickstein said. 'It was too risky. I couldn't guarantee it would be possible, especially in bad weather.'

'We could still do it if the good weather holds.'

'Yes, but now that we have identical sister ships it will be easier to switch names than cargoes.'

Ish said lugubriously, 'Anyway, the good weather won't hold.'

The fourth man at the table was Porush, a crewcut youngster with a chest like a barrel of ale, who happened to be married to Abbas's sister. He said, 'If it's going to be so easy, what are all of us tough guys doing here?'

Dickstein said, 'I've been running around the world for the past six months setting up this thing. Once or twice I've bumped into people from the other side – inevitably. I don't *think* they know what we're about to do ... but if they do, we may find out just how tough we are.'

One of the officers came in with a piece of paper

and approached Dickstein. 'Signal from Tel Aviv, sir. The *Coparelli* just passed Gibraltar.'

'That's it,' said Dickstein, standing up. 'We sail in the morning.'

Suza Ashford and Al Cortone changed planes in Rome and arrived in Sicily early in the morning. Two of Cortone's cousins were at the airport to meet him. There was a long argument between them: not acrimonious, but nevertheless loudly excitable. Suza could not follow the rapid dialect properly, but she gathered the cousins wanted to accompany Cortone and he was insisting that this was something he had to do alone because it was a debt of honour.

Cortone seemed to win the argument. They left the airport, without the cousins, in a big white Fiat. Suza drove. Cortone directed her on to the coast road. For the hundredth time she played over in her mind the reunion scene with Nathaniel: she saw his slight, angular body; he looked up; he recognized her and his face split in a smile of joy; she ran to him; they threw their arms around each other; he squeezed her so hard it hurt; she said, 'Oh, I love you,' and kissed his cheek, his nose, his mouth. But she was guilty and frightened too, and there was another scene she played less often in which he stared at her stony-faced and said, 'What the hell do you think you're doing here?'

It was a little like the time she had behaved badly on Christmas Eve, and her mother got angry and told her Santa Claus would put stones in her Christmas stocking instead of toys and candy. She had not known whether to believe this or not, and she had lain awake, alternately wishing for and dreading the morning.

She glanced across at Cortone in the seat beside her. The transatlantic journey tired him. Suza found it difficult to think of him as being the same age as Nat, he was so fat and bald and ... well, he had an air of weary depravity that might have been amusing but in fact was merely elderly.

The island was pretty when the sun came out. Suza looked at the scenery, trying to distract herself so that the time would pass more quickly. The road twisted along the edge of the sea from town to town, and on her right-hand side there were views of rocky beaches and the sparkling Mediterranean.

Cortone lit a cigar. 'I used to do this kind of thing a lot when I was young,' he said. 'Get on a plane, go somewhere with a pretty girl, drive around, see places. Not any more. I've been stuck in Buffalo for years, it seems like. That's the thing with business – you get rich, but there's always something to worry about. So you never go places, you have people come to you, bring you stuff. You get too lazy to have fun.'

'You chose it,' Suza said. She felt more sympathy for Cortone than she showed: he was a man who had worked hard for all the wrong things.

'I chose it,' Cortone admitted. 'Young people have no mercy.' He gave a rare half smile and puffed on his cigar.

For the third time Suza saw the same blue car in her

rearview mirror. 'We're being followed,' she said, trying to keep her voice calm and normal.

'The Arab?'

'Must be.' She could not see the face behind the windshield. 'What will we do? You said you'd handle it.'

'I will.'

He was silent. Expecting him to say more, Suza glanced across at him. He was loading a pistol with ugly brown-black bullets. She gasped: she had never seen a real-life gun.

Cortone looked up at her, then ahead. 'Christ, watch the goddamn road!'

She looked ahead, and braked hard for a sharp bend. 'Where did you get that thing?' she said.

'From my cousin.'

Suza felt more and more as if she were in a nightmare. She had not slept in a bed for four days. From the moment when she had heard her father talking so calmly about killing Nathaniel she had been running: fleeing from the awful truth about Hassan and her father, to the safety of Dickstein's wiry arms; and, as in a nightmare, the destination seemed to recede as fast as she ran.

'Why don't you tell me where we're going?' she asked Cortone.

'I guess I can, now. Nat asked me for the loan of a house with a mooring and protection from snooping police. We're going to that house.'

Suza's heart beat faster. 'How far?'

'Couple of miles.'

A minute later Cortone said, 'We'll get there, don't rush, we don't want to die on the way.'

She realized she had unconsciously put her foot down. She eased off the accelerator but she could not slow her thoughts. Any minute now, to see him and touch his face, to kiss him hello, to feel his hands on her shoulders—

'Turn in there, on the right.'

She drove through an open gateway and along a short gravel drive overgrown with weeds to a large ruined villa of white stone. When she pulled up in front of the pillared portico she expected Nathaniel to come running out to greet her.

There were no signs of life on this side of the house.

They got out of the car and climbed the broken stone staircase to the front entrance. The great wooden door was closed but not locked. Suza opened it and they went in.

There was a great hall with a floor of smashed marble. The ceiling sagged and the walls were blotched with damp. In the centre of the hall was a great fallen chandelier sprawled on the floor like a dead eagle.

Cortone called out, 'Hello, anybody here?'

There was no reply.

Suza thought: It's a big place, he must be here, it's just that he can't hear, maybe he's out in the garden.

They crossed the hall, skirting the chandelier. They entered a cavernous bare drawing room, their footsteps echoing loudly, and went out through the glassless french doors at the back of the building.

A short garden ran down to the edge of the cliff. They walked that far and saw a long stairway cut into the rock zigzagging down to the sea.

There was no one in sight.

He's not here, Suza thought; this time, Santa really did leave me stones.

'Look.' Cortone was pointing out to sea with one fat hand. Suza looked, and saw two vessels: a ship and a motorboat. The motorboat was coming toward them fast, jumping the waves and slicing the water with its sharp prow: there was one man in it. The ship was sailing out of the bay, leaving a broad wake.

'Looks like we just missed them,' Cortone said.

Suza ran down the steps, shouting and waving insanely, trying to attract the attention of the people on the ship, knowing it was impossible, they were too far away. She slipped on the stones and fell heavily on her bottom. She began to cry.

Cortone ran down after her, his heavy body jerking on the steps. 'It's no good,' he said. He pulled her to her feet.

'The motorboat,' she said desperately. 'Maybe we can take the motorboat and catch up with the ship—'

'No way. By the time the boat gets here the ship will be too far away, much too far, and going faster than the boat can.'

He led her back up the steps. She had run a long way down, and the climb back taxed him heavily. Suza hardly noticed: she was full of misery.

Her mind was a blank as they walked up the slope of the garden and back into the house.

389

'Have to sit down,' Cortone said as they crossed the drawing room.

Suza looked at him. He was breathing hard, and his face was grey and covered with perspiration. Suddenly she realized it had all been too much for his overweight body. For a moment she forgot her own awful disappointment. 'The stairs,' she said.

They went into the ruined hall. She led Cortone to the wide curving staircase and sat him on the second step. He went down heavily. He closed his eyes and rested his head on the wall beside him.

'Listen,' he said, 'you can call ships . . . or send them a wire . . . we can still reach him . . .'

'Sit quietly for a minute,' she said. 'Don't talk.'

'Ask my cousins – who's there?'

Suza spun around. There had been a clink of chandelier shards, and now she saw what had caused it.

Yasif Hassan walked toward them across the hall.

Suddenly, with a massive effort, Cortone stood up.

Hassan stopped.

Cortone's breath was coming in ragged gulps. He fumbled in his pocket.

Suza said, 'No—'

Cortone pulled out the gun.

Hassan was rooted to the spot, frozen.

Suza screamed. Cortone staggered, the gun in his hand weaving about in the air.

Cortone pulled the trigger. The gun went off twice, with a huge, deafening double bang. The shots went wild. Cortone sank to the ground, his face as dark as death. The gun fell from his fingers and hit the cracked marble floor.

Yasif Hassan threw up.

Suza knelt beside Cortone.

He opened his eyes. 'Listen,' he said hoarsely.

Hassan said, 'Leave him, let's go.'

Suza turned her head to face him. At the top of her voice she shouted, 'Just fuck *off*.' Then she turned back to Cortone.

'I've killed a lot of men,' Cortone said. Suza bent closer to hear. 'Eleven men. I killed myself ... I fornicated with a lot of women ...' His voice trailed off, his eyes closed, and then he made a huge effort to speak again. 'All my goddamn life I been a thief and a bully. But I died for my friend, right? This counts for something, it has to, doesn't it?'

'Yes,' she said. 'This really counts for something.'

'Okay,' he said.

Then he died.

Suza had never seen a man die. It was awful. Suddenly there was nothing there, nothing but a body; the person had vanished. She thought: No wonder death makes us cry. She realized her own face was streaked with tears. I didn't even like him, she thought, until just now.

Hassan said, 'You did very well, now let's get out of here.'

Suza did not understand. I did well? she thought. And then she understood. Hassan did not know she had told Cortone an Arab had been following them. As far as Hassan was concerned she had done just what he wanted her to: she had led him here. Now she must try to keep up the pretence that she was on his side until she could find a way to contact Nat.

I can't lie and cheat any more, I can't, it's too much, I'm tired, she thought.

Then: *You can phone a ship, or at least send a cable,* Cortone said.

She could still warn Nat.

Oh, God, when can I sleep?

She stood up. 'What are we waiting for?'

They went out through the high derelict entrance. 'We'll take my car,' Hassan told her.

She thought of trying to run away from him then, but it was a foolish idea. He would let her go soon. She had done what he'd asked, hadn't she? Now he would send her home.

She got into the car.

'Wait,' Hassan said. He ran to Cortone's car, took out the keys, and threw them into the bushes. He got into his own car. 'So the man in the motorboat can't follow,' he explained.

As they drove off he said, 'I'm disappointed in your attitude. That man was helping our enemies. You should rejoice, not weep, when an enemy dies.'

She covered her eyes with her hand. 'He was helping his friend.'

Hassan patted her knee. 'You've done well, I shouldn't criticize you. You got the information I wanted.'

She looked at him. 'Did I?'

'Sure. That big ship we saw leaving the bay – that

was the *Stromberg*. I know her time of departure and her maximum speed, so now I can figure out the earliest possible moment at which she could meet up with the *Coparelli*. And I can have my men there a day earlier.' He patted her knee again, this time letting his hand rest on her thigh.

'Don't touch me,' she said.

He took his hand away.

She closed her eyes and tried to think. She had achieved the worst possible outcome by what she had done: she had led Hassan to Sicily but she'd failed to warn Nat. She must find out how to send a telegram to a ship, and do it as soon as she and Hassan parted company. There was only one other chance – the airplane steward who had promised to call the Israeli consulate in Rome.

She said, 'Oh, God, I'll be glad to get back to Oxford.'

'Oxford?' Hassan laughed. 'Not yet. You'll have to stay with me until the operation is over.'

She thought: Dear God, I can't stand it. 'But I'm so tired,' she said.

'We'll rest soon. I couldn't let you go. Security, you know. Anyway, you wouldn't want to miss seeing the dead body of Nat Dickstein.'

At the Alitalia desk in the airport three men approached Yasif Hassan. Two of them were young and thuggish, the third was a tall sharp-faced man in his fifties.

The older man said to Hassan, 'You damn fool, you deserve to be shot.'

Hassan looked up at him, and Suza saw naked fear in his eyes as he said, 'Rostov!'

Suza thought: Oh God, what now?

Rostov took hold of Hassan's arm. It seemed for a moment that Hassan would resist, and jerk his arm away. The two young thugs moved closer. Suza and Hassan were enclosed. Rostov led Hassan away from the ticket desk. One of the thugs took Suza's arm and they followed.

They went into a quiet corner. Rostov was obviously blazing with fury but kept his voice low. 'You might have blown the whole thing if you hadn't been a few minutes late.'

'I don't know what you mean,' Hassan said desperately.

'You think I don't know you've been running around the world looking for Dickstein? You think I can't have you followed just like any other bloody imbecile? I've been getting hourly reports on your movements ever since you left Cairo. And what made you think you could trust her?' He jerked a thumb at Suza.

'She led me here.'

'Yes, but you didn't know that then.'

Suza stood still, silent and frightened. She was hopelessly confused. The multiple shocks of the morning – missing Nat, watching Cortone die, now this – had paralyzed her ability to think. Keeping the lies straight had been difficult enough when she had been deceiving Hassan and telling Cortone a truth that Hassan thought was a lie. Now there was this Rostov, to whom Hassan was lying, and she could not even begin to think about whether what she said to Rostov should be the truth or another, different lie.

Hassan was saying, 'How did you get here?'

'On the *Karla*, of course. We were only forty or fifty miles off Sicily when I got the report that you had landed here. I also obtained permission from Cairo to order you to return there immediately and directly.'

'I still think I did the right thing,' said Hassan.

'Get out of my sight.'

Hassan walked away. Suza began to follow him but Rostov said, 'Not you.' He took her arm and began to walk.

She went with him, thinking: What do I do now?

'I know you've proved your loyalty to us, Miss Ashford, but in the middle of a project like this we can't allow newly recruited people simply to go home. On the other hand I have no people here in Sicily other than those I need with me on the ship, so I can't have you escorted somewhere else. I'm afraid you're going to have to come aboard the *Karla* with me until this business is over. I hope you don't mind. Do you know, you look exactly like your mother.'

They had walked out of the airport to a waiting car. Rostov opened the door for her. Now was the time she should run: after this it might be too late. She hesitated. One of the thugs stood beside her. His jacket fell open slightly and she saw the butt of his gun. She remembered the awful bang Cortone's gun had made in the ruined villa, and how she had screamed; and suddenly she was afraid to die, to become a lump of clay like poor fat Cortone; she was terrified of that gun and that bang and the bullet entering her body, and she began to shake.

'What is it?' Rostov said.

'Al Cortone died.'

'We know,' Rostov said. 'Get in the car.'

Suza got in the car.

Pierre Borg drove out of Athens and parked his car at one end of a stretch of beach where occasional lovers strolled. He got out and walked along the shoreline until he met Kawash coming the other way. They stood side by side, looking out to sea, wavelets lapping sleepily at their feet. Borg could see the handsome face of the tall Arab double agent by starlight. Kawash was not his usual confident self.

'Thank you for coming,' Kawash said.

Borg did not know why he was being thanked. If anyone should say thank you, it was he. And then he realized that Kawash had been making precisely that point. The man did everything with subtlety, including insults.

'The Russians suspect there is a leak out of Cairo,' Kawash said. 'They are playing their cards very close to their collective Communist chest, so to speak.' Kawash smiled thinly. Borg did not see the joke. 'Even when Yasif Hassan came back to Cairo for debriefing we didn't learn much – and *I* didn't get all the information Hassan gave.'

Borg belched loudly: he had eaten a big Greek dinner. 'Don't waste time with excuses, please. Just tell me what you do know.'

'All right,' Kawash said mildly. 'They know that Dickstein is to steal some uranium.'

'You told me that last time.'

'I don't think they know any of the details. Their intention is to let it happen, then expose it afterwards. They've put a couple of ships into the Mediterranean, but they don't know where to send them.'

A plastic bottle floated in on the tide and landed at Borg's feet. He kicked it back into the water. 'What about Suza Ashford?'

'Definitely working for the Arab side. Listen. There was an argument between Rostov and Hassan. Hassan wanted to find out exactly where Dickstein was, and Rostov thought it was unnecessary.'

'Bad news. Go on.'

'Afterwards Hassan went out on a limb. He got the Ashford girl to help him look for Dickstein. They went to a place called Buffalo, in the U.S., and met a gangster called Cortone who took them to Sicily. They missed Dickstein, but only just: they saw the *Stromberg* leave. Hassan is in considerable trouble over this. He has been ordered back to Cairo but he hasn't turned up yet.'

'But the girl led them to where Dickstein had been?'

'Exactly.'

'Jesus Christ, this is bad.' Borg thought of the message that had arrived in the Rome consulate for Nat Dickstein from his 'girl friend'. He told Kawash about it. 'Hassan has told me everything and he and I are coming to see you.' What the hell did it mean? Was it intended to warn Dickstein, or to delay him, or to confuse him? Or was it a double bluff – an attempt to make him think she was being coerced into leading Hassan to him?

'A double bluff, I should say,' Kawash said. 'She knew her role in this would eventually be exposed, so she tried for a longer lease on Dickstein's trust. You won't pass the message on . . . '

'Of course not.' Borg's mind turned to another tack. 'If they went to Sicily they know about the *Stromberg*. What conclusions can they draw from that?'

'That the *Stromberg* will be used in the uranium theft?'

'Exactly. Now, if I were Rostov, I'd follow the *Stromberg*, let the hijack take place, then attack. Damn, damn, damn. I think this will have to be called off.' He dug the toe of his shoe into the soft sand. 'What's the situation at Qattara?'

'I was saving the worst news until last. All tests have been completed satisfactorily. The Russians are supplying uranium. The reactor goes on stream three weeks from today.'

Borg stared out to sea, and he was more wretched, pessimistic and depressed than he had ever been in the whole of his unhappy life. 'You know what this fucking means don't you? It means we can't call it off. It means I can't stop Dickstein. It means that Dickstein is Israel's last chance.'

Kawash was silent. After a moment Borg looked at

him. The Arab's eyes were closed. 'What are you doing?' Borg said.

The silence went on for a few moments. Finally Kawash opened his eyes, looked at Borg, and gave his polite little half smile. 'Praying,' he said.

TEL AVIV TO MV STROMBERG
PERSONAL BORG TO DICKSTEIN EYES ONLY
MUST BE DECODED BY THE ADDRESSEE
BEGINS SUZA ASHFORD CONFIRMED ARAB AGENT
STOP SHE PERSUADED CORTONE TO TAKE HER AND
HASSAN TO SICILY STOP THEY ARRIVED AFTER YOU
LEFT STOP CORTONE NOW DEAD STOP THIS AND
OTHER DATA INDICATES STRONG POSSIBILITY YOU
WILL BE ATTACKED AT SEA STOP NO FURTHER
ACTION WE CAN TAKE AT THIS END STOP YOU
FUCKED IT UP ALL ON YOUR OWN NOW GET OUT OF
IT ALONE ENDS

The clouds which had been massing over the western Mediterranean for the previous few days finally burst that night, drenching the *Stromberg* with rain. A brisk wind blew up, and the shortcomings of the ship's design became apparent as she began to roll and yaw in the burgeoning waves.

Nat Dickstein did not notice the weather.

He sat alone in his little cabin, at the table which was screwed to the bulkhead, a pencil in hand and a pad, a codebook and a signal in front of him, transcribing Borg's message word by crucifying word.

He read it over and over again, and finally sat staring at the blank steel wall in front of him.

It was pointless to speculate about why she might have done this, to invent far-fetched hypotheses that Hassan had coerced or blackmailed her, to imagine that she had acted from mistaken beliefs or confused motives: Borg had said she was a spy, and he had been right. She had been a spy all along. That was why she had made love to him.

She had a big future in the intelligence business, that girl.

Dickstein put his face in his hands and pressed his eyeballs with his fingertips, but still he could see her, naked except for her high-heeled shoes, leaning against the cupboard in the kitchen of that little flat, reading the morning paper while she waited for a kettle to boil.

The worst of it was, he loved her still. Before he met her he had been a cripple, an emotional amputee with an empty sleeve hanging where he should have had love; and she had performed a miracle, making him whole again. Now she had betrayed him, taking away what she had given, and he would be more handicapped than ever. He had written her a love letter. Dear God, he thought, what did she do when she read that letter? Did she laugh? Did she show it to Yasif Hassan and say, 'See how I've got him hooked?'

If you took a blind man, and gave him back his sight, and then, after a day made him blind again during the night while he was sleeping, this was how he would feel when he woke up.

He had told Borg he would kill Suza if she were an

agent, but now he knew that he had been lying. He could never hurt her, no matter what she did.

It was late. Most of the crew were asleep except for those taking watches. He left the cabin and went up on deck without seeing anyone. Walking from the hatch to the gunwale he got soaked to the skin, but he did not notice. He stood at the rail, looking into the darkness, unable to see where the black sea ended and the black sky began, letting the rain stream across his face like tears.

He would never kill Suza, but Yasif Hassan was a different matter.

If ever a man had an enemy, he had one in Hassan. He had loved Eila, only to see her in a sensual embrace with Hassan. Now he had fallen in love with Suza, only to find that she had already been seduced by the same old rival. And Hassan had also used Suza in his campaign to take away Dickstein's homeland.

Oh, yes, he would kill Yasif Hassan, and he would do it with his bare hands if he could. And the others. The thought brought him up out of the depths of despair in a fury: he wanted to hear bones snap, he wanted to see bodies crumple, he wanted the smell of fear and gunfire, he wanted death all around him.

Borg thought they would be attacked at sea. Dickstein stood gripping the rail as the ship sawed through the unquiet sea; the wind rose momentarily and lashed his face with cold, hard rain; and he thought, So be it; and then he opened his mouth and shouted into the wind: 'Let them come – let the bastards come!'

CHAPTER FIFTEEN

HASSAN DID not go back to Cairo, then or ever.

Exultation filled him as his plane took off from Palermo. It had been close, but he had outwitted Rostov again! He could hardly believe it when Rostov had said, 'Get out of my sight.' He had felt sure he would be forced to board the *Karla* and consequently miss the hijack by the Fedayeen. But Rostov completely believed that Hassan was merely over-enthusiastic, impulsive, and inexperienced. It had never occurred to him that Hassan might be a traitor. But then, why should it? Hassan was the representative of Egyptian Intelligence on the team and he was an Arab. If Rostov had toyed with suspicions about his loyalty, he might have considered whether he was working for the Israelis, for they were the opposition – the Palestinians, if they entered the picture at all, could be assumed to be on the Arab side.

It was wonderful. Clever, arrogant, patronizing Colonel Rostov and the might of the notorious KGB had been fooled by a lousy Palestinian refugee, a man they thought was a nobody.

But it was not over yet. He still had to join forces with the Fedayeen.

The flight from Palermo took him to Rome, where he tried to get a plane to Annaba or Constantine, both near the Algerian coast. The nearest the airlines could offer was Algiers or Tunis. He went to Tunis.

There he found a young taxi driver with a newish Renault and thrust in front of the man's face more money in American dollars than he normally earned in a year. The taxi took him across the hundred-mile breadth of Tunisia, over the border into Algeria, and dropped him off at a fishing village with a small natural harbour. One of the Fedayeen was waiting for him. Hassan found him on the beach, sitting under a propped-up dinghy, sheltering from the rain and playing backgammon with a fisherman. The three men got into the fisherman's boat and cast off.

The sea was rough as they headed out in the last of the day. Hassan, no seaman, worried that the little motorboat would capsize, but the fisherman grinned cheerfully through it all.

The trip took them less than a half hour. As they approached the looming hulk of the ship, Hassan felt again the rising sense of triumph. A ship . . . they had a *ship*.

He clambered up on to the deck while the man who had met him paid off the fisherman. Mahmoud was waiting for him on deck. They embraced, and Hassan said, 'We should weigh anchor immediately – things are moving very fast now.'

'Come to the bridge with me.'

Hassan followed Mahmoud forward. The ship was a small coaster of about one thousand tons, quite new and in good condition. She was sleek, with most of her accommodations below deck. There was a hatch for one hold. She had been designed to carry small loads quickly and to manoeuvre in local North African ports.

They stood on the foredeck for a moment, looking about.

'She's just what we need,' Hassan said joyfully.

'I have renamed her the *Nablus*,' Mahmoud told him. 'She is the first ship of the Palestine Navy.'

Hassan felt tears start to his eyes.

They climbed the ladder. Mahmoud said, 'I got her from a Libyan businessman who wanted to save his soul.'

The bridge was compact and tidy. There was only one serious lack: radar. Many of these small coastal vessels still managed without it, and there had been no time to buy the equipment and fit it.

Mahmoud introduced the captain, also a Libyan – the businessman had provided a crew as well as a ship; none of the Fedayeen were sailors. The captain gave orders to weigh anchor and start engines.

The three men bent over a chart as Hassan told what he had learned in Sicily. 'The *Stromberg* left the south coast of Sicily at midday today. The *Coparelli* was due to pass through the Strait of Gibraltar late last night, heading for Genoa. They are sister ships, with the same top speed, so the earliest they can meet is twelve hours east of the midpoint between Sicily and Gibraltar.'

The captain made some calculations and looked at

another chart. 'They will meet south-east of the island of Minorca.'

'We should intercept the *Coparelli* no less than eight hours earlier.'

The captain ran his finger back along the trade route. 'That would put her just south of the island of Ibiza at dusk tomorrow.'

'Can we make it?'

'Yes, with a little time to spare, unless there is a storm.'

'Will there be a storm?'

'Sometime in the next few days, yes. But not tomorrow, I think.'

'Good. Where is the radio operator?'

'Here. This is Yaacov.'

Hassan turned to see a small, smiling man with tobacco-stained teeth and told him, 'There is a Russian aboard the *Coparelli*, a man called Tyrin, who will be sending signals to a Polish ship, the *Karla*. You must listen on this wavelength.' He wrote it down. 'Also, there is a radio beacon on the *Stromberg* that sends a simple thirty-second tone every half hour. If we listen for that every time we will be sure the *Stromberg* is not outrunning us.'

The captain was giving a course. Down on the deck the first officer had the hands making ready. Mahmoud was speaking to one of the Fedayeen about an arms inspection. The radio operator began to question Hassan about the *Stromberg*'s beacon. Hassan was not really listening. He was thinking: Whatever happens, it will be glorious.

The ship's engines roared, the deck tilted, the prow broke water and they were on their way.

Dieter Koch, the new engineer officer of the *Coparelli*, lay in his bunk in the middle of the night thinking: but what do I say if somebody sees me?

What he had to do now was simple. He had to get up, go to the aft engineering store, take out the spare oil pump and get rid of it. It was almost certain he could do this without being seen, for his cabin was close to the store, most of the crew were asleep, and those that were awake were on the bridge and in the engine room and likely to stay there. But 'almost certain' was not enough in an operation of this importance. If anyone should suspect, now or later, what he was really up to . . .

He put on a sweater, trousers, sea boots and an oilskin. The thing had to be done, and it had to be done now. He pocketed the key to the store, opened his cabin door and went out. As he made his way along the gangway he thought: I'll say I couldn't sleep so I'm checking the stores.

He unlocked the door to the store, turned on the light, went in and closed it behind him. Engineering spares were racked and shelved all around him – gaskets, valves, plugs, cable, bolts, filters . . . given a cylinder block, you could build a whole engine out of these parts.

He found the spare oil pump in a box on a high shelf. He lifted it down – it was not bulky but it was heavy – and then spent five minutes double-checking that there was not a second spare oil pump.

Now for the difficult part.

. . . I couldn't sleep, sir, so I was checking the spares. Very good, everything in order? Yes, sir. And what's that you've got under your arm? A bottle of whisky, sir. A cake my mother sent me. The spare oil pump, sir, I'm going to throw it overboard . . .

He opened the storeroom door and looked out.

Nobody.

He killed the light, went out, closed the door behind him and locked it. He walked along the gangway and out on deck.

Nobody.

It was still raining. He could see only a few yards, which was good, because it meant others could see only that far.

He crossed the deck to the gunwale, leaned over the rail, dropped the oil pump into the sea, turned, and bumped into someone.

A cake my mother sent me, it was so dry . . .

'Who's that?' a voice said in accented English.

'Engineer. You?' As Koch spoke, the other man turned so that his profile was visible in the deck light, and Koch recognized the rotund figure and big-nosed face of the radio operator.

'I couldn't sleep,' the radio operator said. 'I was . . . getting some air.'

He's as embarrassed as I am, Koch thought. I wonder why?

'Lousy night,' Koch said. 'I'm going in.'

'Goodnight.'

Koch went inside and made his way to his cabin. Strange fellow, that radio operator. He was not one of the regular crew. He had been taken on in Cardiff after the original radioman broke his leg. Like Koch, he was something of an outsider here. A good thing he had bumped into him rather than one of the others.

Inside his cabin he took off his wet outer clothes and lay on his bunk. He knew he would not sleep. His plan for tomorrow was all worked out, there was no point in going over it again, so he tried to think of other things: of his mother, who made the best potato kugel in the world; of his fiancée, who gave the best head in the world; of his mad father now in an institution in Tel Aviv; of the magnificent tapedeck he would buy with his back pay after this assignment; of his fine apartment in Haifa; of the children he would have, and how they would grow up in an Israel safe from war.

He got up two hours later. He went aft to the galley for some coffee. The cook's apprentice was there, standing in a couple of inches of water, frying bacon for the crew.

'Lousy weather,' Koch said.

'It will get worse.'

Koch drank his coffee, then refilled the mug and a second one and took them up to the bridge. The first officer was there. 'Good morning,' Koch said.

'Not really,' said the first officer, looking out into a curtain of rain.

'Coffee?'

'Good of you. Thank you.'

Koch handed him the mug. 'Where are we?'

'Here.' The officer showed him their position on a chart. 'Dead on schedule, in spite of the weather.'

Koch nodded. That meant he had to stop the ship in fifteen minutes. 'See you later,' he said. He left the bridge and went below to the engine room.

His number two was there, looking quite fresh, as if he had taken a good long nap during his night's duty. 'How's the oil pressure?' Koch asked him.

'Steady.'

'It was going up and down a bit yesterday.'

'Well, there was no sign of trouble in the night,' the number two said. He was a little too firm about it, as if he was afraid of being accused of sleeping while the gauge oscillated.

'Good,' Koch said. 'Perhaps it's repaired itself.' He put his mug down on a level cowling, then picked it up quickly as the ship rolled. 'Wake Larsen on your way to bed.'

'Right.'

'Sleep well.'

The number two left, and Koch drank down his coffee and went to work.

The oil pressure gauge was located in a bank of dials aft of the engine. The dials were set into a thin metal casing, painted matt black and secured by four self-tapping screws. Using a large screwdriver, Koch removed the four screws and pulled the casing away. Behind it was a mass of many-coloured wires leading to the different gauges. Koch swapped his large screw-driver for a small electrical one with an insulated handle. With a few turns he disconnected one of the wires to the oil pressure gauge. He wrapped a couple of inches of insulating tape around the bare end of the wire, then taped it to the back of the dial so that only a close inspection would reveal that it was not connected to the terminal. Then he replaced the casing and secured it with the four screws.

When Larsen came in he was topping up the transmission fluid.

'Can I do that, sir?' Larsen said. He was a donkeyman greaser, and lubrication was his province.

'I've done it now,' Koch said. He replaced the filler cap and stowed the can in a locker.

Larsen rubbed his eyes and lit a cigarette. He looked over the dials, did a double take and said, 'Sir! Oil pressure zero!'

'Zero?'

'Yes!'

'Stop engines!'

'Aye, aye, sir.'

Without oil, friction between the engine's metal parts would cause a very rapid build-up of heat until the metal melted, the parts fused and the engines stopped, never to go again. So dangerous was the sudden absence of oil pressure that Larsen might well have stopped the engines on his own initiative, without asking Koch.

Everyone on the ship heard the engine die and felt the *Coparelli* lose way; even those dayworkers who were still asleep in their bunks heard it through their dreams and woke up. Before the engine was completely still the first officer's voice came down the pipe. 'Bridge! What's going on below?'

Koch spoke into the voice-pipe. 'Sudden loss of oil pressure.'

'Any idea why?'

'Not yet.'

'Keep me posted.'

'Aye, aye, sir.'

Koch turned to Larsen. 'We're going to drop the sump,' he said. Larsen picked up a toolbox and followed Koch down a half deck to where they could get at the engine from underneath. Koch told him, 'If the main bearings or the big end bearings were worn the drop in oil pressure would have been gradual. A sudden drop means a failure in the oil supply. There's plenty of oil in the system – I checked earlier – and there are no signs of leaks. So there's probably a blockage.'

Koch released the sump with a power spanner and the two of them lowered it to the deck. They checked the sump strainer, the full flow filter, the filter relief valve and the main relief valve without finding any obstructions.

'If there's no blockage, the fault must be in the pump,' Koch said. 'Break out the spare oil pump.'

'That will be in the store on the main deck,' Larsen said.

Koch handed him the key, and Larsen went above.

Now Koch had to work very quickly. He took the casing off the oil pump, exposing two broad-toothed meshing gear wheels. He took the spanner off the power drill and fitted a bit, then attacked the cogs of the gear wheels with the drill, chipping and breaking them until they were all but useless. He put down the drill, picked up a crowbar and a hammer, and forced the bar in between the two wheels, prising them apart until he heard something give with a loud, dull crack. Finally he took out of his pocket a small nut made of toughened steel, battered and chipped. He had brought it with him when he had boarded the ship. He dropped the nut into the sump.

Done.

Larsen came back.

Koch realized he had not taken the bit off the power drill: when Larsen left there had been a spanner attachment on the tool. Don't look at the drill! he thought.

Larsen said, 'The pump isn't there, sir.'

Koch fished the nut out of the sump. 'Look at this,' he said, distracting Larsen's eye from the incriminating power drill. 'This is the cause of the trouble.' He showed Larsen the ruined gear wheels of the oil pump. 'The nut must have been dropped in the last time the filters were changed. It got into the pump and it's been going round and round in those gear wheels ever since. I'm surprised we didn't hear the noise, even over the sound of the engine. Anyway, the oil pump is beyond repair, so you'll have to find that spare. Get a few hands to help you look for it.'

Larsen went out. Koch took the bit off the power drill and put back the spanner attachment. He ran up the steps to the main engine room to remove the other piece of incriminating evidence. Working at top speed in case someone else should come in, he removed the casing on the gauges and reconnected the oil pressure gauge. Now it would genuinely read zero. He replaced the casing and threw away the insulating tape.

It was finished. Now to pull the wool over the captain's eyes.

As soon as the search party admitted defeat Koch went up to the bridge. He told the captain, 'A mechanic must have dropped a nut into the oil sump last time the engine was serviced, sir.' He showed the captain the nut. 'At some point – maybe while the ship was pitching so steeply – the nut got into the oil pump. After that it was just a matter of time. The nut went around in the gear wheels until it had totally ruined them. I'm afraid we can't make gear wheels like that on board. The ship should carry a spare oil pump, but it doesn't.'

The captain was furious. 'There will be hell to pay when I find out who's responsible for this.'

'It's the engineer's job to check the spares, but as you know, sir, I came on board at the last minute.'

'That means it's Sarne's fault.'

'There may be an explanation—'

'Indeed. Such as he spent too much time chasing Belgian whores to look after his engine. Can we limp along?'

'Absolutely not, sir. We wouldn't move half a cable before she seized.'

'Damnation. Where's that radio operator?'

The first officer said, 'I'll find him, sir,' and went out.

'You're certain you can't put something together?' the captain asked Koch.

'I'm afraid you can't make an oil pump out of spare parts and string. That's why we have to carry a spare pump.'

The first officer came back with the radio operator. The captain said, 'Where the devil have you been?'

The radio operator was the rotund, big-nosed man Koch had bumped into on the deck during the night. He looked hurt. 'I was helping to search the for'ard store for the oil pump, sir, then I went to wash my hands.' He glanced at Koch, but there was no hint of suspicion in his look: Koch was not sure how much he had seen during that little confrontation on the deck, but if he had made any connection between a missing spare and a package thrown overboard by the engineer, he wasn't saying.

'All right,' the captain said. 'Make a signal to the owners: Report engine breakdown at... What's our exact position, number one?'

The first officer gave the radio operator the position.

The captain continued: 'Require new oil pump or tow to port. Please instruct.'

Koch's shoulders slumped a little. He had done it.

Eventually the reply came from the owners: COPA-RELLI SOLD TO SAVILE SHIPPING OF ZURICH. YOUR MESSAGED PASSED TO NEW OWNERS. STAND BY FOR THEIR INSTRUCTIONS.

Almost immediately afterward there was a signal from Savile Shipping: OUR VESSEL GIL HAMILTON IN YOUR WATERS. SHE WILL COME ALONGSIDE AT APPROXI-

MATELY NOON. PREPARE TO DISEMBARK ALL CREW
EXCEPT ENGINEER. GIL HAMILTON WILL TAKE CREW TO
MARSEILLES. ENGINEER WILL AWAIT NEW OIL PUMP.
PAPAGOPOLOUS.

The exchange of signals was heard sixty miles away by
Solly Weinberg, the master of the *Gil Hamilton* and a
commander in the Israeli Navy. He muttered, 'Right on
schedule. Well done, Koch.' He set a course for the
Coparelli and ordered full speed ahead.

It was *not* heard by Yasif Hassan and Mahmoud aboard
the *Nablus* 150 miles away. They were in the captain's
cabin, bent over a sketch plan Hassan had drawn of the
Coparelli, and they were deciding exactly how they
would board her and take over. Hassan had instructed
the *Nablus*'s radio operator to listen out on two wave-
lengths: the one on which the *Stromberg*'s radio beacon
broadcast and the one Tyrin was using for his clandestine signals from the *Coparelli* to Rostov aboard
the *Karla*. Because the messages were sent on the
Coparelli's regular wavelength, the *Nablus* did not
pick them up. It would be some time before the
Fedayeen realized they were hijacking an almost abandoned ship.

The exchange was heard 200 miles away on the bridge
of the *Stromberg*. When the *Coparelli* acknowledged the

signal from Papagopolous, the officers on the bridge cheered and clapped. Nat Dickstein, leaning against a bulkhead with a mug of black coffee in his hand, staring ahead at the rain and the heaving sea, did not cheer. His body was hunched and tense, his face stiff, his brown eyes slitted behind the plastic spectacles. One of the others noticed his silence and made a remark about getting over the first big hurdle. Dickstein's muttered reply was uncharacteristically peppered with the strongest of obscenities. The cheerful officer turned away, and later in the mess observed that Dickstein looked like the kind of man who would stick a knife in you if you stepped on his toe.

And it was heard by David Rostov and Suza Ashford 300 miles away aboard the *Karla*.

Suza had been in a daze as she walked across the gangplank from the Sicilian quayside on to the Polish vessel. She had hardly noticed what was happening as Rostov showed her to her cabin – an officer's room with its own head – and said he hoped she would be comfortable. She sat on the bed. She was still there, in the same position, an hour later when a sailor brought some cold food on a tray and set it down on her table without speaking. She did not eat it. When it got dark she began to shiver, so she got into the bed and lay there with her eyes wide open, staring at nothing, still shivering.

Eventually she had slept – fitfully at first, with strange

meaningless nightmares, but in the end deeply. Dawn woke her.

She lay still, feeling the motion of the ship and looking blankly at the cabin around her; and then she realized where she was. It was like waking up and remembering the blind terror of a nightmare, except that instead of thinking: Oh, thank God it was a dream, she realized it was all true and it was still going on.

She felt horribly guilty. She had been fooling herself, she could see that now. She had convinced herself that she had to find Nat to warn him, no matter the risk: but the truth was she would have reached for any excuse to go and see him. The disastrous consequences of what she had done followed naturally from the confusion of her motives. It was true that Nat had been in danger; but he was in worse danger now, and it was Suza's fault.

She thought of that, and she thought of how she was at sea in a Polish ship commanded by Nat's enemies and surrounded by Russian thugs, and she closed her eyes tightly and pushed her head under the pillow and fought the hysteria that bubbled up in her throat.

And then she began to feel angry, and that was what saved her sanity.

She thought of her father, and how he wanted to use her to further his political ideas, and she felt angry with him. She thought of Hassan, manipulating her father, putting his hand on her knee, and she wished she had slapped his face while she had the chance. Finally she thought of Rostov, with his hard, intelligent face and his cold smile, and how he intended to ram Nat's ship and kill him, and she got mad as hell.

Dickstein was her man. He was funny, and he was strong, and he was oddly vulnerable, and he wrote love letters and stole ships, and he was the only man she had ever loved like *this*; and she was not going to lose him.

She was in the enemy camp, a prisoner, but only from *her* point of view. They thought she was on their side; they trusted her. Perhaps she would have a chance to throw a wrench in their works. She must look for it. She would move about the ship, concealing her fear, talking to her enemies, consolidating her position in their confidence, pretending to share their ambitions and concerns, until she saw her opportunity.

The thought made her tremble. Then she told herself: If I don't do this, I lose him; and if I lose him I don't want to live.

She got out of bed. She took off the clothes she had slept in, washed and put on clean sweater and pants from her suitcase. She sat at the small nailed-down table and ate some of the sausage and cheese that had been left there the day before. She brushed her hair and, just to boost her morale a little, put on a trace of make-up.

She tried her cabin door. It was not locked.

She went out.

She walked along a gangway and followed the smell of food to the galley. She went in and looked swiftly about.

Rostov sat alone, eating eggs slowly with a fork. He

looked up and saw her. Suddenly his face seemed icily evil, his narrow mouth hard, his eyes without emotion. Suza hesitated, then forced herself to walk toward him. Reaching his table, she leaned briefly on a chair, for her legs felt weak.

Rostov said, 'Sit down.'

She dropped into the chair.

'How did you sleep?'

She was breathing too quickly, as if she had been walking very fast. 'Fine,' she said. Her voice shook.

His sharp, sceptical eyes seemed to bore into her brain. 'You seem upset.' He spoke evenly, without sympathy or hostility.

'I . . .' Words seemed to stick in her throat, choking her. 'Yesterday . . . was confusing.' It was true, anyway: it was easy to say this. 'I never saw someone die.'

'Ah.' At last a hint of human feeling showed in Rostov's expression: perhaps he remembered the first time he watched a man die. He reached for a coffee pot and poured her a cup. 'You're very young,' he said. 'You can't be much older than my first son.'

Suza sipped at the hot coffee gratefully, hoping he would go on talking in this fashion – it would help her to calm down.

'Your son?' she said.

'Yuri Davidovitch, he's twenty.'

'What does he do?'

Rostov's smile was not as chilly as before. 'Unfortunately he spends most of his time listening to decadent music. He doesn't study as hard as he should. Not like his brother.'

Suza's breathing was slowing to normal, and her hand no longer shook when she picked up her cup. She knew that this man was no less dangerous just because he had a family; but he *seemed* less frightening when he talked like this. 'And your other son?' she asked. 'The younger one?'

Rostov nodded. 'Vladimir.' Now he was not frightening at all: he was staring over Suza's shoulder with a fond, indulgent expression on his face. 'He's very gifted. He will be a great mathematician if he gets the right schooling.'

'That shouldn't be a problem,' she said, watching him. 'Soviet education is the best in the world.'

It seemed like a safe thing to say, but must have had some special significance for him, because the faraway look disappeared and his face turned hard and cold again. 'No,' he said. 'It shouldn't be a problem.' He continued eating his eggs.

Suza thought urgently: He was becoming friendly, I mustn't lose him now. She cast about desperately for something to say. What did they have in common, what could they talk about? Then she was inspired. 'I wish I could remember you from when you were at Oxford.'

'You were very small.' He poured himself some coffee. 'Everyone remembers your mother. She was easily the most beautiful woman around. And you're exactly like her.'

That's better, Suza thought. She asked him, 'What did you study?'

'Economics.'

'Not an exact science in those days, I imagine.'

'And not much better today.'

Suza put on a faintly solemn expression. 'We speak of bourgeois economics, of course.'

'Of course.' Rostov looked at her as if he could not tell whether she were serious or not. He seemed to decide she was.

An officer came into the galley and spoke to him in Russian. Rostov looked at Suza regretfully. 'I must go up to the bridge.'

She had to go with him. She forced herself to speak calmly. 'May I come?'

He hesitated. Suza thought: He *should* let me. He's enjoyed talking to me, he believes I'm on his side, and if I learn any secrets how could he imagine I could use them, stuck here on a KGB ship?

Rostov said: 'Why not?'

He walked away. Suza followed.

Up in the radio room Rostov smiled as he read through the messages and translated them for Suza's benefit. He seemed delighted with Dickstein's ingenuity. 'The man is smart as hell,' he said.

'What's Savile Shipping?' Suza asked.

'A front for Israeli Intelligence. Dickstein is eliminating all the people who have reason to be interested in what happens to the uranium. The shipping company isn't interested because they no longer own the ship. Now he's taking off the captain and crew. No doubt he has some kind of hold over the people who actually own the uranium. It's a beautiful scheme.'

This was what Suza wanted. Rostov was talking to her like a colleague, she was at the centre of events; she

must be able to find a way to foul things up for him.
She said, 'I suppose the breakdown was rigged?'

'Yes. Now Dickstein can take over the ship without
firing a shot.'

Suza thought fast. When she 'betrayed' Dickstein she
had proved her loyalty to the Arab side. Now the Arab
side had split into two camps: in one were Rostov, the
KGB and Egyptian Intelligence; in the other Hassan
and the Fedayeen. Now Suza could prove her loyalty to
Rostov's side by betraying Hassan.

She said, as casually as she possibly could, 'And so
can Yasif Hassan, of course.'

'What?'

'Hassan can also take over the *Coparelli* without firing
a shot.'

Rostov stared at her. The blood seemed to drain
from his thin face. Suza was shocked to see him
suddenly lose all his poise and confidence. He said,
'Hassan intends to hijack the *Coparelli*?'

Suza pretended to be shocked. 'Are you telling me
that you didn't *know*?'

'But who? Not the Egyptians, surely!'

'The Fedayeen. Hassan said this was *your* plan.'

Rostov banged the bulkhead with his fist, looking
very uncool and Russian for a moment. 'Hassan is a liar
and a traitor!'

This was Suza's chance, she knew. She thought: Give
me strength. She said: 'Maybe we can stop him . . .'

Rostov looked at her. 'What's his plan?'

'To hijack the *Coparelli* before Dickstein gets there,
then ambush the Israeli team, and sail to . . . he didn't

tell me exactly, somewhere in North Africa. What was your plan?'

'To ram the ship after Dickstein had stolen the uranium—'

'Can't we still do that?'

'No. We're too far away, we'd never catch them.'

Suza knew that if she did not do the next bit exactly right, both she and Dickstein would die. She crossed her arms to stop the shaking. She said, 'Then there is only one thing we can do.'

Rostov looked up at her. 'There is?'

'We must warn Dickstein of the Fedayeen ambush so that he can take back the *Coparelli*.'

There. She had said it. She watched Rostov's face. He must swallow it, it was logical, it was the right thing for him to do!

Rostov was thinking hard. He said, 'Warn Dickstein so that he can take the *Coparelli* back from the Fedayeen. Then he can proceed according to his plan and we can proceed according to ours.'

'Yes!' said Suza. 'That's the only way! Isn't it? Isn't it?'

FROM: SAVILE SHIPPING, ZURICH

TO: ANGELUZZI E BIANCO, GENOA

YOUR YELLOWCAKE CONSIGNMENT FROM F.A. PEDLER INDEFINITELY DELAYED DUE TO ENGINE TROUBLE AT SEA. WILL ADVISE SOONEST OF NEW DELIVERY DATES. PAPAGOPOLOUS.

*

As the *Gil Hamilton* came into view, Pyotr Tyrin cornered Ravlo, the addict, in the 'tweendecks of the *Coparelli*. Tyrin acted with a confidence he did not feel. He adopted a bullying manner and grabbed hold of Ravlo's sweater. Tyrin was a bulky man, and Ravlo was somewhat wasted. Tyrin said, 'Listen, you're going to do something for me.'

'Sure, anything you say.'

Tyrin hesitated. It would be risky. Still, there was no alternative. 'I need to stay on board ship when the rest of you go on the *Gil Hamilton*. If I'm missed, you will say that you have seen me go over.'

'Right, okay, sure.'

'If I'm discovered, and I have to board the *Gil Hamilton*, you can be sure I'll tell them your secret.'

'I'll do everything I can.'

'You'd better.'

Tyrin let him go. He was not reassured: a man like that would promise you anything, but when it came to the crunch he might fall to pieces.

All hands were summoned on deck for the change-over. The sea was too rough for the *Gil Hamilton* to come alongside, so she sent a launch. Everyone had to wear lifebelts for the crossing. The officers and crew of the *Coparelli* stood quietly in the pouring rain while they were counted, then the first sailor went over the side and down the ladder, jumped into the well of the launch.

The boat would be too small to take the whole crew – they would have to go over in two or three detachments, Tyrin realized. While everyone's attention was on the first men to go over the rail, Tyrin whispered to Ravlo, 'Try and be last to go.'

'All right.'

The two of them edged out to the back of the crowd on deck. The officers were peering over the side at the launch. The men were standing, waiting, facing toward the *Gil Hamilton*.

Tyrin slipped back behind a bulkhead.

He was two steps from a lifeboat whose cover he had loosened earlier. The stem of the boat could be seen from the deck amidships, where the sailors were standing, but the stern could not. Tyrin moved to the stern, lifted the cover, got in and from inside put the cover back in place.

He thought: If I'm discovered now I've had it.

He was a big man, and the life jacket made him bigger. With some difficulty he crawled the length of the boat to a position from which he could see the deck through an eyelet in the tarpaulin. Now it was up to Ravlo.

He watched as a second detachment of men went down the ladder to the launch, then heard the first officer say, 'Where's that radio operator?'

Tyrin looked for Ravlo and located him. Speak. damn you!

Ravlo hesitated. 'He went over with the first lot, sir.'

Good boy!

'Are you sure?'

'Yes, sir. I saw him.'

The officer nodded and said something about not being able to tell one from another in this filthy rain.

The captain called to Koch, and the two men stood talking in the lee of a bulkhead, close to Tyrin's hiding place. The captain said, 'I've never heard of Savile Shipping, have you?'

'No, sir.'

'This is all wrong, selling a ship while she's at sea, then leaving the engineer in charge of her and taking the captain off.'

'Yes, sir. I imagine they're not seafaring people, these new owners.'

'They're surely not, or they'd know better. Probably accountants.' There was a pause. 'You could refuse to stay alone, of course, then I would have to stay with you. I'd back you up afterwards.'

'I'm afraid I'd lose my ticket.'

'Right, I shouldn't have suggested it. Well, good luck.'

'Thank you, sir.'

The third group of seamen had boarded the launch. The first officer was at the top of the ladder waiting for the captain, who was still muttering about accountants as he turned around, crossed the deck and followed the first officer over the side.

Tyrin turned his attention to Koch, who now thought he was the only man aboard the *Coparelli*. The engineer watched the launch go across to the *Gil Hamilton*, then climbed the ladder to the bridge.

Tyrin cursed aloud. He wanted Koch to go below so

that he could get to the for'ard store and radio to the *Karla*. He watched the bridge, and saw Koch's face appear from time to time behind the glass. If Koch stayed there, Tyrin would have to wait until dark before he could contact Rostov and report.

It looked very much as if Koch planned to remain on the bridge all day.

Tyrin settled down for a long wait.

When the *Nablus* reached the point south of Ibiza where Hassan expected to encounter the *Coparelli*, there was not a single ship in sight.

They circled the point in a widening spiral while Hassan scanned the desolate rainswept horizon through binoculars.

Mahmoud said, 'You have made a mistake.'

'Not necessarily.' Hassan was determined he would not appear panicked. 'This was just the earliest point at which we could meet her. She doesn't have to travel at top speed.'

'Why should she be delayed?'

Hassan shrugged, seeming less worried than he was. 'Perhaps the engine isn't running well. Perhaps they've had worse weather than we have. A lot of reasons.'

'What do you suggest, then?'

Mahmoud was also very uneasy, Hassan realized. On this ship he was not in control, only Hassan could make the decisions. 'We travel south-west, backing along the *Coparelli*'s route. We must meet her sooner or later.'

'Give the order to the captain,' Mahmoud said, and

went below to his troops, leaving Hassan on the bridge with the captain.

Mahmoud burned with the irrational anger of tension. So did his troops, Hassan had observed. They had been expecting a fight at midday, and now they had to wait, dawdling about in the crew quarters and the galley, cleaning weapons, playing cards, and bragging about past battles. They were hyped up for combat, and inclined to play dangerous knife-throwing games to prove their courage to each other and to themselves. One of them had quarrelled with two seamen over an imaginary insult, and had cut them both about the face with a broken glass before the fight was broken up. Now the crew were staying well away from the Fedayeen.

Hassan wondered how he would handle them if he were Mahmoud. He had thought along these lines a lot recently. Mahmoud was still the commander, but he was the one who had done all the important work: discovered Dickstein, brought the news of his plan, conceived the counter-hijack, and established the *Stromberg*'s whereabouts. He was beginning to wonder what would be his position in the movement when all this was over.

Clearly, Mahmoud was wondering the same thing.

Well. If there was to be a power struggle between the two of them, it would have to wait. First they had to hijack the *Coparelli* and ambush Dickstein. Hassan felt a little nauseous when he thought about that. It was all very well for the battle-hardened men below to convince themselves they looked forward to a fight, but

Hassan had never been in war, never even had a gun pointed at him except by Cortone in the ruined villa. He was afraid, and he was even more afraid of disgracing himself by showing his fear, by turning and running away, by throwing up as he had done in the villa. But he also felt excited, for if they won – if they won!

There was a false alarm at four-thirty in the afternoon when they sighted another ship coming toward them, but after examining her through binoculars Hassan announced she was not the *Coparelli*, and as she passed they were able to read the name on her side: *Gil Hamilton*.

As daylight began to fade Hassan became worried. In this weather, even with navigation lights, two ships could pass within half a mile of one another at night without seeing each other. And there had been not a sound out of the *Coparelli*'s secret radio all afternoon, although Yaacov had reported that Rostov was trying to raise Tyrin. To be certain that the *Coparelli* did not pass the *Nablus* in the night they would have to go about and spend the night travelling toward Genoa at the *Coparelli*'s speed, then resume searching in the morning. But by that time the *Stromberg* would be close by and the Fedayeen might lose the chance of springing a trap on Dickstein.

Hassan was about to explain this to Mahmoud – who had just returned to the bridge – when a single white light winked on in the distance.

'She's at anchor,' said the captain.

'How can you tell?' Mahmoud asked.

'That's what a single white light means.'

Hassan said, 'That would explain why she wasn't off Ibiza when we expected her. If that's the *Coparelli*, you should prepare to board.'

'I agree,' said Mahmoud, and went off to tell his men.

'Turn out your navigation lights,' Hassan told the captain.

As the *Nablus* closed with the other ship, night fell.

'I'm almost certain that's the *Coparelli*,' Hassan said.

The captain lowered his binoculars. 'She has three cranes on deck, and all her upperworks are aft of the hatches.'

'Your eyesight is better than mine,' Hassan said. 'She's the *Coparelli*.'

He went below to the galley, where Mahmoud was addressing his troops. Mahmoud looked at him as he stepped inside. Hassan nodded. 'This is it.'

Mahmoud turned back to his men. 'We do not expect much resistance. The ship is crewed by ordinary seamen, and there is no reason for them to be armed. We go in two boats, one to attack the port side and one the starboard. On board our first task is to take the bridge and prevent the crew from using the radio. Next we round up the crew on deck.' He paused and turned to Hassan. 'Tell the captain to get as close as possible to the *Coparelli* and then stop engines.'

Hassan turned. Suddenly he was errand boy again: Mahmoud was demonstrating that he was still the battle leader. Hassan felt the humiliation bring a rush of blood to his cheeks.

'Yasif.'

He turned back.

'Your weapon.' Mahmoud threw him a gun. Hassan caught it. It was a small pistol, almost a toy, the kind of gun a woman might carry in her handbag. The Fedayeen roared with laughter.

Hassan thought: I can play these games too. He found what looked like the safety catch and released it. He pointed the gun at the floor and pulled the trigger. The report was very loud. He emptied the gun into the deck.

There was a silence.

Hassan said, 'I thought I saw a mouse.' He threw the gun back to Mahmoud.

The Fedayeen laughed even louder.

Hassan went out. He went back up to the bridge, passed the message to the captain, and returned to the deck. It was very dark now. For a time all that could be seen of the *Coparelli* was its light. Then, as he strained his eyes, a silhouette of solid black became distinguishable against the wash of dark grey.

The Fedayeen, quiet now, had emerged from the galley and stood on deck with the crew. The *Nablus*'s engines died. The crew lowered the boats.

Hassan and his Fedayeen went over the side.

Hassan was in the same boat as Mahmoud. The little launch bobbed on the waves, which now seemed immense. They approached the sheer side of the *Coparelli*. There was no sign of activity on the ship. Surely, Hassan thought, the officer on watch must hear the sound of two engines approaching? But no alarms sounded, no lights flooded the deck, no one shouted orders or came to the rail.

Mahmoud was first up the ladder.

By the time Hassan reached the *Coparelli*'s deck the other team was swarming over the starboard gunwale.

Men poured down the companionways and up the ladders. Still there was no sign of the *Coparelli*'s crew. Hassan had a dreadful premonition that something had gone terribly wrong.

He followed Mahmoud up to the bridge. Two of the men were already there. Hassan asked, 'Did they have time to use the radio?'

'Who?' Mahmoud said.

They went back down to the deck. Slowly the men were emerging from the bowels of the boat, looking puzzled, their cold guns in their hands.

Mahmoud said: 'The wreck of the *Marie Celeste*.'

Two men came across the deck with a frightened looking sailor between them.

Hassan spoke to the sailor in English. 'What's happened here?'

The sailor replied in some other language.

Hassan had a sudden terrifying thought. 'Let's check the hold,' he said to Mahmoud.

They found a companionway leading below and went down into the hold. Hassan found a light switch and turned it on.

The hold was full of large oil drums, sealed and secured with wooden wedges. The drums had the word PLUMBAT stencilled on their sides.

'That's it,' said Hassan. 'That's the uranium.'

They looked at the drums, then at each other. For a moment all rivalry was forgotten.

'We did it,' said Hassan. 'By God, we did it.'

As darkness fell Tyrin had watched the engineer go forward to switch on the white light. Coming back, he had not gone up to the bridge but had walked farther aft and entered the galley. He was going to get something to eat. Tyrin was hungry too. He would give his arm for a plate of salted herring and a loaf of brown bread. Sitting cramped in his lifeboat all afternoon, waiting for Koch to move, he had had nothing to think about but his hunger, and he had tortured himself with thoughts of caviar, smoked salmon, marinated mushrooms and most of all brown bread.

Not yet, Pyotr, he told himself.

As soon as Koch had disappeared from sight, Tyrin got out of the lifeboat, his muscles protesting as he stretched, and hurried along the deck to the for'ard store.

He had shifted the boxes and junk in the main store so that they concealed the entrance to his small radio room. Now he had to get down on hands and knees, pull away one box, and crawl through a little tunnel to get in.

The set was repeating a short two-letter signal. Tyrin checked the code book and found it meant he was to switch to another wavelength before acknowledging. He set the radio to transmit and followed his instructions.

Rostov immediately replied. CHANGE OF PLAN. HASSAN WILL ATTACK COPARELLI.

Tyrin frowned in puzzlement, and made: REPEAT PLEASE.

HASSAN IS A TRAITOR, FEDAYEEN WILL ATTACK COPARELLI.

Tyrin said aloud: 'Jesus, what's going on?' The *Coparelli* was *here*, he was on it ... Why would Hassan ... for the uranium, of course.

Rostov was still signalling. HASSAN PLANS TO AMBUSH DICKSTEIN. FOR OUR PLAN TO PROCEED WE MUST WARN DICKSTEIN OF THE AMBUSH.

Tyrin frowned as he decoded this, then his face cleared as he understood. 'Then we'll be back to square one,' he said to himself. 'That's clever. But what do I do?'

He made: HOW?

YOU WILL CALL STROMBERG ON COPARELLI'S REGU-LAR WAVELENGTH AND SEND FOLLOWING MESSAGE PRE-CISELY REPEAT PRECISELY. QUOTE COPARELLI TO STROMBERG I AM BOARDED ARABS I THINK. WATCH UNQUOTE.

Tyrin nodded. Dickstein would think that Koch had time to get a few words off before the Arabs killed him. Forewarned, Dickstein should be able to take the *Coparelli*. Then Rostov's *Karla* could collide with Dick-stein's ship as planned. Tyrin thought: But what about me?

He made: UNDERSTOOD. He heard a distant bump, as if something had hit the ship's hull. At first he ignored it, then he remembered there was nobody aboard but him and Koch. He went to the door of the for'ard store and looked out.

The Fedayeen had arrived.

He closed the door and hurried back to his transmitter. He made: HASSAN IS HERE.

Rostov replied, SIGNAL DICKSTEIN NOW.

WHAT DO I DO THEN?

HIDE.

Thanks very much, Tyrin thought. He signed off and tuned to the regular wavelength to signal the *Stromberg*.

The morbid thought occurred to him that he might never eat salted herring again.

'I've heard of being armed to the teeth, but this is ridiculous,' said Nat Dickstein, and they all laughed.

The message from the *Coparelli* had altered his mood. At first he had been shocked. How had the opposition managed to learn so much of his plan that they had been able to hijack the *Coparelli* first? Somewhere he must have made terrible errors of judgment. Suza...? But there was no point now in castigating himself. There was a fight ahead. His black depression vanished. The tension was still there, coiled tight inside him like a steel spring, but now he could ride it and use it, now he had something to do with it.

The twelve men in the mess room of the *Stromberg* sensed the change in Dickstein and they caught his eagerness for the battle, although they knew some of them would die soon.

Armed to the teeth they were. Each had an Uzi 9-mm

submachine gun, a reliable, compact firearm weighing nine pounds when loaded with the 25-round magazine and only an inch over two feet long with its metal stock extended. They had three spare magazines each. Each man had a 9-mm Luger in a belt holster – the pistol would take the same cartridges as the machine gun – and a clip of four grenades on the opposite side of his belt. Almost certainly, they all had extra weapons of their own choice: knives, blackjacks, bayonets, knuckle-dusters and others more exotic, carried superstitiously, more like lucky charms than fighting implements.

Dickstein knew their mood, knew they had caught it from him. He had felt it before with men before a fight. They were afraid, and – paradoxically – the fear made them eager to get started, for the waiting was the worst part, the battle itself was anaesthetic, and afterwards you had either survived or you were dead and did not care any more.

Dickstein had figured his battle plan in detail and briefed them. The *Coparelli* was designed like a miniature tanker, with holds forward and amidships, the main superstructure on the afterdeck, and a secondary superstructure in the stern. The main superstructure contained the bridge, the officers' quarters and the mess; below it were crew's quarters. The stern superstructure contained the galley, below that stores, and below these the engine room. The two superstructures were separate above deck, but below deck they were connected by gangways.

They were to go over in three teams. Abbas's would

attack the bows. The other two, led by Bader and Gibli, would go up the port and starboard ladders at the stern.

The two stern teams were detailed to go below and work forward, flushing out the enemy amidships where they could be mown down by Abbas and his men from the prow. The strategy was likely to leave a pocket of resistance at the bridge, so Dickstein planned to take the bridge himself.

The attack would be by night; otherwise they would never get aboard – they would be picked off as they came over the rails. That left the problem of how to avoid shooting at one another as well as the enemy. For this he provided a recognition signal, the word *Aliyah*, and the attack plan was designed so that they were not expected to confront one another until the very end.

Now they were waiting.

They sat in a loose circle in the galley of the *Stromberg*, identical to the galley of the *Coparelli* where they would soon be fighting and dying. Dickstein was speaking to Abbas: 'From the bows you'll control the foredeck, an open field of fire. Deploy your men behind cover and stay there. When the enemy on deck reveal their positions, pick them off. Your main problem is going to be hailing fire from the bridge.'

Slumped in his chair, Abbas looked even more like a tank than usual. Dickstein was glad Abbas was on his side. 'And we hold our fire at first.'

Dickstein nodded. 'Yes. You've a good chance of getting aboard unseen. No point in shooting until you know the rest of us have arrived.'

Abbas nodded. 'I see Porush is on my team. You know he's my brother-in-law.'

'Yes. I also know he's the only married man here. I thought you might want to take care of him.'

'Thanks.'

Feinberg looked up from the knife he was cleaning. The lanky New Yorker was not grinning for once. 'How do you figure these Arabs?'

Dickstein shook his head. 'They could be regular army or Fedayeen.'

Feinberg grinned. 'Let's hope they're regular army – we make faces, they surrender.'

It was a lousy joke, but they all laughed anyway.

Ish, always pessimistic, sitting with his feet on a table and his eyes closed, said, 'Going over the rail will be the worst part. We'll be naked as babes.'

Dickstein said, 'Remember that they believe we're expecting to take over a deserted boat. Their ambush is supposed to be a big surprise for us. They're looking for an easy victory – but we're prepared. And it will be dark—'

The door opened and the captain came in. 'We've sighted the *Coparelli*.'

Dickstein stood up. 'Let's go. Good luck, and don't take any prisoners.'

CHAPTER SIXTEEN

THE THREE boats pulled away from the *Stromberg* in the last few minutes before dawn.

Within seconds the ship behind them was invisible. She had no navigation lights, and deck lights and cabin lamps had been extinguished, even below the water-line, to ensure that no light escaped to warn the *Coparelli*.

The weather had worsened during the night. The captain of the *Stromberg* said it was still not bad enough to be called a storm, but the rain was torrential, the wind strong enough to blow a steel bucket clattering along the deck, the waves so high that now Dickstein was obliged to cling tightly to his bench seat in the well of the motorboat.

For a while they were in limbo, with nothing visible ahead or behind. Dickstein could not even see the faces of the four men in the boat with him. Feinberg broke the silence: 'I still say we should have postponed this fishing trip until tomorrow.'

Whistling past the graveyard.

Dickstein was as superstitious as the rest: underneath his oilskin and his life jacket he wore his father's old striped waistcoat with a smashed fob watch in the pocket over his heart. The watch had once stopped a German bullet.

Dickstein was thinking logically, but in a way he knew he had gone a little crazy. His affair with Suza, and her betrayal, had turned him upside down: his old values and motivations had been jolted, and the new ones he had acquired with her had turned to dust in his hands. He still cared for some things: he wanted to win this battle, he wanted Israel to have the uranium, and he wanted to kill Yasif Hassan; the one thing he did not care about was himself. He had no fear, suddenly, of bullets and pain and death. Suza had betrayed him, and he had no burning desire to live a long life with that in his past. So long as Israel got its bomb, Esther would die peacefully, Mottie would finish *Treasure Island*, and Yigael would look after the grapes.

He gripped the barrel of the machine gun beneath his oilskin.

They crested a wave and suddenly, there in the next trough, was the *Coparelli*.

Switching from forward to reverse several times in rapid succession, Levi Abbas edged his boat closer to the bows of the *Coparelli*. The white light above them enabled him to see quite clearly, while the outward-curving hull shielded his boat from the sight of anyone on deck or on the bridge. When the boat was close enough to the ladder Abbas took a rope and tied it around his waist under the oilskin. He hesitated a moment, then shucked off the oilskin, unwrapped his gun and slung the gun over his neck. He stood with one foot in the boat and one on the gunwale, waited for his moment, and jumped.

He hit the ladder with both feet and both hands. He untied the rope around his waist and secured it to a rung of the ladder. He went up the ladder almost to the top, then stopped. They should go over the rail as close together as possible.

He looked back down. Sharrett and Sapir were already on the ladder below him. As he looked, Porush made his jump, landed awkwardly and missed his grip, and for a moment Abbas's breath caught in his throat; but Porush slipped down only one rung before he manged to hook an arm around the side of the ladder and arrest his descent.

Abbas waited for Porush to come up close behind Sapir, then he went over the rail. He landed softly on all fours and crouched low beside the gunwale. The others followed swiftly: one, two, three. The white light was above them and they were very exposed.

Abbas looked about. Sharrett was the smallest and he could wriggle like a snake. Abbas touched his shoulder and pointed across the deck. 'Take cover on the port side.'

Sharret bellied across two yards of open deck, then he was partly concealed by the raised edge of the for'ard hatch. He inched forward.

Abbas looked up and down the deck. At any moment they could be spotted; they would know nothing until a hail of bullets tore into them. Quick, quick! Up in the stem was the winding gear for the anchor, with a large pile of slack chain. 'Sapir.' Abbas pointed, and Sapir crawled along the deck to the position.

'I like the crane,' Porush said.

Abbas looked at the derrick towering over them, dominating the whole of the foredeck. The control cabin was some ten feet above deck level. It would be a dangerous position, but it made good tactical sense. 'Go,' he said.

Porush crawled forward, following Sharrett's route. Watching, Abbas thought: He's got a fat ass – my sister feeds him too well. Porush gained the foot of the crane and began to climb the ladder. Abbas held his breath – if one of the enemy should happen to look this way now, while Porush was on the ladder – then he reached the cabin.

Behind Abbas, in the prow, was a companion head over a short flight of steps leading down to a door. The area was not big enough to be called a fo'c'sle, and there was almost certainly no proper accommodation in there – it was simply a for'ard store. He crawled to it, crouched at the foot of the steps in the little well, and gently cracked the door. It was dark inside. He closed the door and turned around, resting his gun on the head of the steps, satisfied that he was alone.

There was very little light at the stern end, and Dickstein's boat had to get very close to the *Coparelli*'s starboard ladder. Gibli, the team leader, found it difficult to keep the boat in position. Dickstein found a boathook in the well of the launch and used it to hold the boat steady, pulling toward the *Coparelli* when the sea tried to part them and pushing away when the boat and the ship threatened to collide broadside.

Gibli, who was ex-army, insisted on adhering to the Israeli tradition that the officers lead their men from in front, not from behind: he had to go first. He always wore a hat to conceal his receding hairline, and now he sported a beret. He crouched at the edge of the boat while it slid down a wave: then, in the trough when boat and ship moved closer together, he jumped. He landed well and moved upward.

On the edge, waiting for his moment, Feinberg said, 'Now, then – I count to three, then open my parachute, right?' Then he jumped.

Katzen went next, then Raoul Dovrat. Dickstein dropped the boathook and followed. On the ladder, he leaned back and looked up through the streaming rain to see Gibli reach the level of the gunwale then swing one leg over the rail.

Dickstein looked back over his shoulder and saw a faint band of lighter grey in the distant sky, the first sign of dawn.

Then there was a sudden shocking burst of machine-gun fire and a shout.

Dickstein looked up again to see Gibli falling slowly backward off the top of the ladder. His beret came off and was whipped away by the wind, disappearing into the darkness. Gibli fell down, down past Dickstein and into the sea.

Dickstein shouted, 'Go, go, go!'

Feinberg flew over the rail. He would hit the deck

rolling, Dickstein knew, then – yes, there was the sound of his gun as he gave covering fire for the others—

And Katzen was over and there were four, five, many guns crackling, and Dickstein was scampering up the ladder and pulling the pin from a grenade with his teeth and hurling it up and over the rail some thirty yards forward, where it would cause a diversion without injuring any of his men already on deck, and then Dovrat was over the rail and Dickstein saw him hit the deck rolling, gain his feet, dive for cover behind the stern superstructure and Dickstein yelled, 'Here I come you fuckers' and went over in a high-jumper's roll, landed on hands and knees, bent double under a sheet of covering fire and scampered to the stern.

'Where are they?' he yelled.

Feinberg stopped shooting to answer him. 'In the galley,' he said, jerking a thumb toward the bulkhead beside them. 'In the lifeboats, and in the doorways amidships.'

'All right.' Dickstein got to his feet. 'We hold this position until Bader's group makes the deck. When you hear them open fire, move. Dovrat and Katzen, hit the galley door and head below. Feinberg, cover them, then work your way forward along this edge of the deck. I'll make for the first lifeboat. Meantime give them something to distract their attention from the port stern ladder and Bader's team. Fire at will.'

Hassan and Mahmoud were interrogating the sailor when the shooting started. They were in the chartroom, aft of the bridge. The sailor would speak only German, but Hassan spoke German. His story was that the *Coparelli* had broken down and the crew had been taken off, leaving him to wait in the ship until a spare part arrived. He knew nothing of uranium or hijacks or Dickstein. Hassan did not believe him, for – as he pointed out to Mahmoud – if Dickstein could arrange for the ship to break down, he could surely arrange for one of his own men to be left aboard it. The sailor was tied to a chair, and now Mahmoud was cutting off his fingers one by one in an attempt to make him tell a different story.

They heard one quick burst of firing, then a silence, then a second burst followed by a barrage. Mahmoud sheathed his knife and went down the stairs which led from the chartroom to the officers' quarters.

Hassan tried to assess the situation. The Fedayeen were grouped in three places – the lifeboats, the galley and the main amidships superstructure. From where he was Hassan could see both port and starboard sides of the deck, and if he went forward from the chartroom to the bridge he could see the foredeck. Most of the Israelis seemed to have boarded the ship at the stern. The Fedayeen, both those immediately below Hassan and those in the lifeboats at either side, were firing toward the stern. There was no firing from the galley, which must mean the Israelis had taken it. They must have gone below, but they had left two men on deck, one on either side, to guard their rear.

Mahmoud's ambush had failed, then. The Israelis were supposed to be mown down as they came over the rail. In fact they had succeeded in reaching cover, and now the battle was even.

The fighting on deck was stalemated, with both sides shooting at each other from good cover. That was the Israelis' intention, Hassan assumed: to keep the opposition busy on deck while they made their progress below. They would attack the Fedayeen stronghold, the amidships superstructure, from below, after making their way the length of the 'tweendecks gangways.

Where was the best place to be? Right where he was, Hassan decided. To reach him the Israelis had to fight their way along the 'tweendecks, then up through the officers' quarters, then up again to the bridge and chartroom. It was a tough position to take.

There was a huge explosion from the bridge. The heavy door separating bridge and chartroom rattled, sagged on its hinges and fell slowly inward. Hassan looked through.

A grenade had landed in the bridge. The bodies of three Fedayeen were spread across the bulkheads. All the glass of the bridge was smashed. The grenade must have come from the foredeck, which meant that there was another group of Israelis in the prow. As if to confirm his supposition, a burst of gunfire came from the for'ard crane.

Hassan picked up a submachine gun from the floor, rested it on the window frame, and began to shoot back.

*

Levi Abbas watched Porush's grenade sail through the air and into the bridge, then saw the explosion shatter what remained of the glass. The guns from that quarter were briefly silenced, and then a new one started up. For a minute Abbas could not figure out what the new gun was shooting at, for none of the bullets landed near him. He looked at either side. Sapir and Sharrett were both shooting at the bridge, and neither seemed to be under fire. Abbas looked up at the crane. Porush – it was Porush who was under fire. There was a burst from the cabin of the crane as Porush fired back.

The shooting from the bridge was amateurish, wild and inaccurate – the man was just spraying bullets. But he had a good position. He was high, and well protected by the walls of the bridge. He would hit something sooner or later. Abbas took out a grenade and lobbed it, but it fell short. Only Porush was close enough to throw into the bridge, and he had used all his grenades – only the fourth had landed on target.

Abbas fired again, then looked up at the control cabin of the crane. As he looked, he saw Porush come toppling backward out of the control cabin, turn over in the air, and fall like a dead weight to the deck.

Abbas thought: And how will I tell my sister?

The gunman in the bridge stopped firing, then resumed with a burst in Sharrett's direction. Unlike Abbas and Sapir, Sharrett had very little cover: he was squeezed between a capstan and the gunwale. Abbas and Sapir both shot at the bridge. The unseen sniper was improving: bullets stitched a seam in the deck toward Sharrett's capstan; then Sharrett screamed, jumped sideways, and jerked as if electrocuted while more bullets thudded into his body, until at last he lay still and the screaming stopped.

The situation was bad. Abbas's team was supposed to command the foredeck, but at the moment the man on the bridge was doing that. Abbas had to take him out.

He threw another grenade. It landed short of the bridge and exploded; the flash might dazzle the sniper for a second or two. When the bang came Abbas was on his feet and running for the crane, the crash of Sapir's covering fire in his ears. He made the foot of the ladder and started firing before the sniper on the bridge saw him. Then bullets were clanging on the girders all around him. It seemed to take him an age to climb each step. Some lunatic part of his mind began to count the steps: seven-eight-nine-ten—

He was hit by a ricochet. The bullet entered his thigh just below the hip bone. It did not kill him, but the shock of it seemed to paralyze the muscles in the lower half of his body. His feet slipped from the rungs of the ladder. He had a moment of confused panic as he discovered that his legs would not work. Instinctively he grabbed for the ladder with his hands, but he missed and fell. He turned partly over and landed awkwardly, breaking his neck; and he died.

The door to the for'ard store opened slightly and a wide-eyed, frightened Russian face looked out; but nobody saw it, and it went back inside; and the door closed.

As Katzen and Dovrat rushed the galley, Dickstein took advantage of Feinberg's covering fire to move forward. He ran, bent double, past the point at which they had boarded the ship and past the galley door, to throw himself behind the first of the lifeboats, one that had already been grenaded. From there, in the faint but increasing light, he could make out the lines of the amidships superstructure, shaped like a flight of three steps rising forward. At the main deck level was the officers' mess, the officers' dayroom, the sick bay and a passenger cabin used as a dry store. On the next level up were officers' cabins, heads, and the captain's quarters. On the top deck was the bridge with adjoining chartroom and radio booth.

Most of the enemy would now be at deck level in the mess and the dayroom. He could bypass them by climbing a ladder alongside the funnel to the walkway around the second deck, but the only way to the bridge was through the second deck. He would have to take out any soldiers in the cabins on his own.

He looked back. Feinberg had retreated behind the galley, perhaps to reload. He waited until Feinberg started shooting again, then got to his feet. Firing wildly from the hip, he broke from behind the lifeboat and dashed across the afterdeck to the ladder. Without breaking stride, he jumped on to the fourth rung and scrambled up, conscious that for a few seconds he made an easy target, hearing a clutch of bullets rattle on the funnel beside him, until he reached the level of the upper deck and flung himself across the walkway to fetch up, breathing hard and shaking with effort, lying against the door to the officers' quarters.

'Stone the bloody crows,' he muttered.

He reloaded his gun. He put his back to the door and slowly slid upright to a porthole in the door at eye level. He risked a look. He saw a passage with three doors on either side and, at the far end, ladders going down to the mess and up to the chartroom. He knew that the bridge could be reached by either of two outside ladders leading up from the main deck as well as by way of the chartroom. However, the Arabs still controlled that part of the deck and could cover the outside ladders; therefore the only way to the bridge was this way.

He opened the door and stepped in. He crept along the passage to the first cabin door, opened it, and threw in a grenade. He saw one of the enemy begin to turn around, and closed the door. He heard the grenade explode in the small space. He ran to the next door on the same side, opened it, and threw in another grenade. It exploded into empty space.

There was one more door on this side, and he had no more grenades.

He ran to the door, threw it open, and went in firing. There was one man here. He had been firing through the porthole, but now he was easing his gun

450

out of the hole and turning around. Dickstein's burst of bullets sliced him in half.

Dickstein turned and faced the open door, waiting. The door of the opposite cabin flew open and Dickstein shot down the man behind it.

Dickstein stepped into the gangway, firing blind. There were two more cabins to account for. The door of the nearer one opened as Dickstein was spraying it, and a body fell out.

One to go. Dickstein watched. The door opened a crack, then closed again. Dickstein ran down the gangway, and kicked open the door, sprayed the cabin. There was no return fire. He stepped inside: the occupant had been hit by a ricochet and lay bleeding on the bunk.

Dickstein was seized with a kind of mad exultation: he had taken the entire deck on his own.

Next, the bridge. He ran forward along the gangway. At the far end the companionway led up to the chartroom and down to the officers' mess. He stepped on to the ladder, looked up, and threw himself down and away as the snout of a gun poked down at him and began to fire.

His grenades were gone. The man in the chartroom was impregnable to gunfire. He could stay behind the edge of the companionhead and fire blind down the ladder. Dickstein had to get on the ladder, for he wanted to go up.

· He went into one of the forward cabins to overlook the deck and try to assess the situation. He was appalled when he saw what had happened on the foredeck: only one of the four men of Abbas's team was still firing, and Dickstein could just make out three bodies. Two or three guns seemed to be firing from the bridge at the remaining Israeli, trapping him behind a stack of anchor chain.

Dickstein looked to the side. Feinberg was still well aft – he had not managed to progress forward. And there was still no sign of the men who had gone below.

The Fedayeen were well entrenched in the mess below him. From their superior position they were able to keep at bay the men on deck and the men in the 'tweendecks below them. The only way to take the mess would be to attack it from all sides at once – including from above. But that meant taking the bridge first. And the bridge was impregnable.

Dickstein ran back along the gangway and out of the aft door. It was still pouring with rain, but there was a dim cold light in the sky. He could make out Feinberg on one side and Dovrat on the other. He called out their names until he caught their attention, then pointed at the galley. He jumped from the walkway to the afterdeck, raced across it, and dived into the galley.

They had got his meaning. A moment later they followed him in. Dickstein said, 'We have to take the mess.'

'I don't see how,' said Feinberg.

'Shut up and I'll tell you. We rush it from all sides at once: port, starboard, below and above. First we have to take the bridge. I'm going to do that. When I get there I'll sound the foghorn. That will be the signal: I want you both to go below and tell the men there.'

'How will you reach the bridge?' Feinberg said.

Dickstein said, 'Over the roof.'

On the bridge, Yasif Hassan had been joined by Mahmoud and two more of his Fedayeen, who took up firing positions while the leaders sat on the floor and conferred.

'They can't win,' Mahmoud said. 'From here we control too much deck. They can't attack the mess from below, because the companionway is easy to dominate from above. They can't attack from the sides or the front because we can fire down on them from here. They can't attack from above because we control the down companion. We just keep shooting until they surrender.'

Hassan said, 'One of them tried to take this companion a few minutes ago. I stopped him.'

'You were on your own up here?'

'Yes.'

He put his hands on Hassan's shoulders. 'You are now one of the Fedayeen,' he said.

Hassan voiced the thought that was on both their minds. 'After this?'

Mahmoud nodded. 'Equal partners.'

They clasped hands.

Hassan repeated, 'Equal partners.'

Mahmoud said, 'And now, I think they will try for that companionway again – it's their only hope.'

'I'll cover it from the chartroom,' Hassan said.

They both stood up; then a stray bullet from the

foredeck came in through the glassless windows and entered Mahmoud's brain, and he died instantly.

And Hassan was the leader of the Fedayeen.

Lying on his belly, arms and legs spread wide for traction, Dickstein inched his way across the roof. It was curved, and totally without handholds, and it was slick with rain. As the *Coparelli* heaved and shifted in the waves, the roof tilted forward, backward, and from side to side. All Dickstein could do was press himself to the metal and try to slow his slide.

At the forward end of the roof was a navigation light. When he reached that he would be safe, for he could hold on to it. His progress toward it was painfully slow. He got within a foot of it, then the ship rolled to port and he slid away. It was a long roll, and it took him all the way to the edge of the roof. For a moment he hung with one arm and a leg over a thirty-foot drop to the deck. The ship rolled a little more, the rest of his leg went over and he tried to dig the fingernails of his right hand into the painted metal of the roof.

There was an agonizing pause.

The *Coparelli* rolled back.

Dickstein let himself go with the roll, sliding faster and faster toward the navigation light.

But the ship pitched up, the roof tilted backward, and he slid in a long curve, missing the light by a yard. Once again he pressed his hands and feet into the metal, trying to slow himself down; once again he went all the way to the edge; once again he hung over the drop to the deck; but this time it was his right arm which dangled over the edge, and his machine gun slipped off his right shoulder and fell into a lifeboat.

She rolled back and pitched forward, and Dickstein found himself sliding with increasing speed toward the navigation light. This time he reached it. He grabbed with both hands. The light was about a foot from the forward edge of the roof. Immediately below the edge were the front windows of the bridge. their glass smashed out long ago, and two gun barrels poking out through them.

Dickstein held on to the light, but he could not stop his slide. His body swung about in a wide sweep, heading for the edge. He saw that the front of the roof, unlike the sides, had a narrow steel gutter to take away the rain from the glass below. As his body swung over the edge he released his grip on the navigation light, let himself slide forward with the pitch of the ship, grabbed the steel gutter with his fingertips, and swung his legs down and in. He came flying through the broken windows feet first to land in the middle of the bridge. He bent his knees to take the shock of landing, then straightened up. His submachine gun had been lost and he had no time to draw his pistol or his knife. There were two Arabs on the bridge, one on either side of him, both holding machine guns and firing down on to the deck. As Dickstein straightened up they began to turn toward him, their faces a picture of amazement.

Dickstein was fractionally nearer the one on the port side. He lashed out with a kick which, more by luck than by judgment, landed on the point of the man's elbow, momentarily paralyzing his gun arm. Then Dickstein jumped for the other man. His machine gun was swinging toward Dickstein just a split second too late: Dickstein got inside its swing. He brought up his right hand in the most vicious two-stroke blow he knew: the heel of his hand hit the point of the Arab's chin, snapping his head back for the second stroke as Dickstein's hand, fingers stiffened for a karate chop, came down hard into the exposed flesh of the soft throat.

Before the man could fall Dickstein grabbed him by the jacket and swung him around between himself and the other Arab. The other man was bringing up his gun. Dickstein lifted the dead man and hurled him across the bridge as the machine gun opened up. The dead body took the bullets and crashed into the other Arab, who lost his balance, went backward out through the open doorway and fell to the deck below.

There was a third man in the chartroom, guarding the companionway leading down. In the three seconds during which Dickstein had been on the bridge the man had stood up and turned around; and now Dickstein recognized Yasif Hassan.

Dickstein dropped to a crouch, stuck out a leg, kicked at the broken door which lay on the floor between himself and Hassan. The door slid along the deck, striking Hassan's feet. It was only enough to throw him off balance, but as he spread his arms to recover his equilibrium Dickstein moved.

Until this moment Dickstein had been like a machine, reacting reflexively to everything that confronted him, letting his nervous system plan every move without conscious thought, allowing training and instinct to guide him; but now it was more than that. Now, faced with the enemy of all he had ever loved, he was possessed by blind hatred and mad rage.

It gave him added speed and power.

He took hold of Hassan's gun arm by the wrist and shoulder, and with a downward pull broke the arm over his knee. Hassan screamed and the gun dropped from his useless hand. Turning slightly, Dickstein brought his elbow back in a blow which caught Hassan just under the ear. Hassan turned away, falling. Dickstein grabbed his hair from behind, pulling the head backward; and as Hassan sagged away from him he lifted his foot high and kicked. His heel struck the back of Hassan's neck at the moment he jerked the head. There was a snap as all the tension went out of the man's muscles and his head lolled, unsupported, on his shoulders.

Dickstein let go and the body crumpled.

He stared at the harmless body with exultation ringing in his ears.

Then he saw Koch.

The engineer was tied to a chair, slumped over, pale as death but conscious. There was blood on his clothes. Dickstein drew his knife and cut the ropes that bound Koch. Then saw the man's hands.

He said, 'Christ.'

'I'll live,' Koch muttered. He did not get up from the chair.

Dickstein picked up Hassan's machine gun and

checked the magazine. It was almost full. He moved out on to the bridge and located the foghorn.

'Koch,' he said, 'can you get out of that chair?'

Koch got up, swaying unsteadily until Dickstein stepped across and supported him, leading him through to the bridge. 'See this button? I want you to count slowly to ten, then lean on it.'

Koch shook his head to clear it. 'I think I can handle it.'

'Start. Now.'

'One,' Koch said. 'Two.'

Dickstein went down the companionway and came out on the second deck, the one he had cleared himself. It was still empty, He went on down, and stopped just before the ladder emerged into the mess. He figured all the remaining Fedayeen must be here, lined against the walls, shooting out through portholes and doorways; one or two perhaps watching the companionway. There was no safe, careful way to take such a strong defensive position.

Come on, Koch!

Dickstein had intended to spend a second or two hiding in the companionway. At any moment one of the Arabs might look up it to check. If Koch had collapsed he would have to go back up there and—

The foghorn sounded.

Dickstein jumped. He was firing before he landed. There were two men close to the foot of the ladder. He shot them first. The firing from outside went into a crescendo. Dickstein turned in a rapid half circle, dropped to one knee to make a smaller target, and sprayed the Fedayeen along the walls. Suddenly there was another gun as Ish came up from below; then Feinberg was at one door, shooting; and Dovrat, wounded, came in through another door. And then, as if by signal, they all stopped shooting, and the silence was like thunder.

All the Fedayeen were dead.

Dickstein, still kneeling, bowed his head in exhaustion. After a moment he stood up and looked at his men. 'Where are the others?' he said.

Feinberg gave him a peculiar look. 'There's someone on the foredeck, Sapir I think.'

'And the rest?'

'That's it,' Feinberg said. 'All the others are dead.'

Dickstein slumped against a bulkhead. 'What a price,' he said quietly.

Looking out through the smashed porthole he saw that it was day.

CHAPTER SEVENTEEN

A YEAR earlier the BOAC jet in which Suza
Ashford was serving dinner had abruptly begun
to lose height for no apparent reason over the Atlantic
Ocean. The pilot had switched on the seat-belt lights.
Suza had walked up and down the aisle, saying, 'Just a
little turbulence,' and helping people fasten their seat
belts, all the time thinking: We're going to die, we're
all going to die.

She felt like that now.

There had been a short message from Tyrin: *Israel is
attacking* – then silence. At this moment Nathaniel was
being shot at. He might be wounded, he might have
been captured, he might be dead; and while Suza
seethed with nervous tension she had to give the radio
operator the BOAC Big Smile and say. 'It's quite a
setup you've got here.'

The *Karla*'s radio operator was a big grey-haired man
from Odessa. His name was Aleksandr, and he spoke
passable English. 'It cost one hundred thousand dollar,'
he said proudly. 'You know about radio?'

'A little ... I used to be an air hostess.' She had
said 'used to be' without forethought, and now she
wondered whether that life really was gone. 'I've

seen the air crew using their radios. I know the basics.'

'Really, this is four radios,' Aleksandr explained. 'One picks up the *Stromberg* beacon. One listens to Tyrin on *Coparelli*. One listens to *Coparelli*'s regular wave-length. And this one wanders. Look.'

He showed her a dial whose pointer moved around slowly. 'It seeks a transmitter, stops when it finds one,' Aleksandr said.

'That's incredible. Did you invent that?'

'I am an operator, not inventor, sadly.'

'And you can broadcast on any of the sets, just by switching to TRANSMIT?'

'Yes, Morse code or speech. But of course, on this operation nobody uses speech.'

'Did you have to go through long training to become a radio operator?'

'Not long. Learning Morse is easy. But to be a ship's radioman you must know how to repair the set.' He lowered his voice. 'And to be a KGB operator, you must go to spy school.' He laughed, and Suza laughed with him, thinking: come on, Tyrin; and then her wish was granted.

The message began, Aleksandr started writing and at the same time said to Suza, 'Tyrin. Get Rostov, please.'

Suza left the bridge reluctantly; she wanted to know what was in the message. She hurried to the mess, expecting to find Rostov there drinking strong black coffee, but the room was empty. She went down another deck and made her way to his cabin. She knocked on the door.

His voice in Russian said something which might have meant come in.

She opened the door. Rostov stood there in his shorts, washing in a bowl.

'Tyrin's coming through,' Suza said. She turned to leave.

'Suza.'

She turned back. 'What would you say if I surprised you in your underwear?'

'I'd say piss off,' she said.

'Wait for me outside.'

She closed the door, thinking: That's done it.

When he came out she said, 'I'm sorry.'

He gave a tight smile. 'I should not have been so unprofessional. Let's go.'

She followed him up to the radio room, which was immediately below the bridge in what should have been the captain's cabin. Because of the mass of extra equipment, Aleksandr had explained, it was not possible to put the radio operator adjacent to the bridge, as was customary. Suza had figured out for herself that this arrangement had the additional advantage of segregating the radio from the crew when the ship carried a mixture of ordinary seamen and KGB agents.

Aleksandr had transcribed Tyrin's signal. He handed it to Rostov, who read it in English. 'Israelis have taken *Coparelli. Stromberg* alongside. Dickstein alive.'

Suza went limp with relief. She had to sit down. She slumped into a chair.

No one noticed. Rostov was already composing his reply to Tyrin: 'We will hit at six A.M. tomorrow.'

The tide of relief went out for Suza and she thought: Oh, God, what do I do now?

Nat Dickstein stood in silence, wearing a borrowed seaman's cap, as the captain of the *Stromberg* read the words of the service for the dead, raising his voice against the noise of wind, rain and sea. One by one the canvas-wrapped bodies were tipped over the rail into the black water: Abbas, Sharrett, Porush, Gibli, Bader, Remez, and Jabotinsky. Seven of the twelve had died. Uranium was the most costly metal in the world.

There had been another funeral earlier. Four Fedayeen had been left alive – three wounded, one who had lost his nerve and hidden – and after they had been disarmed Dickstein had allowed them to bury their dead. Theirs had been a bigger funeral – they had dropped twenty-five bodies into the sea. They had hurried through their ceremony under the watchful eyes – and guns – of three surviving Israelis, who understood that this courtesy should be extended to the enemy but did not have to like it.

Meanwhile, the *Stromberg*'s captain had brought aboard all his ship's papers. The team of fitters and joiners, which had come along in case it was necessary to alter the *Coparelli* to match the *Stromberg*, was set to work repairing the battle damage. Dickstein told them to concentrate on what was visible from the deck: the rest would have to wait until they reached port. They set about filling holes, repairing furniture, and replacing panes of glass and metal fittings with spares cannibalized from the doomed *Stromberg*. A painter went down a ladder to remove the name *Coparelli* from the hull and replace it with the stencilled letters S-T-R-O-M-B-E-R-G. When he had finished he set about painting over the repaired bulkheads and woodwork on deck. All the *Coparelli*'s lifeboats, damaged beyond repair, were chopped up and thrown over the side, and the *Stromberg*'s boats were brought over to replace them. The new oil pump, which the *Stromberg* had carried on Koch's instructions, was installed in the *Coparelli*'s engine.

Work had stopped for the burial. Now, as soon as the captain had uttered the final words, it began again. Towards the end of the afternoon the engine rumbled to life. Dickstein stood on the bridge with the captain while the anchor was raised. The crew of the *Stromberg* quickly found their way round the new ship, which was identical to their old one. The captain set a course and ordered full speed ahead.

It was almost over, Dickstein thought. The *Coparelli* had disappeared: for all intents and purposes the ship in which he now sailed was the *Stromberg*, and the *Stromberg* was legally owned by Savile Shipping. Israel had her uranium, and nobody knew how she had got it. Everyone in the chain of operation was now taken care of – except Pedler, still the legal owner of the yellowcake. He was the one man who could ruin the whole scheme if he should become either curious or hostile. Papagopolous would be handling him right now: Dickstein silently wished him luck.

'We're clear,' the captain said.

The explosives expert in the chartroom pulled a lever on his radio detonator, then everybody watched the empty *Stromberg*, now more than a mile away.

There was a loud, dull thud, like thunder, and the *Stromberg* seemed to sag in the middle. Her fuel tanks caught fire and the stormy evening was lit by a gout of flame reaching for the sky. Dickstein felt elation and faint anxiety at the sight of such great destruction. The *Stromberg* began to sink, slowly at first and then faster. Her stern went under; seconds later her bows followed; her funnel poked up above the water for a moment like the raised arm of a drowning man, and then she was gone.

Dickstein smiled faintly and turned away.

He heard a noise. The captain heard it too. They went to the side of the bridge and looked out, and then they understood.

Down on the deck, the men were cheering.

Franz Albrecht Pedler sat in his office on the outskirts of Wiesbaden and scratched his snowy-white head. The telegram from Angeluzzi e Bianco in Genoa, translated from the Italian by Pedler's multilingual secretary, was perfectly plain and at the same time totally incomprehensible. It said: PLEASE ADVISE SOONEST OF NEW EXPECTED DELIVERY DATE OF YELLOWCAKE.

As far as Pedler knew there was nothing wrong with the old expected delivery date, which was a couple of days away. Clearly Angeluzzi e Bianco knew something he did not. He had already wired the shippers: IS

YELLOWCAKE DELAYED? He felt a little annoyed with them. Surely they should have informed him as well as the receiving company if there was a delay. But maybe the Italians had their wires crossed. Pedler had formed the opinion during the war that you could never trust Italians to do what they were told. He had thought they might be different nowadays, but perhaps they were the same.

He stood at his window, watching the evening gather over his little cluster of factory buildings. He could almost wish he had not bought the uranium. The deal with the Israeli Army, all signed, sealed and delivered, would keep his company in profit for the rest of his life, and he no longer needed to speculate.

His secretary came in with the reply from the shippers, already translated: COPARELLI SOLD TO SAVILE SHIPPING OF ZURICH WHO NOW HAVE RESPONSIBILITY FOR YOUR CARGO. WE ASSURE YOU OF COMPLETE RELIABILITY OF PURCHASERS. There followed the phone number of Savile Shipping and the words SPEAK TO PAPAGOPOLOUS.

Pedler gave the telegram back to the secretary. 'Would you call that number in Zurich and get this Papagopolous on the line please?'

She came back a few minutes later. 'Papagopolous will call you back.'

Pedler looked at his watch. 'I suppose I'd better wait for his call. I might as well get to the bottom of this now that I've started.'

Papagopolous came through ten minutes later. Pedler said to him, 'I'm told you are now responsible for my cargo on board the *Coparelli*. I've had a cable from the Italians asking for a new delivery date – is there some delay?'

'Yes, there is,' Papagopolous said. 'You should have been informed – I'm terribly sorry.' The man spoke excellent German but it was still clear he was not a German. It was also clear he was not really terribly sorry. He went on, 'The *Coparelli*'s oil pump broke down at sea and she is becalmed. We're making arrangements to have your cargo delivered as early as possible.'

'Well, what am I to say to Angeluzzi e Bianco?'

'I have told them that I will let them know the new date just as soon as I know it myself,' Papagopolous said. 'Please leave it to me. I will keep you both informed.'

'Very well. Goodbye.'

Odd, Pedler thought as he hung up the phone. Looking out of the window, he saw that all the workers had left. The staff car parking lot was empty except for his Mercedes and his secretary's Volkswagen. What the hell, time to go home. He put on his coat. The uranium was insured. If it was lost he would get his money back. He turned out the office lights and helped his secretary on with her coat, then he got into his car and drove home to his wife.

Suza Ashford did not close her eyes all night.

Once again, Nat Dickstein's life was in danger. Once again, she was the only one who could warn him. And this time she could not deceive others into helping her.

She had to do it alone.

It was simple. She had to go to the *Karla*'s radio room, get rid of Aleksandr, and call the *Coparelli*.

I'll never do it, she thought. The ship is full of KGB. Aleksandr is a big man. I want to go to sleep. For ever. It's impossible. I can't do it.

Oh, Nathaniel.

At four A.M. she put on jeans, a sweater, boots and an oilskin. The full bottle of vodka she had taken from the mess – 'to help me sleep' – went in the inside pocket of the oilskin.

She had to know the *Karla*'s position.

She went up to the bridge. The first officer smiled at her. 'Can't sleep?' he said in English.

'The suspense is too much,' she told him. The BOAC Big Smile. Is your seat belt fastened, sir? Just a little turbulence, nothing to worry about. She asked the first officer, 'Where are we?'

He showed her their position on the map, and the estimated position of the *Coparelli*.

'What's that in numbers?' she said.

He told her the coordinates, the course, and the speed of the *Karla*. She repeated the numbers once aloud and twice more in her head, trying to burn them into her brain. 'It's fascinating,' she said brightly. 'Everyone on a ship has a special skill . . . Will we reach the *Coparelli* on time, do you think?'

'Oh, yes,' he said. 'Then – boom.'

She looked outside. It was completely black – there

were no stars and no ships' lights in sight. The weather was getting worse.

'You're shivering,' the first officer said. 'Are you cold?'

'Yes,' she said, though it was not the weather making her shiver. 'When is Colonel Rostov getting up?'

'He's to be called at five.'

'I think I'll try to get another hour's sleep.'

She went down to the radio room. Aleksandr was there. 'Couldn't you sleep, either?' she asked him.

'No. I've sent my number two to bed.'

She looked over the radio equipment. 'Aren't you listening to the *Stromberg* any more?'

'The signal stopped. Either they found the beacon, or they sank the ship. We think they sank her.'

Suza sat down and took out the bottle of vodka. She unscrewed the cap. 'Have a drink.' She handed him the bottle.

'Are you cold?'

'A little.'

'Your hand is shaking.' He took the bottle and put it to his lips, taking a long swallow. 'Ah, thank you.' He handed it back to her.

Suza drank a mouthful for courage. It was rough Russian vodka, and it burned her throat, but it had the desired effect. She screwed down the cap and waited for Aleksandr to turn his back on her.

'Tell me about life in England,' he said conversationally. 'Is it true that the poor starve while the rich get fat?'

'Not many people starve,' she said. Turn around,

damn it, turn *around*. I can't do this facing you. 'But there is great inequality.'

'Are there different laws for rich and poor?'

'There's a saying: "The law forbids rich and poor alike to steal bread and sleep under bridges."'

Aleksandr laughed. 'In the Soviet Union people are equal, but some have privileges. Will you live in Russia now?'

'I don't know.' Suza opened the bottle and passed it to him again.

He took a long swallow and gave it back. 'In Russia you won't have such clothes.'

The time was passing too quickly, she had to do it now. She stood up to take the bottle. Her oilskin was open down the front. Standing before him, she tilted her head back to drink from the bottle, knowing he would stare at her breasts as they jutted out. She allowed him a good look, then shifted her grip on the bottle and brought it down as hard as she could on top of his head.

There was a sickening thud as it hit him. He stared at her dazedly. She thought: You're supposed to be knocked out! His eyes would not shut. What do I do? She hesitated, then she gritted her teeth and hit him again.

His eyes closed and he slumped in the chair. Suza got hold of his feet and pulled. As he came off the chair his head hit the deck, making Suza wince, but then she thought: It's just as well, he'll stay out longer.

She dragged him to a cupboard. She was breathing fast, from fear as well as exertion. From her jeans pocket she took a long piece of baling twine she had picked up in the stern. She tied Aleksandr's feet, then turned him over and bound his hands behind his back.

She had to get him into the cupboard. She glanced at the door. Oh, God, don't let anyone come in now! She put his feet in, then straddled his unconscious body and tried to lift him. He was a heavy man. She got him half upright, but when she tried to shift him into the cupboard he slipped from her grasp. She got behind him to try again. She grasped him beneath the armpits and lifted. This way was better: she could lean his weight against her chest while she shifted her grip. She got him half upright again, then wrapped her arms around his chest and inched sideways. She had to go into the cupboard with him, let him go, then wriggle out from underneath him.

He was in a sitting position now, his feet against one side of the cupboard, his knees bent, and his back against the opposite side. She checked his bonds: still tight. But he could still shout! She looked about for something to stuff in his mouth to gag him. She could see nothing. She could not leave the room to search for something because he might come round in the meantime. The only thing that she could think of was her pantyhose.

It seemed to take her for ever to do it. She had to pull off her borrowed sea boots, take off her jeans, pull her pantyhose off, put her jeans on, get into her boots, then crumple the nylon cloth into a ball and stuff it between his slack jaws.

She could not close the cupboard door. 'Oh, God!'

she said out loud. It was Aleksandr's elbow that was in the way. His bound hands rested on the floor of the cupboard, and because of his slumped position his arms were bent outward. No matter how she pushed and shoved at the door that elbow stopped it from closing. Finally she had to get back into the cupboard with him and turn him slightly sideways so that he leaned into the corner. Now his elbow was out of the way.

She looked at him a moment longer. How long did people stay knocked out? She had no idea. She knew she should hit him again, but she was afraid of killing him. She went and got the bottle, and even lifted it over her head; but at the last moment she lost her nerve, put the bottle down, and slammed the cupboard door.

She looked at her wristwatch and gave a cry of dismay: it was ten minutes to five. The *Coparelli* would soon appear on the *Karla*'s radar screen, and Rostov would be here, and she would have lost her chance.

She sat down at the radio desk, switched the lever to TRANSMIT, selected the set that was already tuned to the *Coparelli*'s wavelength and leaned over the microphone.

'Calling *Coparelli*, come in please.'

She waited.

Nothing.

'Damn you to hell, Nat Dickstein, *speak* to me. Nathaniel!'

Nat Dickstein stood in the amidships hold of the *Coparelli*, staring at the drums of sandy metallic ore that had cost so much. They looked nothing special – just large black oil drums with the word PLUMBAT stencilled on their sides. He would have liked to open one and feel the stuff, just to know what it was like, but the lids were heavily sealed.

He felt suicidal. Instead of the elation of victory, he had only bereavement. He could not rejoice over the terrorists he had killed, he could only mourn for his own dead.

He went over the battle again, as he had been doing throughout a sleepless night. If he had told Abbas to open fire as soon as he got aboard it might have distracted the Fedayeen long enough for Gibli to get over the rail without being shot. If he had gone with three men to take out the bridge with grenades at the very start of the fight the mess might have been taken earlier and lives would have been saved. If . . . but there were a hundred things he would have done differently if he had been able to see into the future, or if he were just a wiser man.

Well, Israel would now have atom bombs to protect her for ever.

Even that thought gave him no joy. A year ago it would have thrilled him. But a year ago he had not met Suza Ashford.

He heard a noise and looked up. It sounded as if people were running around on deck. Some nautical crisis, no doubt.

Suza had changed him. She had taught him to expect more out of life than victory in battle. When he had anticipated this day, when he had thought about what it would feel like to have pulled off this tremendous coup, she had always been in his daydream, waiting for him somewhere, ready to share his triumph. But she would not be there. Nobody else would do. And there was no joy in a solitary celebration.

He had stared long enough. He climbed the ladder out of the hold, wondering what to do with the rest of his life. He emerged on deck. A rating peered at him. 'Mr Dickstein?'

'Yes. What do you want?'

'We've been searching the ship for you, sir . . . It's the radio, someone is calling the *Coparelli*. We haven't answered, sir, because we're not supposed to be the *Coparelli*, are we? But she says—'

'She?'

'Yes, sir. She's coming over clear – speech, not Morse code. She sounds close. And she's upset. "Speak to me, Nathaniel," she says, stuff like that, sir.'

Dickstein grabbed the rating by his peajacket. 'Nathaniel?' he shouted. 'Did she say Nathaniel?'

'Yes, sir, I'm sorry, if—'

But Dickstein was heading for the bridge at a run.

The voice of Nat Dickstein came over the radio: 'Who is calling *Coparelli*?'

She found her voice. 'Oh, Nat, at last.'

'Suza? Is that Suza?'

'Yes, yes.'

'Where are you?'

She gathered her thoughts. 'I'm with David Rostov

474

on a Russian ship called the *Karla*. Make a note of this.'
She gave him the position, course and speed just as the
first officer had told them to her. 'That was at four-ten
this morning. Nat, this ship is going to ram yours at six
A.M.'

'Ram? Why? Oh, I see . . .'

'Nat, they'll catch me at the radio any minute, what
are we going to do, quickly—'

'Can you create a diversion of some kind at precisely
five-thirty?'

'Diversion?'

'Start a fire, shout "man overboard", anything to
keep them all very busy for a few minutes.'

'Well – I'll try—'

'Do your best. I want them all running around,
nobody quite sure what's going on or what to do – are
they all KGB?'

'Yes.'

'Okay, now—'

The door of the radio room opened – Suza flipped
the switch to TRANSMIT and Dickstein's voice was
silenced and David Rostov walked in. He said, 'Where's
Aleksandr?'

Suza tried to smile. 'He went for coffee. I'm minding
the shop.'

'The damn fool . . .' His curses switched into Russian
as he stormed out.

Suza moved the lever to RECEIVE.

Nat said, 'I heard that. You'd better make yourself
scarce until five-thirty—'

'Wait,' she shouted. 'What are you going to do?'

'Do?' he said. 'I'm coming to get you.'

'Oh,' she said. 'Oh, thank you.'

'I love you.'

As she switched off, Morse began to come through on another set. Tyrin would have heard every word of her conversation, and now he would be trying to warn Rostov. She had forgotten to tell Nat about Tyrin.

She could try to contact Nat again, but it would be very risky, and Tyrin would get his message through to Rostov in the time it took Nat's men to search the *Coparelli*, locate Tyrin and destroy his equipment. And when Tyrin's message got to Rostov, he would know Nat was coming, and he would be prepared.

She had to block that message.

She also had to get away.

She decided to wreck the radio.

How? All the wiring must be behind the panels. She would have to take a panel off. She needed a screwdriver. Quickly, quickly before Rostov gives up looking for Aleksandr! She found Aleksandr's tools in a corner and picked out a small screwdriver. She undid the screws on two corners of the panel. Impatient, she pocketed the screwdriver and forced the panel out with her hands. Inside was a mass of wires like psychedelic spaghetti. She grabbed a fistful and pulled. Nothing happened: she had pulled too many at once. She selected one, and tugged: it came out. Furiously she pulled wires until fifteen or twenty were hanging loose. Still the Morse code chattered. She poured the remains of the vodka into the innards of the radio. The Morse stopped, and every light on the panel went out.

There was a thump from inside the cupboard. Aleksandr must be coming round. Well, they would know everything as soon as they saw the radio now anyway.

She went out, closing the door behind her.

She went down the ladder and out on to the deck, trying to figure out where she could hide and what kind of diversion she could create. No point now in shouting 'man overboard' – they certainly would not believe her after what she had done to their radio and their radio operator. Let down the anchor? She would not know where to begin.

What was Rostov likely to do now? He would look for Aleksandr in the galley, the mess, and his cabin. Not finding him, he would return to the radio room, and then would start a shipwide search for her.

He was a methodical man. He would start at the prow and work backwards along the main deck, then send one party to search the upperworks and another to sweep below, deck by deck, starting at the top and working down.

What was the lowest part of the ship? The engine room. That would have to be her hiding place. She went inside and found her way to a downward companionway. She had her foot on the top rung of the ladder when she saw Rostov.

And he saw her.

She had no idea where her next words came from. 'Aleksandr's come back to the radio room. I'll be back in a moment.'

Rostov nodded grimly, and went off in the direction of the radio room.

She headed straight down through two decks and emerged into the engine room. The second engineer was on duty at night. He stared at her as she came in and approached him.

'This is the only warm place on the ship,' she said cheerfully. 'Mind if I keep you company?'

He looked mystified, and said slowly, 'I cannot . . . speak English . . . please.'

'You don't speak English?'

He shook his head.

'I'm cold,' she said, and mimed a shiver. She held her hands out toward the throbbing engine. 'Okay?'

He was more than happy to have this beautiful girl for company in his engine room. 'Okay,' he said, nodding vigorously.

He continued to stare at her, with a pleased look on his face, until it occurred to him that he should perhaps show some hospitality. He looked about, then pulled a pack of cigarettes from his pocket and offered her one.

'I don't usually, but I think I will,' she said, and took a cigarette. It had a small cardboard tube for a filter. The engineer lit it for her. She looked up at the hatch, half expecting to see Rostov. She looked at her watch. It could not be five-twenty-five already! She had no time to think. Diversion, start a diversion. Shout 'man overboard', drop the anchor, light a fire—

Light a fire.

With what?

Petrol, there must be petrol, or diesel fuel, or something, right here in the engine room.

She looked over the engine. Where did the petrol

come in? The thing was a mass of tubes and pipes. Concentrate, concentrate! She wished she had learned more about the engine of her car. Were boat engines the same? No, sometimes they used truck fuel. Which kind was this? It was supposed to be a fast ship, so perhaps it used petrol, she remembered vaguely that petrol engines were more expensive to run but faster. If it was a petrol engine it would be similar to the engine of her car. Were there cables leading to spark plugs? She had changed a spark plug once.

She stared. Yes, it was like her car. There were six plugs, with leads from them to a round cap like a distributor. Somewhere there had to be a carburettor. The petrol went through the carburettor. It was a small thing that sometimes got blocked—

The voice-pipe barked in Russian, and the engineer walked toward it to answer. His back was to Suza.

She had to do it now.

There was something about the size of a coffee tin with a lid held on by a central nut. It could be the carburettor. She stretched herself across the engine and tried to undo the nut with her fingers. It would not budge. A heavy plastic pipe led into it. She grabbed it and tugged. She could not pull it out. She remembered she had put Aleksandr's screwdriver into her oilskin pocket. She took it out and jabbed at the pipe with the sharp end. The plastic was thick and tough. She stabbed the screwdriver into it with all her might. It made a small cut in the surface of the pipe. She stuck the point of the screwdriver into the cut and worked it.

The engineer reached the voice-pipe and spoke into it in Russian.

Suza felt the screwdriver break through the plastic. She tugged it out. A spray of clear liquid jetted out of the little hole, and the air was filled with the unmistakable smell of petrol. She dropped the screwdriver and ran toward the ladder.

She heard the engineer answer yes in Russian and nod his head to a question from the voice-pipe. An order followed. The voice was angry. As she reached the foot of the ladder she looked back. The engineer's smiling face had been transformed into a mask of malice. She went up the ladder as he ran across the engine-room deck after her.

At the top of the ladder she turned around. She saw a pool of petrol spreading over the deck, and the engineer stepping on the bottom rung of the ladder. In her hand she still held the cigarette he had given her. She threw it toward the engine, aiming at the place where the petrol was squirting out of the pipe.

She did not wait to see it land. She carried on up the ladder. Her head and shoulders were emerging on to the next deck when there was a loud *whooosh*, a bright red light from below, and a wave of scorching heat. Suza screamed as her trousers caught fire and the skin of her legs burned. She jumped the last few inches of the ladder and rolled. She beat at her trousers, then struggled out of her oilskin and managed to wrap it around her legs. The fire was killed, but the pain got worse.

She wanted to collapse. She knew if she lay down she

would pass out and the pain would go, but she had to get away from the fire, and she had to be somewhere where Nat could find her. She forced herself to stand up. Her legs felt as if they were still burning. She looked down to see bits like burned paper falling off, and she wondered if they were bits of trouser or bits of leg.

She took a step.

She could walk.

She staggered along the gangway. The fire alarm began to sound all over the ship. She reached the end of the gangway and leaned on the ladder.

Up, she had to go up.

She raised one foot, placed it on the bottom rung, and began the longest climb of her life.

CHAPTER EIGHTEEN

FOR THE second time in twenty-four hours Nat Dickstein was crossing huge seas in a small boat to board a ship held by the enemy. He was dressed as before, with life jacket, oilskin, and sea boots; and armed as before with submachine gun, pistol and grenades; but this time he was alone, and he was terrified.

There had been an argument aboard the *Coparelli* about what to do after Suza's radio message. Her dialogue with Dickstein had been listened to by the captain, Feinberg, and Ish. They had seen the jubilation in Nat's face, and they had felt entitled to argue that his judgment was now distorted by personal involvement.

'It's a trap,' argued Feinberg. 'They can't catch us, so they want us to turn and fight.'

'I know Rostov,' Dickstein said hotly. 'This is exactly how his mind works: he waits for you to make a break, then he pounces. This ramming idea has his name written all over it.'

Feinberg got angry. 'This isn't a game, Dickstein.'

'Listen, Nat,' Ish said more reasonably, 'let's us carry on and be ready to fight if and when they catch us. What have we got to gain by sending a boarding party?'

'I'm not suggesting a boarding party. I'm going alone.'

'Don't be a damn fool,' Ish said. 'If you go, so do we – you can't take a ship alone.'

'Look,' Dickstein said, trying to pacify them. 'If I make it, the *Karla* will never catch this ship. If I don't, the rest of you can still fight when the *Karla* gets to you. And if the *Karla* really can't catch you, and it's a trap, then I'm the only one who falls into it. It's the best way.'

'I don't think it's the best way,' Feinberg said.

'Nor do I,' Ish said.

Dickstein smiled. 'Well, I do, and it's my life, and besides, I'm the senior officer here and it's my decision, so to hell with all of you.'

So he had dressed and armed himself, and the captain had shown him how to operate the launch's radio and how to maintain an interception course with the *Karla*, and they had lowered the launch, and he had climbed down into it and pulled away.

And he was terrified.

It was impossible for him to overcome a whole boat-load of KGB all on his own. However, he was not planning that. He would not fight with any of them if he could help it. He would get aboard, hide himself until Suza's diversion began, and then look for her; and when he had found her, he would get off the *Karla* with her and flee. He had a small magnetic mine with him that he would fix to the *Karla*'s side before boarding. Then, whether he managed to escape or not, whether the whole thing was a trap or genuine, the *Karla* would have a hole blown in her side big enough to keep her from catching the *Coparelli*.

He was sure it was not a trap. He knew she was there, he knew that somehow she had been in their power and had been forced to help them, he knew she had risked her life to save his. He knew that she loved him.

And *that* was why he was terrified.

Suddenly he wanted to live. The blood-lust was gone: he was no longer interested in killing his enemies, defeating Rostov, frustrating the schemes of the Fedayeen or outwitting Egyptian Intelligence. He wanted to find Suza, and take her home, and spend the rest of his life with her. He was afraid to die.

He concentrated on steering his boat. Finding the *Karla* at night was not easy. He could keep a steady course but he had to estimate and make allowance for how much the wind and the waves were carrying him sideways. After fifteen minutes he knew he should have reached her, but she was nowhere to be seen. He began to zigzag in a search pattern, wondering desperately how far off course he was.

He was contemplating radioing the *Coparelli* for a new fix when suddenly the *Karla* appeared out of the night alongside him. She was moving fast, faster than his launch could go, and he had to reach the ladder at her bows before she was past, and at the same time avoid a collision. He gunned the launch forward, swerved away as the *Karla* rolled toward him, then turned back, homing in, while she rolled the other way.

He had the rope tied around his waist ready. The ladder came within reach. He flipped the engine of his launch into idle, stepped on the gunwale, and jumped. The *Karla* began to pitch forward as he landed on the ladder. He clung on while her prow went down into the waves. The sea came up to his waist, up to his shoulders. He took a deep breath as his head went under. He seemed to be under water for ever. The *Karla* just kept on going down. When he felt his lungs would burst she hesitated, and at last began to come up; and that seemed to take even longer. At last he broke surface and gulped lungfuls of air. He went up the ladder a few steps, untied the rope around his waist and made it fast to the ladder, securing the boat to the *Karla* for his escape. The magnetic mine was hanging from a rope across his shoulders. He took it off and slapped it on to the *Karla*'s hull.

The uranium was safe.

He shed his oilskin and climbed up the ladder.

The sound of the launch engine was inaudible in the noise of the wind, the sea, and the *Karla*'s own engines, but something must have attracted the attention of the man who looked over the rail just as Dickstein came up level with the deck. For a moment the man stared at Dickstein, his face registering amazement. Then Dickstein reached out his hand for a pull as he climbed over the rail. Automatically, with a natural instinct to help someone trying to get aboard out of the raging sea, the other man grabbed his arm. Dickstein got one leg over the rail, used his other hand to grab the outstretched arm, and threw the other man overboard and into the sea. His cry was lost in the wind. Dickstein brought the other leg over the rail and crouched down on the deck.

It seemed nobody had seen the incident.

The *Karla* was a small ship, much smaller than the *Coparelli*. There was only one superstructure, located amidships, two decks high. There were no cranes. The foredeck had a big hatch over the for'ard hold, but there was no aft hold: the crew accommodations and the engine room must occupy all the below-deck space aft, Dickstein concluded.

He looked at his watch. It was five-twenty-five. Suza's diversion should begin any moment, if she could do it.

He began to walk along the deck. There was some light from the ship's lamps, but one of the crew would have to look twice at him before being sure he was not one of them. He took his knife out of the sheath at his belt: he did not want to use his gun unless he had to, for the noise would start a hue and cry.

As he drew level with the superstructure a door opened, throwing a wedge of yellow light on to the rain-spattered deck. He dodged around the corner, flattening himself against the for'ard bulkhead. He heard two voices speaking Russian. The door slammed, and the voices receded as the men walked aft in the rain.

In the lee of the superstructure he crossed to the port side and continued toward the stern. He stopped at the corner and, looking cautiously around it, saw the two men cross the afterdeck and speak to a third man in the stern. He was tempted to take all three out with a burst from his submachine gun – three men was probably one fifth of the opposition – but decided not to: it was too early, Suza's diversion had not yet started and he had no idea where she was.

The two men came back along the starboard deck and went inside. Dickstein walked up to the remaining man in the stern, who seemed to be on guard. The man spoke to him in Russian. Dickstein grunted something unintelligible, the man replied with a question, then Dickstein was close enough and he jumped forward and cut the man's throat.

He threw the body overboard and retraced his steps. Two dead, and still they did not know he was on board. He looked at his watch. The luminous hands showed five-thirty. It was time to go inside.

He opened a door and saw an empty gangway and a companionway leading up, presumably to the bridge. He climbed the ladder. Loud voices came from the bridge. As he emerged through the companionhead he saw three men – the captain, the first officer and the second sublieutenant, he guessed. The first officer was shouting into the voice-pipe. A strange noise was coming back. As Dickstein brought his gun level, the captain pulled a lever and an alarm began to sound all over the ship. Dickstein pulled the trigger. The loud chatter of the gun was partly smothered by the wailing klaxon of the fire alarm. The three men were killed where they stood.

Dickstein hurried back down the ladder. The alarm must mean that Suza's diversion had started. Now all he had to do was stay alive until he found her.

The companionway from the bridge met the deck at

a junction of two gangways – a lateral one, which Dickstein had used, and another running the length of the superstructure. In response to the alarm doors were opening and men emerging all down both gangways. None of them seemed to be armed: this was a fire alarm, not a call to battle stations. Dickstein decided to run a bluff, and shoot only if it failed. He proceeded briskly along the central gangway, pushing his way through the milling men, shouting, 'Get out of the way' in German. They stared at him, not knowing who he was or what he was doing, except that he seemed to be in authority and there was a fire. One or two spoke to him. He ignored them. There was a rasping order from somewhere, and the men began to move purposefully. Dickstein reached the end of the gangway and was about to go down the ladder when the officer who had given the order came into sight and pointed at him, shouting a question.

Dickstein dropped down.

On the lower deck things were better organized. The men were running in one direction, toward the stern, and a group of three hands under the supervision of an officer was breaking out fire-fighting gear. There, in a place where the gangway widened for access to hoses, Dickstein saw something which made him temporarily unhinged, and brought a red mist of hatred to his eyes.

Suza was on the floor, her back to the bulkhead. Her legs were stretched out in front of her, her trousers torn. He could see her scorched and blackened skin through the tatters. He heard Rostov's voice, shouting at her over the sound of the alarm: 'What did you tell Dickstein?'

Dickstein jumped from the ladder onto the deck. One of the hands moved in front of him. Dickstein knocked him to the deck with an elbow blow to the face, and jumped on Rostov.

Even in his rage, he realized that he could not use the gun in this confined space while Rostov was so close to Suza. Besides, he wanted to kill the man with his hands.

He grabbed Rostov's shoulder and spun him around. Rostov saw his face. 'You!' Dickstein hit him in the stomach first, a pile-driving blow that buckled him at the waist and made him gasp for air. As his head came down Dickstein brought a knee up fast and hard, snapping Rostov's chin up and breaking his jaw; then, continuing the motion, he put all his strength behind a kick into the throat that smashed Rostov's neck and drove him backward into the bulkhead.

Before Rostov had completed his fall Dickstein turned quickly around, went down on one knee to bring his machine gun off his shoulder, and with Suza behind him and to one side opened fire on three hands who appeared in the gangway.

He turned again, picking Suza up in a fireman's lift, trying not to touch her charred flesh. He had a moment to think, now. Clearly the fire was in the stern, the direction in which all the men had been running. If he went forward now he was less likely to be seen.

He ran the length of the gangway, then carried her up the ladder. He could tell by the feel of her body on his shoulder that she was still conscious. He came off the top of the ladder to the main deck level, found a door and stepped out.

There was some confusion out on deck. A man ran past him, heading for the stern; another ran off in the opposite direction. Somebody was in the prow. Down in the stern a man lay on the deck with two others bending over him; presumably he had been injured in the fire.

Dickstein ran forward to the ladder that he had used to board. He eased his gun on to his shoulder, shifted Suza a little on the other shoulder, and stepped over the rail.

Looking about the deck as he started to go down, he knew that they had seen him.

It was one thing to see a strange face on board ship, wonder who he was, and delay asking questions until later because there was a fire alarm; but it was quite another to see someone leaving the ship with a body over his shoulder.

He was not quite halfway down the ladder when they began to shoot at him.

A bullet pinged off the hull beside his head. He looked up to see three men leaning over the rail, two of them with pistols. Holding on to the ladder with his left hand, he put his right hand to his gun, pointed up and fired. His aim was hopeless but the men pulled back.

And he lost his balance.

As the prow of the ship pitched up, he swayed to the left, dropped his gun into the sea and grabbed hold of the ladder with his right hand. His right foot slipped off the rung – and then, to his horror, Suza began to slip from his left shoulder.

'Hold on to me,' he yelled at her, no longer sure whether she was conscious or not. He felt her hands clutch at his sweater, but she continued to slip away, and now her unbalanced weight was pulling him even more to the left.

'No!' he yelled.

She slipped off his shoulder and went plunging into the sea.

Dickstein turned, saw the launch, and jumped, landing with a jarring shock in the well of the boat.

He called her name into the black sea all around him, swinging from one side of the boat to the other, his desperation increasing with every second she failed to surface. And then he heard, over the noise of the wind, a scream. Turning toward the sound he saw her head just above the surface, between the side of the boat and the hull of the *Karla*.

She was out of his reach.

She screamed again.

The launch was tied to the *Karla* by the rope, most of which was piled on the deck of the boat. Dickstein cut the rope with his knife, letting go of the end that was tied to the *Karla*'s ladder and throwing the other end toward Suza.

As she reached for the rope the sea rose again and engulfed her.

Up on the deck of the *Karla* they started shooting over the rail again.

He ignored the gunfire.

Dickstein's eyes swept the sea. With the ship and the boat pitching and rolling in different directions the chances of a hit were relatively slim.

After a few seconds that seemed hours, Suza surfaced again. Dickstein threw her the rope. This time she was able to grab it. Swiftly he pulled it, bringing her closer and closer until he was able to lean over the gunwale of the launch perilously and take hold of her wrists.

He had her now, and he would never let her go.

He pulled her into the well of the launch. Up above a machine gun opened fire. Dickstein threw the launch into gear, then fell on top of Suza, covering her body with his own. The launch moved away from the *Karla*, undirected, riding the waves like a lost surfboard.

The shooting stopped. Dickstein looked back. The *Karla* was out of sight.

Gently he turned Suza over, fearing for her life. Her eyes were closed. He took the wheel of the launch, looked at the compass, and set an approximate course. He turned on the boat's radio and called the *Coparelli*. Waiting for them to come in, he lifted Suza toward him and cradled her in his arms.

A muffled thud came across the water like a distant explosion: the magnetic mine.

The *Coparelli* replied. Dickstein said, 'The *Karla* is on fire. Turn back and pick me up. Have the sick bay ready for the girl – she's badly burned.' He waited for their acknowledgment, then switched off and stared at Suza's expressionless face. 'Don't die,' he said. 'Please don't die.'

She opened her eyes and looked up at him. She opened her mouth, struggling to speak. He bent his head to her. She said, 'Is it really you?'

'It's me,' he said.

The corners of her mouth lifted in a faint smile. 'I'll make it.'

There was the sound of a tremendous explosion. The fire had reached the fuel tanks of the *Karla*. The sky was lit up for several moments by a sheet of flame, the air was filled with a roaring noise, and the rain stopped. The noise and the light died, and so did the *Karla*.

'She's gone down,' Dickstein said to Suza. He looked at her. Her eyes were closed, she was unconscious again, but she was still smiling.

EPILOGUE

NATHANIEL DICKSTEIN resigned from the Mossad, and his name passed into legend. He married Suza and took her back to the kibbutz, where they tended grapes by day and made love half the night. In his spare time he organized a political campaign to have the laws changed so that his children could be classified Jewish; or, better still, to abolish classification.

They did not have children for a while. They were prepared to wait: Suza was young, and he was in no hurry. Her burns never healed completely. Sometimes, in bed, she would say, 'My legs are horrible,' and he would kiss her knees and tell her, 'They're beautiful, they saved my life.'

When the opening of the Yom Kippur War took the Israeli armed forces by surprise, Pierre Borg was blamed for the lack of advance intelligence, and he resigned. The truth was more complicated. The fault lay with a Russian intelligence officer called David Rostov – an elderly-looking man who had to wear a neck brace every moment of his life. He had gone to Cairo and, beginning with the interrogation and death of an Israeli agent called Towfik early in 1968, he had investigated all the events of that year and concluded that Kawash was a double agent. Instead of having Kawash tried and hanged for espionage, Rostov had told the Egyptians how to feed him disinformation, which Kawash, in all innocence, duly passed on to Pierre Borg.

The result was that Nat Dickstein came out of retirement to take over Pierre Borg's job for the duration of the war. On Monday, October 8, 1973, he attended a crisis meeting of the Cabinet. After three days of war the Israelis were in deep trouble. The Egyptians had crossed the Suez Canal and pushed the Israelis back into Sinai with heavy casualties. On the other front, the Golan Heights, the Syrians were pushing forward, again with heavy losses to the Israeli side. The proposal before the Cabinet was to drop atom bombs on Cairo and Damascus. Not even the most hawkish ministers actually relished the idea; but the situation was desperate and the Americans were dragging their heels over the arms airlift which might save the day.

The meeting was coming around to accepting the idea of using nuclear weapons when Nat Dickstein made his only contribution to the discussion: 'Of course, we could *tell* the Americans that we plan to drop these bombs – on Wednesday, say – unless they start the airlift immediately . . .'

And that is exactly what they did.

The airlift turned the tide of the war, and later a similar crisis meeting took place in Cairo. Once again, nobody was in favour of nuclear war in the Middle East; once again, the politicians gathered around the table began to persuade one another that there was no alternative; and once again, the proposal was stopped by an unexpected contribution.

This time it was the military that stepped in. Knowing of the proposal that would be before the assembled presidents, they had run checks on their nuclear strike force in readiness for a positive decision; and they had found that all the plutonium in the bombs had been taken out and replaced with iron filings. It was assumed that the Russians had done this, as they had mysteriously rendered unworkable the nuclear reactor in Qattara, before being expelled from Egypt in 1972.

That night, one of the presidents talked to his wife for five minutes before falling asleep in his chair. 'It's all over,' he told her. 'Israel has won – permanently. They have the bomb, and we do not, and that single fact will determine the course of history in our region for the rest of the century.'

'What about the Palestine refugees?' his wife said.

The president shrugged and began to light his last pipe of the day. 'I remember reading a story in the London *Times* . . . this must be five years ago, I suppose. It said that the Free Wales Army had put a bomb in the police station in Cardiff.'

'Wales?' said his wife. 'Where is Wales?'

'It is a part of England, more or less.'

'I remember,' she said. 'They have coal mines and choirs.'

'That's right. Have you any idea how long ago the Anglo-Saxons conquered the Welsh?'

'None at all.'

'Nor have I, but it must be more than a thousand years ago, because the Norman French conquered the Anglo-Saxons nine hundred years ago. You see? A thousand years, and they are still bombing police stations! The Palestinians will be like the Welsh... They can bomb Israel for a thousand years, but they will always be the losers.'

His wife looked up at him. All these years they had been together, and still he was capable of surprising her. She had thought she would never hear words like this from him.

'I will tell you something else,' he went on. 'There will have to be peace. We cannot possibly win, now, so we will have to make peace. Not now; perhaps not for five or ten years. But the time will come, and then I will have to go to Jerusalem and say, "No more war." I may even get some credit for it, when the dust settles. It is not how I planned to go down in history, but it's not such a bad way, for all that. "The man who brought peace to the Middle East." What would you say to that?'

His wife got up from her chair and came across to hold his hands. There were tears in her eyes. 'I would give thanks to God,' she said.

Franz Albrecht Pedler died in 1974. He died content. His life had seen some ups and downs – he had, after all, lived through the most ignominious period in the history of his nation – but he had survived and ended his days happily.

He had guessed what had happened to the uranium. One day early in 1969 his company had received a cheque for two million dollars, signed by A. Papagopolous, with a statement from Savile Shipping which read: 'To lost cargo.' The next day a representative of the Israeli Army had called, bringing the payment for the first shipment of cleaning materials. As he left, the army man had said, 'On the matter of your lost cargo, we would be happy if you were not to pursue any further inquiries.'

Pedler began to understand then. 'But what if Euratom asks me questions?'

'Tell them the truth,' the man said. 'The cargo was lost, and when you tried to discover what had happened to it, you found that Savile Shipping had gone out of business.'

'Have they?'

'They have.'

And that was what Pedler told Euratom. They sent an investigator to see him, and he repeated his story, which was completely true, if not truly complete. He said to the investigator, 'I suppose there will be publicity about all this soon.'

'I doubt it,' the investigator told him. 'It reflects badly on us. I don't suppose we'll broadcast the story unless we get more information.'

They did not get more information, of course; at least, not in Pedler's lifetime.

On Yom Kippur in 1974 Suza Dickstein went into labour.

In accordance with the custom of this particular